Poetry to Read in a Graveyard
Published by NRM Books.

ISBN: 978-1-965179-51-2

CREDITS

Decorations, Cover Redesign & Layout:
Nathan Reese Maher

COPYRIGHT

TABLE OF CONTENTS

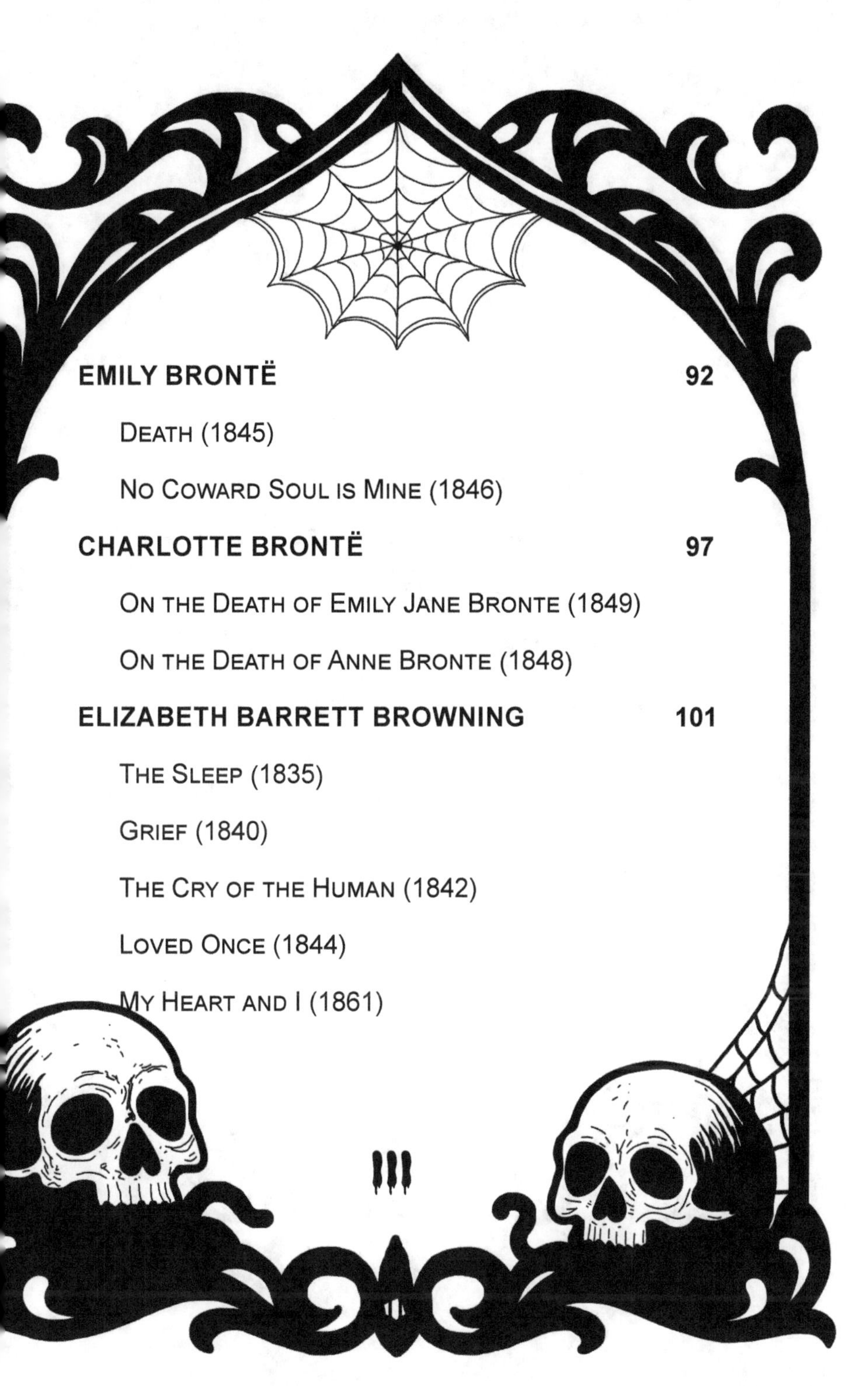

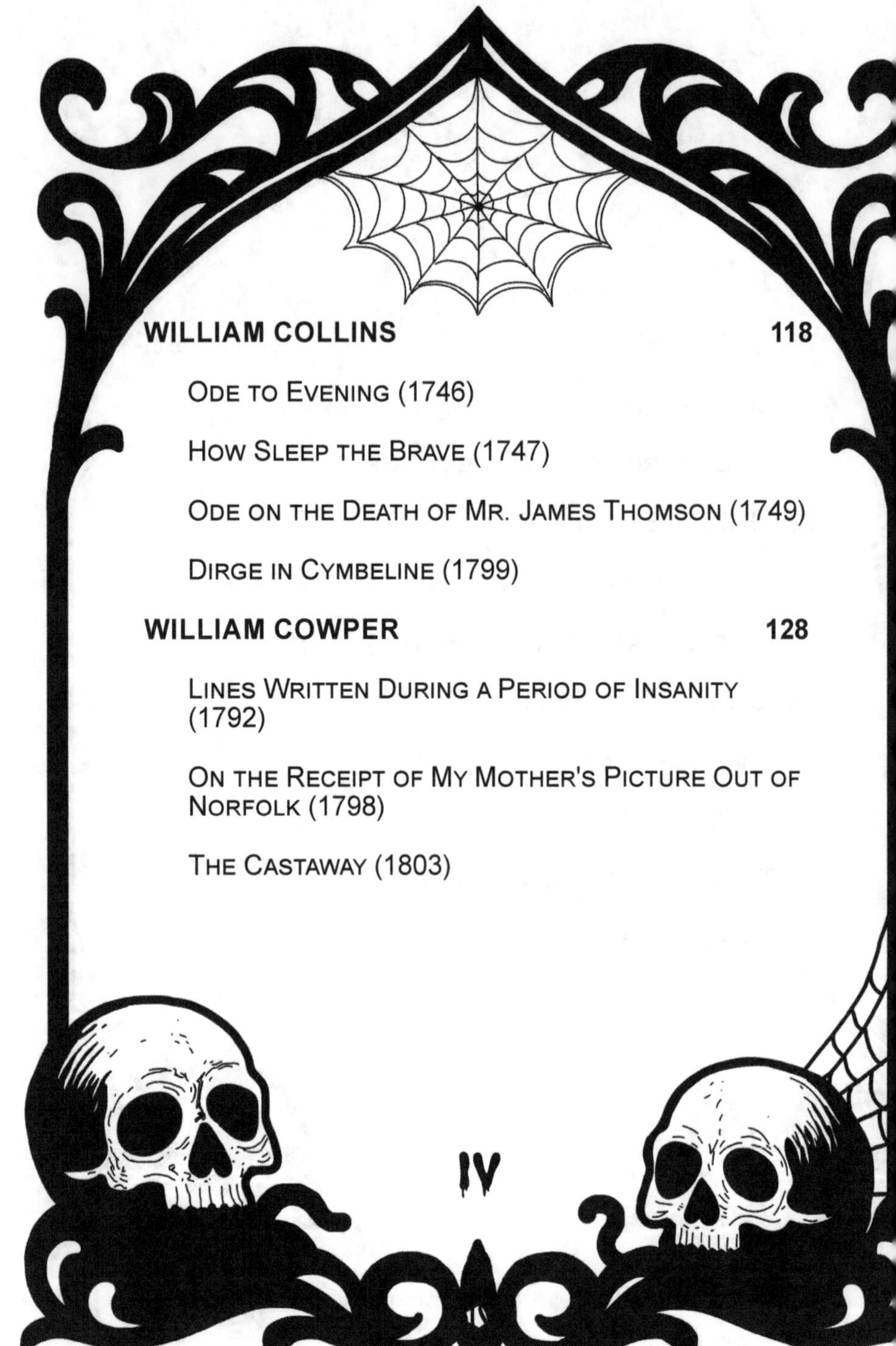

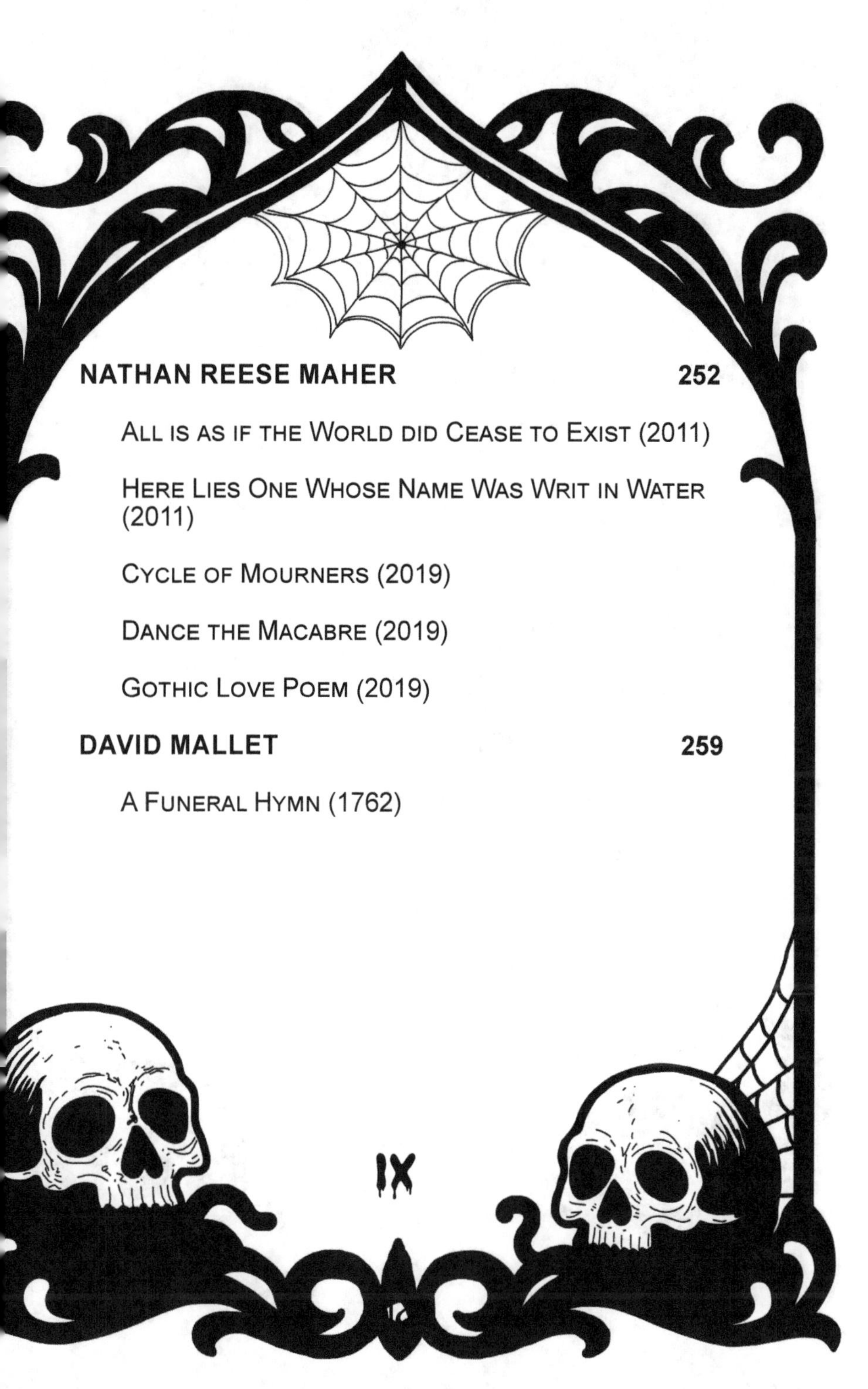

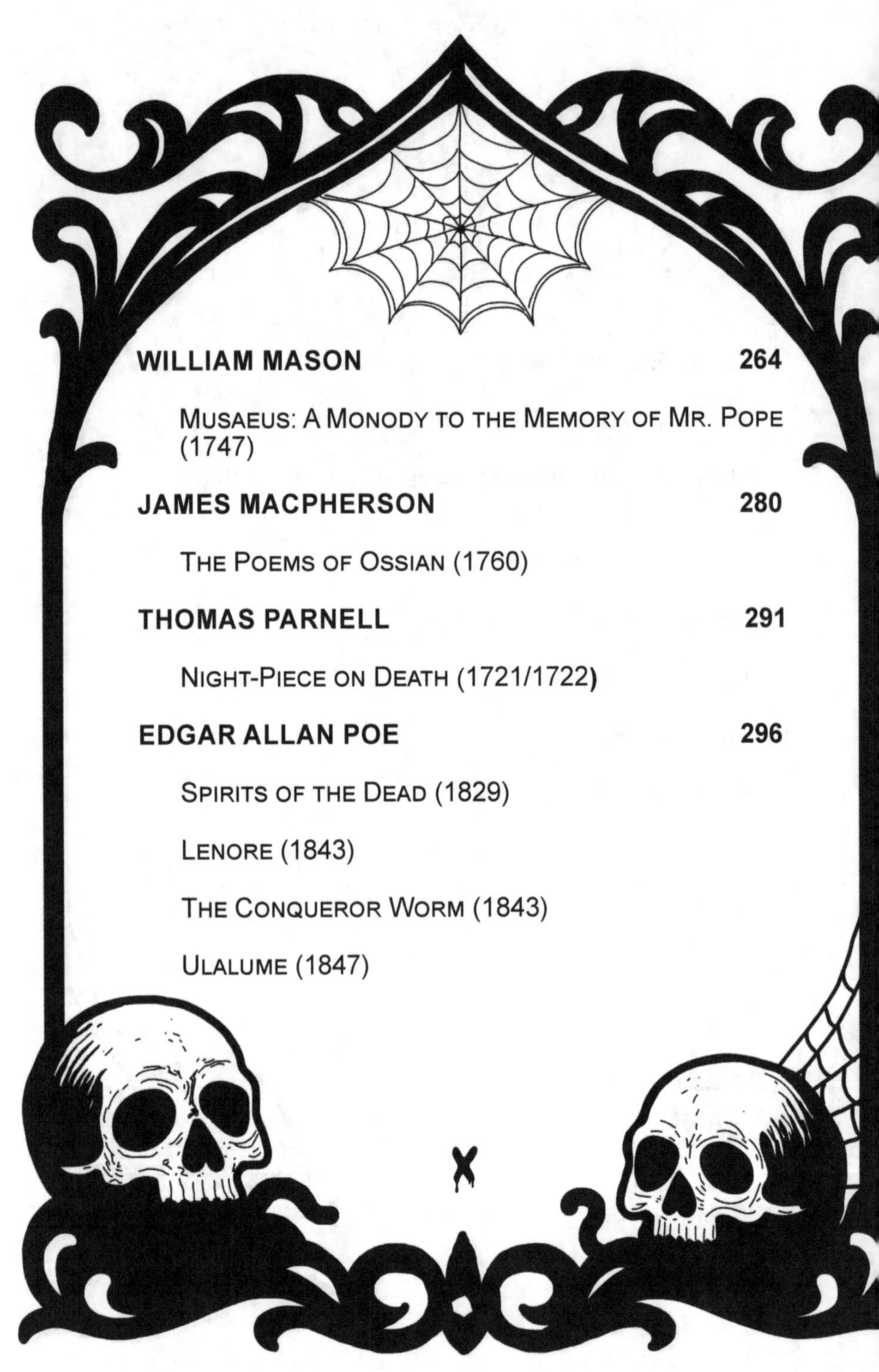

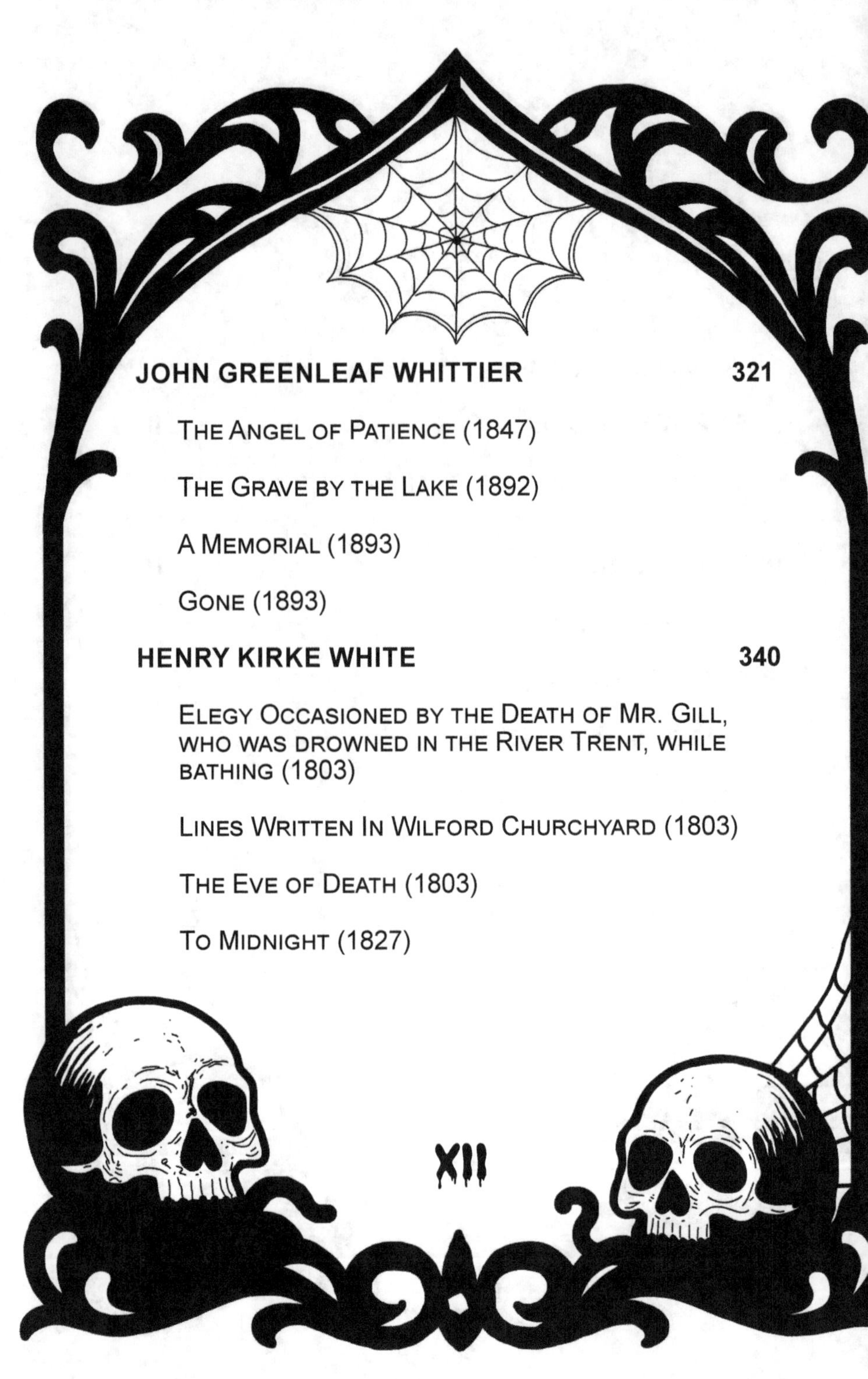

DEDICATION

To all who find solace strolling amongst headstones.

To the melancholy.

To the outcasts.

To all those who make their way through the labyrinth of death and find its mysteries a curiosity, rather than meeting it with fear.

Mark Akenside

HYMN TO THE NAIADS.

O'ER yonder eastern hill the twilight throws
Her dusky mantle; and the God of day,
With bright Astraea seated by his side,
Waits yet to leave the ocean. Tarry, Nymphs,
Ye Nymphs, ye blue-ey'd progeny of Thames,
Who now the mazes of this rugged heath
Trace with your fleeting steps; who all night long
Repeat, amid the cool and tranquil air,
Your lonely murmurs, tarry: and receive
My offer'd lay. To pay you homage due,
I leave the gates of sleep; nor shall my lyre
Too far into the splendid hours of morn
Ingage your audience: my observant hand
Shall close the strain ere any sultry beam
Approach you. To your subterranean haunts
Ye then may timely steal; to pace with care
The humid sands; to loosen from the soil
The bubbling sources; to direct the rills
To meet in wider channels; or beneath

Some grotto's dripping arch, at height of noon
To slumber, shelter'd from the burning heaven.
Where shall my song begin, ye Nymphs? or end?
Wide is your praise and copious — First of things,
First of the lonely powers, ere Time arose,
Were Love and Chaos. Love, the fire of Fate;
Elder than Chaos. Born of Fate was Time,
Who many sons and many comely births
Devour'd, relentless father: till the child
Of Rhea drove him from the upper sky,
And quell'd his deadly might. Then social reign'd
The kindred powers, Tethys, and reverend Ops,
And spotless Vesta; while supreme of sway
Remain'd the cloud-compeller. From the couch
Of Tethys sprang the sedgy-crowned race,
Who from a thousand urns, o'er every clime,
Send tribute to their parent; and from them
Are ye, O Naiads: Arethusa fair,
And tuneful Aganippe; that sweet name,
Bandusia; that soft family which dwelt
With Syrian Daphne; and the honour'd tribes

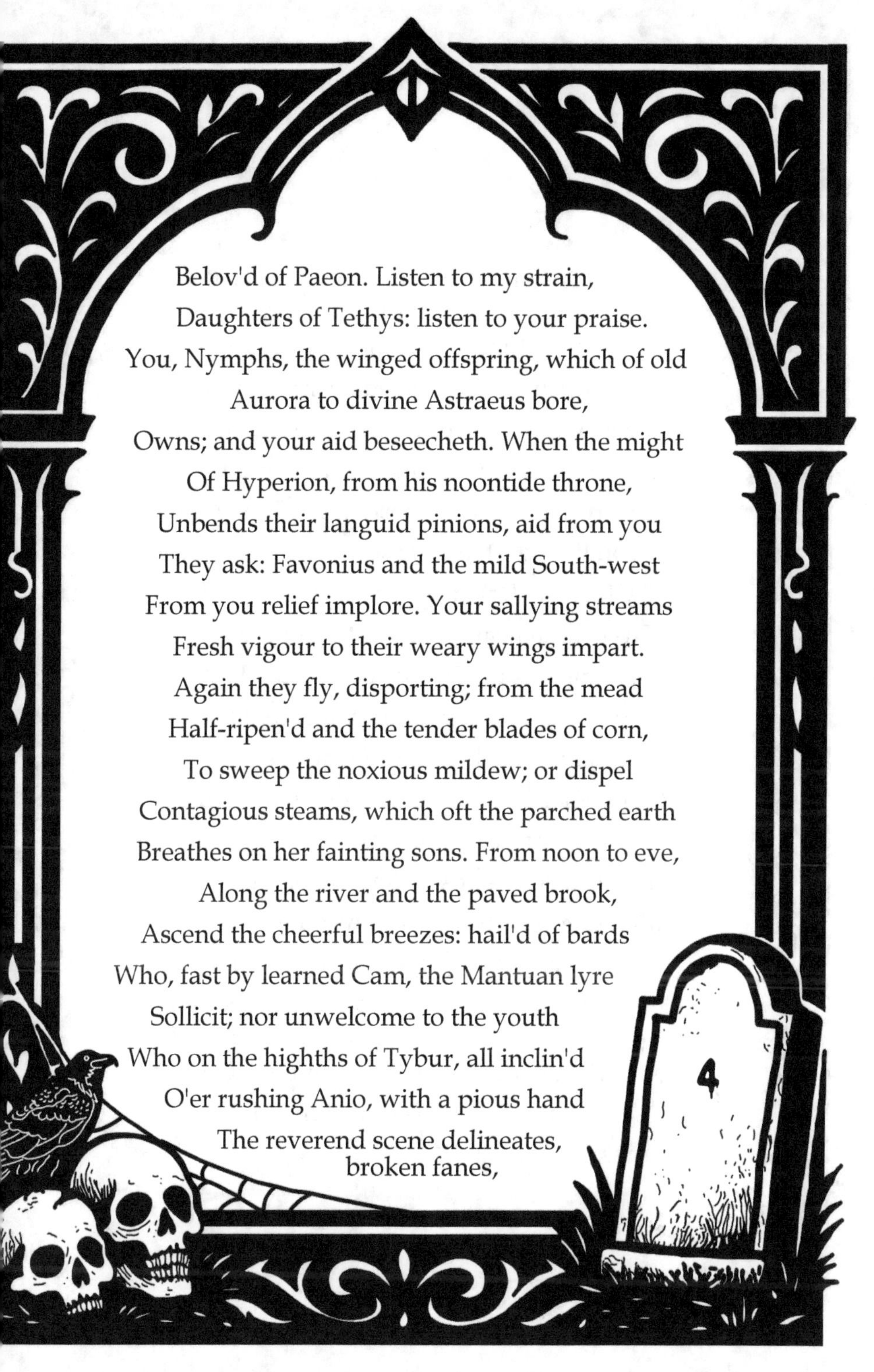

Belov'd of Paeon. Listen to my strain,
Daughters of Tethys: listen to your praise.
You, Nymphs, the winged offspring, which of old
Aurora to divine Astraeus bore,
Owns; and your aid beseecheth. When the might
Of Hyperion, from his noontide throne,
Unbends their languid pinions, aid from you
They ask: Favonius and the mild South-west
From you relief implore. Your sallying streams
Fresh vigour to their weary wings impart.
Again they fly, disporting; from the mead
Half-ripen'd and the tender blades of corn,
To sweep the noxious mildew; or dispel
Contagious steams, which oft the parched earth
Breathes on her fainting sons. From noon to eve,
Along the river and the paved brook,
Ascend the cheerful breezes: hail'd of bards
Who, fast by learned Cam, the Mantuan lyre
Sollicit; nor unwelcome to the youth
Who on the highths of Tybur, all inclin'd
O'er rushing Anio, with a pious hand
The reverend scene delineates,
broken fanes,

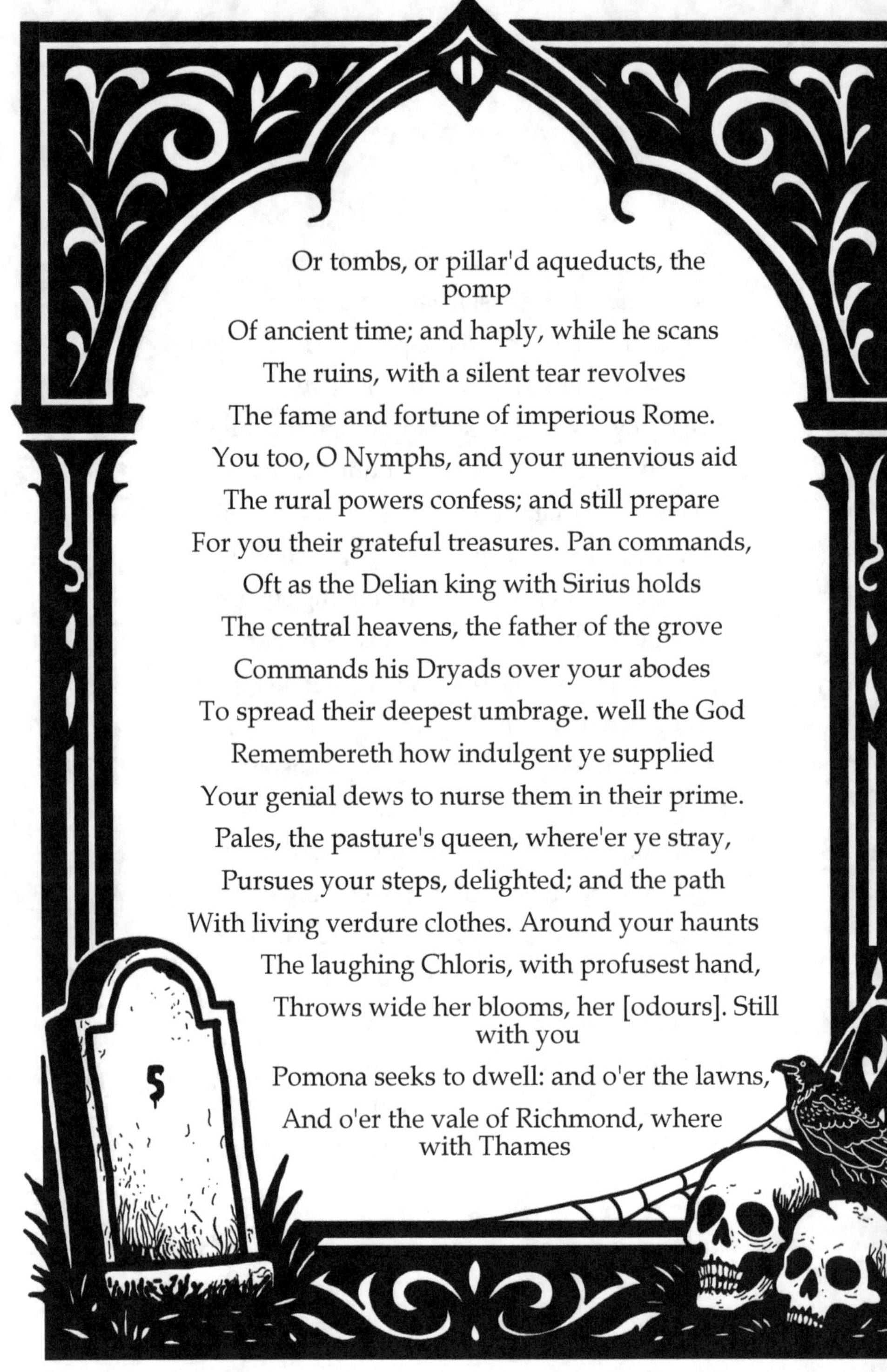

Or tombs, or pillar'd aqueducts, the pomp
Of ancient time; and haply, while he scans
The ruins, with a silent tear revolves
The fame and fortune of imperious Rome.
You too, O Nymphs, and your unenvious aid
The rural powers confess; and still prepare
For you their grateful treasures. Pan commands,
Oft as the Delian king with Sirius holds
The central heavens, the father of the grove
Commands his Dryads over your abodes
To spread their deepest umbrage. well the God
Remembereth how indulgent ye supplied
Your genial dews to nurse them in their prime.
Pales, the pasture's queen, where'er ye stray,
Pursues your steps, delighted; and the path
With living verdure clothes. Around your haunts
The laughing Chloris, with profusest hand,
Throws wide her blooms, her [odours]. Still with you
Pomona seeks to dwell: and o'er the lawns,
And o'er the vale of Richmond, where with Thames

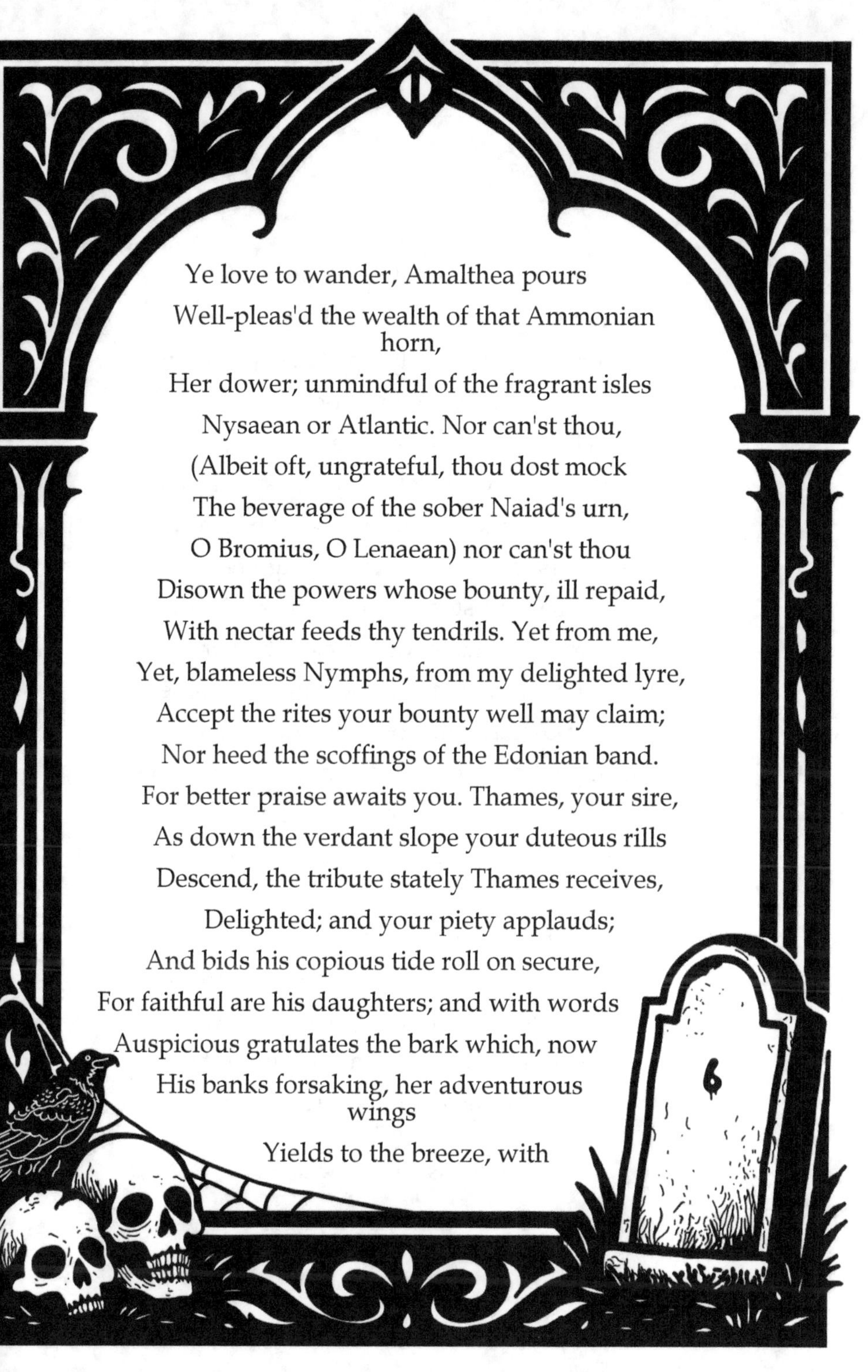

Ye love to wander, Amalthea pours
Well-pleas'd the wealth of that Ammonian horn,
Her dower; unmindful of the fragrant isles
Nysaean or Atlantic. Nor can'st thou,
(Albeit oft, ungrateful, thou dost mock
The beverage of the sober Naiad's urn,
O Bromius, O Lenaean) nor can'st thou
Disown the powers whose bounty, ill repaid,
With nectar feeds thy tendrils. Yet from me,
Yet, blameless Nymphs, from my delighted lyre,
Accept the rites your bounty well may claim;
Nor heed the scoffings of the Edonian band.
For better praise awaits you. Thames, your sire,
As down the verdant slope your duteous rills
Descend, the tribute stately Thames receives,
Delighted; and your piety applauds;
And bids his copious tide roll on secure,
For faithful are his daughters; and with words
Auspicious gratulates the bark which, now
His banks forsaking, her adventurous wings
Yields to the breeze, with

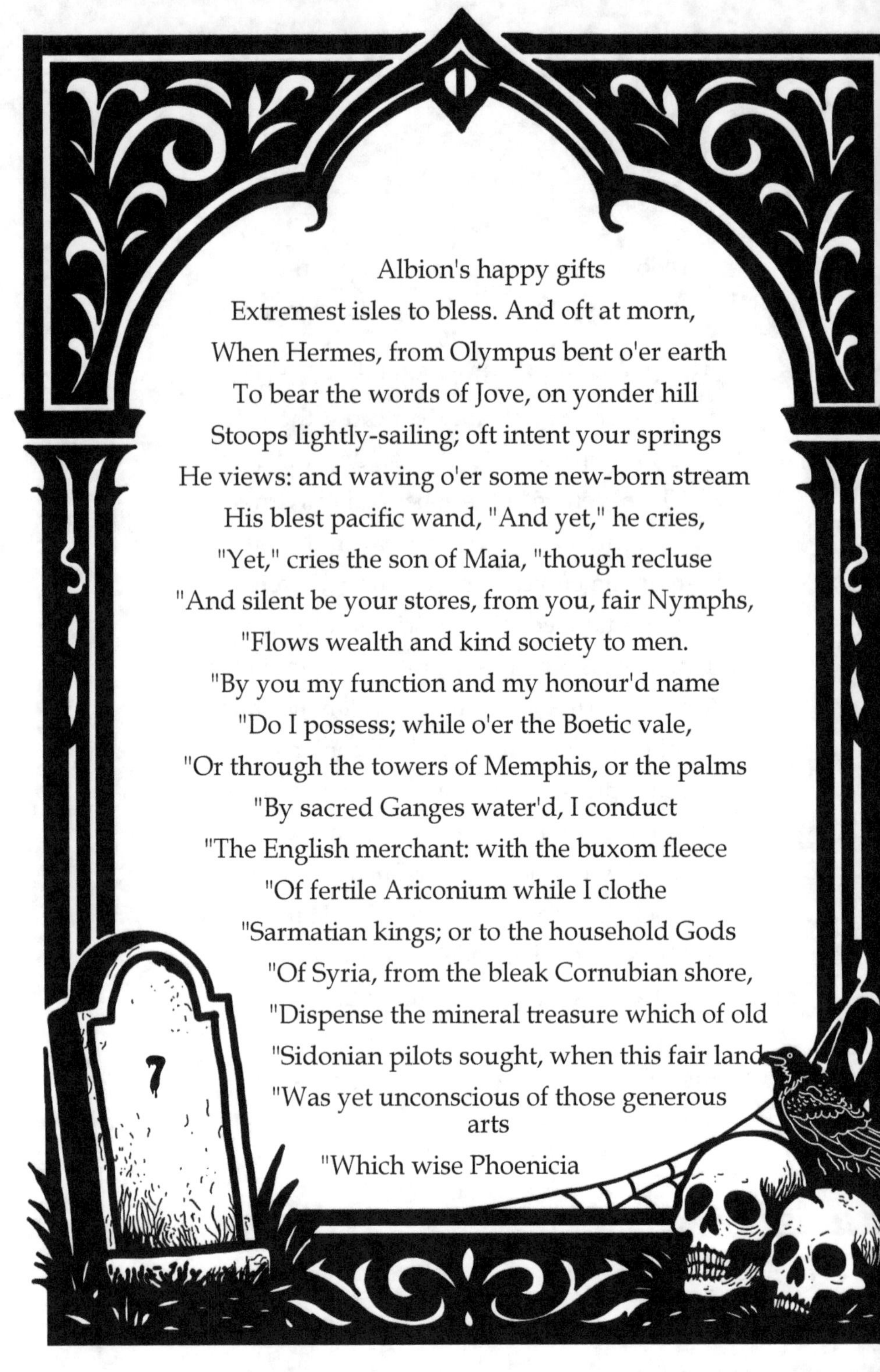

Albion's happy gifts
Extremest isles to bless. And oft at morn,
When Hermes, from Olympus bent o'er earth
To bear the words of Jove, on yonder hill
Stoops lightly-sailing; oft intent your springs
He views: and waving o'er some new-born stream
His blest pacific wand, "And yet," he cries,
"Yet," cries the son of Maia, "though recluse
"And silent be your stores, from you, fair Nymphs,
"Flows wealth and kind society to men.
"By you my function and my honour'd name
"Do I possess; while o'er the Boetic vale,
"Or through the towers of Memphis, or the palms
"By sacred Ganges water'd, I conduct
"The English merchant: with the buxom fleece
"Of fertile Ariconium while I clothe
"Sarmatian kings; or to the household Gods
"Of Syria, from the bleak Cornubian shore,
"Dispense the mineral treasure which of old
"Sidonian pilots sought, when this fair land
"Was yet unconscious of those generous arts
"Which wise Phoenicia

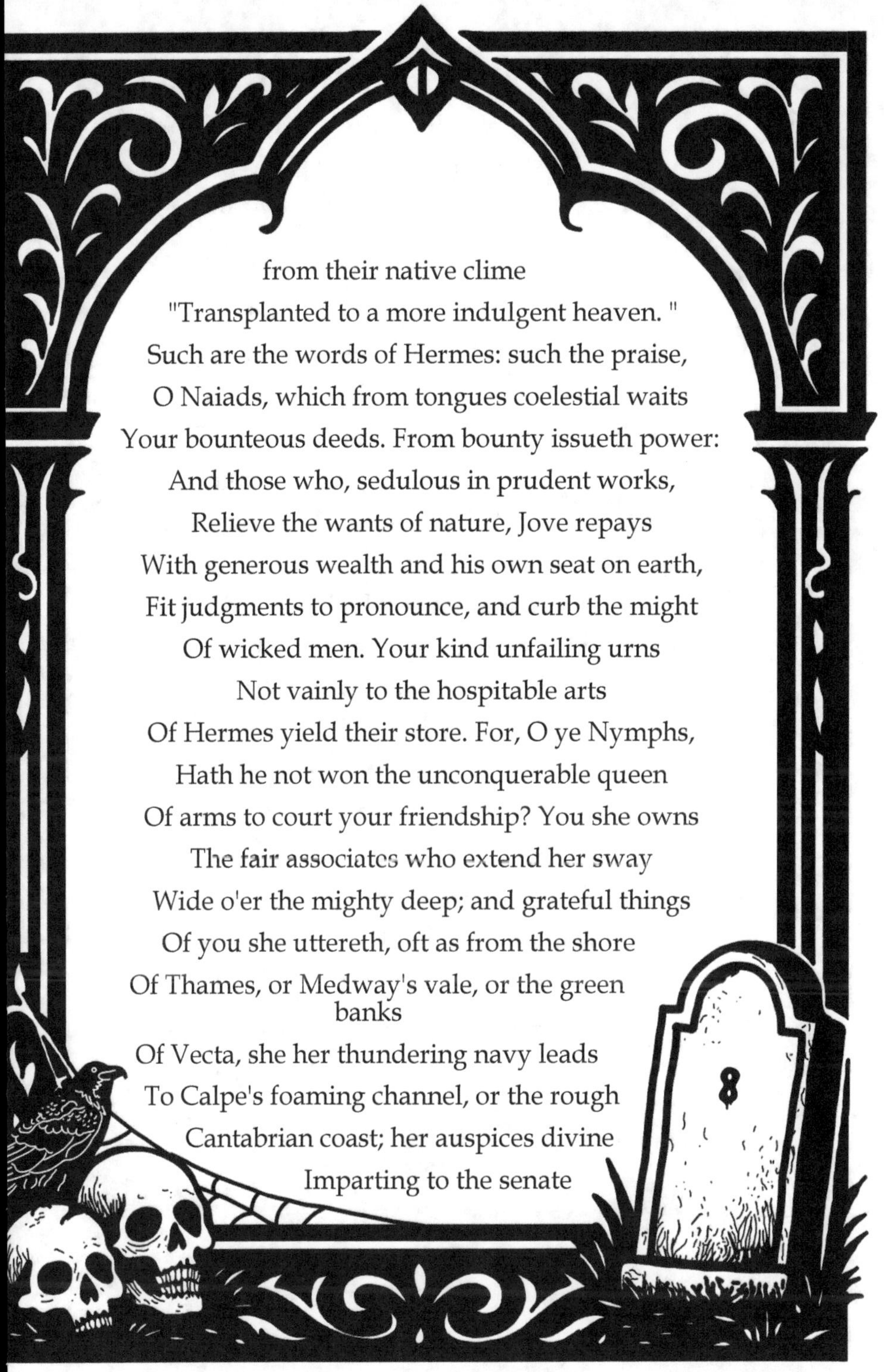

from their native clime
"Transplanted to a more indulgent heaven."
Such are the words of Hermes: such the praise,
O Naiads, which from tongues coelestial waits
Your bounteous deeds. From bounty issueth power:
And those who, sedulous in prudent works,
Relieve the wants of nature, Jove repays
With generous wealth and his own seat on earth,
Fit judgments to pronounce, and curb the might
Of wicked men. Your kind unfailing urns
Not vainly to the hospitable arts
Of Hermes yield their store. For, O ye Nymphs,
Hath he not won the unconquerable queen
Of arms to court your friendship? You she owns
The fair associates who extend her sway
Wide o'er the mighty deep; and grateful things
Of you she uttereth, oft as from the shore
Of Thames, or Medway's vale, or the green banks
Of Vecta, she her thundering navy leads
To Calpe's foaming channel, or the rough
Cantabrian coast; her auspices divine
Imparting to the senate

and the prince
Of Albion, to dismay barbaric kings,
The Iberian, or the Celt. The pride of kings
Was ever scorn'd by Pallas: and of old
Rejoic'd the virgin, from the brazen prow
Of Athens o'er Aegina's gloomy surge,
To drive her clouds and storms; o'erwhelming all
The Persian's promis'd glory, when the realms
Of Indus and the soft Ionian clime,
When Lybia's torrid champain and the rocks
Of cold Imaüs join'd their servile bands,
To sweep the sons of liberty from earth.
In vain: Minerva on the brazen prow
Of Athens stood, and with the thunder's voice
Denounc'd her terrours on their impious heads,
And shook her burning Aegis. Xerxes saw:
From Heracleum, on the mountain's highth
Thron'd in his golden car, he knew the sign
Coelestial; felt unrighteous hope forsake
His faltering heart, and turn'd his face with shame.

Hail, ye who share the stern Minerva's power;

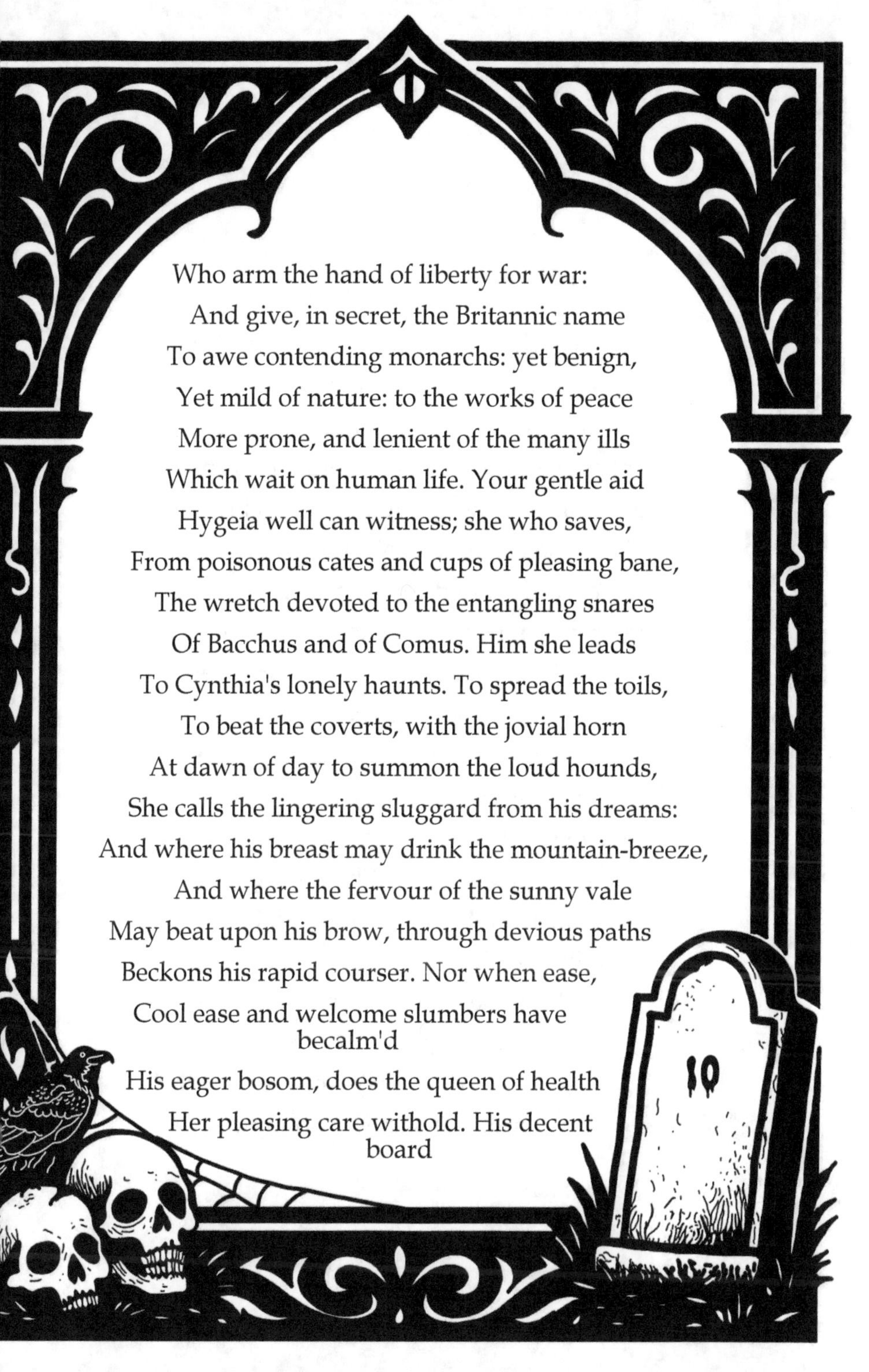

Who arm the hand of liberty for war:
And give, in secret, the Britannic name
To awe contending monarchs: yet benign,
Yet mild of nature: to the works of peace
More prone, and lenient of the many ills
Which wait on human life. Your gentle aid
Hygeia well can witness; she who saves,
From poisonous cates and cups of pleasing bane,
The wretch devoted to the entangling snares
Of Bacchus and of Comus. Him she leads
To Cynthia's lonely haunts. To spread the toils,
To beat the coverts, with the jovial horn
At dawn of day to summon the loud hounds,
She calls the lingering sluggard from his dreams:
And where his breast may drink the mountain-breeze,
And where the fervour of the sunny vale
May beat upon his brow, through devious paths
Beckons his rapid courser. Nor when ease,
Cool ease and welcome slumbers have becalm'd
His eager bosom, does the queen of health
Her pleasing care withold. His decent board

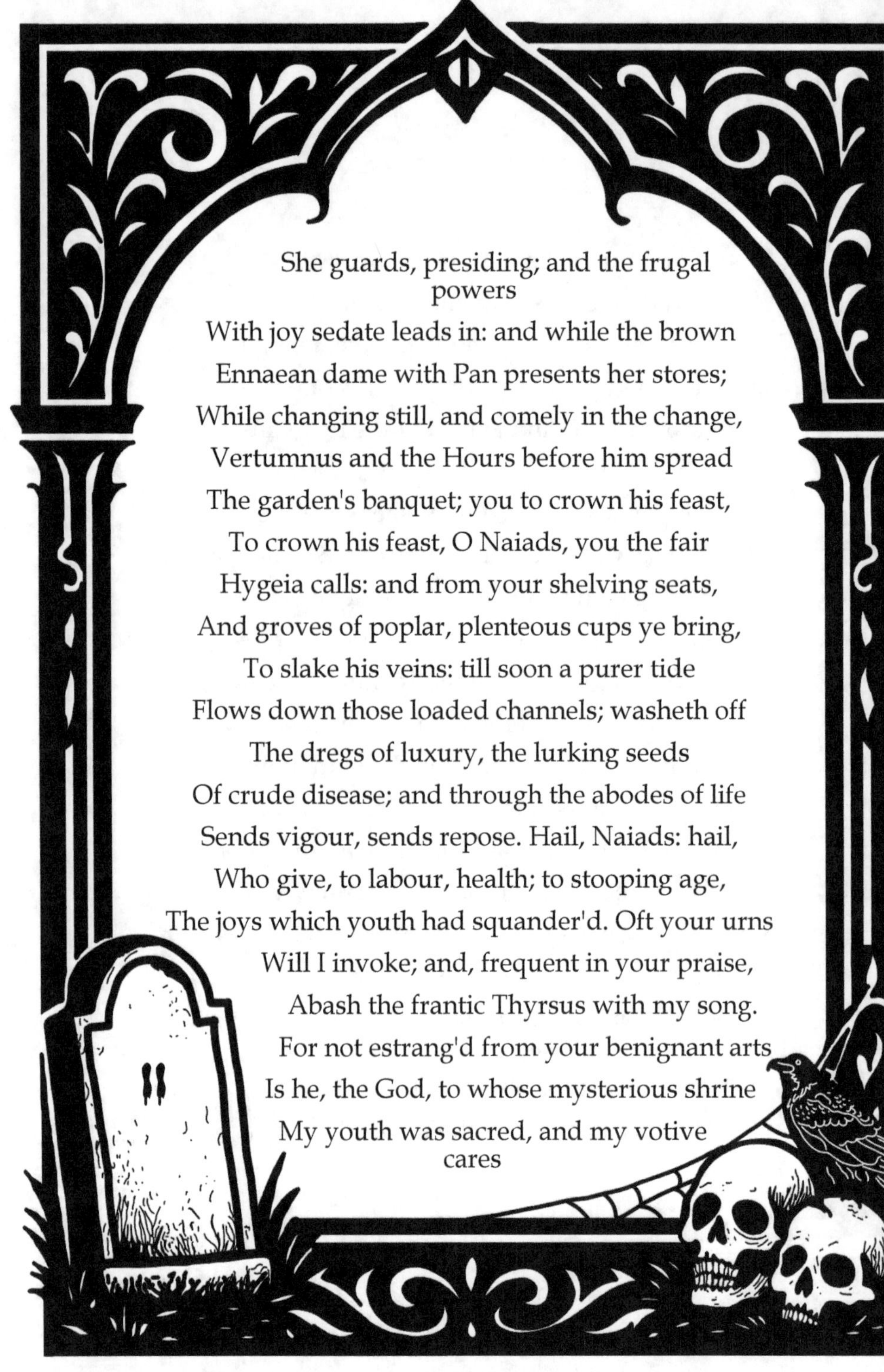

She guards, presiding; and the frugal powers
With joy sedate leads in: and while the brown
Ennaean dame with Pan presents her stores;
While changing still, and comely in the change,
Vertumnus and the Hours before him spread
The garden's banquet; you to crown his feast,
To crown his feast, O Naiads, you the fair
Hygeia calls: and from your shelving seats,
And groves of poplar, plenteous cups ye bring,
To slake his veins: till soon a purer tide
Flows down those loaded channels; washeth off
The dregs of luxury, the lurking seeds
Of crude disease; and through the abodes of life
Sends vigour, sends repose. Hail, Naiads: hail,
Who give, to labour, health; to stooping age,
The joys which youth had squander'd. Oft your urns
Will I invoke; and, frequent in your praise,
Abash the frantic Thyrsus with my song.
For not estrang'd from your benignant arts
Is he, the God, to whose mysterious shrine
My youth was sacred, and my votive cares

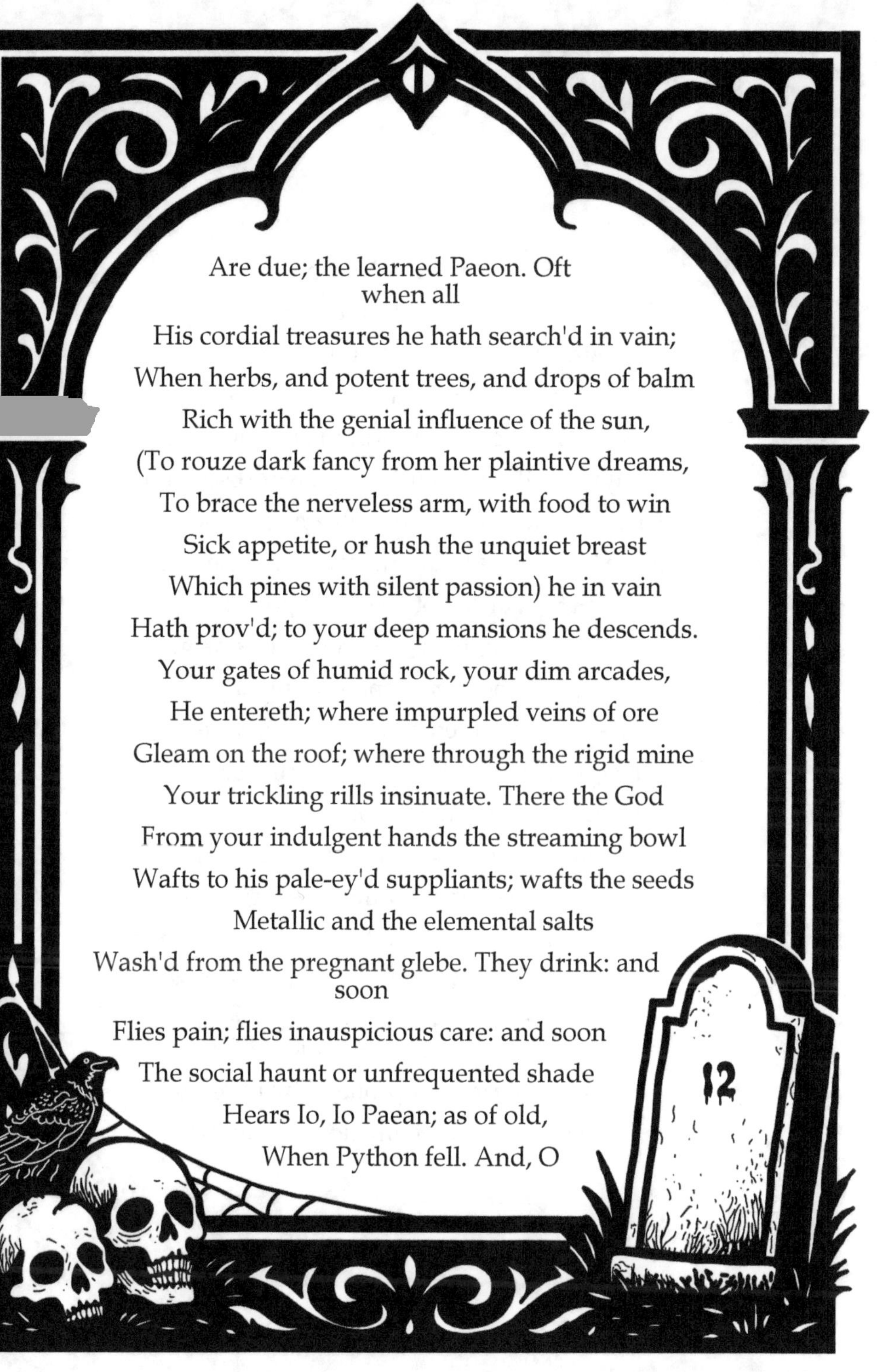

Are due; the learned Paeon. Oft when all
His cordial treasures he hath search'd in vain;
When herbs, and potent trees, and drops of balm
Rich with the genial influence of the sun,
(To rouze dark fancy from her plaintive dreams,
To brace the nerveless arm, with food to win
Sick appetite, or hush the unquiet breast
Which pines with silent passion) he in vain
Hath prov'd; to your deep mansions he descends.
Your gates of humid rock, your dim arcades,
He entereth; where impurpled veins of ore
Gleam on the roof; where through the rigid mine
Your trickling rills insinuate. There the God
From your indulgent hands the streaming bowl
Wafts to his pale-ey'd suppliants; wafts the seeds
Metallic and the elemental salts
Wash'd from the pregnant glebe. They drink: and soon
Flies pain; flies inauspicious care: and soon
The social haunt or unfrequented shade
Hears Io, Io Paean; as of old,
When Python fell. And, O

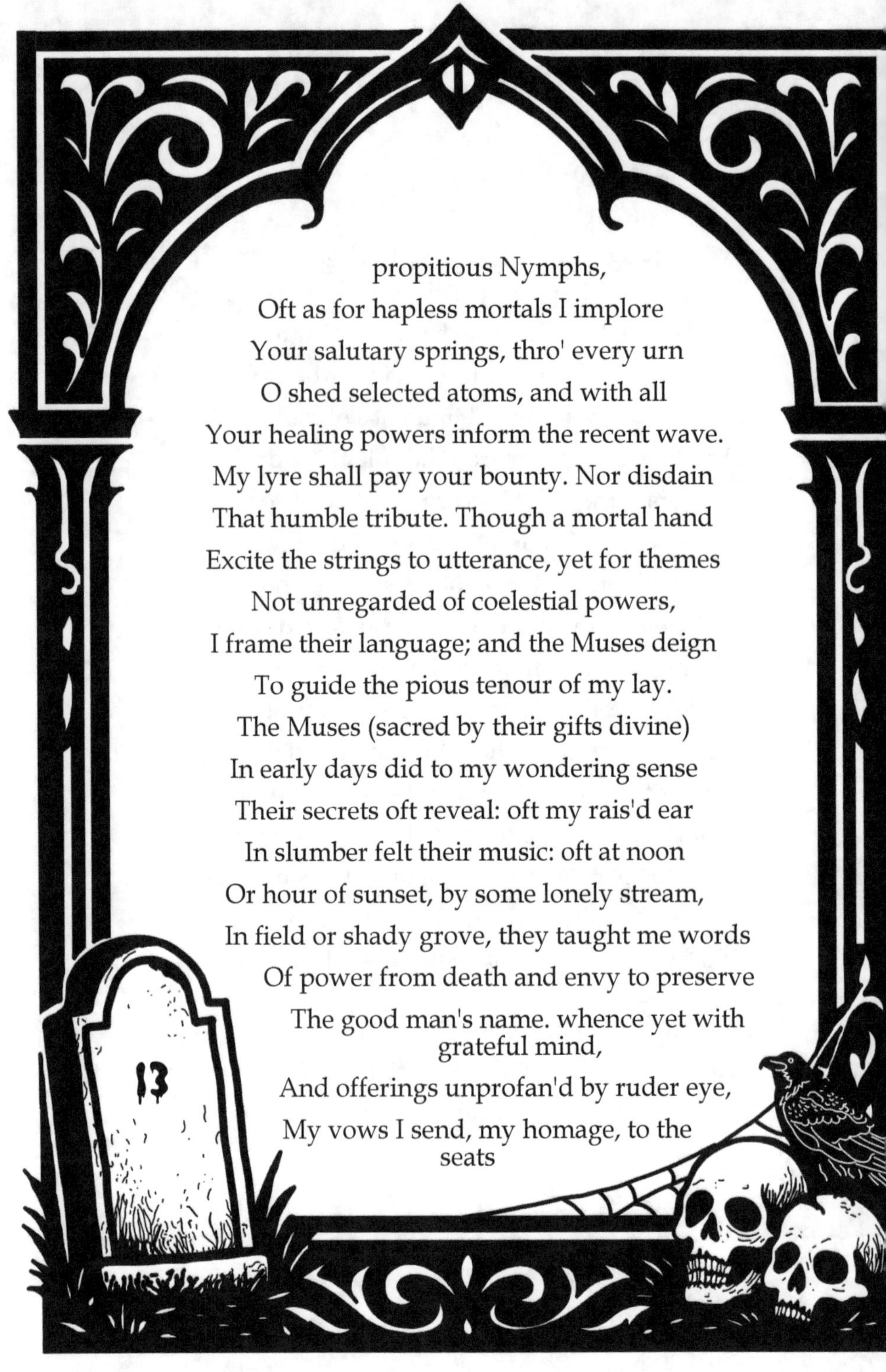

propitious Nymphs,
Oft as for hapless mortals I implore
Your salutary springs, thro' every urn
O shed selected atoms, and with all
Your healing powers inform the recent wave.
My lyre shall pay your bounty. Nor disdain
That humble tribute. Though a mortal hand
Excite the strings to utterance, yet for themes
Not unregarded of coelestial powers,
I frame their language; and the Muses deign
To guide the pious tenour of my lay.
The Muses (sacred by their gifts divine)
In early days did to my wondering sense
Their secrets oft reveal: oft my rais'd ear
In slumber felt their music: oft at noon
Or hour of sunset, by some lonely stream,
In field or shady grove, they taught me words
Of power from death and envy to preserve
The good man's name. whence yet with grateful mind,
And offerings unprofan'd by ruder eye,
My vows I send, my homage, to the seats

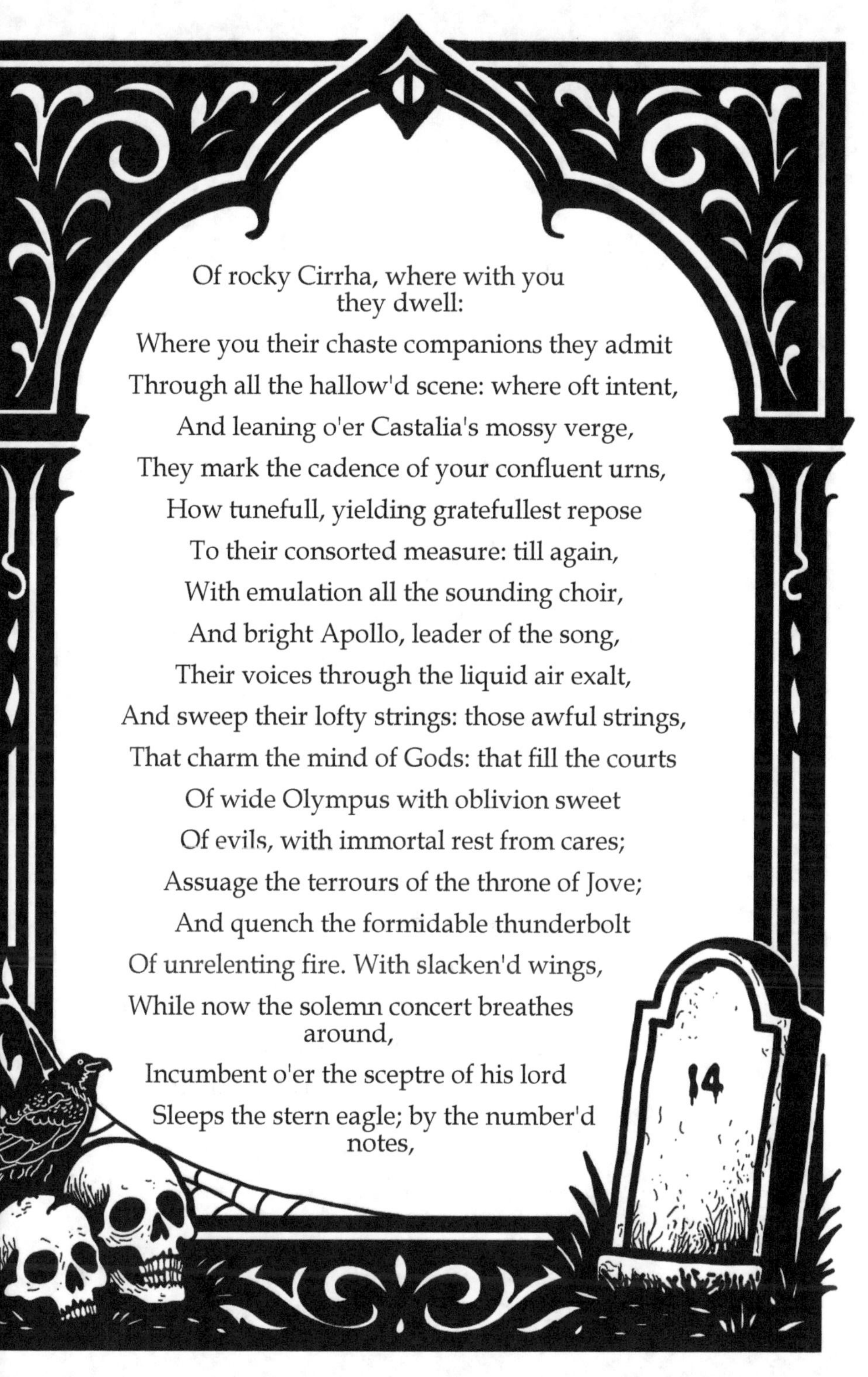

Of rocky Cirrha, where with you they dwell:
Where you their chaste companions they admit
Through all the hallow'd scene: where oft intent,
And leaning o'er Castalia's mossy verge,
They mark the cadence of your confluent urns,
How tunefull, yielding gratefullest repose
To their consorted measure: till again,
With emulation all the sounding choir,
And bright Apollo, leader of the song,
Their voices through the liquid air exalt,
And sweep their lofty strings: those awful strings,
That charm the mind of Gods: that fill the courts
Of wide Olympus with oblivion sweet
Of evils, with immortal rest from cares;
Assuage the terrours of the throne of Jove;
And quench the formidable thunderbolt
Of unrelenting fire. With slacken'd wings,
While now the solemn concert breathes around,
Incumbent o'er the sceptre of his lord
Sleeps the stern eagle; by the number'd notes,

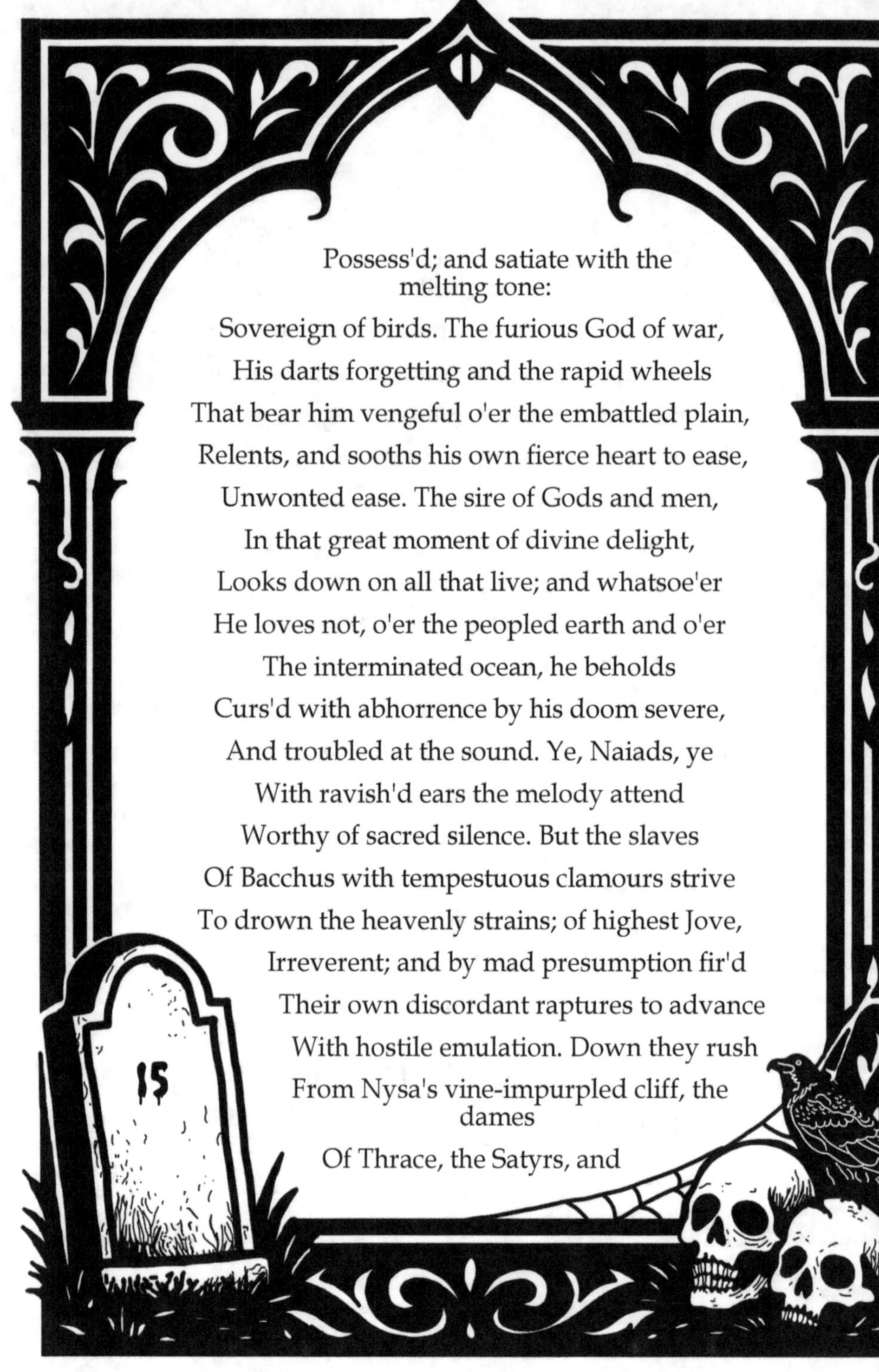

Possess'd; and satiate with the melting tone:
Sovereign of birds. The furious God of war,
His darts forgetting and the rapid wheels
That bear him vengeful o'er the embattled plain,
Relents, and sooths his own fierce heart to ease,
Unwonted ease. The sire of Gods and men,
In that great moment of divine delight,
Looks down on all that live; and whatsoe'er
He loves not, o'er the peopled earth and o'er
The interminated ocean, he beholds
Curs'd with abhorrence by his doom severe,
And troubled at the sound. Ye, Naiads, ye
With ravish'd ears the melody attend
Worthy of sacred silence. But the slaves
Of Bacchus with tempestuous clamours strive
To drown the heavenly strains; of highest Jove,
Irreverent; and by mad presumption fir'd
Their own discordant raptures to advance
With hostile emulation. Down they rush
From Nysa's vine-impurpled cliff, the dames
Of Thrace, the Satyrs, and

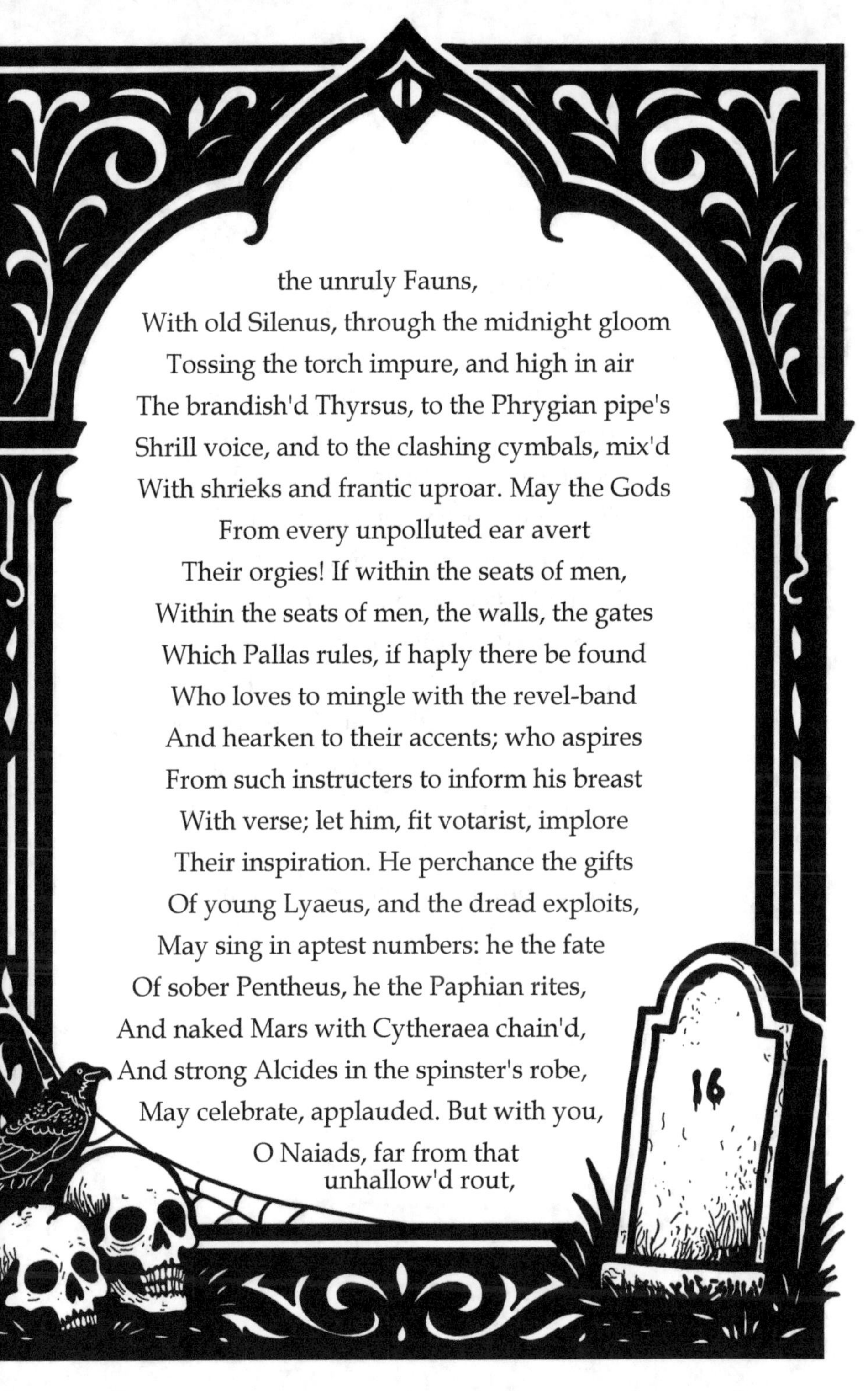

the unruly Fauns,
With old Silenus, through the midnight gloom
Tossing the torch impure, and high in air
The brandish'd Thyrsus, to the Phrygian pipe's
Shrill voice, and to the clashing cymbals, mix'd
With shrieks and frantic uproar. May the Gods
From every unpolluted ear avert
Their orgies! If within the seats of men,
Within the seats of men, the walls, the gates
Which Pallas rules, if haply there be found
Who loves to mingle with the revel-band
And hearken to their accents; who aspires
From such instructers to inform his breast
With verse; let him, fit votarist, implore
Their inspiration. He perchance the gifts
Of young Lyaeus, and the dread exploits,
May sing in aptest numbers: he the fate
Of sober Pentheus, he the Paphian rites,
And naked Mars with Cytheraea chain'd,
And strong Alcides in the spinster's robe,
May celebrate, applauded. But with you,
O Naiads, far from that
unhallow'd rout,

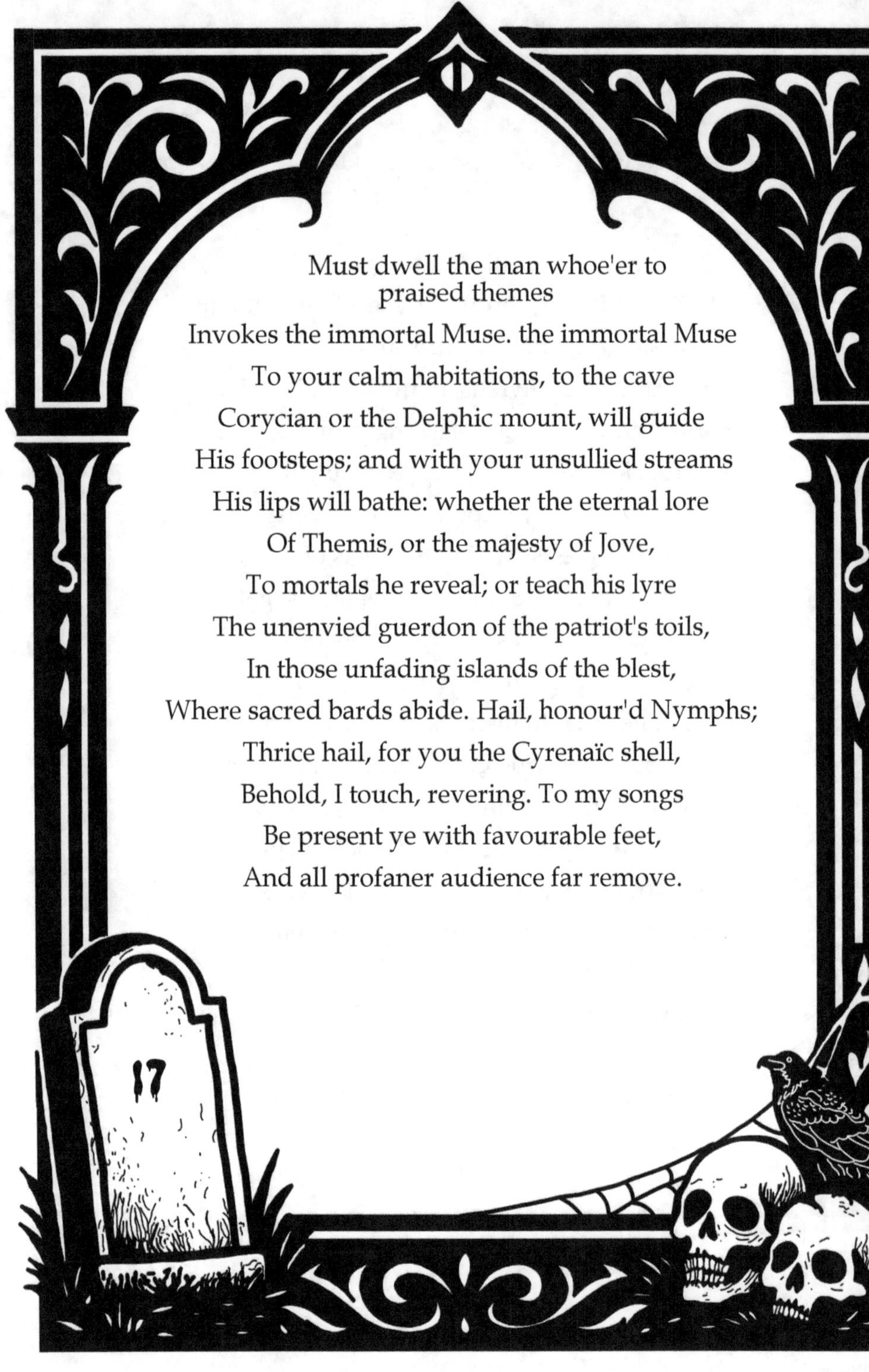

Must dwell the man whoe'er to
praised themes
Invokes the immortal Muse. the immortal Muse
To your calm habitations, to the cave
Corycian or the Delphic mount, will guide
His footsteps; and with your unsullied streams
His lips will bathe: whether the eternal lore
Of Themis, or the majesty of Jove,
To mortals he reveal; or teach his lyre
The unenvied guerdon of the patriot's toils,
In those unfading islands of the blest,
Where sacred bards abide. Hail, honour'd Nymphs;
Thrice hail, for you the Cyrenaïc shell,
Behold, I touch, revering. To my songs
Be present ye with favourable feet,
And all profaner audience far remove.

Charles Baudelaire

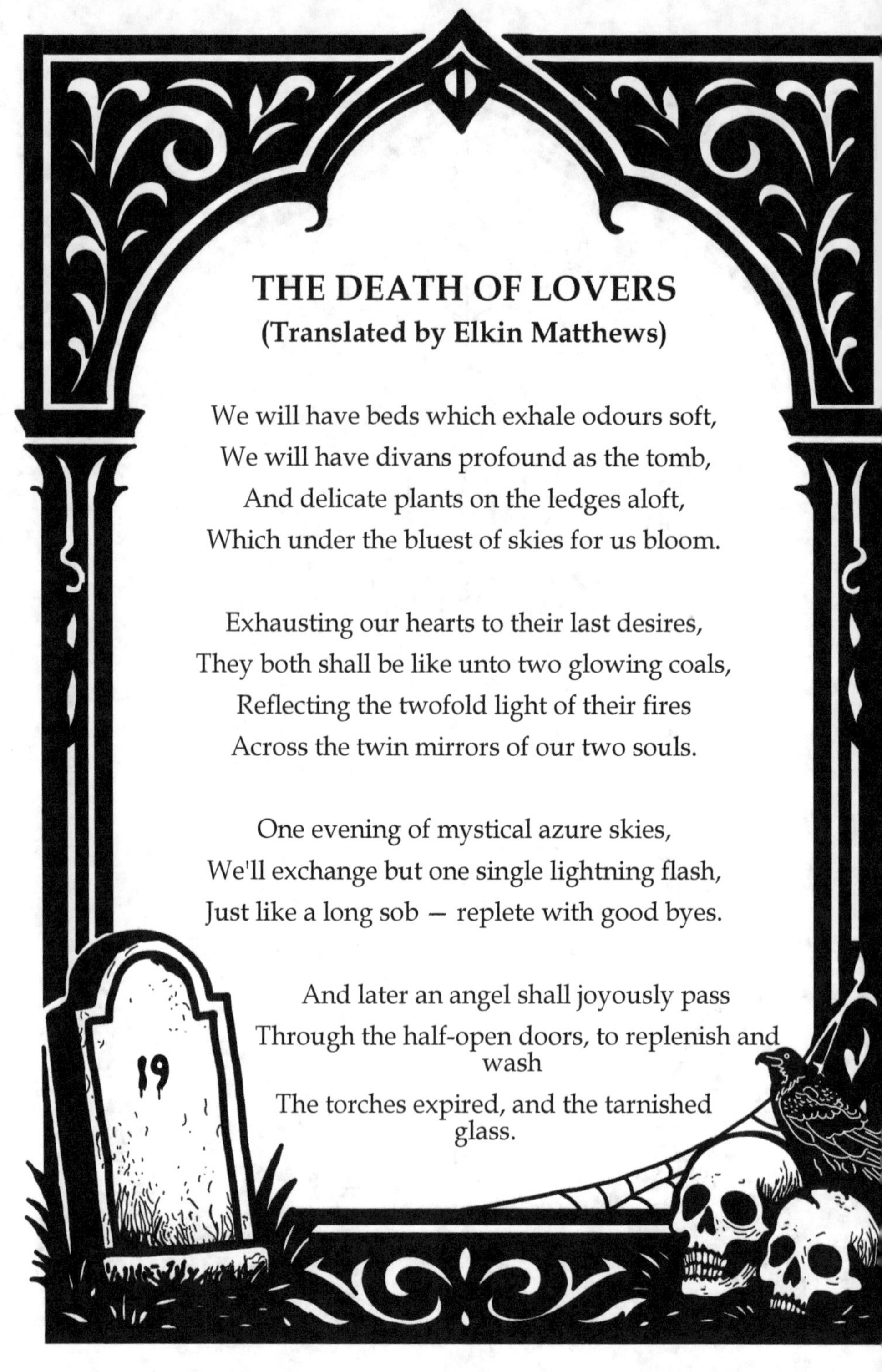

THE DEATH OF LOVERS

(Translated by Elkin Matthews)

We will have beds which exhale odours soft,
We will have divans profound as the tomb,
And delicate plants on the ledges aloft,
Which under the bluest of skies for us bloom.

Exhausting our hearts to their last desires,
They both shall be like unto two glowing coals,
Reflecting the twofold light of their fires
Across the twin mirrors of our two souls.

One evening of mystical azure skies,
We'll exchange but one single lightning flash,
Just like a long sob — replete with good byes.

And later an angel shall joyously pass
Through the half-open doors, to replenish and wash
The torches expired, and the tarnished glass.

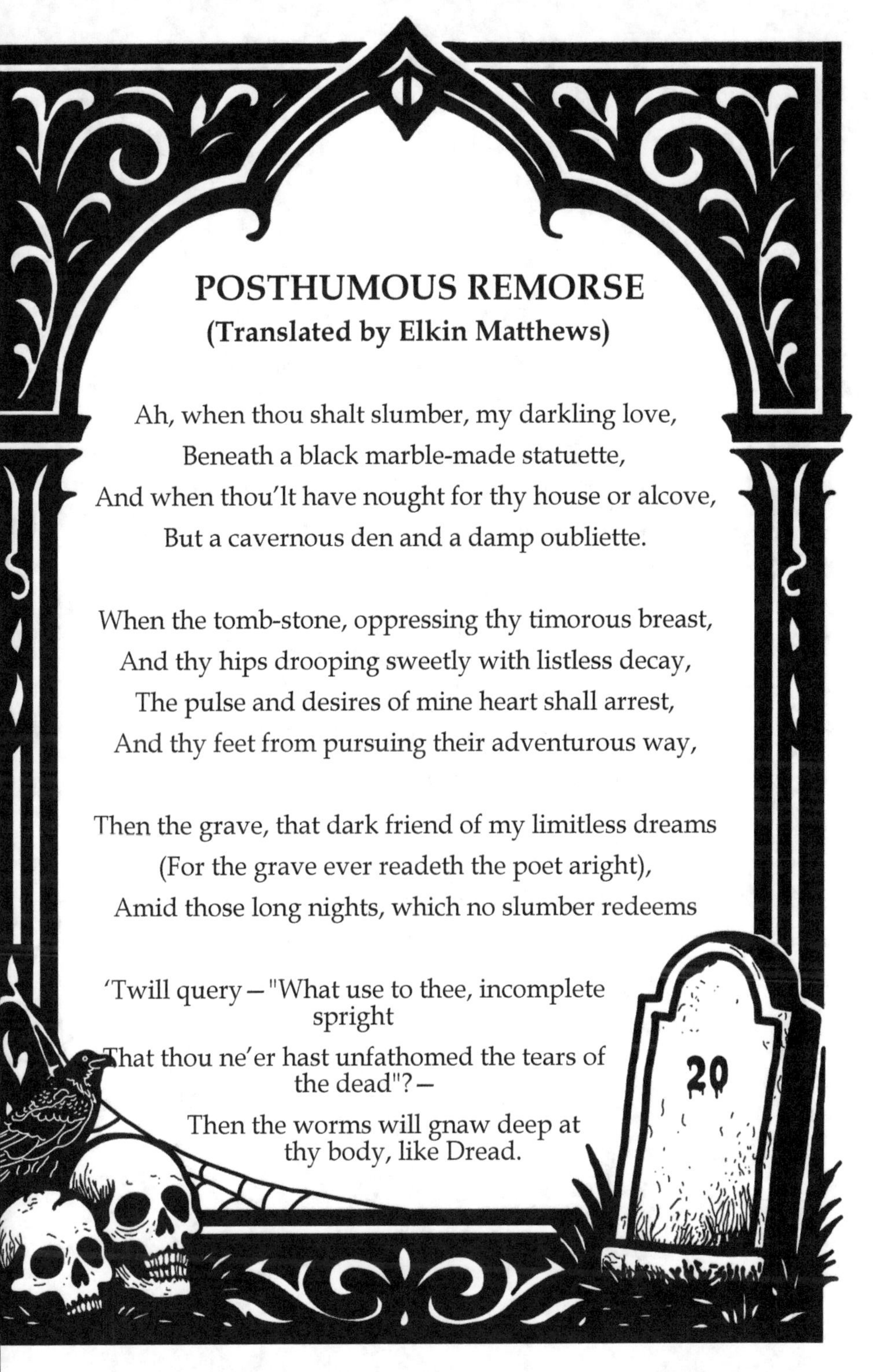

POSTHUMOUS REMORSE

(Translated by Elkin Matthews)

Ah, when thou shalt slumber, my darkling love,
Beneath a black marble-made statuette,
And when thou'lt have nought for thy house or alcove,
But a cavernous den and a damp oubliette.

When the tomb-stone, oppressing thy timorous breast,
And thy hips drooping sweetly with listless decay,
The pulse and desires of mine heart shall arrest,
And thy feet from pursuing their adventurous way,

Then the grave, that dark friend of my limitless dreams
(For the grave ever readeth the poet aright),
Amid those long nights, which no slumber redeems

'Twill query—"What use to thee, incomplete spright
That thou ne'er hast unfathomed the tears of the dead"?—
Then the worms will gnaw deep at thy body, like Dread.

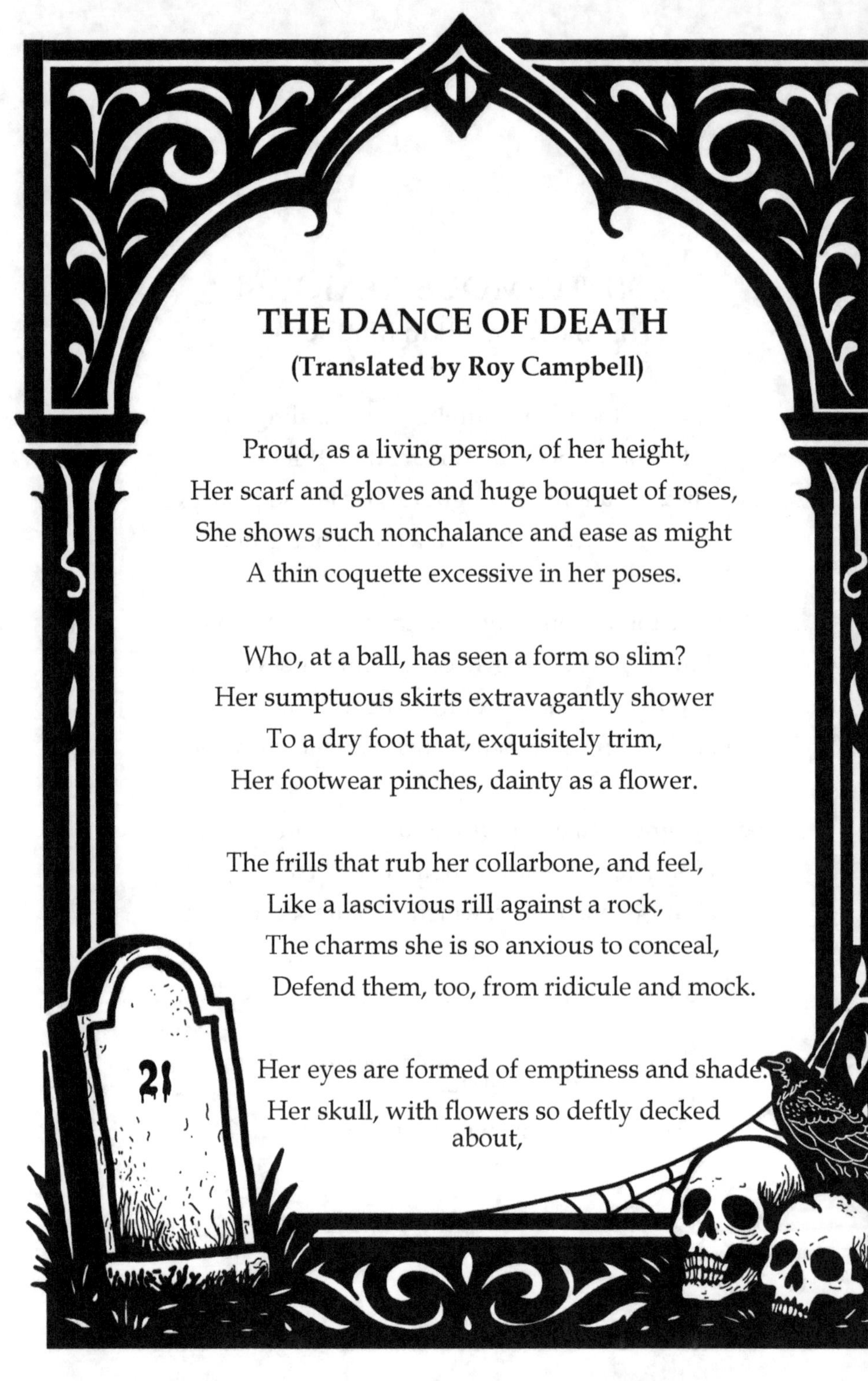

THE DANCE OF DEATH

(Translated by Roy Campbell)

Proud, as a living person, of her height,
Her scarf and gloves and huge bouquet of roses,
She shows such nonchalance and ease as might
A thin coquette excessive in her poses.

Who, at a ball, has seen a form so slim?
Her sumptuous skirts extravagantly shower
To a dry foot that, exquisitely trim,
Her footwear pinches, dainty as a flower.

The frills that rub her collarbone, and feel,
Like a lascivious rill against a rock,
The charms she is so anxious to conceal,
Defend them, too, from ridicule and mock.

Her eyes are formed of emptiness and shade.
Her skull, with flowers so deftly decked about,

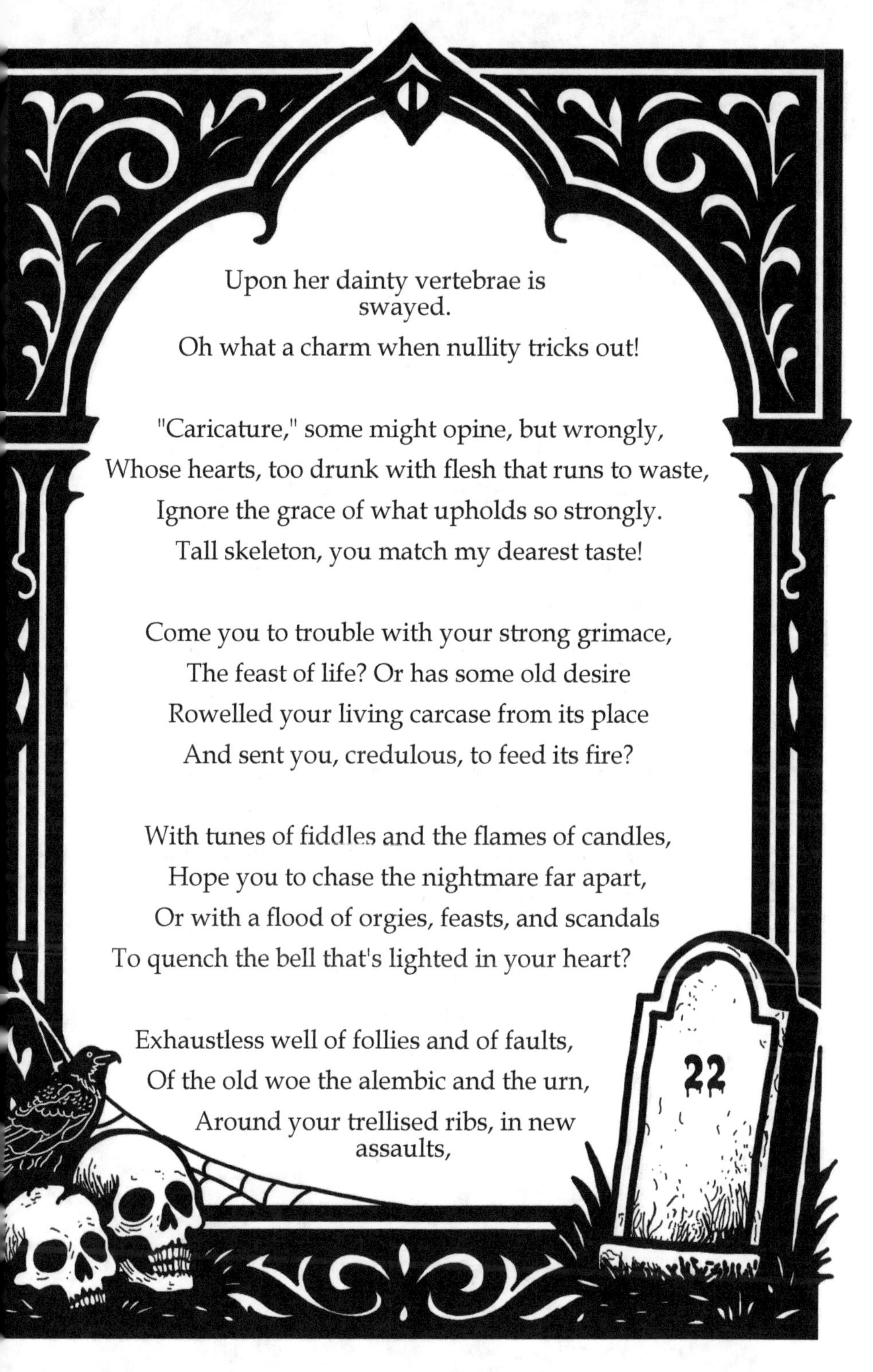

Upon her dainty vertebrae is
swayed.
Oh what a charm when nullity tricks out!

"Caricature," some might opine, but wrongly,
Whose hearts, too drunk with flesh that runs to waste,
Ignore the grace of what upholds so strongly.
Tall skeleton, you match my dearest taste!

Come you to trouble with your strong grimace,
The feast of life? Or has some old desire
Rowelled your living carcase from its place
And sent you, credulous, to feed its fire?

With tunes of fiddles and the flames of candles,
Hope you to chase the nightmare far apart,
Or with a flood of orgies, feasts, and scandals
To quench the bell that's lighted in your heart?

Exhaustless well of follies and of faults,
Of the old woe the alembic and the urn,
Around your trellised ribs, in new
assaults,

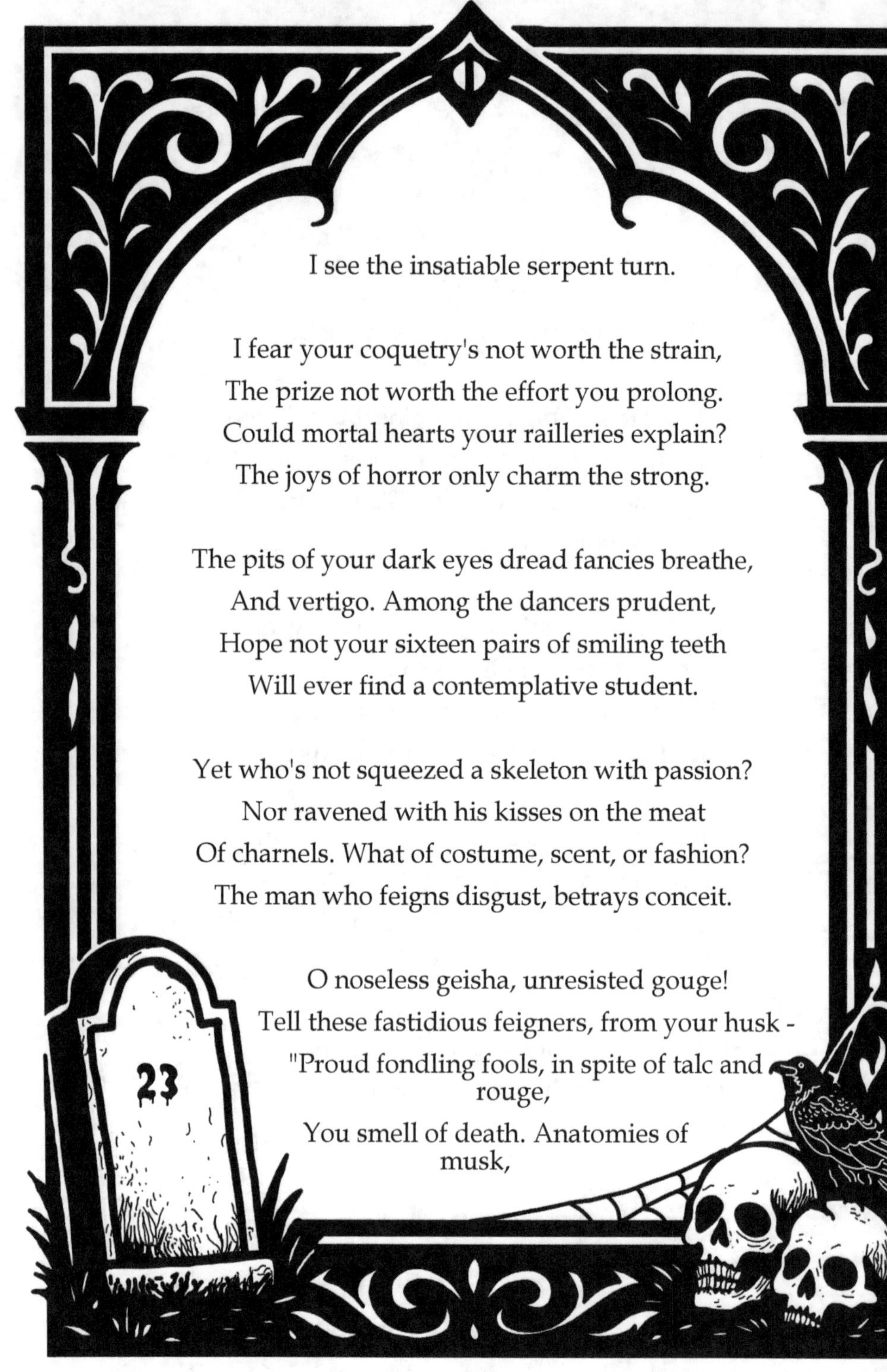

I see the insatiable serpent turn.

I fear your coquetry's not worth the strain,
The prize not worth the effort you prolong.
Could mortal hearts your railleries explain?
The joys of horror only charm the strong.

The pits of your dark eyes dread fancies breathe,
And vertigo. Among the dancers prudent,
Hope not your sixteen pairs of smiling teeth
Will ever find a contemplative student.

Yet who's not squeezed a skeleton with passion?
Nor ravened with his kisses on the meat
Of charnels. What of costume, scent, or fashion?
The man who feigns disgust, betrays conceit.

O noseless geisha, unresisted gouge!
Tell these fastidious feigners, from your husk -
"Proud fondling fools, in spite of talc and rouge,
You smell of death. Anatomies of musk,

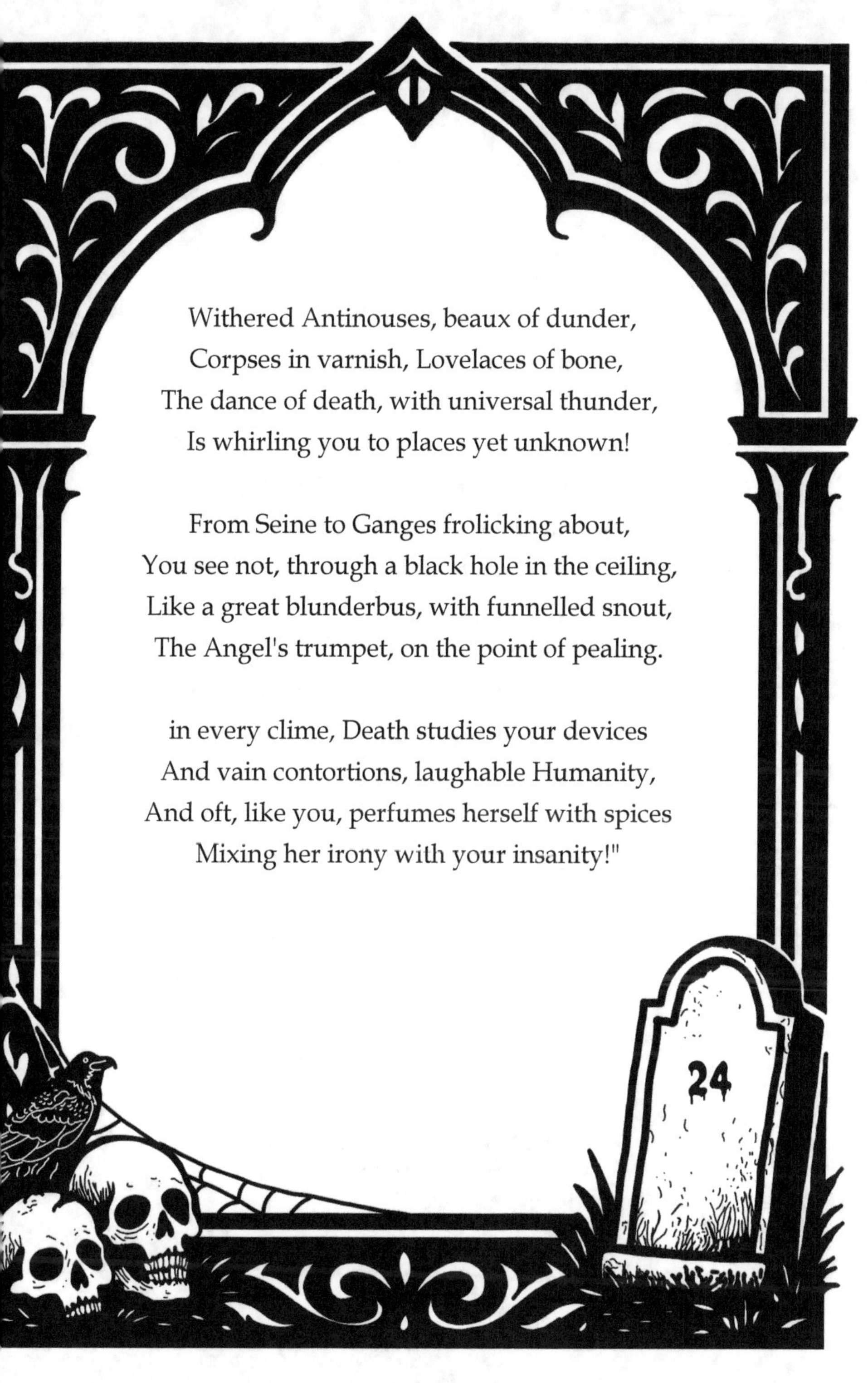

Withered Antinouses, beaux of dunder,
Corpses in varnish, Lovelaces of bone,
The dance of death, with universal thunder,
Is whirling you to places yet unknown!

From Seine to Ganges frolicking about,
You see not, through a black hole in the ceiling,
Like a great blunderbus, with funnelled snout,
The Angel's trumpet, on the point of pealing.

in every clime, Death studies your devices
And vain contortions, laughable Humanity,
And oft, like you, perfumes herself with spices
Mixing her irony with your insanity!"

SPLEEN

(Translated by Jack Collings Squire)

When the low heavy sky weighs like a lid
Upon the spirit aching for the light,
And all the wide horizon's line is hid
By a black day sadder than any night;

When the changed earth is but a dungeon dank
Where batlike Hope goes blindly fluttering
And, striking wall and roof and mouldered plank,
Bruises his tender head and timid wing;

When like grim prison-bars stretch down the thin,
Straight, rigid pillars of the endless rain,
And the dumb throngs of infamous spiders spin
Their meshes in the caverns of the brain; –

Suddenly, bells leap forth into the air,
Hurling a hideous uproar to the sky
As 'twere a band of homeless
spirits who fare

Through the strange heavens,
wailing stubbornly.

And hearses, without drum or instrument,
File slowly through my soul; crushed, sorrowful,
Weeps Hope, and Grief, fierce and omnipotent,
Plants his black banner on my drooping skull.

James Beattie

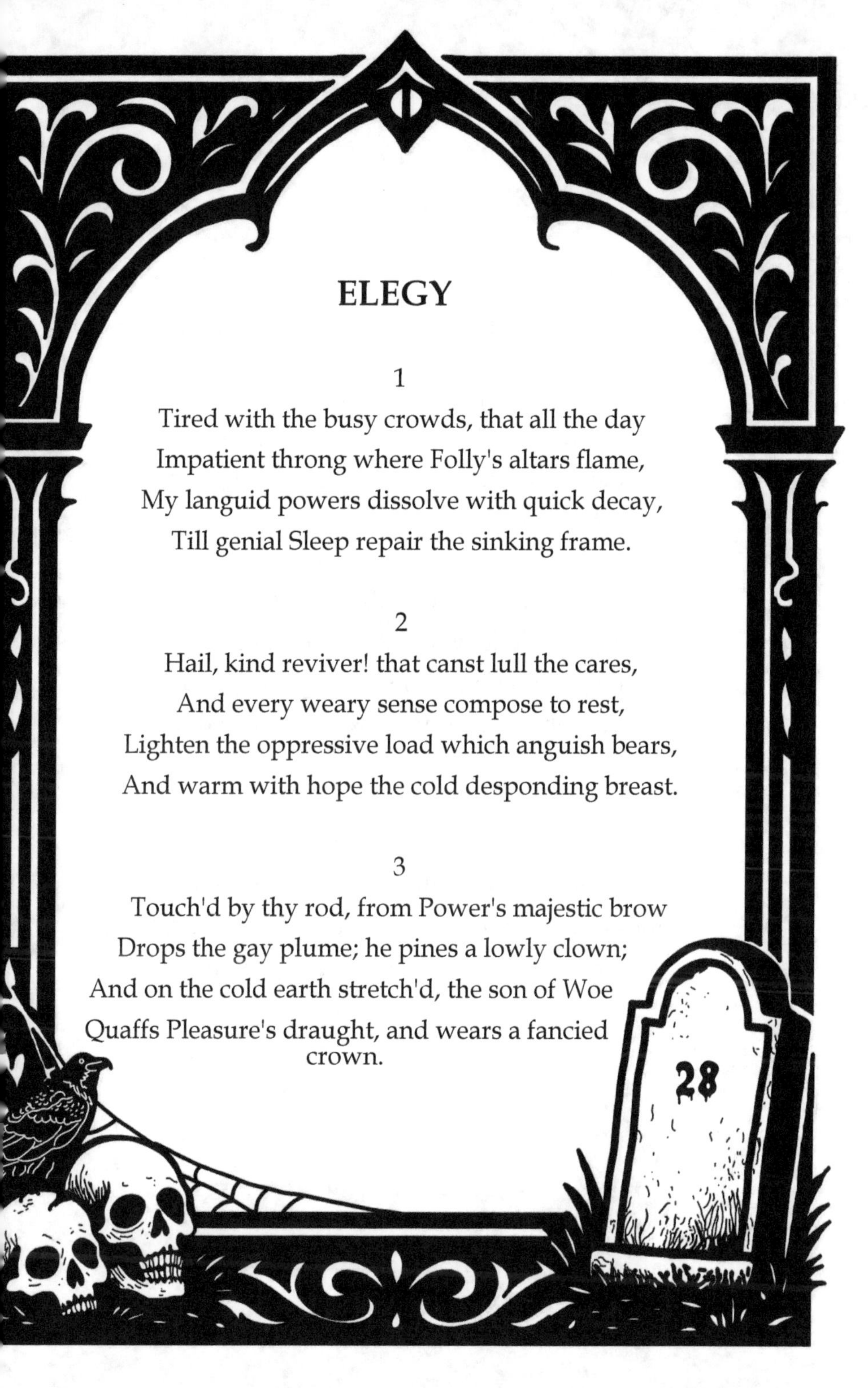

ELEGY

1

Tired with the busy crowds, that all the day
Impatient throng where Folly's altars flame,
My languid powers dissolve with quick decay,
Till genial Sleep repair the sinking frame.

2

Hail, kind reviver! that canst lull the cares,
And every weary sense compose to rest,
Lighten the oppressive load which anguish bears,
And warm with hope the cold desponding breast.

3

Touch'd by thy rod, from Power's majestic brow
Drops the gay plume; he pines a lowly clown;
And on the cold earth stretch'd, the son of Woe
Quaffs Pleasure's draught, and wears a fancied crown.

4

When roused by thee, on boundless pinions borne,
Fancy to fairy scenes exults to rove,
Now scales the cliff gay-gleaming on the morn,
Now sad and silent treads the deepening grove;

5

Or skims the main, and listens to the storms,
Marks the long waves roll far remote away;
Or, mingling with ten thousand glittering forms,
Floats on the gale, and basks in purest day.

6

Haply, ere long, pierced by the howling blast,
Through dark and pathless deserts I shall roam,
Plunge down the unfathom'd deep, or shrink aghast
Where bursts the shrieking spectre from the tomb:

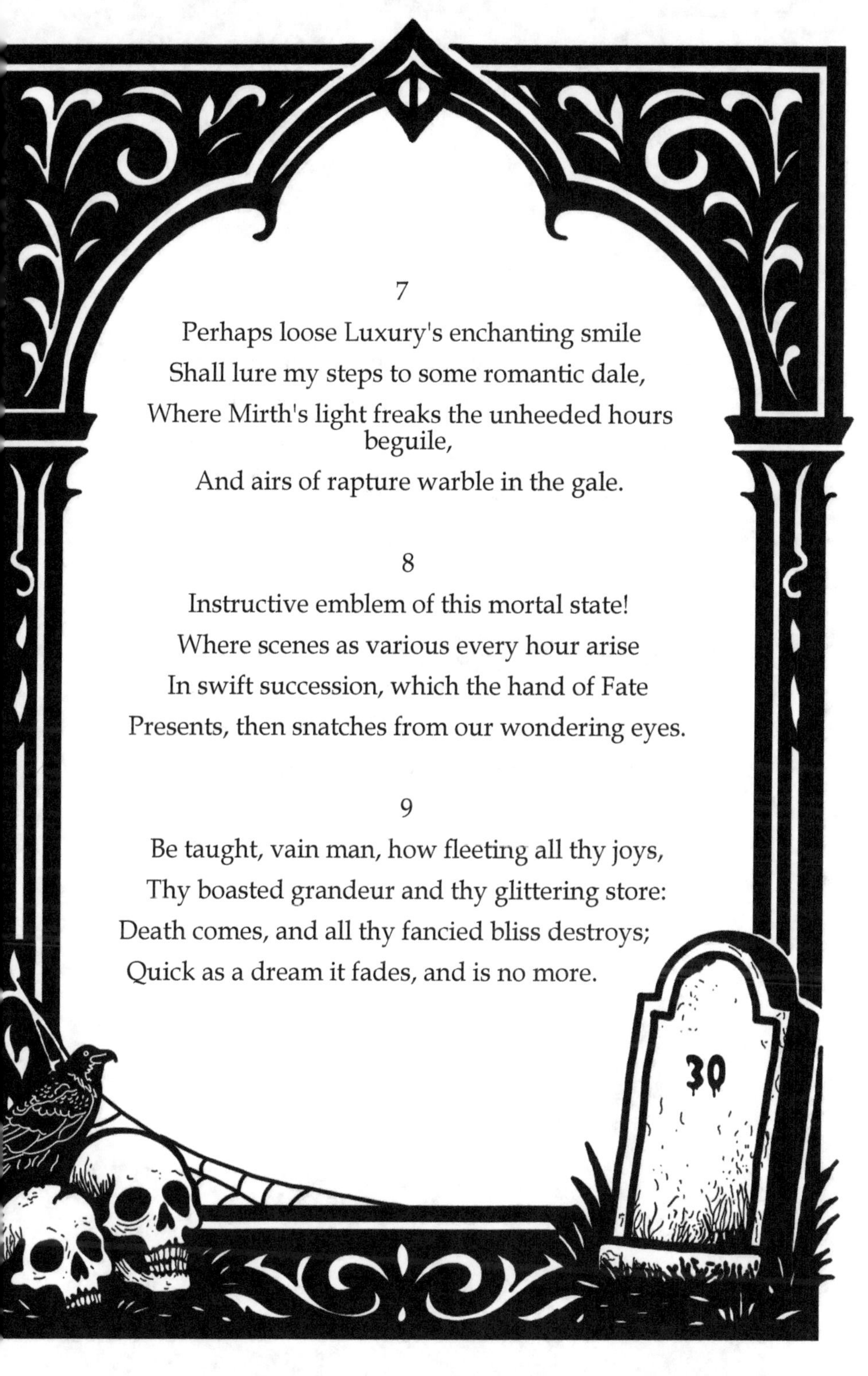

7

Perhaps loose Luxury's enchanting smile
Shall lure my steps to some romantic dale,
Where Mirth's light freaks the unheeded hours beguile,
And airs of rapture warble in the gale.

8

Instructive emblem of this mortal state!
Where scenes as various every hour arise
In swift succession, which the hand of Fate
Presents, then snatches from our wondering eyes.

9

Be taught, vain man, how fleeting all thy joys,
Thy boasted grandeur and thy glittering store:
Death comes, and all thy fancied bliss destroys;
Quick as a dream it fades, and is no more.

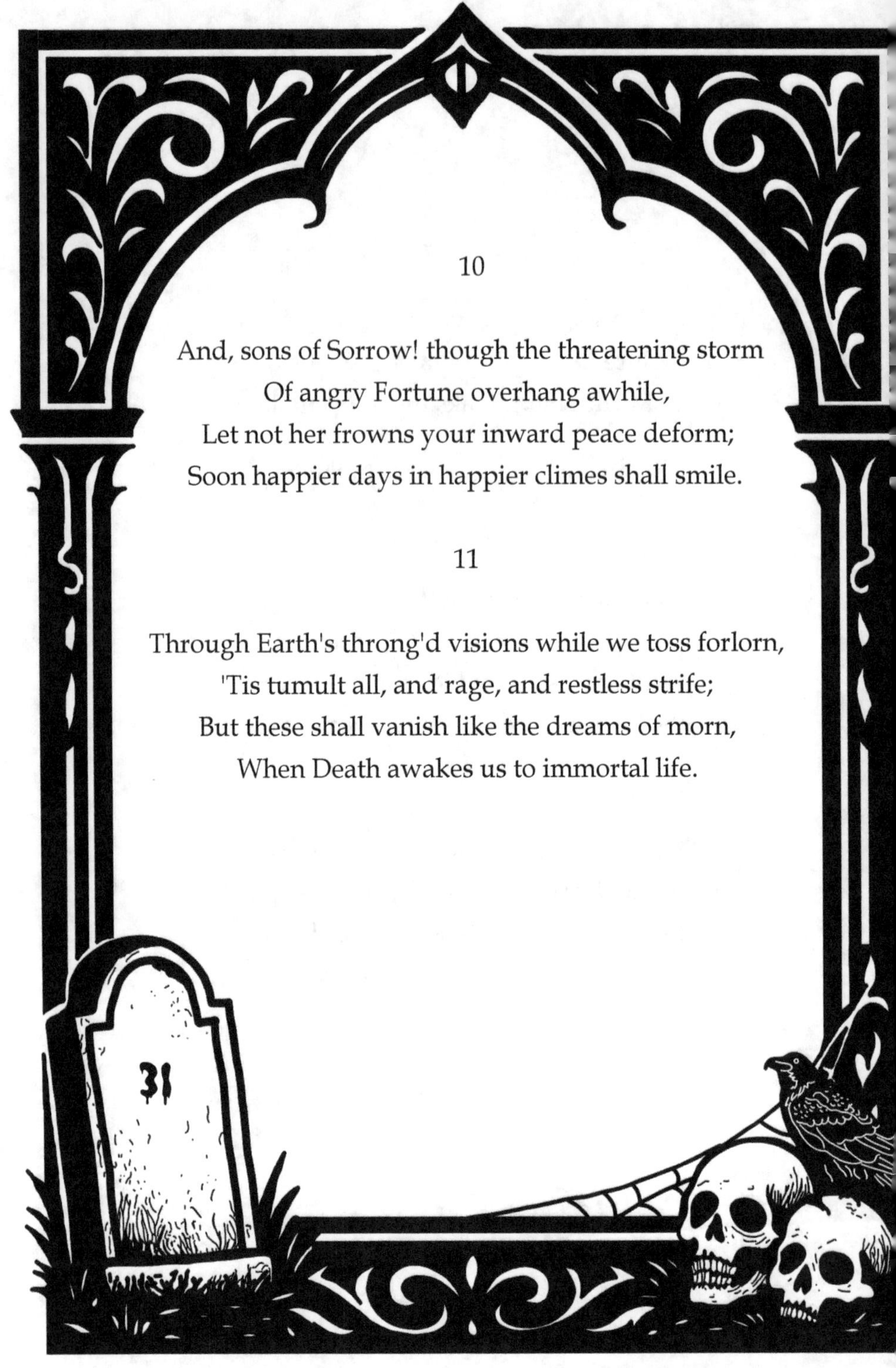

10

And, sons of Sorrow! though the threatening storm
Of angry Fortune overhang awhile,
Let not her frowns your inward peace deform;
Soon happier days in happier climes shall smile.

11

Through Earth's throng'd visions while we toss forlorn,
'Tis tumult all, and rage, and restless strife;
But these shall vanish like the dreams of morn,
When Death awakes us to immortal life.

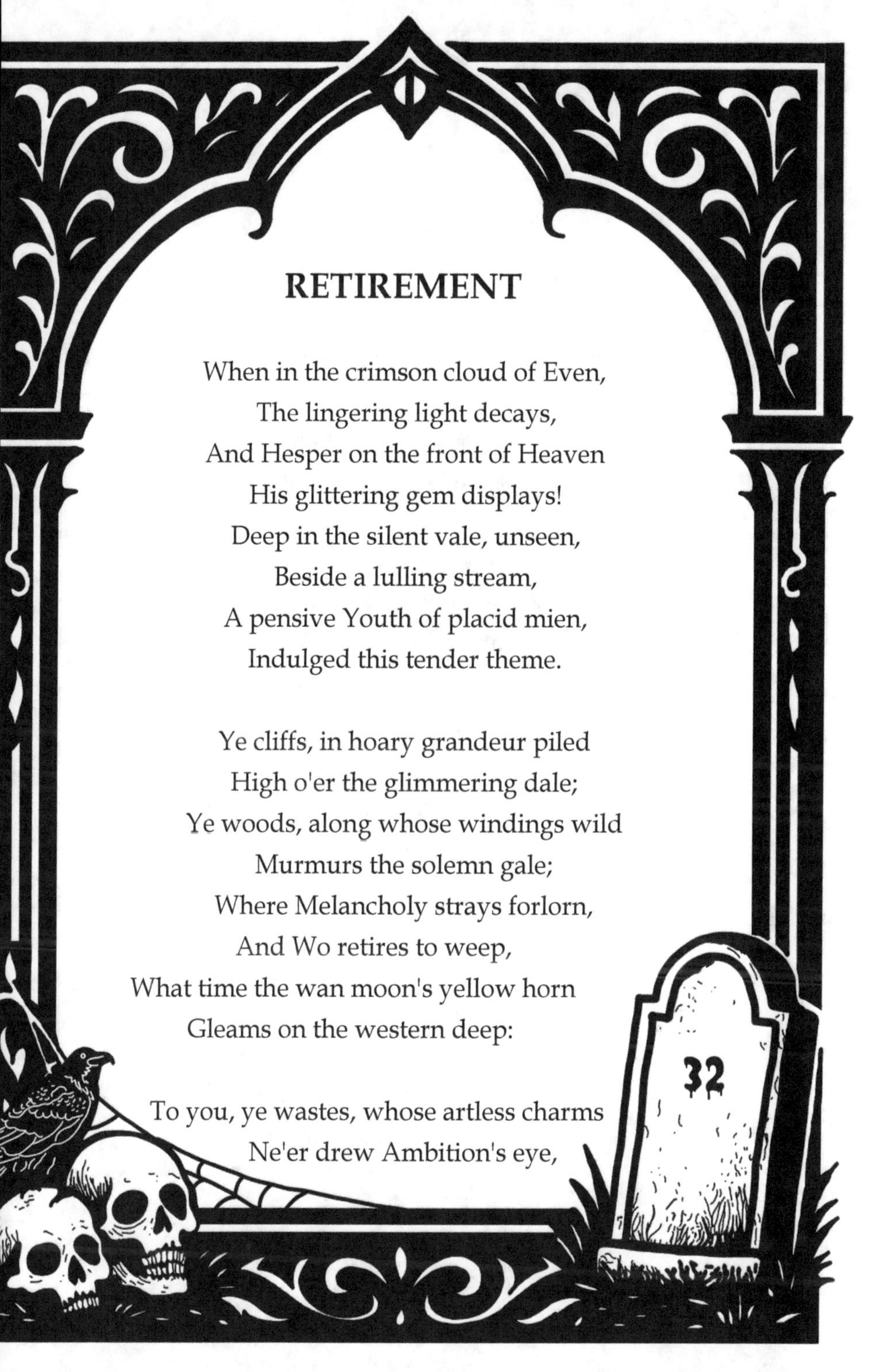

RETIREMENT

When in the crimson cloud of Even,
The lingering light decays,
And Hesper on the front of Heaven
His glittering gem displays!
Deep in the silent vale, unseen,
Beside a lulling stream,
A pensive Youth of placid mien,
Indulged this tender theme.

Ye cliffs, in hoary grandeur piled
High o'er the glimmering dale;
Ye woods, along whose windings wild
Murmurs the solemn gale;
Where Melancholy strays forlorn,
And Wo retires to weep,
What time the wan moon's yellow horn
Gleams on the western deep:

To you, ye wastes, whose artless charms
Ne'er drew Ambition's eye,

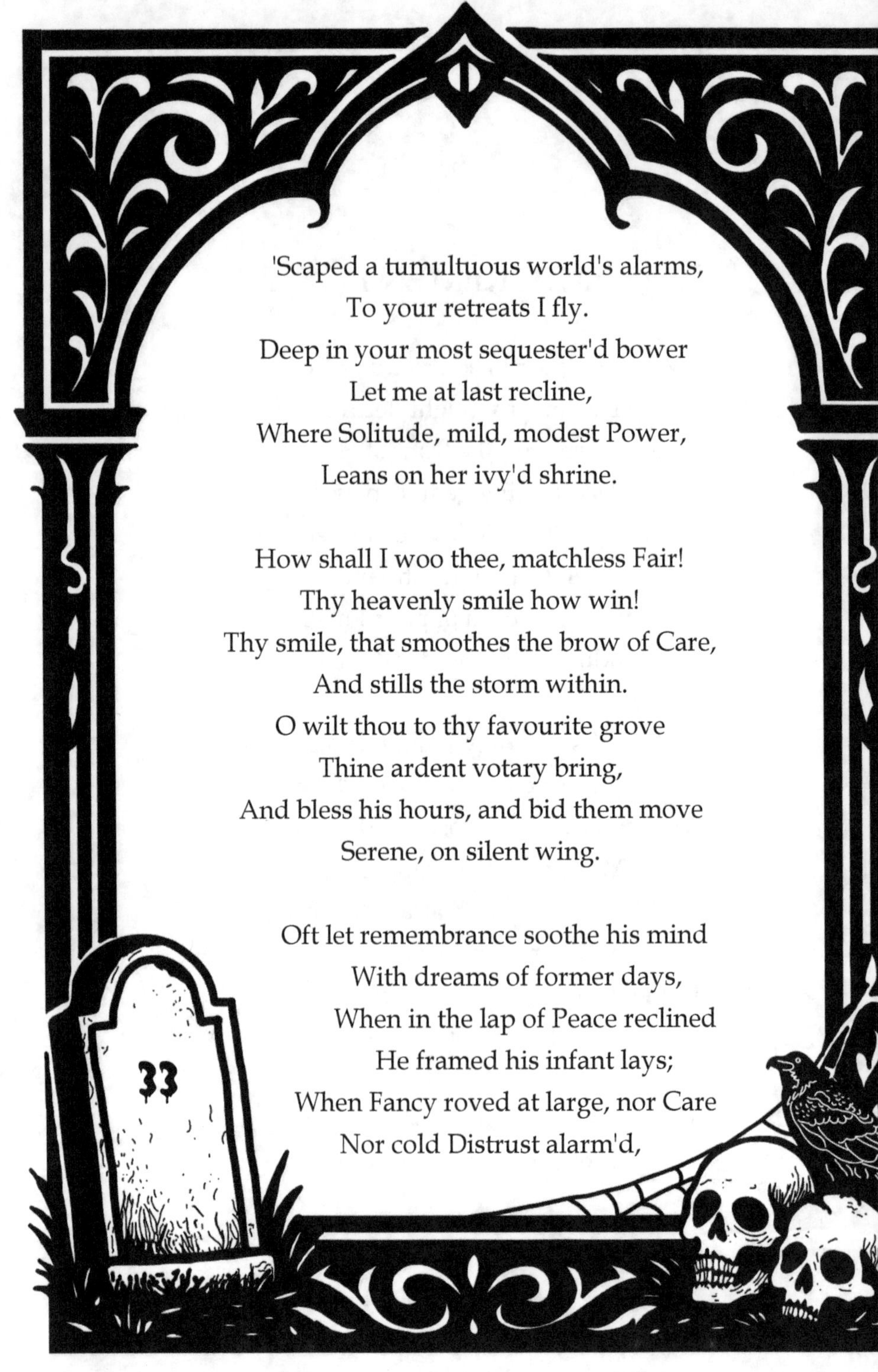

'Scaped a tumultuous world's alarms,
To your retreats I fly.
Deep in your most sequester'd bower
Let me at last recline,
Where Solitude, mild, modest Power,
Leans on her ivy'd shrine.

How shall I woo thee, matchless Fair!
Thy heavenly smile how win!
Thy smile, that smoothes the brow of Care,
And stills the storm within.
O wilt thou to thy favourite grove
Thine ardent votary bring,
And bless his hours, and bid them move
Serene, on silent wing.

Oft let remembrance soothe his mind
With dreams of former days,
When in the lap of Peace reclined
He framed his infant lays;
When Fancy roved at large, nor Care
Nor cold Distrust alarm'd,

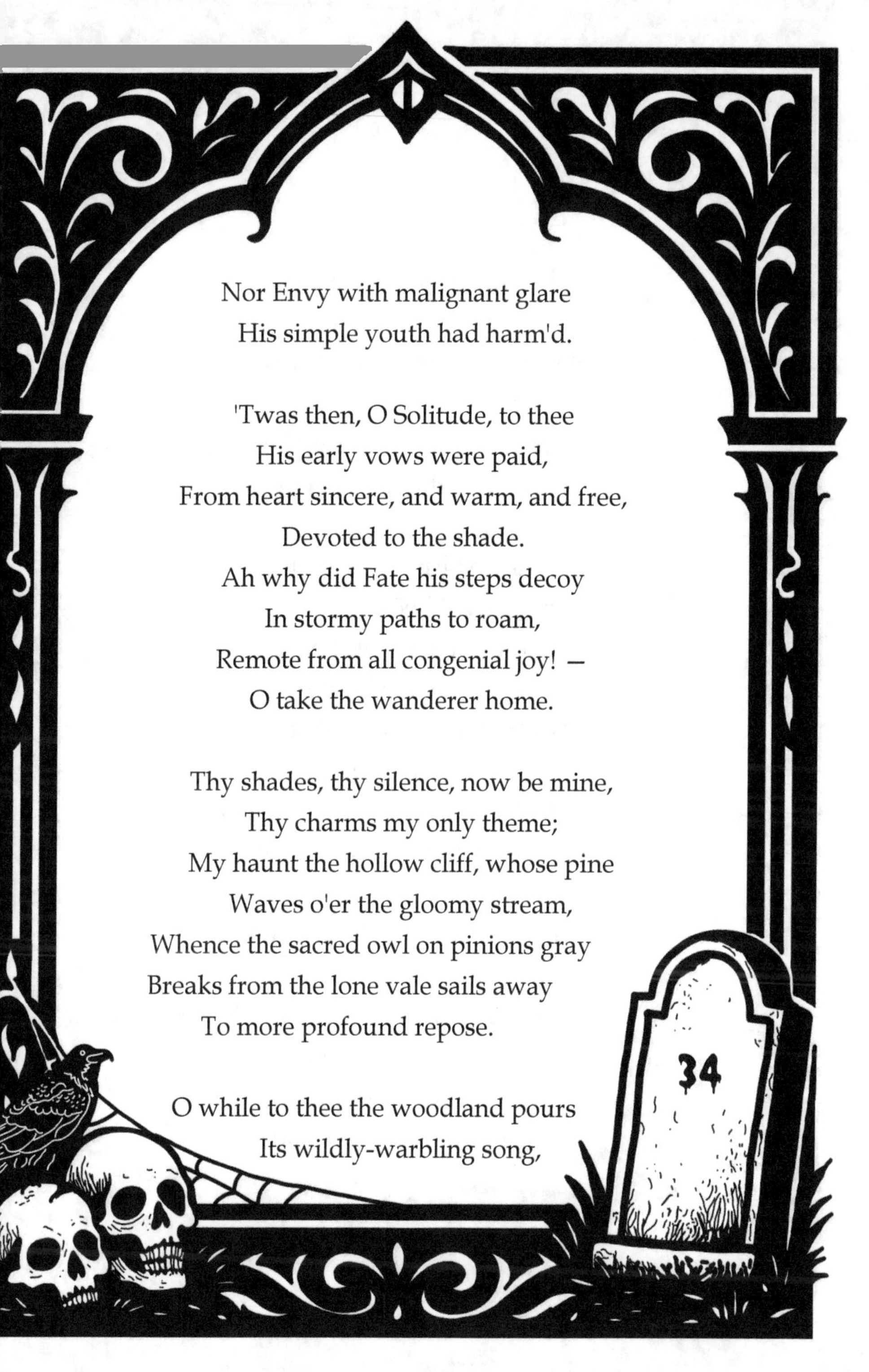

Nor Envy with malignant glare
His simple youth had harm'd.

'Twas then, O Solitude, to thee
His early vows were paid,
From heart sincere, and warm, and free,
Devoted to the shade.
Ah why did Fate his steps decoy
In stormy paths to roam,
Remote from all congenial joy! –
O take the wanderer home.

Thy shades, thy silence, now be mine,
Thy charms my only theme;
My haunt the hollow cliff, whose pine
Waves o'er the gloomy stream,
Whence the sacred owl on pinions gray
Breaks from the lone vale sails away
To more profound repose.

O while to thee the woodland pours
Its wildly-warbling song,

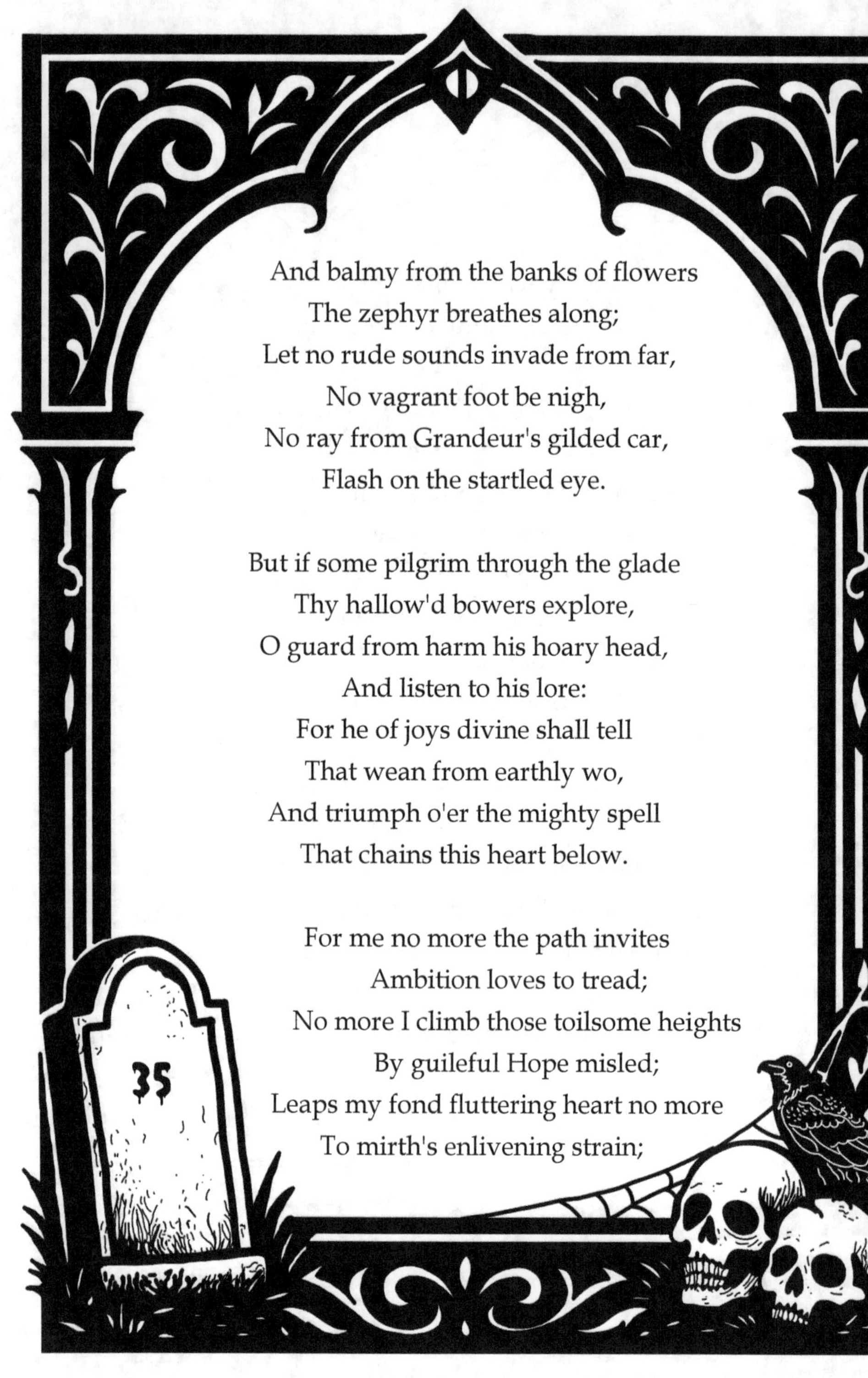

And balmy from the banks of flowers
The zephyr breathes along;
Let no rude sounds invade from far,
No vagrant foot be nigh,
No ray from Grandeur's gilded car,
Flash on the startled eye.

But if some pilgrim through the glade
Thy hallow'd bowers explore,
O guard from harm his hoary head,
And listen to his lore:
For he of joys divine shall tell
That wean from earthly wo,
And triumph o'er the mighty spell
That chains this heart below.

For me no more the path invites
Ambition loves to tread;
No more I climb those toilsome heights
By guileful Hope misled;
Leaps my fond fluttering heart no more
To mirth's enlivening strain;

For present pleasure soon is o'er,
And all the past is vain.

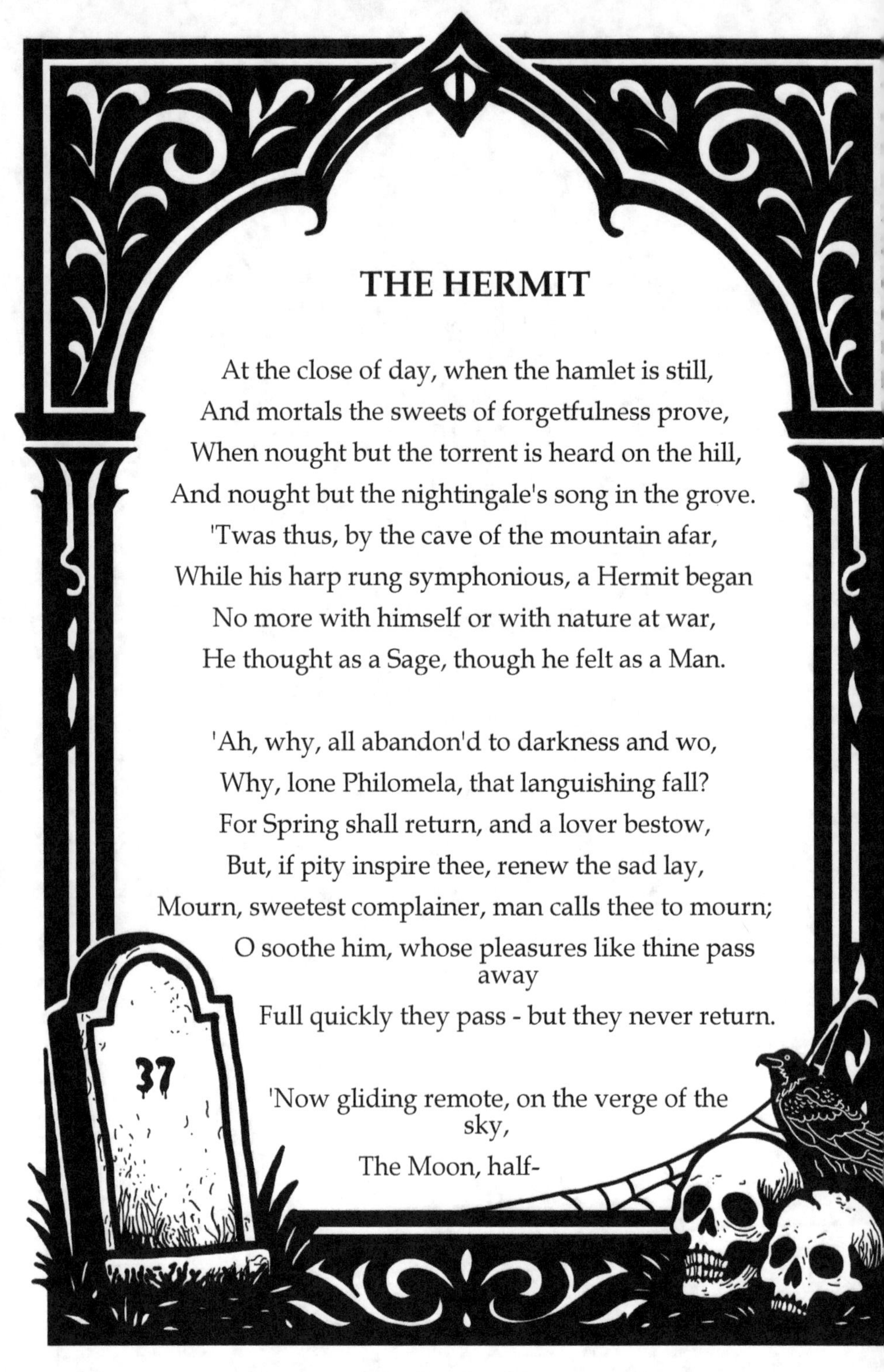

THE HERMIT

At the close of day, when the hamlet is still,
And mortals the sweets of forgetfulness prove,
When nought but the torrent is heard on the hill,
And nought but the nightingale's song in the grove.
'Twas thus, by the cave of the mountain afar,
While his harp rung symphonious, a Hermit began
No more with himself or with nature at war,
He thought as a Sage, though he felt as a Man.

'Ah, why, all abandon'd to darkness and wo,
Why, lone Philomela, that languishing fall?
For Spring shall return, and a lover bestow,
But, if pity inspire thee, renew the sad lay,
Mourn, sweetest complainer, man calls thee to mourn;
O soothe him, whose pleasures like thine pass away
Full quickly they pass - but they never return.

'Now gliding remote, on the verge of the sky,
The Moon, half-

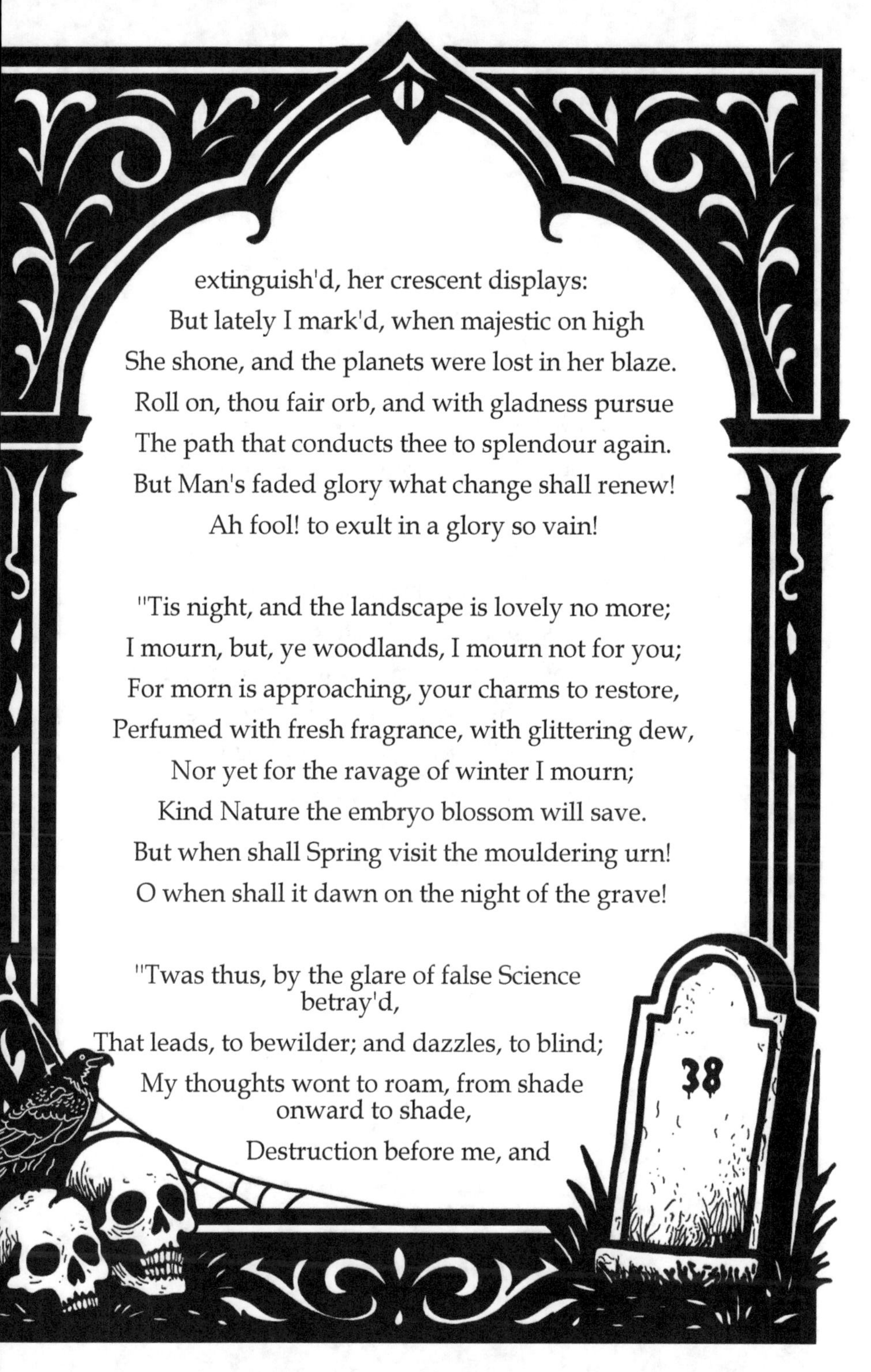

extinguish'd, her crescent displays:
But lately I mark'd, when majestic on high
She shone, and the planets were lost in her blaze.
Roll on, thou fair orb, and with gladness pursue
The path that conducts thee to splendour again.
But Man's faded glory what change shall renew!
Ah fool! to exult in a glory so vain!

"Tis night, and the landscape is lovely no more;
I mourn, but, ye woodlands, I mourn not for you;
For morn is approaching, your charms to restore,
Perfumed with fresh fragrance, with glittering dew,
Nor yet for the ravage of winter I mourn;
Kind Nature the embryo blossom will save.
But when shall Spring visit the mouldering urn!
O when shall it dawn on the night of the grave!

"Twas thus, by the glare of false Science betray'd,
That leads, to bewilder; and dazzles, to blind;
My thoughts wont to roam, from shade onward to shade,
Destruction before me, and

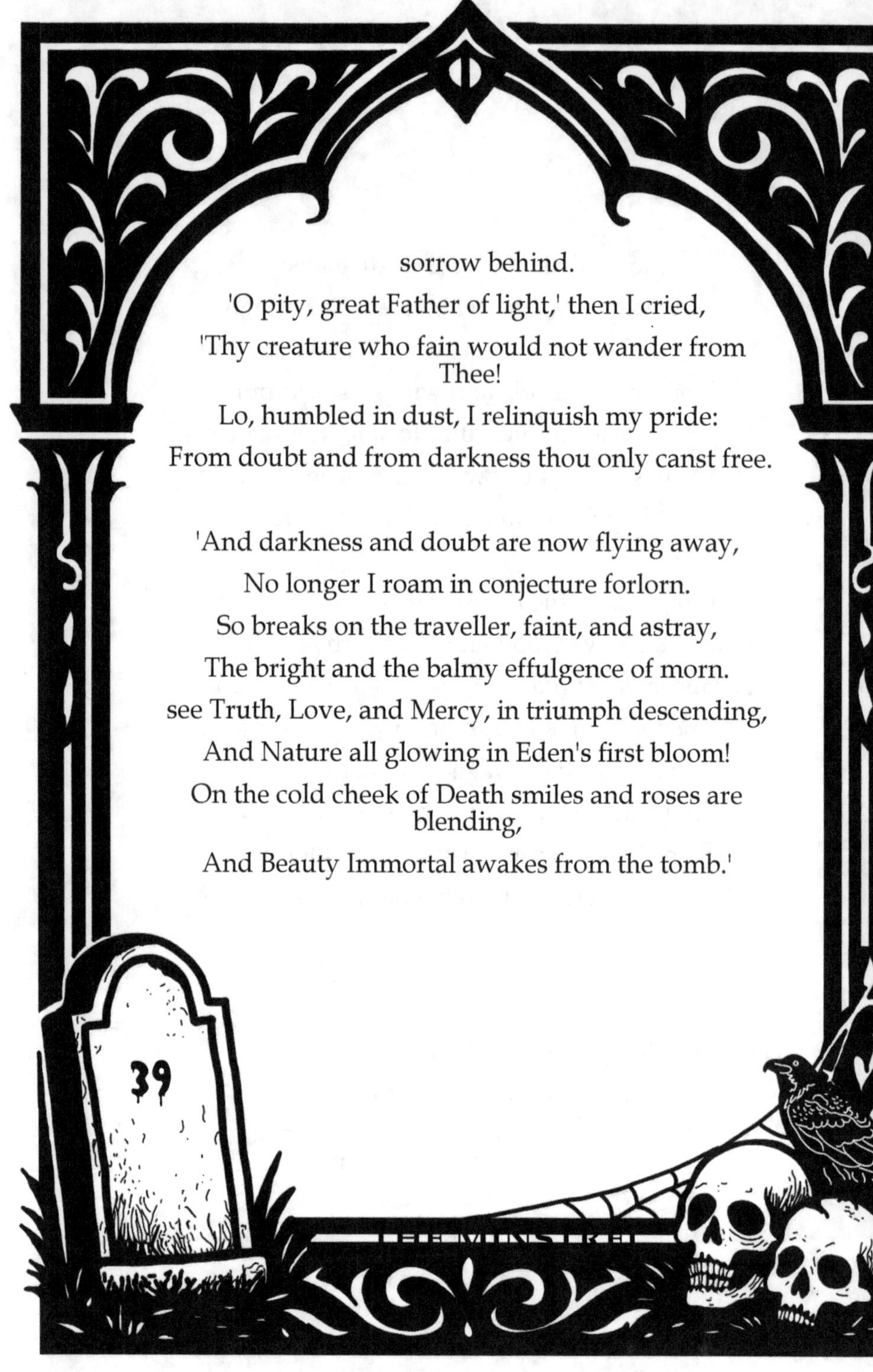

sorrow behind.

'O pity, great Father of light,' then I cried,
'Thy creature who fain would not wander from Thee!
Lo, humbled in dust, I relinquish my pride:
From doubt and from darkness thou only canst free.

'And darkness and doubt are now flying away,
No longer I roam in conjecture forlorn.
So breaks on the traveller, faint, and astray,
The bright and the balmy effulgence of morn.
see Truth, Love, and Mercy, in triumph descending,
And Nature all glowing in Eden's first bloom!
On the cold cheek of Death smiles and roses are blending,
And Beauty Immortal awakes from the tomb.'

Robert Blair

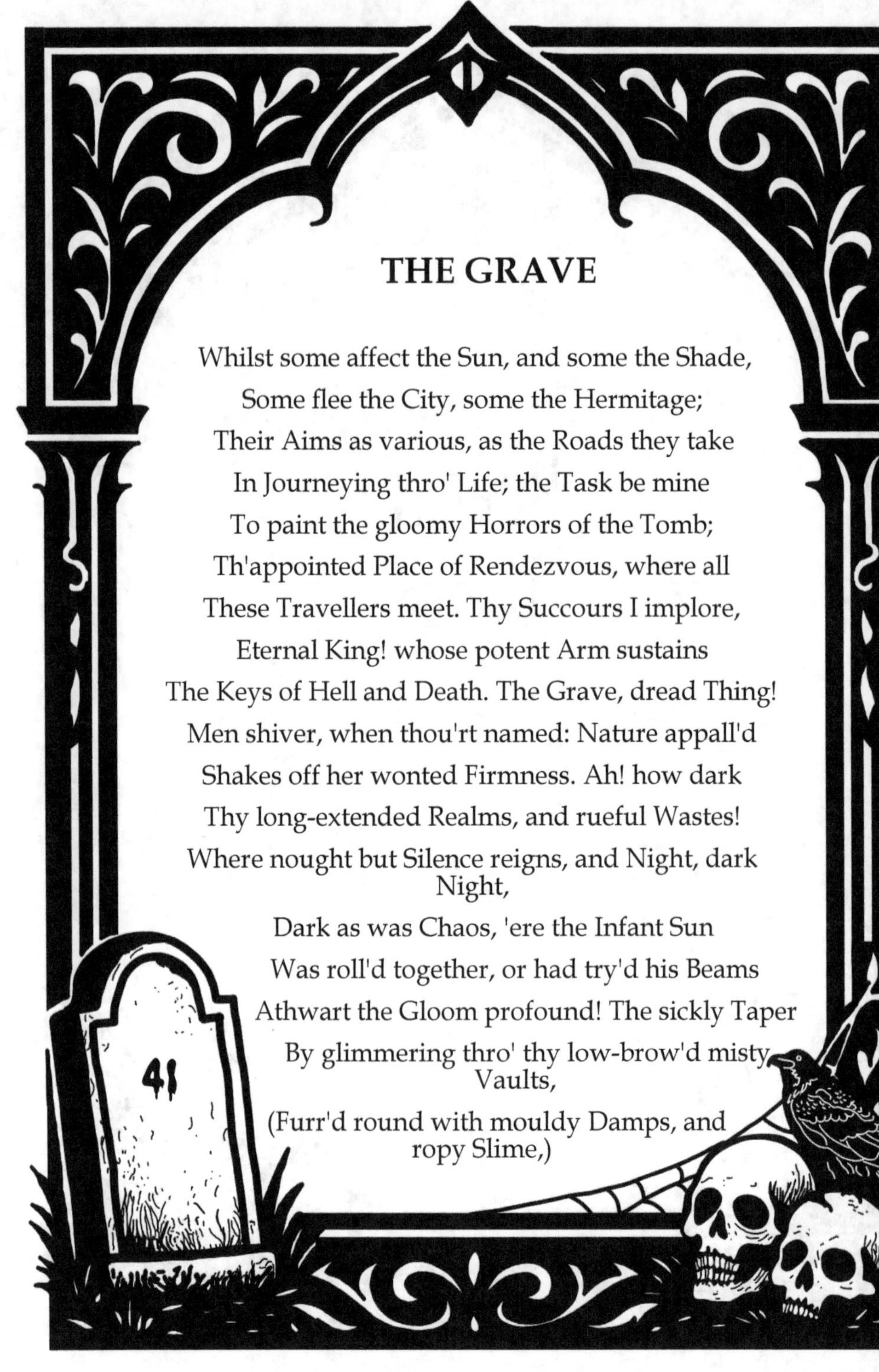

THE GRAVE

Whilst some affect the Sun, and some the Shade,
Some flee the City, some the Hermitage;
Their Aims as various, as the Roads they take
In Journeying thro' Life; the Task be mine
To paint the gloomy Horrors of the Tomb;
Th'appointed Place of Rendezvous, where all
These Travellers meet. Thy Succours I implore,
Eternal King! whose potent Arm sustains
The Keys of Hell and Death. The Grave, dread Thing!
Men shiver, when thou'rt named: Nature appall'd
Shakes off her wonted Firmness. Ah! how dark
Thy long-extended Realms, and rueful Wastes!
Where nought but Silence reigns, and Night, dark Night,
Dark as was Chaos, 'ere the Infant Sun
Was roll'd together, or had try'd his Beams
Athwart the Gloom profound! The sickly Taper
By glimmering thro' thy low-brow'd misty Vaults,
(Furr'd round with mouldy Damps, and ropy Slime,)

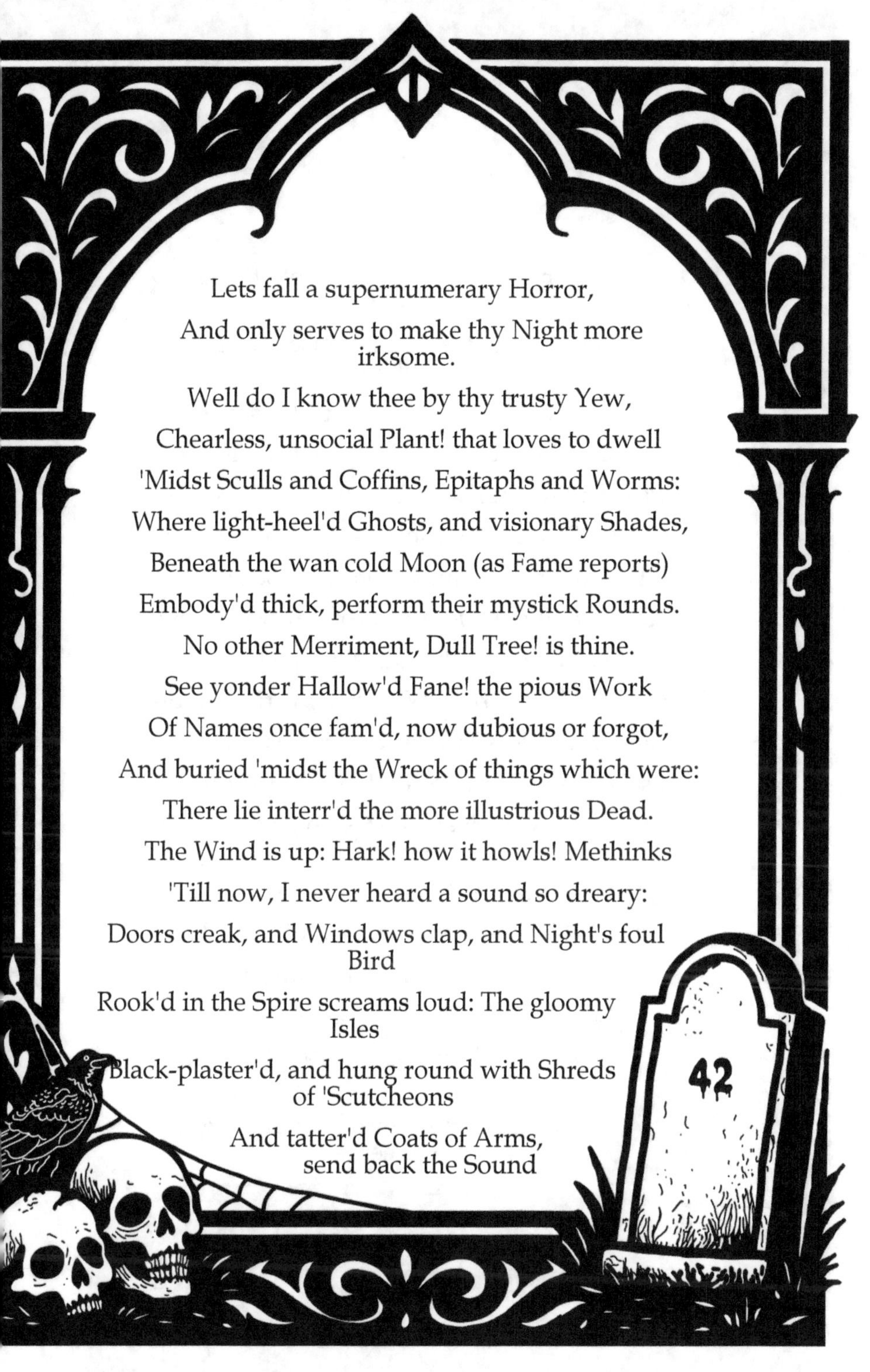

Lets fall a supernumerary Horror,
And only serves to make thy Night more irksome.
Well do I know thee by thy trusty Yew,
Chearless, unsocial Plant! that loves to dwell
'Midst Sculls and Coffins, Epitaphs and Worms:
Where light-heel'd Ghosts, and visionary Shades,
Beneath the wan cold Moon (as Fame reports)
Embody'd thick, perform their mystick Rounds.
No other Merriment, Dull Tree! is thine.
See yonder Hallow'd Fane! the pious Work
Of Names once fam'd, now dubious or forgot,
And buried 'midst the Wreck of things which were:
There lie interr'd the more illustrious Dead.
The Wind is up: Hark! how it howls! Methinks
'Till now, I never heard a sound so dreary:
Doors creak, and Windows clap, and Night's foul Bird
Rook'd in the Spire screams loud: The gloomy Isles
Black-plaster'd, and hung round with Shreds of 'Scutcheons
And tatter'd Coats of Arms, send back the Sound

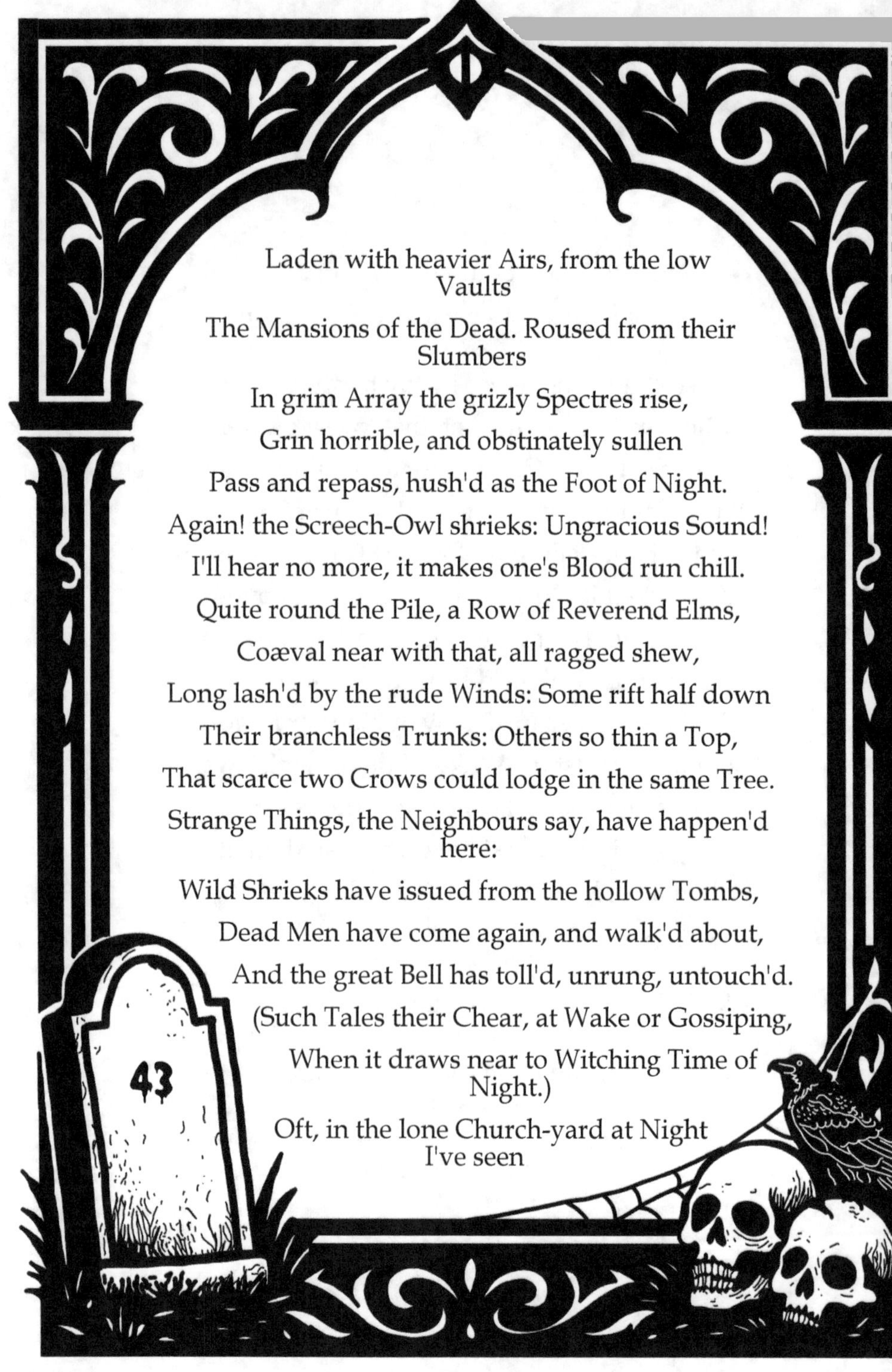

Laden with heavier Airs, from the low Vaults

The Mansions of the Dead. Roused from their Slumbers

In grim Array the grizly Spectres rise,

Grin horrible, and obstinately sullen

Pass and repass, hush'd as the Foot of Night.

Again! the Screech-Owl shrieks: Ungracious Sound!

I'll hear no more, it makes one's Blood run chill.

Quite round the Pile, a Row of Reverend Elms,

Coæval near with that, all ragged shew,

Long lash'd by the rude Winds: Some rift half down

Their branchless Trunks: Others so thin a Top,

That scarce two Crows could lodge in the same Tree.

Strange Things, the Neighbours say, have happen'd here:

Wild Shrieks have issued from the hollow Tombs,

Dead Men have come again, and walk'd about,

And the great Bell has toll'd, unrung, untouch'd.

(Such Tales their Chear, at Wake or Gossiping,

When it draws near to Witching Time of Night.)

Oft, in the lone Church-yard at Night I've seen

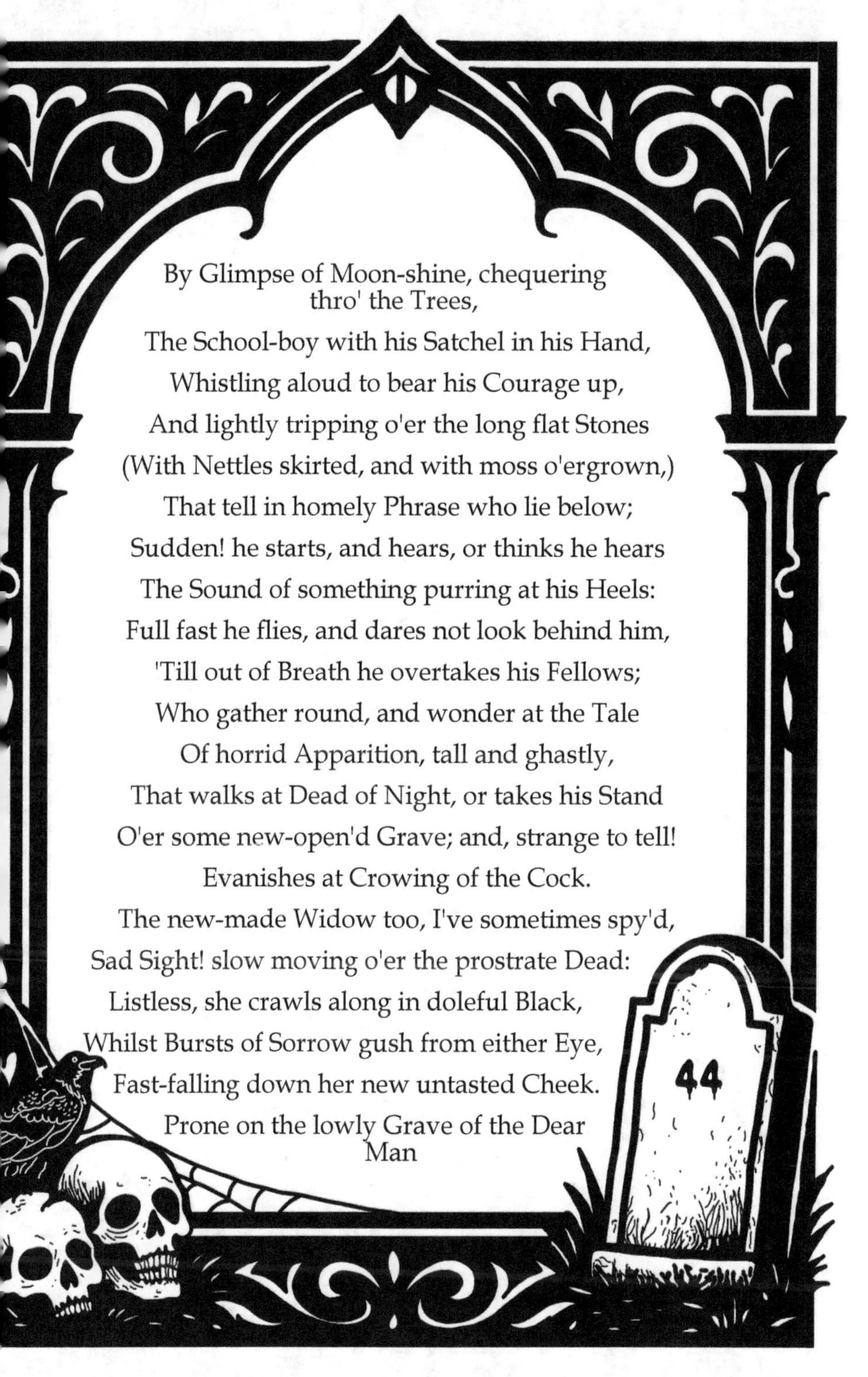

By Glimpse of Moon-shine, chequering thro' the Trees,
The School-boy with his Satchel in his Hand,
Whistling aloud to bear his Courage up,
And lightly tripping o'er the long flat Stones
(With Nettles skirted, and with moss o'ergrown,)
That tell in homely Phrase who lie below;
Sudden! he starts, and hears, or thinks he hears
The Sound of something purring at his Heels:
Full fast he flies, and dares not look behind him,
'Till out of Breath he overtakes his Fellows;
Who gather round, and wonder at the Tale
Of horrid Apparition, tall and ghastly,
That walks at Dead of Night, or takes his Stand
O'er some new-open'd Grave; and, strange to tell!
Evanishes at Crowing of the Cock.
The new-made Widow too, I've sometimes spy'd,
Sad Sight! slow moving o'er the prostrate Dead:
Listless, she crawls along in doleful Black,
Whilst Bursts of Sorrow gush from either Eye,
Fast-falling down her new untasted Cheek.
Prone on the lowly Grave of the Dear Man

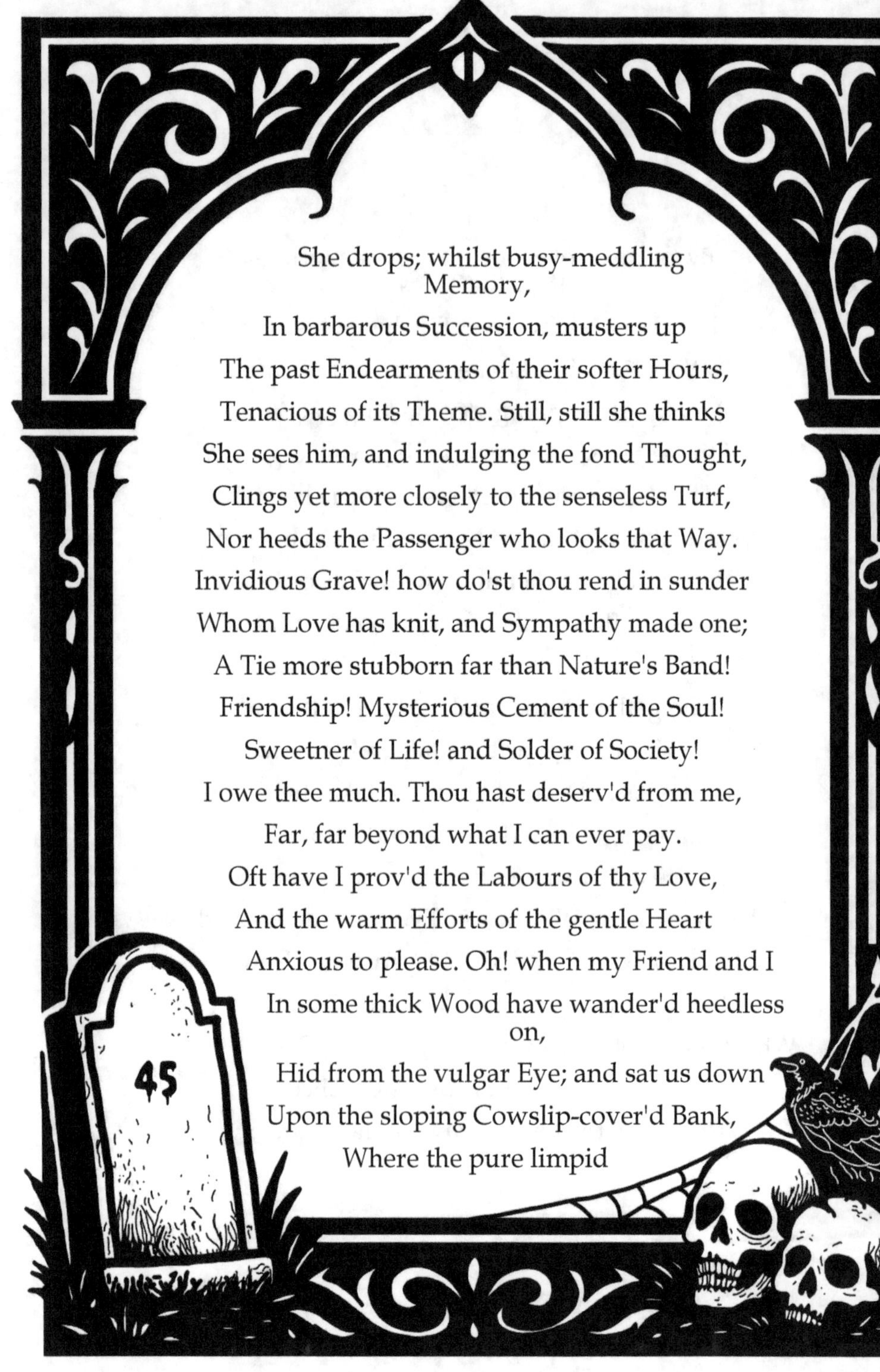

She drops; whilst busy-meddling Memory,
In barbarous Succession, musters up
The past Endearments of their softer Hours,
Tenacious of its Theme. Still, still she thinks
She sees him, and indulging the fond Thought,
Clings yet more closely to the senseless Turf,
Nor heeds the Passenger who looks that Way.
Invidious Grave! how do'st thou rend in sunder
Whom Love has knit, and Sympathy made one;
A Tie more stubborn far than Nature's Band!
Friendship! Mysterious Cement of the Soul!
Sweetner of Life! and Solder of Society!
I owe thee much. Thou hast deserv'd from me,
Far, far beyond what I can ever pay.
Oft have I prov'd the Labours of thy Love,
And the warm Efforts of the gentle Heart
Anxious to please. Oh! when my Friend and I
In some thick Wood have wander'd heedless on,
Hid from the vulgar Eye; and sat us down
Upon the sloping Cowslip-cover'd Bank,
Where the pure limpid

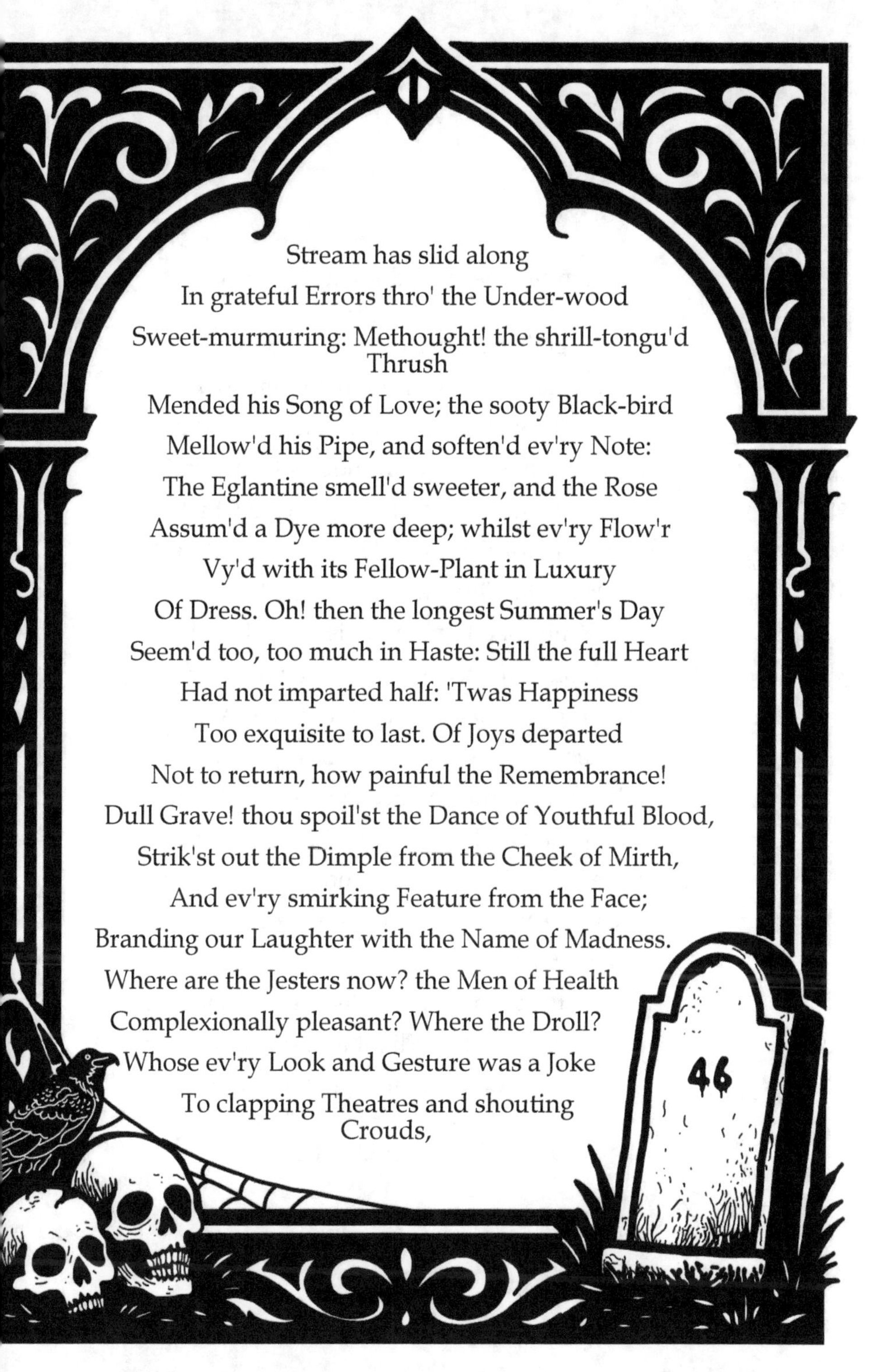

Stream has slid along
In grateful Errors thro' the Under-wood
Sweet-murmuring: Methought! the shrill-tongu'd Thrush
Mended his Song of Love; the sooty Black-bird
Mellow'd his Pipe, and soften'd ev'ry Note:
The Eglantine smell'd sweeter, and the Rose
Assum'd a Dye more deep; whilst ev'ry Flow'r
Vy'd with its Fellow-Plant in Luxury
Of Dress. Oh! then the longest Summer's Day
Seem'd too, too much in Haste: Still the full Heart
Had not imparted half: 'Twas Happiness
Too exquisite to last. Of Joys departed
Not to return, how painful the Remembrance!
Dull Grave! thou spoil'st the Dance of Youthful Blood,
Strik'st out the Dimple from the Cheek of Mirth,
And ev'ry smirking Feature from the Face;
Branding our Laughter with the Name of Madness.
Where are the Jesters now? the Men of Health
Complexionally pleasant? Where the Droll?
Whose ev'ry Look and Gesture was a Joke
To clapping Theatres and shouting Crouds,

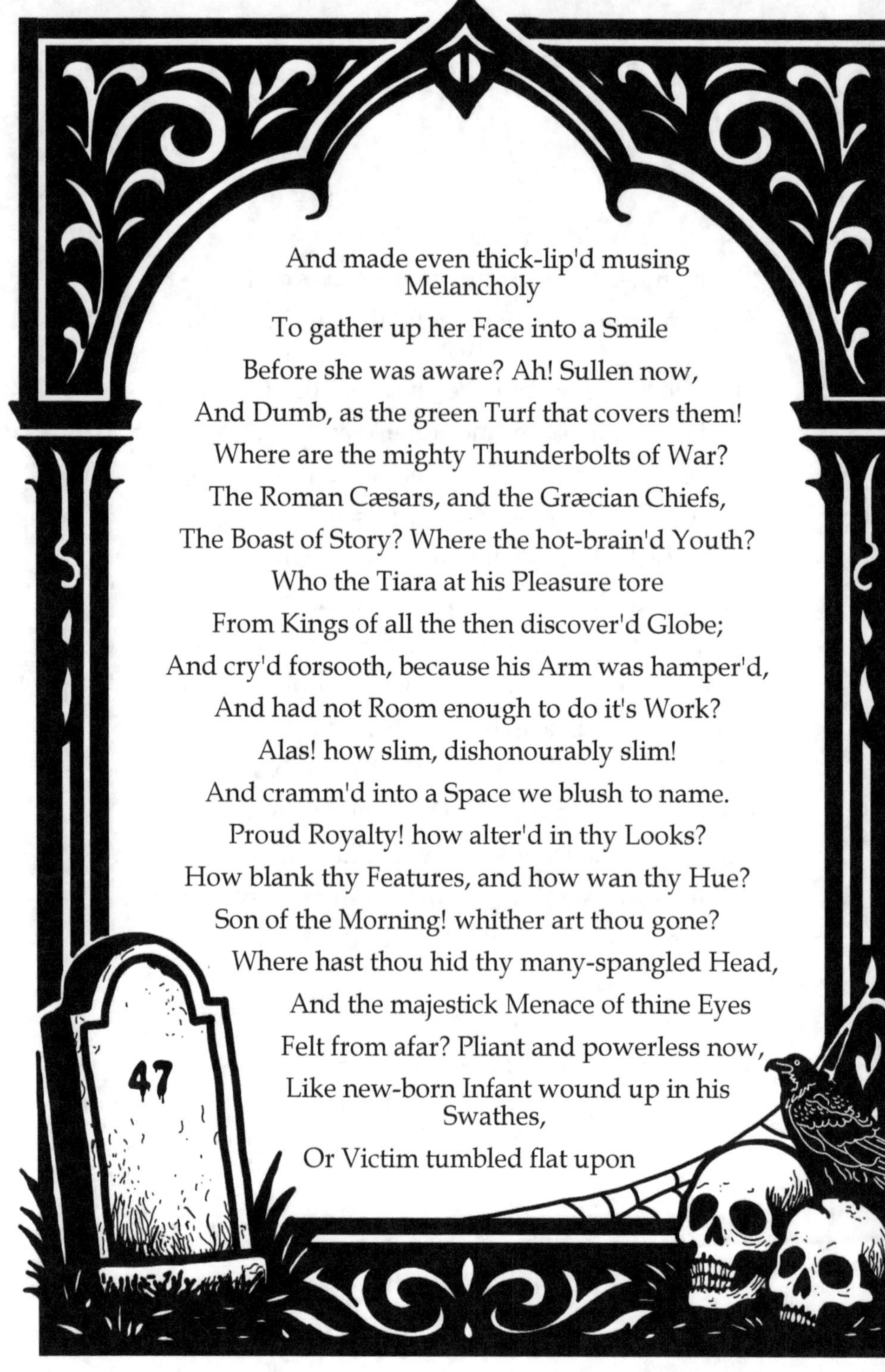

And made even thick-lip'd musing Melancholy
To gather up her Face into a Smile
Before she was aware? Ah! Sullen now,
And Dumb, as the green Turf that covers them!
Where are the mighty Thunderbolts of War?
The Roman Cæsars, and the Græcian Chiefs,
The Boast of Story? Where the hot-brain'd Youth?
Who the Tiara at his Pleasure tore
From Kings of all the then discover'd Globe;
And cry'd forsooth, because his Arm was hamper'd,
And had not Room enough to do it's Work?
Alas! how slim, dishonourably slim!
And cramm'd into a Space we blush to name.
Proud Royalty! how alter'd in thy Looks?
How blank thy Features, and how wan thy Hue?
Son of the Morning! whither art thou gone?
Where hast thou hid thy many-spangled Head,
And the majestick Menace of thine Eyes
Felt from afar? Pliant and powerless now,
Like new-born Infant wound up in his Swathes,
Or Victim tumbled flat upon

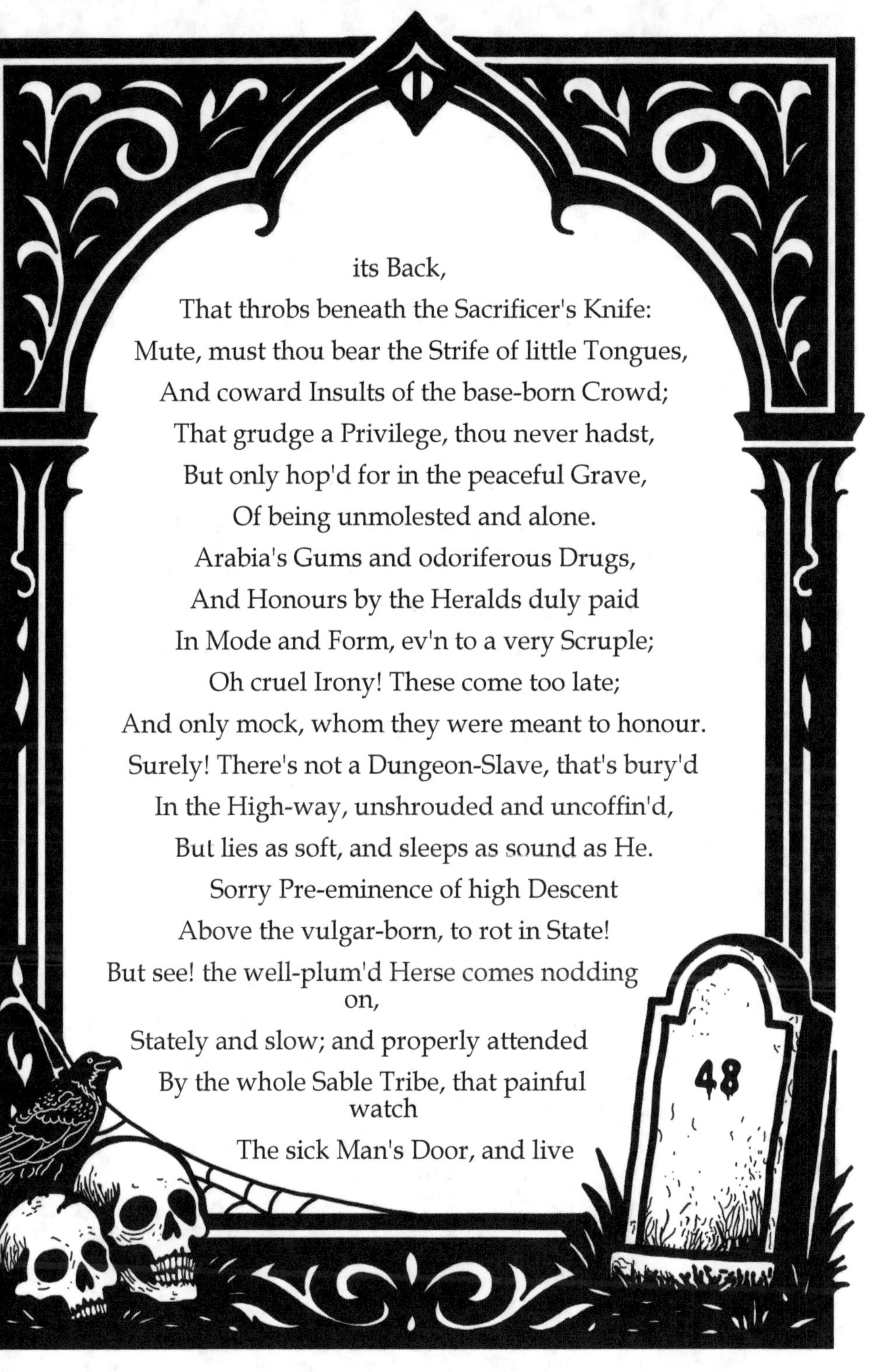

its Back,
That throbs beneath the Sacrificer's Knife:
Mute, must thou bear the Strife of little Tongues,
And coward Insults of the base-born Crowd;
That grudge a Privilege, thou never hadst,
But only hop'd for in the peaceful Grave,
Of being unmolested and alone.
Arabia's Gums and odoriferous Drugs,
And Honours by the Heralds duly paid
In Mode and Form, ev'n to a very Scruple;
Oh cruel Irony! These come too late;
And only mock, whom they were meant to honour.
Surely! There's not a Dungeon-Slave, that's bury'd
In the High-way, unshrouded and uncoffin'd,
But lies as soft, and sleeps as sound as He.
Sorry Pre-eminence of high Descent
Above the vulgar-born, to rot in State!
But see! the well-plum'd Herse comes nodding on,
Stately and slow; and properly attended
By the whole Sable Tribe, that painful watch
The sick Man's Door, and live

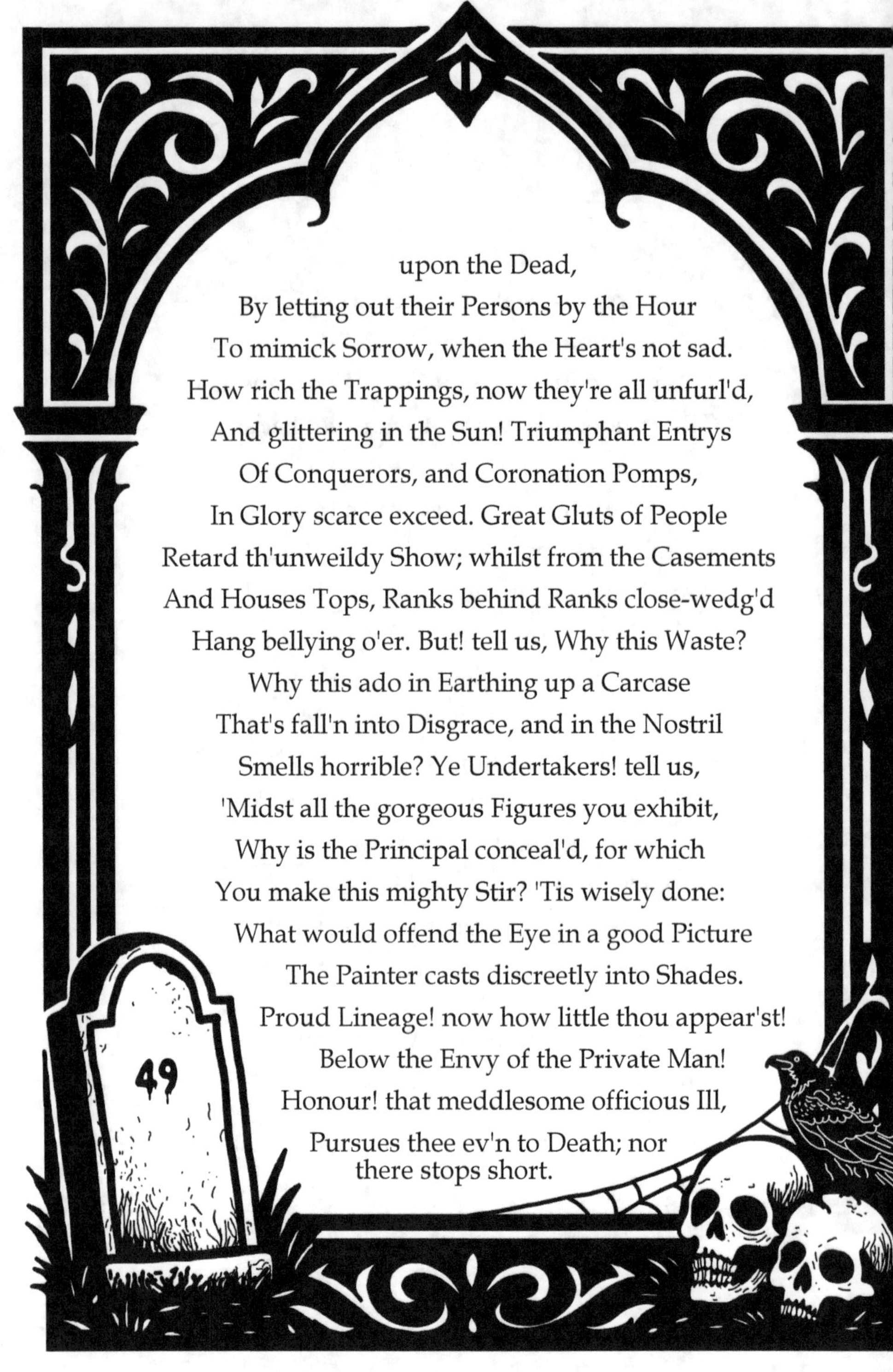

upon the Dead,
By letting out their Persons by the Hour
To mimick Sorrow, when the Heart's not sad.
How rich the Trappings, now they're all unfurl'd,
And glittering in the Sun! Triumphant Entrys
Of Conquerors, and Coronation Pomps,
In Glory scarce exceed. Great Gluts of People
Retard th'unweildy Show; whilst from the Casements
And Houses Tops, Ranks behind Ranks close-wedg'd
Hang bellying o'er. But! tell us, Why this Waste?
Why this ado in Earthing up a Carcase
That's fall'n into Disgrace, and in the Nostril
Smells horrible? Ye Undertakers! tell us,
'Midst all the gorgeous Figures you exhibit,
Why is the Principal conceal'd, for which
You make this mighty Stir? 'Tis wisely done:
What would offend the Eye in a good Picture
The Painter casts discreetly into Shades.
Proud Lineage! now how little thou appear'st!
Below the Envy of the Private Man!
Honour! that meddlesome officious Ill,
Pursues thee ev'n to Death; nor
there stops short.

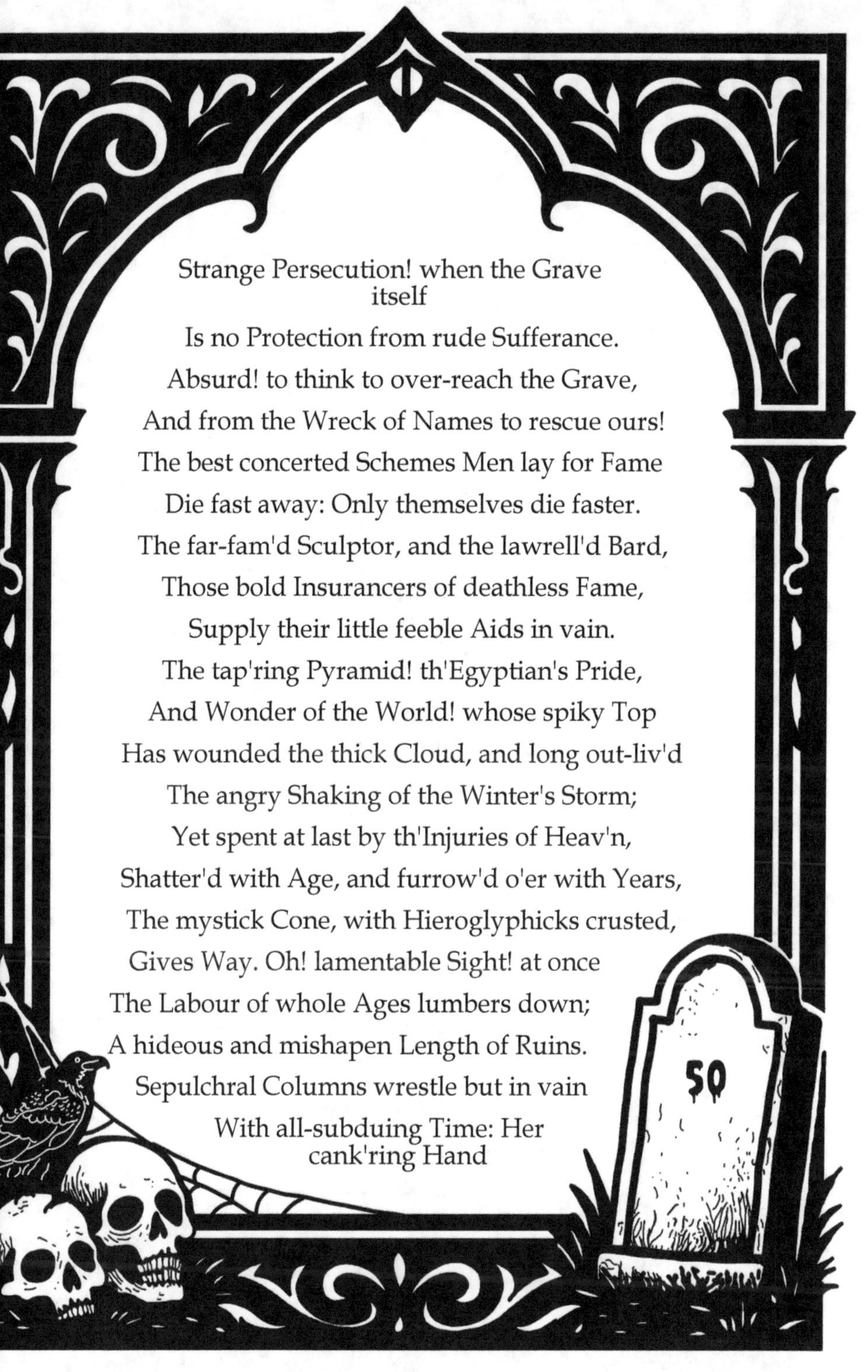

Strange Persecution! when the Grave itself
Is no Protection from rude Sufferance.
Absurd! to think to over-reach the Grave,
And from the Wreck of Names to rescue ours!
The best concerted Schemes Men lay for Fame
Die fast away: Only themselves die faster.
The far-fam'd Sculptor, and the lawrell'd Bard,
Those bold Insurancers of deathless Fame,
Supply their little feeble Aids in vain.
The tap'ring Pyramid! th'Egyptian's Pride,
And Wonder of the World! whose spiky Top
Has wounded the thick Cloud, and long out-liv'd
The angry Shaking of the Winter's Storm;
Yet spent at last by th'Injuries of Heav'n,
Shatter'd with Age, and furrow'd o'er with Years,
The mystick Cone, with Hieroglyphicks crusted,
Gives Way. Oh! lamentable Sight! at once
The Labour of whole Ages lumbers down;
A hideous and mishapen Length of Ruins.
Sepulchral Columns wrestle but in vain
With all-subduing Time: Her cank'ring Hand

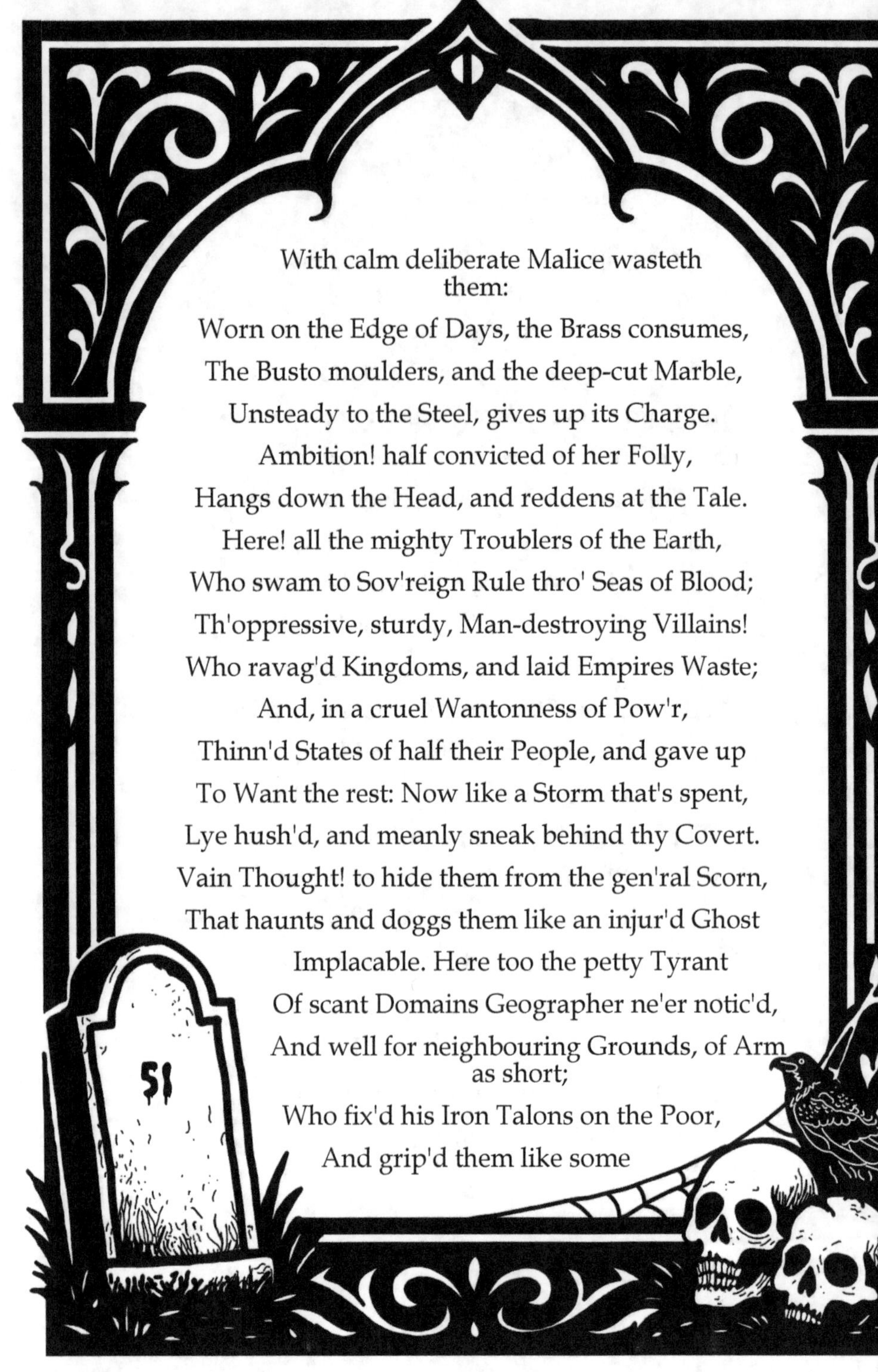

With calm deliberate Malice wasteth them:
Worn on the Edge of Days, the Brass consumes,
The Busto moulders, and the deep-cut Marble,
Unsteady to the Steel, gives up its Charge.
Ambition! half convicted of her Folly,
Hangs down the Head, and reddens at the Tale.
Here! all the mighty Troublers of the Earth,
Who swam to Sov'reign Rule thro' Seas of Blood;
Th'oppressive, sturdy, Man-destroying Villains!
Who ravag'd Kingdoms, and laid Empires Waste;
And, in a cruel Wantonness of Pow'r,
Thinn'd States of half their People, and gave up
To Want the rest: Now like a Storm that's spent,
Lye hush'd, and meanly sneak behind thy Covert.
Vain Thought! to hide them from the gen'ral Scorn,
That haunts and doggs them like an injur'd Ghost
Implacable. Here too the petty Tyrant
Of scant Domains Geographer ne'er notic'd,
And well for neighbouring Grounds, of Arm as short;
Who fix'd his Iron Talons on the Poor,
And grip'd them like some

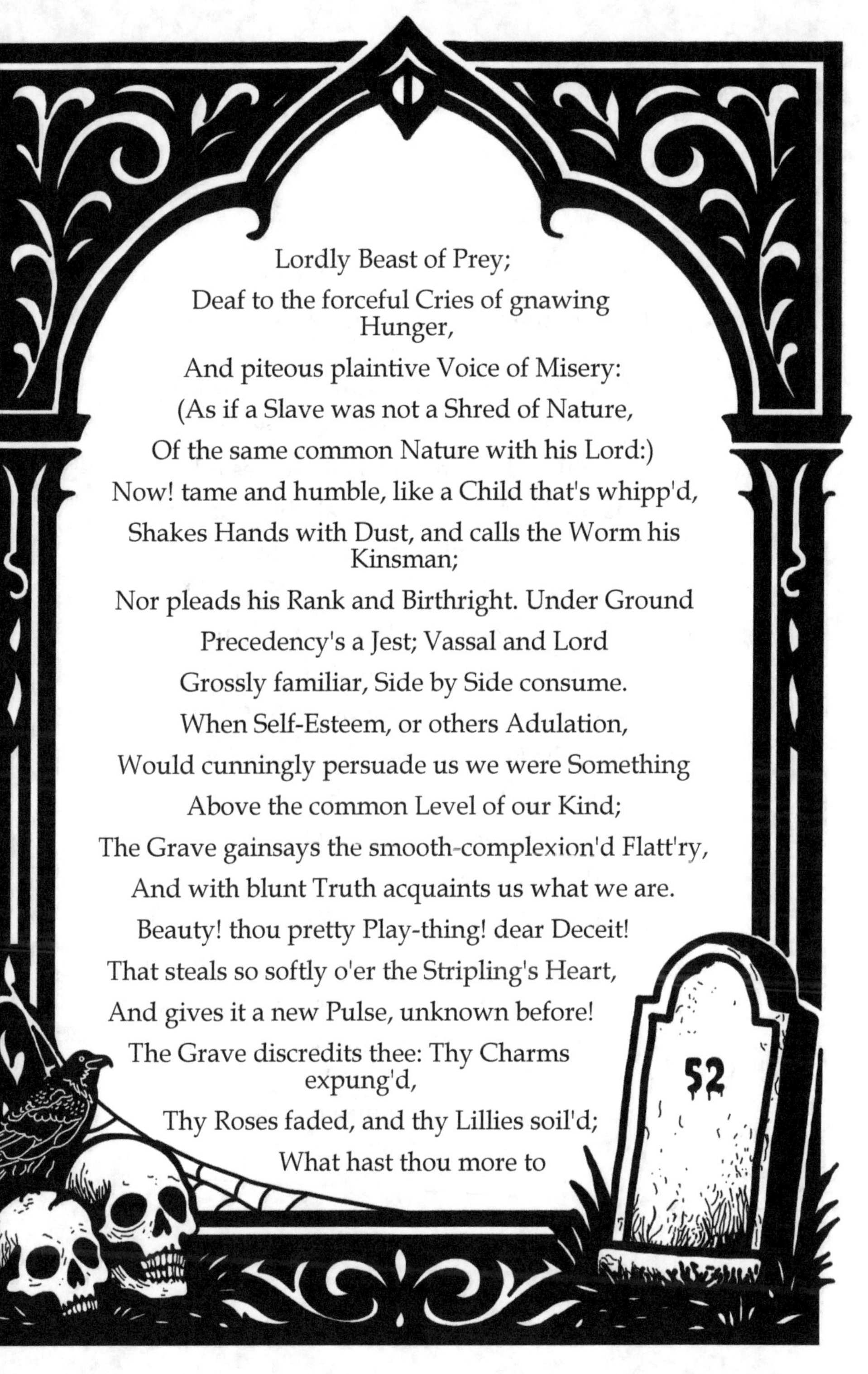

Lordly Beast of Prey;
Deaf to the forceful Cries of gnawing Hunger,
And piteous plaintive Voice of Misery:
(As if a Slave was not a Shred of Nature,
Of the same common Nature with his Lord:)
Now! tame and humble, like a Child that's whipp'd,
Shakes Hands with Dust, and calls the Worm his Kinsman;
Nor pleads his Rank and Birthright. Under Ground
Precedency's a Jest; Vassal and Lord
Grossly familiar, Side by Side consume.
When Self-Esteem, or others Adulation,
Would cunningly persuade us we were Something
Above the common Level of our Kind;
The Grave gainsays the smooth-complexion'd Flatt'ry,
And with blunt Truth acquaints us what we are.
Beauty! thou pretty Play-thing! dear Deceit!
That steals so softly o'er the Stripling's Heart,
And gives it a new Pulse, unknown before!
The Grave discredits thee: Thy Charms expung'd,
Thy Roses faded, and thy Lillies soil'd;
What hast thou more to

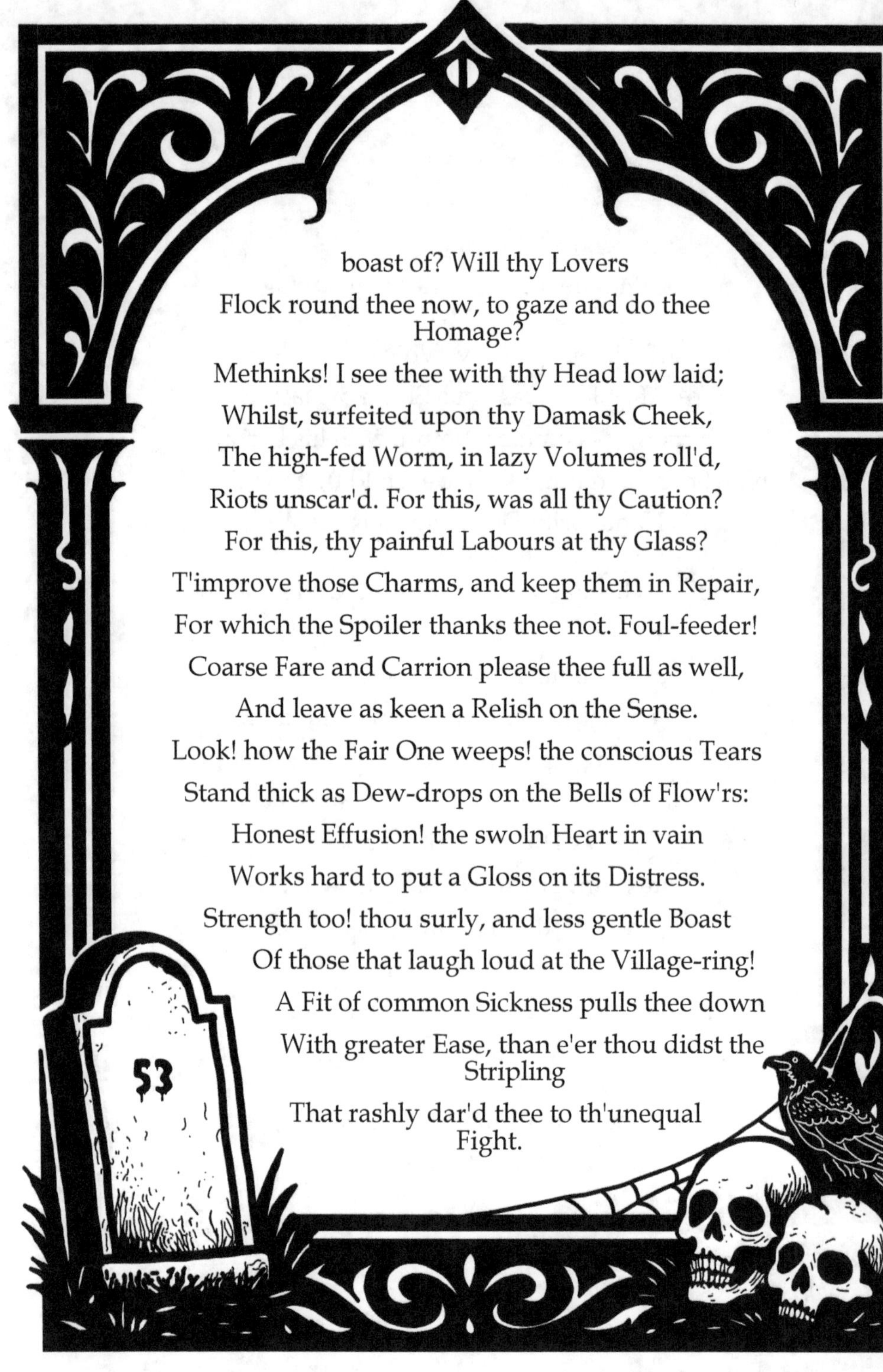

boast of? Will thy Lovers
Flock round thee now, to gaze and do thee Homage?
Methinks! I see thee with thy Head low laid;
Whilst, surfeited upon thy Damask Cheek,
The high-fed Worm, in lazy Volumes roll'd,
Riots unscar'd. For this, was all thy Caution?
For this, thy painful Labours at thy Glass?
T'improve those Charms, and keep them in Repair,
For which the Spoiler thanks thee not. Foul-feeder!
Coarse Fare and Carrion please thee full as well,
And leave as keen a Relish on the Sense.
Look! how the Fair One weeps! the conscious Tears
Stand thick as Dew-drops on the Bells of Flow'rs:
Honest Effusion! the swoln Heart in vain
Works hard to put a Gloss on its Distress.
Strength too! thou surly, and less gentle Boast
Of those that laugh loud at the Village-ring!
A Fit of common Sickness pulls thee down
With greater Ease, than e'er thou didst the Stripling
That rashly dar'd thee to th'unequal Fight.

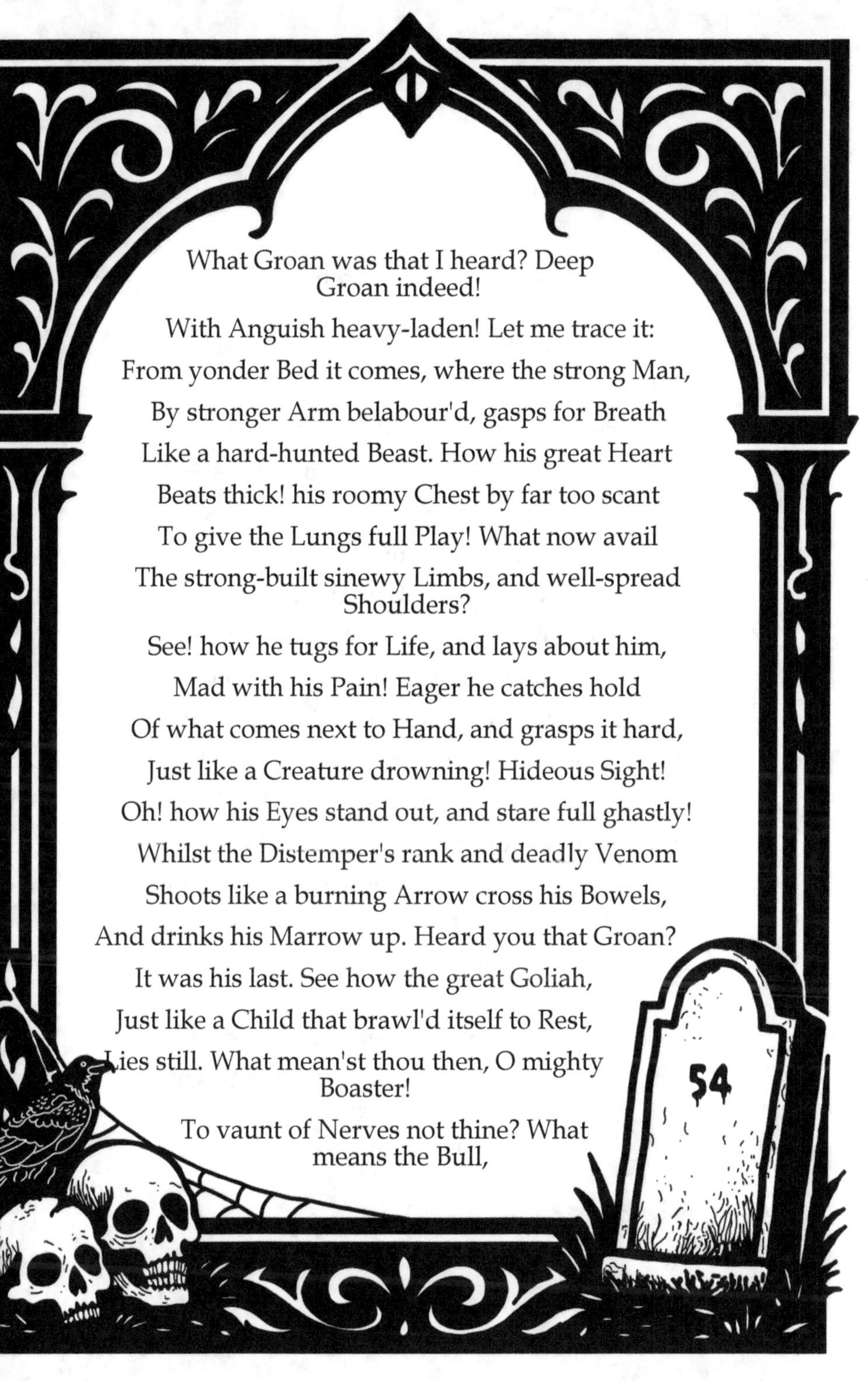

What Groan was that I heard? Deep Groan indeed!
With Anguish heavy-laden! Let me trace it:
From yonder Bed it comes, where the strong Man,
By stronger Arm belabour'd, gasps for Breath
Like a hard-hunted Beast. How his great Heart
Beats thick! his roomy Chest by far too scant
To give the Lungs full Play! What now avail
The strong-built sinewy Limbs, and well-spread Shoulders?
See! how he tugs for Life, and lays about him,
Mad with his Pain! Eager he catches hold
Of what comes next to Hand, and grasps it hard,
Just like a Creature drowning! Hideous Sight!
Oh! how his Eyes stand out, and stare full ghastly!
Whilst the Distemper's rank and deadly Venom
Shoots like a burning Arrow cross his Bowels,
And drinks his Marrow up. Heard you that Groan?
It was his last. See how the great Goliah,
Just like a Child that brawl'd itself to Rest,
Lies still. What mean'st thou then, O mighty Boaster!
To vaunt of Nerves not thine? What means the Bull,

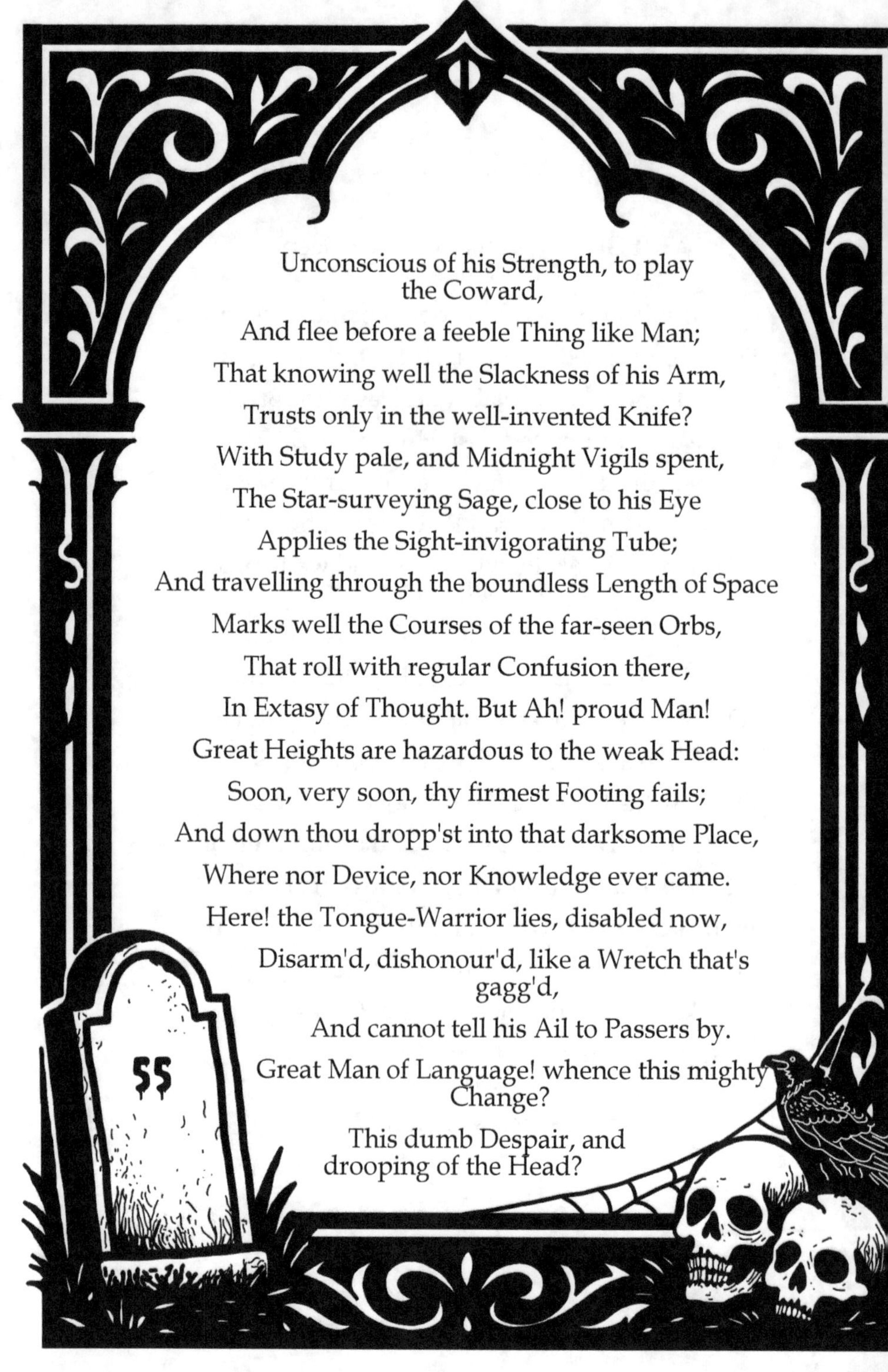

Unconscious of his Strength, to play the Coward,
And flee before a feeble Thing like Man;
That knowing well the Slackness of his Arm,
Trusts only in the well-invented Knife?
With Study pale, and Midnight Vigils spent,
The Star-surveying Sage, close to his Eye
Applies the Sight-invigorating Tube;
And travelling through the boundless Length of Space
Marks well the Courses of the far-seen Orbs,
That roll with regular Confusion there,
In Extasy of Thought. But Ah! proud Man!
Great Heights are hazardous to the weak Head:
Soon, very soon, thy firmest Footing fails;
And down thou dropp'st into that darksome Place,
Where nor Device, nor Knowledge ever came.
Here! the Tongue-Warrior lies, disabled now,
Disarm'd, dishonour'd, like a Wretch that's gagg'd,
And cannot tell his Ail to Passers by.
Great Man of Language! whence this mighty Change?
This dumb Despair, and drooping of the Head?

55

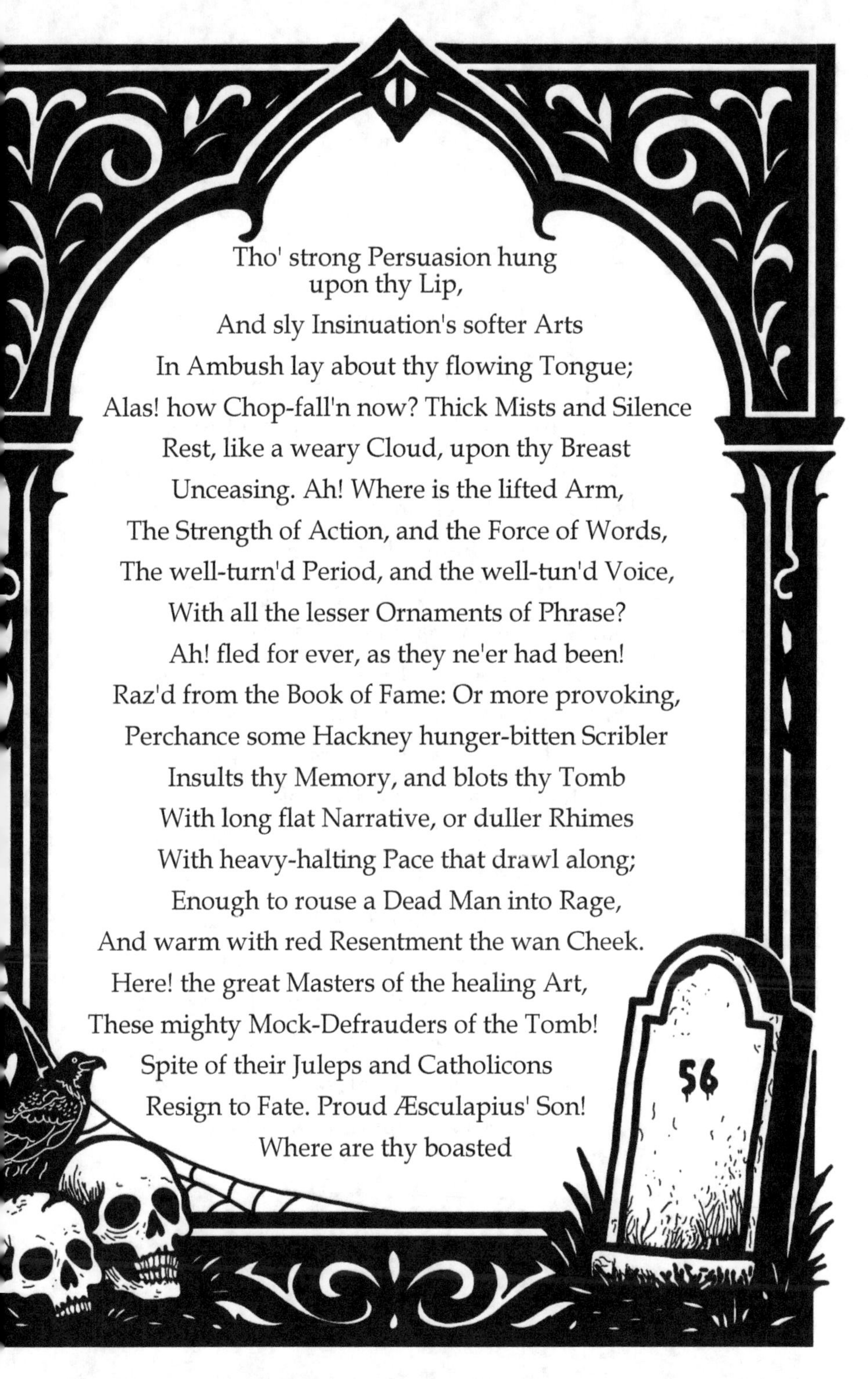

Tho' strong Persuasion hung upon thy Lip,
And sly Insinuation's softer Arts
In Ambush lay about thy flowing Tongue;
Alas! how Chop-fall'n now? Thick Mists and Silence
Rest, like a weary Cloud, upon thy Breast
Unceasing. Ah! Where is the lifted Arm,
The Strength of Action, and the Force of Words,
The well-turn'd Period, and the well-tun'd Voice,
With all the lesser Ornaments of Phrase?
Ah! fled for ever, as they ne'er had been!
Raz'd from the Book of Fame: Or more provoking,
Perchance some Hackney hunger-bitten Scribler
Insults thy Memory, and blots thy Tomb
With long flat Narrative, or duller Rhimes
With heavy-halting Pace that drawl along;
Enough to rouse a Dead Man into Rage,
And warm with red Resentment the wan Cheek.
Here! the great Masters of the healing Art,
These mighty Mock-Defrauders of the Tomb!
Spite of their Juleps and Catholicons
Resign to Fate. Proud Æsculapius' Son!
Where are thy boasted

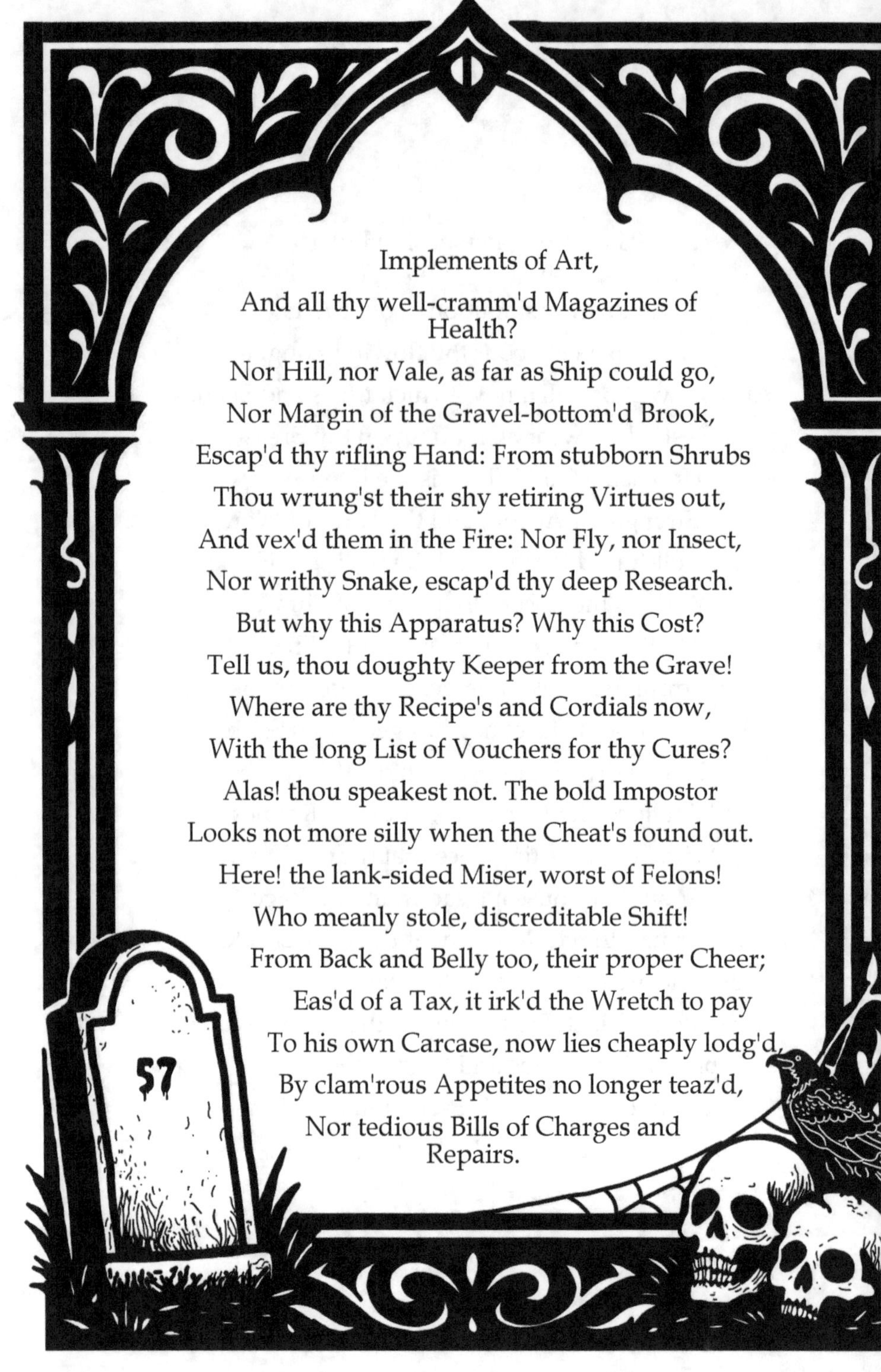

Implements of Art,
And all thy well-cramm'd Magazines of Health?
Nor Hill, nor Vale, as far as Ship could go,
Nor Margin of the Gravel-bottom'd Brook,
Escap'd thy rifling Hand: From stubborn Shrubs
Thou wrung'st their shy retiring Virtues out,
And vex'd them in the Fire: Nor Fly, nor Insect,
Nor writhy Snake, escap'd thy deep Research.
But why this Apparatus? Why this Cost?
Tell us, thou doughty Keeper from the Grave!
Where are thy Recipe's and Cordials now,
With the long List of Vouchers for thy Cures?
Alas! thou speakest not. The bold Impostor
Looks not more silly when the Cheat's found out.
Here! the lank-sided Miser, worst of Felons!
Who meanly stole, discreditable Shift!
From Back and Belly too, their proper Cheer;
Eas'd of a Tax, it irk'd the Wretch to pay
To his own Carcase, now lies cheaply lodg'd,
By clam'rous Appetites no longer teaz'd,
Nor tedious Bills of Charges and Repairs.

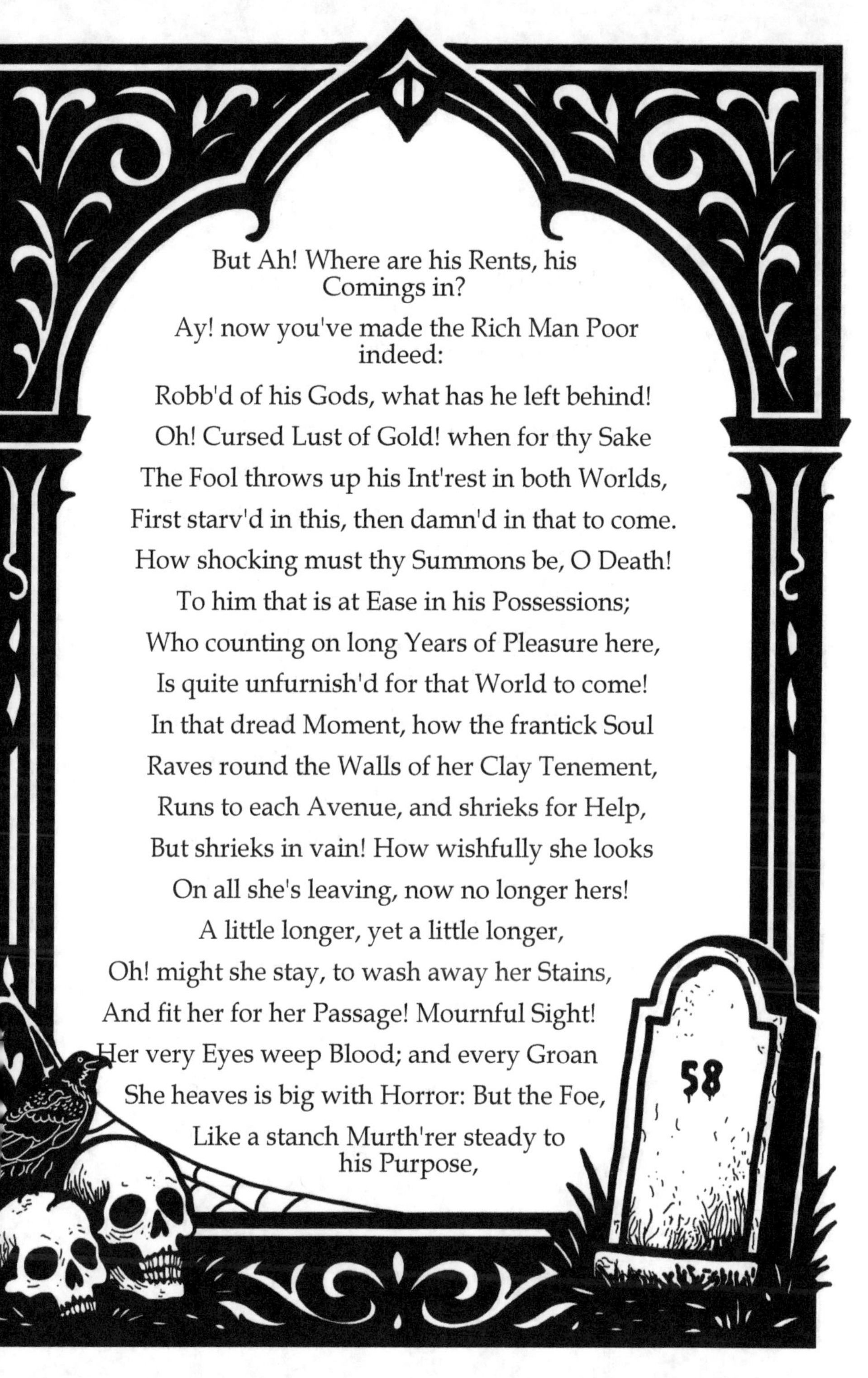

But Ah! Where are his Rents, his Comings in?
Ay! now you've made the Rich Man Poor indeed:
Robb'd of his Gods, what has he left behind!
Oh! Cursed Lust of Gold! when for thy Sake
The Fool throws up his Int'rest in both Worlds,
First starv'd in this, then damn'd in that to come.
How shocking must thy Summons be, O Death!
To him that is at Ease in his Possessions;
Who counting on long Years of Pleasure here,
Is quite unfurnish'd for that World to come!
In that dread Moment, how the frantick Soul
Raves round the Walls of her Clay Tenement,
Runs to each Avenue, and shrieks for Help,
But shrieks in vain! How wishfully she looks
On all she's leaving, now no longer hers!
A little longer, yet a little longer,
Oh! might she stay, to wash away her Stains,
And fit her for her Passage! Mournful Sight!
Her very Eyes weep Blood; and every Groan
She heaves is big with Horror: But the Foe,
Like a stanch Murth'rer steady to his Purpose,

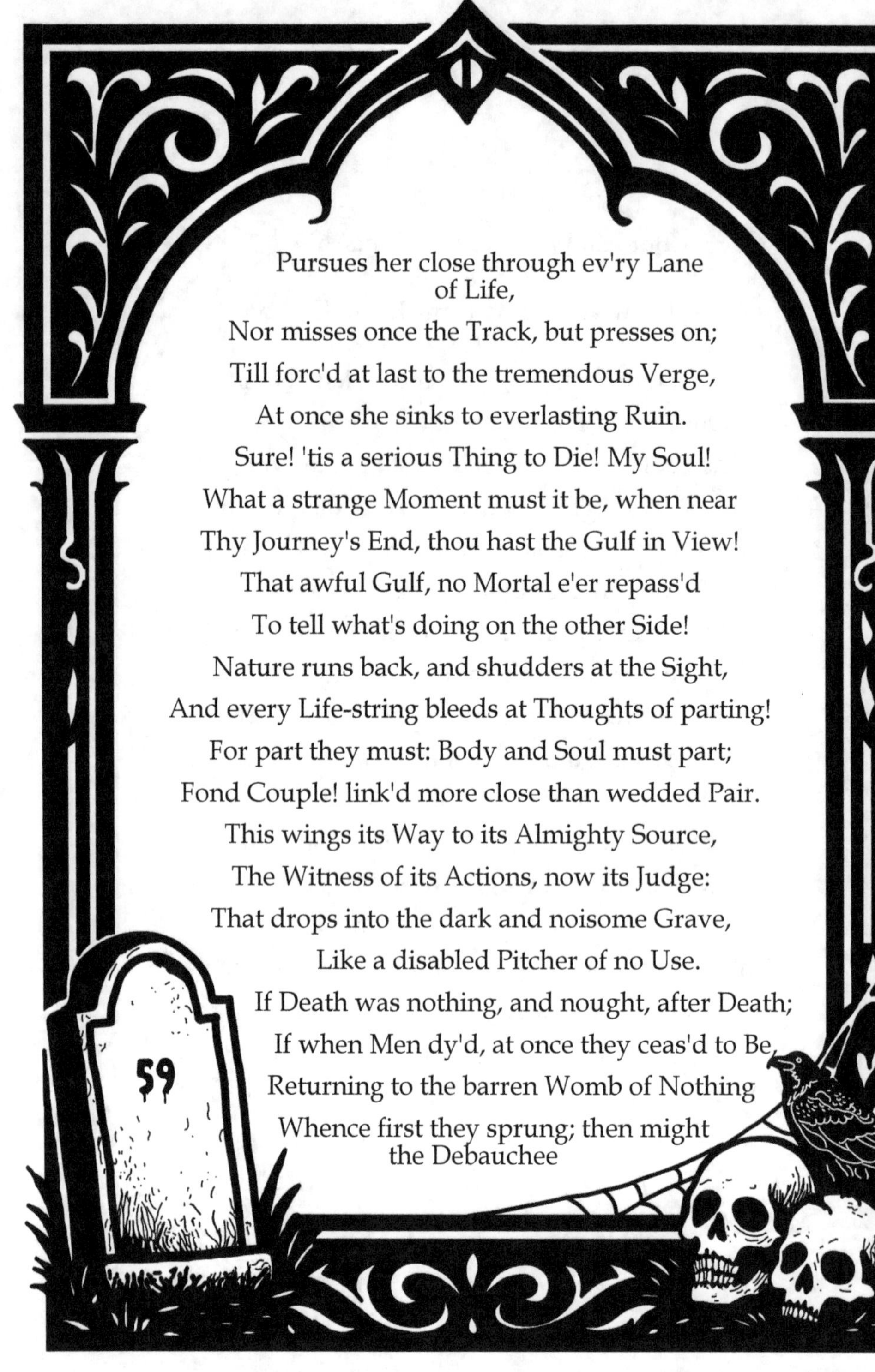

Pursues her close through ev'ry Lane of Life,
Nor misses once the Track, but presses on;
Till forc'd at last to the tremendous Verge,
At once she sinks to everlasting Ruin.
Sure! 'tis a serious Thing to Die! My Soul!
What a strange Moment must it be, when near
Thy Journey's End, thou hast the Gulf in View!
That awful Gulf, no Mortal e'er repass'd
To tell what's doing on the other Side!
Nature runs back, and shudders at the Sight,
And every Life-string bleeds at Thoughts of parting!
For part they must: Body and Soul must part;
Fond Couple! link'd more close than wedded Pair.
This wings its Way to its Almighty Source,
The Witness of its Actions, now its Judge:
That drops into the dark and noisome Grave,
Like a disabled Pitcher of no Use.
If Death was nothing, and nought, after Death;
If when Men dy'd, at once they ceas'd to Be,
Returning to the barren Womb of Nothing
Whence first they sprung; then might the Debauchee

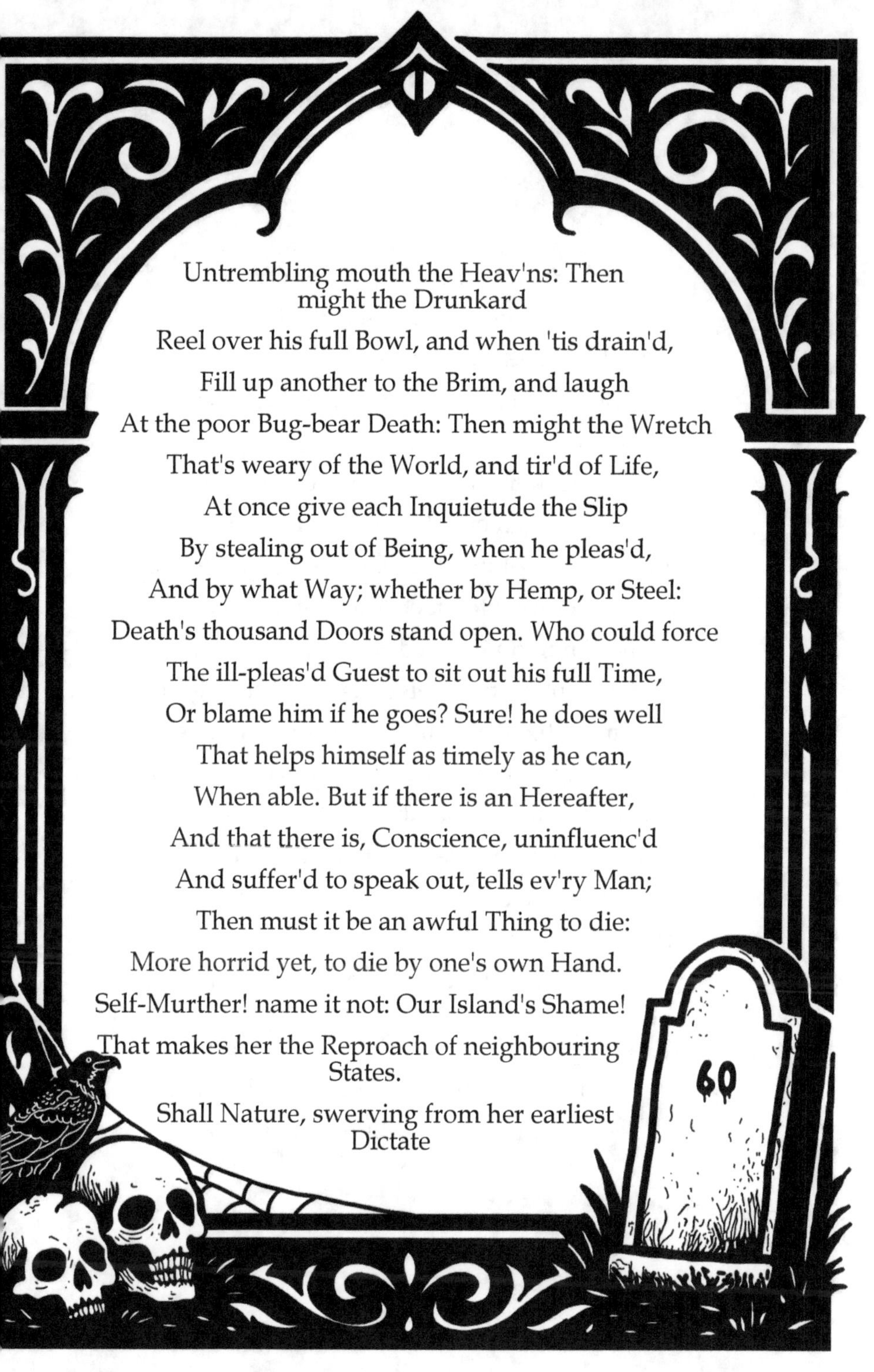

Untrembling mouth the Heav'ns: Then might the Drunkard
Reel over his full Bowl, and when 'tis drain'd,
Fill up another to the Brim, and laugh
At the poor Bug-bear Death: Then might the Wretch
That's weary of the World, and tir'd of Life,
At once give each Inquietude the Slip
By stealing out of Being, when he pleas'd,
And by what Way; whether by Hemp, or Steel:
Death's thousand Doors stand open. Who could force
The ill-pleas'd Guest to sit out his full Time,
Or blame him if he goes? Sure! he does well
That helps himself as timely as he can,
When able. But if there is an Hereafter,
And that there is, Conscience, uninfluenc'd
And suffer'd to speak out, tells ev'ry Man;
Then must it be an awful Thing to die:
More horrid yet, to die by one's own Hand.
Self-Murther! name it not: Our Island's Shame!
That makes her the Reproach of neighbouring States.
Shall Nature, swerving from her earliest Dictate

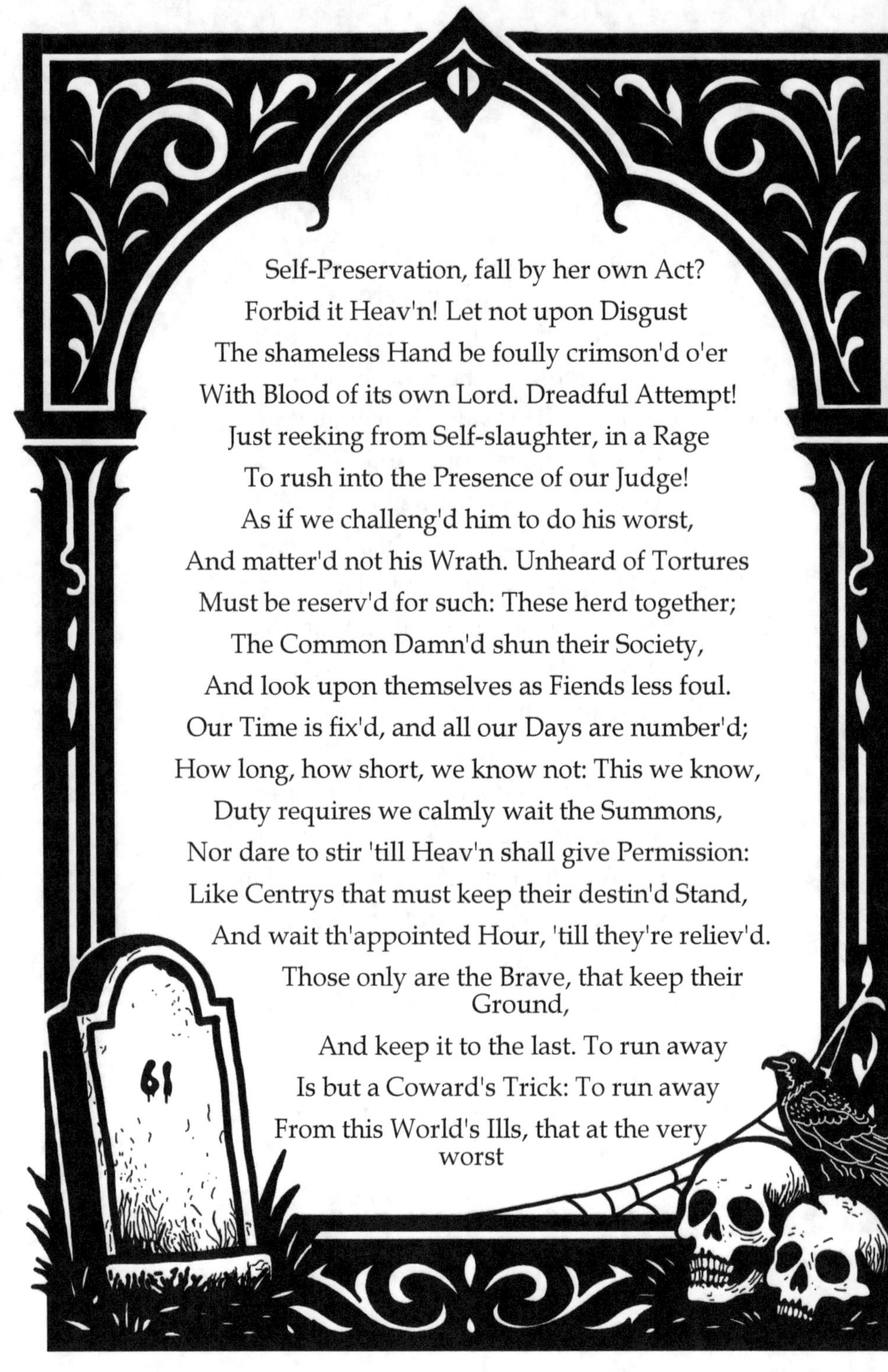

Self-Preservation, fall by her own Act?
Forbid it Heav'n! Let not upon Disgust
The shameless Hand be foully crimson'd o'er
With Blood of its own Lord. Dreadful Attempt!
Just reeking from Self-slaughter, in a Rage
To rush into the Presence of our Judge!
As if we challeng'd him to do his worst,
And matter'd not his Wrath. Unheard of Tortures
Must be reserv'd for such: These herd together;
The Common Damn'd shun their Society,
And look upon themselves as Fiends less foul.
Our Time is fix'd, and all our Days are number'd;
How long, how short, we know not: This we know,
Duty requires we calmly wait the Summons,
Nor dare to stir 'till Heav'n shall give Permission:
Like Centrys that must keep their destin'd Stand,
And wait th'appointed Hour, 'till they're reliev'd.
Those only are the Brave, that keep their Ground,
And keep it to the last. To run away
Is but a Coward's Trick: To run away
From this World's Ills, that at the very worst

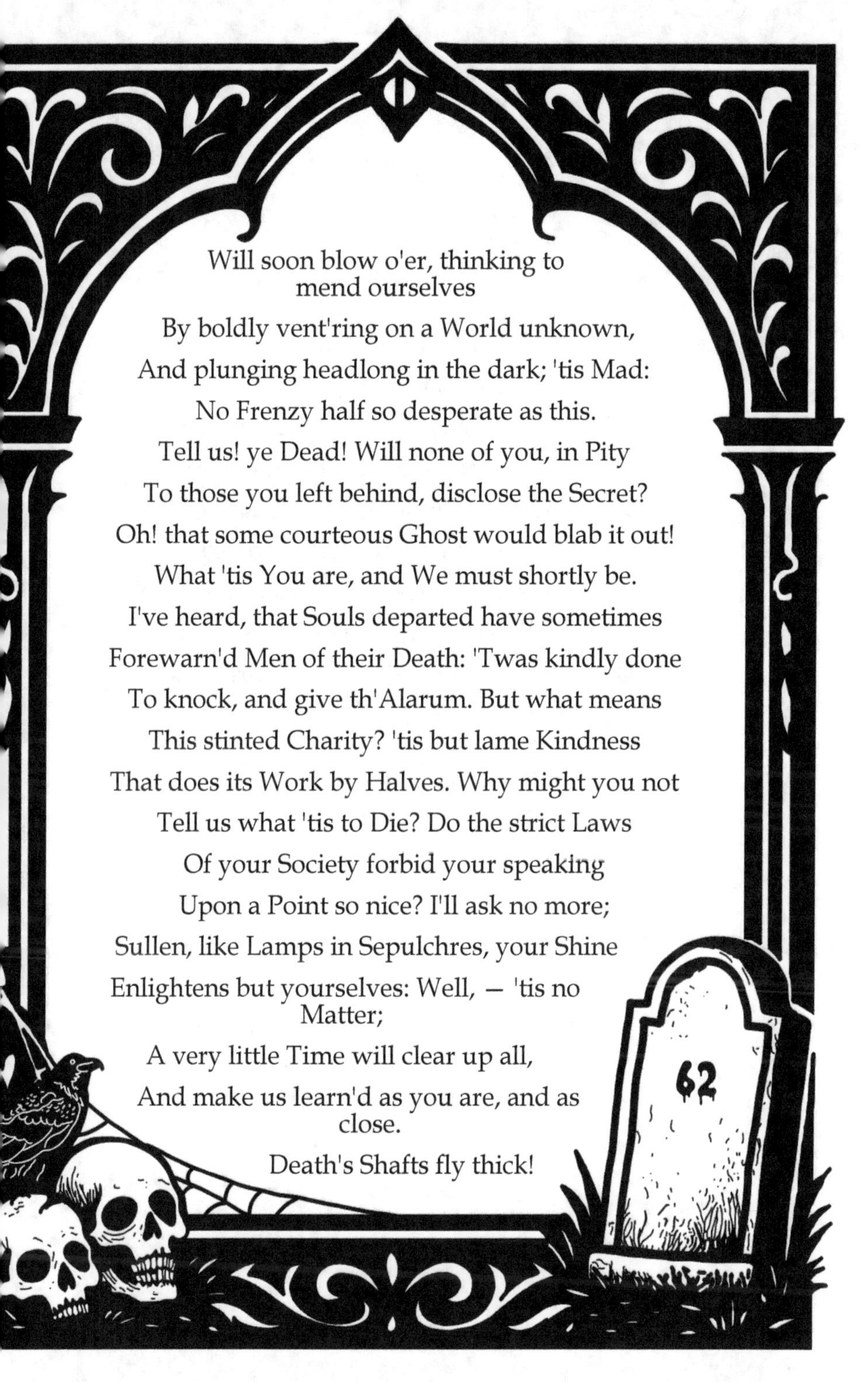

Will soon blow o'er, thinking to mend ourselves
By boldly vent'ring on a World unknown,
And plunging headlong in the dark; 'tis Mad:
No Frenzy half so desperate as this.
Tell us! ye Dead! Will none of you, in Pity
To those you left behind, disclose the Secret?
Oh! that some courteous Ghost would blab it out!
What 'tis You are, and We must shortly be.
I've heard, that Souls departed have sometimes
Forewarn'd Men of their Death: 'Twas kindly done
To knock, and give th'Alarum. But what means
This stinted Charity? 'tis but lame Kindness
That does its Work by Halves. Why might you not
Tell us what 'tis to Die? Do the strict Laws
Of your Society forbid your speaking
Upon a Point so nice? I'll ask no more;
Sullen, like Lamps in Sepulchres, your Shine
Enlightens but yourselves: Well, — 'tis no Matter;
A very little Time will clear up all,
And make us learn'd as you are, and as close.
Death's Shafts fly thick!

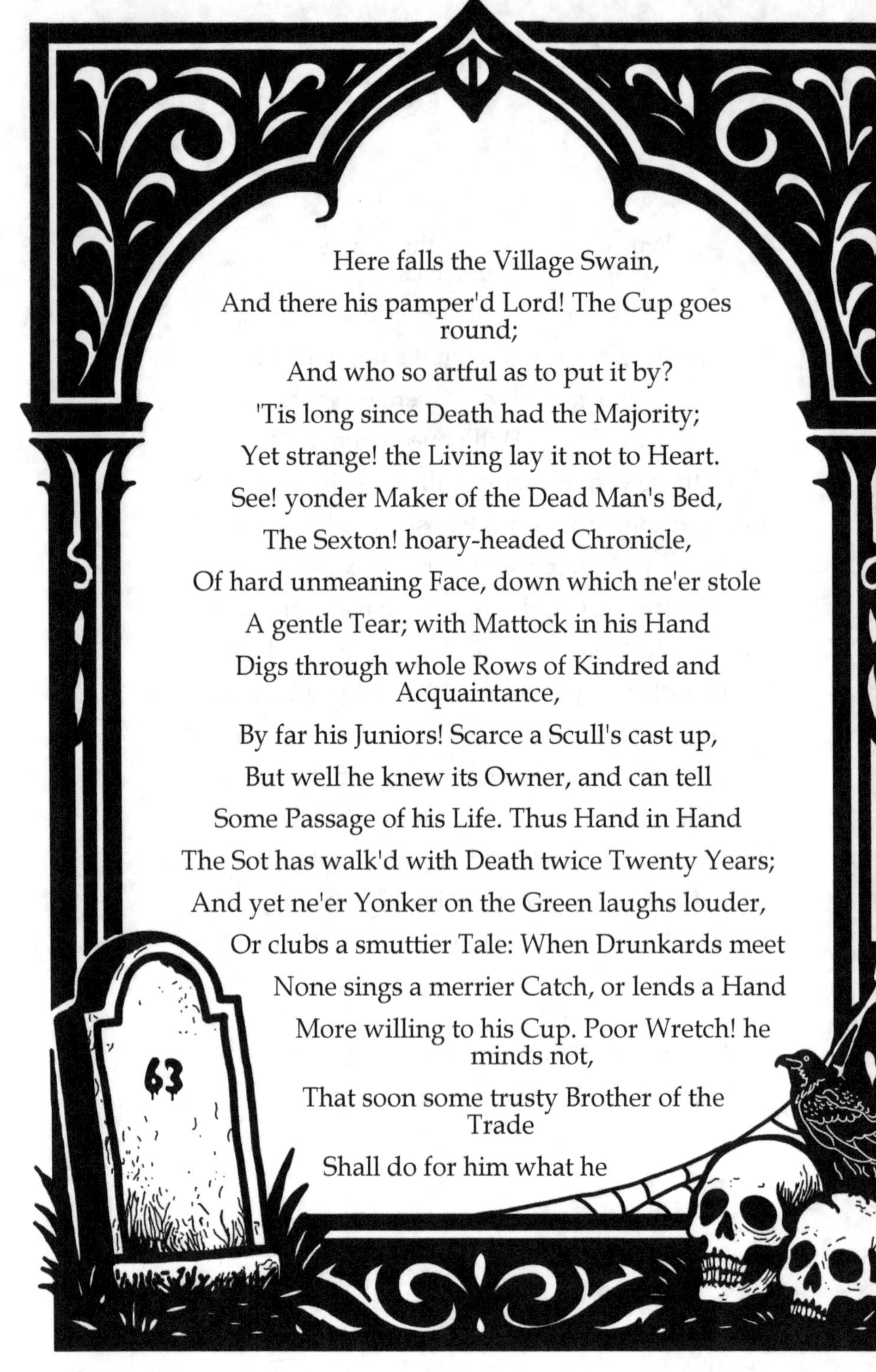

Here falls the Village Swain,
And there his pamper'd Lord! The Cup goes round;
And who so artful as to put it by?
'Tis long since Death had the Majority;
Yet strange! the Living lay it not to Heart.
See! yonder Maker of the Dead Man's Bed,
The Sexton! hoary-headed Chronicle,
Of hard unmeaning Face, down which ne'er stole
A gentle Tear; with Mattock in his Hand
Digs through whole Rows of Kindred and Acquaintance,
By far his Juniors! Scarce a Scull's cast up,
But well he knew its Owner, and can tell
Some Passage of his Life. Thus Hand in Hand
The Sot has walk'd with Death twice Twenty Years;
And yet ne'er Yonker on the Green laughs louder,
Or clubs a smuttier Tale: When Drunkards meet
None sings a merrier Catch, or lends a Hand
More willing to his Cup. Poor Wretch! he minds not,
That soon some trusty Brother of the Trade
Shall do for him what he

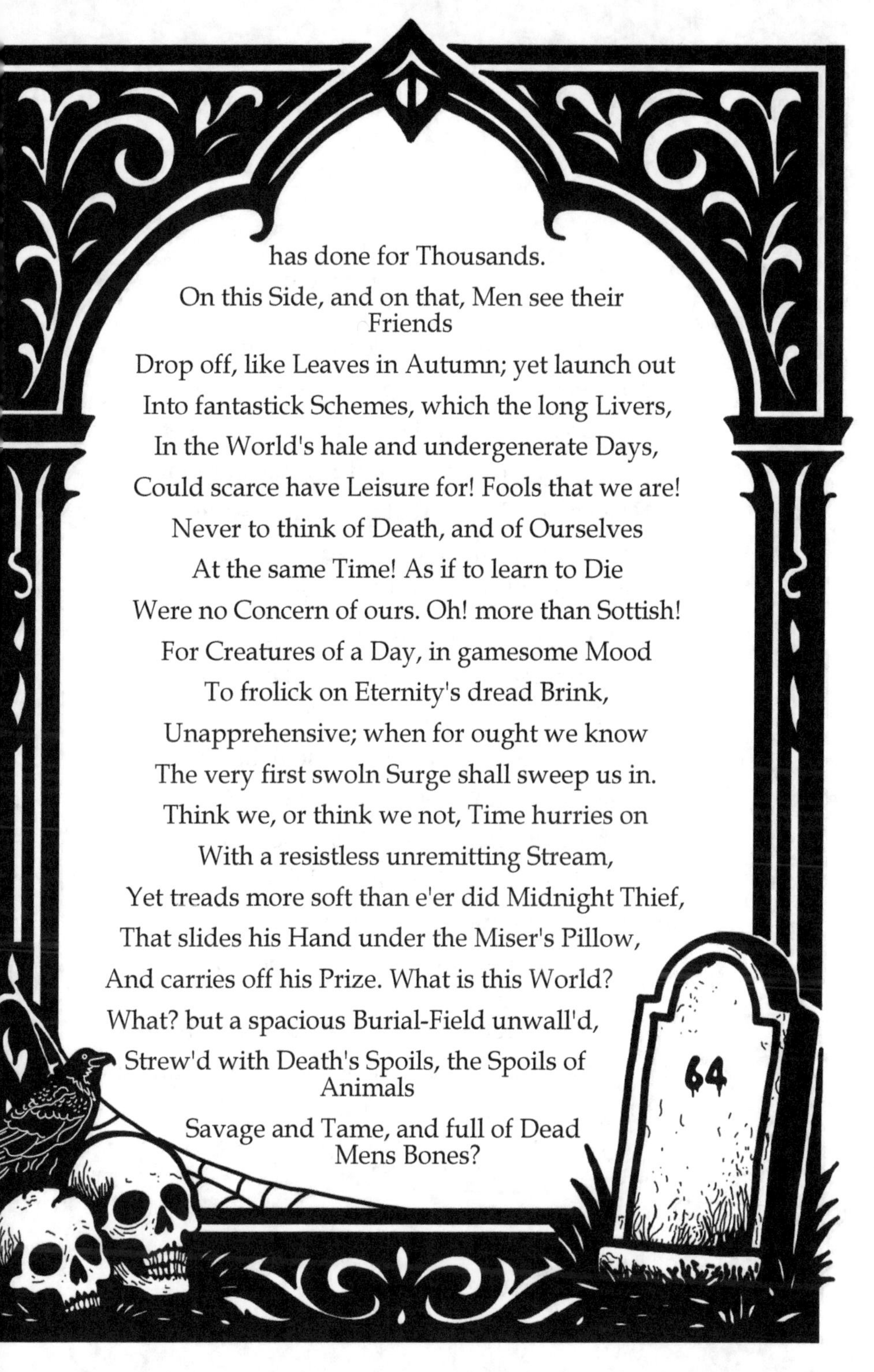

has done for Thousands.
On this Side, and on that, Men see their Friends
Drop off, like Leaves in Autumn; yet launch out
Into fantastick Schemes, which the long Livers,
In the World's hale and undergenerate Days,
Could scarce have Leisure for! Fools that we are!
Never to think of Death, and of Ourselves
At the same Time! As if to learn to Die
Were no Concern of ours. Oh! more than Sottish!
For Creatures of a Day, in gamesome Mood
To frolick on Eternity's dread Brink,
Unapprehensive; when for ought we know
The very first swoln Surge shall sweep us in.
Think we, or think we not, Time hurries on
With a resistless unremitting Stream,
Yet treads more soft than e'er did Midnight Thief,
That slides his Hand under the Miser's Pillow,
And carries off his Prize. What is this World?
What? but a spacious Burial-Field unwall'd,
Strew'd with Death's Spoils, the Spoils of Animals
Savage and Tame, and full of Dead Mens Bones?

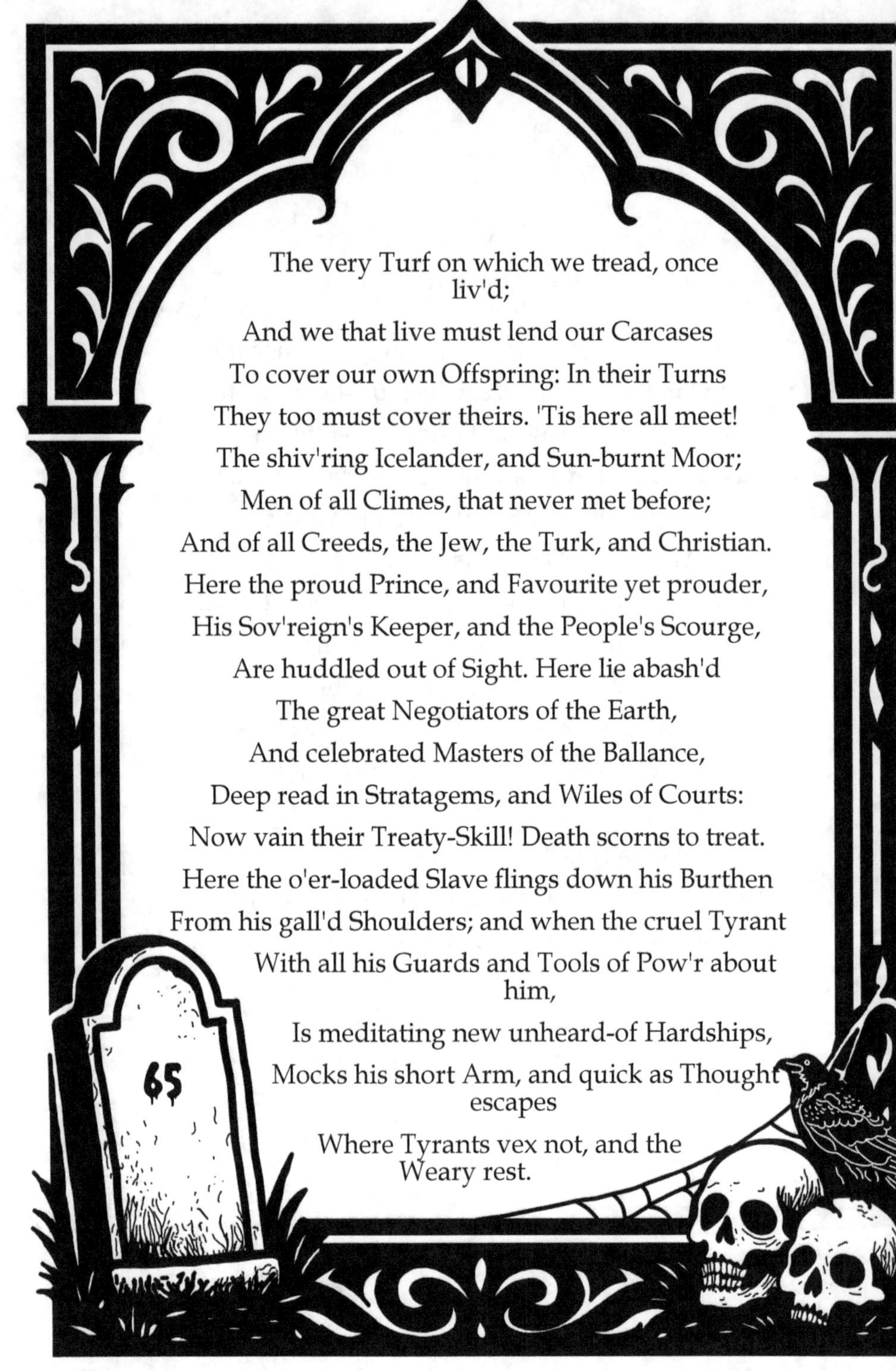

The very Turf on which we tread, once liv'd;
And we that live must lend our Carcases
To cover our own Offspring: In their Turns
They too must cover theirs. 'Tis here all meet!
The shiv'ring Icelander, and Sun-burnt Moor;
Men of all Climes, that never met before;
And of all Creeds, the Jew, the Turk, and Christian.
Here the proud Prince, and Favourite yet prouder,
His Sov'reign's Keeper, and the People's Scourge,
Are huddled out of Sight. Here lie abash'd
The great Negotiators of the Earth,
And celebrated Masters of the Ballance,
Deep read in Stratagems, and Wiles of Courts:
Now vain their Treaty-Skill! Death scorns to treat.
Here the o'er-loaded Slave flings down his Burthen
From his gall'd Shoulders; and when the cruel Tyrant
With all his Guards and Tools of Pow'r about him,
Is meditating new unheard-of Hardships,
Mocks his short Arm, and quick as Thought escapes
Where Tyrants vex not, and the Weary rest.

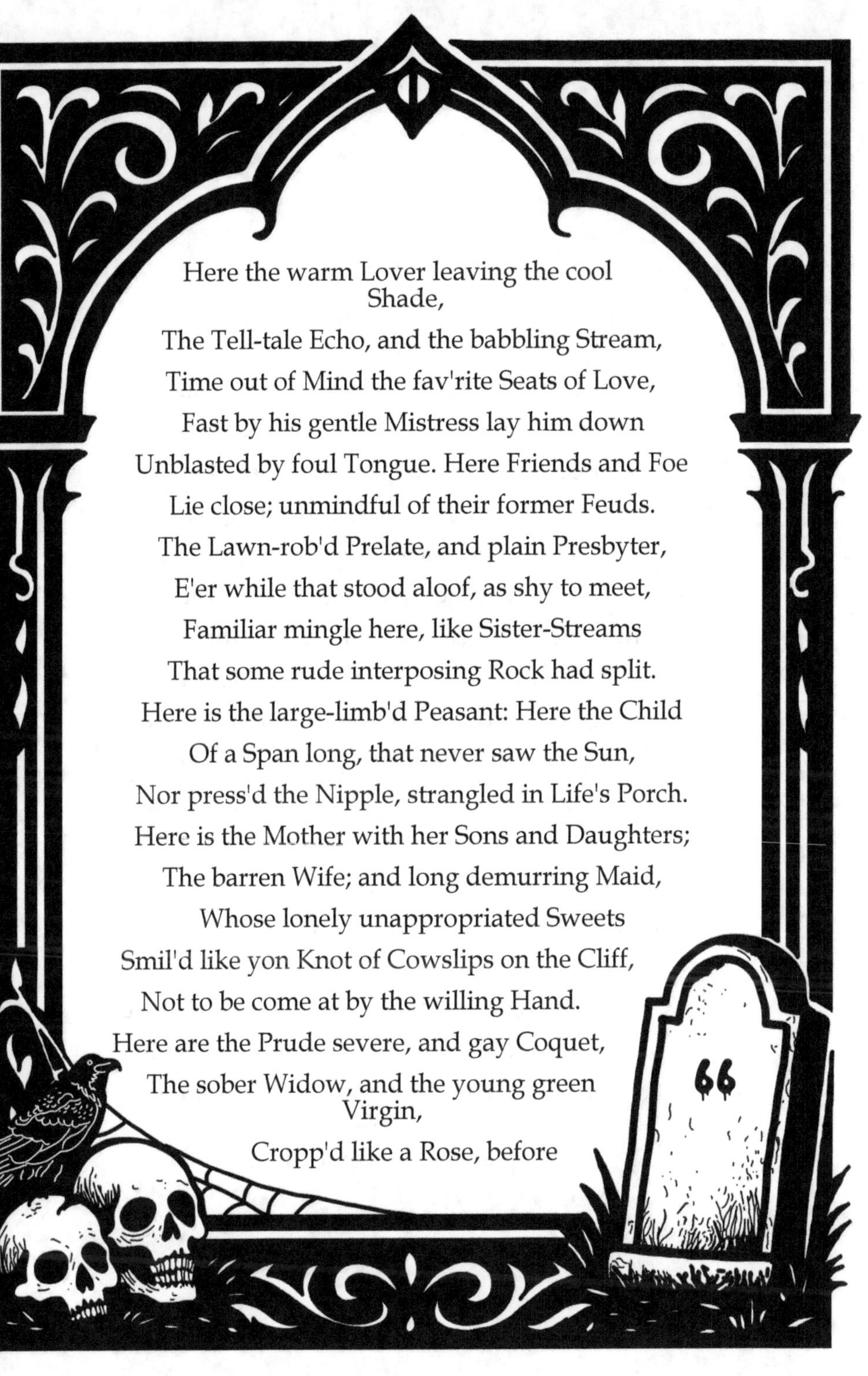

Here the warm Lover leaving the cool Shade,
The Tell-tale Echo, and the babbling Stream,
Time out of Mind the fav'rite Seats of Love,
Fast by his gentle Mistress lay him down
Unblasted by foul Tongue. Here Friends and Foe
Lie close; unmindful of their former Feuds.
The Lawn-rob'd Prelate, and plain Presbyter,
E'er while that stood aloof, as shy to meet,
Familiar mingle here, like Sister-Streams
That some rude interposing Rock had split.
Here is the large-limb'd Peasant: Here the Child
Of a Span long, that never saw the Sun,
Nor press'd the Nipple, strangled in Life's Porch.
Here is the Mother with her Sons and Daughters;
The barren Wife; and long demurring Maid,
Whose lonely unappropriated Sweets
Smil'd like yon Knot of Cowslips on the Cliff,
Not to be come at by the willing Hand.
Here are the Prude severe, and gay Coquet,
The sober Widow, and the young green Virgin,
Cropp'd like a Rose, before

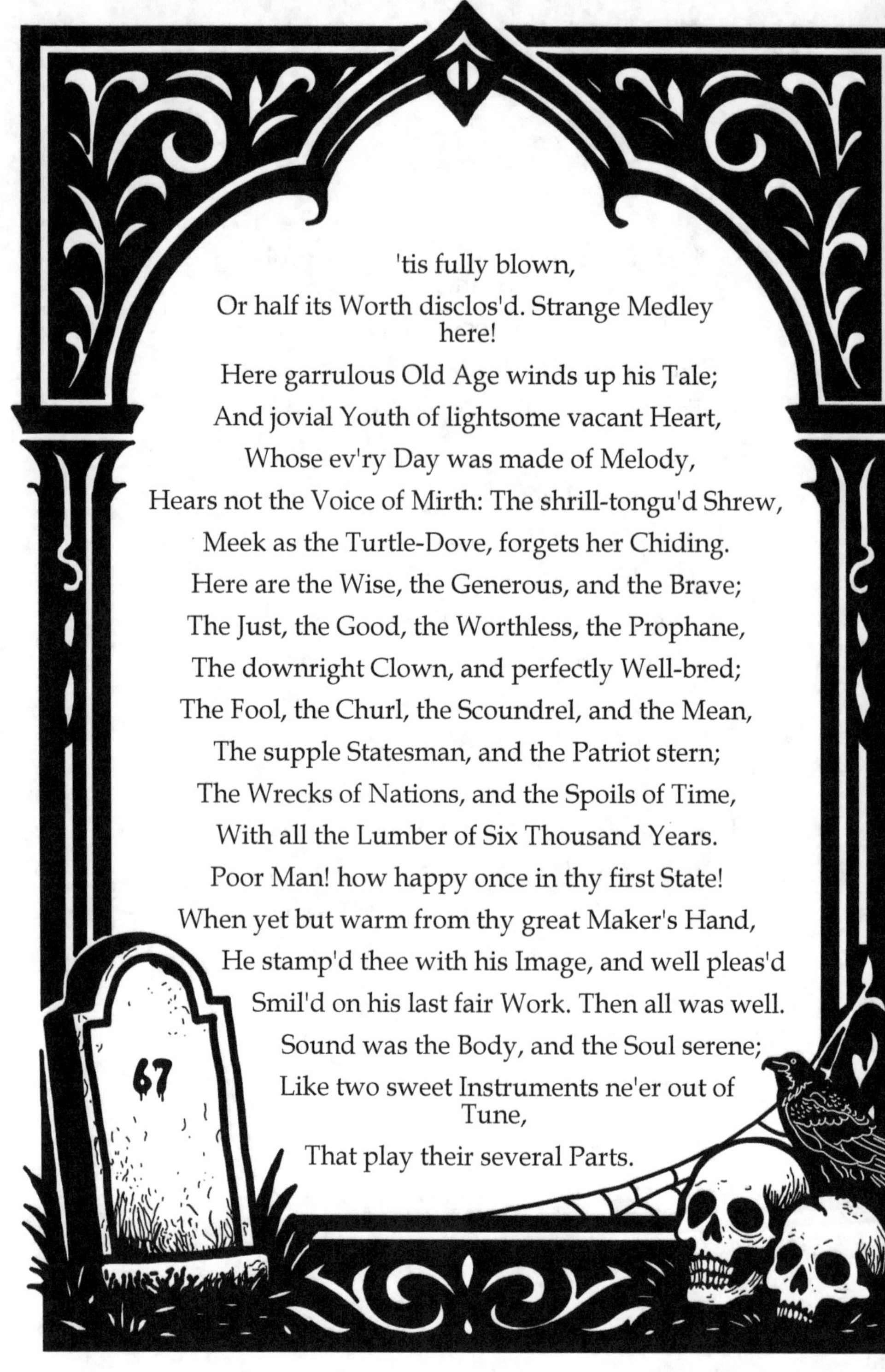

'tis fully blown,
Or half its Worth disclos'd. Strange Medley here!
Here garrulous Old Age winds up his Tale;
And jovial Youth of lightsome vacant Heart,
Whose ev'ry Day was made of Melody,
Hears not the Voice of Mirth: The shrill-tongu'd Shrew,
Meek as the Turtle-Dove, forgets her Chiding.
Here are the Wise, the Generous, and the Brave;
The Just, the Good, the Worthless, the Prophane,
The downright Clown, and perfectly Well-bred;
The Fool, the Churl, the Scoundrel, and the Mean,
The supple Statesman, and the Patriot stern;
The Wrecks of Nations, and the Spoils of Time,
With all the Lumber of Six Thousand Years.
Poor Man! how happy once in thy first State!
When yet but warm from thy great Maker's Hand,
He stamp'd thee with his Image, and well pleas'd
Smil'd on his last fair Work. Then all was well.
Sound was the Body, and the Soul serene;
Like two sweet Instruments ne'er out of Tune,
That play their several Parts.

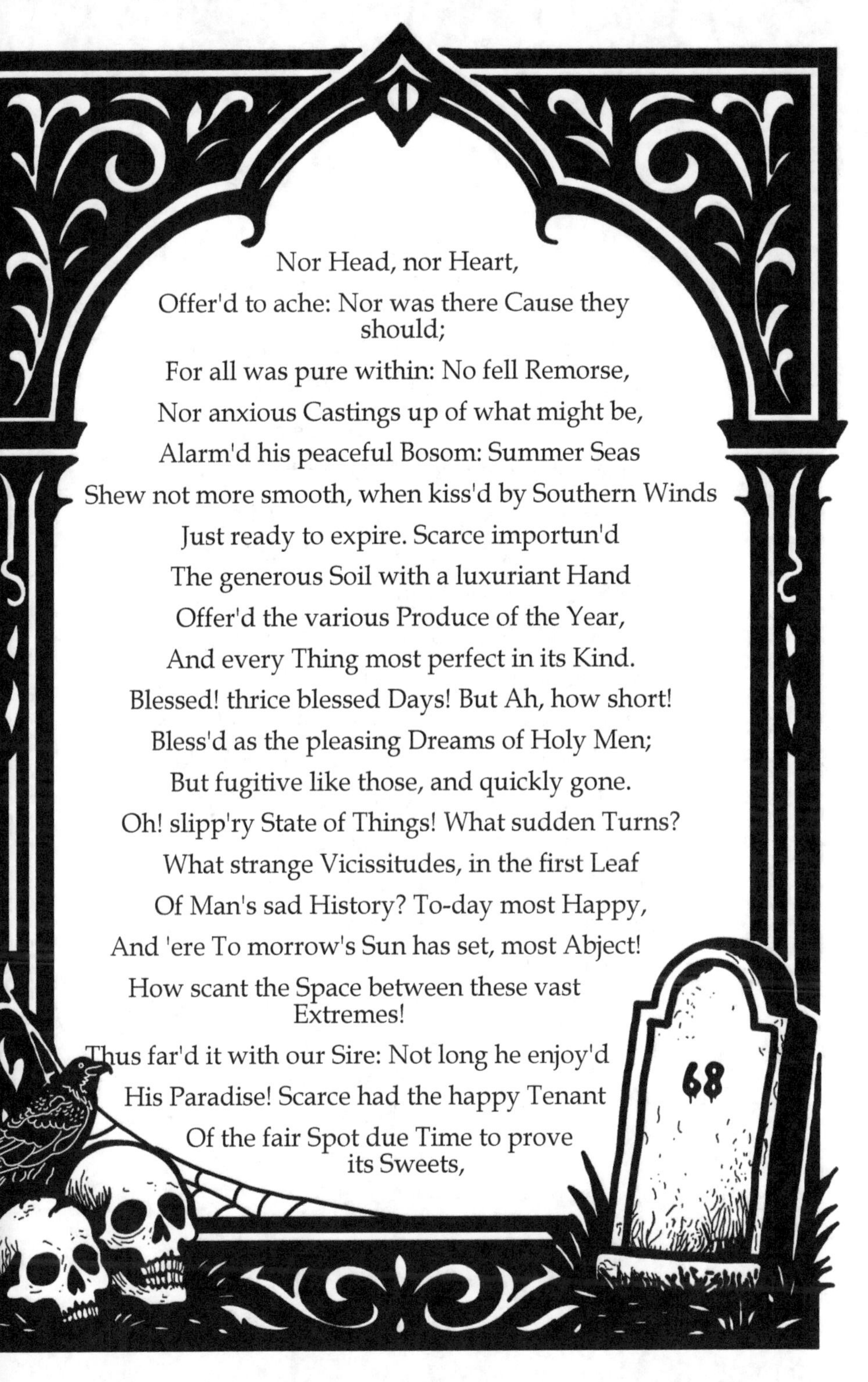

Nor Head, nor Heart,
Offer'd to ache: Nor was there Cause they should;
For all was pure within: No fell Remorse,
Nor anxious Castings up of what might be,
Alarm'd his peaceful Bosom: Summer Seas
Shew not more smooth, when kiss'd by Southern Winds
Just ready to expire. Scarce importun'd
The generous Soil with a luxuriant Hand
Offer'd the various Produce of the Year,
And every Thing most perfect in its Kind.
Blessed! thrice blessed Days! But Ah, how short!
Bless'd as the pleasing Dreams of Holy Men;
But fugitive like those, and quickly gone.
Oh! slipp'ry State of Things! What sudden Turns?
What strange Vicissitudes, in the first Leaf
Of Man's sad History? To-day most Happy,
And 'ere To morrow's Sun has set, most Abject!
How scant the Space between these vast Extremes!
Thus far'd it with our Sire: Not long he enjoy'd
His Paradise! Scarce had the happy Tenant
Of the fair Spot due Time to prove its Sweets,

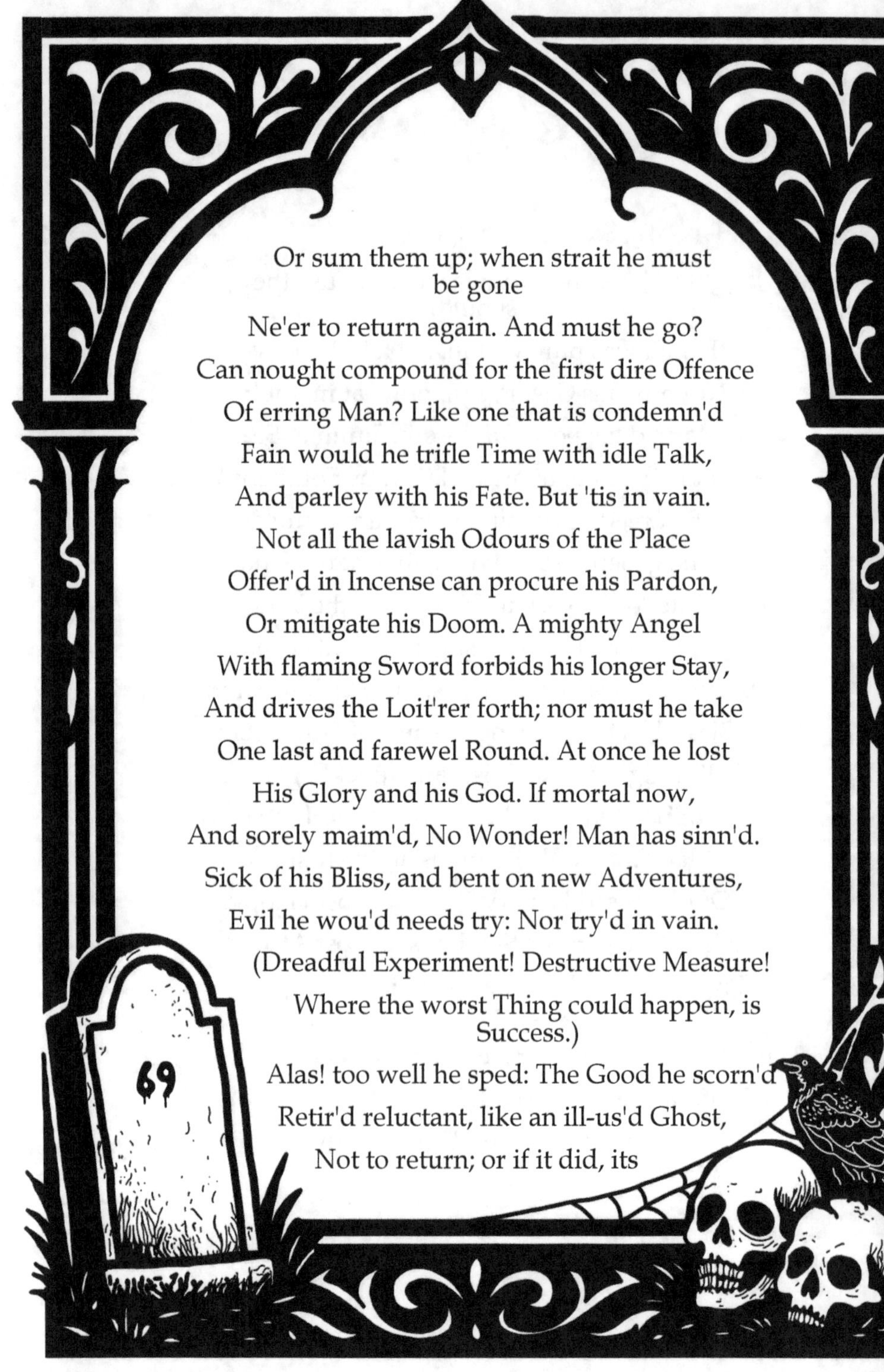

Or sum them up; when strait he must be gone
Ne'er to return again. And must he go?
Can nought compound for the first dire Offence
Of erring Man? Like one that is condemn'd
Fain would he trifle Time with idle Talk,
And parley with his Fate. But 'tis in vain.
Not all the lavish Odours of the Place
Offer'd in Incense can procure his Pardon,
Or mitigate his Doom. A mighty Angel
With flaming Sword forbids his longer Stay,
And drives the Loit'rer forth; nor must he take
One last and farewel Round. At once he lost
His Glory and his God. If mortal now,
And sorely maim'd, No Wonder! Man has sinn'd.
Sick of his Bliss, and bent on new Adventures,
Evil he wou'd needs try: Nor try'd in vain.
(Dreadful Experiment! Destructive Measure!
Where the worst Thing could happen, is Success.)
Alas! too well he sped: The Good he scorn'd
Retir'd reluctant, like an ill-us'd Ghost,
Not to return; or if it did, its

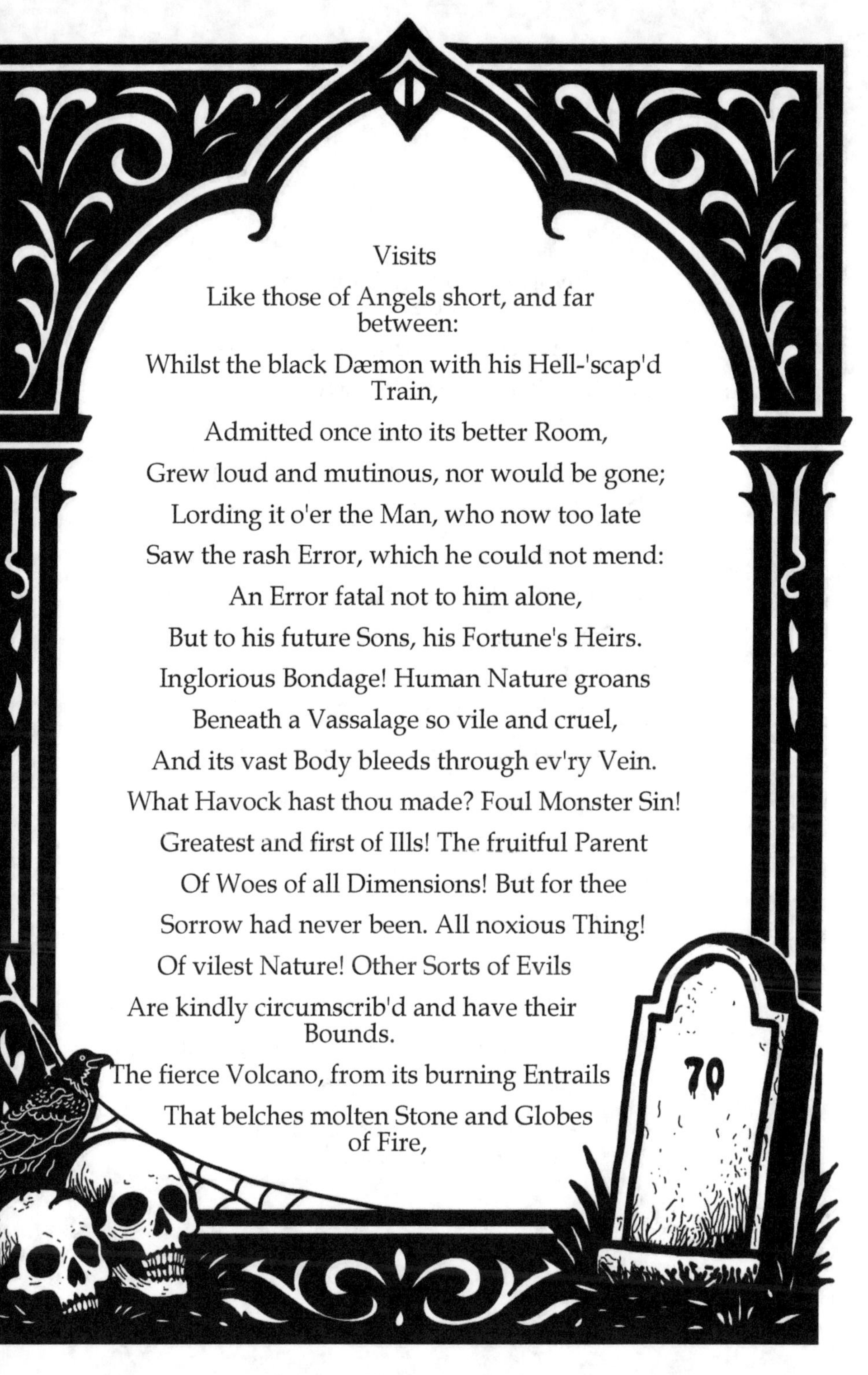

Visits
Like those of Angels short, and far between:
Whilst the black Dæmon with his Hell-'scap'd Train,
Admitted once into its better Room,
Grew loud and mutinous, nor would be gone;
Lording it o'er the Man, who now too late
Saw the rash Error, which he could not mend:
An Error fatal not to him alone,
But to his future Sons, his Fortune's Heirs.
Inglorious Bondage! Human Nature groans
Beneath a Vassalage so vile and cruel,
And its vast Body bleeds through ev'ry Vein.
What Havock hast thou made? Foul Monster Sin!
Greatest and first of Ills! The fruitful Parent
Of Woes of all Dimensions! But for thee
Sorrow had never been. All noxious Thing!
Of vilest Nature! Other Sorts of Evils
Are kindly circumscrib'd and have their Bounds.
The fierce Volcano, from its burning Entrails
That belches molten Stone and Globes of Fire,

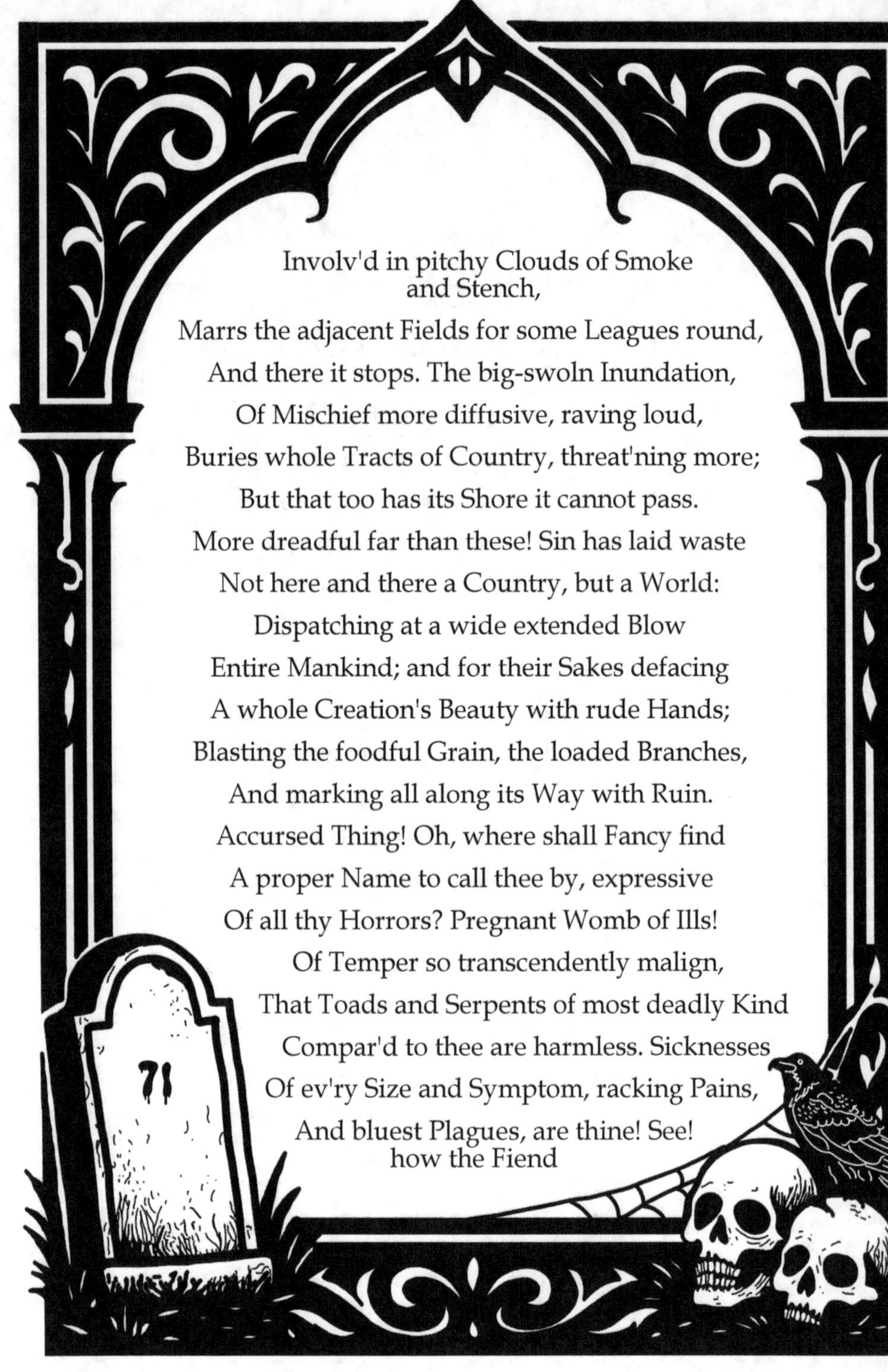

Involv'd in pitchy Clouds of Smoke and Stench,
Marrs the adjacent Fields for some Leagues round,
And there it stops. The big-swoln Inundation,
Of Mischief more diffusive, raving loud,
Buries whole Tracts of Country, threat'ning more;
But that too has its Shore it cannot pass.
More dreadful far than these! Sin has laid waste
Not here and there a Country, but a World:
Dispatching at a wide extended Blow
Entire Mankind; and for their Sakes defacing
A whole Creation's Beauty with rude Hands;
Blasting the foodful Grain, the loaded Branches,
And marking all along its Way with Ruin.
Accursed Thing! Oh, where shall Fancy find
A proper Name to call thee by, expressive
Of all thy Horrors? Pregnant Womb of Ills!
Of Temper so transcendently malign,
That Toads and Serpents of most deadly Kind
Compar'd to thee are harmless. Sicknesses
Of ev'ry Size and Symptom, racking Pains,
And bluest Plagues, are thine! See! how the Fiend

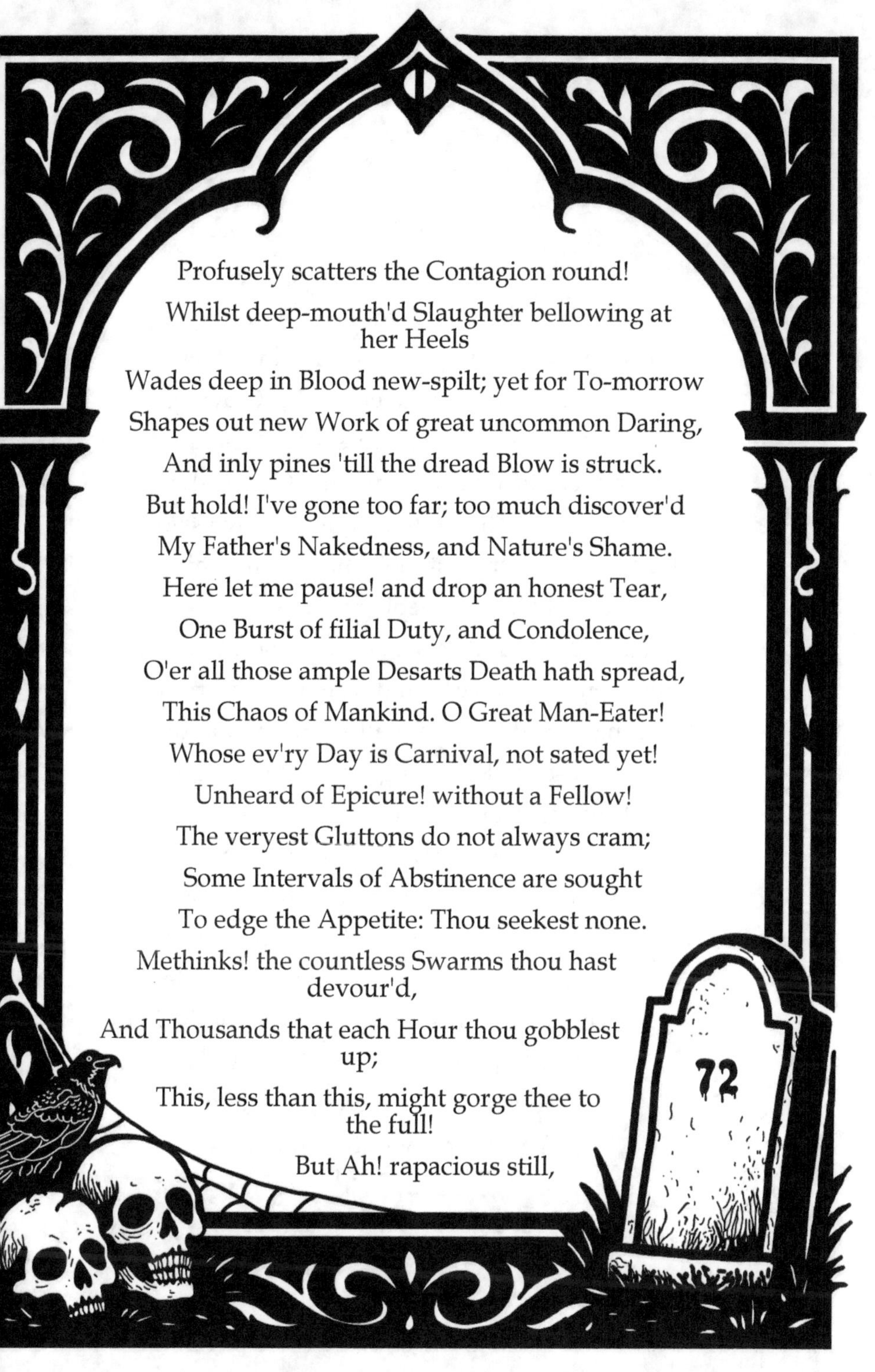

Profusely scatters the Contagion round!
Whilst deep-mouth'd Slaughter bellowing at her Heels
Wades deep in Blood new-spilt; yet for To-morrow
Shapes out new Work of great uncommon Daring,
And inly pines 'till the dread Blow is struck.
But hold! I've gone too far; too much discover'd
My Father's Nakedness, and Nature's Shame.
Here let me pause! and drop an honest Tear,
One Burst of filial Duty, and Condolence,
O'er all those ample Desarts Death hath spread,
This Chaos of Mankind. O Great Man-Eater!
Whose ev'ry Day is Carnival, not sated yet!
Unheard of Epicure! without a Fellow!
The veryest Gluttons do not always cram;
Some Intervals of Abstinence are sought
To edge the Appetite: Thou seekest none.
Methinks! the countless Swarms thou hast devour'd,
And Thousands that each Hour thou gobblest up;
This, less than this, might gorge thee to the full!
But Ah! rapacious still,

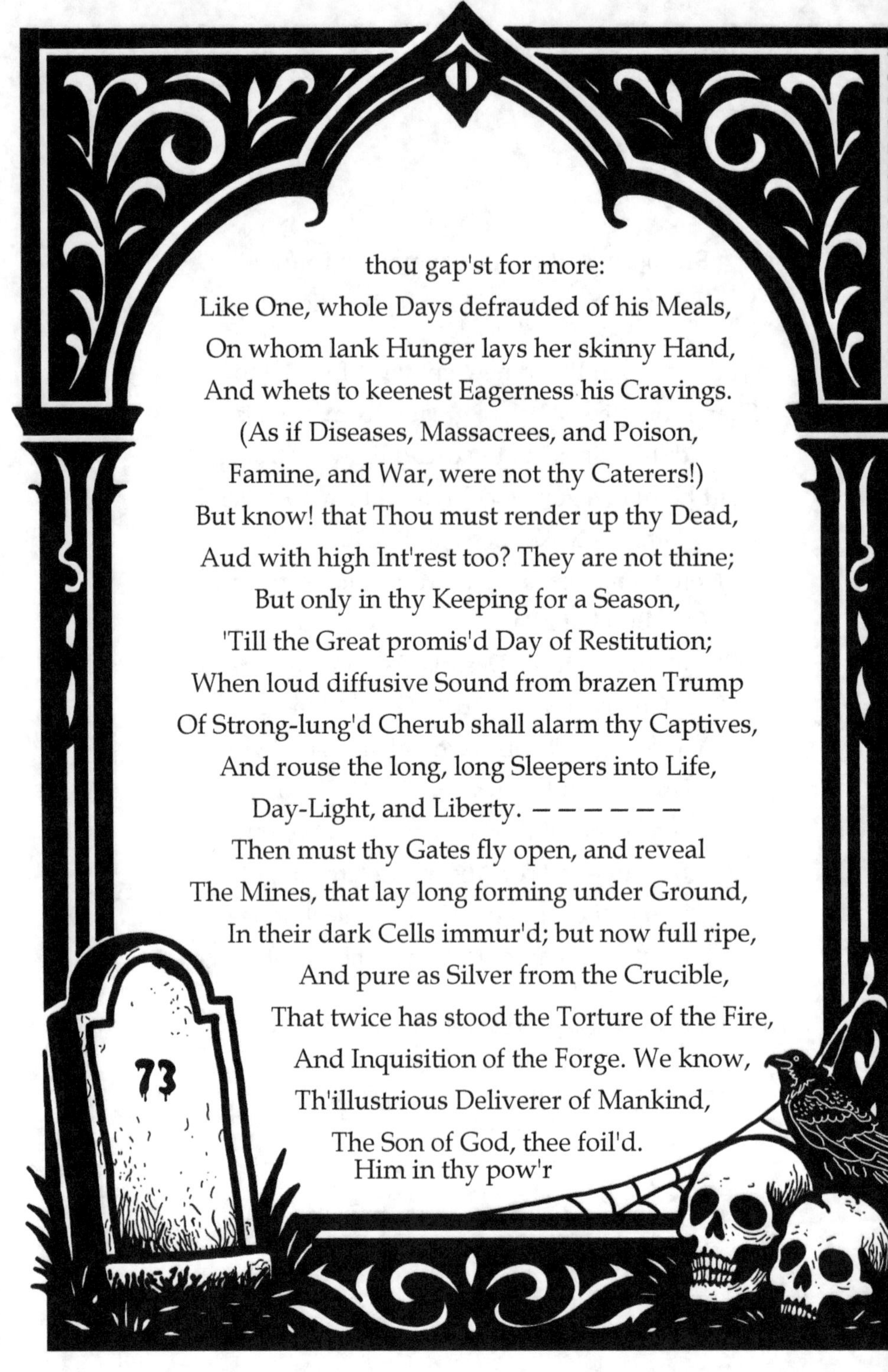

thou gap'st for more:
Like One, whole Days defrauded of his Meals,
On whom lank Hunger lays her skinny Hand,
And whets to keenest Eagerness his Cravings.
(As if Diseases, Massacrees, and Poison,
Famine, and War, were not thy Caterers!)
But know! that Thou must render up thy Dead,
Aud with high Int'rest too? They are not thine;
But only in thy Keeping for a Season,
'Till the Great promis'd Day of Restitution;
When loud diffusive Sound from brazen Trump
Of Strong-lung'd Cherub shall alarm thy Captives,
And rouse the long, long Sleepers into Life,
Day-Light, and Liberty. — — — — — —
Then must thy Gates fly open, and reveal
The Mines, that lay long forming under Ground,
In their dark Cells immur'd; but now full ripe,
And pure as Silver from the Crucible,
That twice has stood the Torture of the Fire,
And Inquisition of the Forge. We know,
Th'illustrious Deliverer of Mankind,
The Son of God, thee foil'd.
Him in thy pow'r

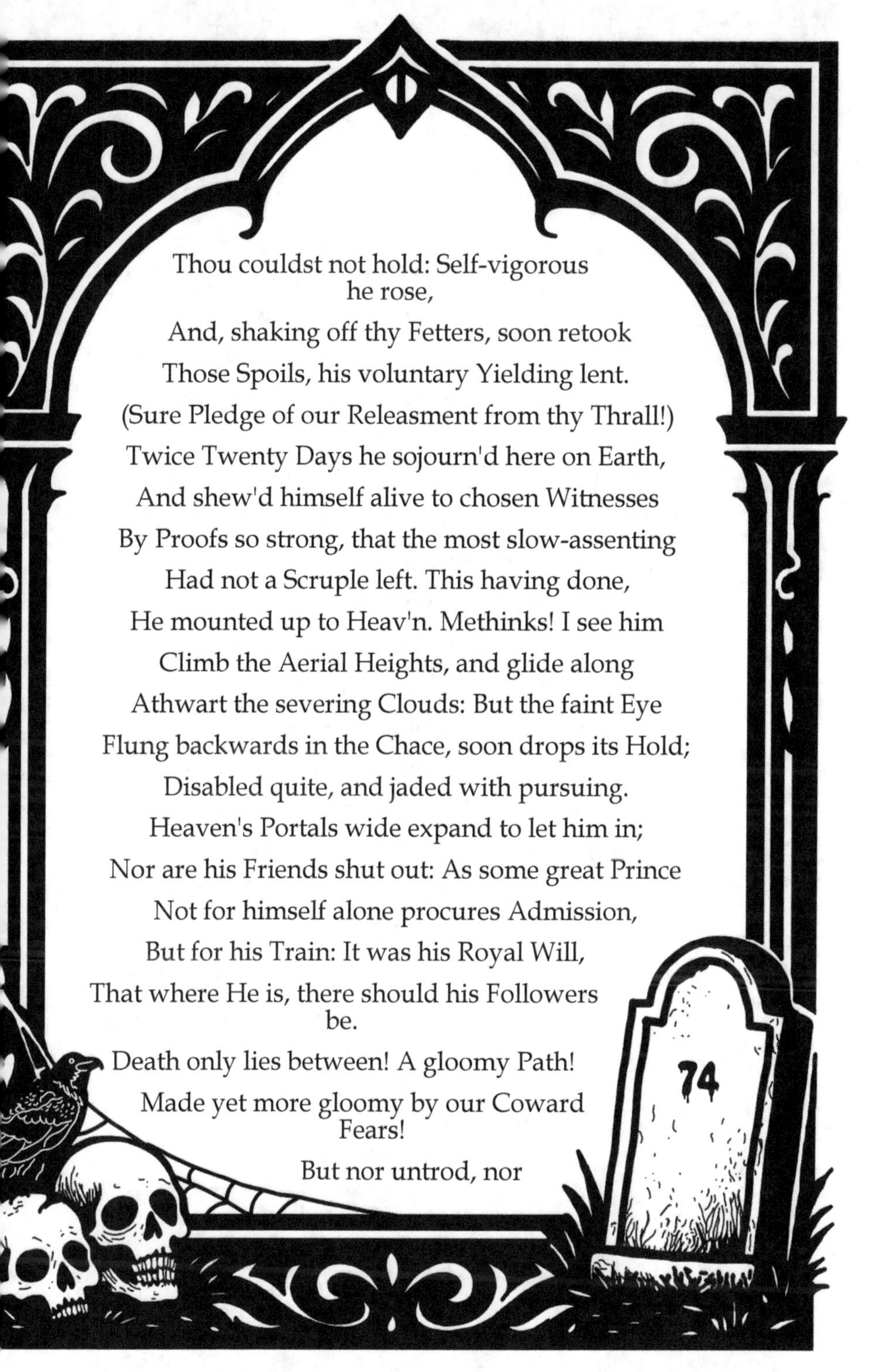

Thou couldst not hold: Self-vigorous he rose,
And, shaking off thy Fetters, soon retook
Those Spoils, his voluntary Yielding lent.
(Sure Pledge of our Releasment from thy Thrall!)
Twice Twenty Days he sojourn'd here on Earth,
And shew'd himself alive to chosen Witnesses
By Proofs so strong, that the most slow-assenting
Had not a Scruple left. This having done,
He mounted up to Heav'n. Methinks! I see him
Climb the Aerial Heights, and glide along
Athwart the severing Clouds: But the faint Eye
Flung backwards in the Chace, soon drops its Hold;
Disabled quite, and jaded with pursuing.
Heaven's Portals wide expand to let him in;
Nor are his Friends shut out: As some great Prince
Not for himself alone procures Admission,
But for his Train: It was his Royal Will,
That where He is, there should his Followers be.
Death only lies between! A gloomy Path!
Made yet more gloomy by our Coward Fears!
But nor untrod, nor

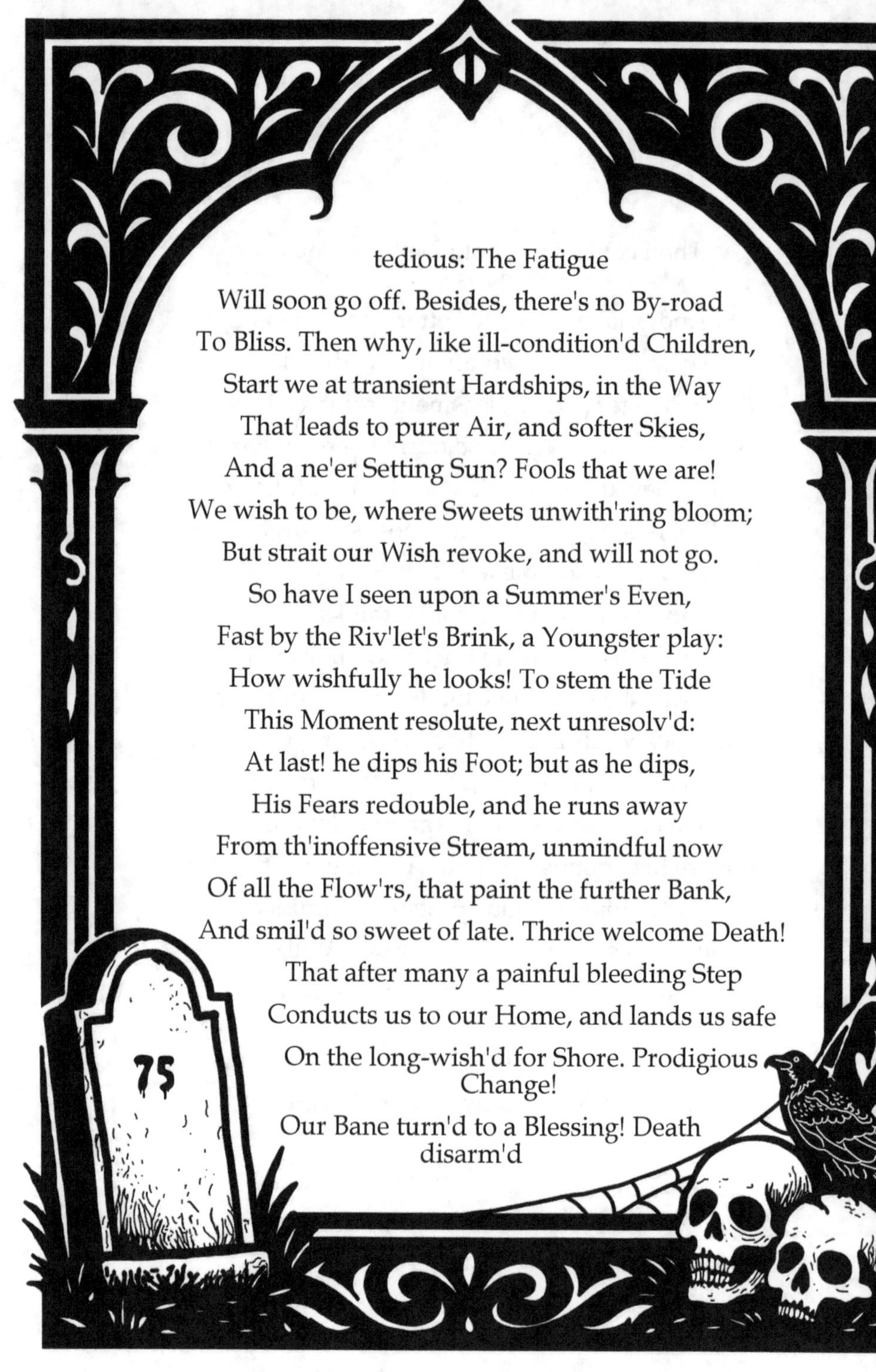

tedious: The Fatigue
Will soon go off. Besides, there's no By-road
To Bliss. Then why, like ill-condition'd Children,
Start we at transient Hardships, in the Way
That leads to purer Air, and softer Skies,
And a ne'er Setting Sun? Fools that we are!
We wish to be, where Sweets unwith'ring bloom;
But strait our Wish revoke, and will not go.
So have I seen upon a Summer's Even,
Fast by the Riv'let's Brink, a Youngster play:
How wishfully he looks! To stem the Tide
This Moment resolute, next unresolv'd:
At last! he dips his Foot; but as he dips,
His Fears redouble, and he runs away
From th'inoffensive Stream, unmindful now
Of all the Flow'rs, that paint the further Bank,
And smil'd so sweet of late. Thrice welcome Death!
That after many a painful bleeding Step
Conducts us to our Home, and lands us safe
On the long-wish'd for Shore. Prodigious Change!
Our Bane turn'd to a Blessing! Death disarm'd

Loses her Fullness quite: All Thanks to him
Who scourg'd the Venom out. Sure! the last End
Of the Good Man is Peace. How calm his Exit!
Night-Dews fall not more gently to the Ground,
Nor weary worn-out Winds expire so soft.
Behold him! in the Evening-Tide of Life,
A Life well-spent, whose early Care it was
His riper Years should not upbraid his Green:
By unperceiv'd Degrees he wears away;
Yet like the Sun seems larger at his Setting!
High in his Faith and Hopes, look! how he reaches
After the Prize in View! and, like a Bird
That's hamper'd struggles hard to get away!
Whilst the glad Gates of Sight are wide expanded
To let new Glories in, the first fair Fruits
Of the fast-coming Harvest. Then! Oh Then!
Each Earth-born Joy grows vile, or disappears,
Shrunk to a Thing of Nought. Oh! how he longs
To have has Passport sign'd, and be dismiss'd!
'Tis done; and now he's Happy: The glad Soul
Has not a Wish uncrown'd. Ev'n the lag Flesh

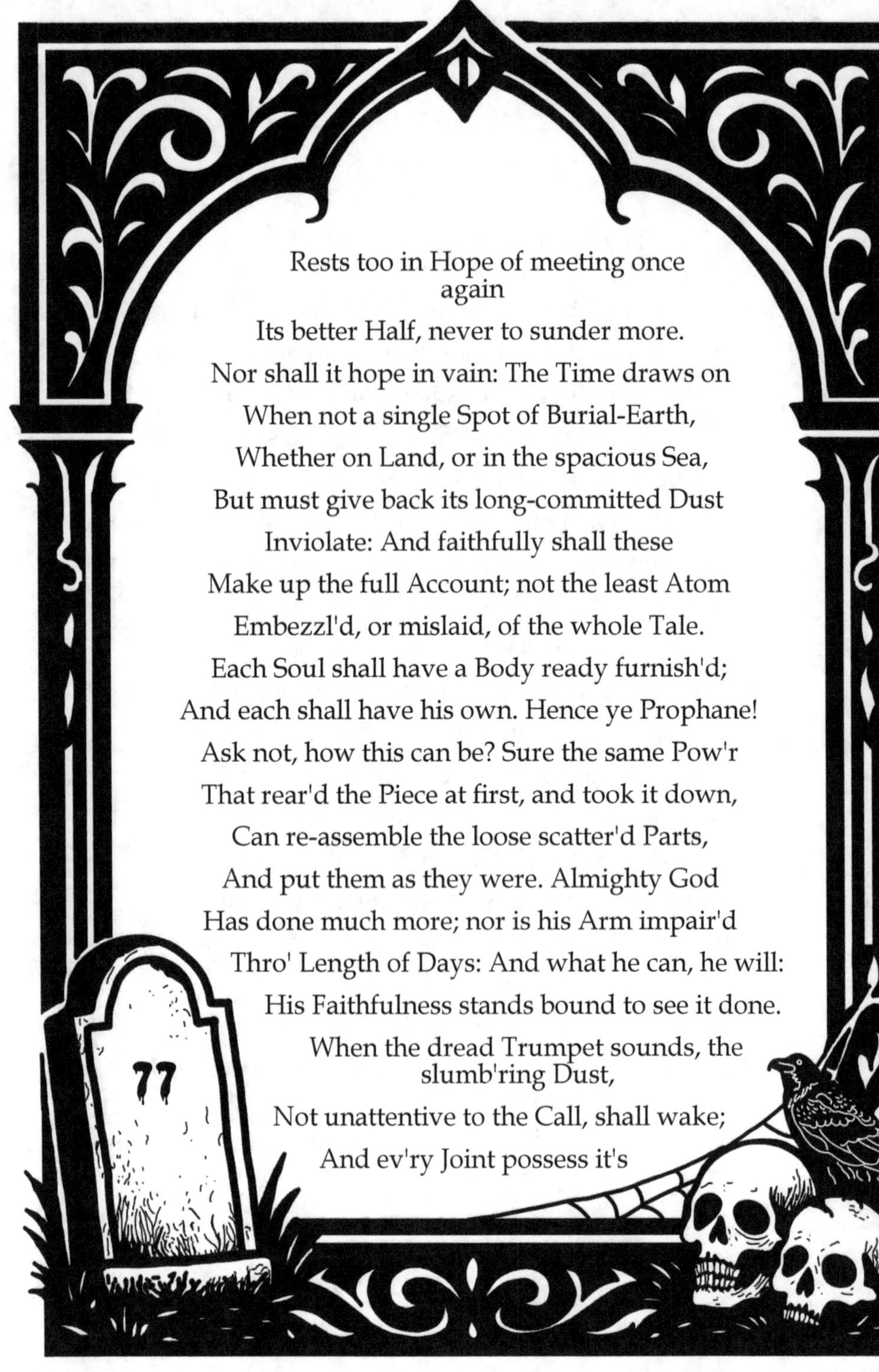

Rests too in Hope of meeting once again
Its better Half, never to sunder more.
Nor shall it hope in vain: The Time draws on
When not a single Spot of Burial-Earth,
Whether on Land, or in the spacious Sea,
But must give back its long-committed Dust
Inviolate: And faithfully shall these
Make up the full Account; not the least Atom
Embezzl'd, or mislaid, of the whole Tale.
Each Soul shall have a Body ready furnish'd;
And each shall have his own. Hence ye Prophane!
Ask not, how this can be? Sure the same Pow'r
That rear'd the Piece at first, and took it down,
Can re-assemble the loose scatter'd Parts,
And put them as they were. Almighty God
Has done much more; nor is his Arm impair'd
Thro' Length of Days: And what he can, he will:
His Faithfulness stands bound to see it done.
When the dread Trumpet sounds, the slumb'ring Dust,
Not unattentive to the Call, shall wake;
And ev'ry Joint possess it's

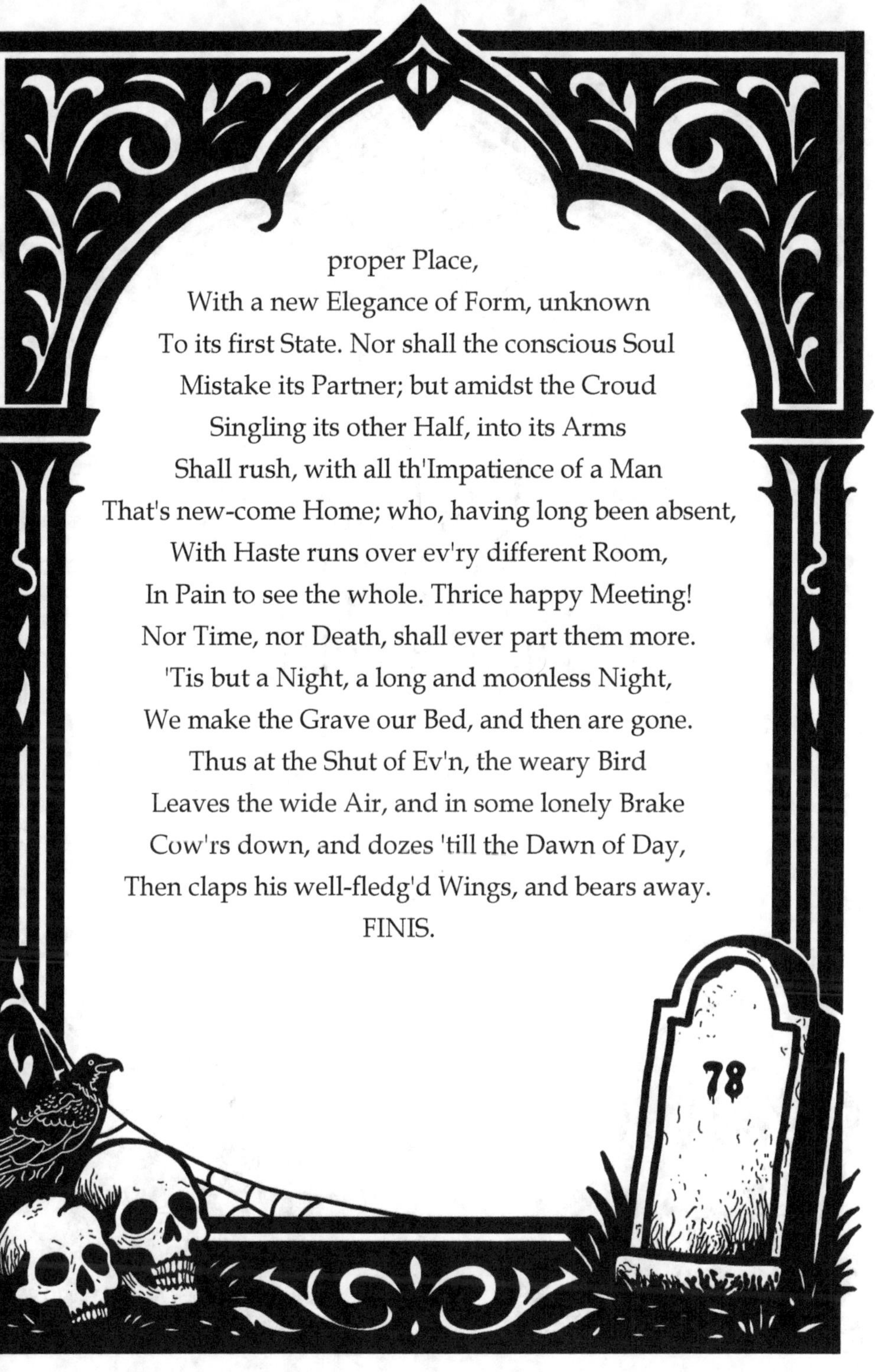

proper Place,
With a new Elegance of Form, unknown
To its first State. Nor shall the conscious Soul
Mistake its Partner; but amidst the Croud
Singling its other Half, into its Arms
Shall rush, with all th'Impatience of a Man
That's new-come Home; who, having long been absent,
With Haste runs over ev'ry different Room,
In Pain to see the whole. Thrice happy Meeting!
Nor Time, nor Death, shall ever part them more.
'Tis but a Night, a long and moonless Night,
We make the Grave our Bed, and then are gone.
Thus at the Shut of Ev'n, the weary Bird
Leaves the wide Air, and in some lonely Brake
Cow'rs down, and dozes 'till the Dawn of Day,
Then claps his well-fledg'd Wings, and bears away.

FINIS.

William Stanley Braithwaite

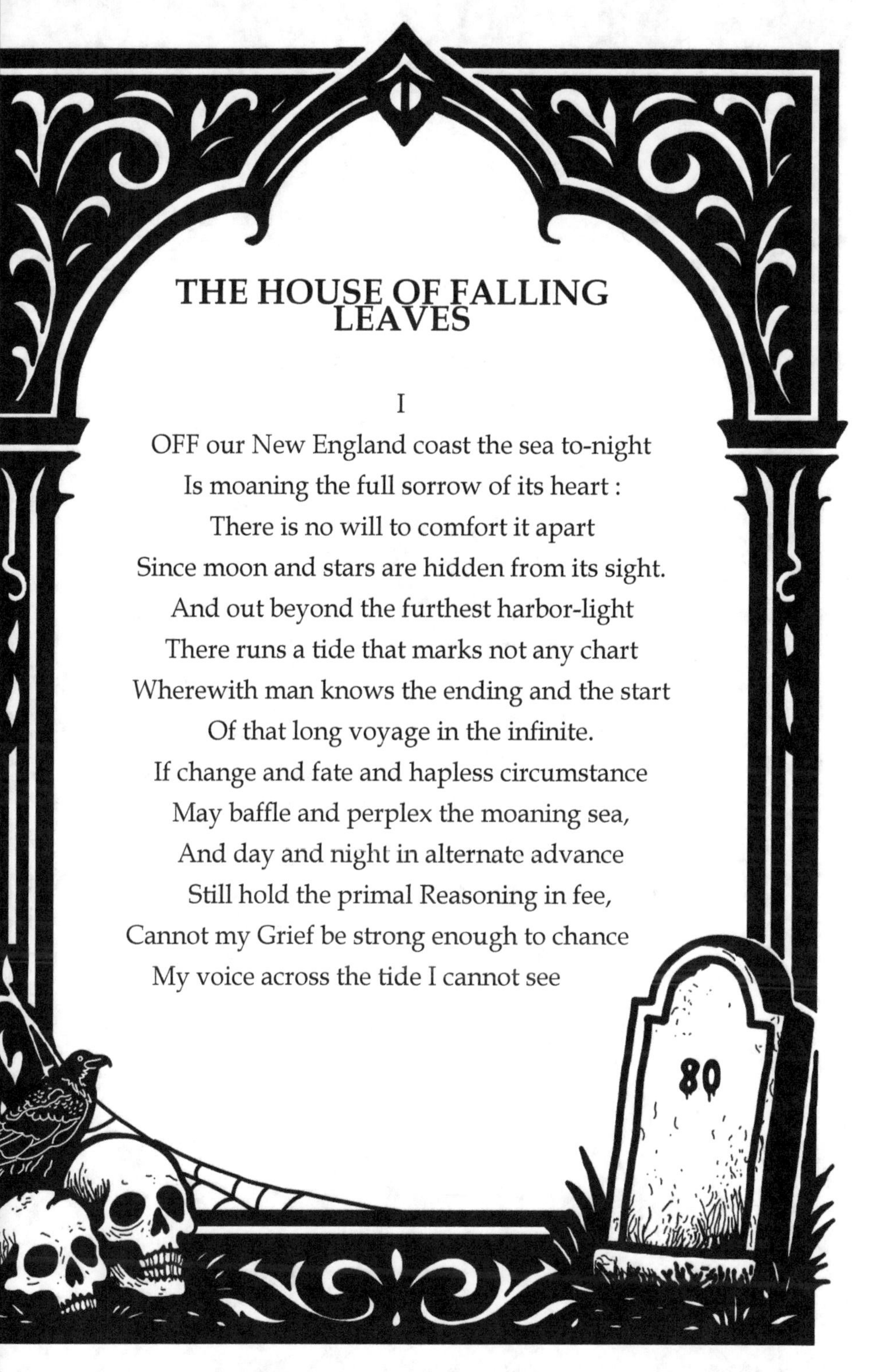

THE HOUSE OF FALLING LEAVES

I

OFF our New England coast the sea to-night
Is moaning the full sorrow of its heart :
There is no will to comfort it apart
Since moon and stars are hidden from its sight.
And out beyond the furthest harbor-light
There runs a tide that marks not any chart
Wherewith man knows the ending and the start
Of that long voyage in the infinite.
If change and fate and hapless circumstance
May baffle and perplex the moaning sea,
And day and night in alternate advance
Still hold the primal Reasoning in fee,
Cannot my Grief be strong enough to chance
My voice across the tide I cannot see

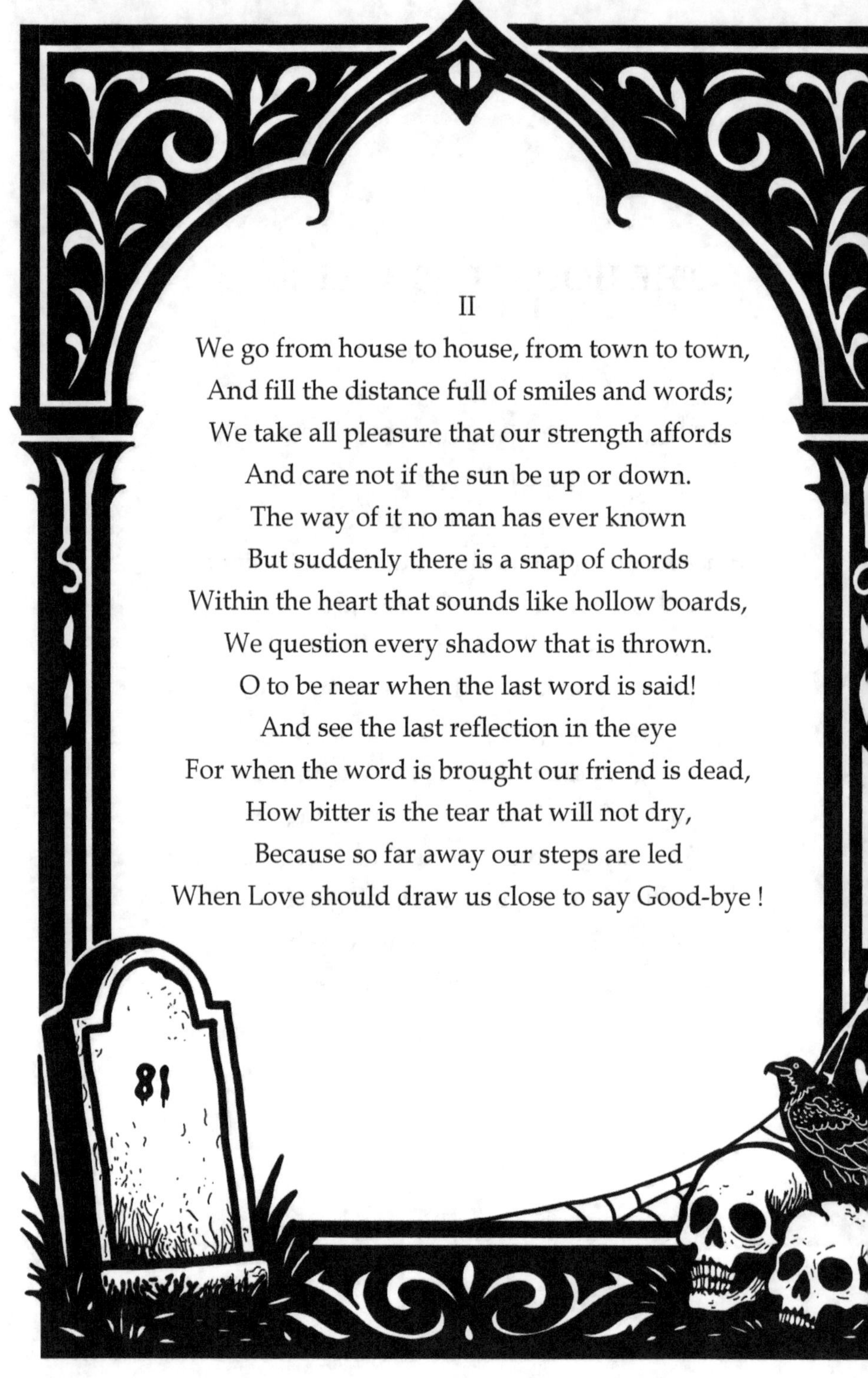

II

We go from house to house, from town to town,
And fill the distance full of smiles and words;
We take all pleasure that our strength affords
And care not if the sun be up or down.
The way of it no man has ever known
But suddenly there is a snap of chords
Within the heart that sounds like hollow boards,
We question every shadow that is thrown.
O to be near when the last word is said!
And see the last reflection in the eye
For when the word is brought our friend is dead,
How bitter is the tear that will not dry,
Because so far away our steps are led
When Love should draw us close to say Good-bye !

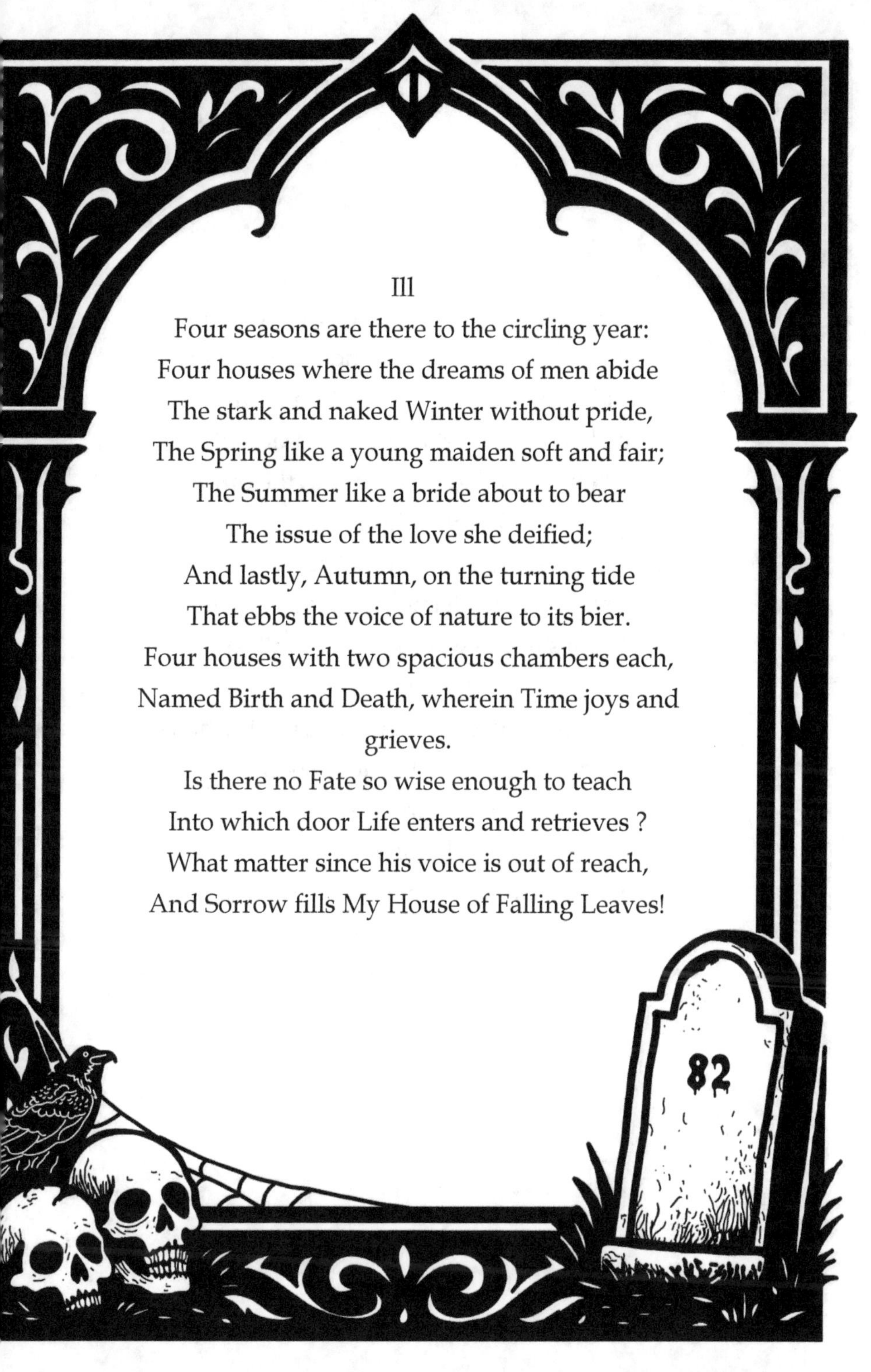

III

Four seasons are there to the circling year:
Four houses where the dreams of men abide
The stark and naked Winter without pride,
The Spring like a young maiden soft and fair;
The Summer like a bride about to bear
The issue of the love she deified;
And lastly, Autumn, on the turning tide
That ebbs the voice of nature to its bier.
Four houses with two spacious chambers each,
Named Birth and Death, wherein Time joys and grieves.
Is there no Fate so wise enough to teach
Into which door Life enters and retrieves ?
What matter since his voice is out of reach,
And Sorrow fills My House of Falling Leaves!

IV

The House of Falling Leaves we entered in
He and I we entered in and found it fair;
At midnight some one called him up the stair,
And closed him in the Room I could not win.
Now must I go alone out in the din
Of hurrying days :
for forth he cannot fare;
I must go on with Time, and leave him there
In Autumn s house where dreams will soon grow
thin.
When Time shall close the door unto the house
And opens that of Winter s soon to be,
And dreams go moving through the ruined
boughs
He who went in comes out a Memory.
From his deep sleep no sound may e er arouse,
The moaning rain, nor wind-embattled sea.

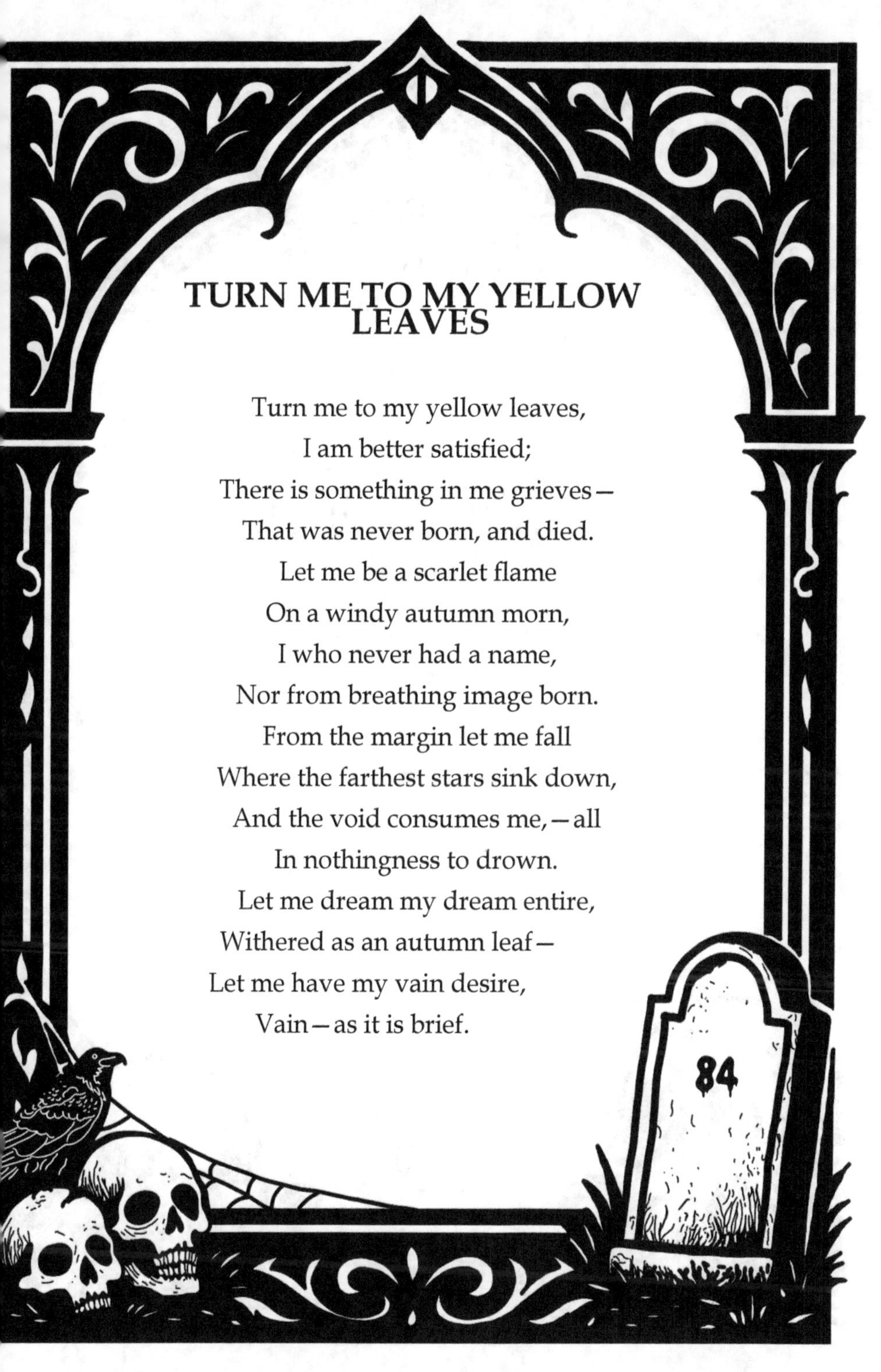

TURN ME TO MY YELLOW LEAVES

Turn me to my yellow leaves,
I am better satisfied;
There is something in me grieves—
That was never born, and died.
Let me be a scarlet flame
On a windy autumn morn,
I who never had a name,
Nor from breathing image born.
From the margin let me fall
Where the farthest stars sink down,
And the void consumes me,—all
In nothingness to drown.
Let me dream my dream entire,
Withered as an autumn leaf—
Let me have my vain desire,
Vain—as it is brief.

Anne Brontë

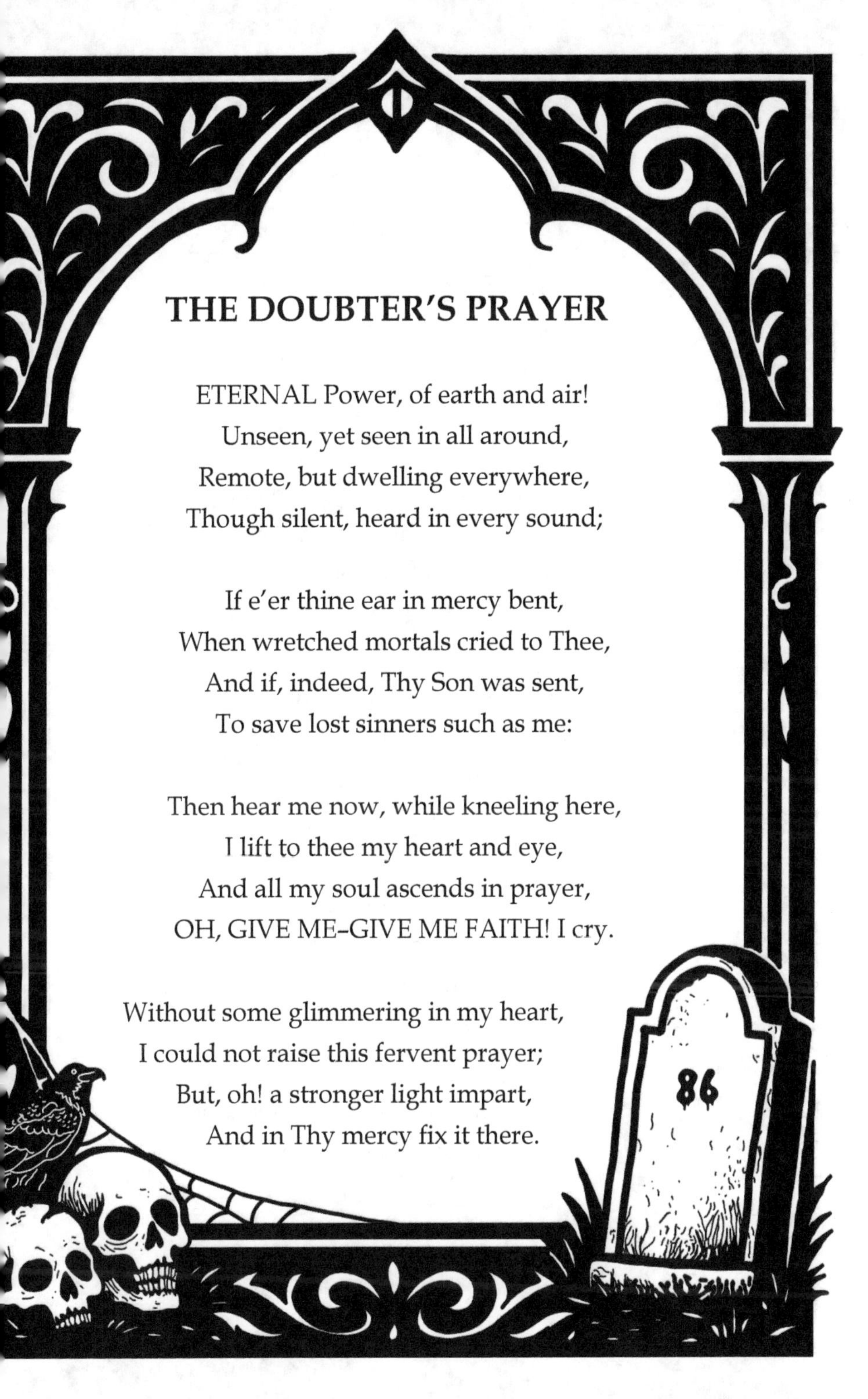

THE DOUBTER'S PRAYER

ETERNAL Power, of earth and air!
Unseen, yet seen in all around,
Remote, but dwelling everywhere,
Though silent, heard in every sound;

If e'er thine ear in mercy bent,
When wretched mortals cried to Thee,
And if, indeed, Thy Son was sent,
To save lost sinners such as me:

Then hear me now, while kneeling here,
I lift to thee my heart and eye,
And all my soul ascends in prayer,
OH, GIVE ME–GIVE ME FAITH! I cry.

Without some glimmering in my heart,
I could not raise this fervent prayer;
But, oh! a stronger light impart,
And in Thy mercy fix it there.

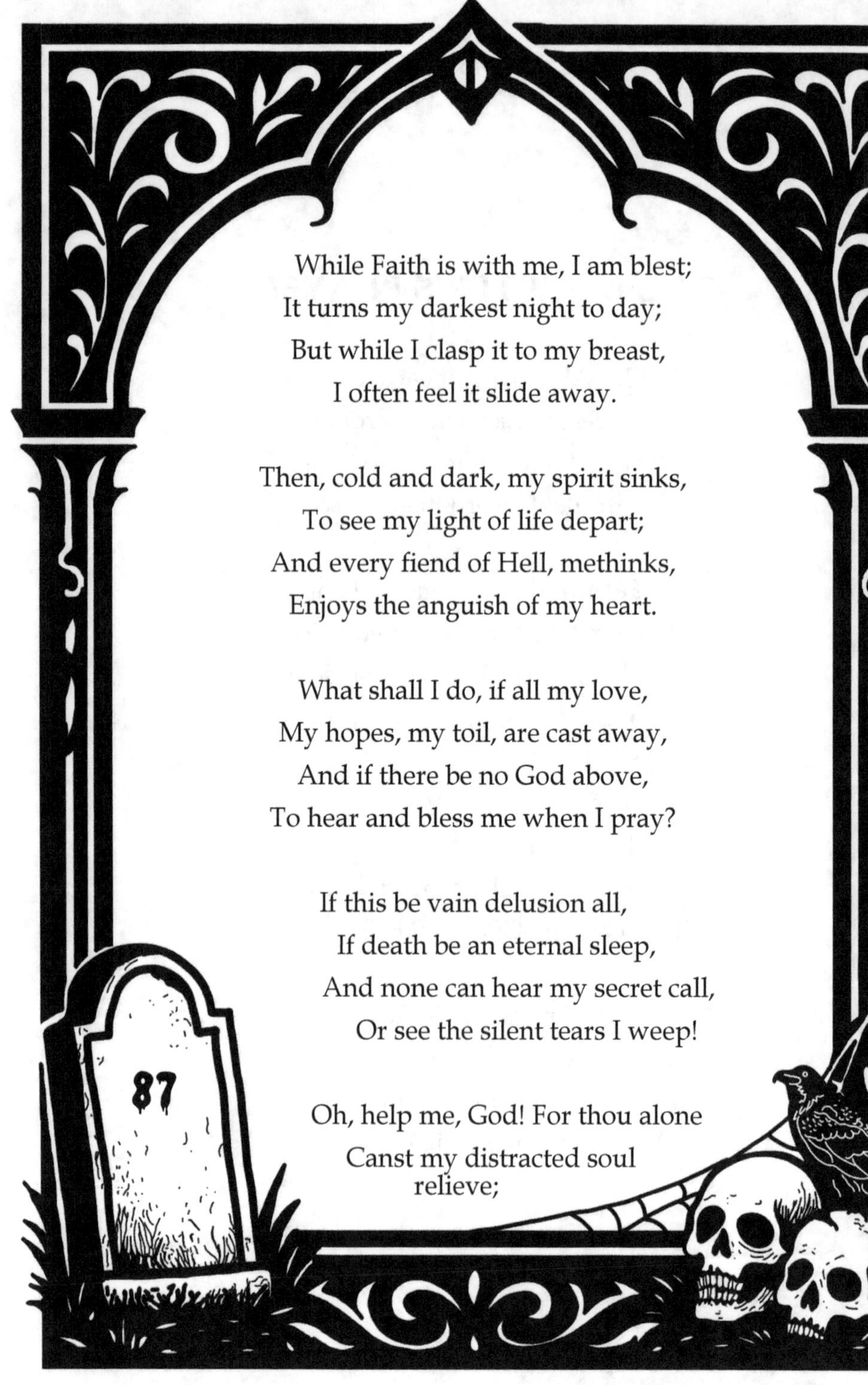

While Faith is with me, I am blest;
It turns my darkest night to day;
But while I clasp it to my breast,
I often feel it slide away.

Then, cold and dark, my spirit sinks,
To see my light of life depart;
And every fiend of Hell, methinks,
Enjoys the anguish of my heart.

What shall I do, if all my love,
My hopes, my toil, are cast away,
And if there be no God above,
To hear and bless me when I pray?

If this be vain delusion all,
If death be an eternal sleep,
And none can hear my secret call,
Or see the silent tears I weep!

Oh, help me, God! For thou alone
Canst my distracted soul relieve;

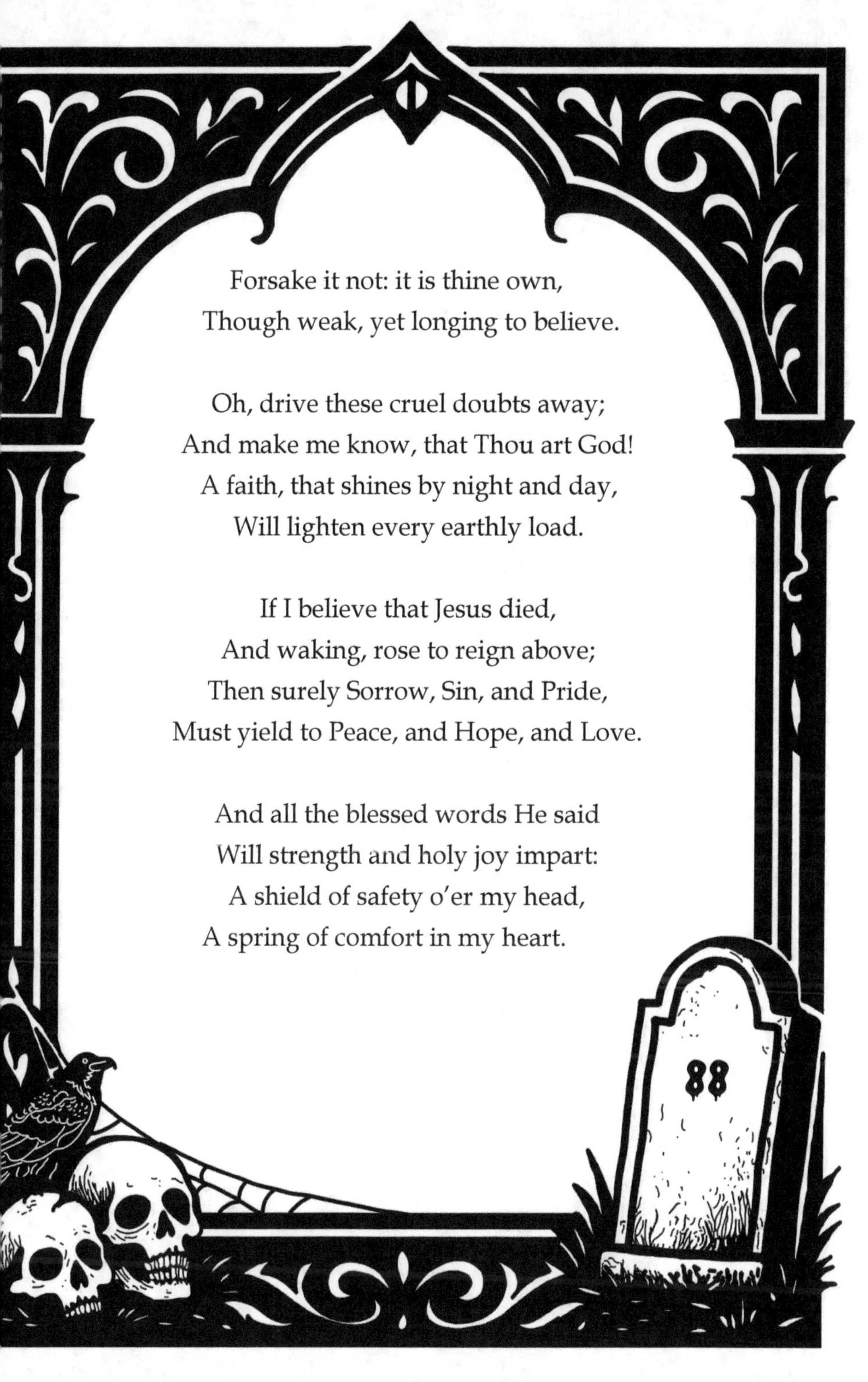

Forsake it not: it is thine own,
Though weak, yet longing to believe.

Oh, drive these cruel doubts away;
And make me know, that Thou art God!
A faith, that shines by night and day,
Will lighten every earthly load.

If I believe that Jesus died,
And waking, rose to reign above;
Then surely Sorrow, Sin, and Pride,
Must yield to Peace, and Hope, and Love.

And all the blessed words He said
Will strength and holy joy impart:
A shield of safety o'er my head,
A spring of comfort in my heart.

THE STUDENT'S SERENADE

I have slept upon my couch,
But my spirit did not rest,
For the labours of the day
Yet my weary soul opprest;
And, before my dreaming eyes
Still the learned volumes lay,
And I could not close their leaves,
And I could not turn away.

But I oped my eyes at last,
And I heard a muffled sound;
'Twas the night-breeze, come to say
That the snow was on the ground.

Then I knew that there was rest
On the mountain's bosom free;
So I left my fevered couch,
And I flew to waken thee!

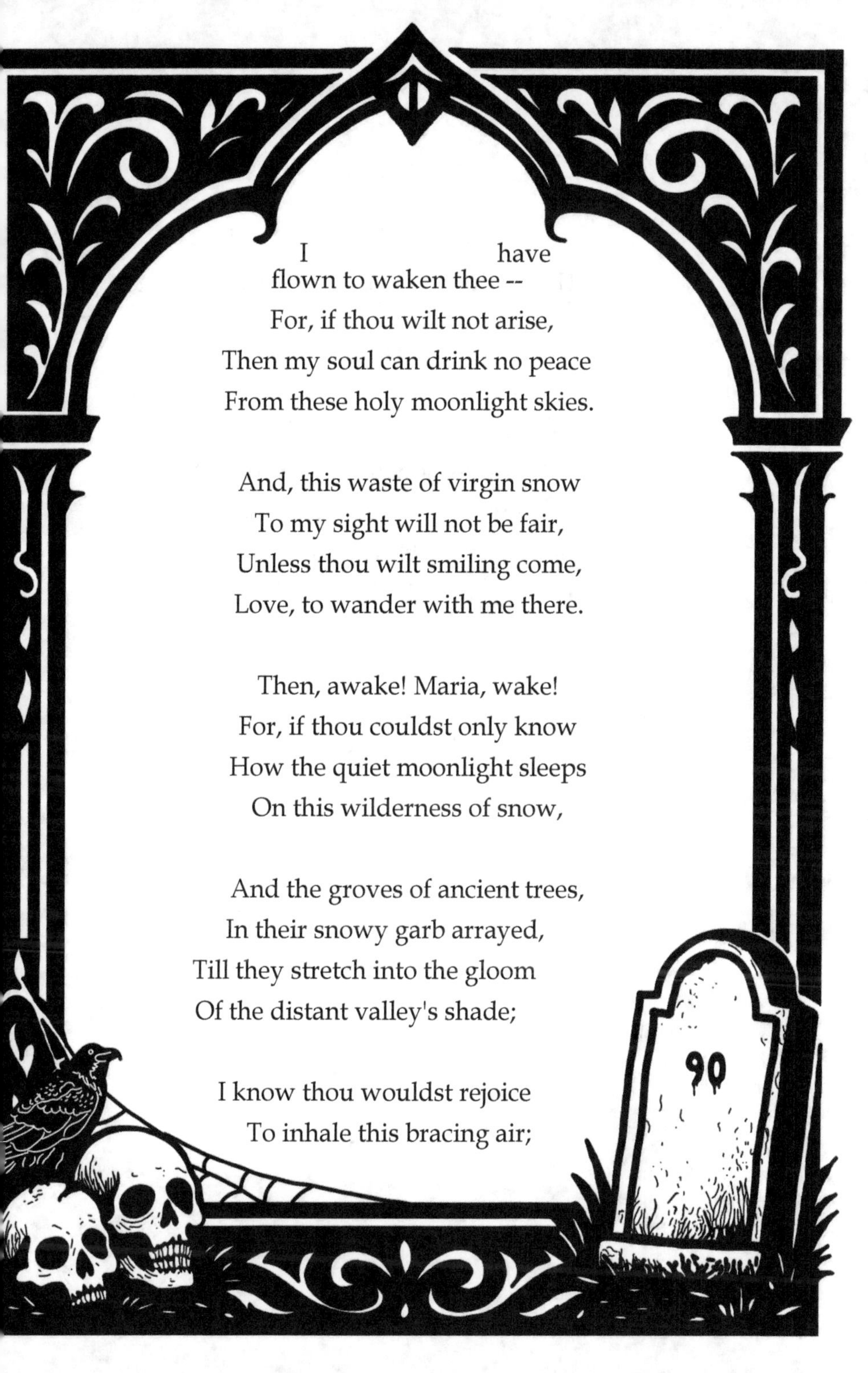

I have
flown to waken thee --
For, if thou wilt not arise,
Then my soul can drink no peace
From these holy moonlight skies.

And, this waste of virgin snow
To my sight will not be fair,
Unless thou wilt smiling come,
Love, to wander with me there.

Then, awake! Maria, wake!
For, if thou couldst only know
How the quiet moonlight sleeps
On this wilderness of snow,

And the groves of ancient trees,
In their snowy garb arrayed,
Till they stretch into the gloom
Of the distant valley's shade;

I know thou wouldst rejoice
To inhale this bracing air;

Thou wouldst break thy sweetest sleep
To behold a scene so fair.

O'er these wintry wilds, alone,
Thou wouldst joy to wander free;
And it will not please thee less,
Though that bliss be shared with me.

Emily Brontë

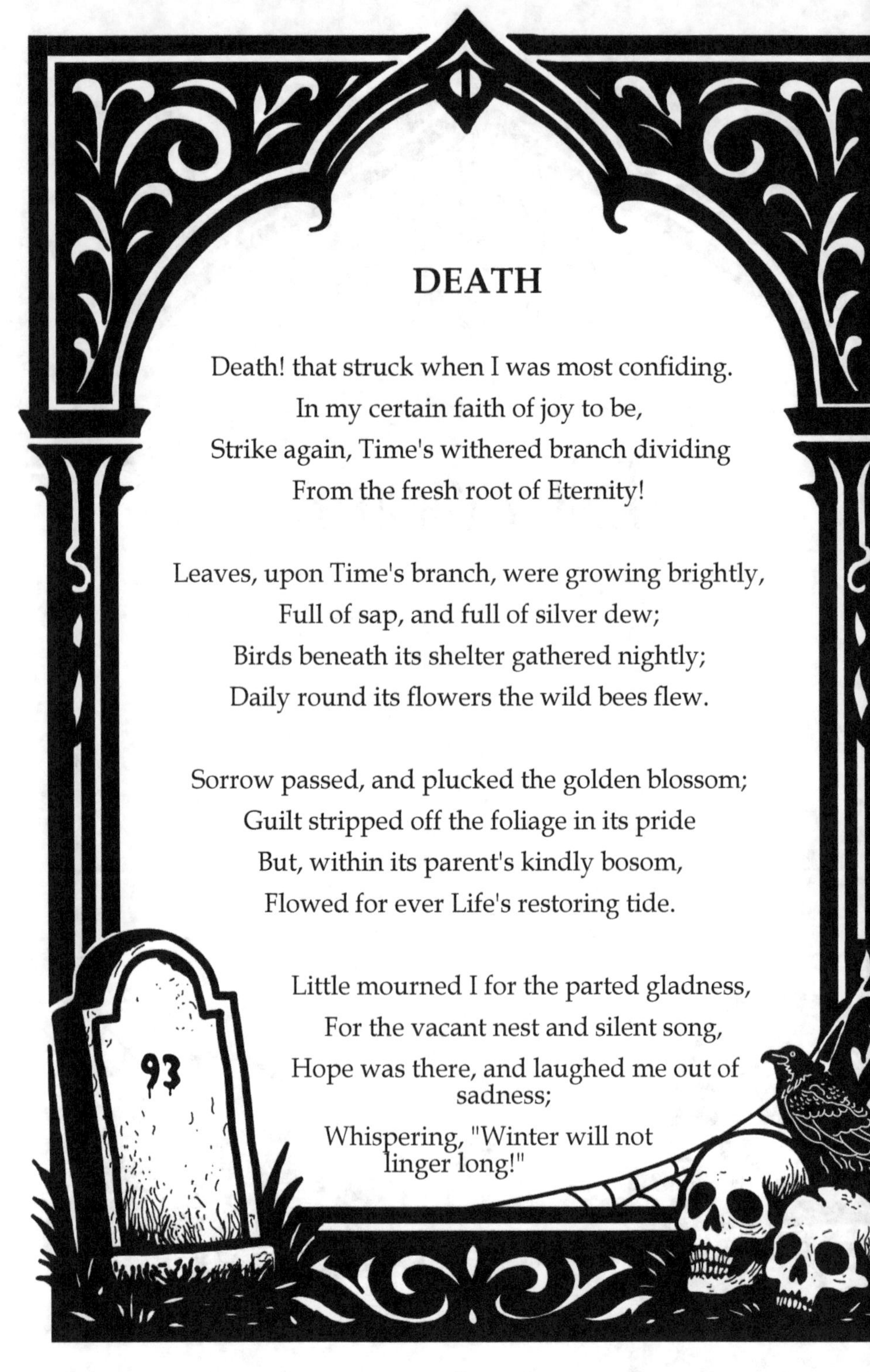

DEATH

Death! that struck when I was most confiding.
In my certain faith of joy to be,
Strike again, Time's withered branch dividing
From the fresh root of Eternity!

Leaves, upon Time's branch, were growing brightly,
Full of sap, and full of silver dew;
Birds beneath its shelter gathered nightly;
Daily round its flowers the wild bees flew.

Sorrow passed, and plucked the golden blossom;
Guilt stripped off the foliage in its pride
But, within its parent's kindly bosom,
Flowed for ever Life's restoring tide.

Little mourned I for the parted gladness,
For the vacant nest and silent song,
Hope was there, and laughed me out of sadness;
Whispering, "Winter will not linger long!"

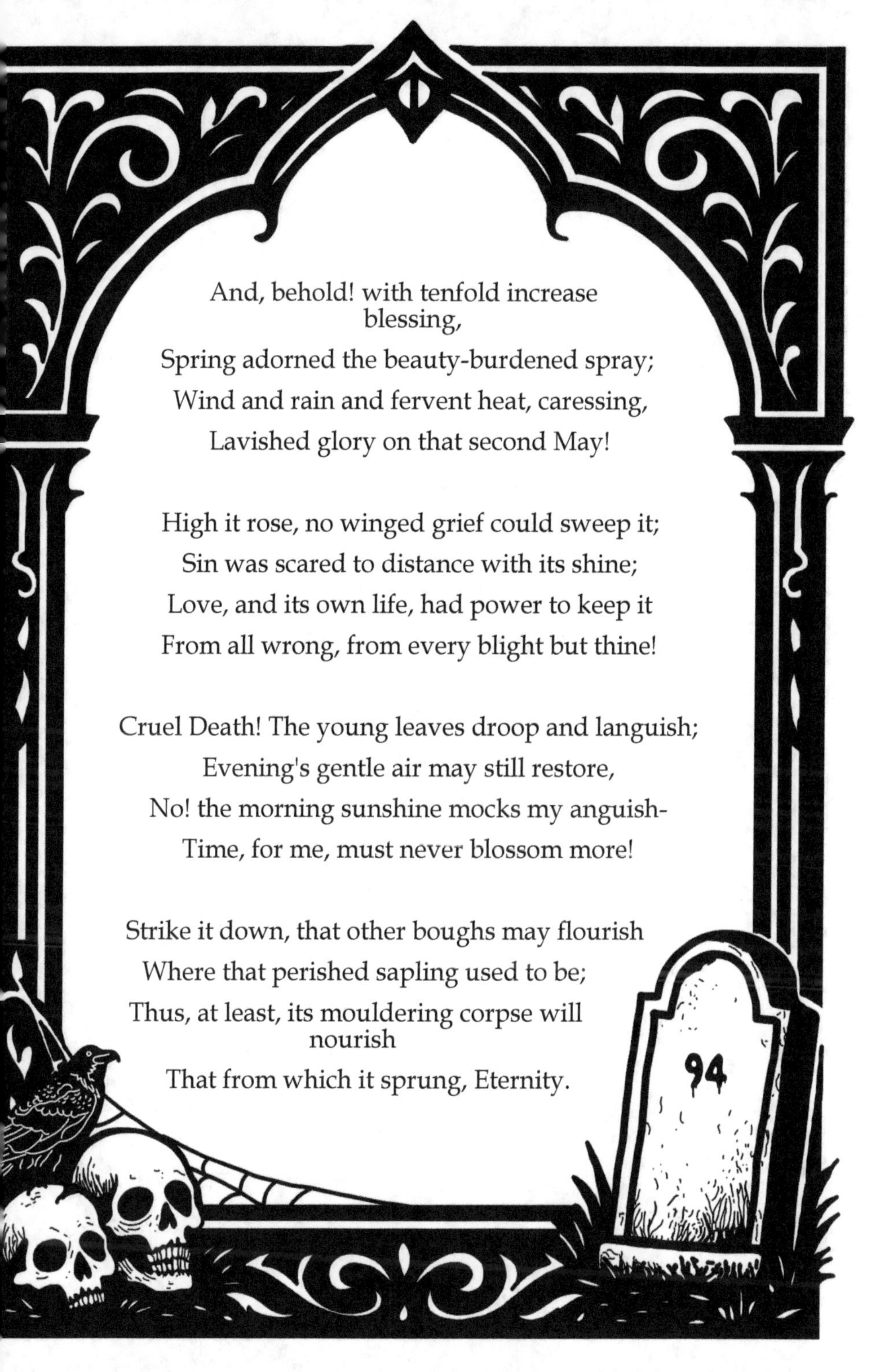

And, behold! with tenfold increase blessing,
Spring adorned the beauty-burdened spray;
Wind and rain and fervent heat, caressing,
Lavished glory on that second May!

High it rose, no winged grief could sweep it;
Sin was scared to distance with its shine;
Love, and its own life, had power to keep it
From all wrong, from every blight but thine!

Cruel Death! The young leaves droop and languish;
Evening's gentle air may still restore,
No! the morning sunshine mocks my anguish-
Time, for me, must never blossom more!

Strike it down, that other boughs may flourish
Where that perished sapling used to be;
Thus, at least, its mouldering corpse will nourish
That from which it sprung, Eternity.

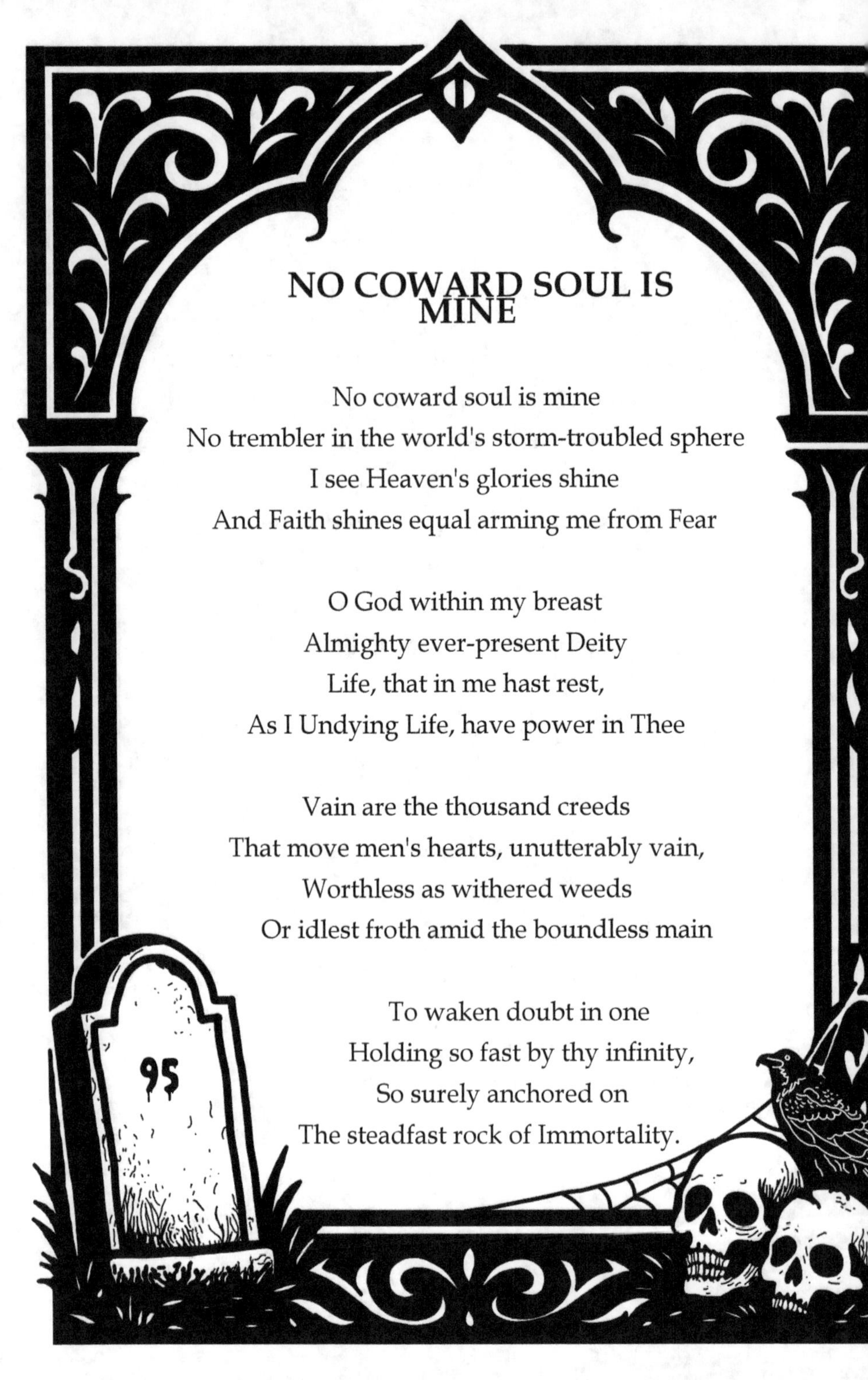

NO COWARD SOUL IS MINE

No coward soul is mine
No trembler in the world's storm-troubled sphere
I see Heaven's glories shine
And Faith shines equal arming me from Fear

O God within my breast
Almighty ever-present Deity
Life, that in me hast rest,
As I Undying Life, have power in Thee

Vain are the thousand creeds
That move men's hearts, unutterably vain,
Worthless as withered weeds
Or idlest froth amid the boundless main

To waken doubt in one
Holding so fast by thy infinity,
So surely anchored on
The steadfast rock of Immortality.

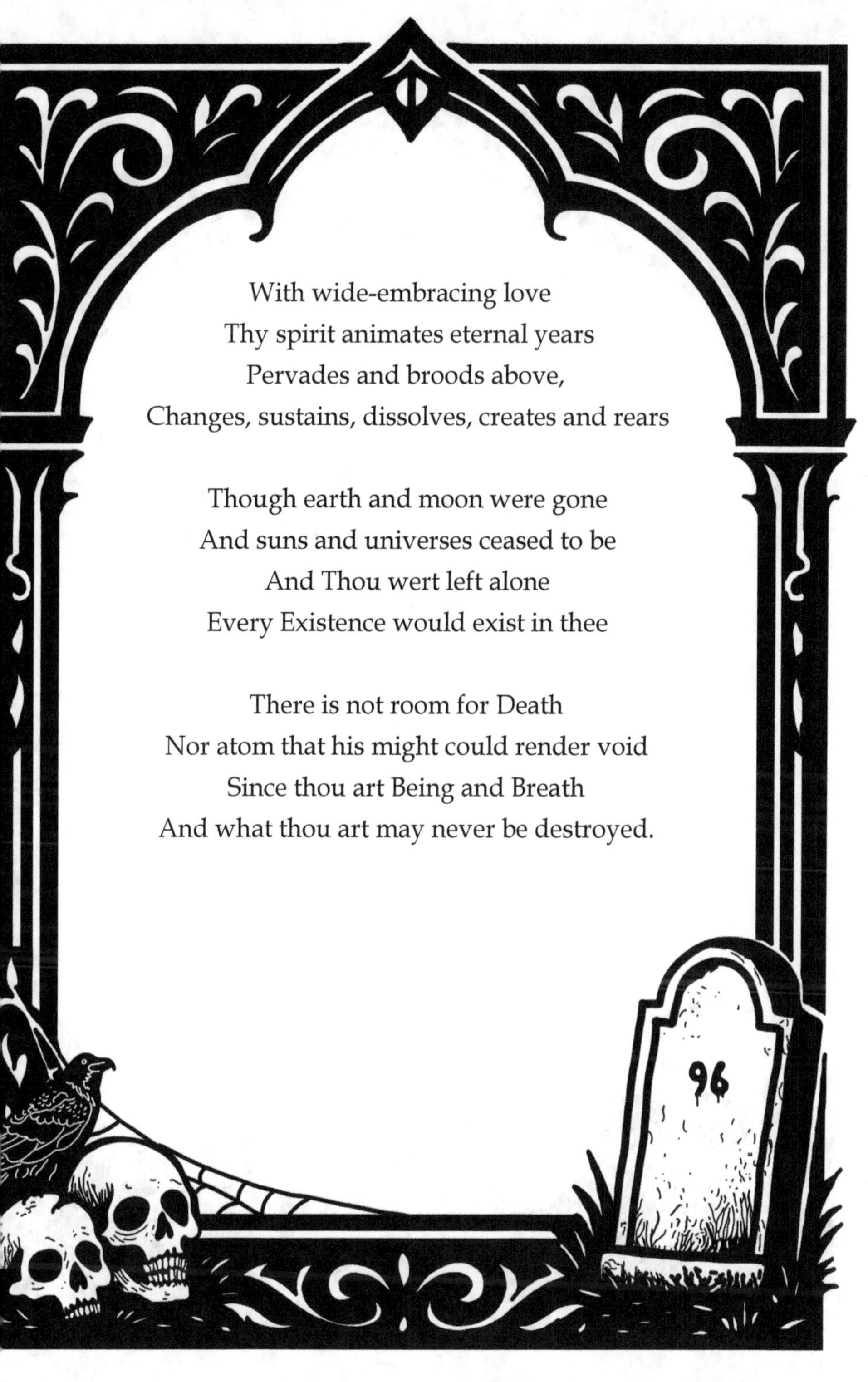

With wide-embracing love
Thy spirit animates eternal years
Pervades and broods above,
Changes, sustains, dissolves, creates and rears

Though earth and moon were gone
And suns and universes ceased to be
And Thou wert left alone
Every Existence would exist in thee

There is not room for Death
Nor atom that his might could render void
Since thou art Being and Breath
And what thou art may never be destroyed.

Charlotte Brontë

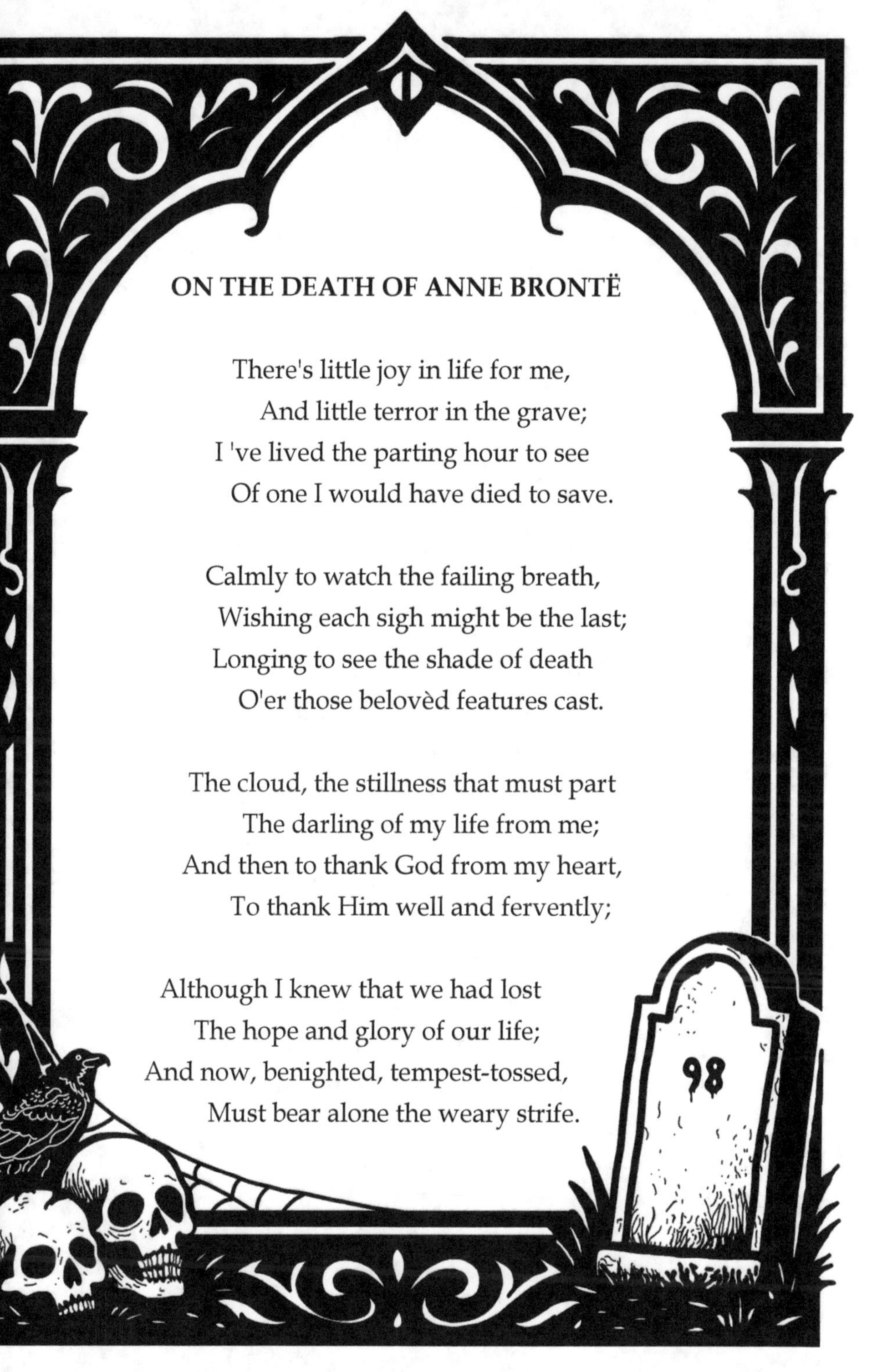

ON THE DEATH OF ANNE BRONTË

There's little joy in life for me,
And little terror in the grave;
I 've lived the parting hour to see
Of one I would have died to save.

Calmly to watch the failing breath,
Wishing each sigh might be the last;
Longing to see the shade of death
O'er those belovèd features cast.

The cloud, the stillness that must part
The darling of my life from me;
And then to thank God from my heart,
To thank Him well and fervently;

Although I knew that we had lost
The hope and glory of our life;
And now, benighted, tempest-tossed,
Must bear alone the weary strife.

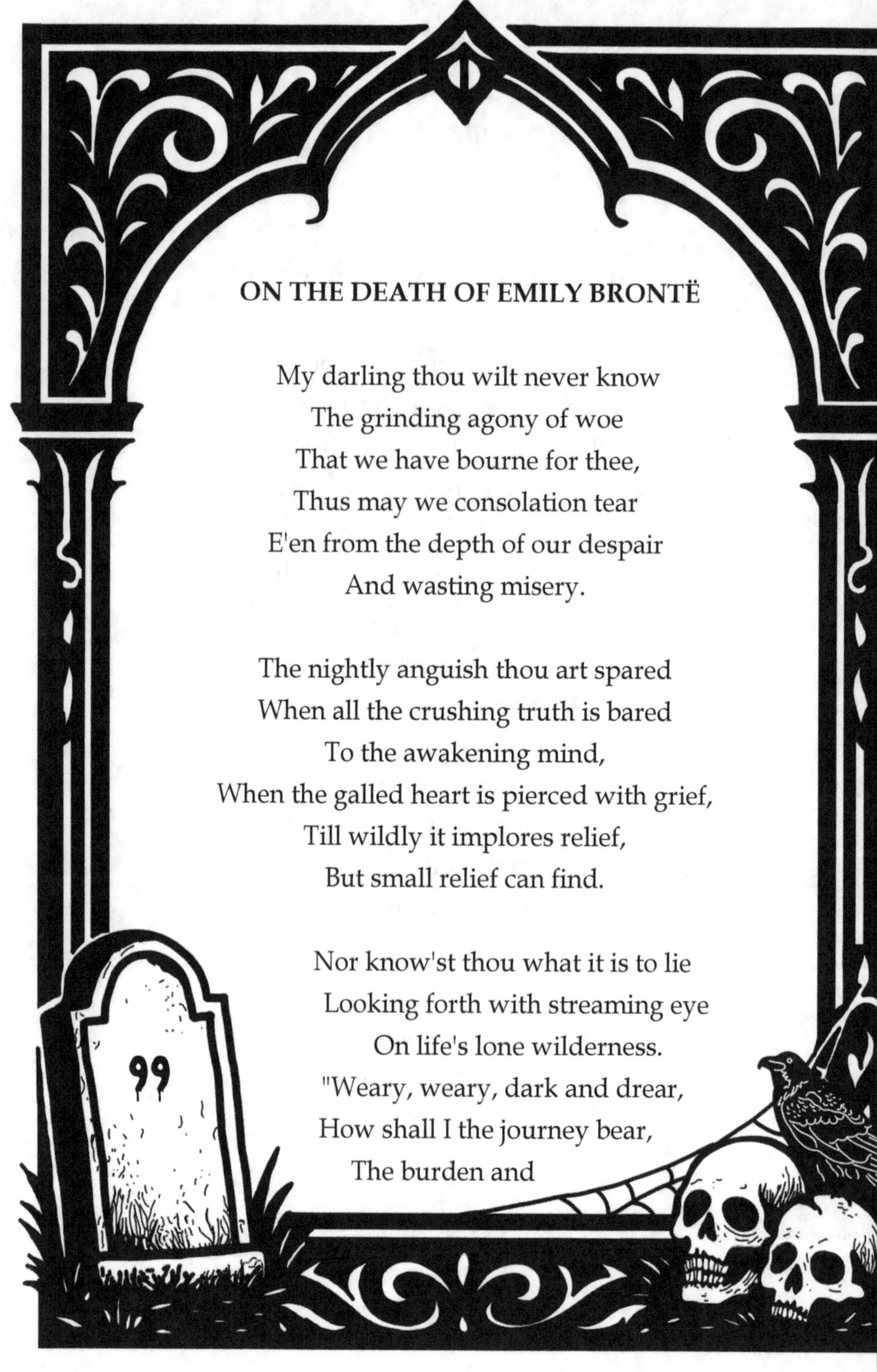

ON THE DEATH OF EMILY BRONTË

My darling thou wilt never know
The grinding agony of woe
That we have bourne for thee,
Thus may we consolation tear
E'en from the depth of our despair
And wasting misery.

The nightly anguish thou art spared
When all the crushing truth is bared
To the awakening mind,
When the galled heart is pierced with grief,
Till wildly it implores relief,
But small relief can find.

Nor know'st thou what it is to lie
Looking forth with streaming eye
On life's lone wilderness.
"Weary, weary, dark and drear,
How shall I the journey bear,
The burden and

distress?"

Then since thou art spared such pain
We will not wish thee here again;
He that lives must mourn.
God help us through our misery
And give us rest and joy with thee
When we reach our bourne!

Elizabeth Barrett Browning

THE SLEEP

Of all the thoughts of God that are
Borne inward unto souls afar,
Along the Psalmist's music deep,
Now tell me if that any is,
For gift or grace, surpassing this—
'He giveth His belovèd sleep'?

What would we give to our beloved?
The hero's heart to be unmoved,
The poet's star-tuned harp, to sweep,
The patriot's voice, to teach and rouse,
The monarch's crown, to light the brows?
He giveth His belovèd, sleep.

What do we give to our beloved?
A little faith all undisproved,
A little dust to overweep,
And bitter memories to make
The whole earth blasted for our sake.
He giveth His belovèd,

sleep.

'Sleep soft, beloved!' we sometimes say,
But have no tune to charm away
Sad dreams that through the eye-lids creep.
But never doleful dream again
Shall break the happy slumber when
He giveth His belovèd, sleep.

O earth, so full of dreary noises!
O men, with wailing in your voices!
O delvèd gold, the wailers heap!
O strife, O curse, that o'er it fall!
God strikes a silence through you all,
He giveth His belovèd, sleep.

His dews drop mutely on the hill;
His cloud above it saileth still,
Though on its slope men sow and reap.
More softly than the dew is shed,
Or cloud is floated overhead,
He giveth His belovèd, sleep.

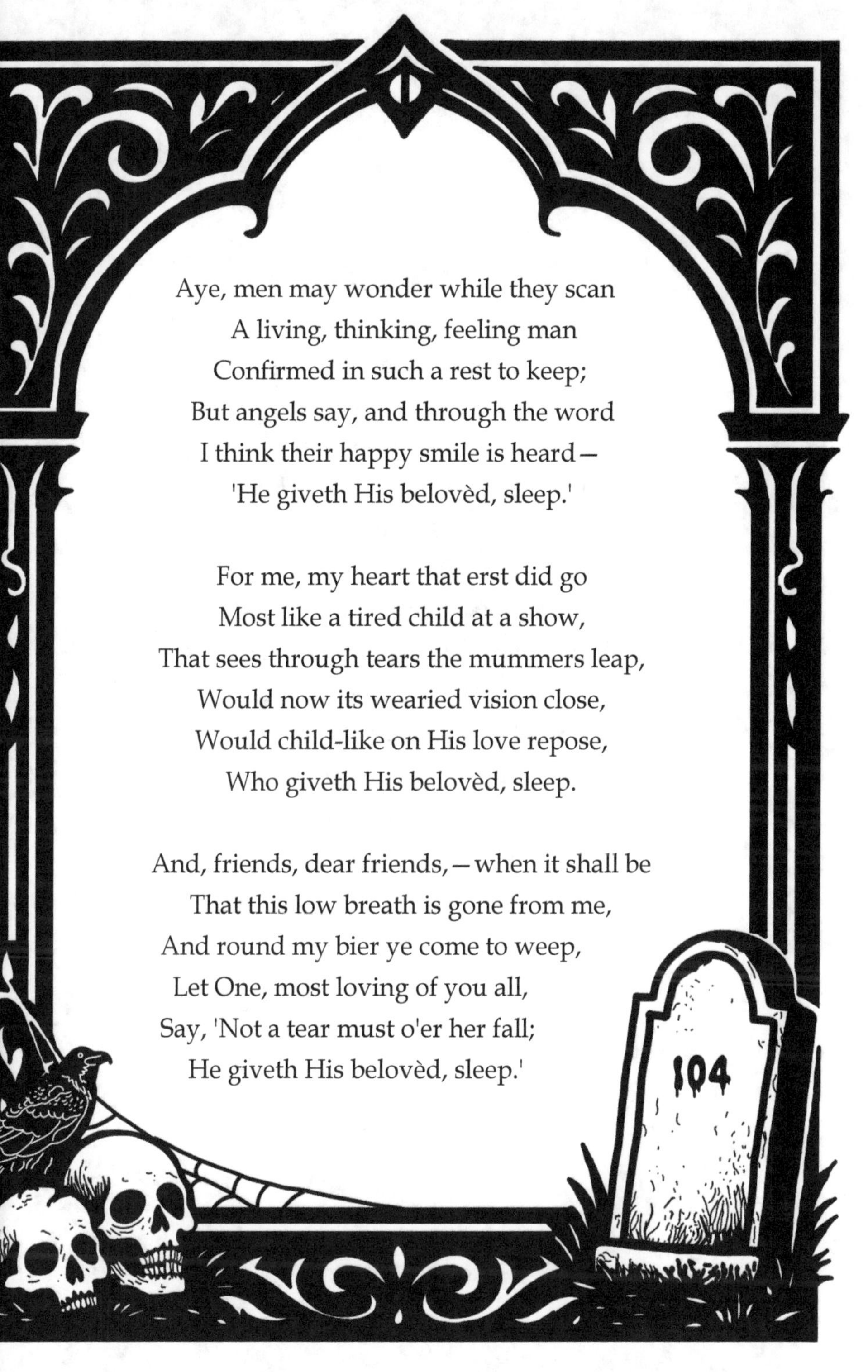

Aye, men may wonder while they scan
A living, thinking, feeling man
Confirmed in such a rest to keep;
But angels say, and through the word
I think their happy smile is heard—
'He giveth His belovèd, sleep.'

For me, my heart that erst did go
Most like a tired child at a show,
That sees through tears the mummers leap,
Would now its wearied vision close,
Would child-like on His love repose,
Who giveth His belovèd, sleep.

And, friends, dear friends,—when it shall be
That this low breath is gone from me,
And round my bier ye come to weep,
Let One, most loving of you all,
Say, 'Not a tear must o'er her fall;
He giveth His belovèd, sleep.'

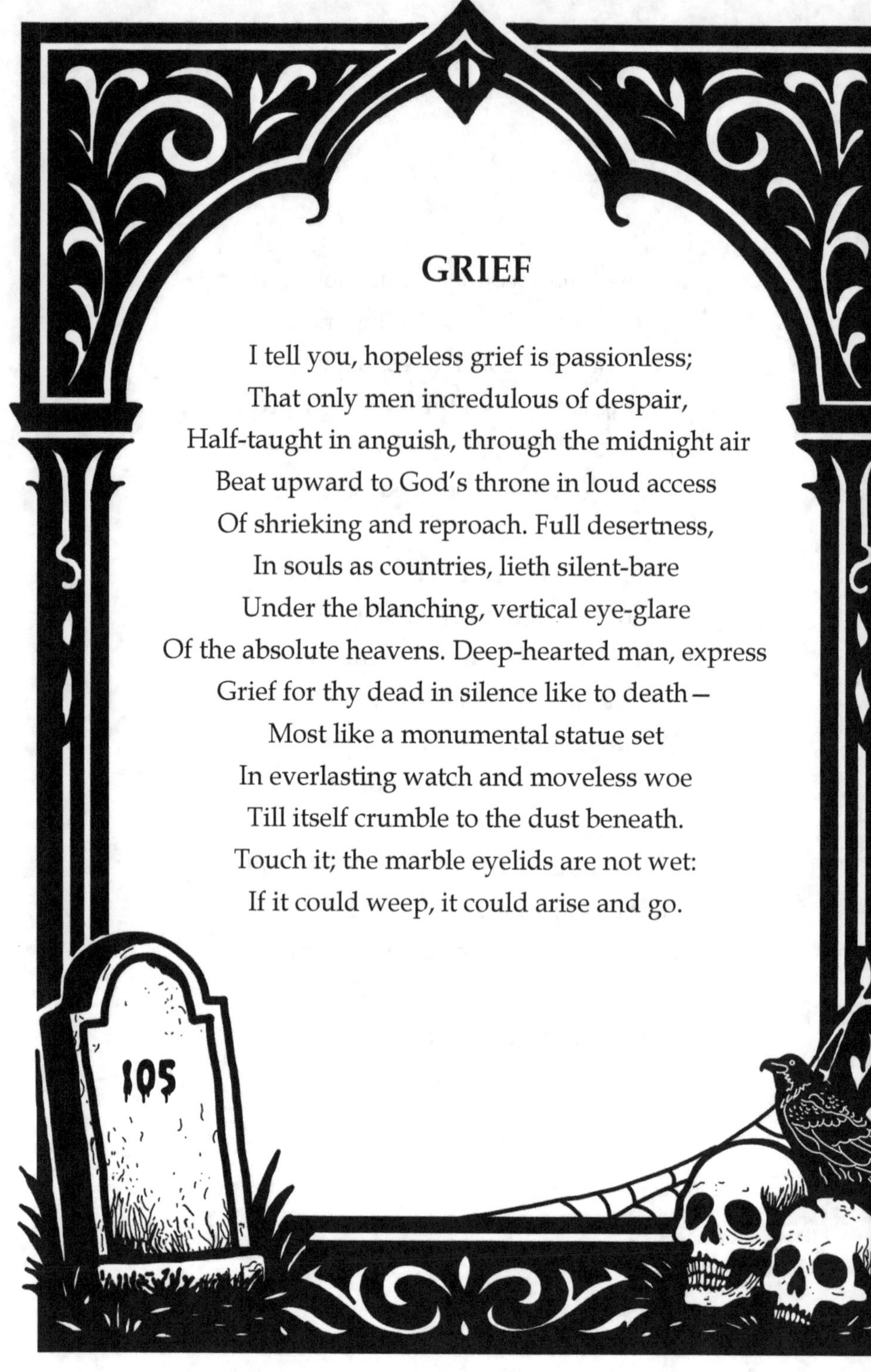

GRIEF

I tell you, hopeless grief is passionless;
That only men incredulous of despair,
Half-taught in anguish, through the midnight air
Beat upward to God's throne in loud access
Of shrieking and reproach. Full desertness,
In souls as countries, lieth silent-bare
Under the blanching, vertical eye-glare
Of the absolute heavens. Deep-hearted man, express
Grief for thy dead in silence like to death—
Most like a monumental statue set
In everlasting watch and moveless woe
Till itself crumble to the dust beneath.
Touch it; the marble eyelids are not wet:
If it could weep, it could arise and go.

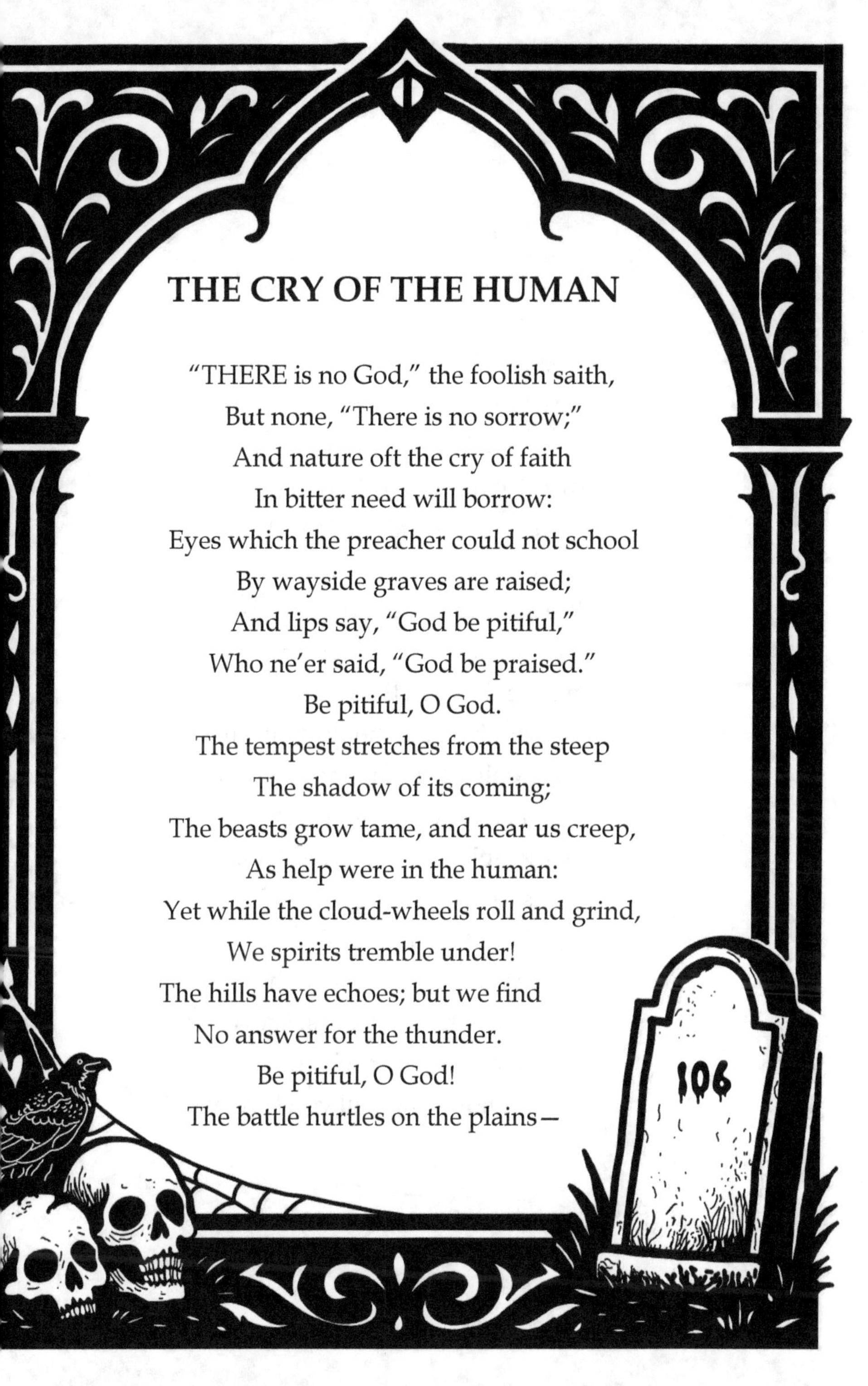

THE CRY OF THE HUMAN

"THERE is no God," the foolish saith,
But none, "There is no sorrow;"
And nature oft the cry of faith
In bitter need will borrow:
Eyes which the preacher could not school
By wayside graves are raised;
And lips say, "God be pitiful,"
Who ne'er said, "God be praised."
Be pitiful, O God.
The tempest stretches from the steep
The shadow of its coming;
The beasts grow tame, and near us creep,
As help were in the human:
Yet while the cloud-wheels roll and grind,
We spirits tremble under!
The hills have echoes; but we find
No answer for the thunder.
Be pitiful, O God!
The battle hurtles on the plains—

Earth feels new scythes upon her:
We reap our brothers for the wains,
And call the harvest—honor.
Draw face to face, front line to line,
One image all inherit:
Then kill, curse on, by that same sign,
Clay, clay,—and spirit, spirit.
Be pitiful, O God!
We meet together at the feast—
To private mirth betake us—
We stare down in the winecup, lest
Some vacant chair should shake us!
We name delight, and pledge it round—
"It shall be ours to-morrow!"
God's seraphs! do your voices sound
As sad in naming sorrow?
Be pitiful, O God!
We sit together, with the skies,
The steadfast skies, above us;
We look into each other's eyes,
"And how long will you love us?"

The eyes grow dim with prophecy,
The voices, low and breathless—
"Till death us part!"—O words, to be
Our best for love the deathless!
Be pitiful, dear God!
We tremble by the harmless bed
Of one loved and departed—
Our tears drop on the lips that said
Last night, "Be stronger-hearted!"
O God,—to clasp those fingers close,
And yet to feel so lonely!—
To see a light upon such brows,
Which is the daylight only!
Be pitiful, O God!
The happy children come to us,
And look up in our faces;
They ask us—Was it thus, and thus,
When we were in their places?
We cannot speak—we see anew
The hills we used to live in,
And feel our mother's smile press through

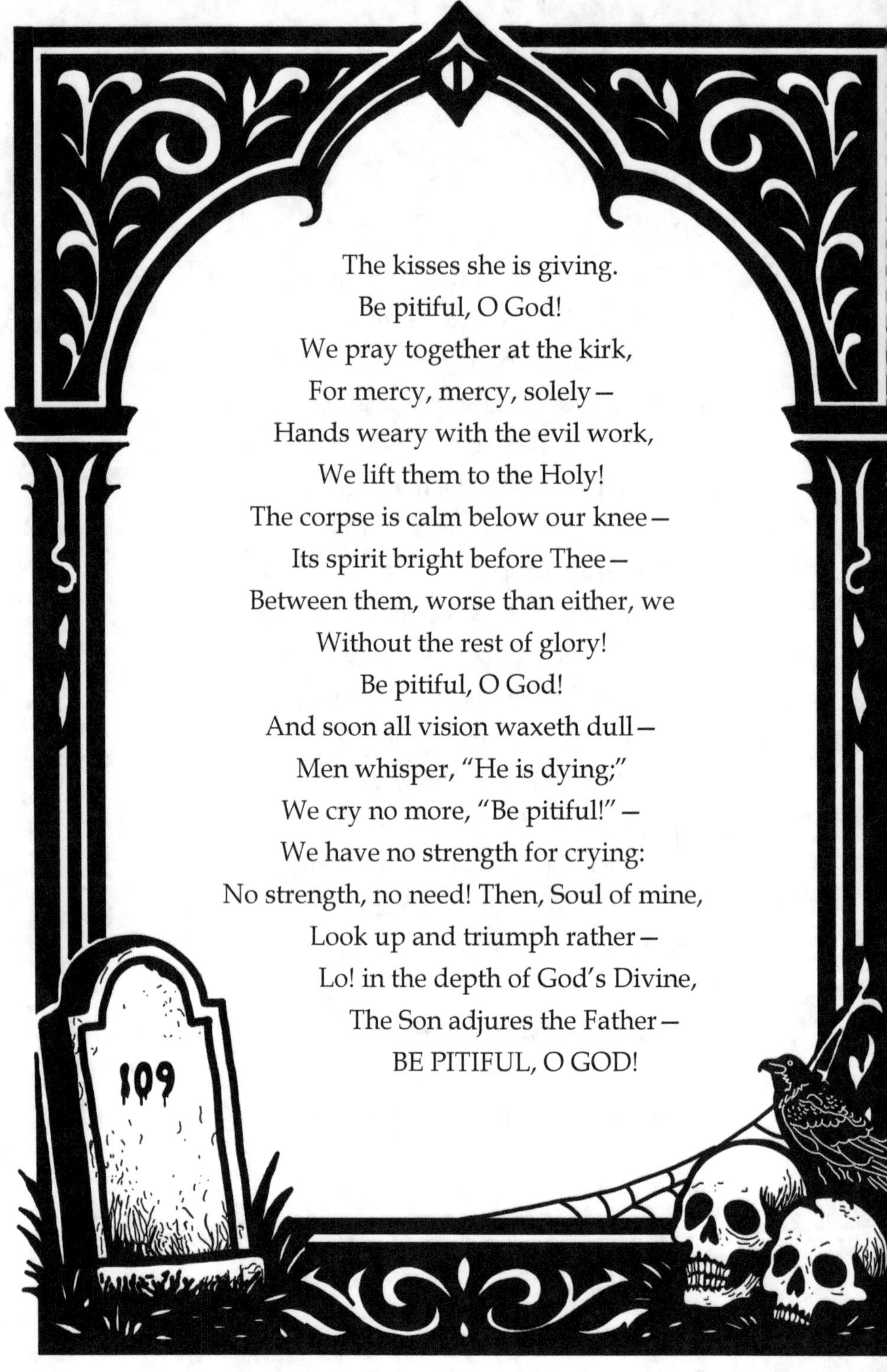

The kisses she is giving.
Be pitiful, O God!
We pray together at the kirk,
For mercy, mercy, solely—
Hands weary with the evil work,
We lift them to the Holy!
The corpse is calm below our knee—
Its spirit bright before Thee—
Between them, worse than either, we
Without the rest of glory!
Be pitiful, O God!
And soon all vision waxeth dull—
Men whisper, "He is dying;"
We cry no more, "Be pitiful!"—
We have no strength for crying:
No strength, no need! Then, Soul of mine,
Look up and triumph rather—
Lo! in the depth of God's Divine,
The Son adjures the Father—
BE PITIFUL, O GOD!

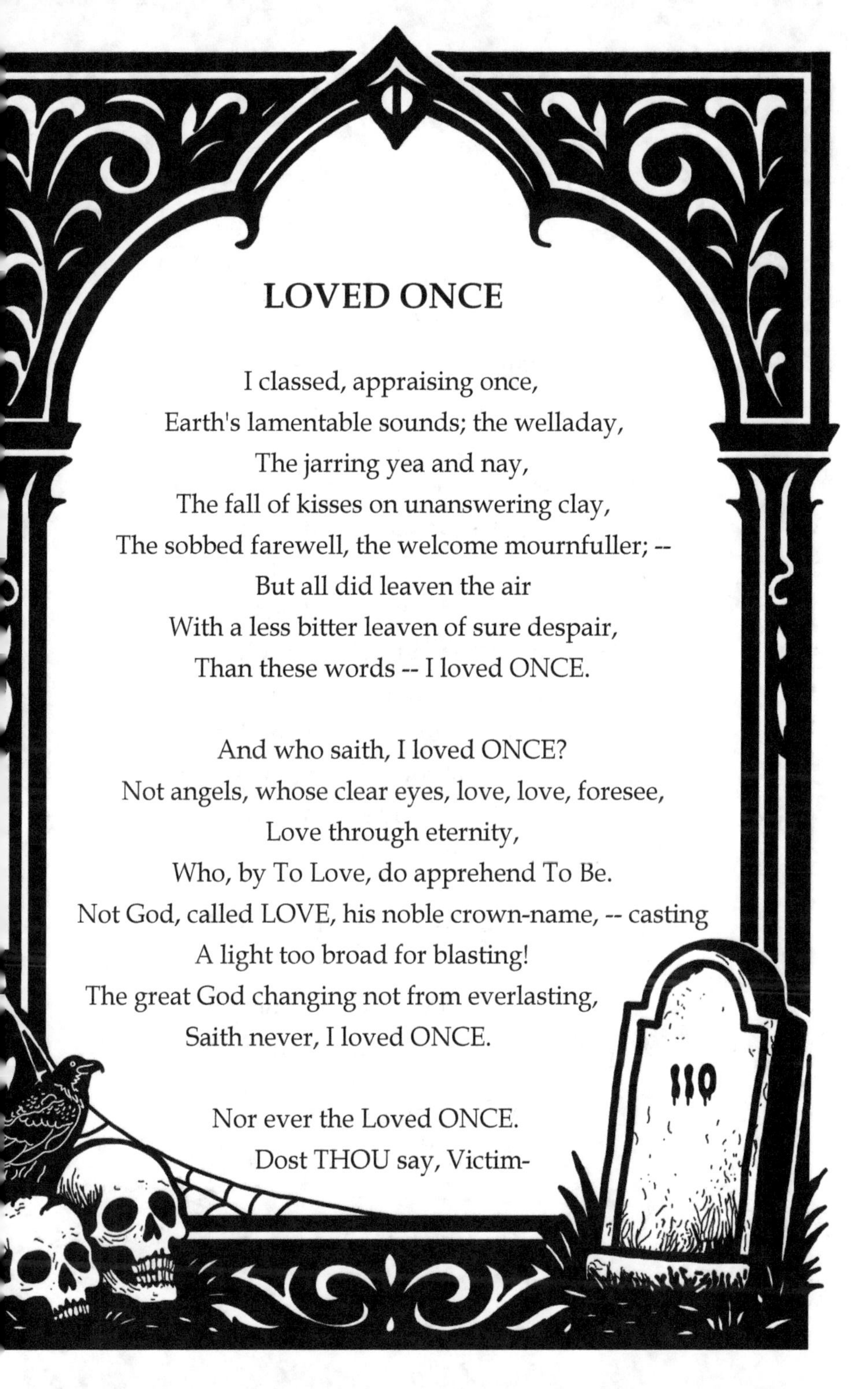

LOVED ONCE

I classed, appraising once,
Earth's lamentable sounds; the welladay,
The jarring yea and nay,
The fall of kisses on unanswering clay,
The sobbed farewell, the welcome mournfuller; --
But all did leaven the air
With a less bitter leaven of sure despair,
Than these words -- I loved ONCE.

And who saith, I loved ONCE?
Not angels, whose clear eyes, love, love, foresee,
Love through eternity,
Who, by To Love, do apprehend To Be.
Not God, called LOVE, his noble crown-name, -- casting
A light too broad for blasting!
The great God changing not from everlasting,
Saith never, I loved ONCE.

Nor ever the Loved ONCE.
Dost THOU say, Victim-

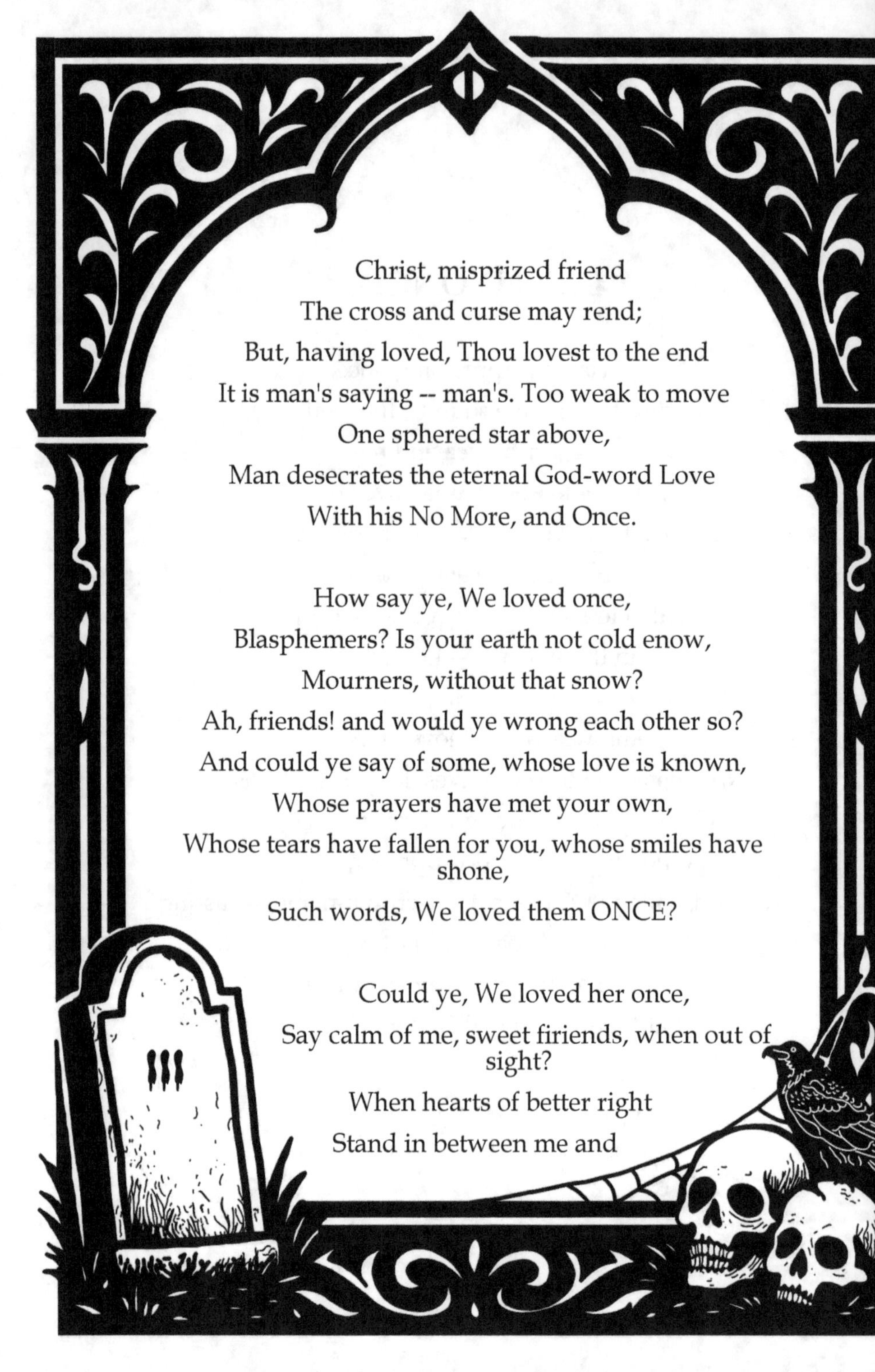

Christ, misprized friend
The cross and curse may rend;
But, having loved, Thou lovest to the end
It is man's saying -- man's. Too weak to move
One sphered star above,
Man desecrates the eternal God-word Love
With his No More, and Once.

How say ye, We loved once,
Blasphemers? Is your earth not cold enow,
Mourners, without that snow?
Ah, friends! and would ye wrong each other so?
And could ye say of some, whose love is known,
Whose prayers have met your own,
Whose tears have fallen for you, whose smiles have shone,
Such words, We loved them ONCE?

Could ye, We loved her once,
Say calm of me, sweet firiends, when out of sight?
When hearts of better right
Stand in between me and

your
happy light?
And when, as flowers kept too long in the shade,
Ye find my colors fade,
And all that is not love in me, decayed?
Such words -- Ye loved me ONCE!

Could ye, We loved her once,
Say cold of me, when further put away
In earth's sepulchral clay?
When mute the lips which deprecate to-day? --
Not so! not then -- least then! When Life is shriven,
And Death's full joy is given, --
Of those who sit and love you up in Heaven,
Say not, We loved them once.

Say never, ye loved ONCE!
God is too near above, the grave, below,
And all our moments go
Too quickly past our souls, for saying so.
The mysteries of Life and Death avenge
Affections light of range --
There comes no change

to justify that chance,
Whatever comes -- loved ONCE!

And yet that word of ONCE
Is humanly acceptive! Kings have said
Shaking a discrowned head,
We ruled once, -- dotards, We once taught and led --
Cripples once danced i' the vines -- and bards approved,
Were once by scornings, moved:
But love strikes one hour -- Love. Those never loved,
Who dream that they loved ONCE.

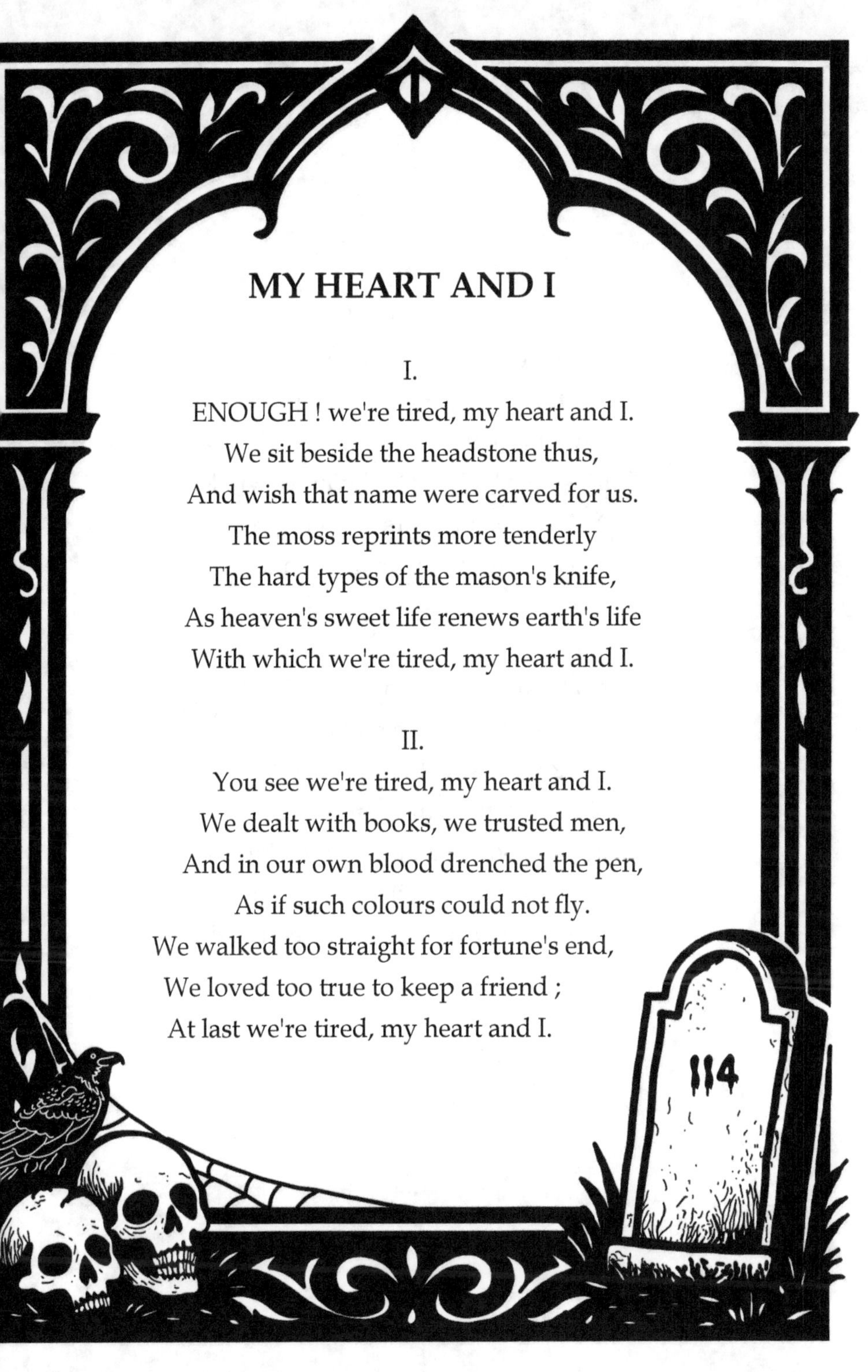

MY HEART AND I

I.

ENOUGH ! we're tired, my heart and I.
We sit beside the headstone thus,
And wish that name were carved for us.
The moss reprints more tenderly
The hard types of the mason's knife,
As heaven's sweet life renews earth's life
With which we're tired, my heart and I.

II.

You see we're tired, my heart and I.
We dealt with books, we trusted men,
And in our own blood drenched the pen,
As if such colours could not fly.
We walked too straight for fortune's end,
We loved too true to keep a friend ;
At last we're tired, my heart and I.

III.

How tired we feel, my heart and I !
We seem of no use in the world ;
Our fancies hang grey and uncurled
About men's eyes indifferently ;
Our voice which thrilled you so, will let
You sleep; our tears are only wet :
What do we here, my heart and I ?

IV.

So tired, so tired, my heart and I !
It was not thus in that old time
When Ralph sat with me 'neath the lime
To watch the sunset from the sky.
Dear love, you're looking tired,' he said;
I, smiling at him, shook my head :
'Tis now we're tired, my heart and I.

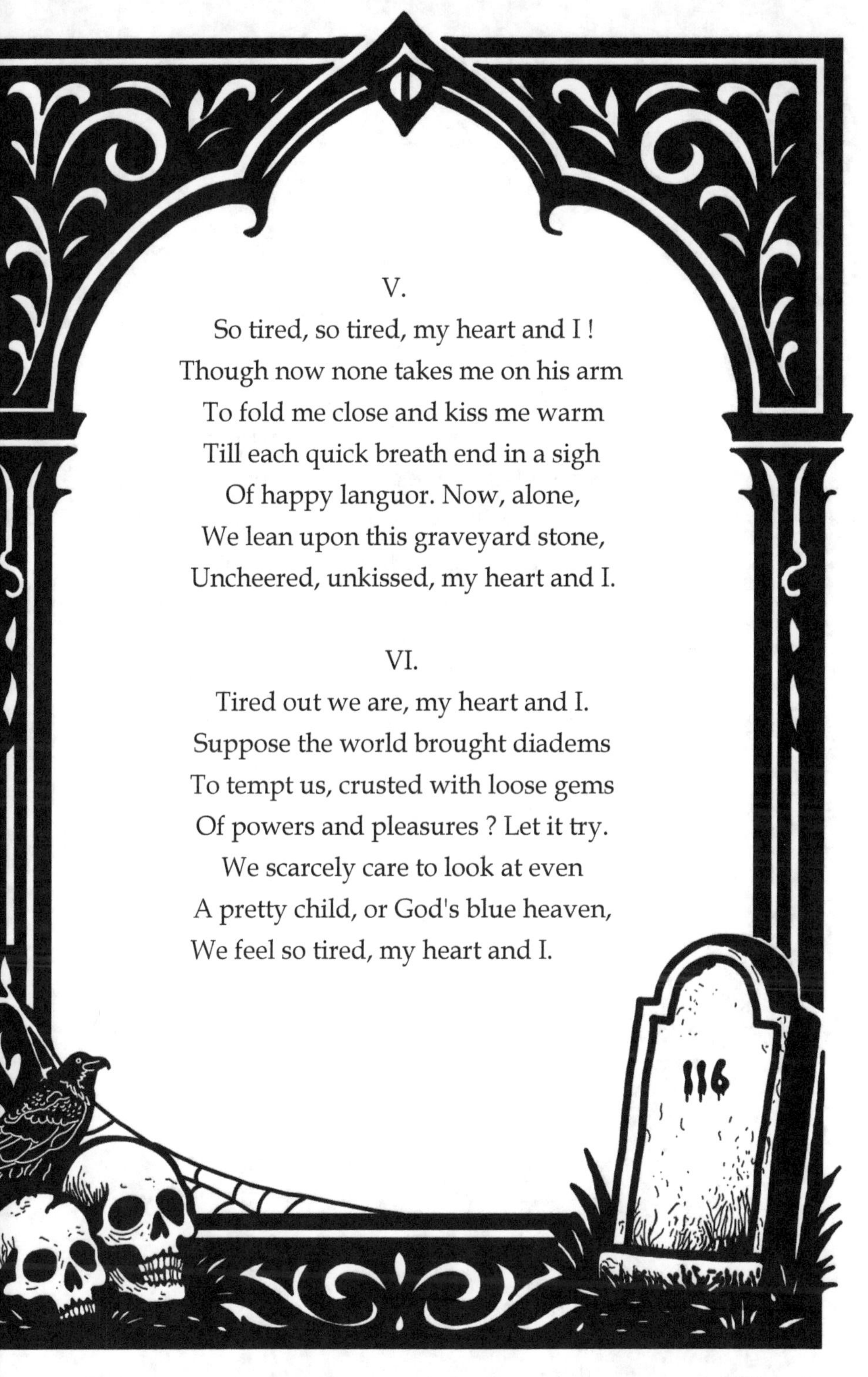

V.

So tired, so tired, my heart and I !
Though now none takes me on his arm
To fold me close and kiss me warm
Till each quick breath end in a sigh
Of happy languor. Now, alone,
We lean upon this graveyard stone,
Uncheered, unkissed, my heart and I.

VI.

Tired out we are, my heart and I.
Suppose the world brought diadems
To tempt us, crusted with loose gems
Of powers and pleasures ? Let it try.
We scarcely care to look at even
A pretty child, or God's blue heaven,
We feel so tired, my heart and I.

VII.

Yet who complains ? My heart and I ?
In this abundant earth no doubt
Is little room for things worn out :
Disdain them, break them, throw them by
And if before the days grew rough
We once were loved, used, — well enough,
I think, we've fared, my heart and I.

William Collins

ODE TO EVENING

If aught of oaten stop, or past'ral song,
May hope, chaste Eve, to soothe thy modest ear,
Like thy own solemn springs,
Thy springs and dying gales,
O nymph reserved, while now the bright-haired sun
Sits in yon western tent, whose cloudy skirts,
With brede ethereal wove,
O'erhang his wavy bed;
Now air is hushed, save where the weak-ey'd bat
With short shrill shriek flits by on leathern wing,
Or where the beetle winds
His small but sullen horn
As oft he rises 'midst the twilight path
Against the pilgrim, borne in heedless hum:
Now teach me, maid composed,
To breathe some softened strain,
Whose numbers stealing through thy dark'ning vale
May not unseemly with its stillness suit,
As musing slow, I hail

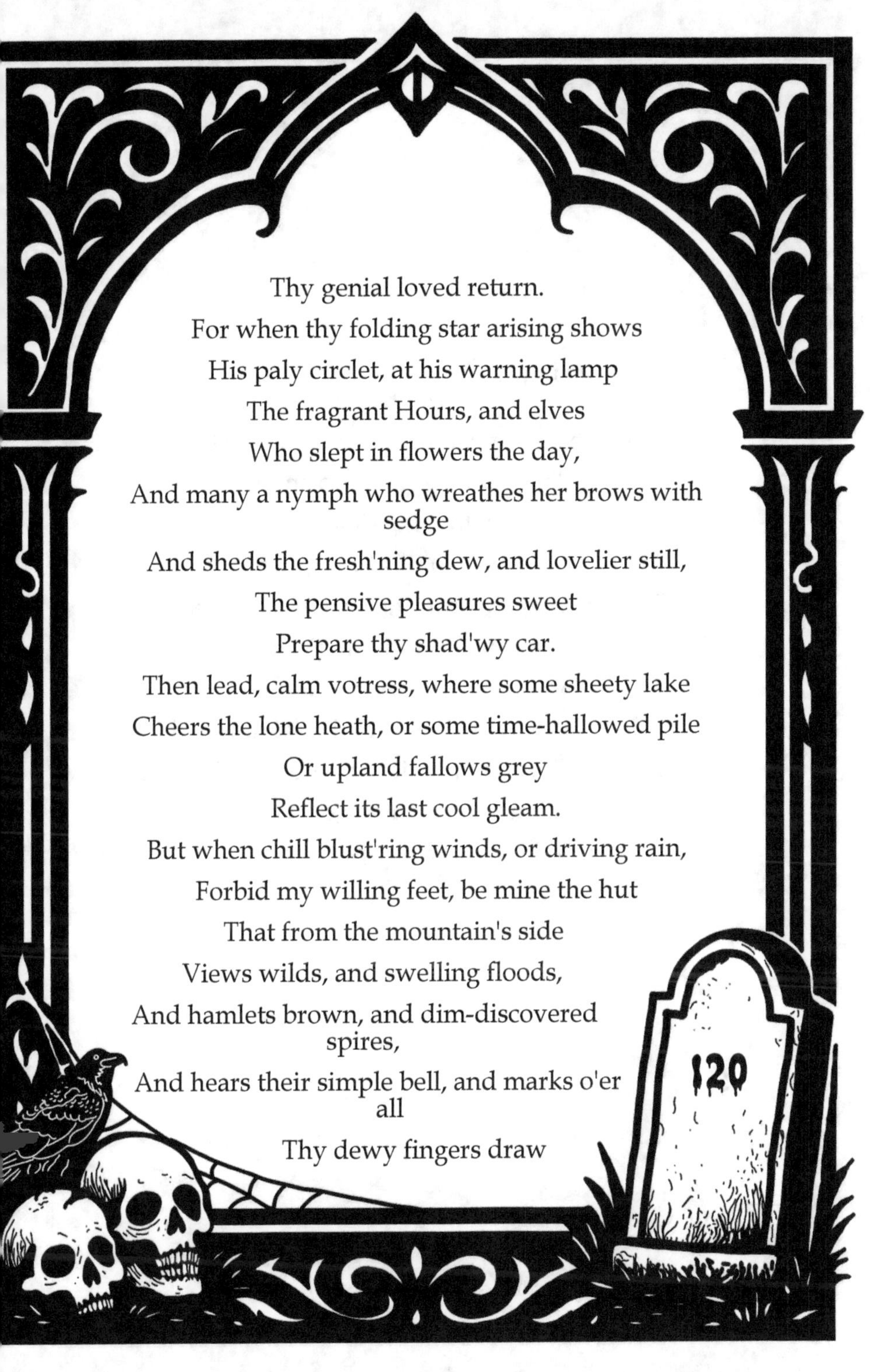

Thy genial loved return.
For when thy folding star arising shows
His paly circlet, at his warning lamp
The fragrant Hours, and elves
Who slept in flowers the day,
And many a nymph who wreathes her brows with sedge
And sheds the fresh'ning dew, and lovelier still,
The pensive pleasures sweet
Prepare thy shad'wy car.
Then lead, calm votress, where some sheety lake
Cheers the lone heath, or some time-hallowed pile
Or upland fallows grey
Reflect its last cool gleam.
But when chill blust'ring winds, or driving rain,
Forbid my willing feet, be mine the hut
That from the mountain's side
Views wilds, and swelling floods,
And hamlets brown, and dim-discovered spires,
And hears their simple bell, and marks o'er all
Thy dewy fingers draw

The gradual dusky veil.

While Spring shall pour his showers, as oft he wont,
And bathe thy breathing tresses, meekest Eve;
While Summer loves to sport
Beneath thy ling'ring light;
While sallow Autumn fills thy lap with leaves;
Or Winter, yelling through the troublous air,
Affrights thy shrinking train
And rudely rends thy robes;
So long, sure-found beneath the sylvan shed,
Shall Fancy, Friendship, Science, rose-lipp'd Health,
Thy gentlest influence own,
And hymn thy fav'rite name!

HOW SLEEP THE BRAVE

How sleep the brave, who sink to rest
By all their country's wishes best!
When Spring, with dewy fingers cold,
Returns to deck their hallow'd mold,
She there shall dress a sweeter sod
Than Fancy's feet have ever trod.

By fairy hands their knell is rung;
By forms unseen their dirge is sung;
There Honor comes, a pilgrim grey,
To bless the turf that wraps their clay;
And Freedom shall awhile repair
To dwell, a weeping hermit, there!

ODE ON THE DEATH OF MR. JAMES THOMSON

IN yonderc grove a Druid lies
Where slowly winds the stealing wave!
The year's best sweets shall duteous rise
To deck its Poet's sylvan grave!
In yon deep bed of whispering reeds
His airy harpd shall now be laid,
That he, whose heart in sorrow bleeds,
May love thro' life the soothing shade.
Then maids and youths shall linger here,
And while its sounds at distance swell,
Shall sadly seem in Pity's ear
To hear the woodland pilgrim's knell.
Remembrance oft shall haunt the shore
When Thames in summer wreaths is drest,
And oft suspend the dashing oar
To bid his gentle spirit rest!
And oft as Ease and Health retire
To breezy lawn, or forest deep,
The friend shall view yon whiteninge spire,

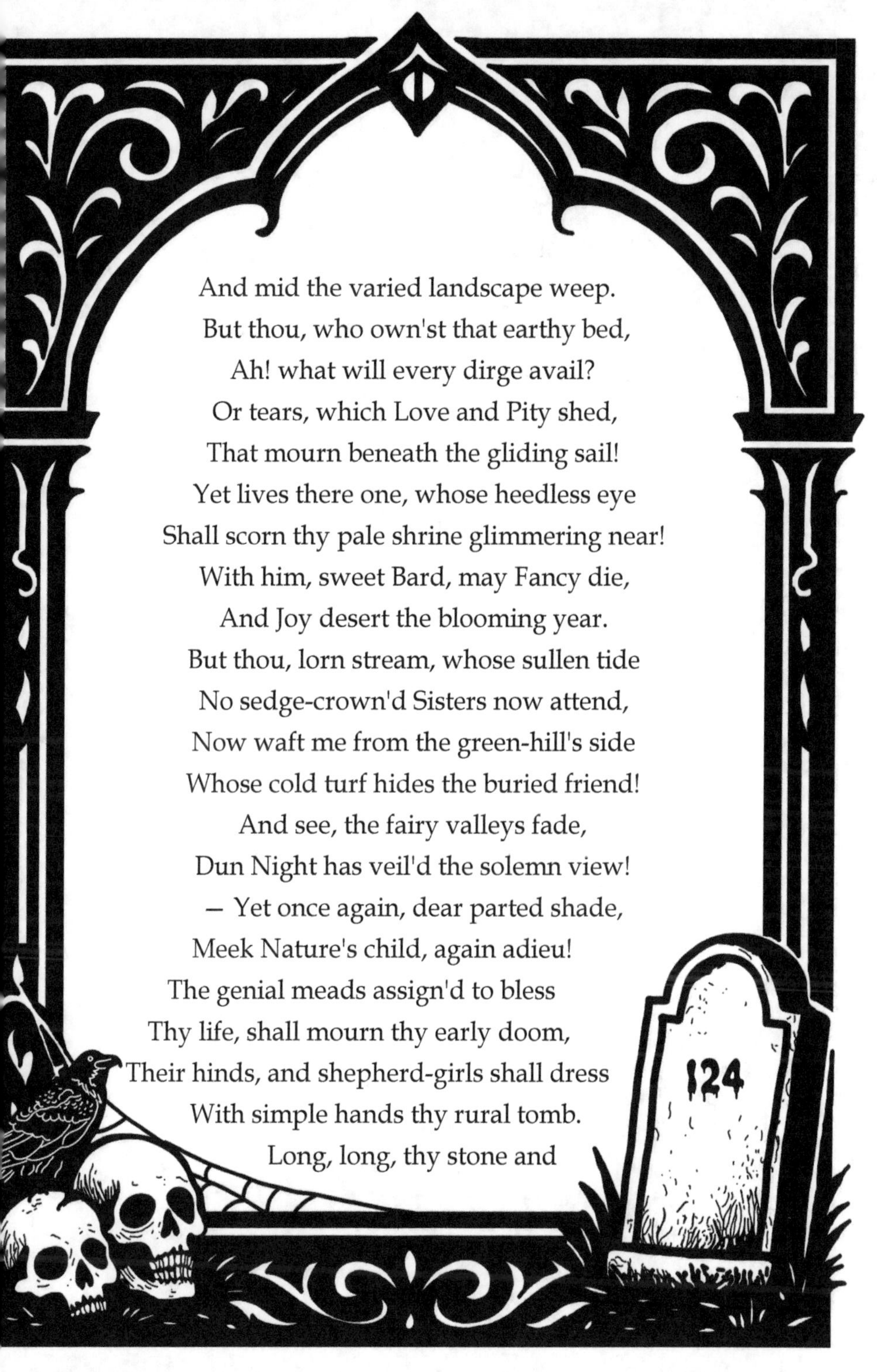

And mid the varied landscape weep.
But thou, who own'st that earthy bed,
Ah! what will every dirge avail?
Or tears, which Love and Pity shed,
That mourn beneath the gliding sail!
Yet lives there one, whose heedless eye
Shall scorn thy pale shrine glimmering near!
With him, sweet Bard, may Fancy die,
And Joy desert the blooming year.
But thou, lorn stream, whose sullen tide
No sedge-crown'd Sisters now attend,
Now waft me from the green-hill's side
Whose cold turf hides the buried friend!
And see, the fairy valleys fade,
Dun Night has veil'd the solemn view!
— Yet once again, dear parted shade,
Meek Nature's child, again adieu!
The genial meads assign'd to bless
Thy life, shall mourn thy early doom,
Their hinds, and shepherd-girls shall dress
With simple hands thy rural tomb.
Long, long, thy stone and

pointed clay

Shall melt the musing Briton's eyes;
O! vales, and wild woods, shall he say,
In yonder grave your Druid lies!

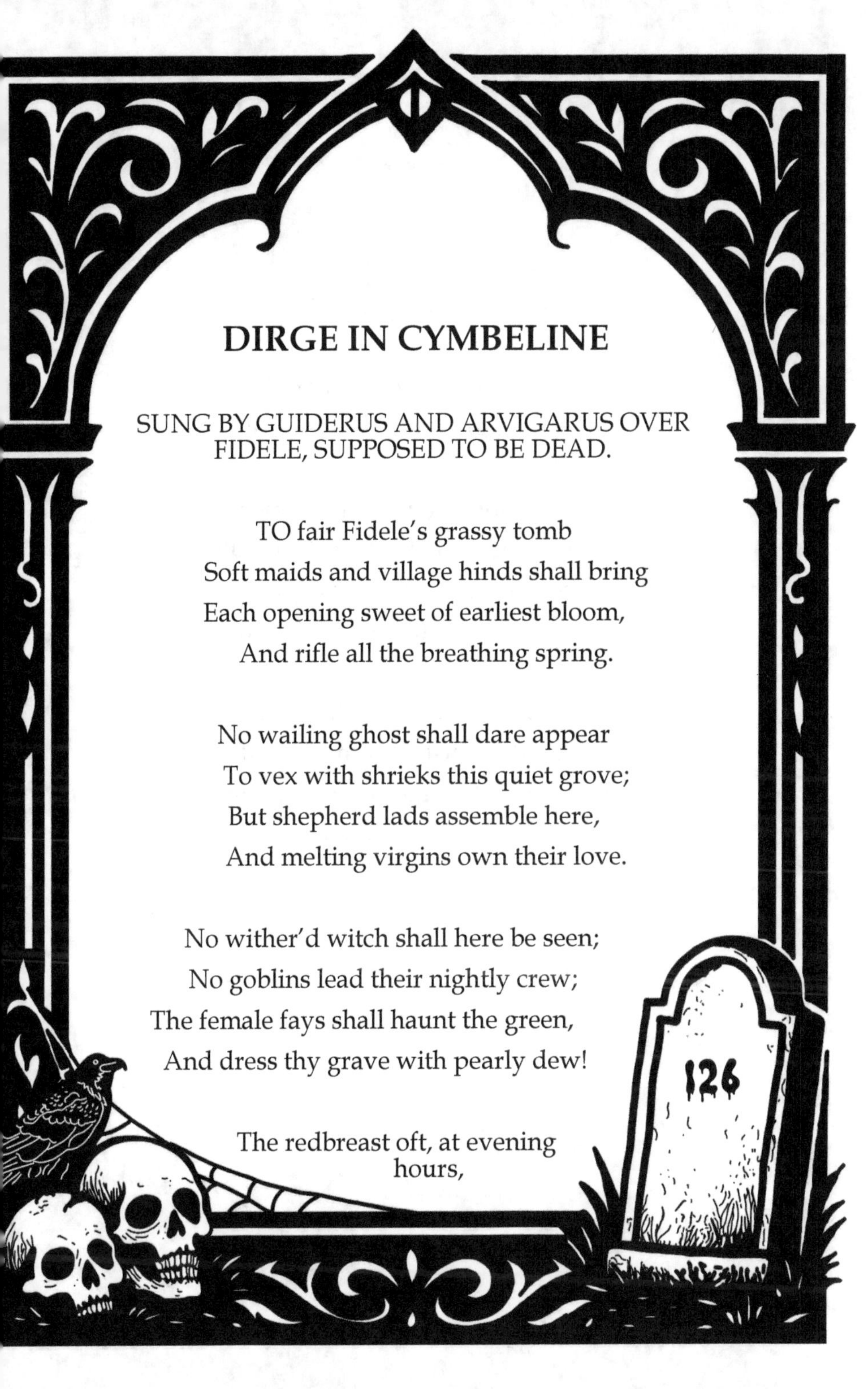

DIRGE IN CYMBELINE

SUNG BY GUIDERUS AND ARVIGARUS OVER FIDELE, SUPPOSED TO BE DEAD.

TO fair Fidele's grassy tomb
Soft maids and village hinds shall bring
Each opening sweet of earliest bloom,
And rifle all the breathing spring.

No wailing ghost shall dare appear
To vex with shrieks this quiet grove;
But shepherd lads assemble here,
And melting virgins own their love.

No wither'd witch shall here be seen;
No goblins lead their nightly crew;
The female fays shall haunt the green,
And dress thy grave with pearly dew!

The redbreast oft, at evening hours,

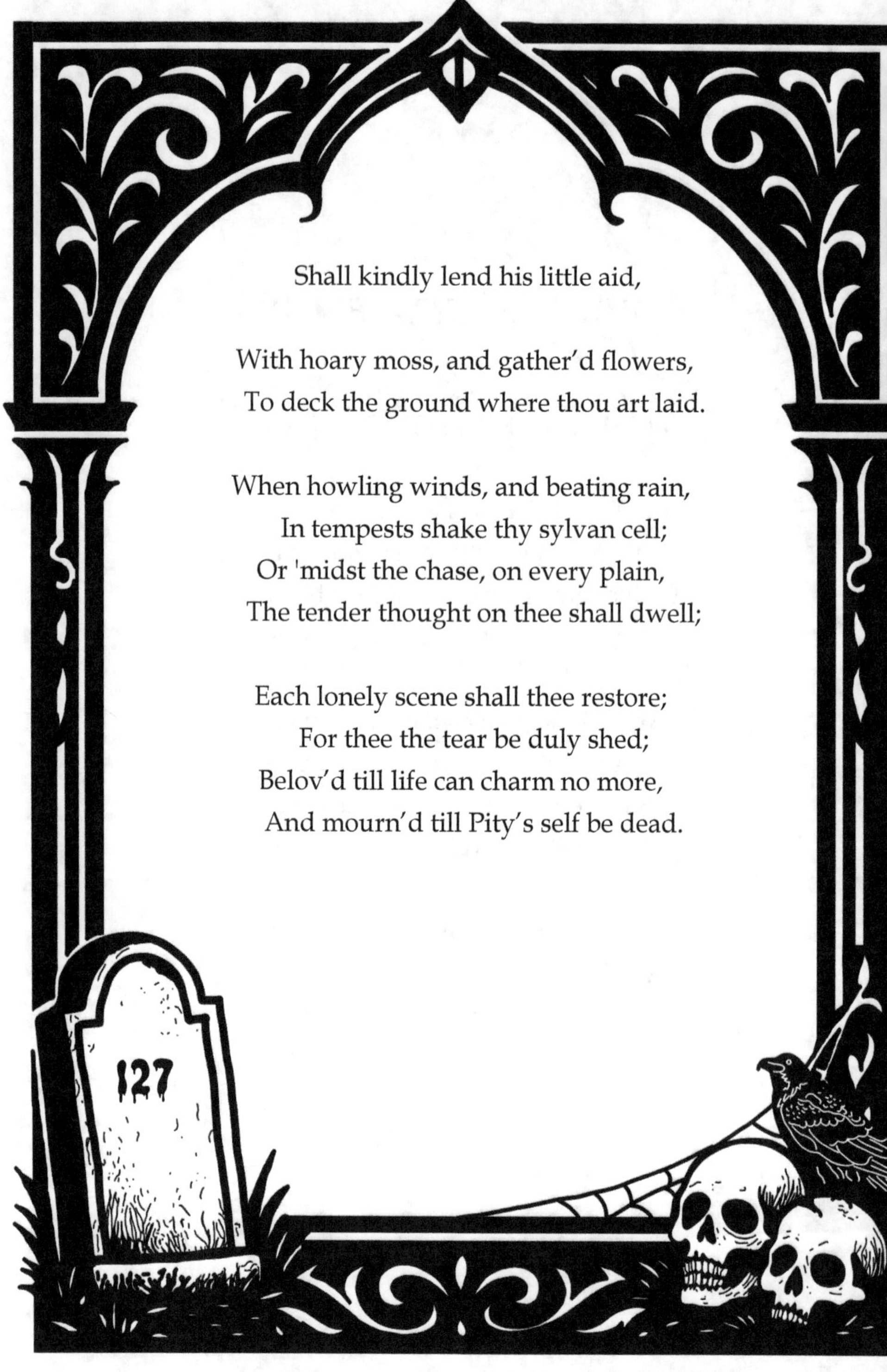

Shall kindly lend his little aid,

With hoary moss, and gather'd flowers,
To deck the ground where thou art laid.

When howling winds, and beating rain,
In tempests shake thy sylvan cell;
Or 'midst the chase, on every plain,
The tender thought on thee shall dwell;

Each lonely scene shall thee restore;
For thee the tear be duly shed;
Belov'd till life can charm no more,
And mourn'd till Pity's self be dead.

William Cowper

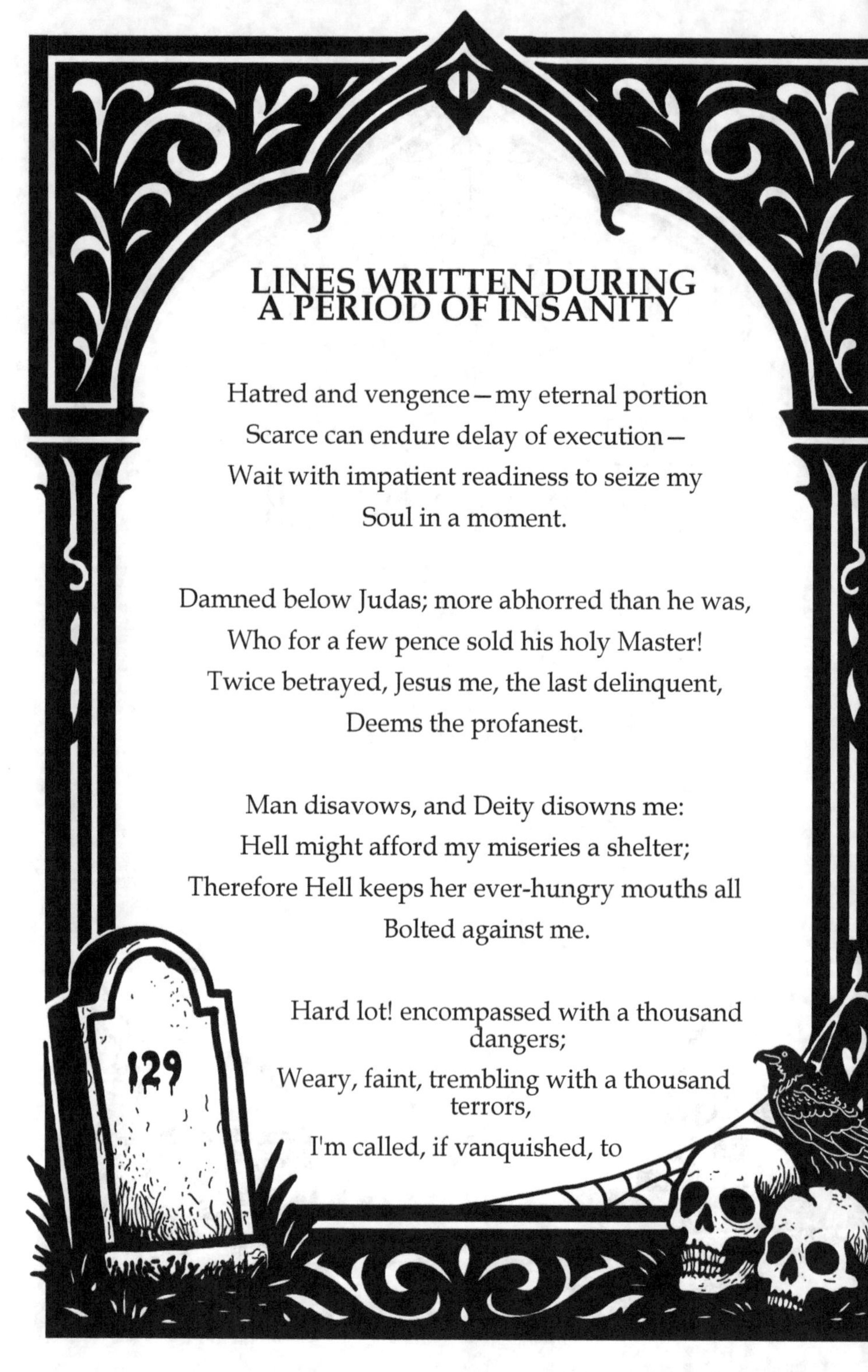

LINES WRITTEN DURING A PERIOD OF INSANITY

Hatred and vengence—my eternal portion
Scarce can endure delay of execution—
Wait with impatient readiness to seize my
Soul in a moment.

Damned below Judas; more abhorred than he was,
Who for a few pence sold his holy Master!
Twice betrayed, Jesus me, the last delinquent,
Deems the profanest.

Man disavows, and Deity disowns me:
Hell might afford my miseries a shelter;
Therefore Hell keeps her ever-hungry mouths all
Bolted against me.

Hard lot! encompassed with a thousand dangers;
Weary, faint, trembling with a thousand terrors,
I'm called, if vanquished, to

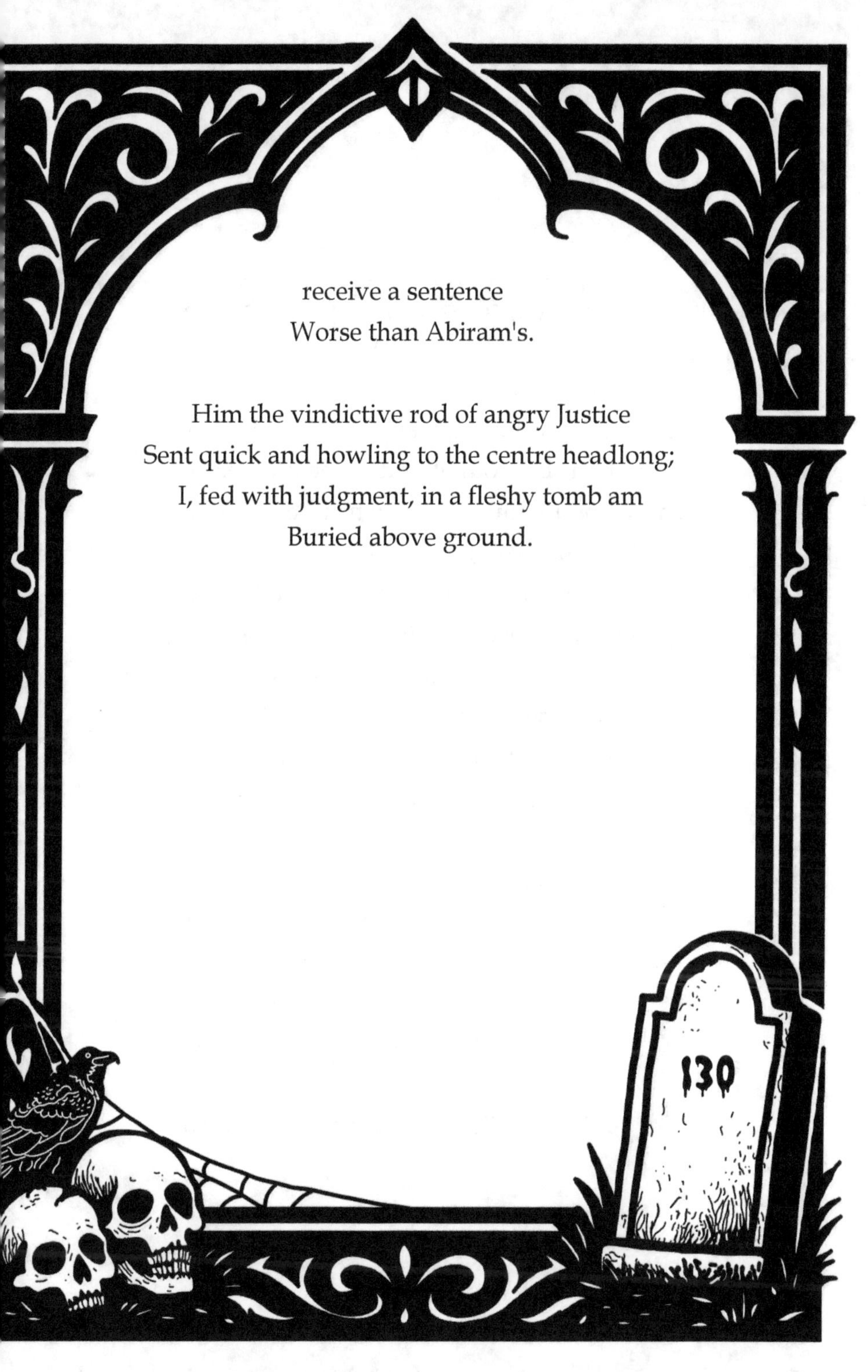

receive a sentence
Worse than Abiram's.

Him the vindictive rod of angry Justice
Sent quick and howling to the centre headlong;
I, fed with judgment, in a fleshy tomb am
Buried above ground.

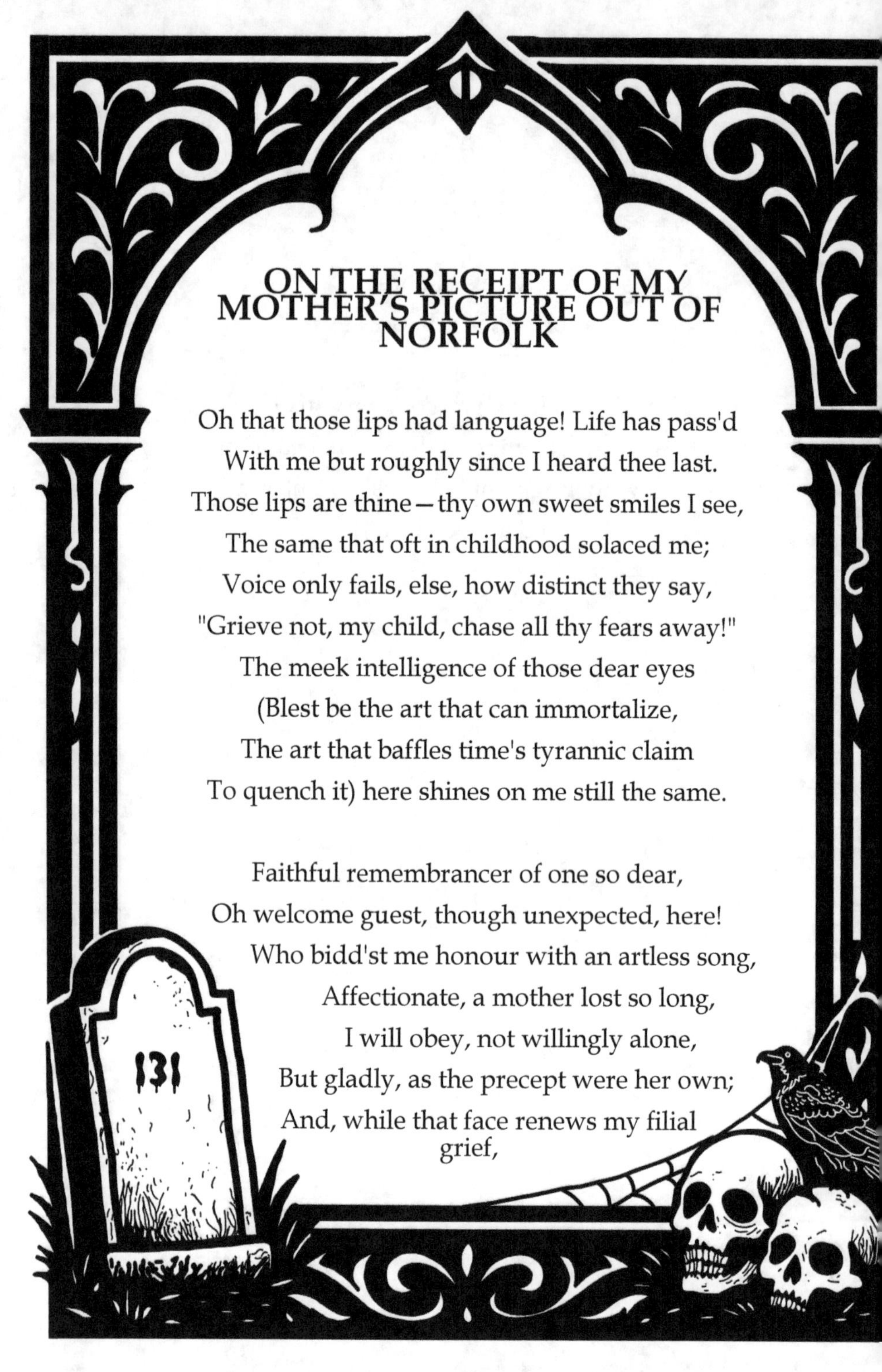

ON THE RECEIPT OF MY MOTHER'S PICTURE OUT OF NORFOLK

Oh that those lips had language! Life has pass'd
With me but roughly since I heard thee last.
Those lips are thine—thy own sweet smiles I see,
The same that oft in childhood solaced me;
Voice only fails, else, how distinct they say,
"Grieve not, my child, chase all thy fears away!"
The meek intelligence of those dear eyes
(Blest be the art that can immortalize,
The art that baffles time's tyrannic claim
To quench it) here shines on me still the same.

Faithful remembrancer of one so dear,
Oh welcome guest, though unexpected, here!
Who bidd'st me honour with an artless song,
Affectionate, a mother lost so long,
I will obey, not willingly alone,
But gladly, as the precept were her own;
And, while that face renews my filial grief,

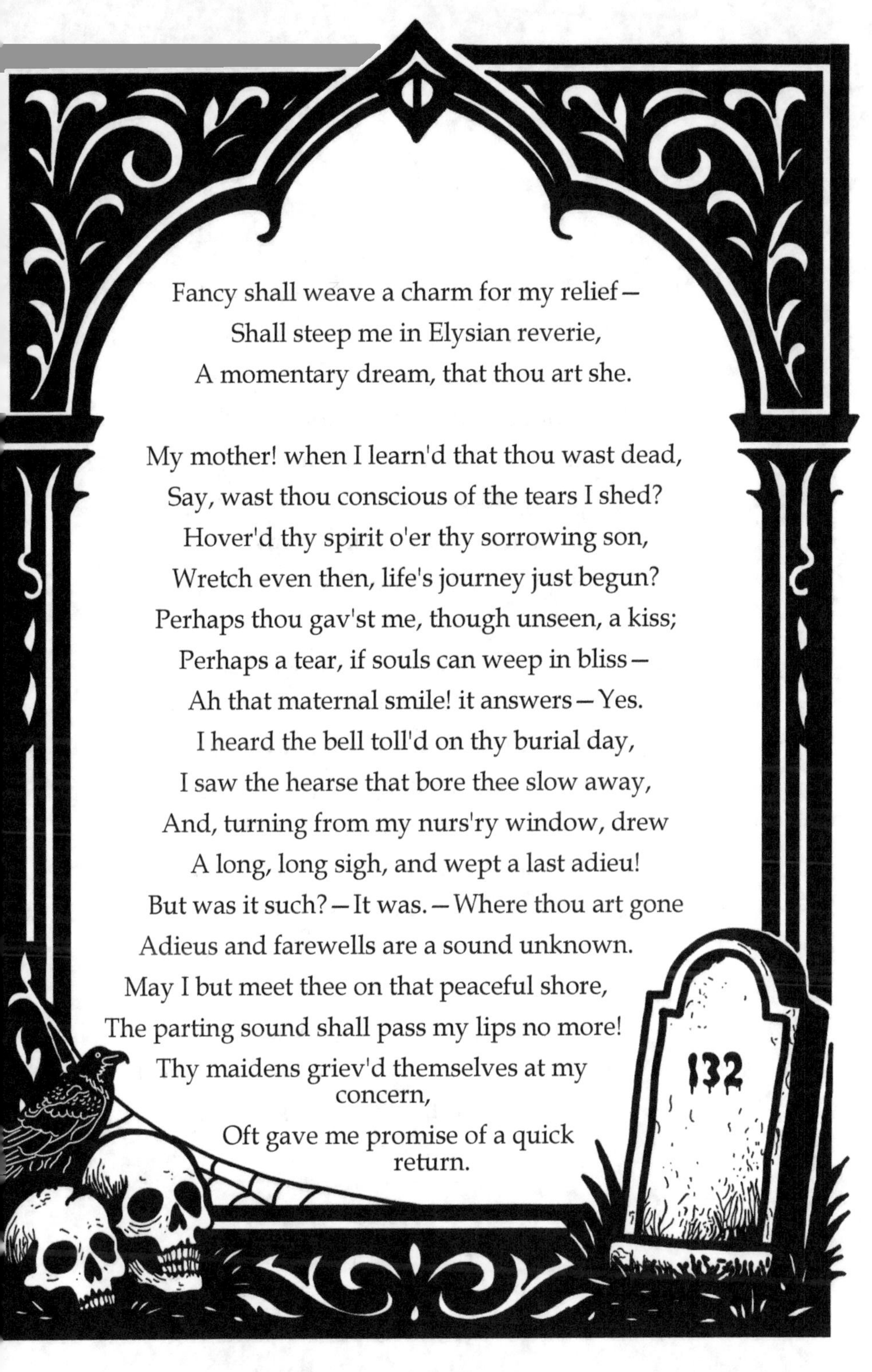

Fancy shall weave a charm for my relief—
Shall steep me in Elysian reverie,
A momentary dream, that thou art she.

My mother! when I learn'd that thou wast dead,
Say, wast thou conscious of the tears I shed?
Hover'd thy spirit o'er thy sorrowing son,
Wretch even then, life's journey just begun?
Perhaps thou gav'st me, though unseen, a kiss;
Perhaps a tear, if souls can weep in bliss—
Ah that maternal smile! it answers—Yes.
I heard the bell toll'd on thy burial day,
I saw the hearse that bore thee slow away,
And, turning from my nurs'ry window, drew
A long, long sigh, and wept a last adieu!
But was it such?—It was.—Where thou art gone
Adieus and farewells are a sound unknown.
May I but meet thee on that peaceful shore,
The parting sound shall pass my lips no more!
Thy maidens griev'd themselves at my concern,
Oft gave me promise of a quick return.

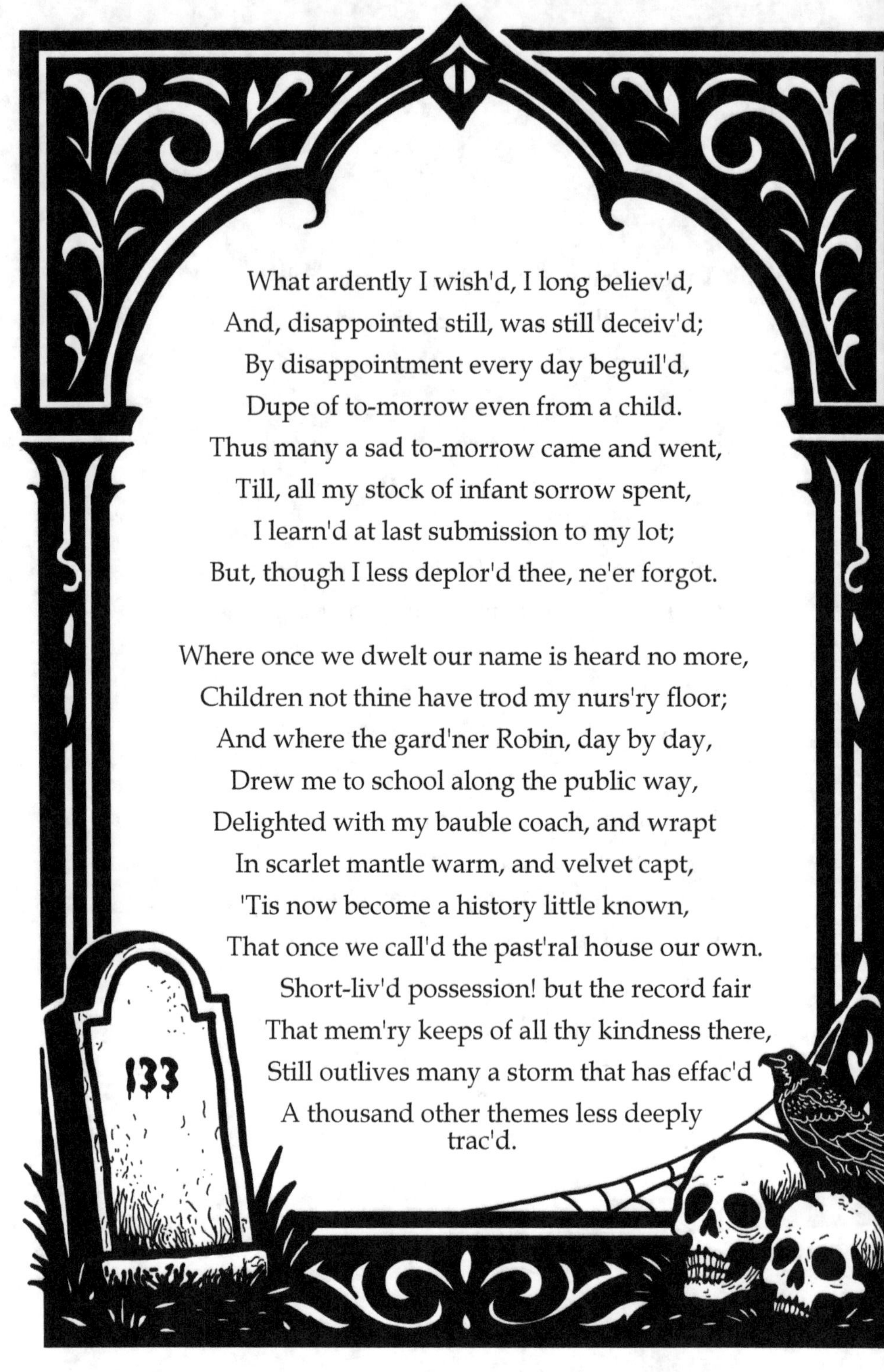

What ardently I wish'd, I long believ'd,
And, disappointed still, was still deceiv'd;
By disappointment every day beguil'd,
Dupe of to-morrow even from a child.
Thus many a sad to-morrow came and went,
Till, all my stock of infant sorrow spent,
I learn'd at last submission to my lot;
But, though I less deplor'd thee, ne'er forgot.

Where once we dwelt our name is heard no more,
Children not thine have trod my nurs'ry floor;
And where the gard'ner Robin, day by day,
Drew me to school along the public way,
Delighted with my bauble coach, and wrapt
In scarlet mantle warm, and velvet capt,
'Tis now become a history little known,
That once we call'd the past'ral house our own.
Short-liv'd possession! but the record fair
That mem'ry keeps of all thy kindness there,
Still outlives many a storm that has effac'd
A thousand other themes less deeply trac'd.

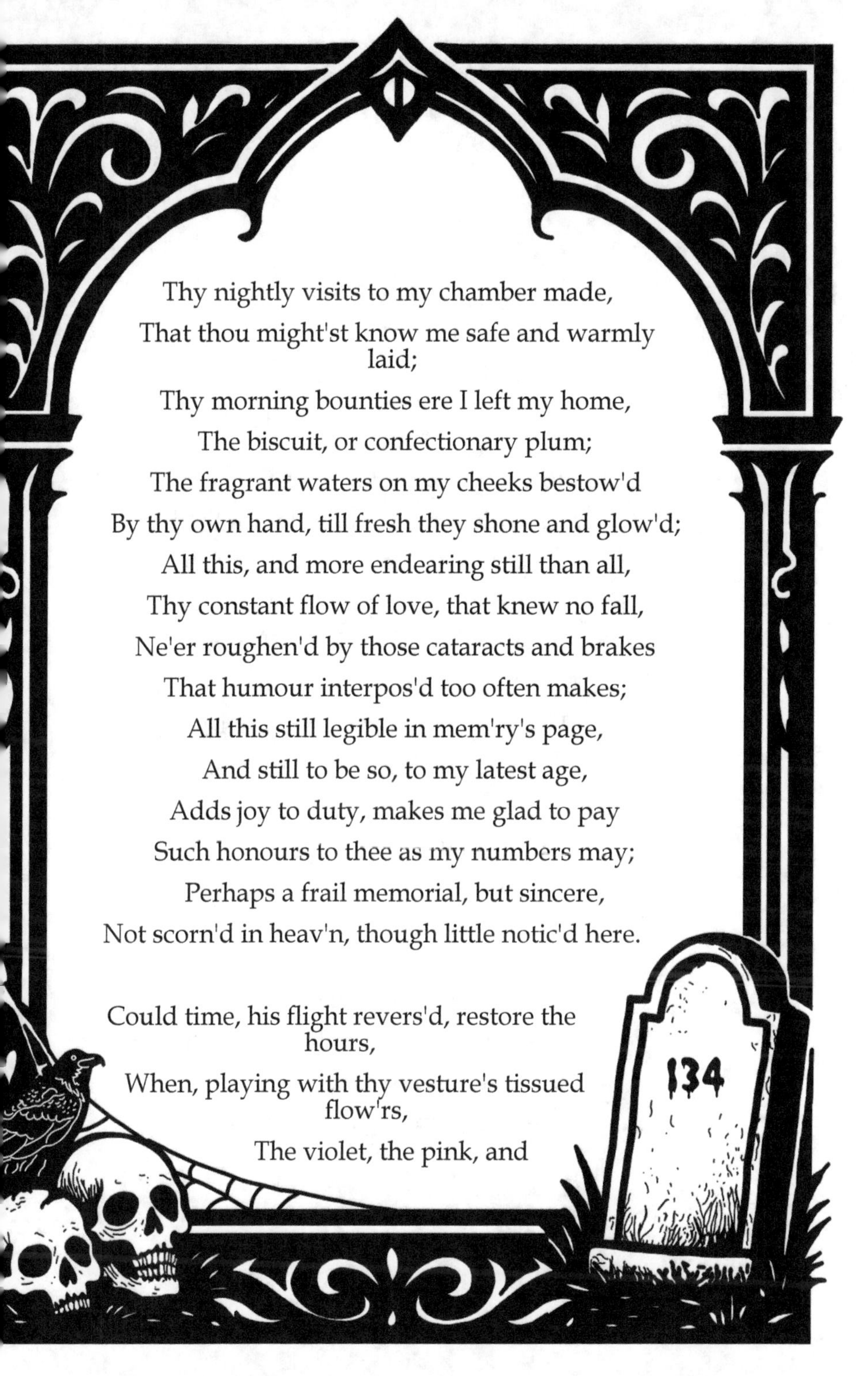

Thy nightly visits to my chamber made,
That thou might'st know me safe and warmly laid;
Thy morning bounties ere I left my home,
The biscuit, or confectionary plum;
The fragrant waters on my cheeks bestow'd
By thy own hand, till fresh they shone and glow'd;
All this, and more endearing still than all,
Thy constant flow of love, that knew no fall,
Ne'er roughen'd by those cataracts and brakes
That humour interpos'd too often makes;
All this still legible in mem'ry's page,
And still to be so, to my latest age,
Adds joy to duty, makes me glad to pay
Such honours to thee as my numbers may;
Perhaps a frail memorial, but sincere,
Not scorn'd in heav'n, though little notic'd here.

Could time, his flight revers'd, restore the hours,
When, playing with thy vesture's tissued flow'rs,
The violet, the pink, and

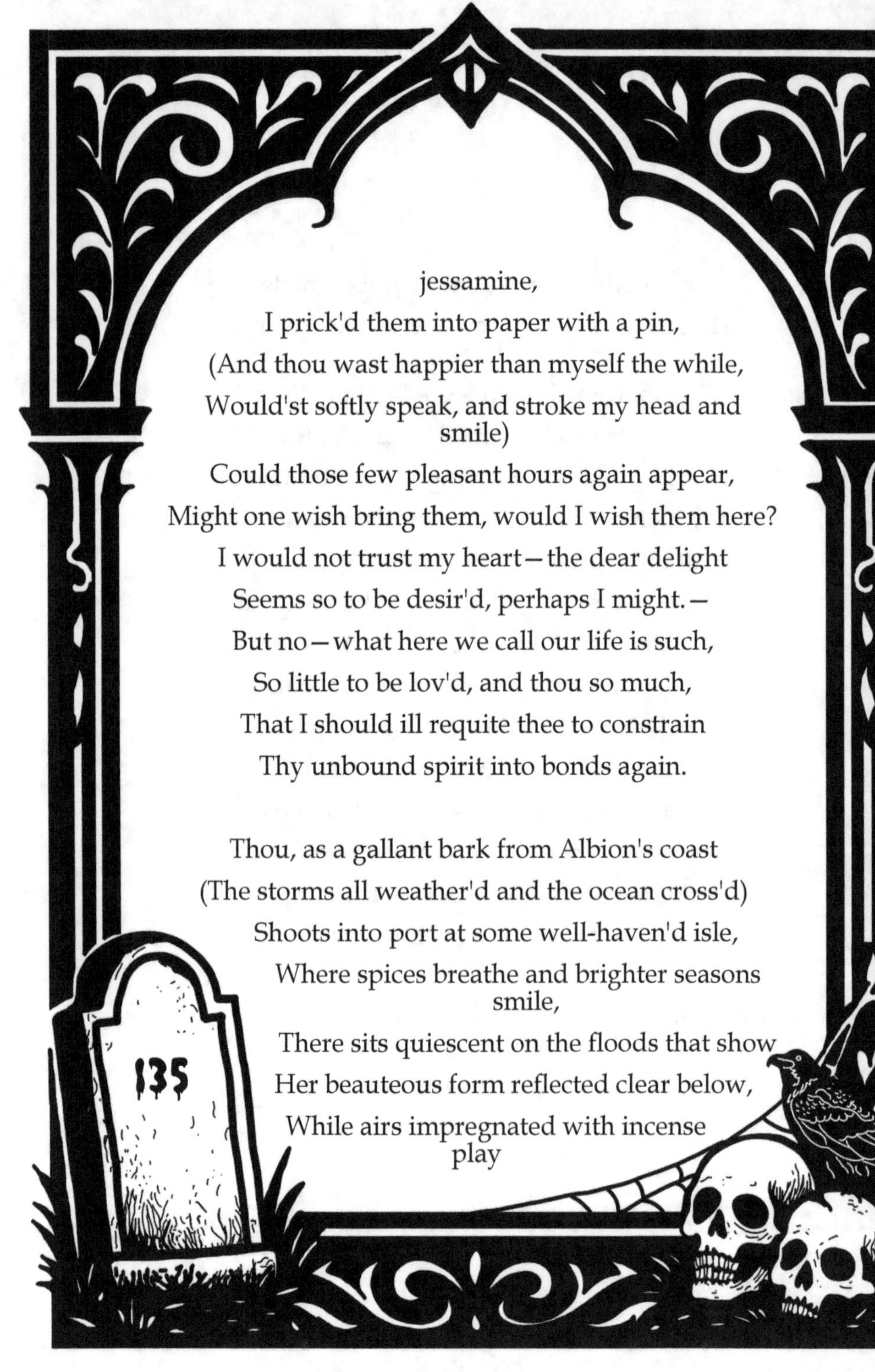

jessamine,
I prick'd them into paper with a pin,
(And thou wast happier than myself the while,
Would'st softly speak, and stroke my head and smile)
Could those few pleasant hours again appear,
Might one wish bring them, would I wish them here?
I would not trust my heart—the dear delight
Seems so to be desir'd, perhaps I might.—
But no—what here we call our life is such,
So little to be lov'd, and thou so much,
That I should ill requite thee to constrain
Thy unbound spirit into bonds again.

Thou, as a gallant bark from Albion's coast
(The storms all weather'd and the ocean cross'd)
Shoots into port at some well-haven'd isle,
Where spices breathe and brighter seasons smile,
There sits quiescent on the floods that show
Her beauteous form reflected clear below,
While airs impregnated with incense play

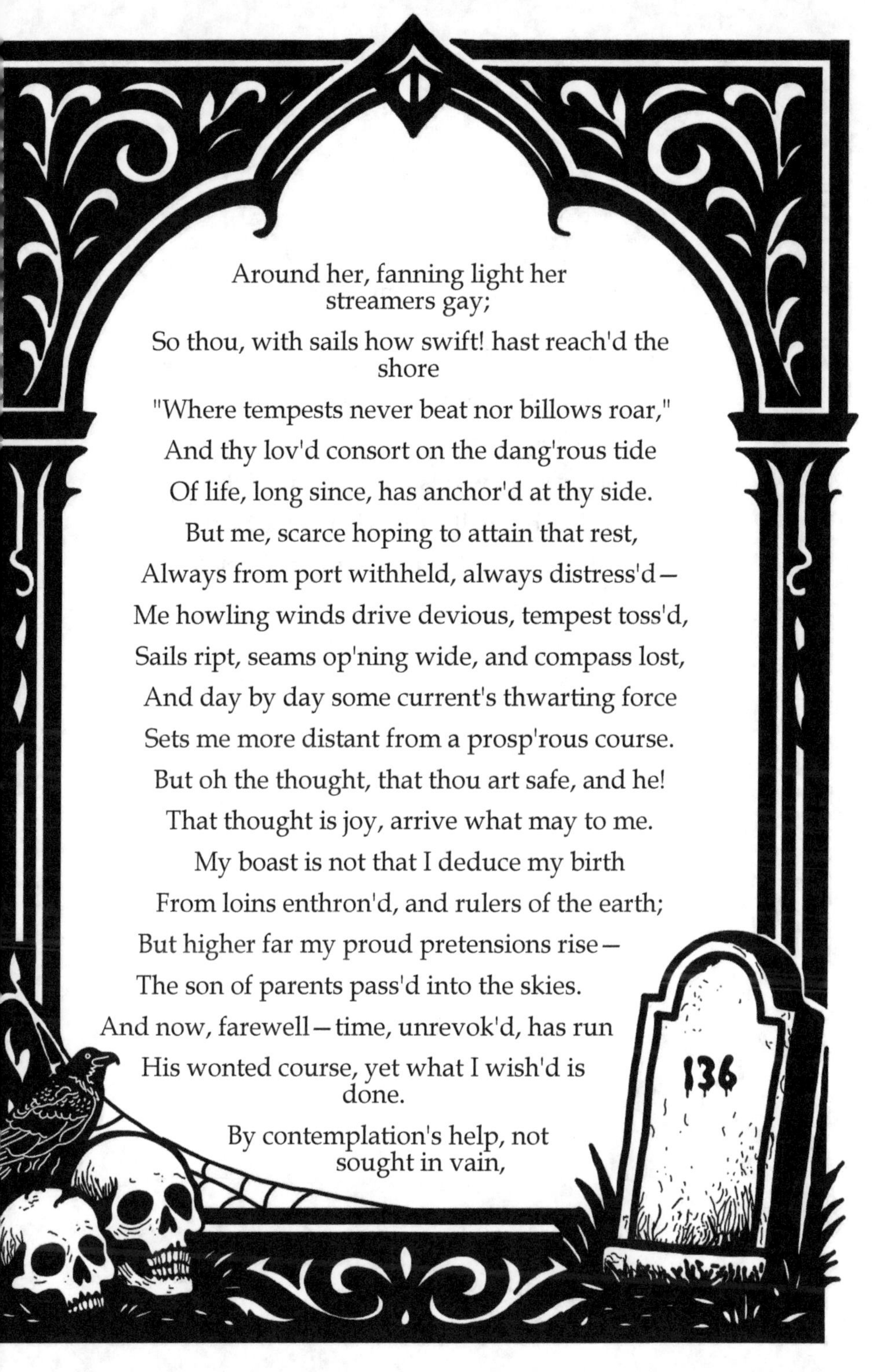

Around her, fanning light her streamers gay;
So thou, with sails how swift! hast reach'd the shore
"Where tempests never beat nor billows roar,"
And thy lov'd consort on the dang'rous tide
Of life, long since, has anchor'd at thy side.
But me, scarce hoping to attain that rest,
Always from port withheld, always distress'd—
Me howling winds drive devious, tempest toss'd,
Sails ript, seams op'ning wide, and compass lost,
And day by day some current's thwarting force
Sets me more distant from a prosp'rous course.
But oh the thought, that thou art safe, and he!
That thought is joy, arrive what may to me.
My boast is not that I deduce my birth
From loins enthron'd, and rulers of the earth;
But higher far my proud pretensions rise—
The son of parents pass'd into the skies.
And now, farewell—time, unrevok'd, has run
His wonted course, yet what I wish'd is done.
By contemplation's help, not sought in vain,

I seem t' have liv'd my childhood o'er again;
To have renew'd the joys that once were mine,
Without the sin of violating thine:
And, while the wings of fancy still are free,
And I can view this mimic shew of thee,
Time has but half succeeded in his theft—
Thyself remov'd, thy power to sooth me left.

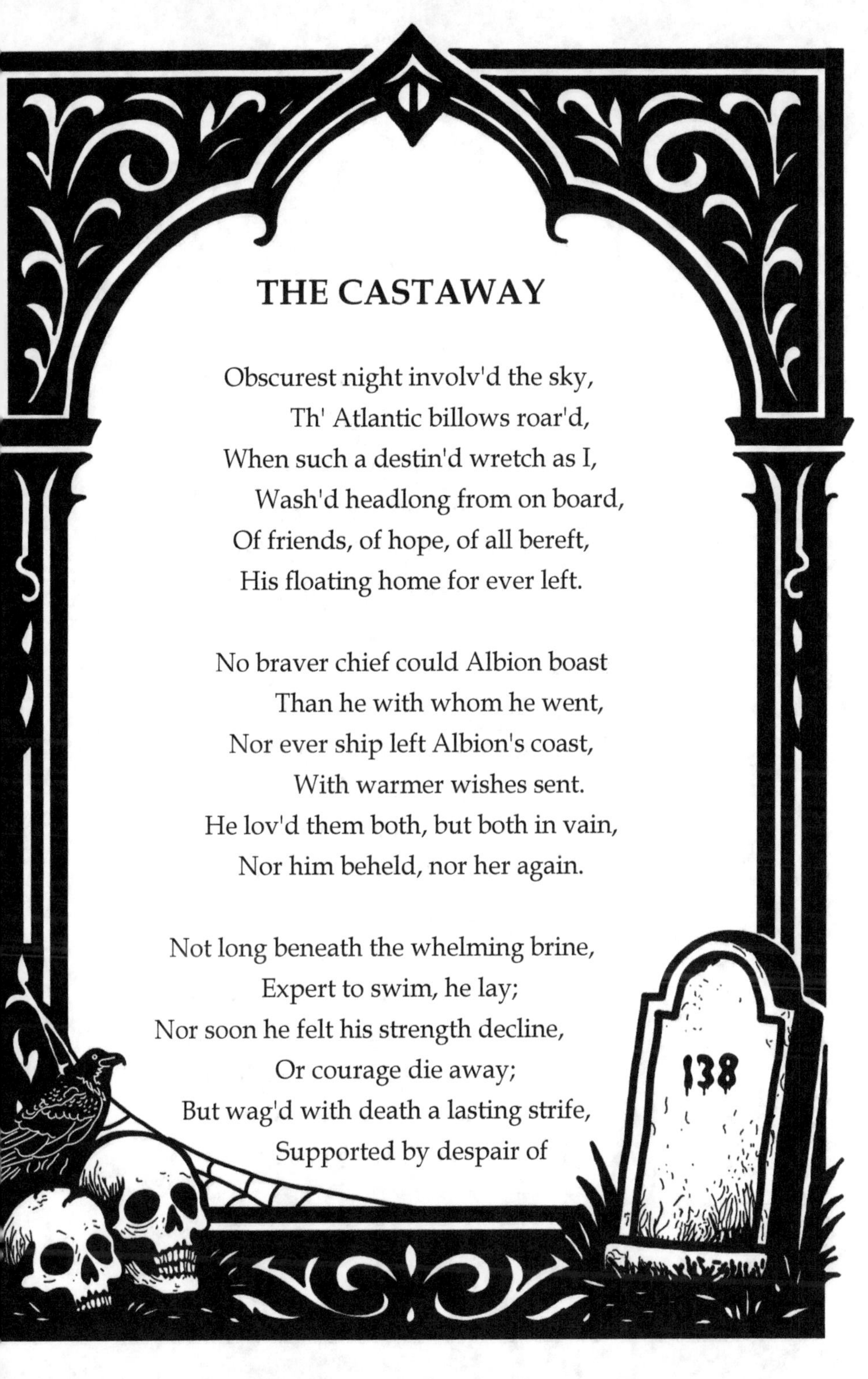

THE CASTAWAY

Obscurest night involv'd the sky,
Th' Atlantic billows roar'd,
When such a destin'd wretch as I,
Wash'd headlong from on board,
Of friends, of hope, of all bereft,
His floating home for ever left.

No braver chief could Albion boast
Than he with whom he went,
Nor ever ship left Albion's coast,
With warmer wishes sent.
He lov'd them both, but both in vain,
Nor him beheld, nor her again.

Not long beneath the whelming brine,
Expert to swim, he lay;
Nor soon he felt his strength decline,
Or courage die away;
But wag'd with death a lasting strife,
Supported by despair of

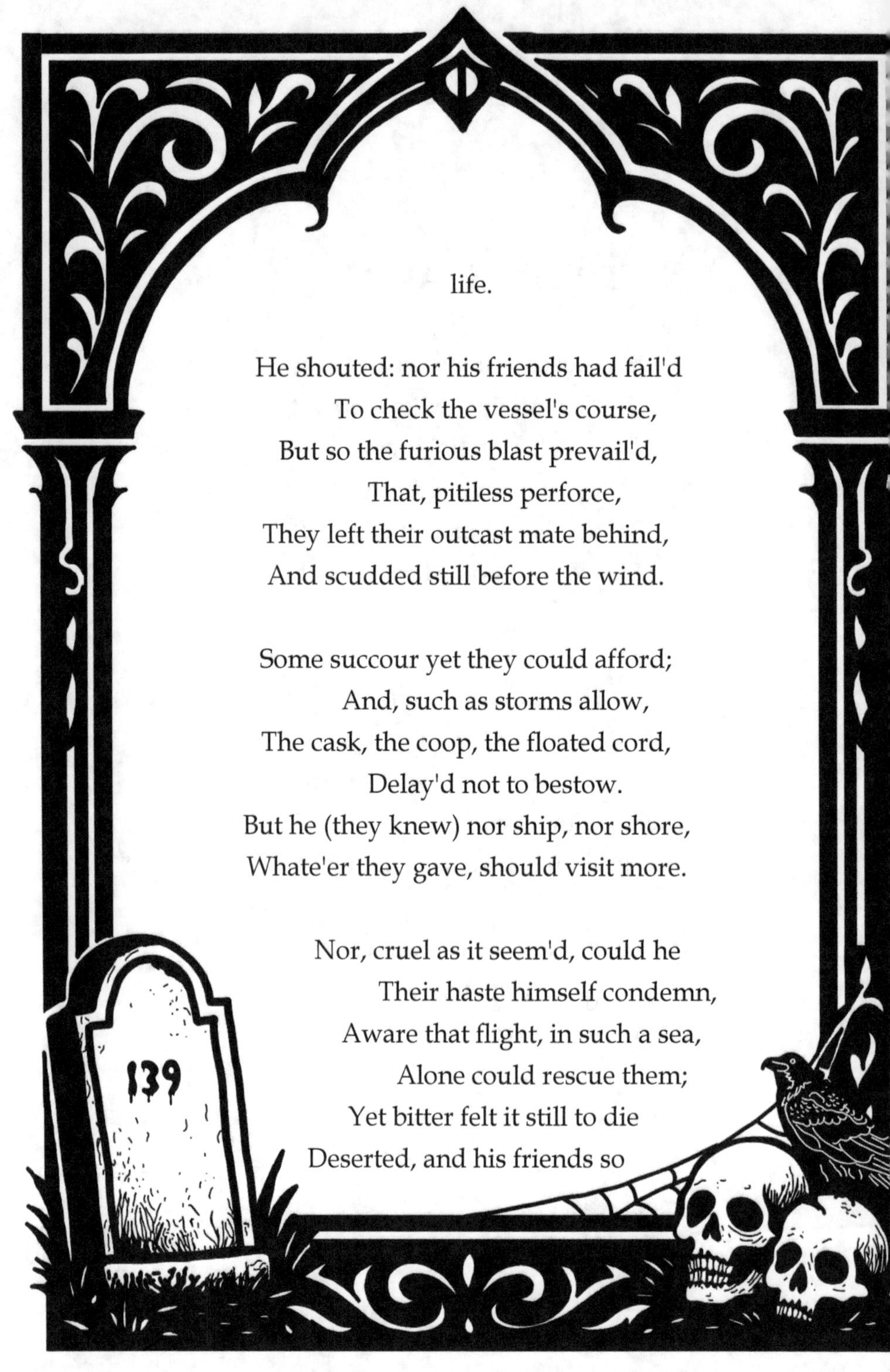

life.

He shouted: nor his friends had fail'd
To check the vessel's course,
But so the furious blast prevail'd,
That, pitiless perforce,
They left their outcast mate behind,
And scudded still before the wind.

Some succour yet they could afford;
And, such as storms allow,
The cask, the coop, the floated cord,
Delay'd not to bestow.
But he (they knew) nor ship, nor shore,
Whate'er they gave, should visit more.

Nor, cruel as it seem'd, could he
Their haste himself condemn,
Aware that flight, in such a sea,
Alone could rescue them;
Yet bitter felt it still to die
Deserted, and his friends so

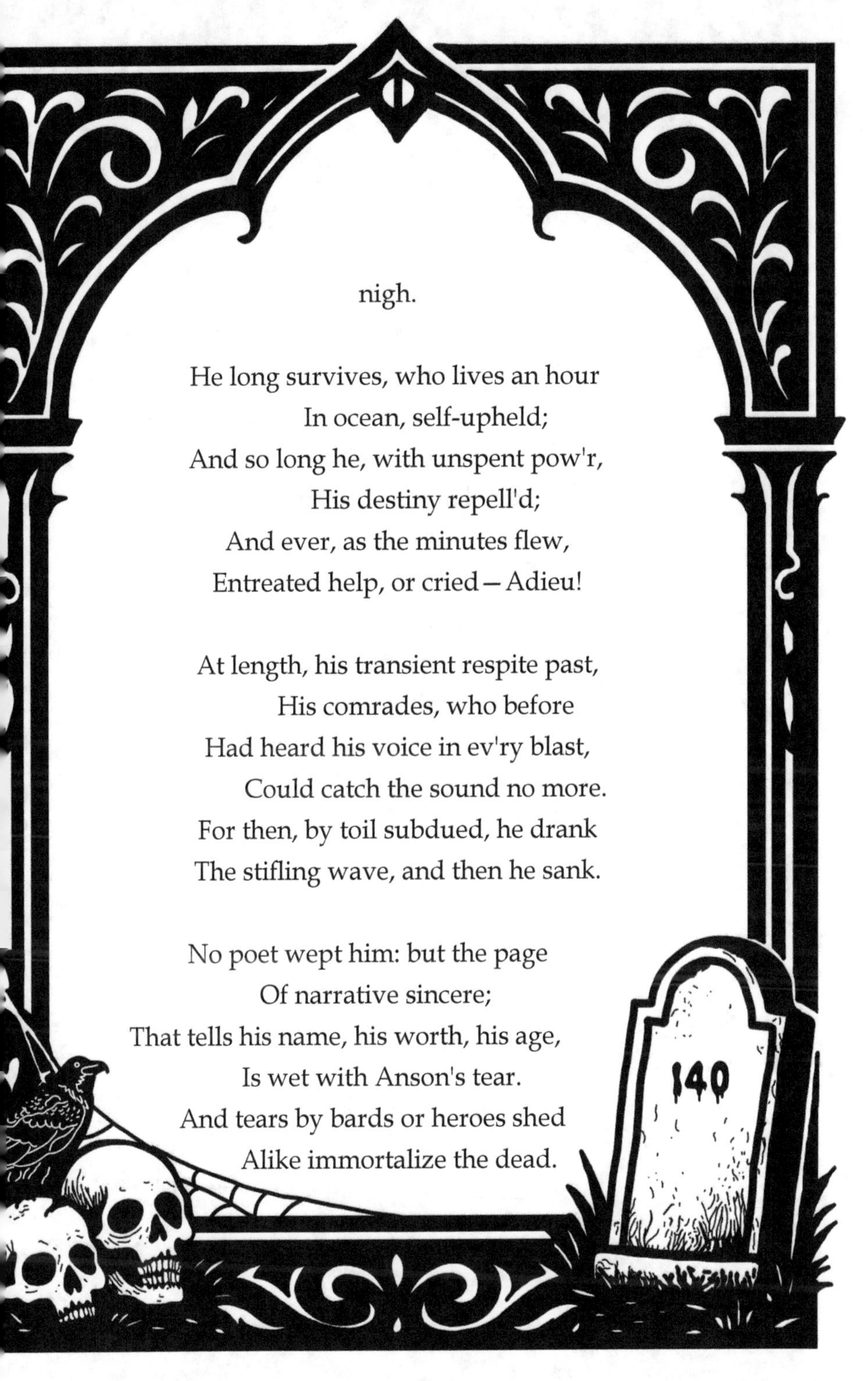

nigh.

He long survives, who lives an hour
In ocean, self-upheld;
And so long he, with unspent pow'r,
His destiny repell'd;
And ever, as the minutes flew,
Entreated help, or cried—Adieu!

At length, his transient respite past,
His comrades, who before
Had heard his voice in ev'ry blast,
Could catch the sound no more.
For then, by toil subdued, he drank
The stifling wave, and then he sank.

No poet wept him: but the page
Of narrative sincere;
That tells his name, his worth, his age,
Is wet with Anson's tear.
And tears by bards or heroes shed
Alike immortalize the dead.

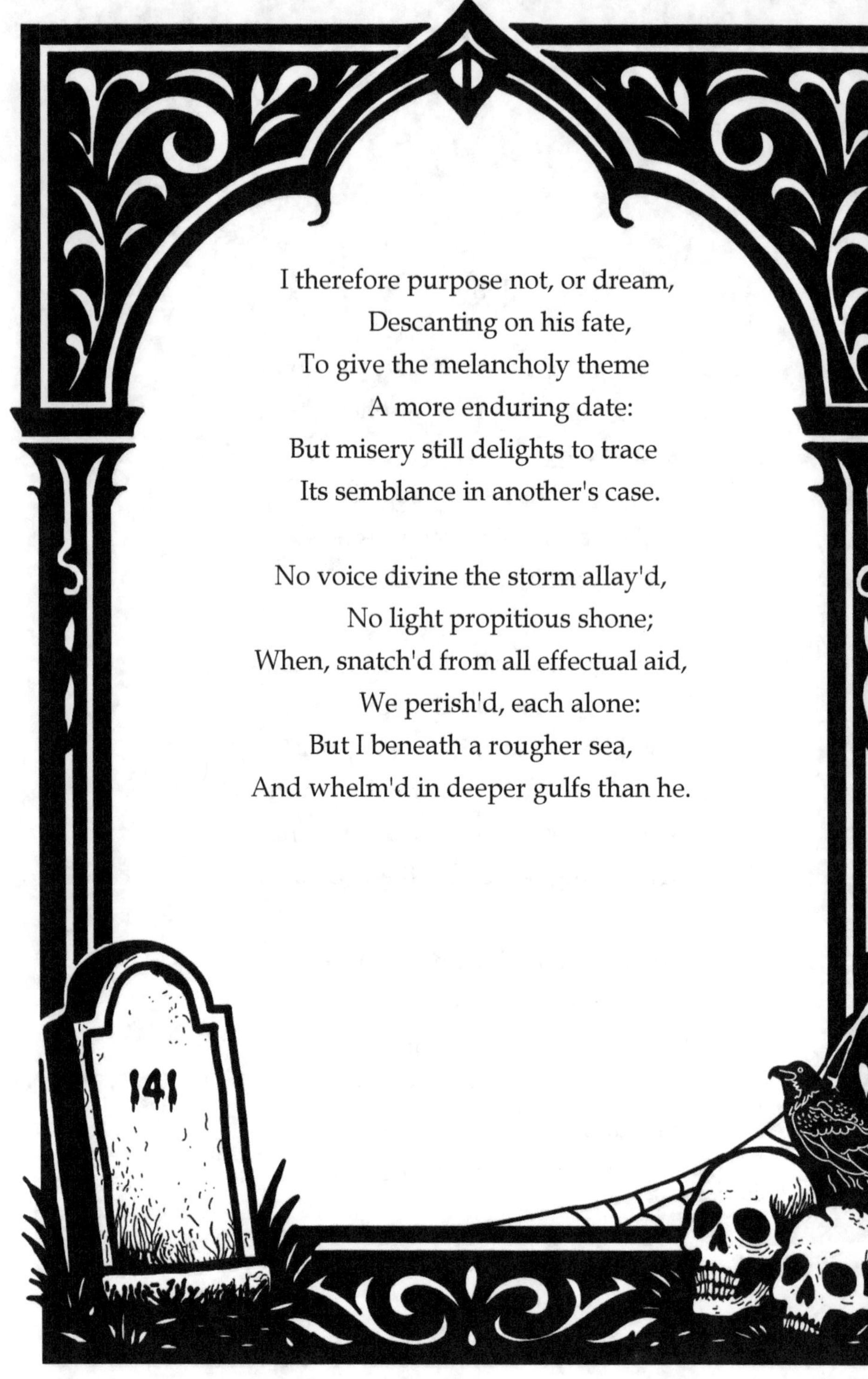

I therefore purpose not, or dream,
Descanting on his fate,
To give the melancholy theme
A more enduring date:
But misery still delights to trace
Its semblance in another's case.

No voice divine the storm allay'd,
No light propitious shone;
When, snatch'd from all effectual aid,
We perish'd, each alone:
But I beneath a rougher sea,
And whelm'd in deeper gulfs than he.

Emily Dickinson

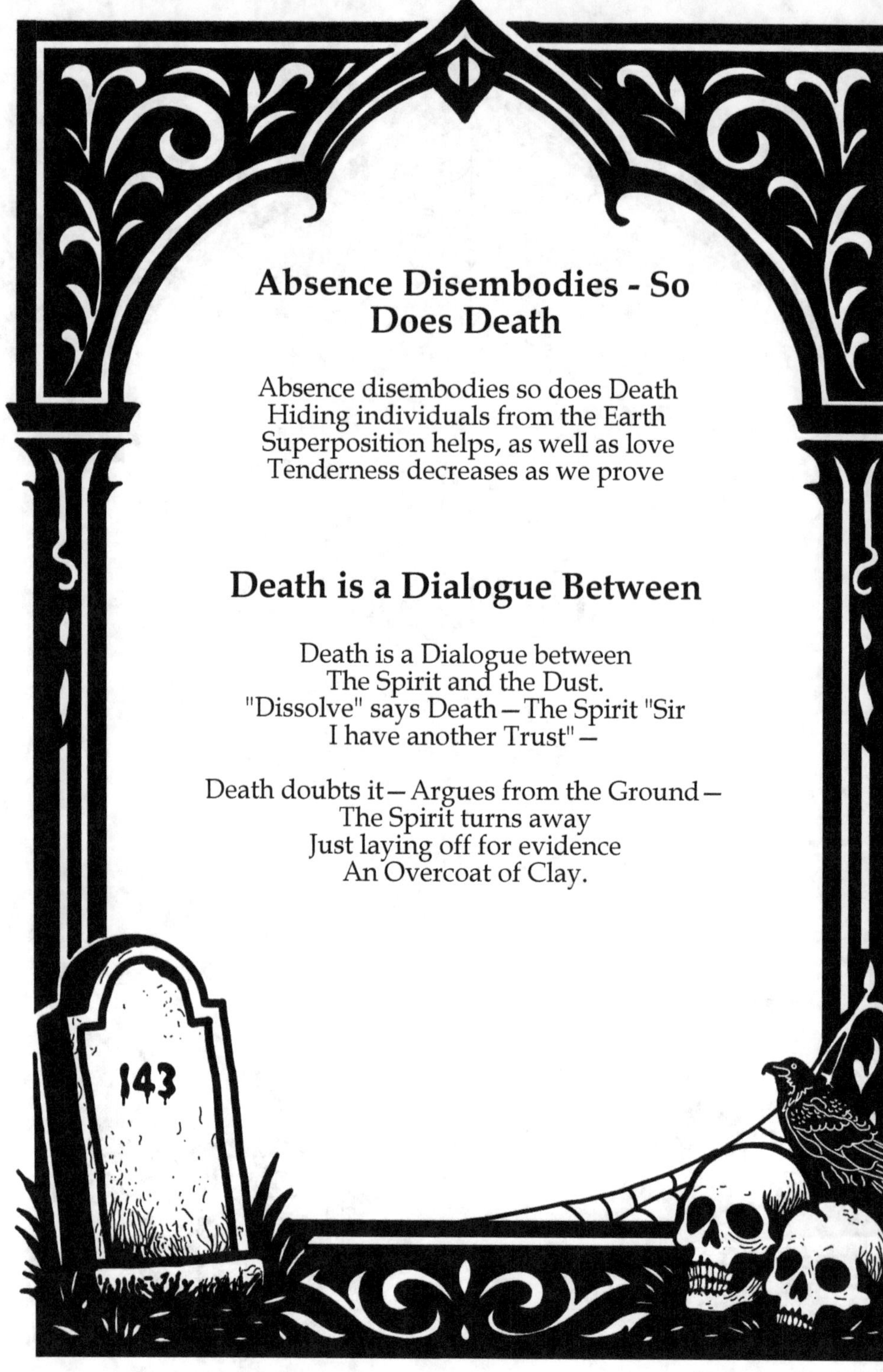

Absence Disembodies - So Does Death

Absence disembodies so does Death
Hiding individuals from the Earth
Superposition helps, as well as love
Tenderness decreases as we prove

Death is a Dialogue Between

Death is a Dialogue between
The Spirit and the Dust.
"Dissolve" says Death—The Spirit "Sir
I have another Trust"—

Death doubts it—Argues from the Ground—
The Spirit turns away
Just laying off for evidence
An Overcoat of Clay.

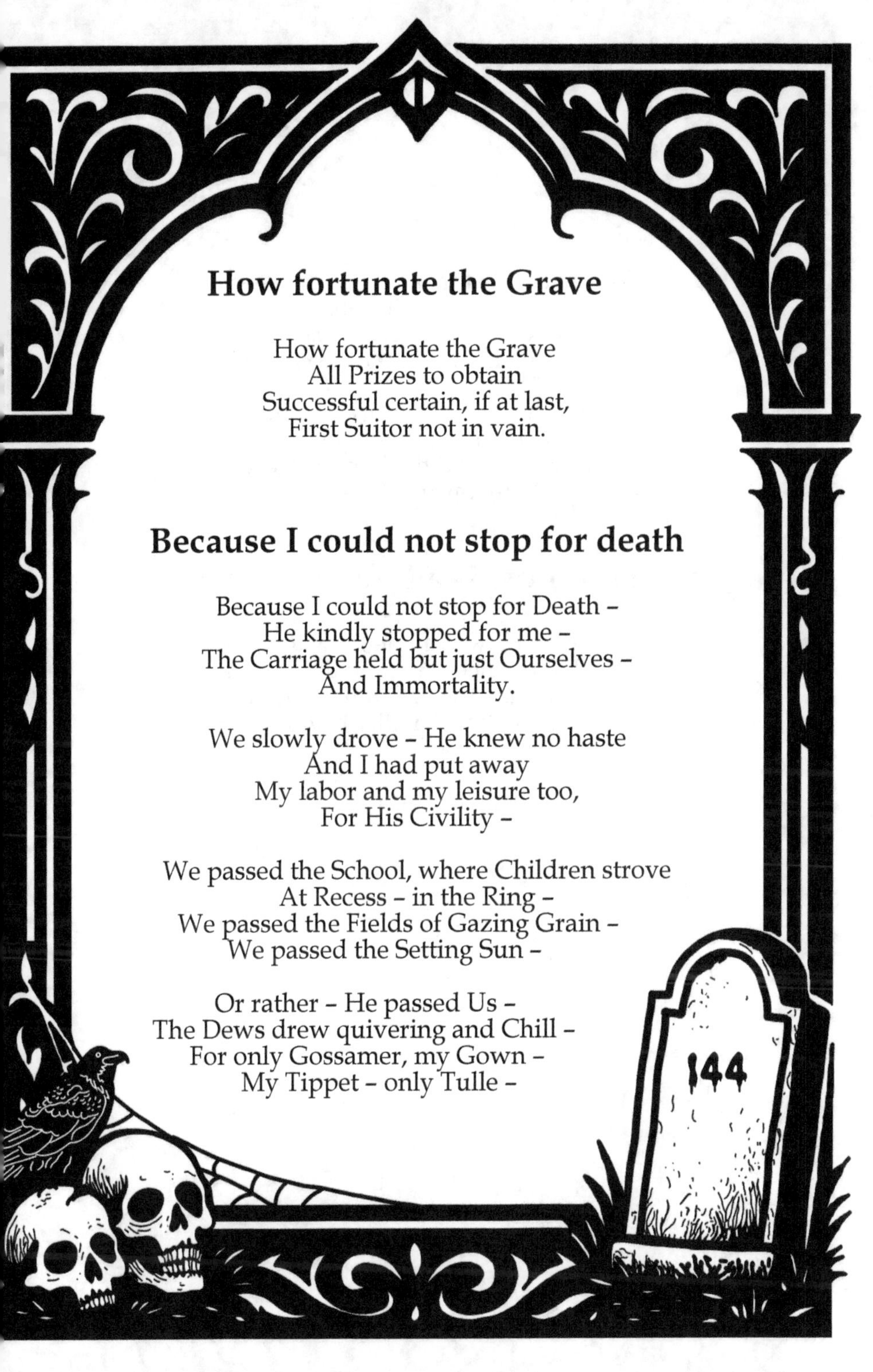

How fortunate the Grave

How fortunate the Grave
All Prizes to obtain
Successful certain, if at last,
First Suitor not in vain.

Because I could not stop for death

Because I could not stop for Death –
He kindly stopped for me –
The Carriage held but just Ourselves –
And Immortality.

We slowly drove – He knew no haste
And I had put away
My labor and my leisure too,
For His Civility –

We passed the School, where Children strove
At Recess – in the Ring –
We passed the Fields of Gazing Grain –
We passed the Setting Sun –

Or rather – He passed Us –
The Dews drew quivering and Chill –
For only Gossamer, my Gown –
My Tippet – only Tulle –

We paused before a House that seemed
A Swelling of the Ground –
The Roof was scarcely visible –
The Cornice – in the Ground –

Since then – 'tis Centuries – and yet
Feels shorter than the Day
I first surmised the Horses' Heads
Were toward Eternity –

A Death Blow is a Life Blow to Some

A Death blow is a Life blow to Some
Who till they died, did not alive become—
Who had they lived, had died but when
They died, Vitality begun.

I Heard a Fly Buzz - when I died

I heard a Fly buzz - when I died -
The Stillness in the Room
Was like the Stillness in the Air -
Between the Heaves of Storm -

The Eyes around - had wrung them dry -
And Breaths were gathering firm
For that last Onset - when the King
Be witnessed - in the Room -

I willed my Keepsakes - Signed away
What portion of me be
Assignable - and then it was
There interposed a Fly -

With Blue - uncertain - stumbling Buzz -
Between the light - and me -
And then the Windows failed - and then
I could not see to see -

I Wonder if the Supulcher

I wonder if the sepulchre
Is not a lonesome way,
When men and boys, and larks and June
Go down the fields to hay!

The Grave my Little Cottage is

The grave my little cottage is,
Where 'Keeping house' for thee
I make my parlor orderly
And lay the marble tea.

For two divided, briefly,
A cycle, it may be,
Till everlasting life unite
In strong society.

Oliver Goldsmith

ELEGY ON THE DEATH OF A MAD DOG

Good people all, of every sort,
Give ear unto my song;
And if you find it wond'rous short,
It cannot hold you long.

In Islington there was a man,
Of whom the world might say,
That still a godly race he ran,
Whene'er he went to pray.

A kind and gentle heart he had,
To comfort friends and foes;
The naked every day he clad,
When he put on his clothes.

And in that town a dog was found,
As many dogs there be,
Both mongrel, puppy, whelp, and hound,
And curs of low degree.

This dog and man at first were friends;
But when a pique began,
The dog, to gain some private ends,
Went mad and bit the man.

Around from all the neighbouring streets
The wond'ring neighbours ran,
And swore the dog had lost his wits,
To bite so good a man.

The wound it seem'd both sore and sad
To every Christian eye;
And while they swore the dog was mad,
They swore the man would die.

But soon a wonder came to light,
That show'd the rogues they lied:
The man recover'd of the bite,
The dog it was that died.

THE HERMIT

'Turn, gentle hermit of the dale,
And guide my lonely way,
To where yon taper cheers the vale,
With hospitable ray.

'For here forlorn and lost I tread,
With fainting steps and slow;
Where wilds immeasurably spread,
Seem lengthening as I go.'

'Forbear, my son,' the hermit cries,
'To tempt the dangerous gloom;
For yonder faithless phantom flies
To lure thee to thy doom.

'Here to the houseless child of want,
My door is open still;
And tho' my portion is but scant,
I give it with good will.

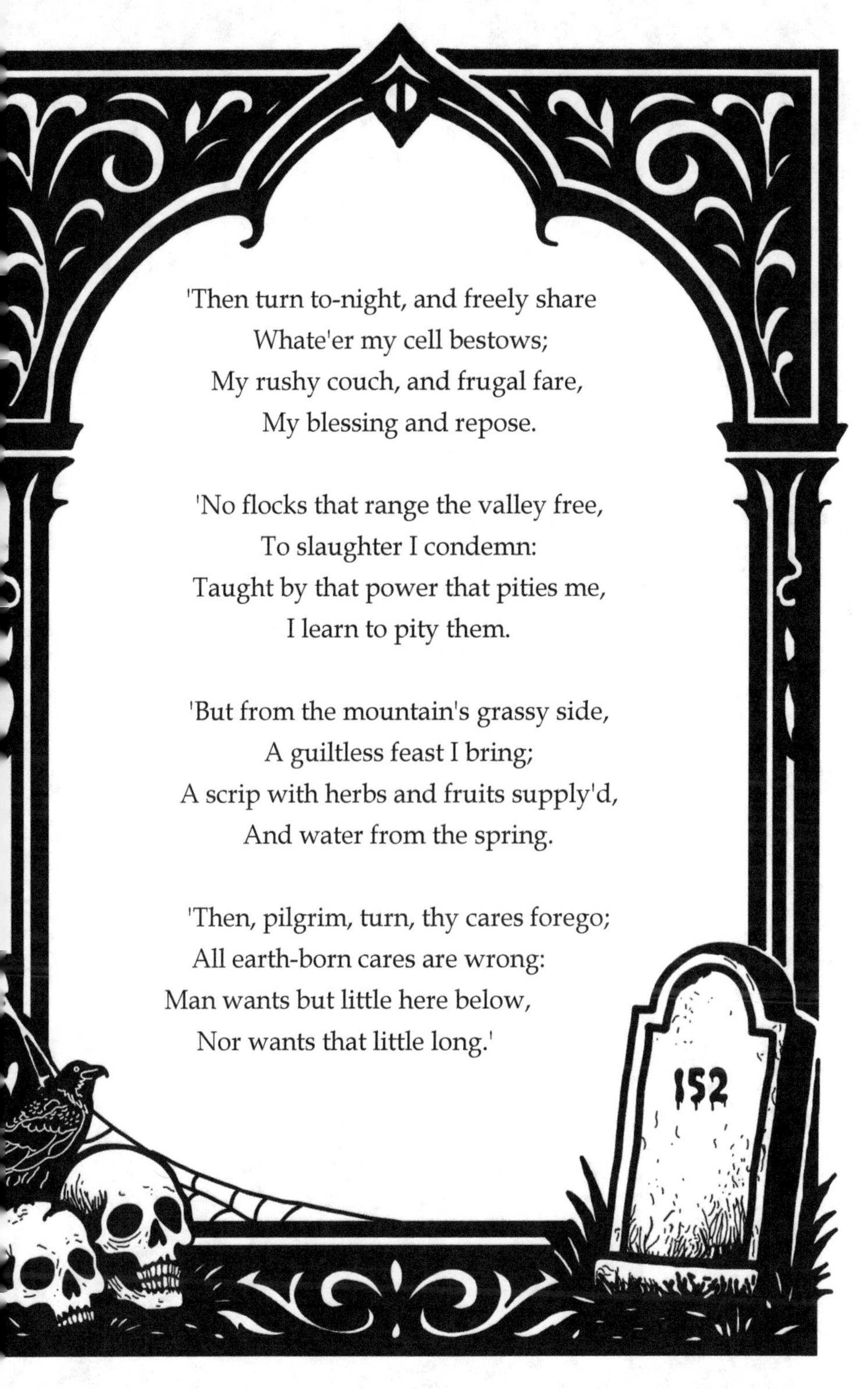

'Then turn to-night, and freely share
Whate'er my cell bestows;
My rushy couch, and frugal fare,
My blessing and repose.

'No flocks that range the valley free,
To slaughter I condemn:
Taught by that power that pities me,
I learn to pity them.

'But from the mountain's grassy side,
A guiltless feast I bring;
A scrip with herbs and fruits supply'd,
And water from the spring.

'Then, pilgrim, turn, thy cares forego;
All earth-born cares are wrong:
Man wants but little here below,
Nor wants that little long.'

Soft as the dew from heav'n descends,
His gentle accents fell:
The modest stranger lowly bends,
And follows to the cell.

Far in a wilderness obscure
The lonely mansion lay;
A refuge to the neighbouring poor,
And strangers led astray.

No stores beneath its humble thatch
Requir'd a master's care;
The wicket opening with a latch,
Receiv'd the harmless pair.

And now when busy crowds retire
To take their evening rest,
The hermit trimm'd his little fire,
And cheer'd his pensive guest:

And spread his vegetable store,
And gayly prest, and smil'd;

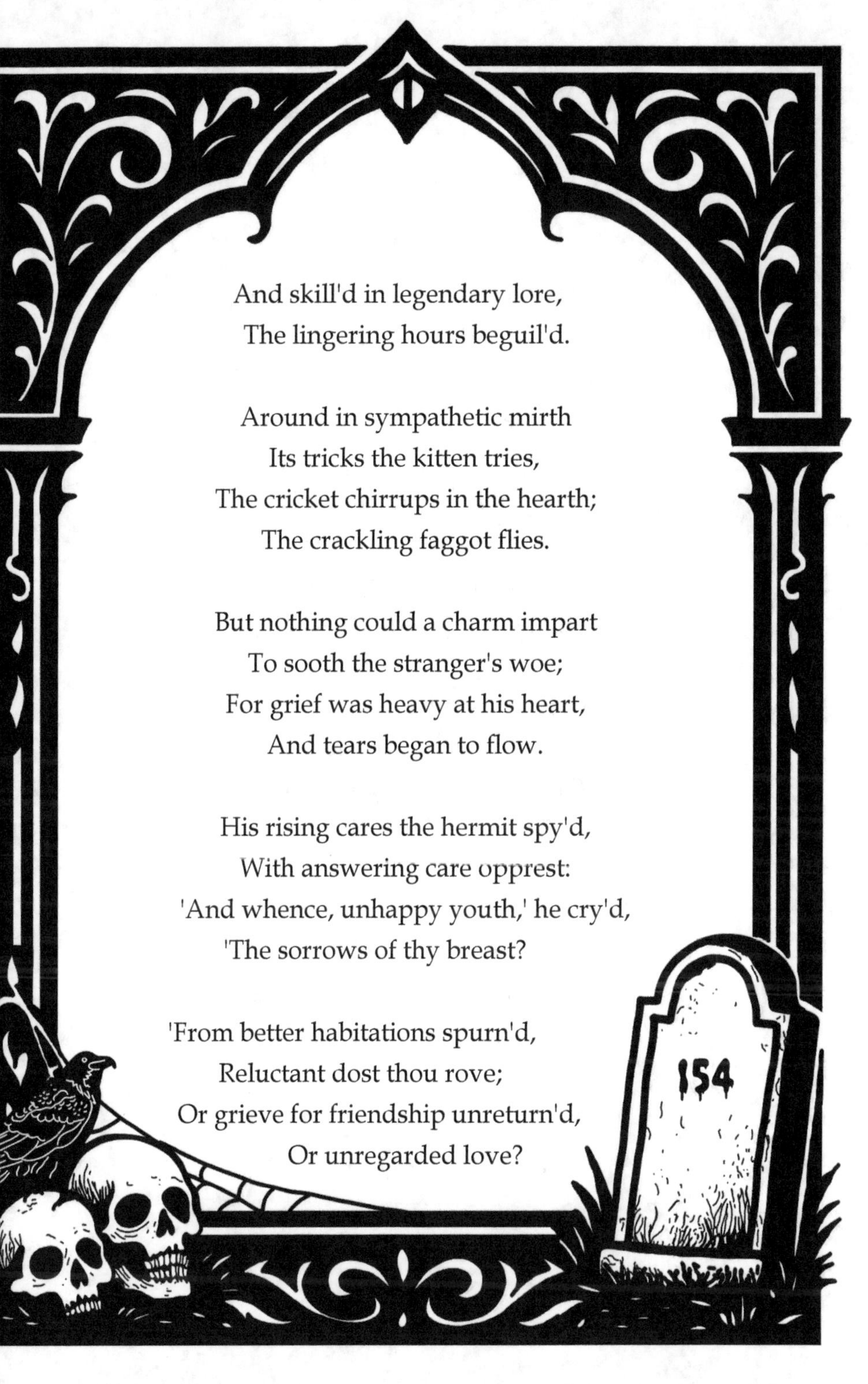

And skill'd in legendary lore,
The lingering hours beguil'd.

Around in sympathetic mirth
Its tricks the kitten tries,
The cricket chirrups in the hearth;
The crackling faggot flies.

But nothing could a charm impart
To sooth the stranger's woe;
For grief was heavy at his heart,
And tears began to flow.

His rising cares the hermit spy'd,
With answering care opprest:
'And whence, unhappy youth,' he cry'd,
'The sorrows of thy breast?

'From better habitations spurn'd,
Reluctant dost thou rove;
Or grieve for friendship unreturn'd,
Or unregarded love?

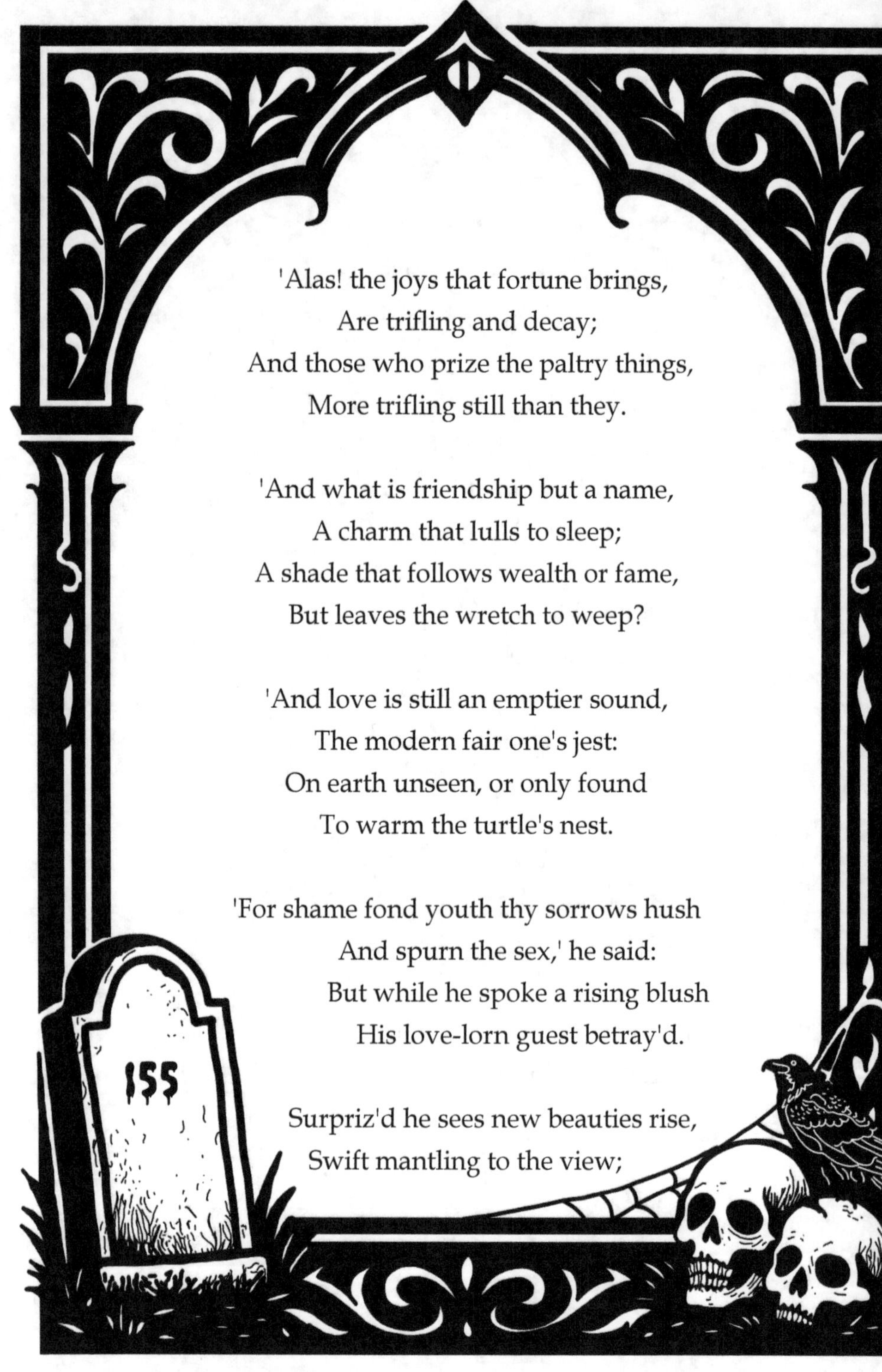

'Alas! the joys that fortune brings,
Are trifling and decay;
And those who prize the paltry things,
More trifling still than they.

'And what is friendship but a name,
A charm that lulls to sleep;
A shade that follows wealth or fame,
But leaves the wretch to weep?

'And love is still an emptier sound,
The modern fair one's jest:
On earth unseen, or only found
To warm the turtle's nest.

'For shame fond youth thy sorrows hush
And spurn the sex,' he said:
But while he spoke a rising blush
His love-lorn guest betray'd.

Surpriz'd he sees new beauties rise,
Swift mantling to the view;

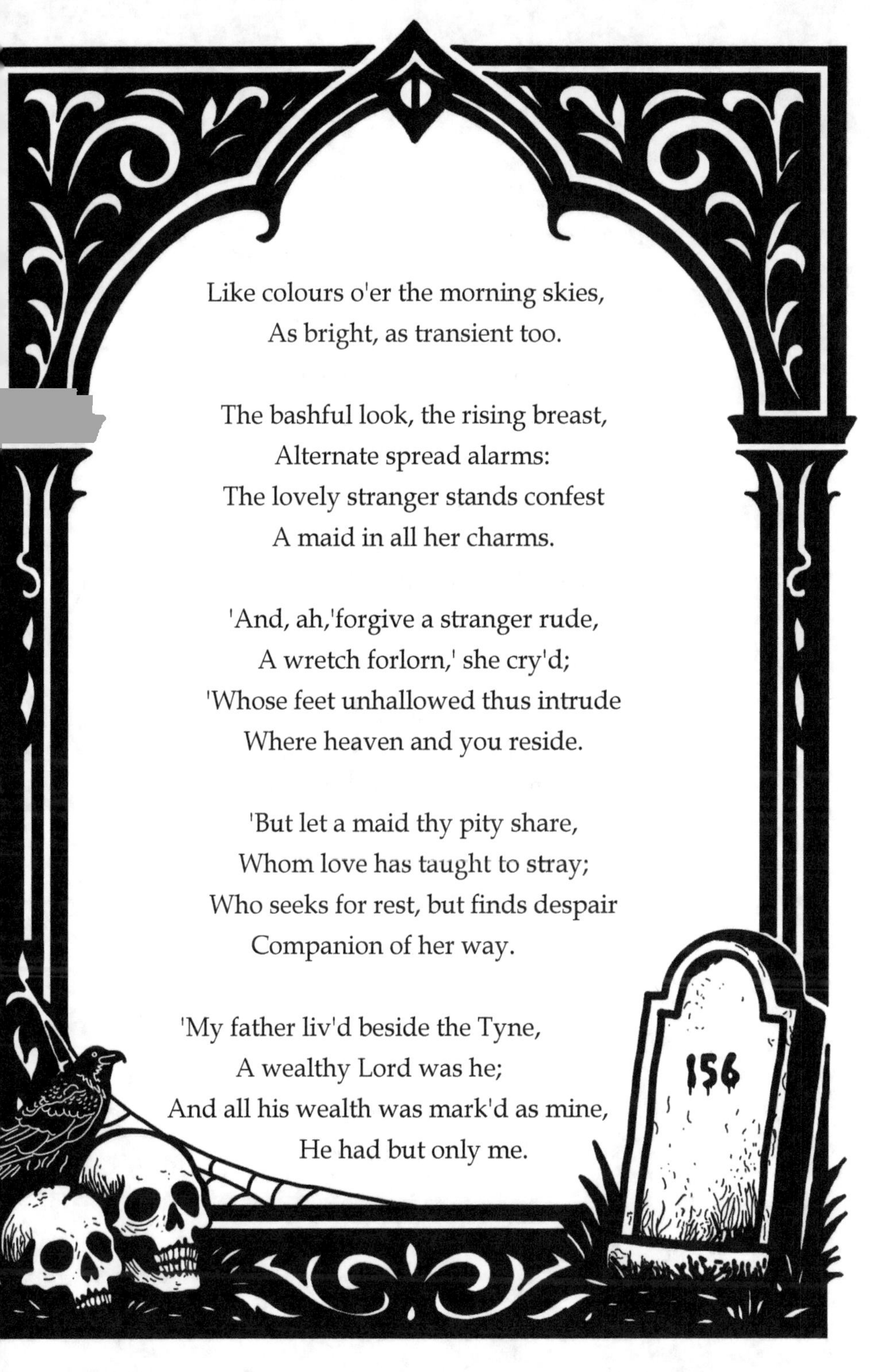

Like colours o'er the morning skies,
As bright, as transient too.

The bashful look, the rising breast,
Alternate spread alarms:
The lovely stranger stands confest
A maid in all her charms.

'And, ah,'forgive a stranger rude,
A wretch forlorn,' she cry'd;
'Whose feet unhallowed thus intrude
Where heaven and you reside.

'But let a maid thy pity share,
Whom love has taught to stray;
Who seeks for rest, but finds despair
Companion of her way.

'My father liv'd beside the Tyne,
A wealthy Lord was he;
And all his wealth was mark'd as mine,
He had but only me.

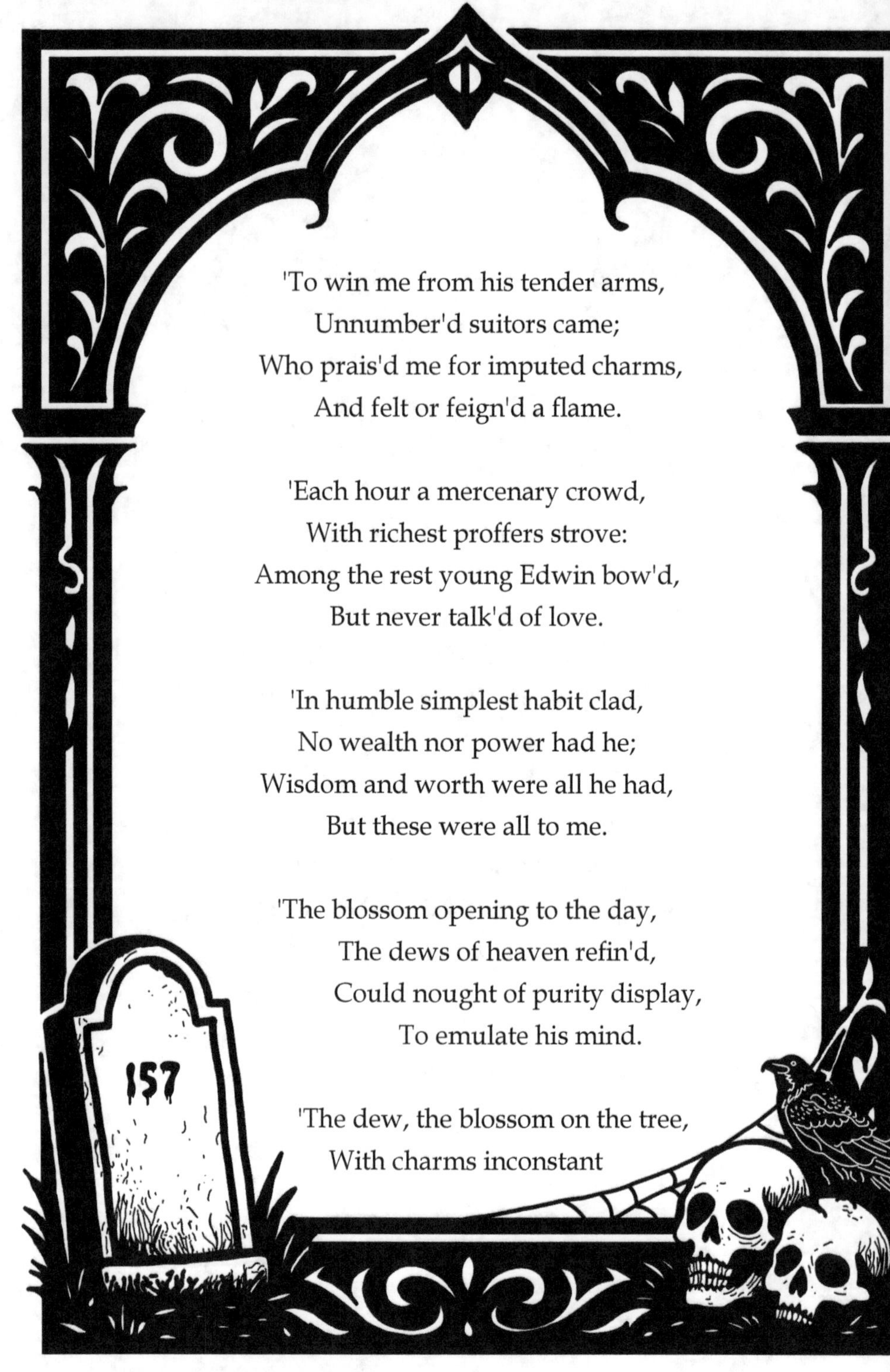

'To win me from his tender arms,
Unnumber'd suitors came;
Who prais'd me for imputed charms,
And felt or feign'd a flame.

'Each hour a mercenary crowd,
With richest proffers strove:
Among the rest young Edwin bow'd,
But never talk'd of love.

'In humble simplest habit clad,
No wealth nor power had he;
Wisdom and worth were all he had,
But these were all to me.

'The blossom opening to the day,
The dews of heaven refin'd,
Could nought of purity display,
To emulate his mind.

'The dew, the blossom on the tree,
With charms inconstant

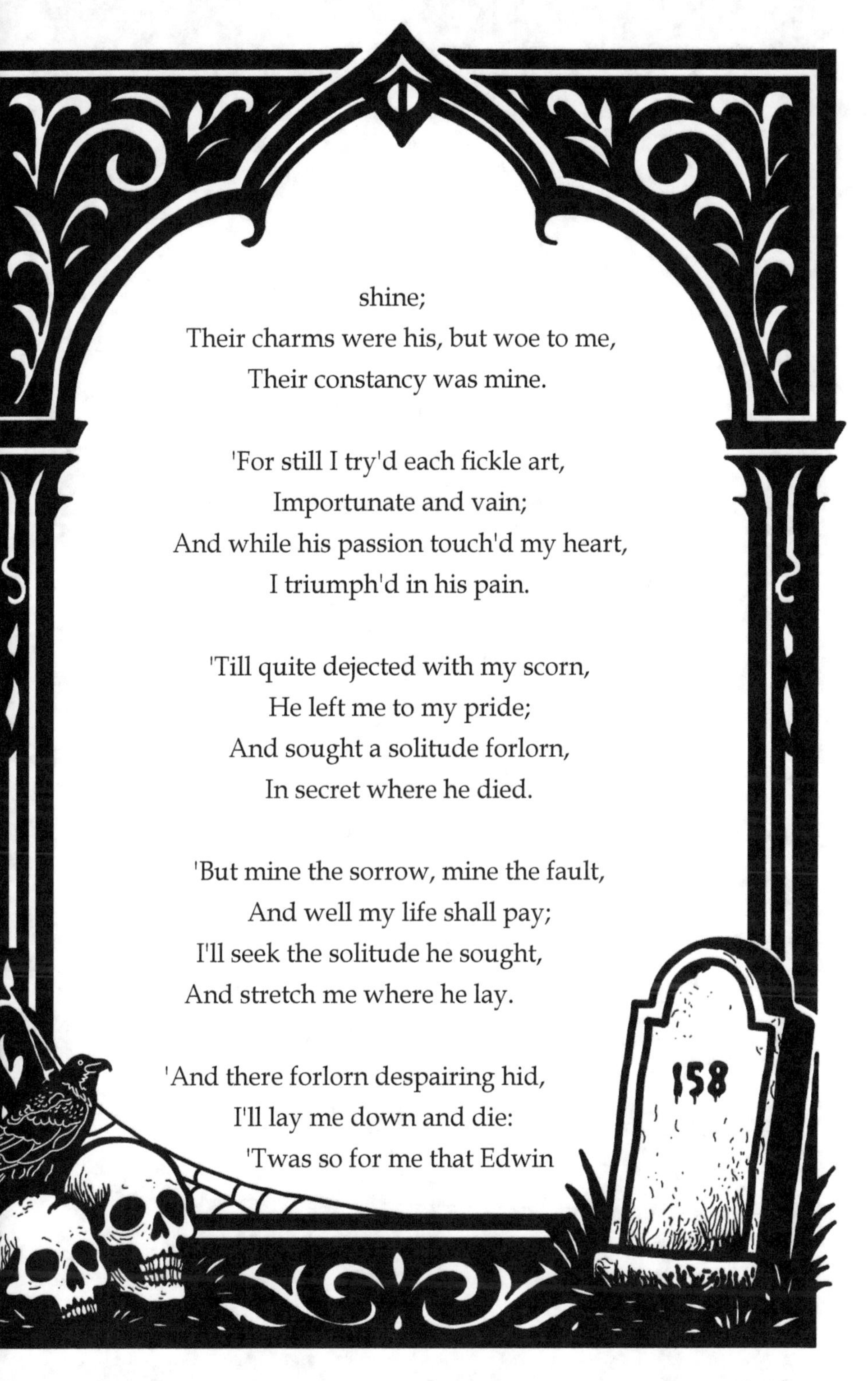

shine;
Their charms were his, but woe to me,
Their constancy was mine.

'For still I try'd each fickle art,
Importunate and vain;
And while his passion touch'd my heart,
I triumph'd in his pain.

'Till quite dejected with my scorn,
He left me to my pride;
And sought a solitude forlorn,
In secret where he died.

'But mine the sorrow, mine the fault,
And well my life shall pay;
I'll seek the solitude he sought,
And stretch me where he lay.

'And there forlorn despairing hid,
I'll lay me down and die:
'Twas so for me that Edwin

did,
And so for him will I.'

'Forbid it heaven!' the hermit cry'd,
And clasp'd her to his breast:
The wondering fair one turn'd to chide,
'Twas Edwin's self that prest.

'Turn, Angelina, ever dear,
My charmer, turn to see,
Thy own, thy long-lost Edwin here,
Restor'd to love and thee.

'Thus let me hold thee to my heart,
And ev'ry care resign:
And shall we never, never part,
My life,--my all that's mine.

'No, never, from this hour to part,
We'll live and love so true;
The sigh that tends thy constant heart,
Shall break thy Edwin's too.'

Hanna Flagg Goud

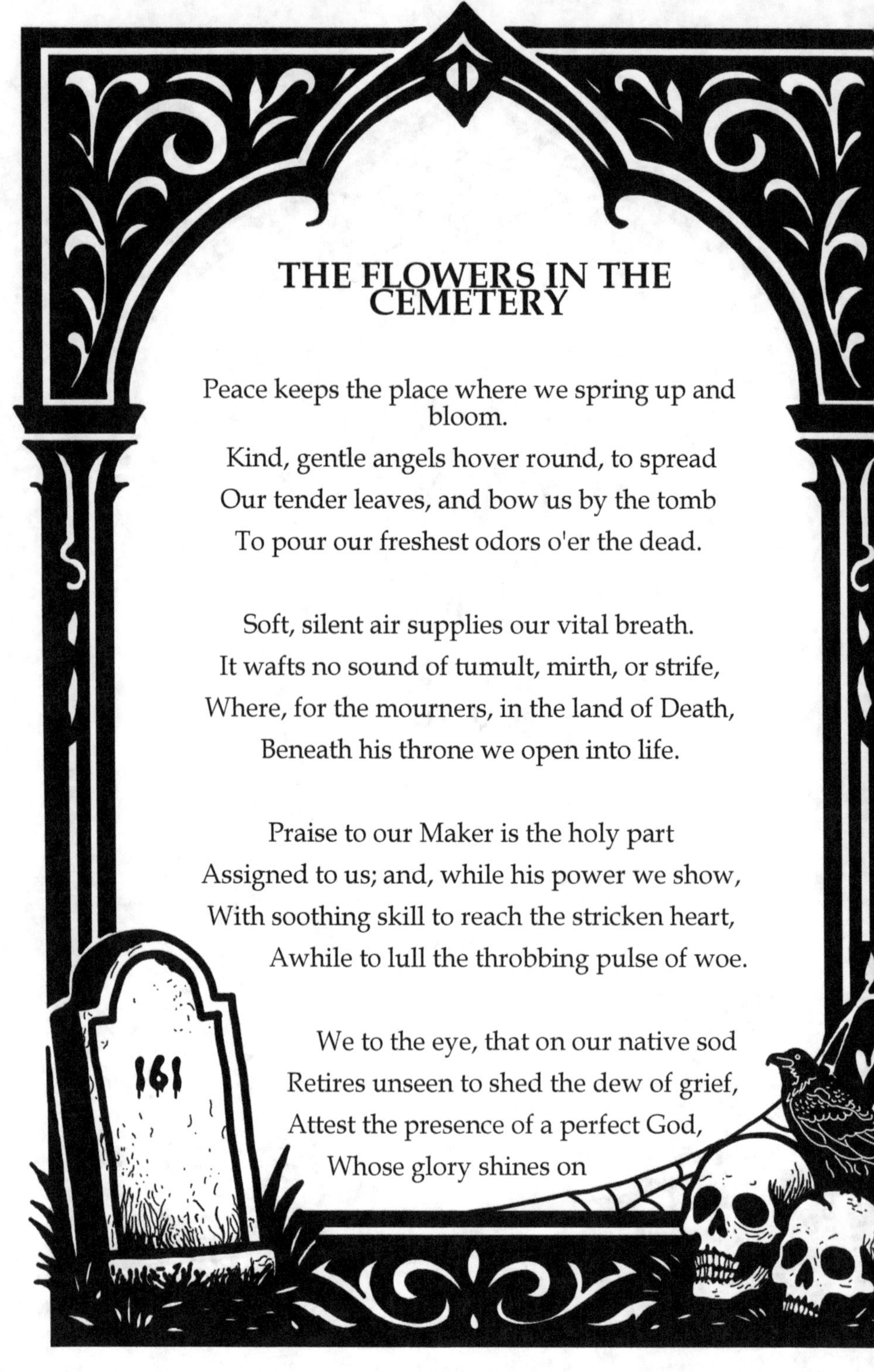

THE FLOWERS IN THE CEMETERY

Peace keeps the place where we spring up and bloom.
Kind, gentle angels hover round, to spread
Our tender leaves, and bow us by the tomb
To pour our freshest odors o'er the dead.

Soft, silent air supplies our vital breath.
It wafts no sound of tumult, mirth, or strife,
Where, for the mourners, in the land of Death,
Beneath his throne we open into life.

Praise to our Maker is the holy part
Assigned to us; and, while his power we show,
With soothing skill to reach the stricken heart,
Awhile to lull the throbbing pulse of woe.

We to the eye, that on our native sod
Retires unseen to shed the dew of grief,
Attest the presence of a perfect God,
Whose glory shines on

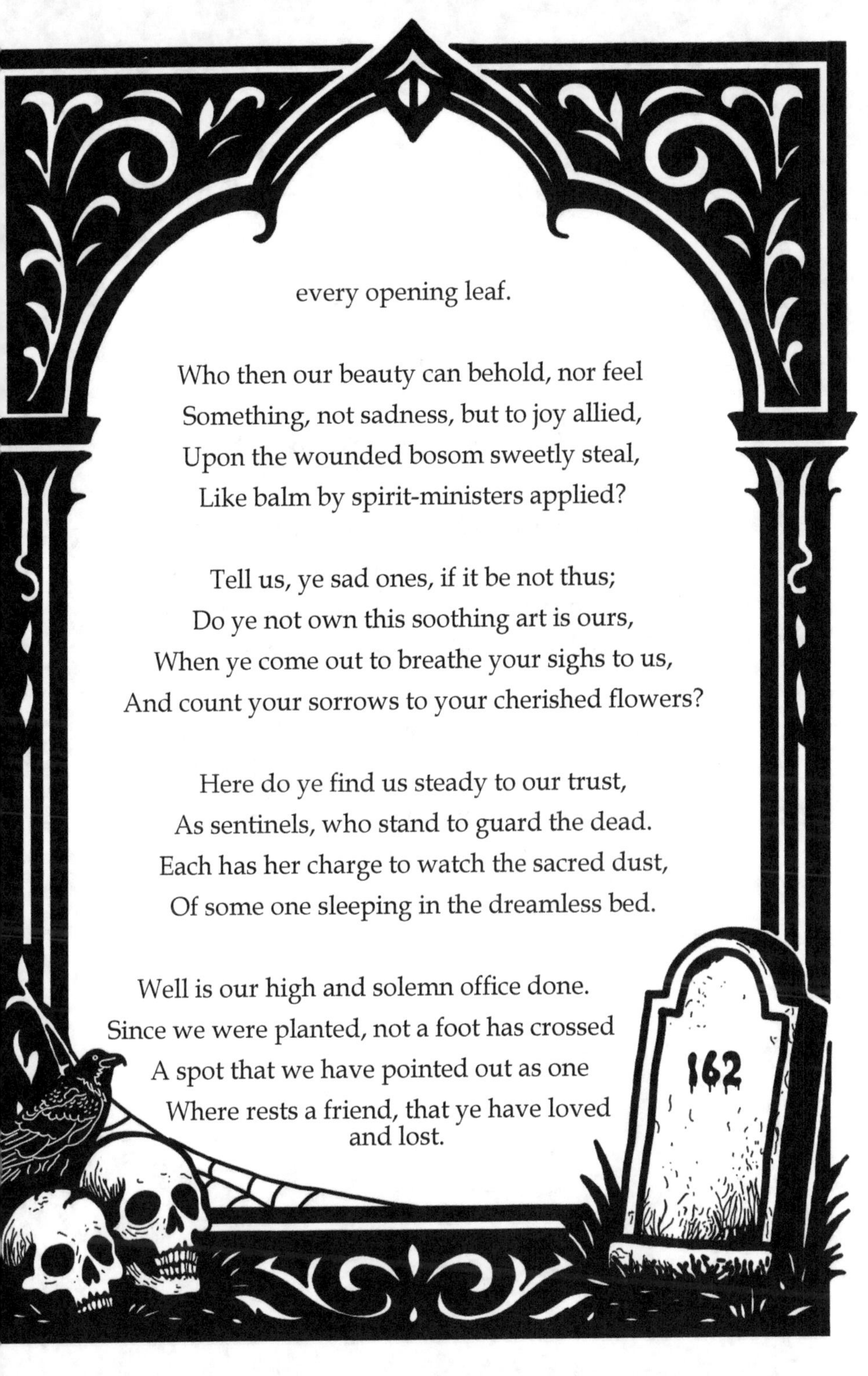

every opening leaf.

Who then our beauty can behold, nor feel
Something, not sadness, but to joy allied,
Upon the wounded bosom sweetly steal,
Like balm by spirit-ministers applied?

Tell us, ye sad ones, if it be not thus;
Do ye not own this soothing art is ours,
When ye come out to breathe your sighs to us,
And count your sorrows to your cherished flowers?

Here do ye find us steady to our trust,
As sentinels, who stand to guard the dead.
Each has her charge to watch the sacred dust,
Of some one sleeping in the dreamless bed.

Well is our high and solemn office done.
Since we were planted, not a foot has crossed
A spot that we have pointed out as one
Where rests a friend, that ye have loved and lost.

Night falls around us, like a mourner's veil;
But, though our beauties in the dimness fade,
Still does the pure, free essence we exhale
Ascend and penetrate the deepest shade.

If thus the better part of those you weep,
From death and darkness, rose to life and light;
Then lift your hearts from all that earth could keep
To that blest world where you may re-unite.

Such is the part that we, the humble Flowers,
Perform; and such the solace we would give
To man, who, while we bloom our few short hours,
Has yet a whole eternity to live!

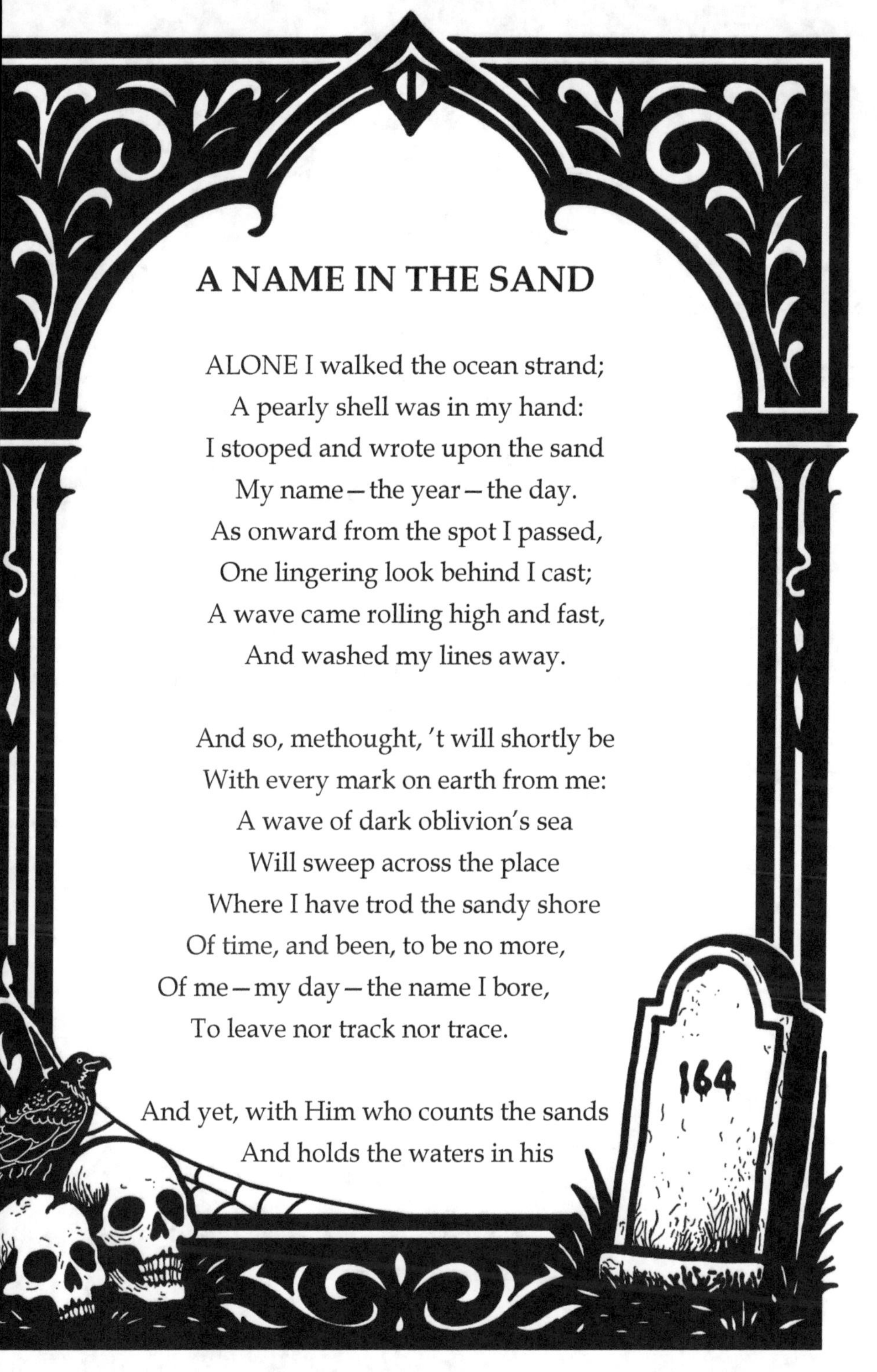

A NAME IN THE SAND

ALONE I walked the ocean strand;
A pearly shell was in my hand:
I stooped and wrote upon the sand
My name — the year — the day.
As onward from the spot I passed,
One lingering look behind I cast;
A wave came rolling high and fast,
And washed my lines away.

And so, methought, 't will shortly be
With every mark on earth from me:
A wave of dark oblivion's sea
Will sweep across the place
Where I have trod the sandy shore
Of time, and been, to be no more,
Of me — my day — the name I bore,
To leave nor track nor trace.

And yet, with Him who counts the sands
And holds the waters in his

hands,
I know a lasting record stands
Inscribed against my name,
Of all this mortal part has wrought,
Of all this thinking soul has thought,
And from these fleeting moments caught
For glory or for shame.

Thomas Grey

ELEGY WRITTEN IN A COUNTRY CHURCHYARD

The curfew tolls the knell of parting day,
The lowing herd wind slowly o'er the lea,
The plowman homeward plods his weary way,
And leaves the world to darkness and to me.

Now fades the glimm'ring landscape on the sight,
And all the air a solemn stillness holds,
Save where the beetle wheels his droning flight,
And drowsy tinklings lull the distant folds;

Save that from yonder ivy-mantled tow'r
The moping owl does to the moon complain
Of such, as wand'ring near her secret bow'r,
Molest her ancient solitary reign.

Beneath those rugged elms, that yew-tree's shade,
Where heaves the turf in many a mould'ring heap,
Each in his narrow cell for

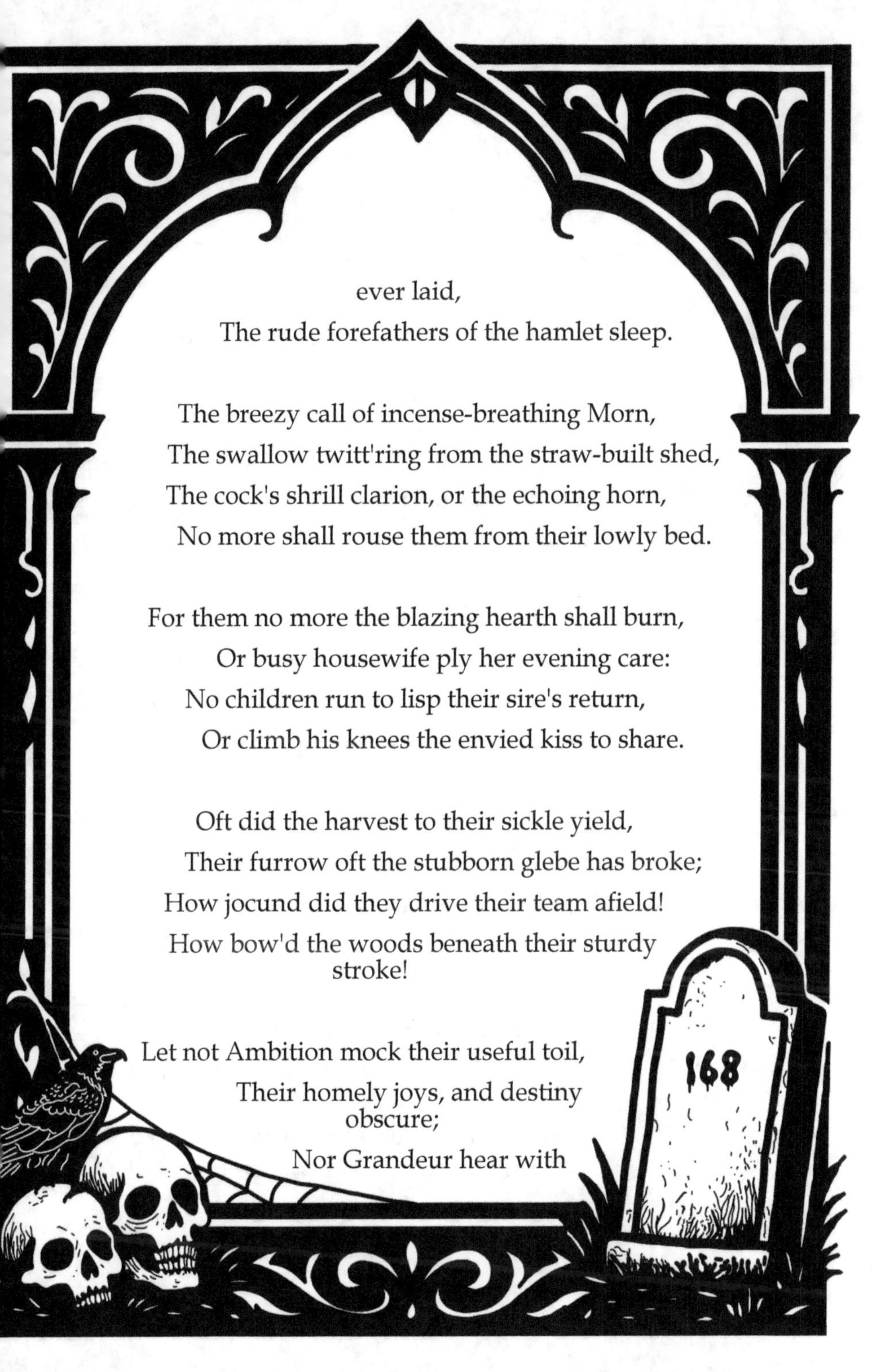

ever laid,
The rude forefathers of the hamlet sleep.

The breezy call of incense-breathing Morn,
The swallow twitt'ring from the straw-built shed,
The cock's shrill clarion, or the echoing horn,
No more shall rouse them from their lowly bed.

For them no more the blazing hearth shall burn,
Or busy housewife ply her evening care:
No children run to lisp their sire's return,
Or climb his knees the envied kiss to share.

Oft did the harvest to their sickle yield,
Their furrow oft the stubborn glebe has broke;
How jocund did they drive their team afield!
How bow'd the woods beneath their sturdy stroke!

Let not Ambition mock their useful toil,
Their homely joys, and destiny obscure;
Nor Grandeur hear with

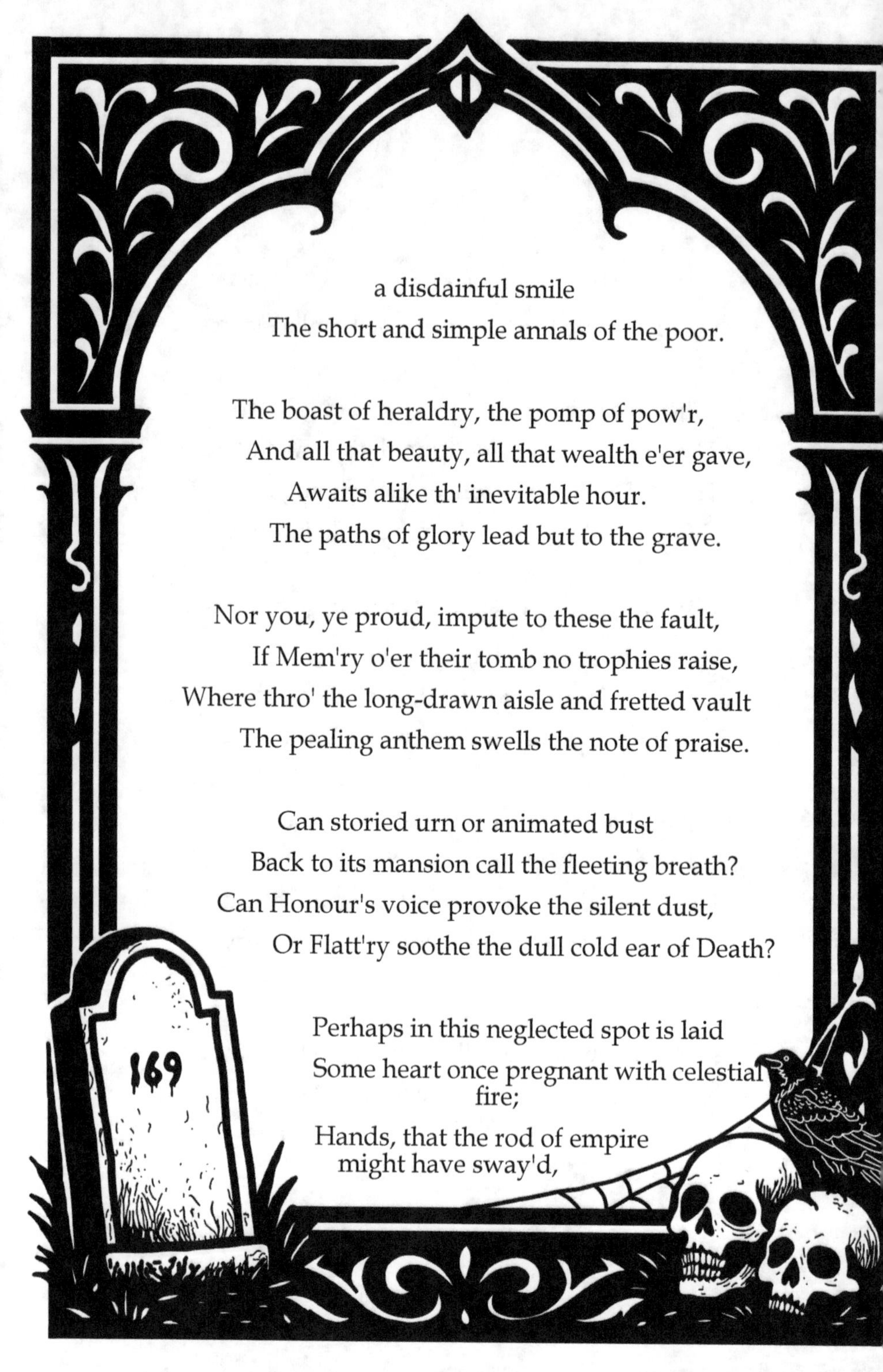

a disdainful smile
The short and simple annals of the poor.

The boast of heraldry, the pomp of pow'r,
And all that beauty, all that wealth e'er gave,
Awaits alike th' inevitable hour.
The paths of glory lead but to the grave.

Nor you, ye proud, impute to these the fault,
If Mem'ry o'er their tomb no trophies raise,
Where thro' the long-drawn aisle and fretted vault
The pealing anthem swells the note of praise.

Can storied urn or animated bust
Back to its mansion call the fleeting breath?
Can Honour's voice provoke the silent dust,
Or Flatt'ry soothe the dull cold ear of Death?

Perhaps in this neglected spot is laid
Some heart once pregnant with celestial fire;
Hands, that the rod of empire might have sway'd,

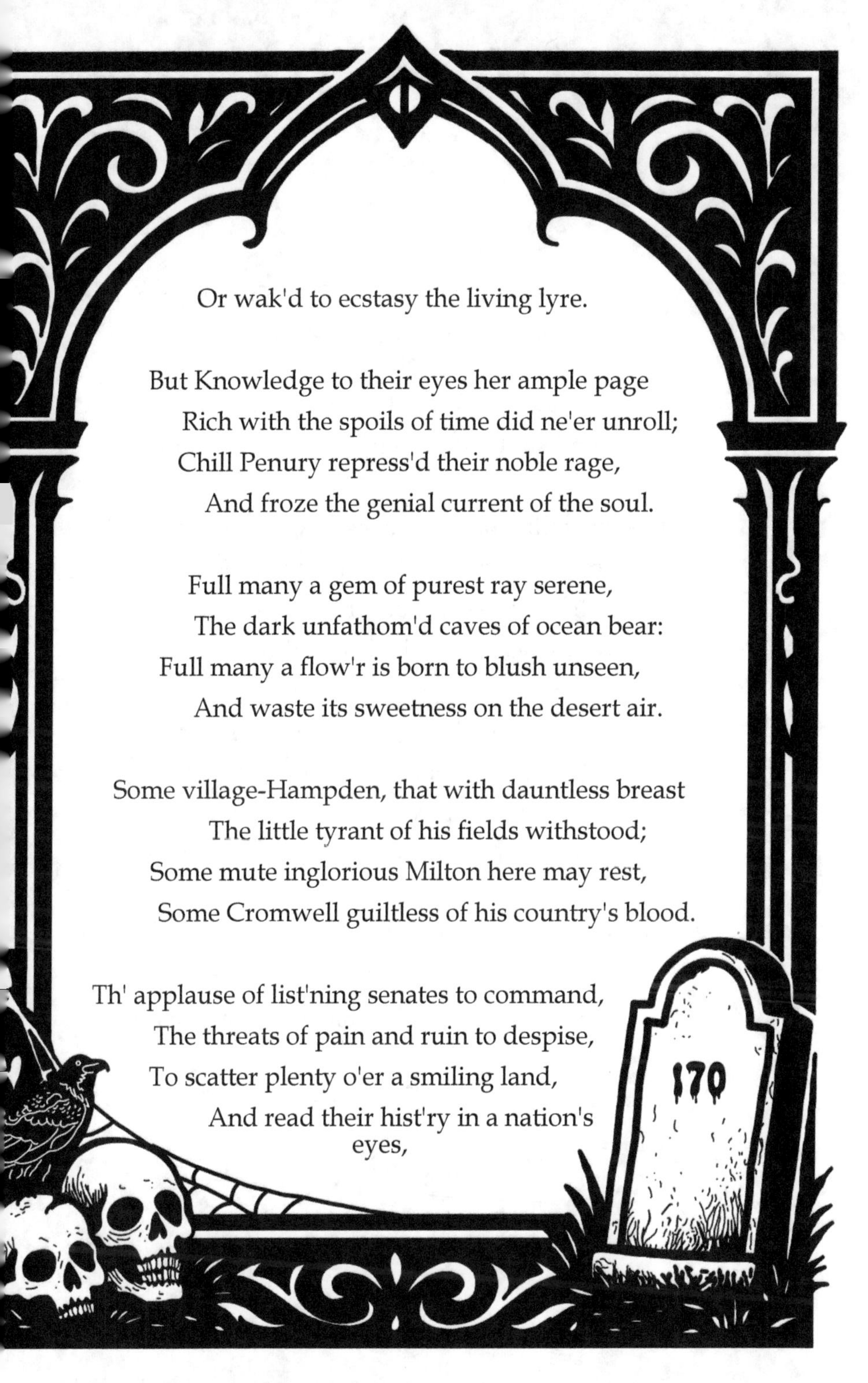

Or wak'd to ecstasy the living lyre.

But Knowledge to their eyes her ample page
Rich with the spoils of time did ne'er unroll;
Chill Penury repress'd their noble rage,
And froze the genial current of the soul.

Full many a gem of purest ray serene,
The dark unfathom'd caves of ocean bear:
Full many a flow'r is born to blush unseen,
And waste its sweetness on the desert air.

Some village-Hampden, that with dauntless breast
The little tyrant of his fields withstood;
Some mute inglorious Milton here may rest,
Some Cromwell guiltless of his country's blood.

Th' applause of list'ning senates to command,
The threats of pain and ruin to despise,
To scatter plenty o'er a smiling land,
And read their hist'ry in a nation's eyes,

Their lot forbade: nor circumscrib'd alone
Their growing virtues, but their crimes confin'd;
Forbade to wade through slaughter to a throne,
And shut the gates of mercy on mankind,

The struggling pangs of conscious truth to hide,
To quench the blushes of ingenuous shame,
Or heap the shrine of Luxury and Pride
With incense kindled at the Muse's flame.

Far from the madding crowd's ignoble strife,
Their sober wishes never learn'd to stray;
Along the cool sequester'd vale of life
They kept the noiseless tenor of their way.

Yet ev'n these bones from insult to protect,
Some frail memorial still erected nigh,
With uncouth rhymes and shapeless sculpture deck'd,
Implores the passing tribute of a sigh.

Their name, their years,

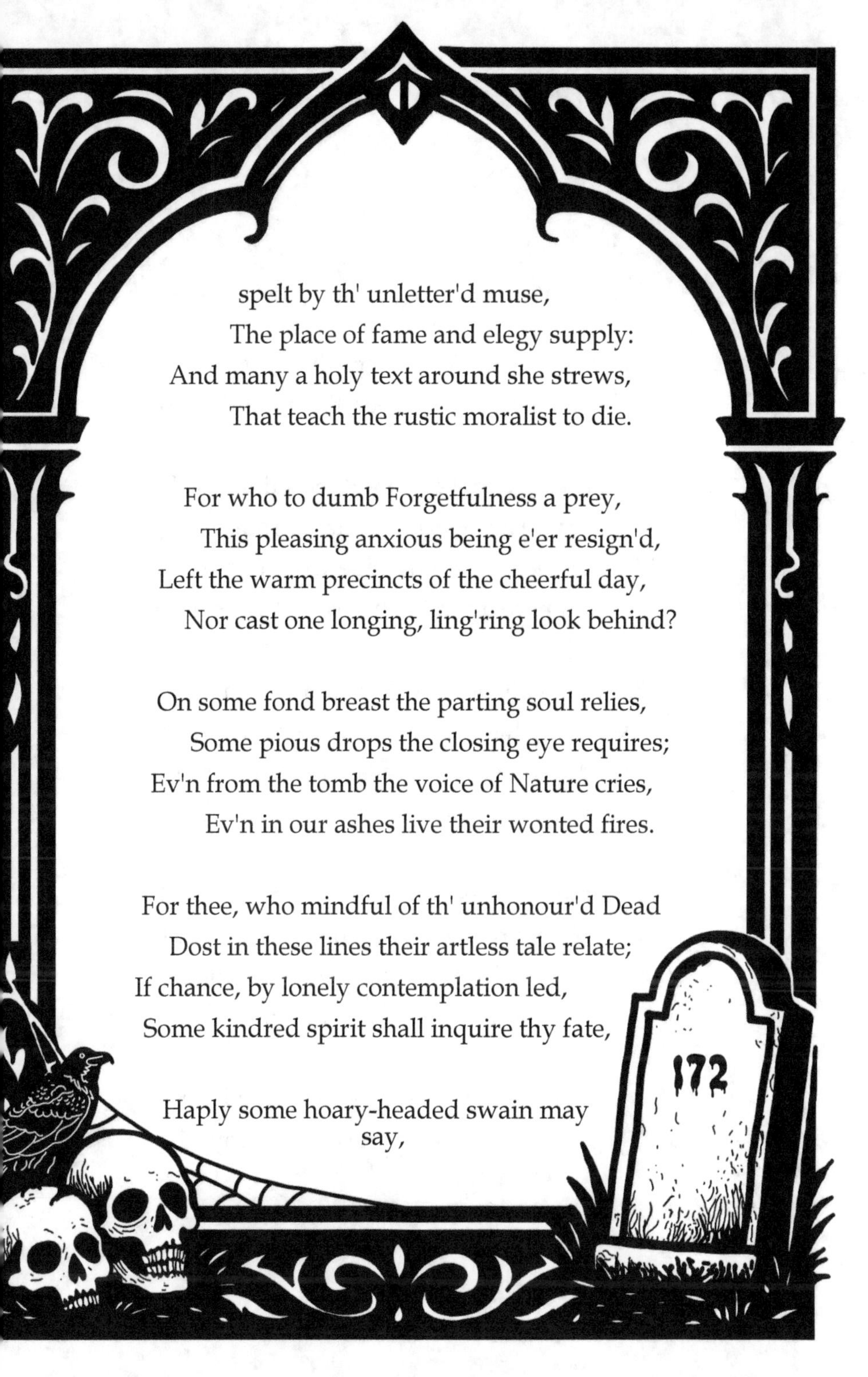

spelt by th' unletter'd muse,
The place of fame and elegy supply:
And many a holy text around she strews,
That teach the rustic moralist to die.

For who to dumb Forgetfulness a prey,
This pleasing anxious being e'er resign'd,
Left the warm precincts of the cheerful day,
Nor cast one longing, ling'ring look behind?

On some fond breast the parting soul relies,
Some pious drops the closing eye requires;
Ev'n from the tomb the voice of Nature cries,
Ev'n in our ashes live their wonted fires.

For thee, who mindful of th' unhonour'd Dead
Dost in these lines their artless tale relate;
If chance, by lonely contemplation led,
Some kindred spirit shall inquire thy fate,

Haply some hoary-headed swain may say,

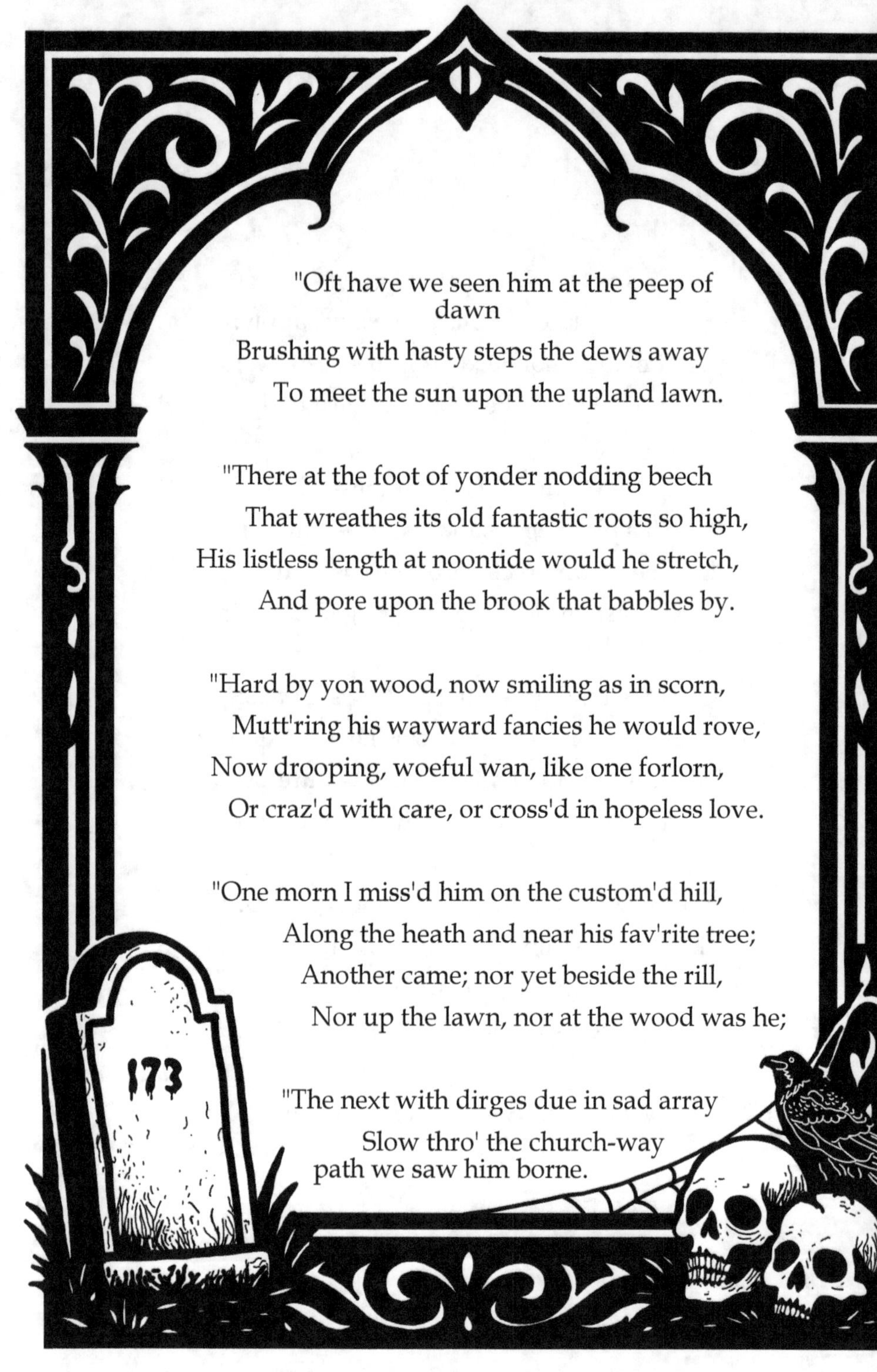

"Oft have we seen him at the peep of dawn
Brushing with hasty steps the dews away
To meet the sun upon the upland lawn.

"There at the foot of yonder nodding beech
That wreathes its old fantastic roots so high,
His listless length at noontide would he stretch,
And pore upon the brook that babbles by.

"Hard by yon wood, now smiling as in scorn,
Mutt'ring his wayward fancies he would rove,
Now drooping, woeful wan, like one forlorn,
Or craz'd with care, or cross'd in hopeless love.

"One morn I miss'd him on the custom'd hill,
Along the heath and near his fav'rite tree;
Another came; nor yet beside the rill,
Nor up the lawn, nor at the wood was he;

"The next with dirges due in sad array
Slow thro' the church-way path we saw him borne.

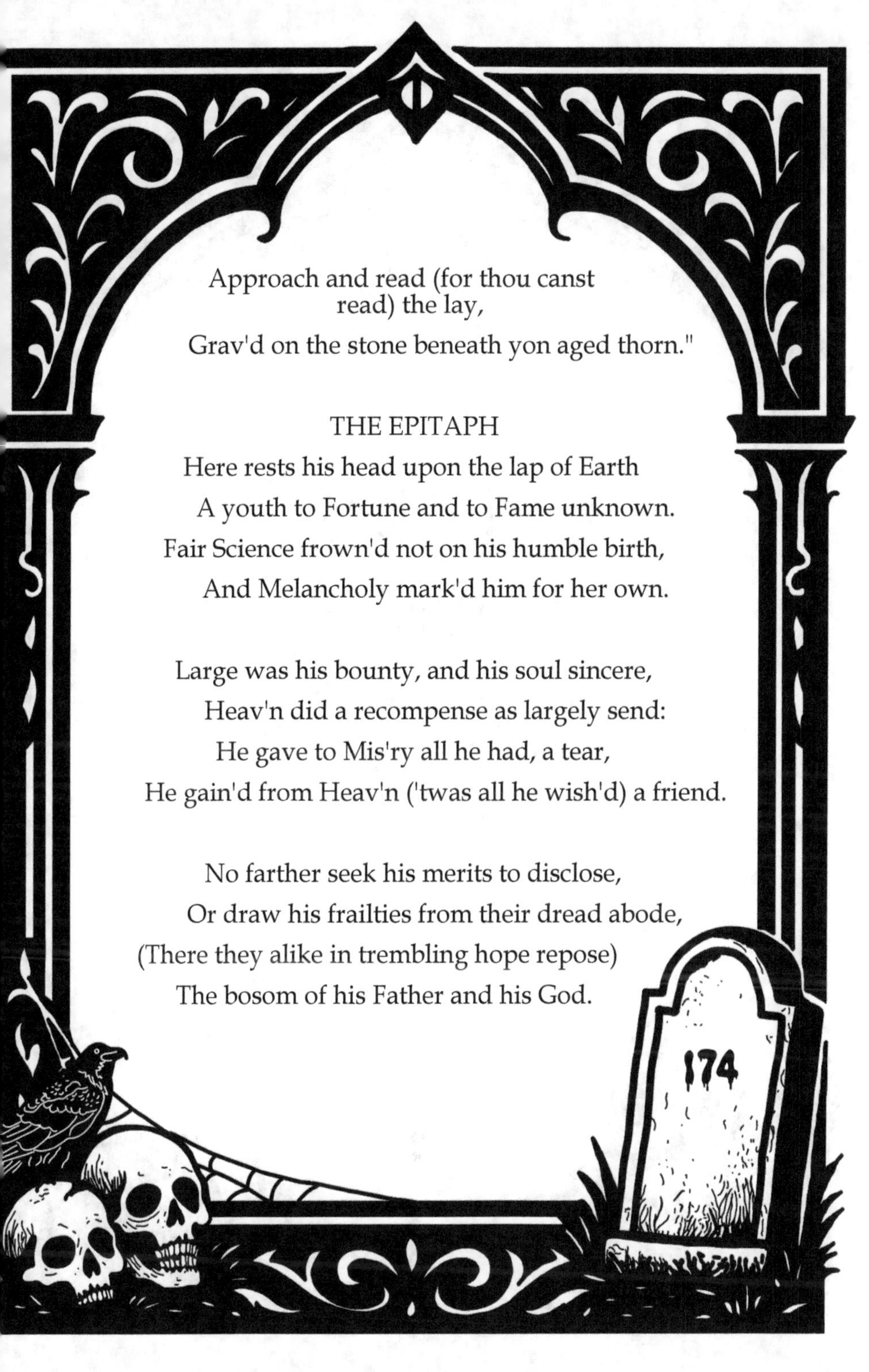

Approach and read (for thou canst read) the lay,
Grav'd on the stone beneath yon aged thorn."

THE EPITAPH

Here rests his head upon the lap of Earth
A youth to Fortune and to Fame unknown.
Fair Science frown'd not on his humble birth,
And Melancholy mark'd him for her own.

Large was his bounty, and his soul sincere,
Heav'n did a recompense as largely send:
He gave to Mis'ry all he had, a tear,
He gain'd from Heav'n ('twas all he wish'd) a friend.

No farther seek his merits to disclose,
Or draw his frailties from their dread abode,
(There they alike in trembling hope repose)
The bosom of his Father and his God.

Thomas Hardy

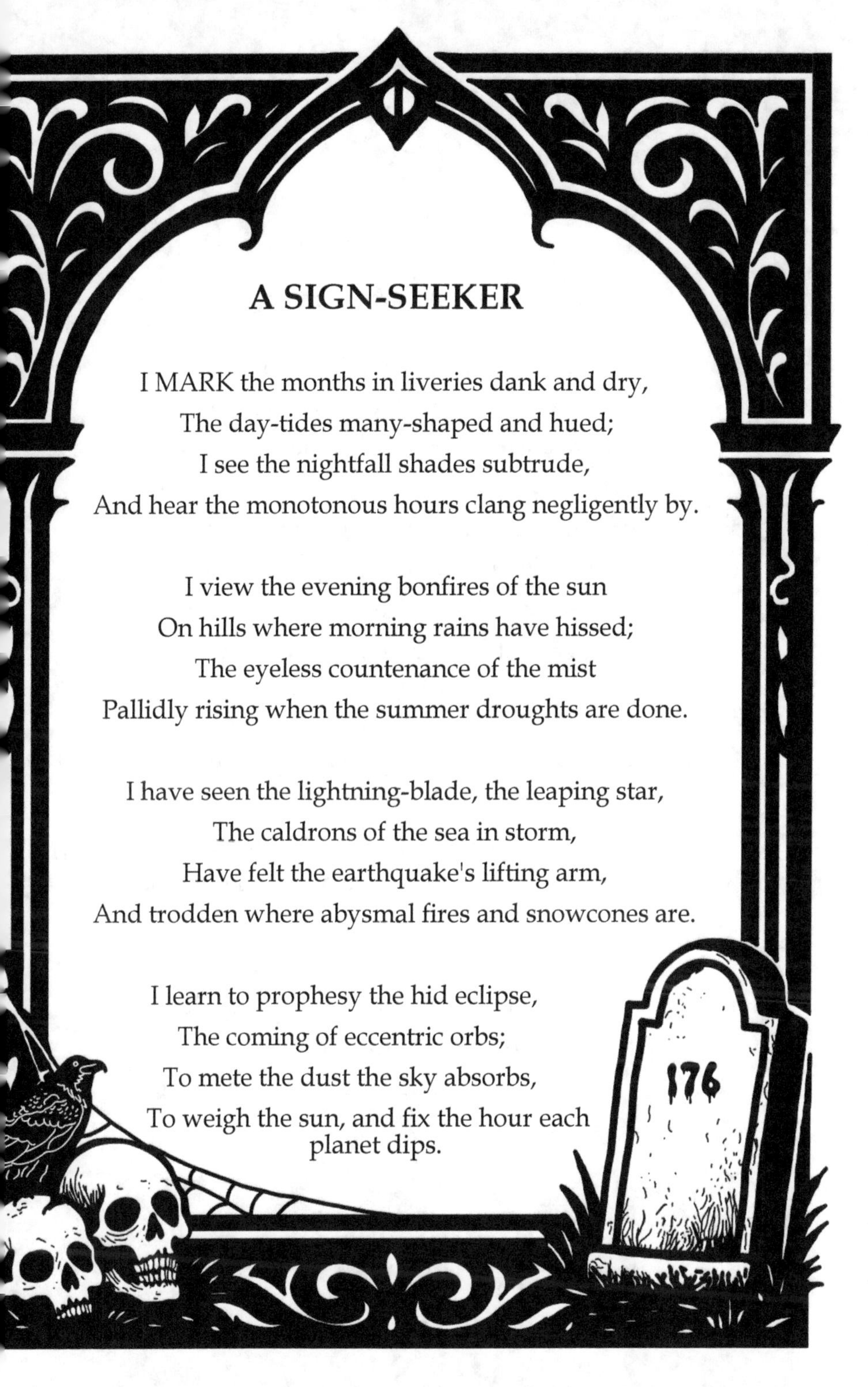

A SIGN-SEEKER

I MARK the months in liveries dank and dry,
The day-tides many-shaped and hued;
I see the nightfall shades subtrude,
And hear the monotonous hours clang negligently by.

I view the evening bonfires of the sun
On hills where morning rains have hissed;
The eyeless countenance of the mist
Pallidly rising when the summer droughts are done.

I have seen the lightning-blade, the leaping star,
The caldrons of the sea in storm,
Have felt the earthquake's lifting arm,
And trodden where abysmal fires and snowcones are.

I learn to prophesy the hid eclipse,
The coming of eccentric orbs;
To mete the dust the sky absorbs,
To weigh the sun, and fix the hour each planet dips.

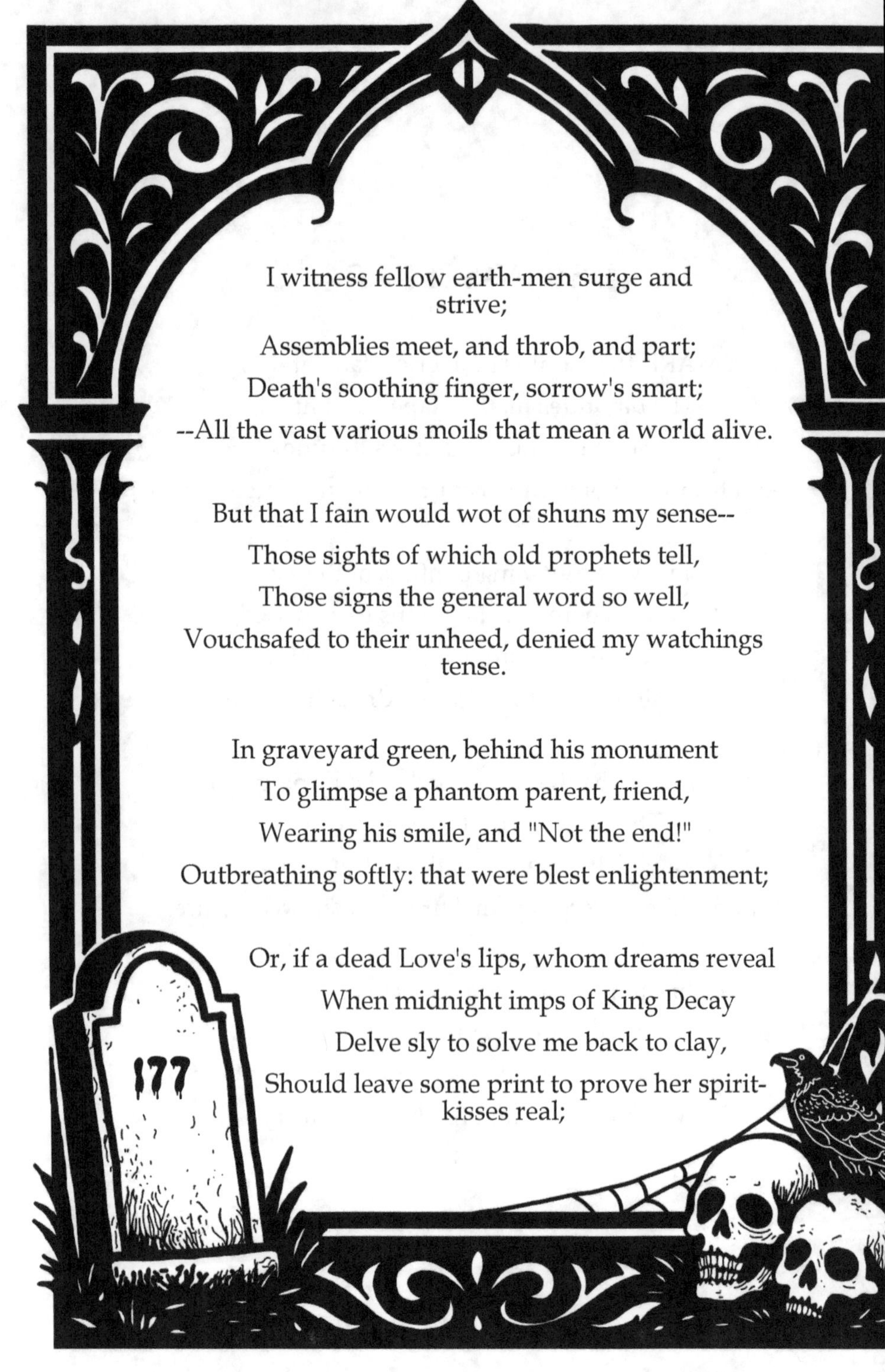

I witness fellow earth-men surge and strive;
Assemblies meet, and throb, and part;
Death's soothing finger, sorrow's smart;
--All the vast various moils that mean a world alive.

But that I fain would wot of shuns my sense--
Those sights of which old prophets tell,
Those signs the general word so well,
Vouchsafed to their unheed, denied my watchings tense.

In graveyard green, behind his monument
To glimpse a phantom parent, friend,
Wearing his smile, and "Not the end!"
Outbreathing softly: that were blest enlightenment;

Or, if a dead Love's lips, whom dreams reveal
When midnight imps of King Decay
Delve sly to solve me back to clay,
Should leave some print to prove her spirit-kisses real;

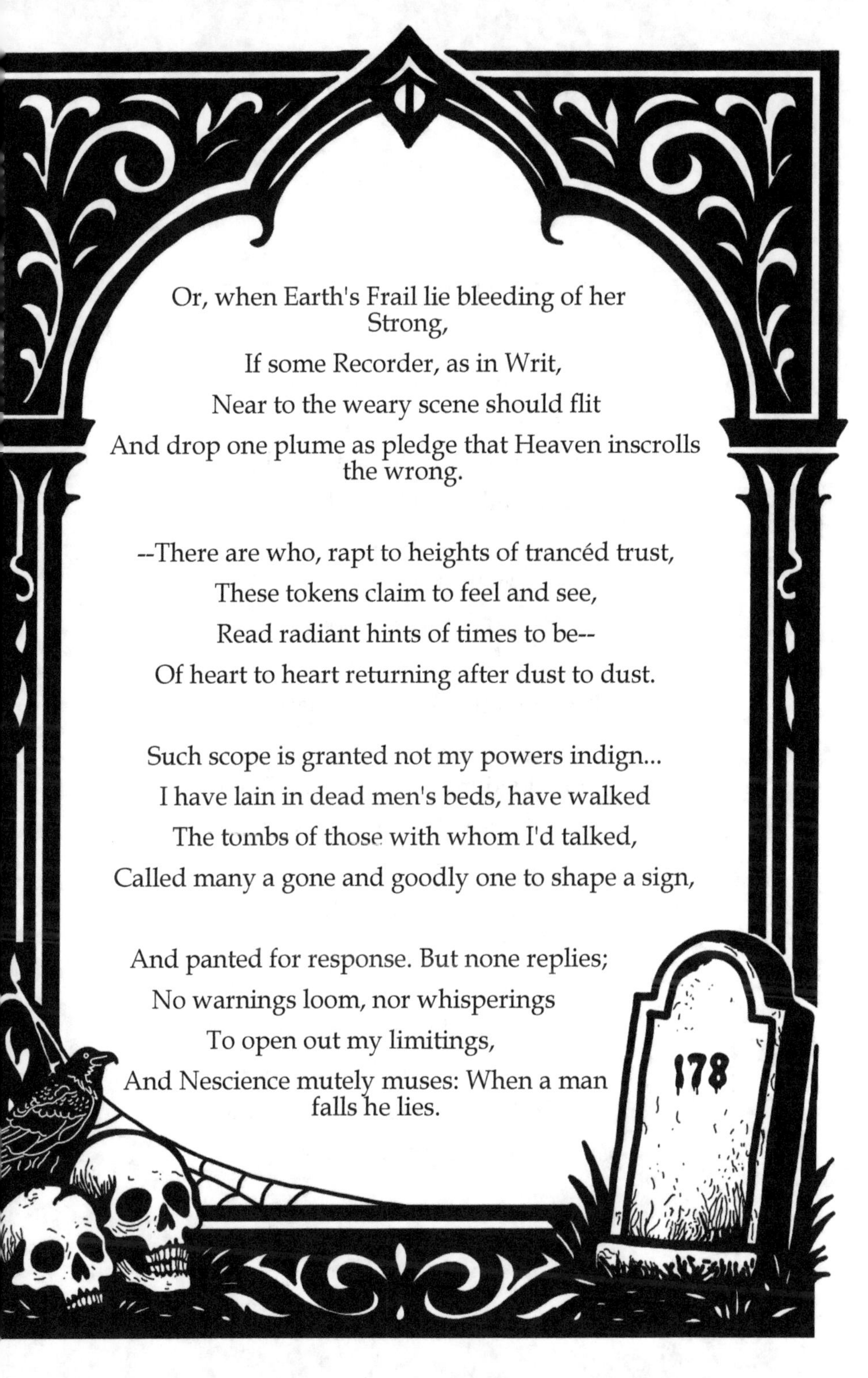

Or, when Earth's Frail lie bleeding of her Strong,
If some Recorder, as in Writ,
Near to the weary scene should flit
And drop one plume as pledge that Heaven inscrolls the wrong.

--There are who, rapt to heights of trancéd trust,
These tokens claim to feel and see,
Read radiant hints of times to be--
Of heart to heart returning after dust to dust.

Such scope is granted not my powers indign...
I have lain in dead men's beds, have walked
The tombs of those with whom I'd talked,
Called many a gone and goodly one to shape a sign,

And panted for response. But none replies;
No warnings loom, nor whisperings
To open out my limitings,
And Nescience mutely muses: When a man falls he lies.

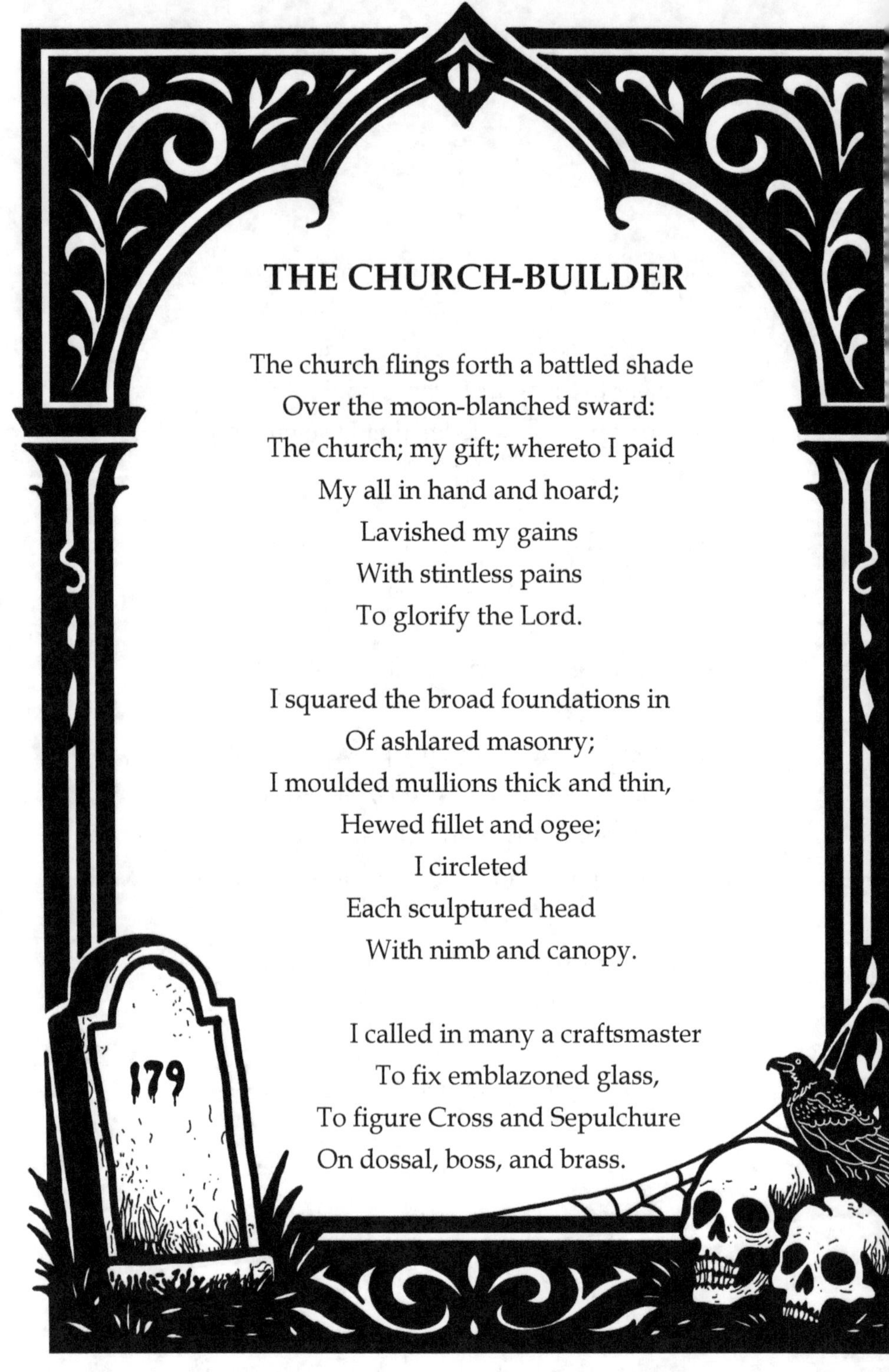

THE CHURCH-BUILDER

The church flings forth a battled shade
Over the moon-blanched sward:
The church; my gift; whereto I paid
My all in hand and hoard;
Lavished my gains
With stintless pains
To glorify the Lord.

I squared the broad foundations in
Of ashlared masonry;
I moulded mullions thick and thin,
Hewed fillet and ogee;
I circleted
Each sculptured head
With nimb and canopy.

I called in many a craftsmaster
To fix emblazoned glass,
To figure Cross and Sepulchure
On dossal, boss, and brass.

My gold all spent,
My jewels went
To gem the cups of Mass.

I borrowed deep to carve the screen
And raise the ivoried Rood;
I parted with my small demesne
To make my owings good.
Heir-looms unpriced
I sacrificed,
Until debt-free I stood.

So closed the task. "Deathless the Creed
Here substanced!" said my soul:
"I heard me bidden to this deed,
And straight obeyed the call.
Illume this fane,
That not in vain
I build it, Lord of all!"

But, as it chanced me, then and there
Did dire misfortunes burst;

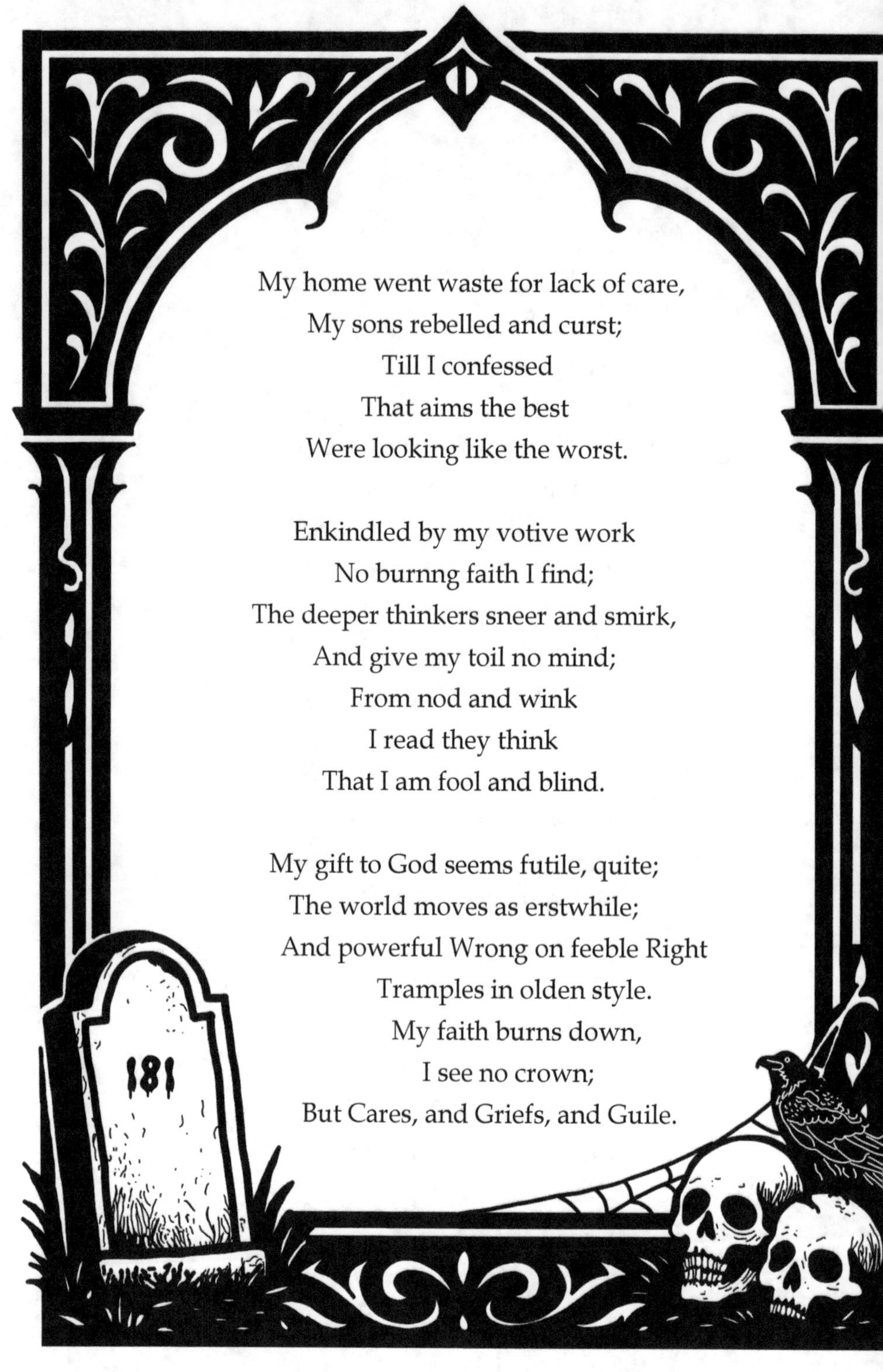

My home went waste for lack of care,
My sons rebelled and curst;
Till I confessed
That aims the best
Were looking like the worst.

Enkindled by my votive work
No burnng faith I find;
The deeper thinkers sneer and smirk,
And give my toil no mind;
From nod and wink
I read they think
That I am fool and blind.

My gift to God seems futile, quite;
The world moves as erstwhile;
And powerful Wrong on feeble Right
Tramples in olden style.
My faith burns down,
I see no crown;
But Cares, and Griefs, and Guile.

So now, the remedy? Yea, this:
I gently swing the door
Here, of my fane--no soul to wis--
And cross the patterned floor
To the rood-screen
That stands between
The nave and inner chore.

The rich red windows dim the moon,
But little light need I;
I mount the prie-dieu, lately hewn
From woods of rarest dye;
Then from below
My garment, so,
I draw this cord, and tie

One end thereof around the beam
Midway 'twixt Cross and truss:
I noose the nethermost extreme,
And in ten seconds thus
I journey hence--
To that land whence

No rumour reaches us.

Well: Here at morn they'll light on one
Dangling in mockery
Of what he spent his substance on
Blindly and uselessly!...
"He might," they'll say,
"Have built, some way,
A cheaper gallows-tree!"

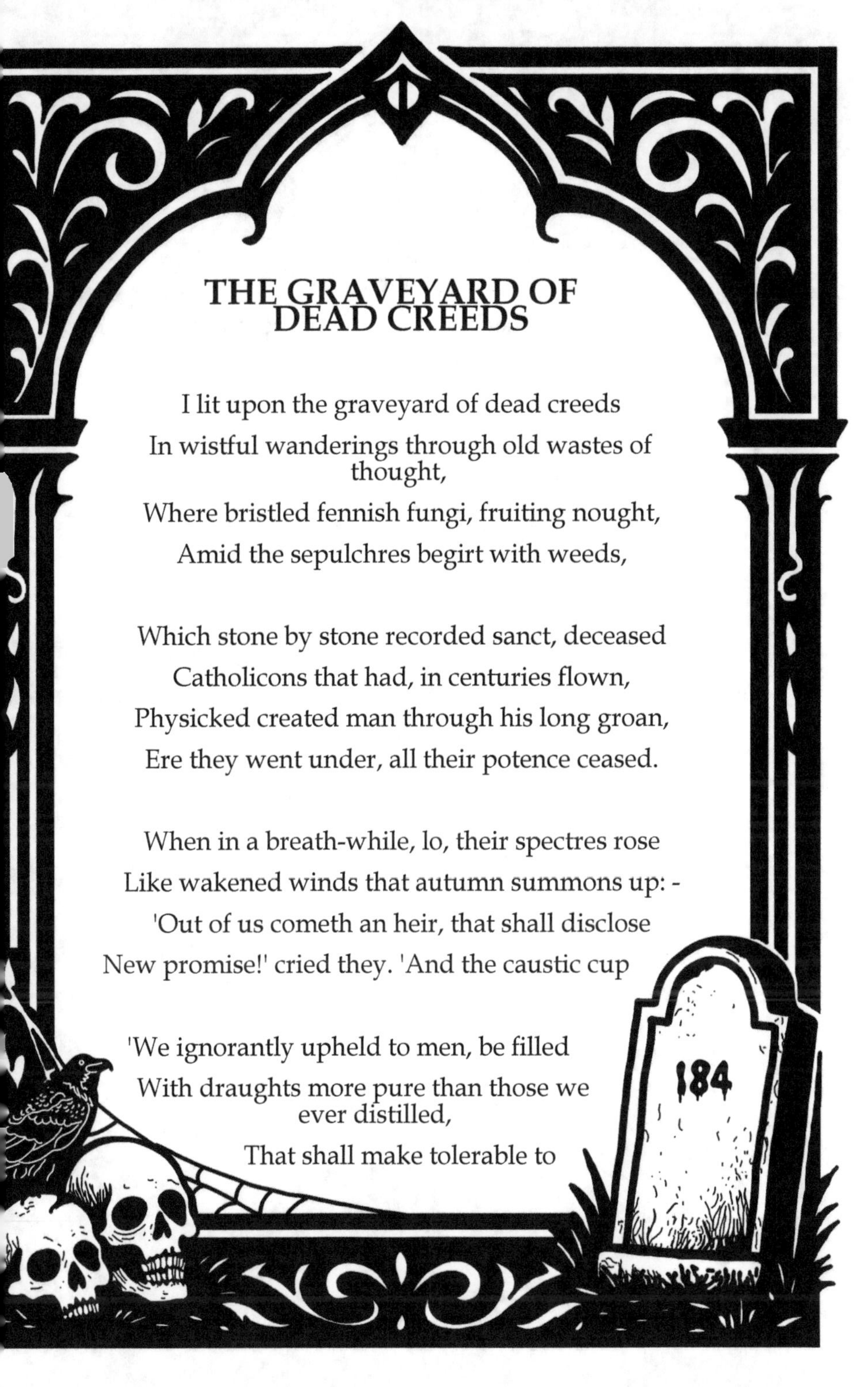

THE GRAVEYARD OF DEAD CREEDS

I lit upon the graveyard of dead creeds
In wistful wanderings through old wastes of thought,
Where bristled fennish fungi, fruiting nought,
Amid the sepulchres begirt with weeds,

Which stone by stone recorded sanct, deceased
Catholicons that had, in centuries flown,
Physicked created man through his long groan,
Ere they went under, all their potence ceased.

When in a breath-while, lo, their spectres rose
Like wakened winds that autumn summons up: -
'Out of us cometh an heir, that shall disclose
New promise!' cried they. 'And the caustic cup

'We ignorantly upheld to men, be filled
With draughts more pure than those we ever distilled,
That shall make tolerable to

sentient seers
The melancholy marching of the years.'

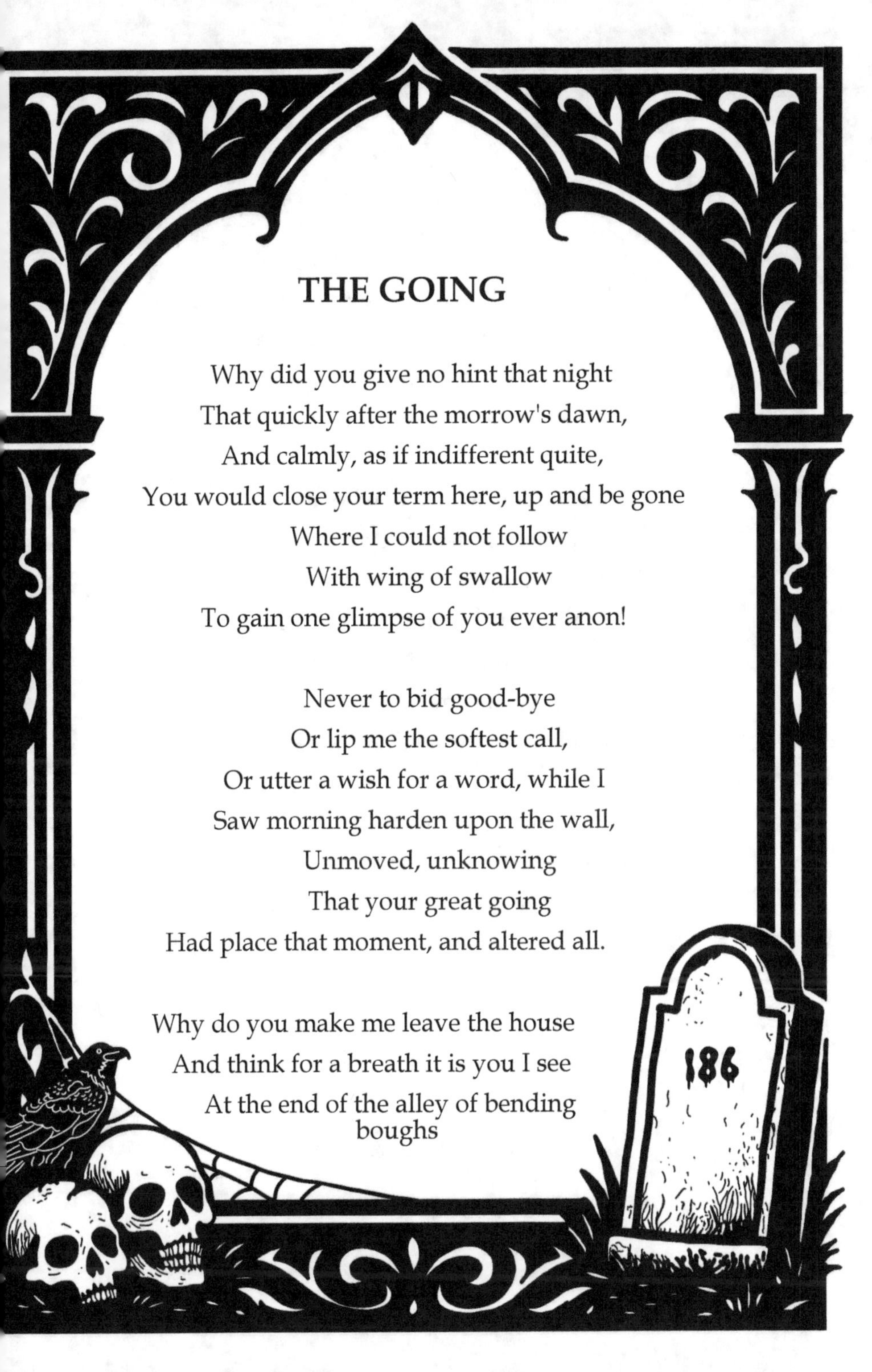

THE GOING

Why did you give no hint that night
That quickly after the morrow's dawn,
And calmly, as if indifferent quite,
You would close your term here, up and be gone
Where I could not follow
With wing of swallow
To gain one glimpse of you ever anon!

Never to bid good-bye
Or lip me the softest call,
Or utter a wish for a word, while I
Saw morning harden upon the wall,
Unmoved, unknowing
That your great going
Had place that moment, and altered all.

Why do you make me leave the house
And think for a breath it is you I see
At the end of the alley of bending boughs

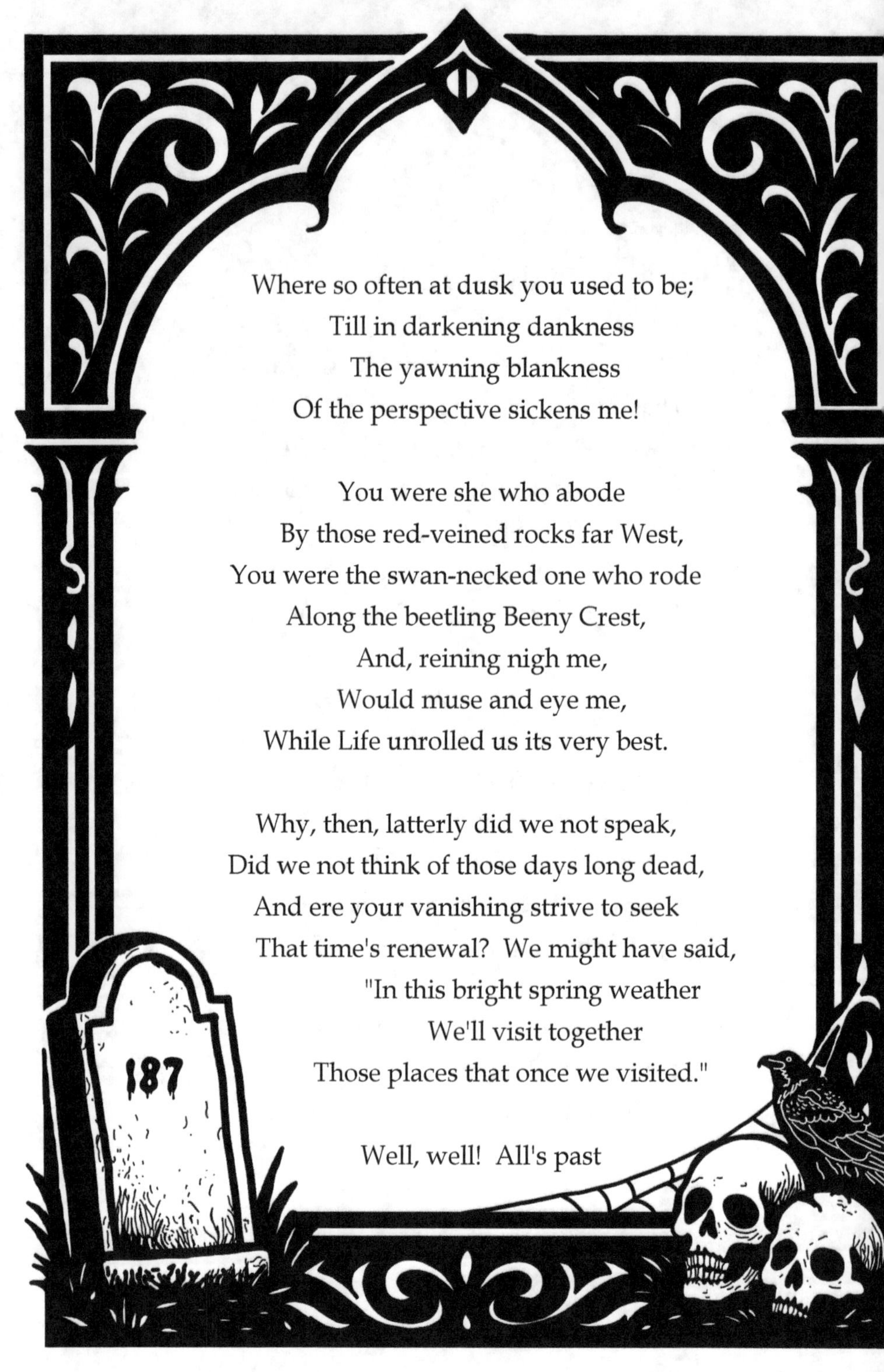

Where so often at dusk you used to be;
Till in darkening dankness
The yawning blankness
Of the perspective sickens me!

You were she who abode
By those red-veined rocks far West,
You were the swan-necked one who rode
Along the beetling Beeny Crest,
And, reining nigh me,
Would muse and eye me,
While Life unrolled us its very best.

Why, then, latterly did we not speak,
Did we not think of those days long dead,
And ere your vanishing strive to seek
That time's renewal? We might have said,
"In this bright spring weather
We'll visit together
Those places that once we visited."

Well, well! All's past

amend,
Unchangeable. It must go.
I seem but a dead man held on end
To sink down soon. . . . O you could not know
That such swift fleeing
No soul foreseeing—
Not even I—would undo me so!

AH, ARE YOU DIGGING ON MY GRAVE?

"Ah, are you digging on my grave,
My loved one? -- planting rue?"
-- "No: yesterday he went to wed
One of the brightest wealth has bred.
'It cannot hurt her now,' he said,
'That I should not be true.'"

"Then who is digging on my grave,
My nearest dearest kin?"
-- "Ah, no: they sit and think, 'What use!
What good will planting flowers produce?
No tendance of her mound can loose
Her spirit from Death's gin.'"

"But someone digs upon my grave?
My enemy? -- prodding sly?"
-- "Nay: when she heard you had passed the Gate
That shuts on all flesh soon or late,
She thought you no

more worth her hate,

And cares not where you lie.

"Then, who is digging on my grave?
Say -- since I have not guessed!"
-- "O it is I, my mistress dear,
Your little dog , who still lives near,
And much I hope my movements here
Have not disturbed your rest?"

"Ah yes! You dig upon my grave...
Why flashed it not to me
That one true heart was left behind!
What feeling do we ever find
To equal among human kind
A dog's fidelity!"

"Mistress, I dug upon your grave
To bury a bone, in case
I should be hungry near this spot
When passing on my daily trot.
I am sorry, but I quite forgot

It was your resting place."

Woman much missed, how you call to me, call to me,
Saying that now you are not as you were
When you had changed from the one who was all to me,
But as at first, when our day was fair.

Can it be you that I hear? Let me view you, then,
Standing as when I drew near to the town
Where you would wait for me: yes, as I knew you then,
Even to the original air-blue gown!

Or is it only the breeze, in its listlessness
Travelling across the wet mead to me here,
You being ever dissolved to wan wistlessness,
Heard no more again far or near?

Thus I; faltering forward,
Leaves around me falling,
Wind oozing thin through the thorn from norward,
And the woman calling.

THE VOICE

Woman much missed, how you call to me, call to me,
Saying that now you are not as you were
When you had changed from the one who was all to me,
But as at first, when our day was fair.

Can it be you that I hear? Let me view you, then,
Standing as when I drew near to the town
Where you would wait for me: yes, as I knew you then,
Even to the original air-blue gown!

Or is it only the breeze, in its listlessness
Travelling across the wet mead to me here,
You being ever dissolved to wan wistlessness,
Heard no more again far or near?

Thus I; faltering forward,
Leaves around me falling,
Wind oozing thin through the thorn from norward,
And the woman calling.

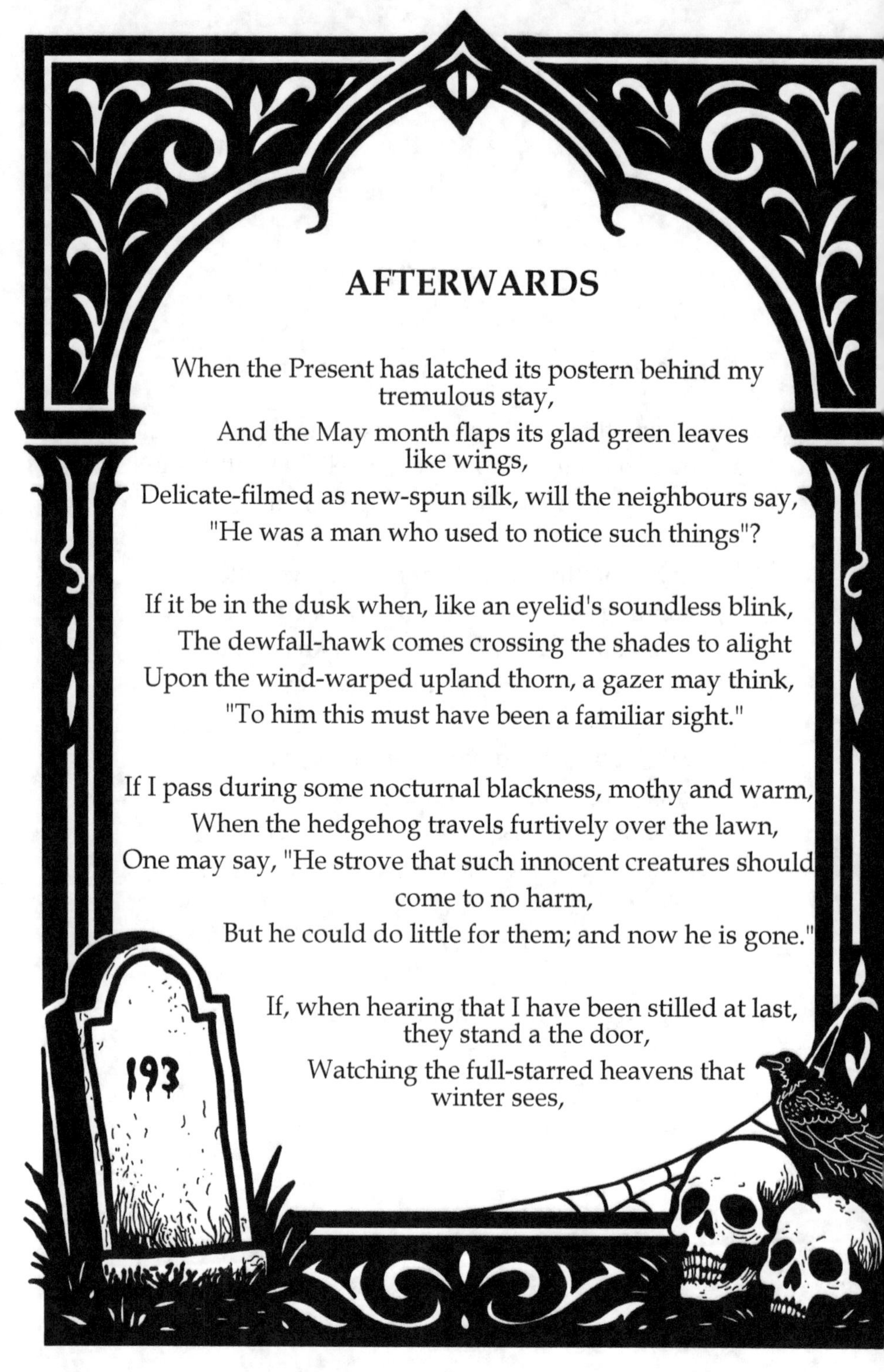

AFTERWARDS

When the Present has latched its postern behind my tremulous stay,
And the May month flaps its glad green leaves like wings,
Delicate-filmed as new-spun silk, will the neighbours say,
"He was a man who used to notice such things"?

If it be in the dusk when, like an eyelid's soundless blink,
The dewfall-hawk comes crossing the shades to alight
Upon the wind-warped upland thorn, a gazer may think,
"To him this must have been a familiar sight."

If I pass during some nocturnal blackness, mothy and warm,
When the hedgehog travels furtively over the lawn,
One may say, "He strove that such innocent creatures should come to no harm,
But he could do little for them; and now he is gone."

If, when hearing that I have been stilled at last, they stand a the door,
Watching the full-starred heavens that winter sees,

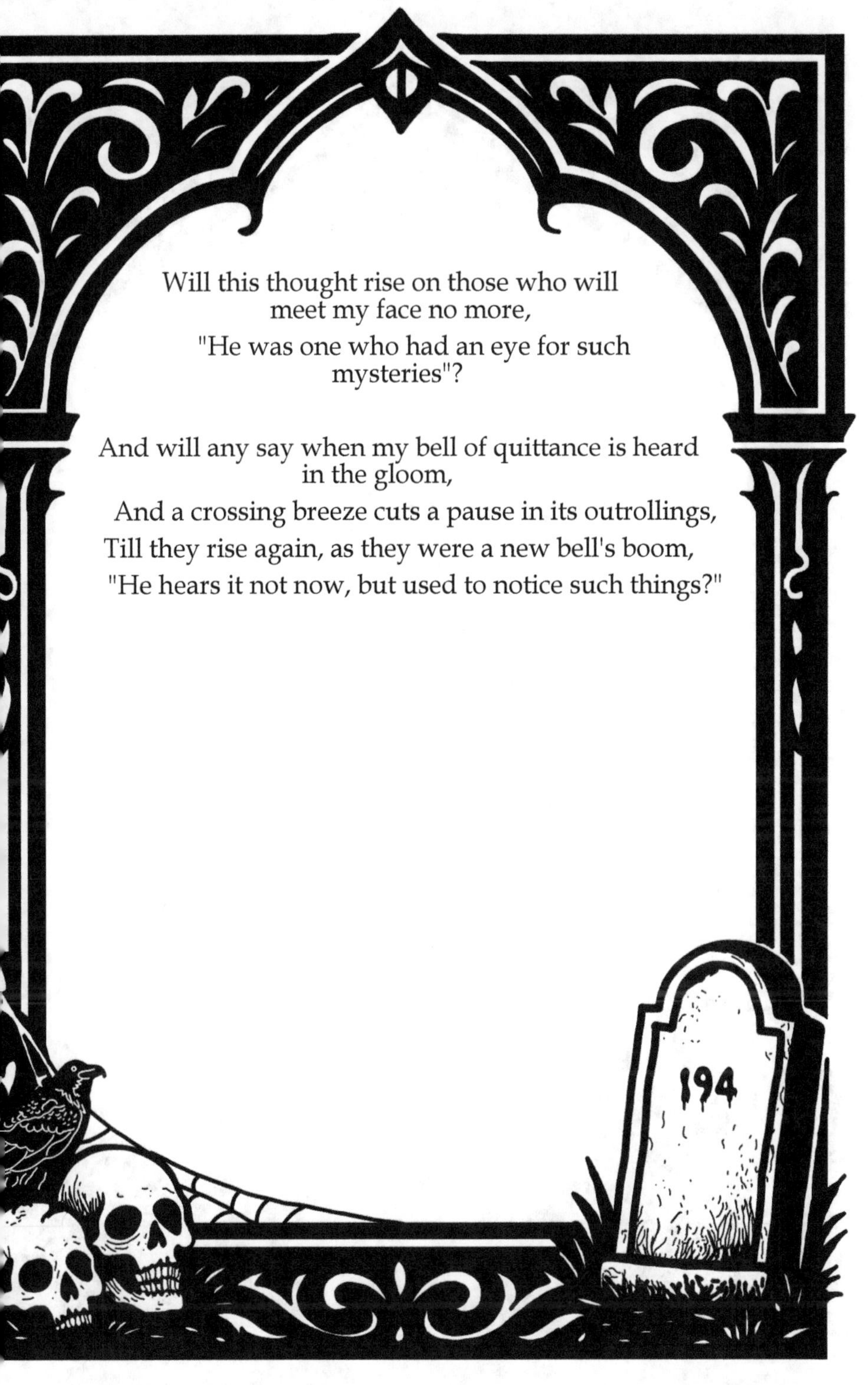

Will this thought rise on those who will
meet my face no more,
"He was one who had an eye for such
mysteries"?

And will any say when my bell of quittance is heard
in the gloom,
And a crossing breeze cuts a pause in its outrollings,
Till they rise again, as they were a new bell's boom,
"He hears it not now, but used to notice such things?"

John Keats

ON DEATH

Can death be sleep, when life is but a dream,
And scenes of bliss pass as a phantom by?
The transient pleasures as a vision seem,
And yet we think the greatest pain's to die.

How strange it is that man on earth should roam,
And lead a life of woe, but not forsake
His rugged path; nor dare he view alone
His future doom which is but to awake.

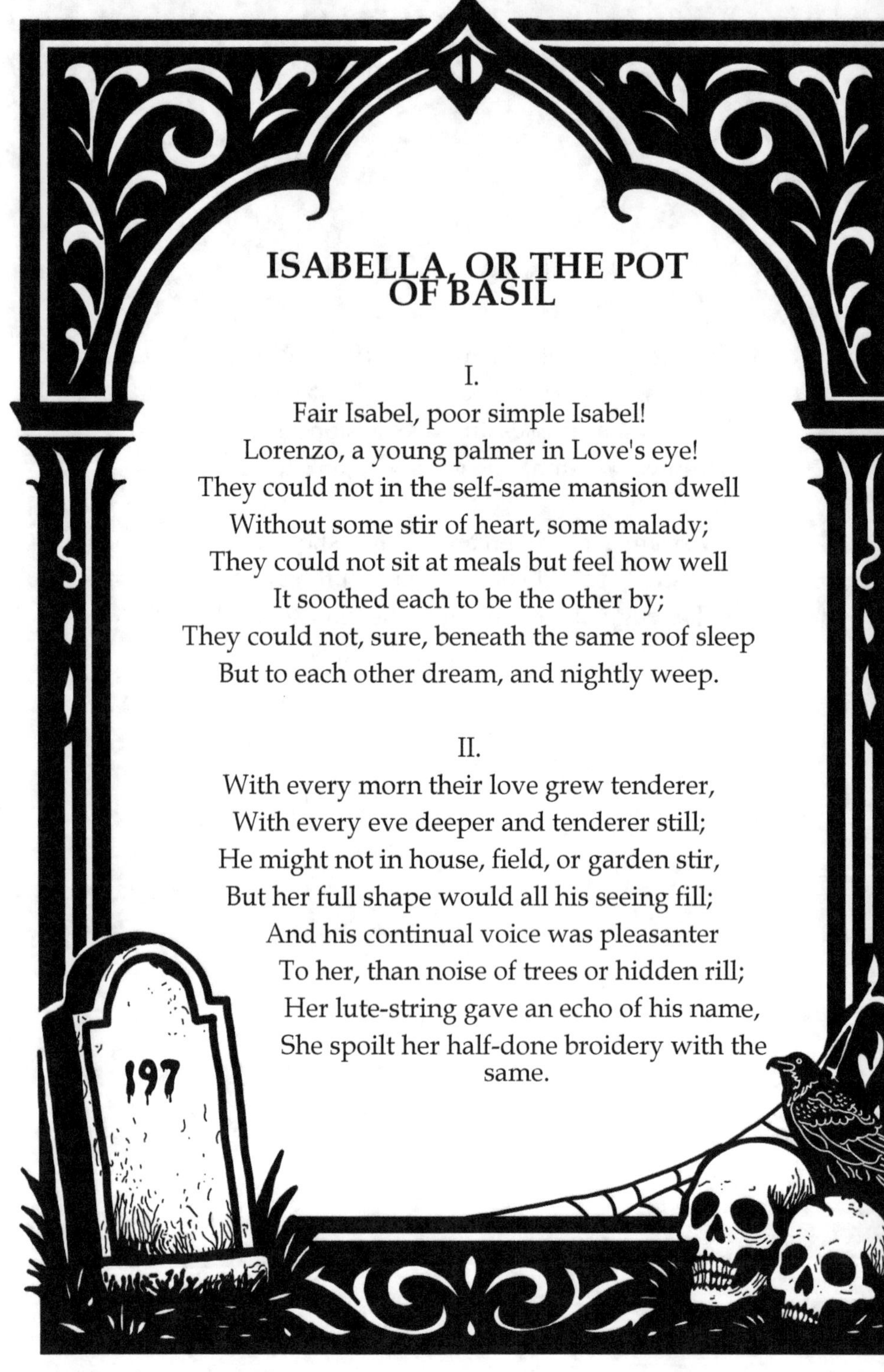

ISABELLA, OR THE POT OF BASIL

I.

Fair Isabel, poor simple Isabel!
Lorenzo, a young palmer in Love's eye!
They could not in the self-same mansion dwell
Without some stir of heart, some malady;
They could not sit at meals but feel how well
It soothed each to be the other by;
They could not, sure, beneath the same roof sleep
But to each other dream, and nightly weep.

II.

With every morn their love grew tenderer,
With every eve deeper and tenderer still;
He might not in house, field, or garden stir,
But her full shape would all his seeing fill;
And his continual voice was pleasanter
To her, than noise of trees or hidden rill;
Her lute-string gave an echo of his name,
She spoilt her half-done broidery with the same.

III.

He knew whose gentle hand was at the latch,
Before the door had given her to his eyes;
And from her chamber-window he would catch
Her beauty farther than the falcon spies;
And constant as her vespers would he watch,
Because her face was turn'd to the same skies;
And with sick longing all the night outwear,
To hear her morning-step upon the stair.

IV.

A whole long month of May in this sad plight
Made their cheeks paler by the break of June:
"To morrow will I bow to my delight,
"To-morrow will I ask my lady's boon."--
"O may I never see another night,
"Lorenzo, if thy lips breathe not love's tune."--
So spake they to their pillows; but, alas,
Honeyless days and days did he let pass;

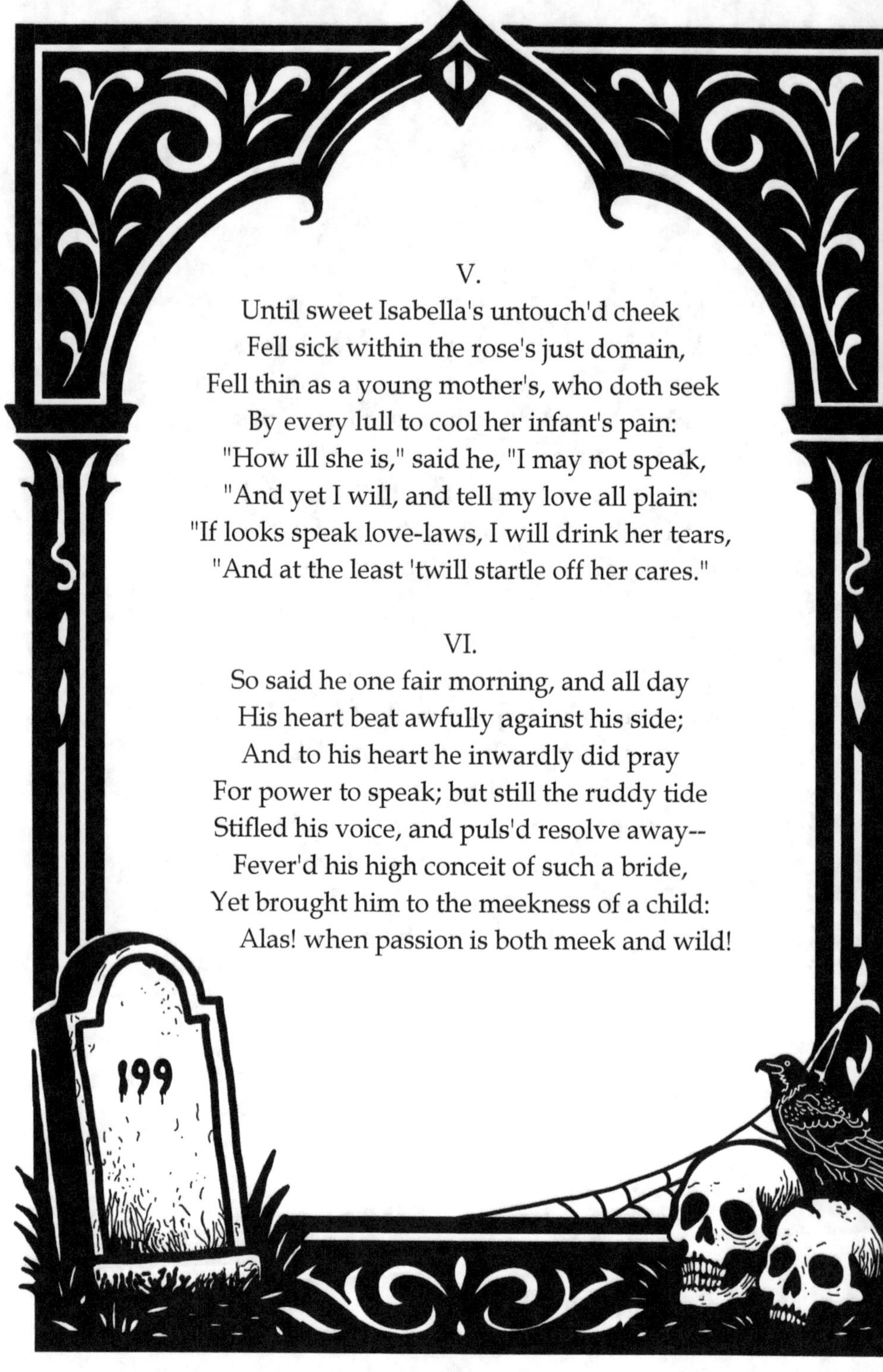

V.

Until sweet Isabella's untouch'd cheek
Fell sick within the rose's just domain,
Fell thin as a young mother's, who doth seek
By every lull to cool her infant's pain:
"How ill she is," said he, "I may not speak,
"And yet I will, and tell my love all plain:
"If looks speak love-laws, I will drink her tears,
"And at the least 'twill startle off her cares."

VI.

So said he one fair morning, and all day
His heart beat awfully against his side;
And to his heart he inwardly did pray
For power to speak; but still the ruddy tide
Stifled his voice, and puls'd resolve away--
Fever'd his high conceit of such a bride,
Yet brought him to the meekness of a child:
Alas! when passion is both meek and wild!

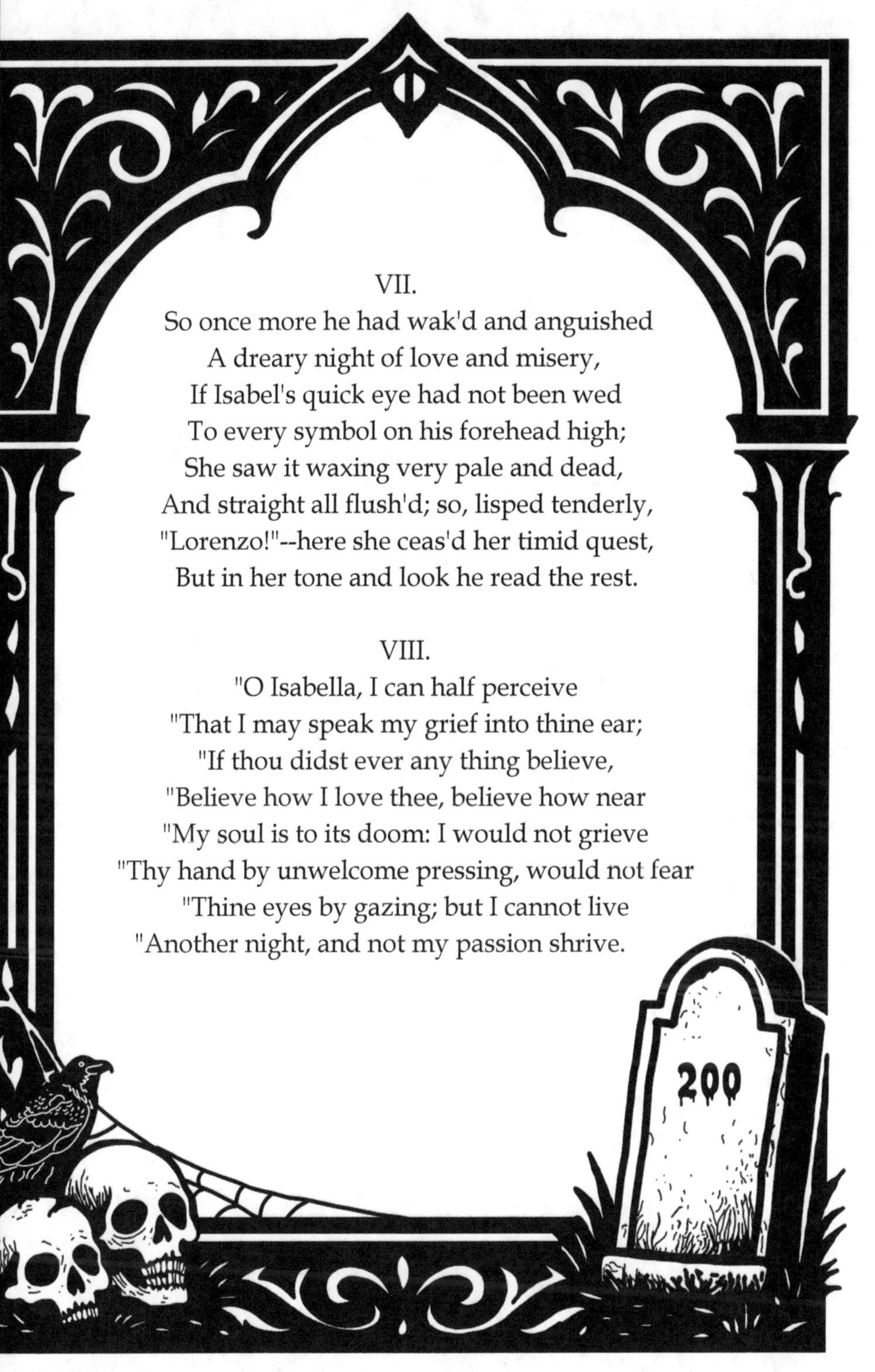

VII.

So once more he had wak'd and anguished
A dreary night of love and misery,
If Isabel's quick eye had not been wed
To every symbol on his forehead high;
She saw it waxing very pale and dead,
And straight all flush'd; so, lisped tenderly,
"Lorenzo!"--here she ceas'd her timid quest,
But in her tone and look he read the rest.

VIII.

"O Isabella, I can half perceive
"That I may speak my grief into thine ear;
"If thou didst ever any thing believe,
"Believe how I love thee, believe how near
"My soul is to its doom: I would not grieve
"Thy hand by unwelcome pressing, would not fear
"Thine eyes by gazing; but I cannot live
"Another night, and not my passion shrive.

IX.

"Love! thou art leading me from wintry cold,
"Lady! thou leadest me to summer clime,
"And I must taste the blossoms that unfold
"In its ripe warmth this gracious morning time."
So said, his erewhile timid lips grew bold,
And poesied with hers in dewy rhyme:
Great bliss was with them, and great happiness
Grew, like a lusty flower in June's caress.

X.

Parting they seem'd to tread upon the air,
Twin roses by the zephyr blown apart
Only to meet again more close, and share
The inward fragrance of each other's heart.
She, to her chamber gone, a ditty fair
Sang, of delicious love and honey'd dart;
He with light steps went up a western hill,
And bade the sun farewell, and joy'd his fill.

XI.

All close they met again, before the dusk
Had taken from the stars its pleasant veil,
All close they met, all eves, before the dusk
Had taken from the stars its pleasant veil,
Close in a bower of hyacinth and musk,
Unknown of any, free from whispering tale.
Ah! better had it been for ever so,
Than idle ears should pleasure in their woe.

XII.

Were they unhappy then?--It cannot be--
Too many tears for lovers have been shed,
Too many sighs give we to them in fee,
Too much of pity after they are dead,
Too many doleful stories do we see,
Whose matter in bright gold were best be read;
Except in such a page where Theseus' spouse
Over the pathless waves towards him bows.

XIII.

But, for the general award of love,
The little sweet doth kill much bitterness;
Though Dido silent is in under-grove,
And Isabella's was a great distress,
Though young Lorenzo in warm Indian clove
Was not embalm'd, this truth is not the less--
Even bees, the little almsmen of spring-bowers,
Know there is richest juice in poison-flowers.

XIV.

With her two brothers this fair lady dwelt,
Enriched from ancestral merchandize,
And for them many a weary hand did swelt
In torched mines and noisy factories,
And many once proud-quiver'd loins did melt
In blood from stinging whip;--with hollow eyes
Many all day in dazzling river stood,
To take the rich-ored driftings of the flood.

XV.

For them the Ceylon diver held his breath,
And went all naked to the hungry shark;
For them his ears gush'd blood; for them in death

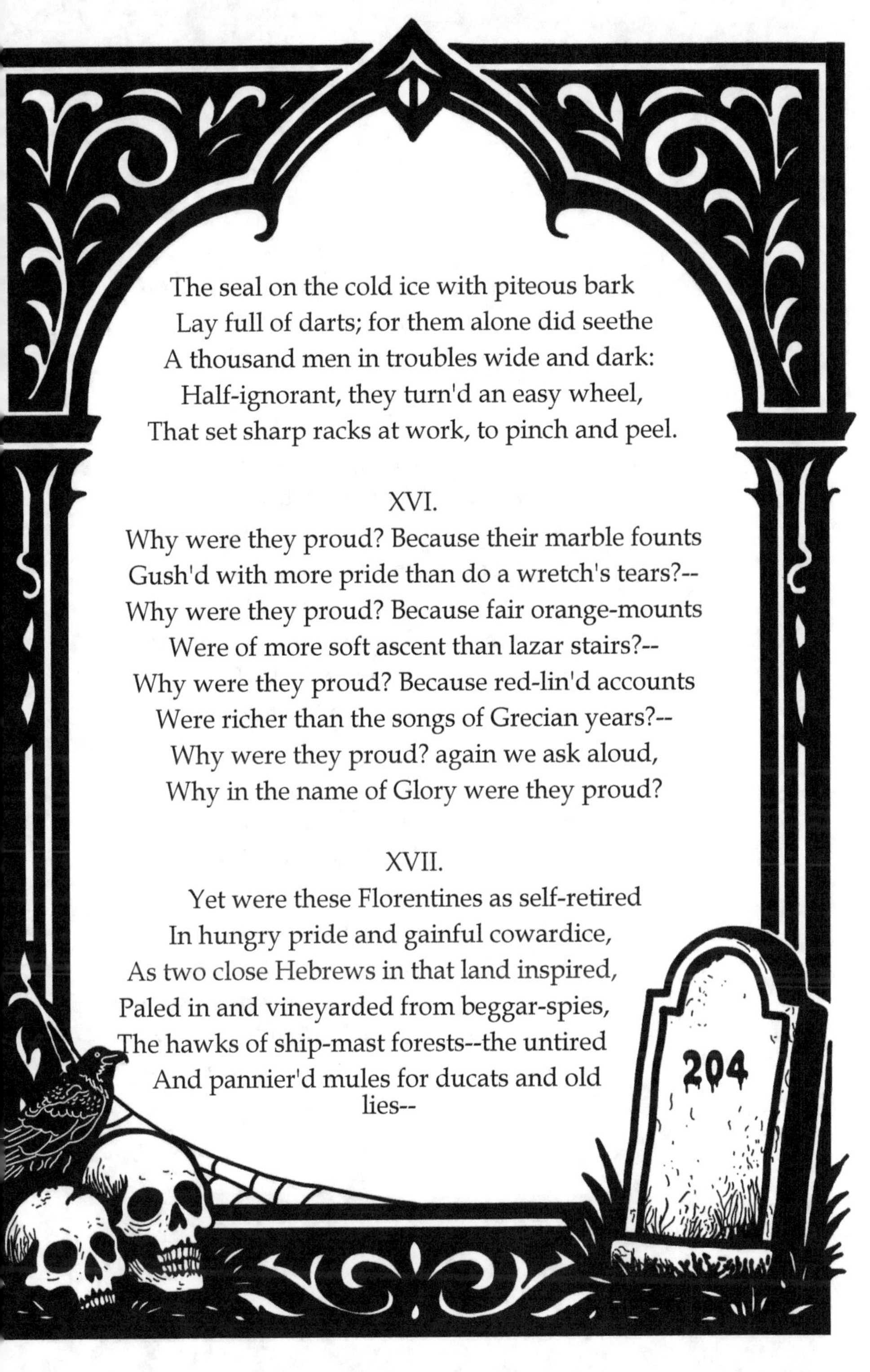

The seal on the cold ice with piteous bark
Lay full of darts; for them alone did seethe
A thousand men in troubles wide and dark:
Half-ignorant, they turn'd an easy wheel,
That set sharp racks at work, to pinch and peel.

XVI.

Why were they proud? Because their marble founts
Gush'd with more pride than do a wretch's tears?--
Why were they proud? Because fair orange-mounts
Were of more soft ascent than lazar stairs?--
Why were they proud? Because red-lin'd accounts
Were richer than the songs of Grecian years?--
Why were they proud? again we ask aloud,
Why in the name of Glory were they proud?

XVII.

Yet were these Florentines as self-retired
In hungry pride and gainful cowardice,
As two close Hebrews in that land inspired,
Paled in and vineyarded from beggar-spies,
The hawks of ship-mast forests--the untired
And pannier'd mules for ducats and old lies--

Quick cat's-paws on the generous stray-
away,--
Great wits in Spanish, Tuscan, and Malay.

XVIII.

How was it these same ledger-men could spy
Fair Isabella in her downy nest?
How could they find out in Lorenzo's eye
A straying from his toil? Hot Egypt's pest
Into their vision covetous and sly!
How could these money-bags see east and west?--
Yet so they did--and every dealer fair
Must see behind, as doth the hunted hare.

XIX.

O eloquent and famed Boccaccio!
Of thee we now should ask forgiving boon,
And of thy spicy myrtles as they blow,
And of thy roses amorous of the moon,
And of thy lilies, that do paler grow
Now they can no more hear thy ghittern's tune,
For venturing syllables that ill beseem
The quiet glooms of such a piteous theme.

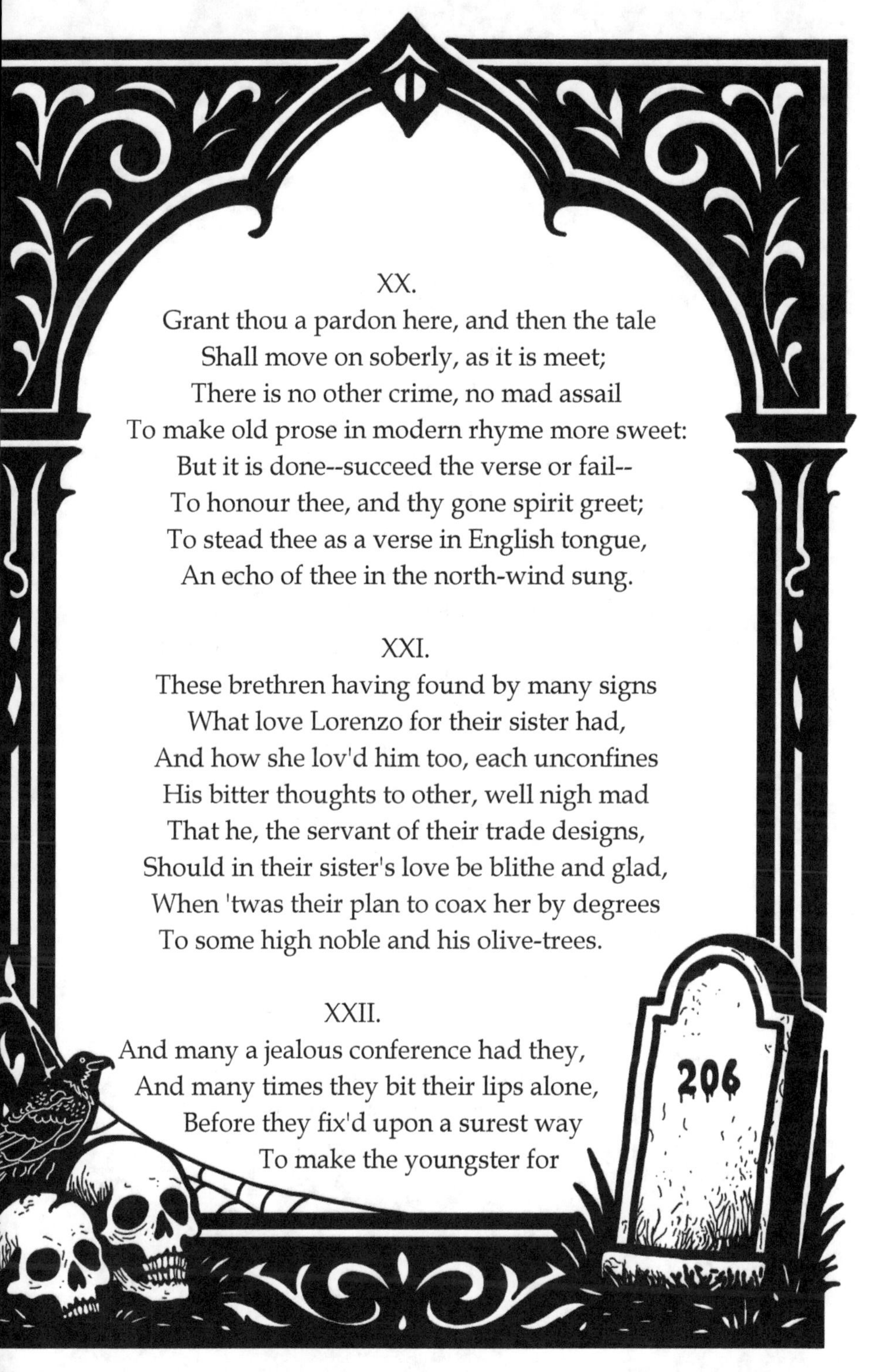

XX.

Grant thou a pardon here, and then the tale
Shall move on soberly, as it is meet;
There is no other crime, no mad assail
To make old prose in modern rhyme more sweet:
But it is done--succeed the verse or fail--
To honour thee, and thy gone spirit greet;
To stead thee as a verse in English tongue,
An echo of thee in the north-wind sung.

XXI.

These brethren having found by many signs
What love Lorenzo for their sister had,
And how she lov'd him too, each unconfines
His bitter thoughts to other, well nigh mad
That he, the servant of their trade designs,
Should in their sister's love be blithe and glad,
When 'twas their plan to coax her by degrees
To some high noble and his olive-trees.

XXII.

And many a jealous conference had they,
And many times they bit their lips alone,
Before they fix'd upon a surest way
To make the youngster for

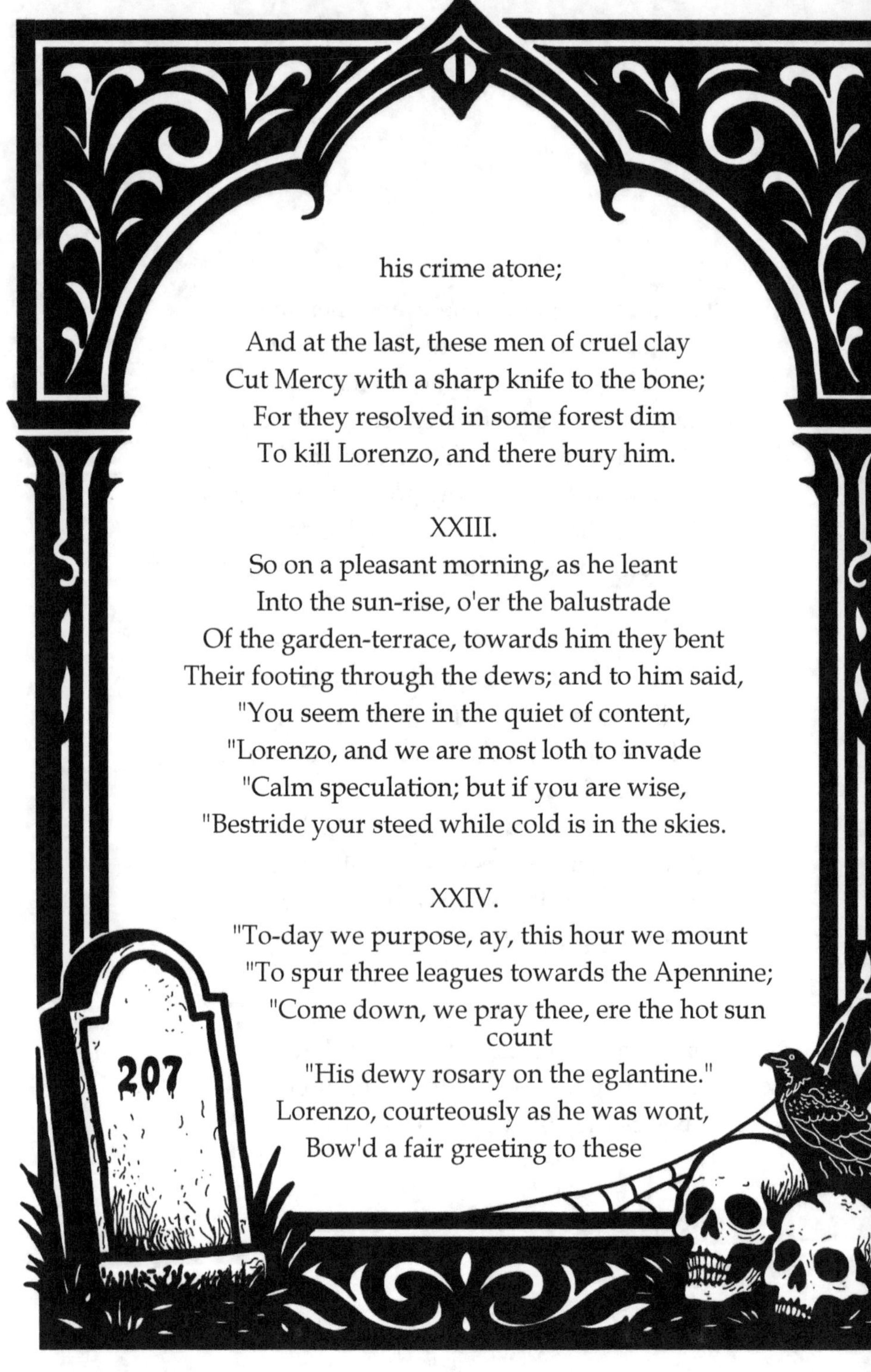

his crime atone;

And at the last, these men of cruel clay
Cut Mercy with a sharp knife to the bone;
For they resolved in some forest dim
To kill Lorenzo, and there bury him.

XXIII.

So on a pleasant morning, as he leant
Into the sun-rise, o'er the balustrade
Of the garden-terrace, towards him they bent
Their footing through the dews; and to him said,
"You seem there in the quiet of content,
"Lorenzo, and we are most loth to invade
"Calm speculation; but if you are wise,
"Bestride your steed while cold is in the skies.

XXIV.

"To-day we purpose, ay, this hour we mount
"To spur three leagues towards the Apennine;
"Come down, we pray thee, ere the hot sun count
"His dewy rosary on the eglantine."
Lorenzo, courteously as he was wont,
Bow'd a fair greeting to these

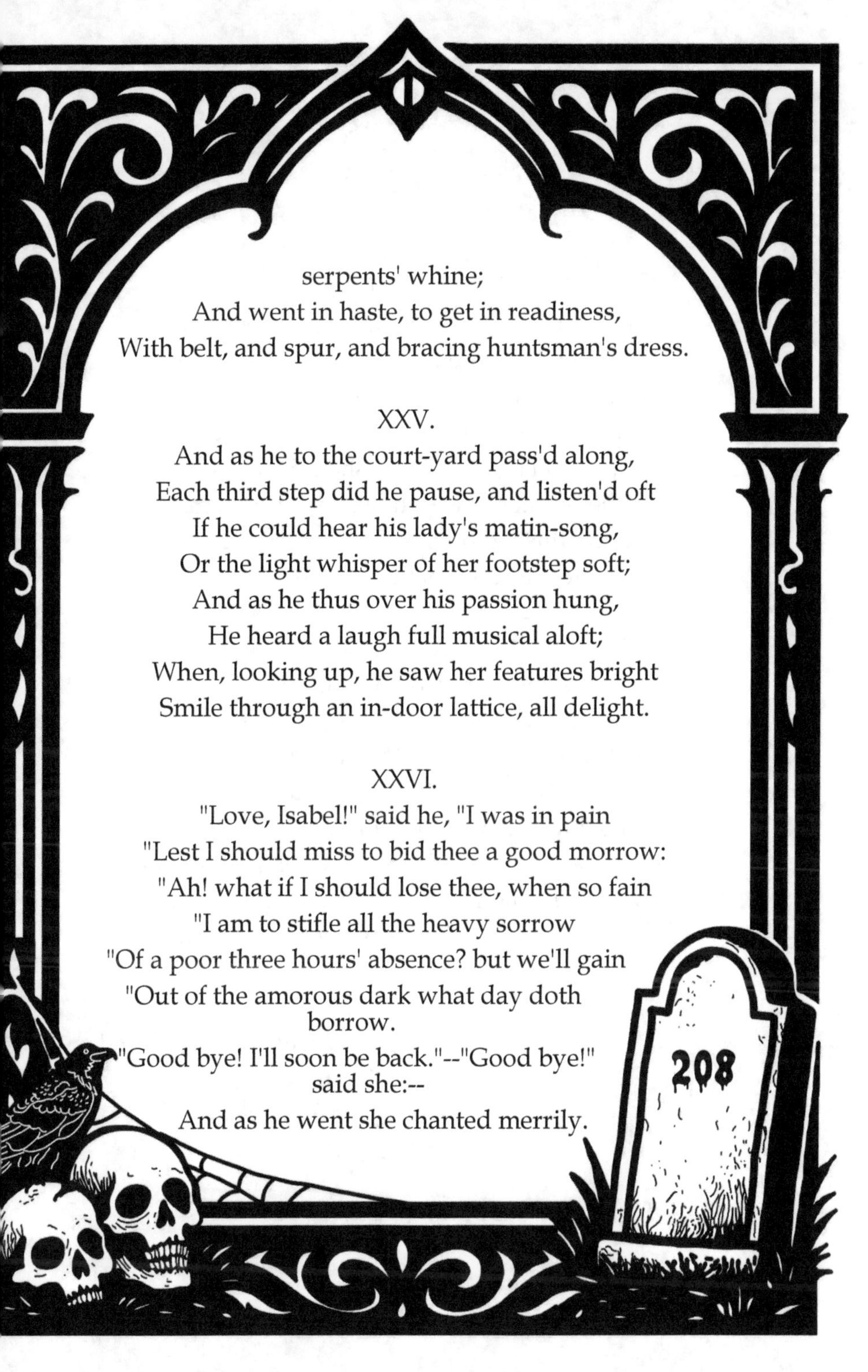

serpents' whine;
And went in haste, to get in readiness,
With belt, and spur, and bracing huntsman's dress.

XXV.

And as he to the court-yard pass'd along,
Each third step did he pause, and listen'd oft
If he could hear his lady's matin-song,
Or the light whisper of her footstep soft;
And as he thus over his passion hung,
He heard a laugh full musical aloft;
When, looking up, he saw her features bright
Smile through an in-door lattice, all delight.

XXVI.

"Love, Isabel!" said he, "I was in pain
"Lest I should miss to bid thee a good morrow:
"Ah! what if I should lose thee, when so fain
"I am to stifle all the heavy sorrow
"Of a poor three hours' absence? but we'll gain
"Out of the amorous dark what day doth borrow.
"Good bye! I'll soon be back."--"Good bye!" said she:--
And as he went she chanted merrily.

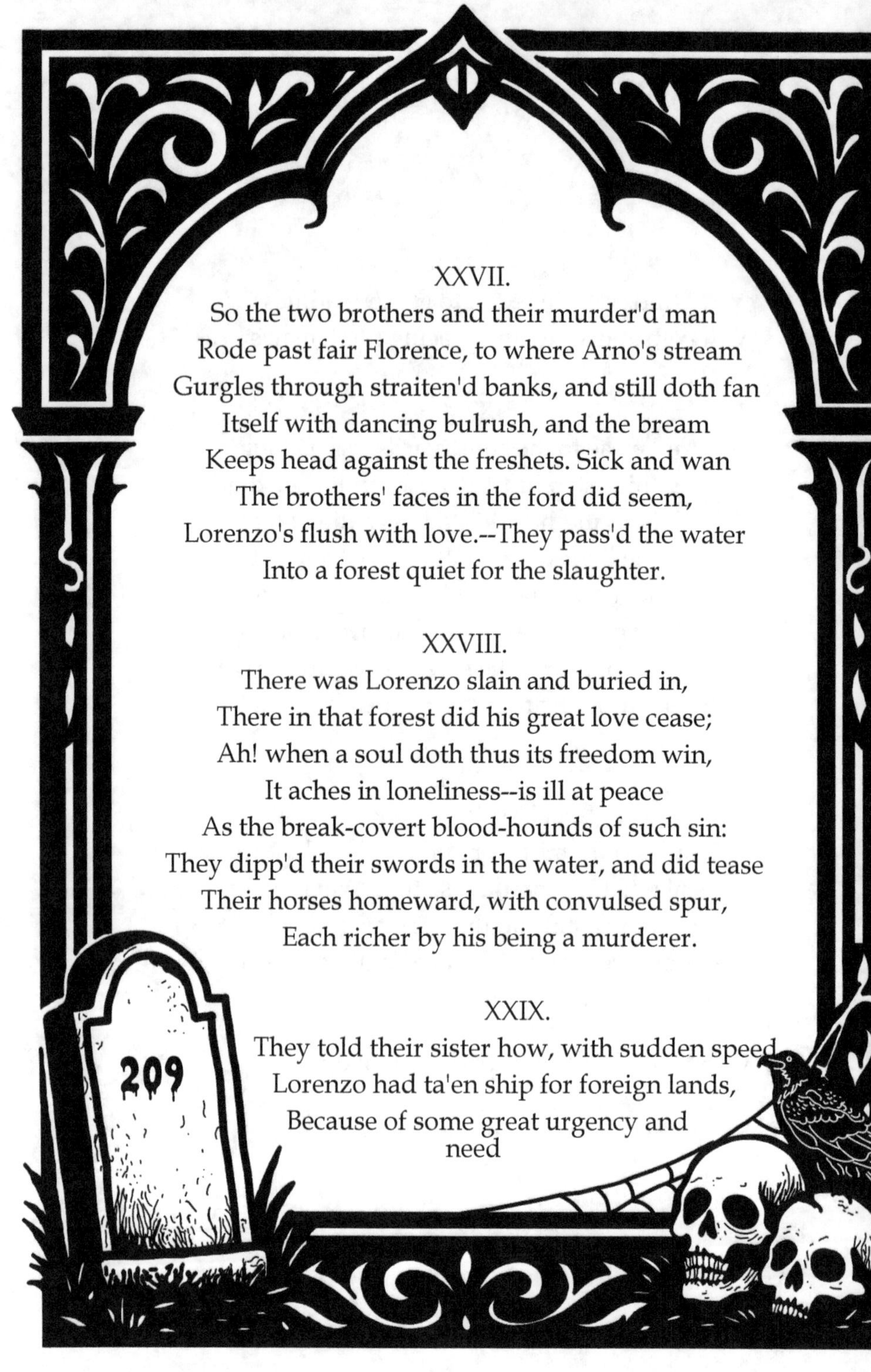

XXVII.

So the two brothers and their murder'd man
Rode past fair Florence, to where Arno's stream
Gurgles through straiten'd banks, and still doth fan
Itself with dancing bulrush, and the bream
Keeps head against the freshets. Sick and wan
The brothers' faces in the ford did seem,
Lorenzo's flush with love.--They pass'd the water
Into a forest quiet for the slaughter.

XXVIII.

There was Lorenzo slain and buried in,
There in that forest did his great love cease;
Ah! when a soul doth thus its freedom win,
It aches in loneliness--is ill at peace
As the break-covert blood-hounds of such sin:
They dipp'd their swords in the water, and did tease
Their horses homeward, with convulsed spur,
Each richer by his being a murderer.

XXIX.

They told their sister how, with sudden speed
Lorenzo had ta'en ship for foreign lands,
Because of some great urgency and need

In their affairs, requiring trusty hands.
Poor Girl! put on thy stifling widow's weed,
And 'scape at once from Hope's accursed bands;
To-day thou wilt not see him, nor to-morrow,
And the next day will be a day of sorrow.

XXX.

She weeps alone for pleasures not to be;
Sorely she wept until the night came on,
And then, instead of love, O misery!
She brooded o'er the luxury alone:
His image in the dusk she seem'd to see,
And to the silence made a gentle moan,
Spreading her perfect arms upon the air,
And on her couch low murmuring, "Where? O where?"

XXXI.

But Selfishness, Love's cousin, held not long
Its fiery vigil in her single breast;
She fretted for the golden hour, and hung
Upon the time with feverish unrest--
Not long--for soon into her heart a throng
Of higher occupants, a richer zest,
Came tragic; passion not to be subdued,
And sorrow for her love in

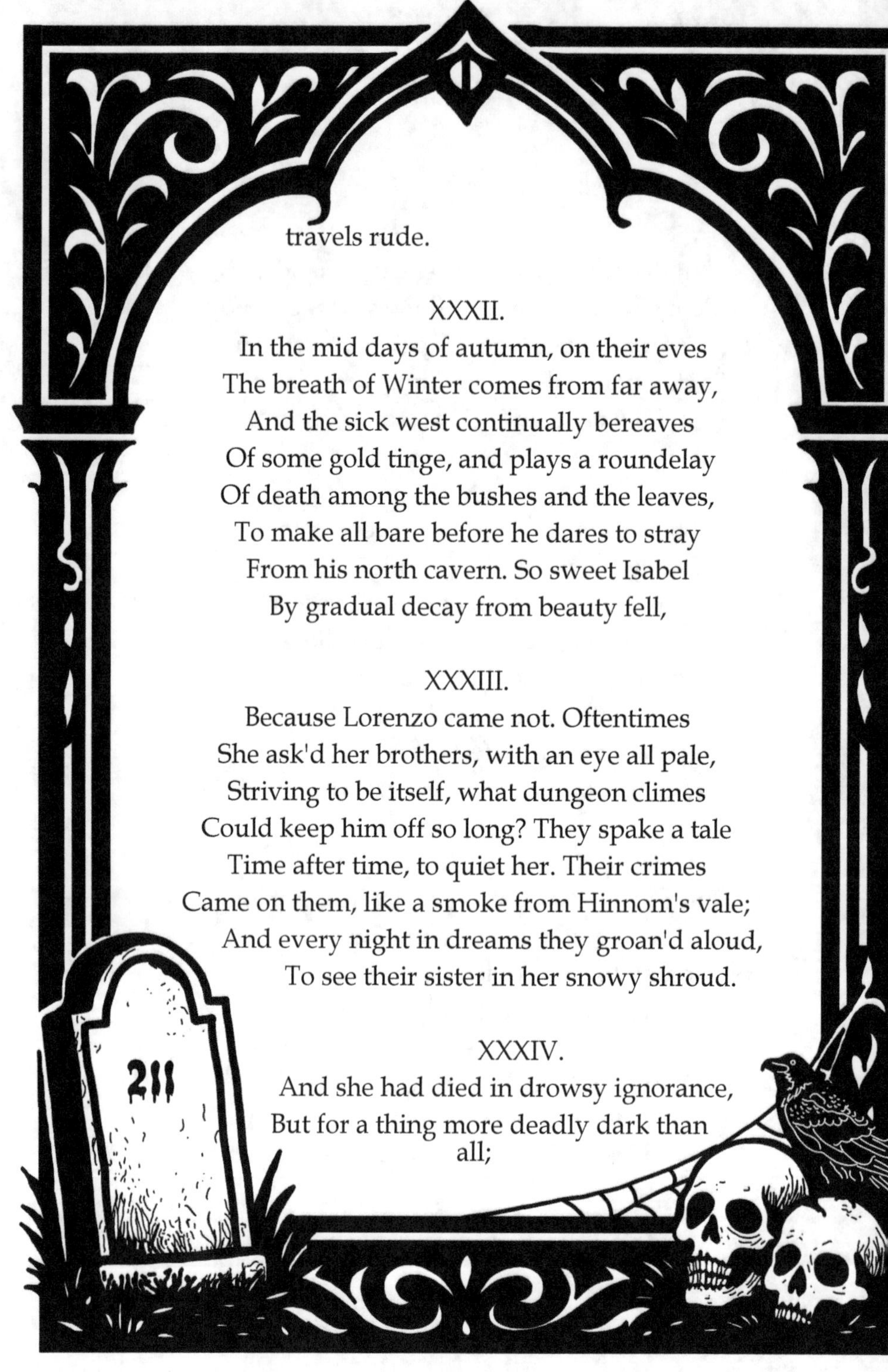

travels rude.

XXXII.

In the mid days of autumn, on their eves
The breath of Winter comes from far away,
And the sick west continually bereaves
Of some gold tinge, and plays a roundelay
Of death among the bushes and the leaves,
To make all bare before he dares to stray
From his north cavern. So sweet Isabel
By gradual decay from beauty fell,

XXXIII.

Because Lorenzo came not. Oftentimes
She ask'd her brothers, with an eye all pale,
Striving to be itself, what dungeon climes
Could keep him off so long? They spake a tale
Time after time, to quiet her. Their crimes
Came on them, like a smoke from Hinnom's vale;
And every night in dreams they groan'd aloud,
To see their sister in her snowy shroud.

XXXIV.

And she had died in drowsy ignorance,
But for a thing more deadly dark than all;

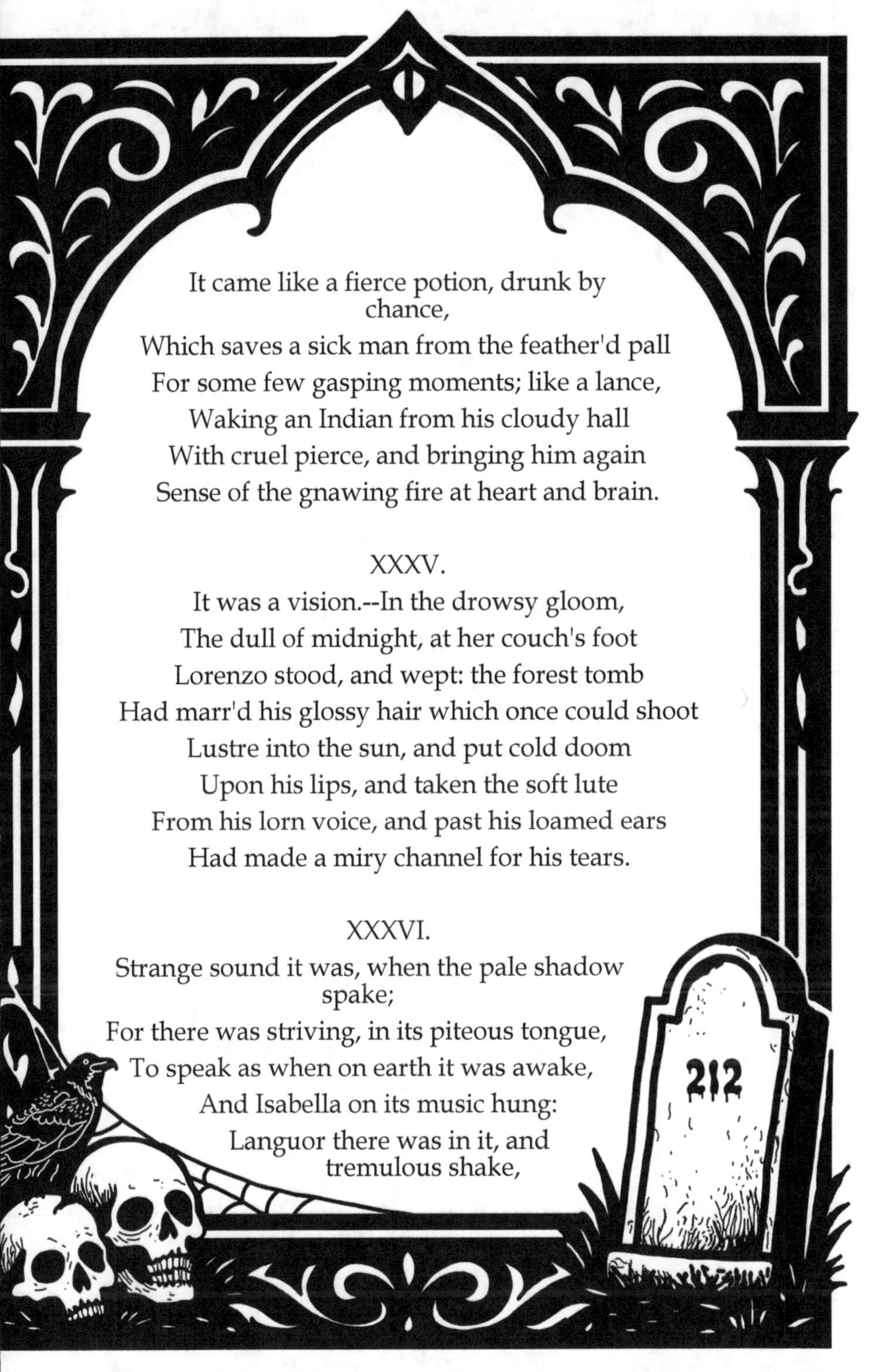

It came like a fierce potion, drunk by chance,
Which saves a sick man from the feather'd pall
For some few gasping moments; like a lance,
Waking an Indian from his cloudy hall
With cruel pierce, and bringing him again
Sense of the gnawing fire at heart and brain.

XXXV.

It was a vision.--In the drowsy gloom,
The dull of midnight, at her couch's foot
Lorenzo stood, and wept: the forest tomb
Had marr'd his glossy hair which once could shoot
Lustre into the sun, and put cold doom
Upon his lips, and taken the soft lute
From his lorn voice, and past his loamed ears
Had made a miry channel for his tears.

XXXVI.

Strange sound it was, when the pale shadow spake;
For there was striving, in its piteous tongue,
To speak as when on earth it was awake,
And Isabella on its music hung:
Languor there was in it, and tremulous shake,

As in a palsied Druid's harp unstrung;
And through it moan'd a ghostly under-song,
Like hoarse night-gusts sepulchral briars among.

XXXVII.

Its eyes, though wild, were still all dewy bright
With love, and kept all phantom fear aloof
From the poor girl by magic of their light,
The while it did unthread the horrid woof
Of the late darken'd time,--the murderous spite
Of pride and avarice,--the dark pine roof
In the forest,--and the sodden turfed dell,
Where, without any word, from stabs he fell.

XXXVIII.

Saying moreover, "Isabel, my sweet!
"Red whortle-berries droop above my head,
"And a large flint-stone weighs upon my feet;
"Around me beeches and high chestnuts shed
"Their leaves and prickly nuts; a sheep-fold bleat
"Comes from beyond the river to my bed:
"Go, shed one tear upon my heather-bloom,
"And it shall comfort me within the tomb.

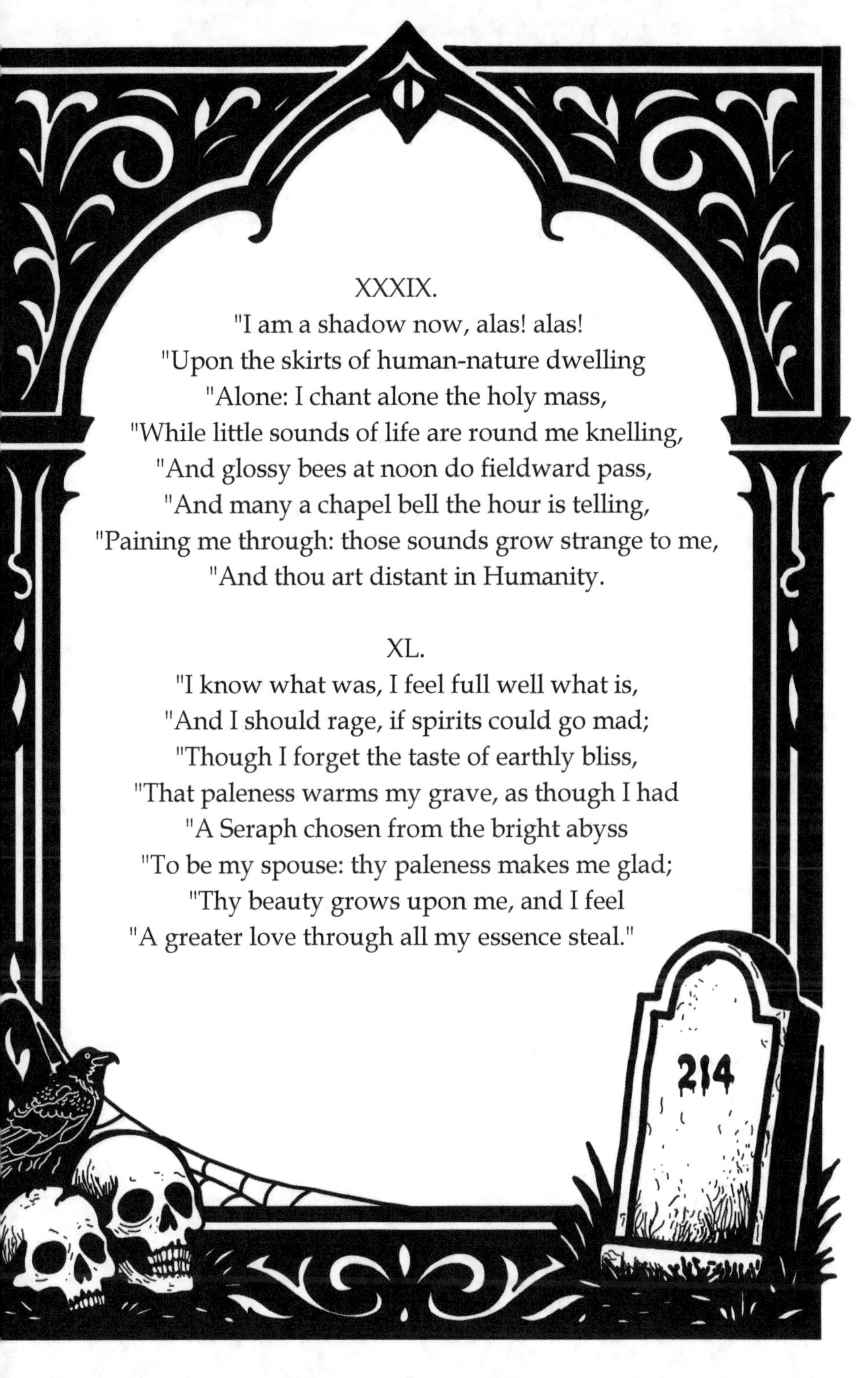

XXXIX.

"I am a shadow now, alas! alas!
"Upon the skirts of human-nature dwelling
"Alone: I chant alone the holy mass,
"While little sounds of life are round me knelling,
"And glossy bees at noon do fieldward pass,
"And many a chapel bell the hour is telling,
"Paining me through: those sounds grow strange to me,
"And thou art distant in Humanity.

XL.

"I know what was, I feel full well what is,
"And I should rage, if spirits could go mad;
"Though I forget the taste of earthly bliss,
"That paleness warms my grave, as though I had
"A Seraph chosen from the bright abyss
"To be my spouse: thy paleness makes me glad;
"Thy beauty grows upon me, and I feel
"A greater love through all my essence steal."

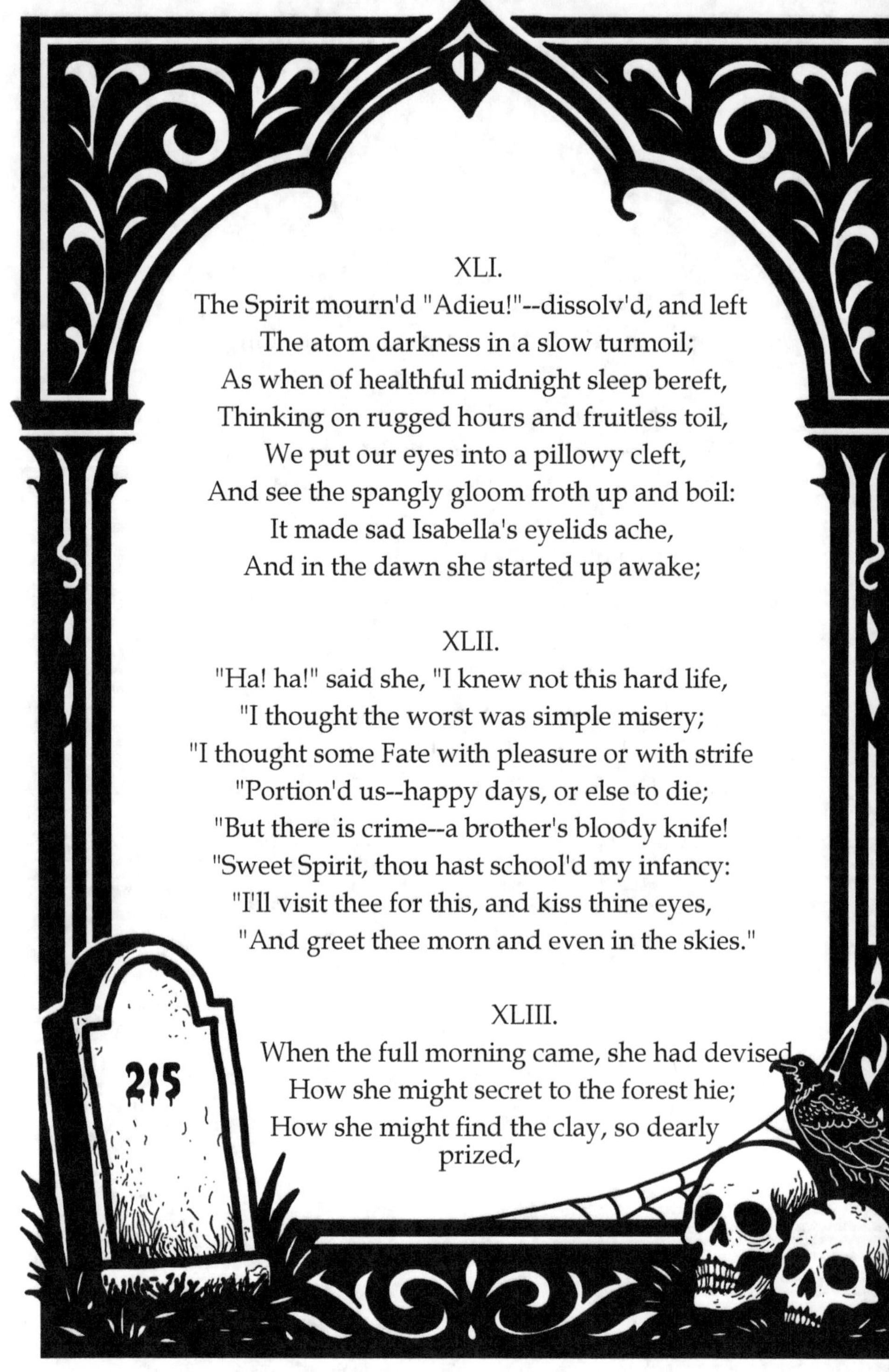

XLI.

The Spirit mourn'd "Adieu!"--dissolv'd, and left
The atom darkness in a slow turmoil;
As when of healthful midnight sleep bereft,
Thinking on rugged hours and fruitless toil,
We put our eyes into a pillowy cleft,
And see the spangly gloom froth up and boil:
It made sad Isabella's eyelids ache,
And in the dawn she started up awake;

XLII.

"Ha! ha!" said she, "I knew not this hard life,
"I thought the worst was simple misery;
"I thought some Fate with pleasure or with strife
"Portion'd us--happy days, or else to die;
"But there is crime--a brother's bloody knife!
"Sweet Spirit, thou hast school'd my infancy:
"I'll visit thee for this, and kiss thine eyes,
"And greet thee morn and even in the skies."

XLIII.

When the full morning came, she had devised
How she might secret to the forest hie;
How she might find the clay, so dearly prized,

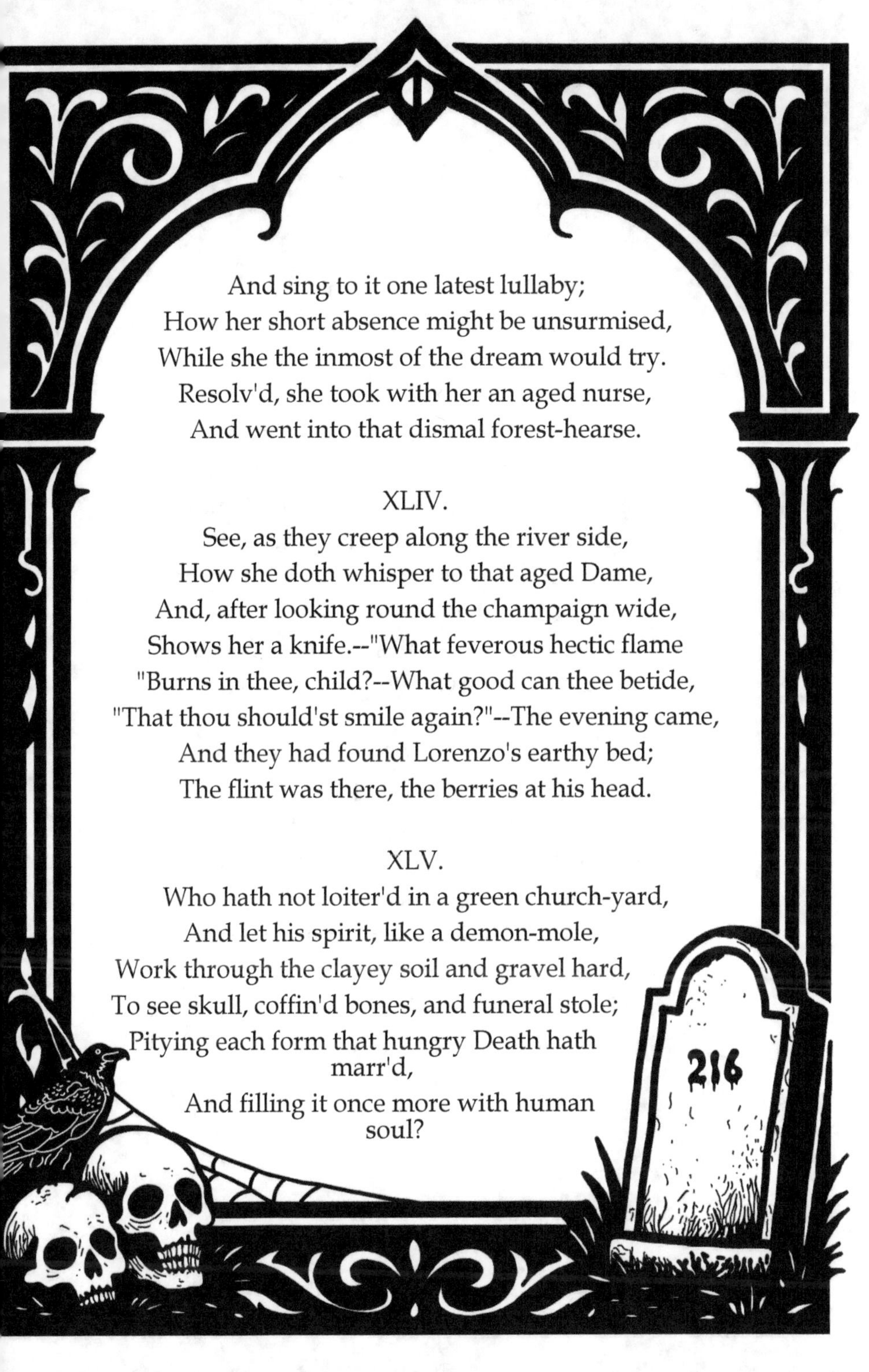

And sing to it one latest lullaby;
How her short absence might be unsurmised,
While she the inmost of the dream would try.
Resolv'd, she took with her an aged nurse,
And went into that dismal forest-hearse.

XLIV.

See, as they creep along the river side,
How she doth whisper to that aged Dame,
And, after looking round the champaign wide,
Shows her a knife.--"What feverous hectic flame
"Burns in thee, child?--What good can thee betide,
"That thou should'st smile again?"--The evening came,
And they had found Lorenzo's earthy bed;
The flint was there, the berries at his head.

XLV.

Who hath not loiter'd in a green church-yard,
And let his spirit, like a demon-mole,
Work through the clayey soil and gravel hard,
To see skull, coffin'd bones, and funeral stole;
Pitying each form that hungry Death hath marr'd,
And filling it once more with human soul?

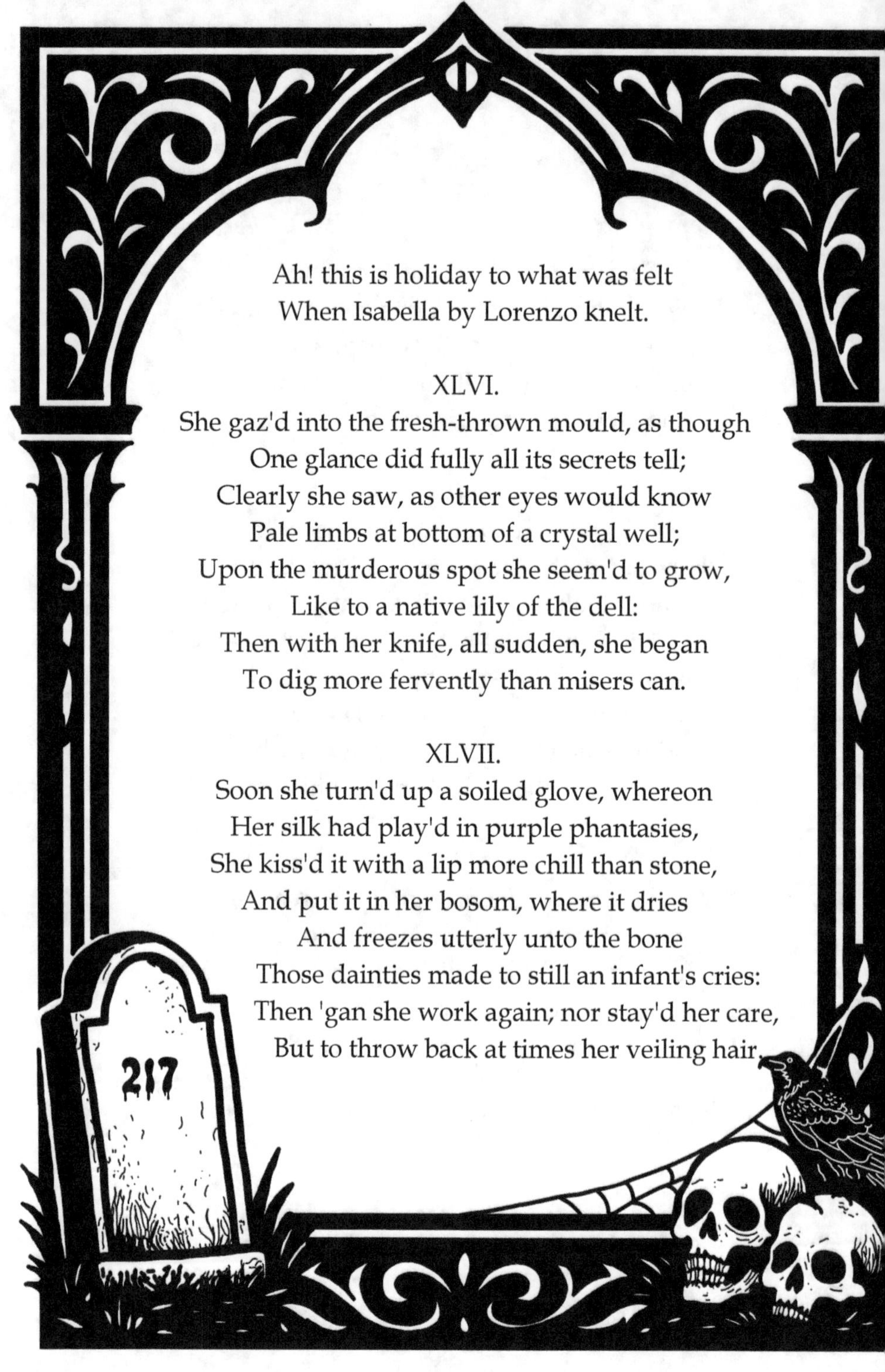

Ah! this is holiday to what was felt
When Isabella by Lorenzo knelt.

XLVI.

She gaz'd into the fresh-thrown mould, as though
One glance did fully all its secrets tell;
Clearly she saw, as other eyes would know
Pale limbs at bottom of a crystal well;
Upon the murderous spot she seem'd to grow,
Like to a native lily of the dell:
Then with her knife, all sudden, she began
To dig more fervently than misers can.

XLVII.

Soon she turn'd up a soiled glove, whereon
Her silk had play'd in purple phantasies,
She kiss'd it with a lip more chill than stone,
And put it in her bosom, where it dries
And freezes utterly unto the bone
Those dainties made to still an infant's cries:
Then 'gan she work again; nor stay'd her care,
But to throw back at times her veiling hair.

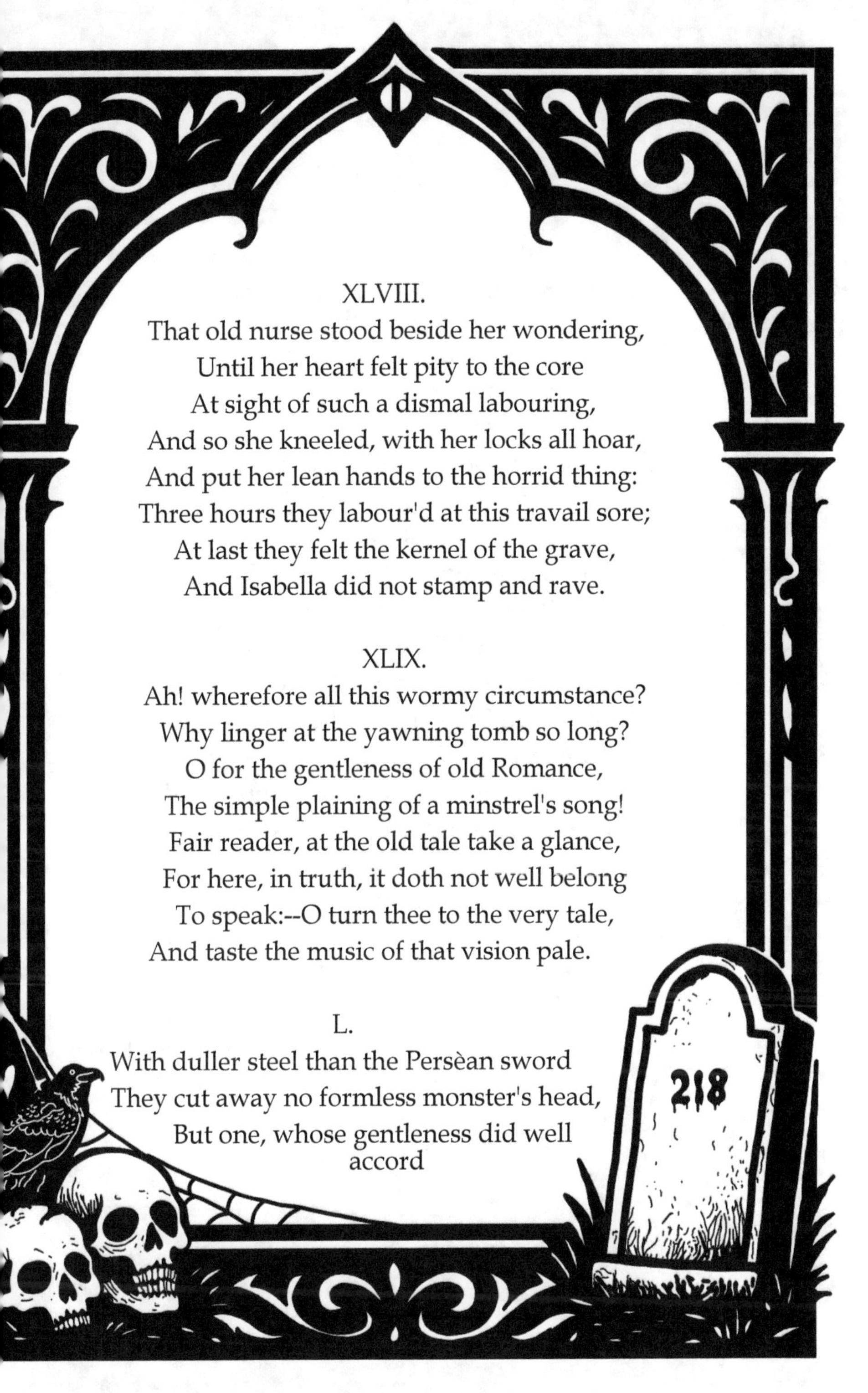

XLVIII.

That old nurse stood beside her wondering,
Until her heart felt pity to the core
At sight of such a dismal labouring,
And so she kneeled, with her locks all hoar,
And put her lean hands to the horrid thing:
Three hours they labour'd at this travail sore;
At last they felt the kernel of the grave,
And Isabella did not stamp and rave.

XLIX.

Ah! wherefore all this wormy circumstance?
Why linger at the yawning tomb so long?
O for the gentleness of old Romance,
The simple plaining of a minstrel's song!
Fair reader, at the old tale take a glance,
For here, in truth, it doth not well belong
To speak:--O turn thee to the very tale,
And taste the music of that vision pale.

L.

With duller steel than the Persèan sword
They cut away no formless monster's head,
But one, whose gentleness did well accord

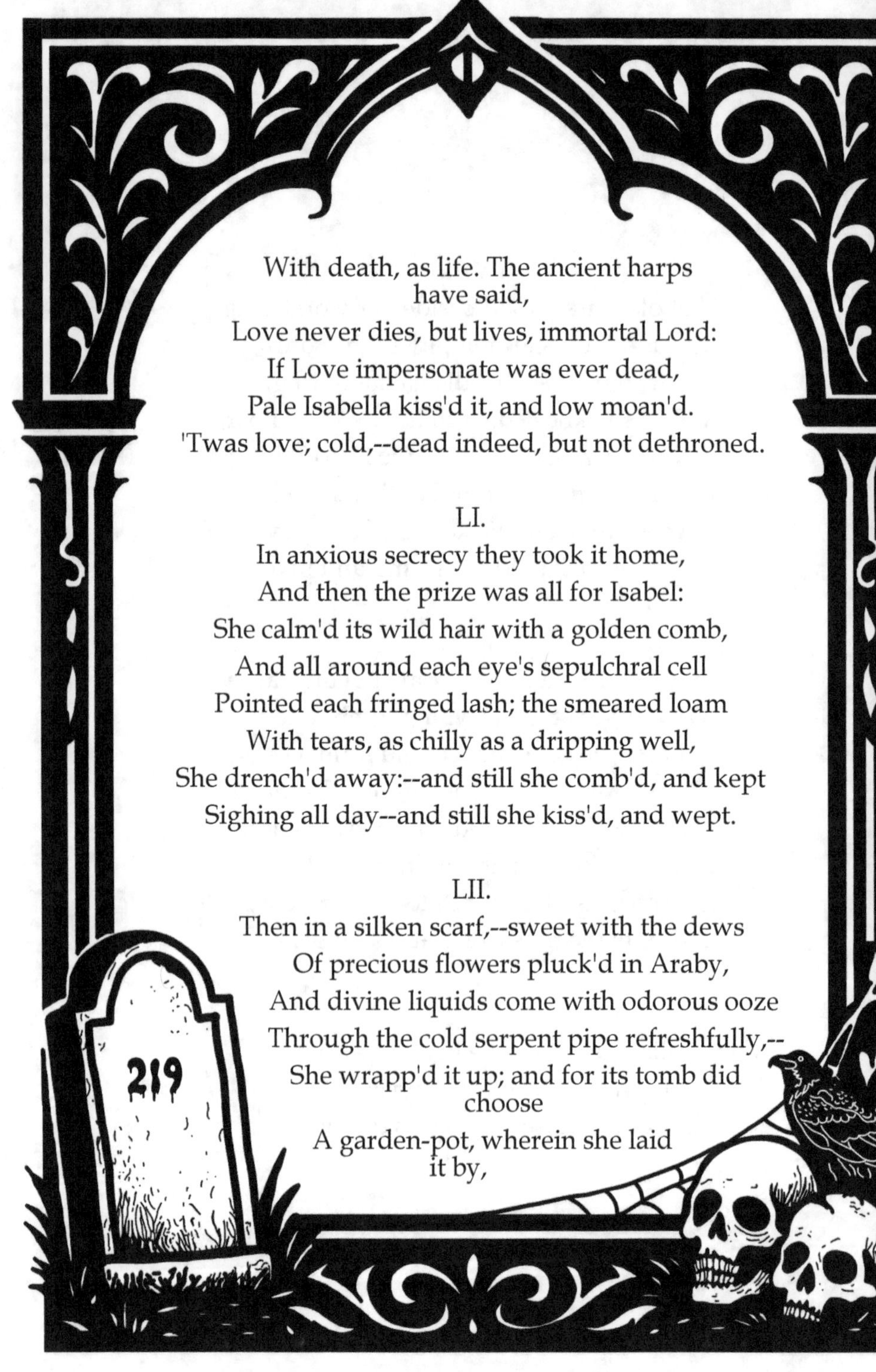

With death, as life. The ancient harps have said,
Love never dies, but lives, immortal Lord:
If Love impersonate was ever dead,
Pale Isabella kiss'd it, and low moan'd.
'Twas love; cold,--dead indeed, but not dethroned.

LI.

In anxious secrecy they took it home,
And then the prize was all for Isabel:
She calm'd its wild hair with a golden comb,
And all around each eye's sepulchral cell
Pointed each fringed lash; the smeared loam
With tears, as chilly as a dripping well,
She drench'd away:--and still she comb'd, and kept
Sighing all day--and still she kiss'd, and wept.

LII.

Then in a silken scarf,--sweet with the dews
Of precious flowers pluck'd in Araby,
And divine liquids come with odorous ooze
Through the cold serpent pipe refreshfully,--
She wrapp'd it up; and for its tomb did choose
A garden-pot, wherein she laid it by,

And cover'd it with mould, and o'er it set
Sweet Basil, which her tears kept ever wet.

LIII.

And she forgot the stars, the moon, and sun,
And she forgot the blue above the trees,
And she forgot the dells where waters run,
And she forgot the chilly autumn breeze;
She had no knowledge when the day was done,
And the new morn she saw not: but in peace
Hung over her sweet Basil evermore,
And moisten'd it with tears unto the core.

LIV.

And so she ever fed it with thin tears,
Whence thick, and green, and beautiful it grew,
So that it smelt more balmy than its peers
Of Basil-tufts in Florence; for it drew
Nurture besides, and life, from human fears,
From the fast mouldering head there shut from view:
So that the jewel, safely casketed,
Came forth, and in perfumed leafits spread.

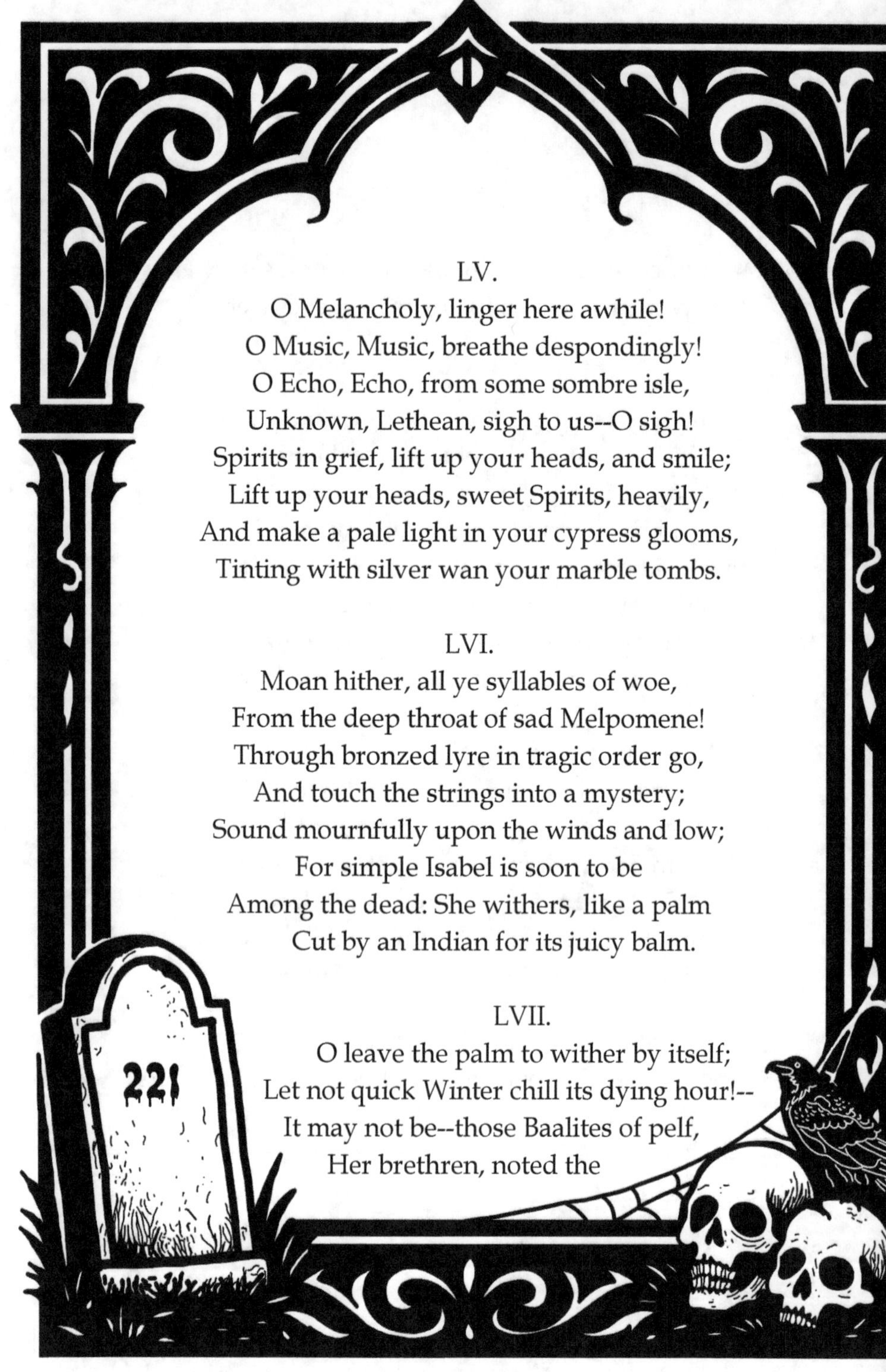

LV.

O Melancholy, linger here awhile!
O Music, Music, breathe despondingly!
O Echo, Echo, from some sombre isle,
Unknown, Lethean, sigh to us--O sigh!
Spirits in grief, lift up your heads, and smile;
Lift up your heads, sweet Spirits, heavily,
And make a pale light in your cypress glooms,
Tinting with silver wan your marble tombs.

LVI.

Moan hither, all ye syllables of woe,
From the deep throat of sad Melpomene!
Through bronzed lyre in tragic order go,
And touch the strings into a mystery;
Sound mournfully upon the winds and low;
For simple Isabel is soon to be
Among the dead: She withers, like a palm
Cut by an Indian for its juicy balm.

LVII.

O leave the palm to wither by itself;
Let not quick Winter chill its dying hour!--
It may not be--those Baalites of pelf,
Her brethren, noted the

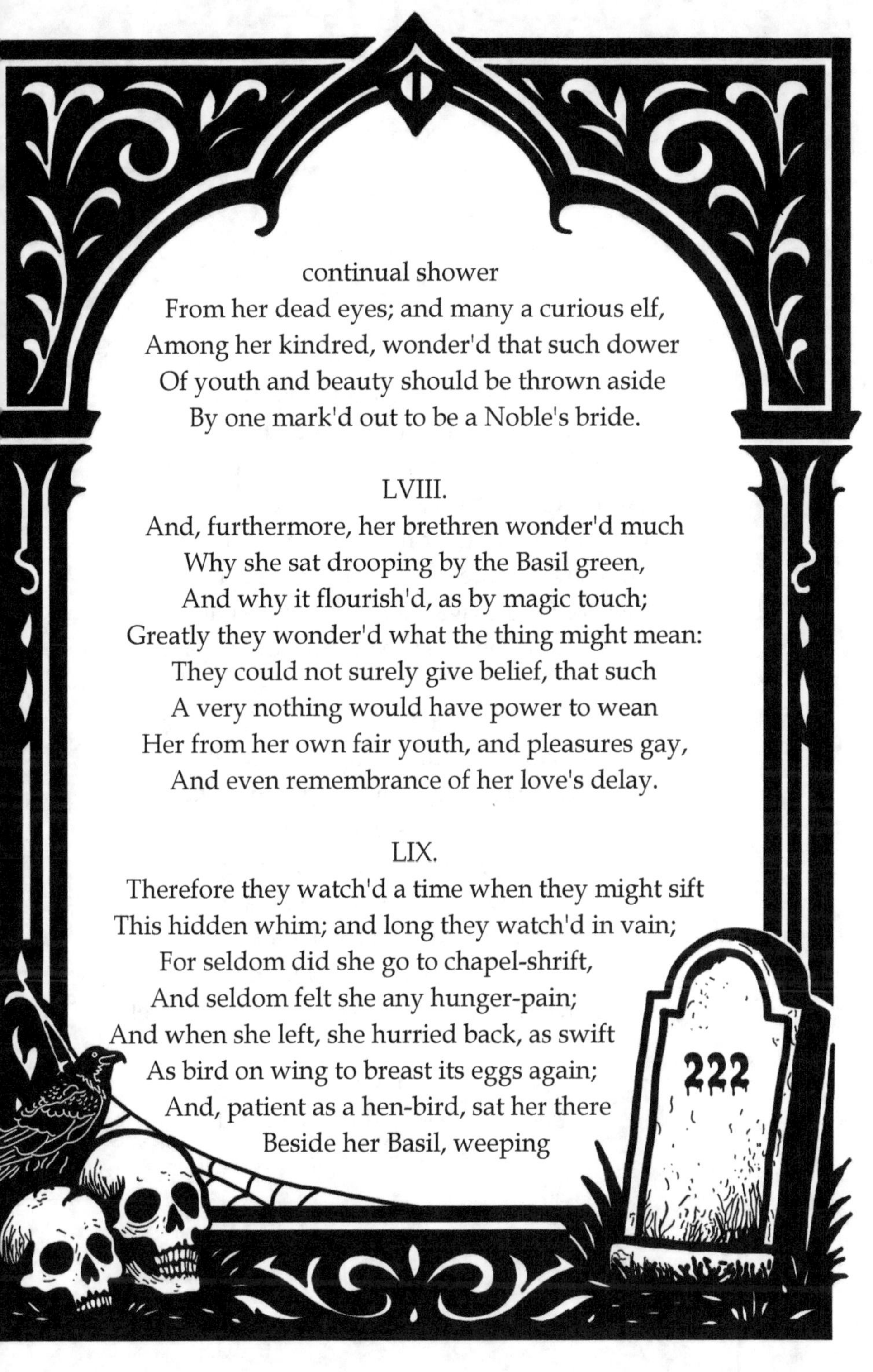

continual shower
From her dead eyes; and many a curious elf,
Among her kindred, wonder'd that such dower
Of youth and beauty should be thrown aside
By one mark'd out to be a Noble's bride.

LVIII.

And, furthermore, her brethren wonder'd much
Why she sat drooping by the Basil green,
And why it flourish'd, as by magic touch;
Greatly they wonder'd what the thing might mean:
They could not surely give belief, that such
A very nothing would have power to wean
Her from her own fair youth, and pleasures gay,
And even remembrance of her love's delay.

LIX.

Therefore they watch'd a time when they might sift
This hidden whim; and long they watch'd in vain;
For seldom did she go to chapel-shrift,
And seldom felt she any hunger-pain;
And when she left, she hurried back, as swift
As bird on wing to breast its eggs again;
And, patient as a hen-bird, sat her there
Beside her Basil, weeping

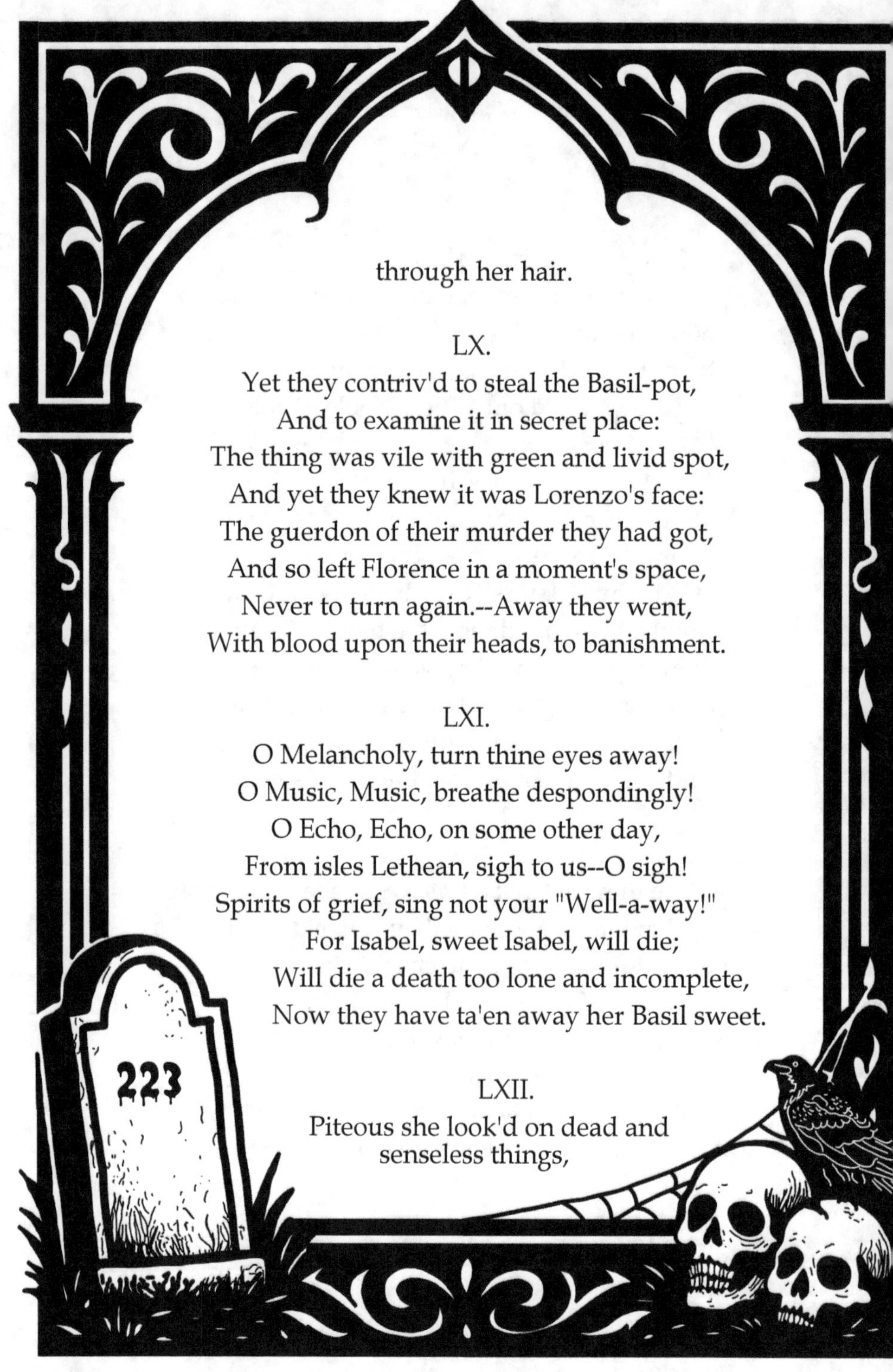

through her hair.

LX.

Yet they contriv'd to steal the Basil-pot,
And to examine it in secret place:
The thing was vile with green and livid spot,
And yet they knew it was Lorenzo's face:
The guerdon of their murder they had got,
And so left Florence in a moment's space,
Never to turn again.--Away they went,
With blood upon their heads, to banishment.

LXI.

O Melancholy, turn thine eyes away!
O Music, Music, breathe despondingly!
O Echo, Echo, on some other day,
From isles Lethean, sigh to us--O sigh!
Spirits of grief, sing not your "Well-a-way!"
For Isabel, sweet Isabel, will die;
Will die a death too lone and incomplete,
Now they have ta'en away her Basil sweet.

LXII.

Piteous she look'd on dead and senseless things,

Asking
for her lost Basil amorously:
And with melodious chuckle in the strings
Of her lorn voice, she oftentimes would cry
After the Pilgrim in his wanderings,
To ask him where her Basil was; and why
'Twas hid from her: "For cruel 'tis," said she,
"To steal my Basil-pot away from me."

LXIII.

And so she pined, and so she died forlorn,
Imploring for her Basil to the last.
No heart was there in Florence but did mourn
In pity of her love, so overcast.
And a sad ditty of this story born
From mouth to mouth through all the country pass'd:
Still is the burthen sung--"O cruelty,
"To steal my Basil-pot away from me!"

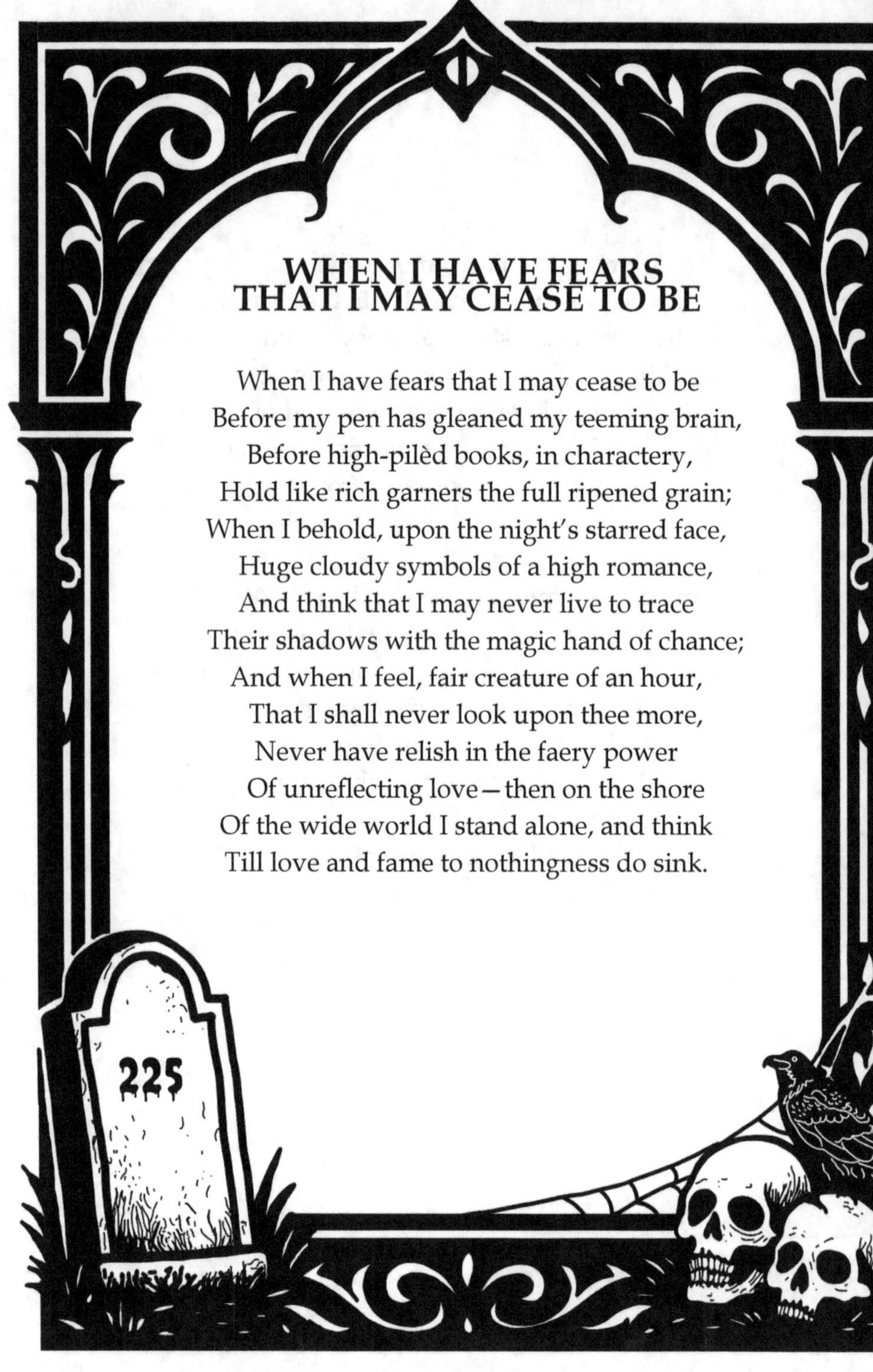

WHEN I HAVE FEARS THAT I MAY CEASE TO BE

When I have fears that I may cease to be
Before my pen has gleaned my teeming brain,
Before high-pilèd books, in charactery,
Hold like rich garners the full ripened grain;
When I behold, upon the night's starred face,
Huge cloudy symbols of a high romance,
And think that I may never live to trace
Their shadows with the magic hand of chance;
And when I feel, fair creature of an hour,
That I shall never look upon thee more,
Never have relish in the faery power
Of unreflecting love—then on the shore
Of the wide world I stand alone, and think
Till love and fame to nothingness do sink.

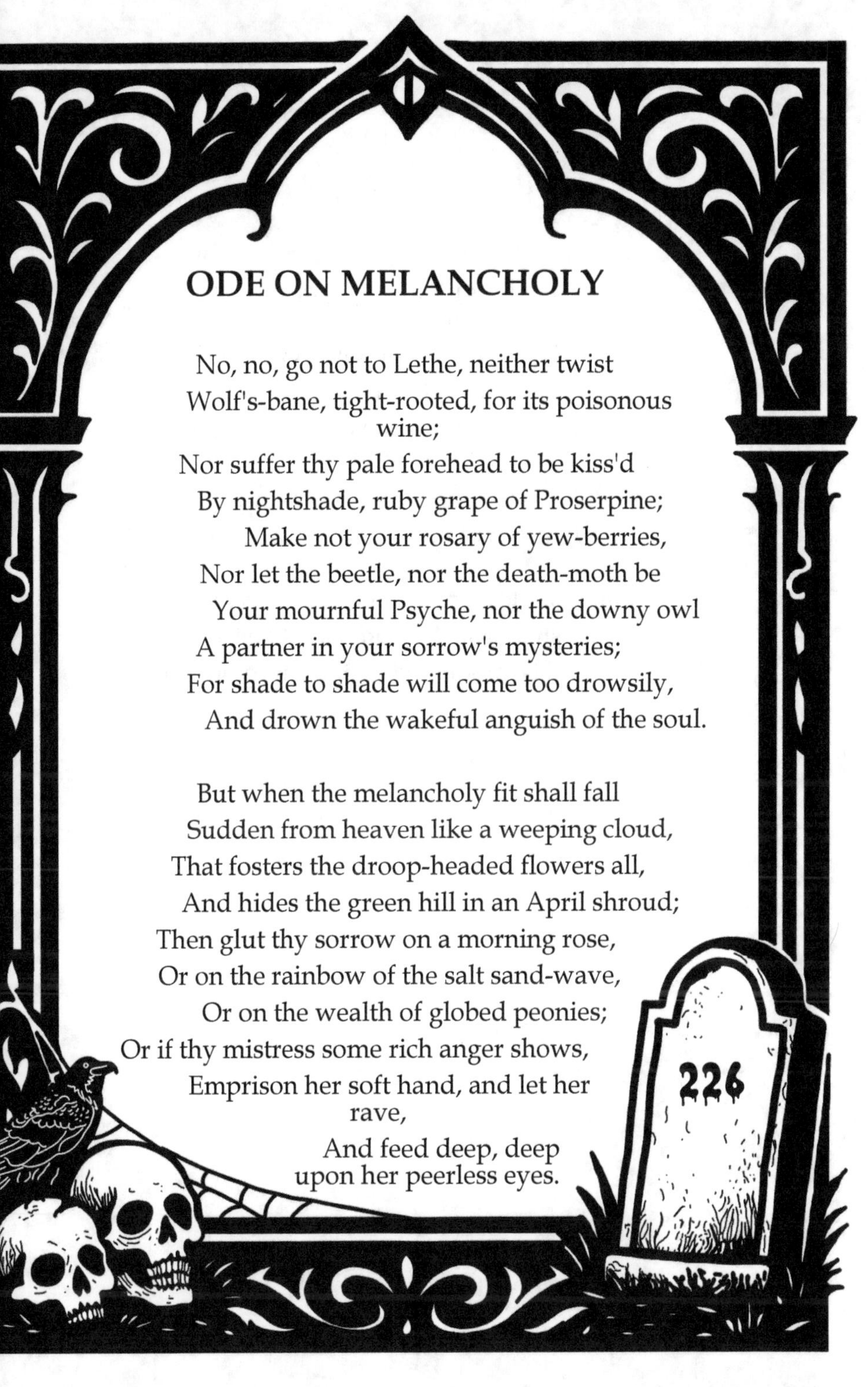

ODE ON MELANCHOLY

No, no, go not to Lethe, neither twist
Wolf's-bane, tight-rooted, for its poisonous wine;
Nor suffer thy pale forehead to be kiss'd
By nightshade, ruby grape of Proserpine;
Make not your rosary of yew-berries,
Nor let the beetle, nor the death-moth be
Your mournful Psyche, nor the downy owl
A partner in your sorrow's mysteries;
For shade to shade will come too drowsily,
And drown the wakeful anguish of the soul.

But when the melancholy fit shall fall
Sudden from heaven like a weeping cloud,
That fosters the droop-headed flowers all,
And hides the green hill in an April shroud;
Then glut thy sorrow on a morning rose,
Or on the rainbow of the salt sand-wave,
Or on the wealth of globed peonies;
Or if thy mistress some rich anger shows,
Emprison her soft hand, and let her rave,
And feed deep, deep upon her peerless eyes.

She dwells with Beauty—Beauty that must die;
And Joy, whose hand is ever at his lips
Bidding adieu; and aching Pleasure nigh,
Turning to poison while the bee-mouth sips:
Ay, in the very temple of Delight
Veil'd Melancholy has her sovran shrine,
Though seen of none save him whose strenuous tongue
Can burst Joy's grape against his palate fine;
His soul shalt taste the sadness of her might,
And be among her cloudy trophies hung.

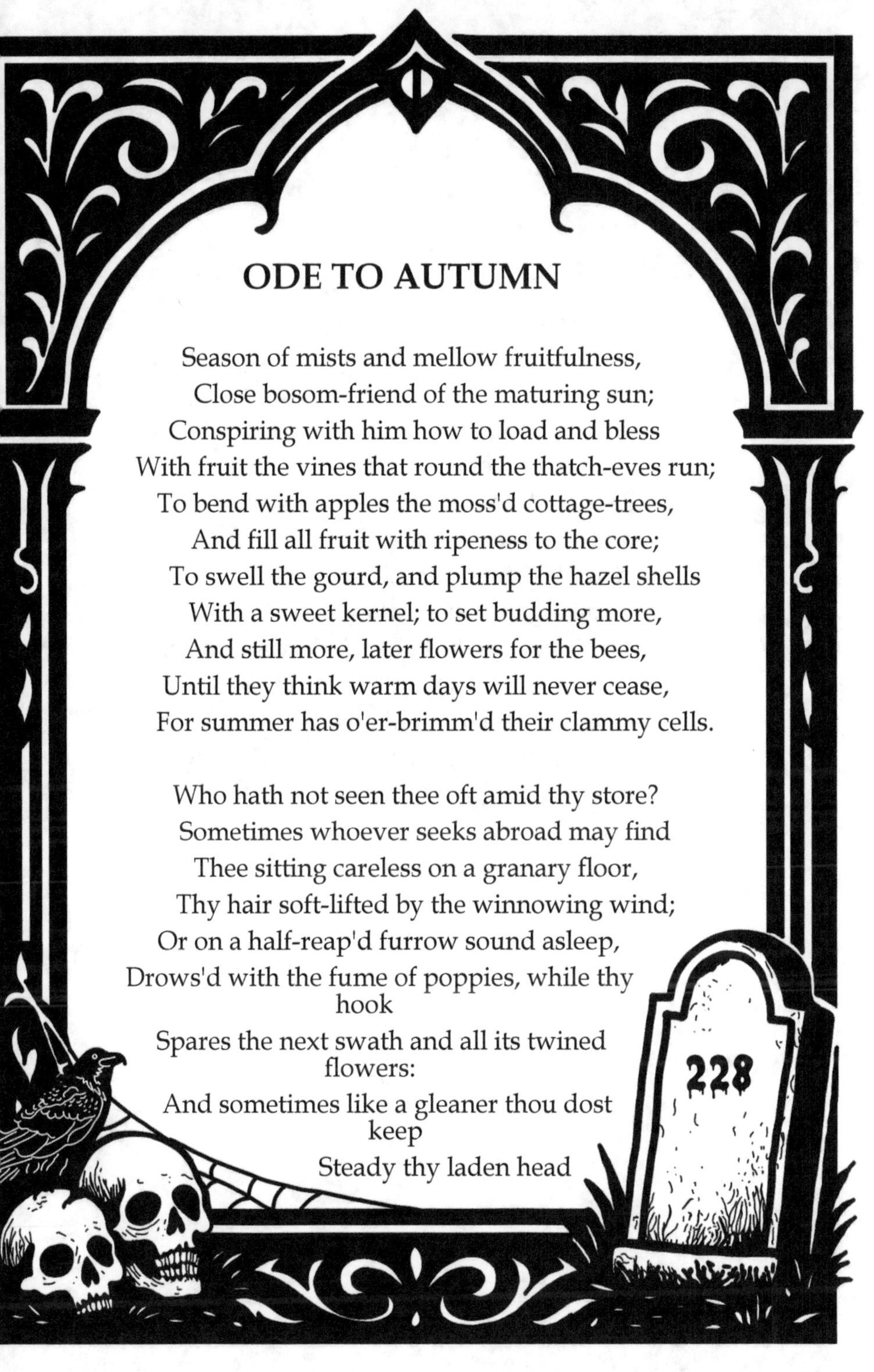

ODE TO AUTUMN

Season of mists and mellow fruitfulness,
Close bosom-friend of the maturing sun;
Conspiring with him how to load and bless
With fruit the vines that round the thatch-eves run;
To bend with apples the moss'd cottage-trees,
And fill all fruit with ripeness to the core;
To swell the gourd, and plump the hazel shells
With a sweet kernel; to set budding more,
And still more, later flowers for the bees,
Until they think warm days will never cease,
For summer has o'er-brimm'd their clammy cells.

Who hath not seen thee oft amid thy store?
Sometimes whoever seeks abroad may find
Thee sitting careless on a granary floor,
Thy hair soft-lifted by the winnowing wind;
Or on a half-reap'd furrow sound asleep,
Drows'd with the fume of poppies, while thy hook
Spares the next swath and all its twined flowers:
And sometimes like a gleaner thou dost keep
Steady thy laden head

across a brook;
Or by a cyder-press, with patient look,
Thou watchest the last oozings hours by hours.

Where are the songs of spring? Ay, Where are they?
Think not of them, thou hast thy music too,—
While barred clouds bloomthe soft-dying day,
And touch the stubble-plains with rosy hue;
Then in a wailful choir the small gnats mourn
Among the river sallows, borne aloft
Or sinking as the light wind lives or dies;
And full-grown lambs loud bleat from hilly bourn;
Hedge-crickets sing; and now with treble soft
The red-breast whistles from a garden-croft;
And gathering swallows twitter in the skies.

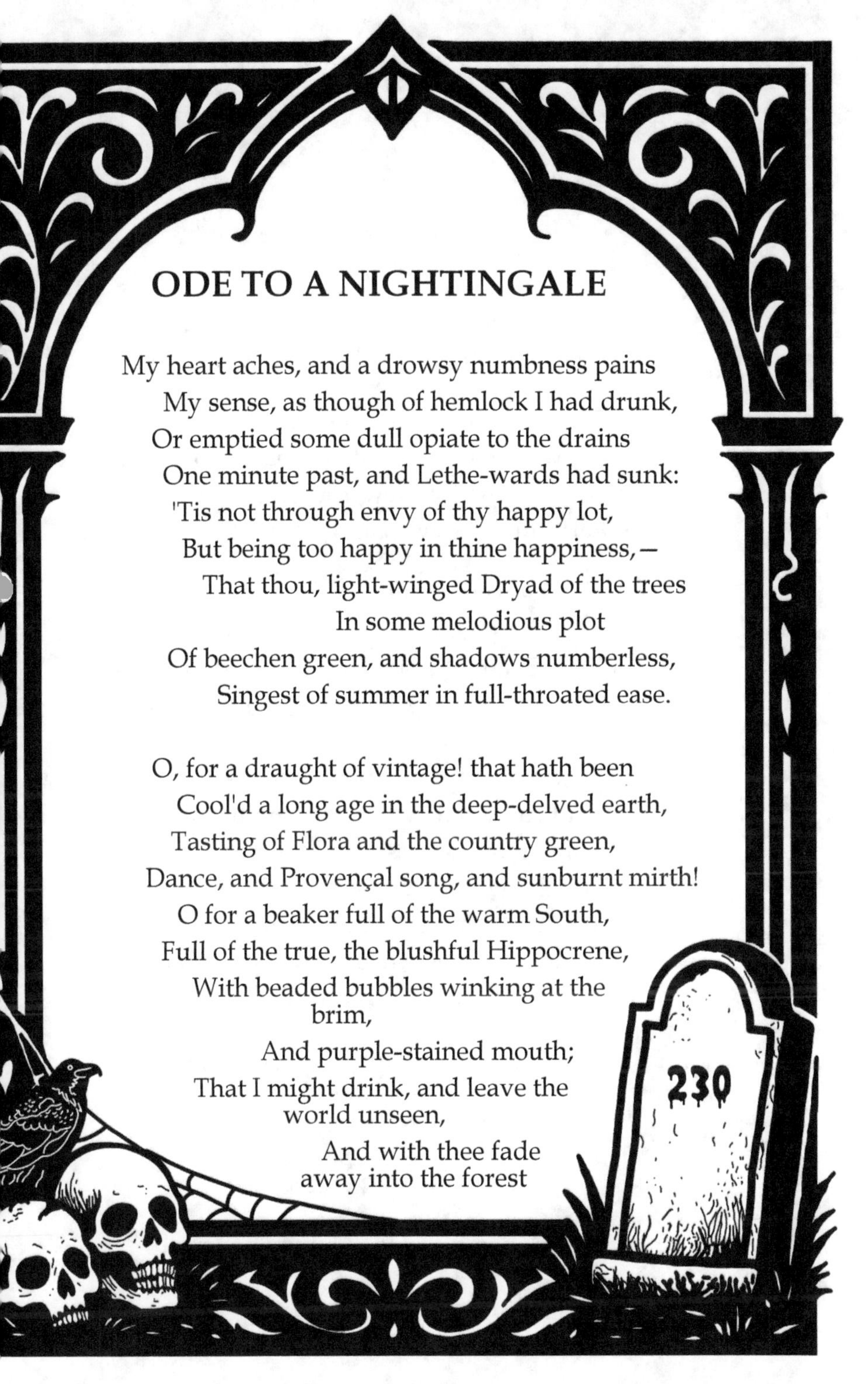

ODE TO A NIGHTINGALE

My heart aches, and a drowsy numbness pains
My sense, as though of hemlock I had drunk,
Or emptied some dull opiate to the drains
One minute past, and Lethe-wards had sunk:
'Tis not through envy of thy happy lot,
But being too happy in thine happiness, –
That thou, light-winged Dryad of the trees
In some melodious plot
Of beechen green, and shadows numberless,
Singest of summer in full-throated ease.

O, for a draught of vintage! that hath been
Cool'd a long age in the deep-delved earth,
Tasting of Flora and the country green,
Dance, and Provençal song, and sunburnt mirth!
O for a beaker full of the warm South,
Full of the true, the blushful Hippocrene,
With beaded bubbles winking at the brim,
And purple-stained mouth;
That I might drink, and leave the world unseen,
And with thee fade away into the forest

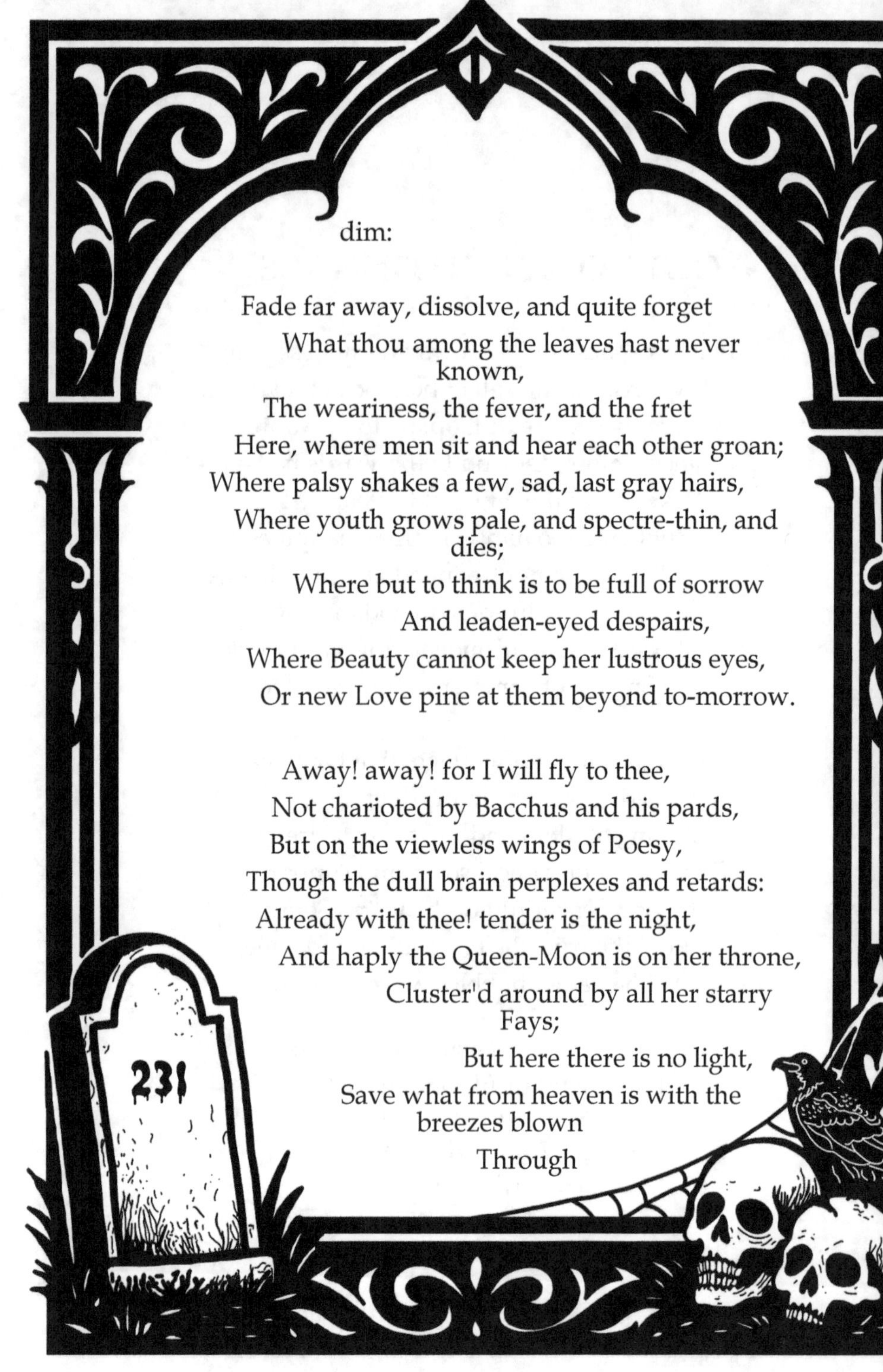

dim:

Fade far away, dissolve, and quite forget
What thou among the leaves hast never known,
The weariness, the fever, and the fret
Here, where men sit and hear each other groan;
Where palsy shakes a few, sad, last gray hairs,
Where youth grows pale, and spectre-thin, and dies;
Where but to think is to be full of sorrow
And leaden-eyed despairs,
Where Beauty cannot keep her lustrous eyes,
Or new Love pine at them beyond to-morrow.

Away! away! for I will fly to thee,
Not charioted by Bacchus and his pards,
But on the viewless wings of Poesy,
Though the dull brain perplexes and retards:
Already with thee! tender is the night,
And haply the Queen-Moon is on her throne,
Cluster'd around by all her starry Fays;
But here there is no light,
Save what from heaven is with the breezes blown
Through

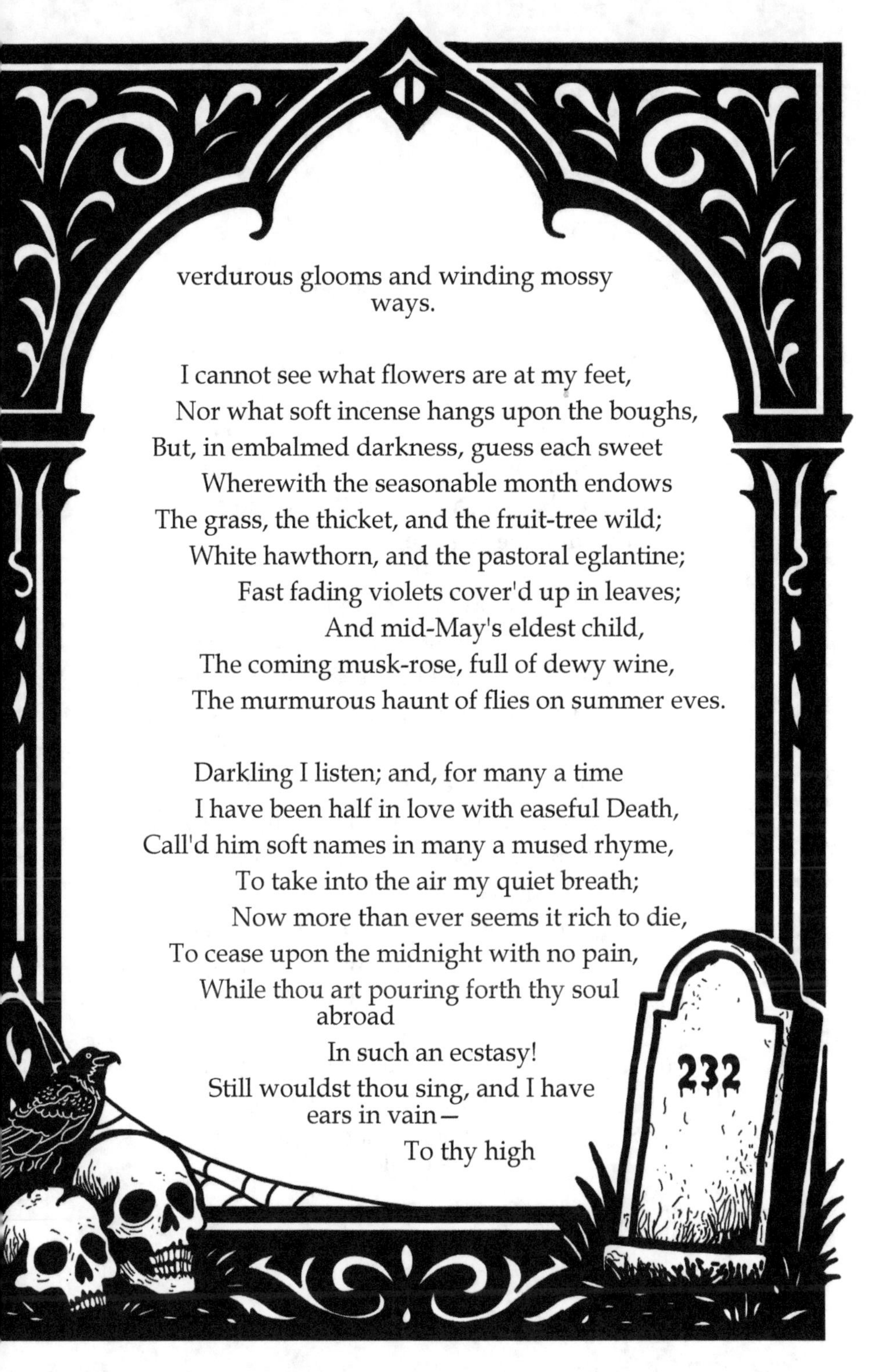

verdurous glooms and winding mossy ways.

I cannot see what flowers are at my feet,
Nor what soft incense hangs upon the boughs,
But, in embalmed darkness, guess each sweet
Wherewith the seasonable month endows
The grass, the thicket, and the fruit-tree wild;
White hawthorn, and the pastoral eglantine;
Fast fading violets cover'd up in leaves;
And mid-May's eldest child,
The coming musk-rose, full of dewy wine,
The murmurous haunt of flies on summer eves.

Darkling I listen; and, for many a time
I have been half in love with easeful Death,
Call'd him soft names in many a mused rhyme,
To take into the air my quiet breath;
Now more than ever seems it rich to die,
To cease upon the midnight with no pain,
While thou art pouring forth thy soul abroad
In such an ecstasy!
Still wouldst thou sing, and I have ears in vain—
To thy high

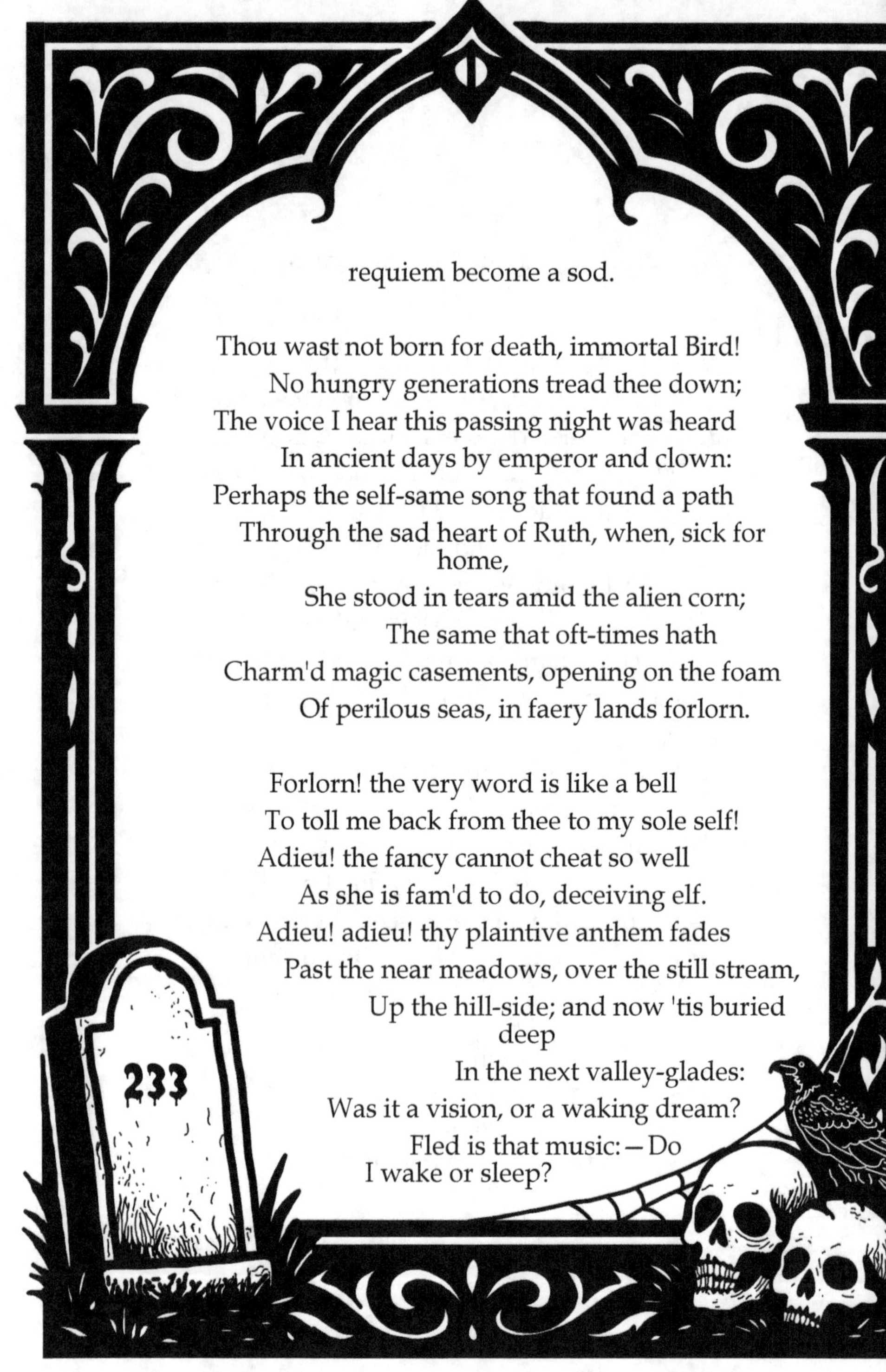

requiem become a sod.

Thou wast not born for death, immortal Bird!
No hungry generations tread thee down;
The voice I hear this passing night was heard
In ancient days by emperor and clown:
Perhaps the self-same song that found a path
Through the sad heart of Ruth, when, sick for home,
She stood in tears amid the alien corn;
The same that oft-times hath
Charm'd magic casements, opening on the foam
Of perilous seas, in faery lands forlorn.

Forlorn! the very word is like a bell
To toll me back from thee to my sole self!
Adieu! the fancy cannot cheat so well
As she is fam'd to do, deceiving elf.
Adieu! adieu! thy plaintive anthem fades
Past the near meadows, over the still stream,
Up the hill-side; and now 'tis buried deep
In the next valley-glades:
Was it a vision, or a waking dream?
Fled is that music:—Do I wake or sleep?

Henry Wadsworth Longfellow

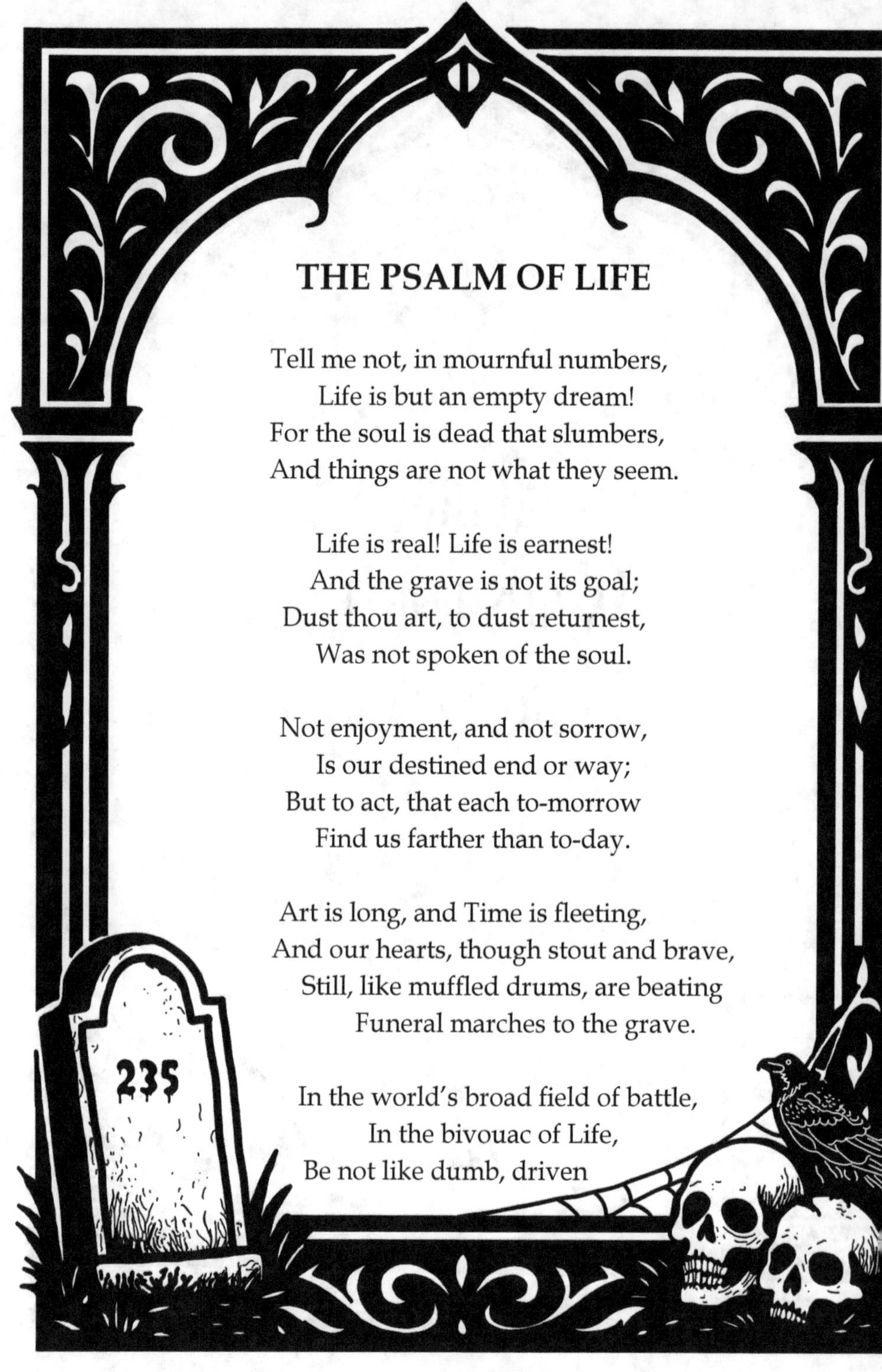

THE PSALM OF LIFE

Tell me not, in mournful numbers,
Life is but an empty dream!
For the soul is dead that slumbers,
And things are not what they seem.

Life is real! Life is earnest!
And the grave is not its goal;
Dust thou art, to dust returnest,
Was not spoken of the soul.

Not enjoyment, and not sorrow,
Is our destined end or way;
But to act, that each to-morrow
Find us farther than to-day.

Art is long, and Time is fleeting,
And our hearts, though stout and brave,
Still, like muffled drums, are beating
Funeral marches to the grave.

In the world's broad field of battle,
In the bivouac of Life,
Be not like dumb, driven

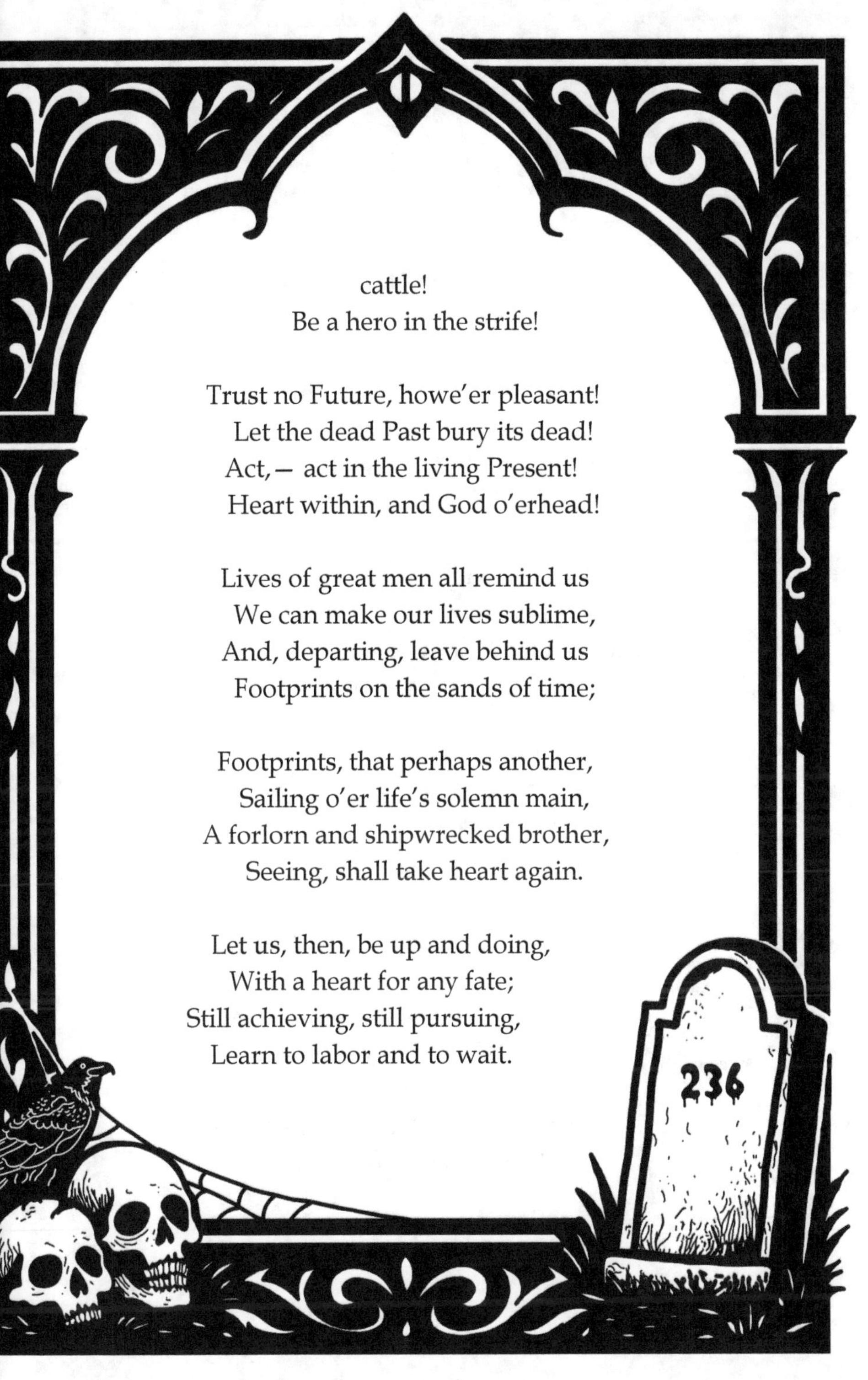

cattle!
Be a hero in the strife!

Trust no Future, howe'er pleasant!
Let the dead Past bury its dead!
Act,— act in the living Present!
Heart within, and God o'erhead!

Lives of great men all remind us
We can make our lives sublime,
And, departing, leave behind us
Footprints on the sands of time;

Footprints, that perhaps another,
Sailing o'er life's solemn main,
A forlorn and shipwrecked brother,
Seeing, shall take heart again.

Let us, then, be up and doing,
With a heart for any fate;
Still achieving, still pursuing,
Learn to labor and to wait.

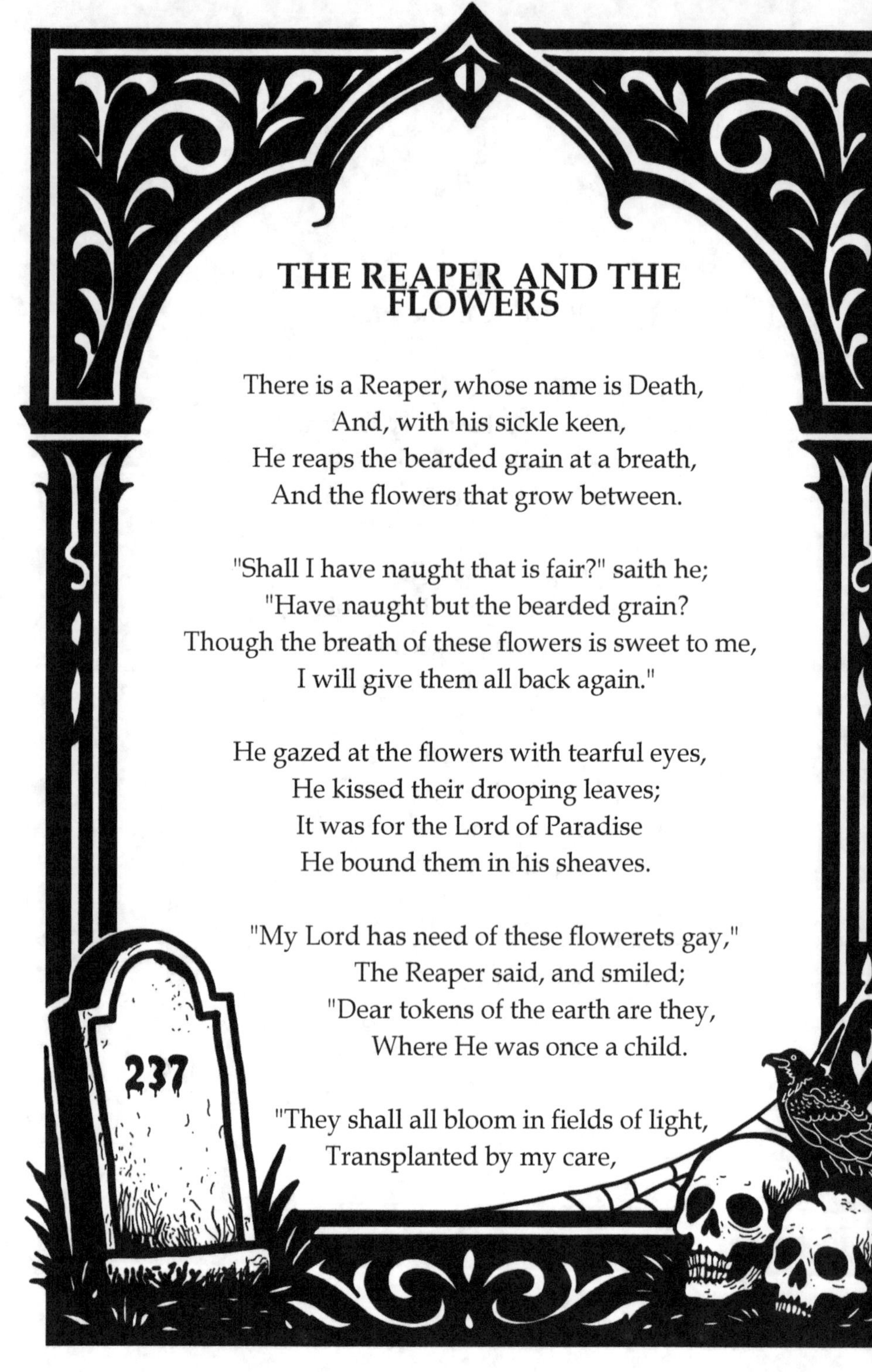

THE REAPER AND THE FLOWERS

There is a Reaper, whose name is Death,
And, with his sickle keen,
He reaps the bearded grain at a breath,
And the flowers that grow between.

"Shall I have naught that is fair?" saith he;
"Have naught but the bearded grain?
Though the breath of these flowers is sweet to me,
I will give them all back again."

He gazed at the flowers with tearful eyes,
He kissed their drooping leaves;
It was for the Lord of Paradise
He bound them in his sheaves.

"My Lord has need of these flowerets gay,"
The Reaper said, and smiled;
"Dear tokens of the earth are they,
Where He was once a child.

"They shall all bloom in fields of light,
Transplanted by my care,

And saints, upon their garments white,
These sacred blossoms wear."

And the mother gave, in tears and pain,
The flowers she most did love;
She knew she should find them all again
In the fields of light above.

Oh, not in cruelty, not in wrath,
The Reaper came that day;
'T was an angel visited the green earth,
And took the flowers away.

THE VILLAGE BLACKSMITH

Under a spreading chestnut-tree
The village smithy stands;
The smith, a mighty man is he,
With large and sinewy hands,
And the muscles of his brawny arms
Are strong as iron bands.

His hair is crisp, and black, and long;
His face is like the tan;
His brow is wet with honest sweat,
He earns whate'er he can,
And looks the whole world in the face,
For he owes not any man.

Week in, week out, from morn till night,
You can hear his bellows blow;
You can hear him swing his heavy sledge,
With measured beat and slow,
Like a sexton ringing the village bell,
When the evening sun is low.

And children coming home

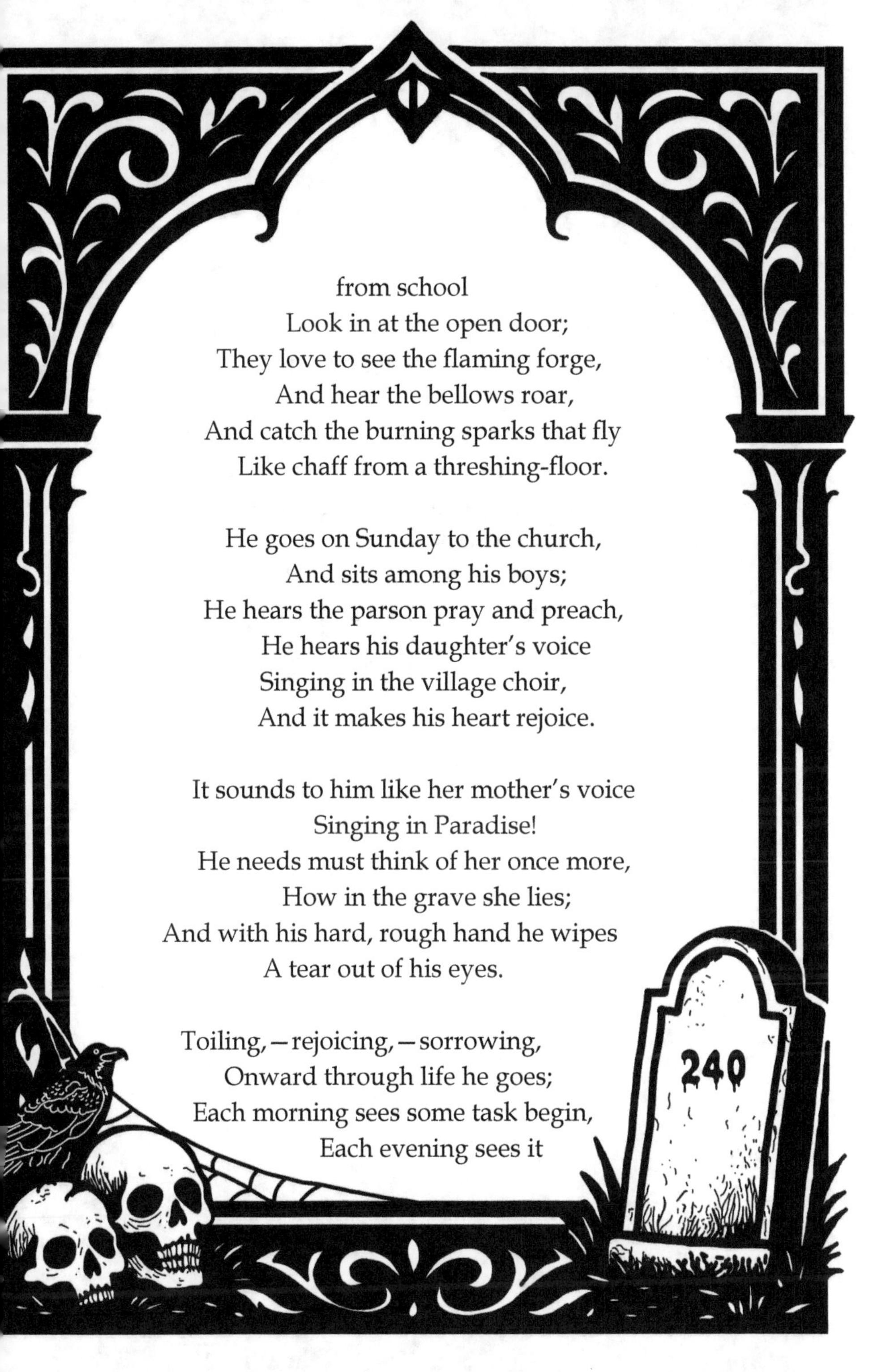

from school
Look in at the open door;
They love to see the flaming forge,
And hear the bellows roar,
And catch the burning sparks that fly
Like chaff from a threshing-floor.

He goes on Sunday to the church,
And sits among his boys;
He hears the parson pray and preach,
He hears his daughter's voice
Singing in the village choir,
And it makes his heart rejoice.

It sounds to him like her mother's voice
Singing in Paradise!
He needs must think of her once more,
How in the grave she lies;
And with his hard, rough hand he wipes
A tear out of his eyes.

Toiling,—rejoicing,—sorrowing,
Onward through life he goes;
Each morning sees some task begin,
Each evening sees it

close;
Something attempted, something done,
Has earned a night's repose.

Thanks, thanks to thee, my worthy friend,
For the lesson thou hast taught!
Thus at the flaming forge of life
Our fortunes must be wrought;
Thus on its sounding anvil shaped
Each burning deed and thought

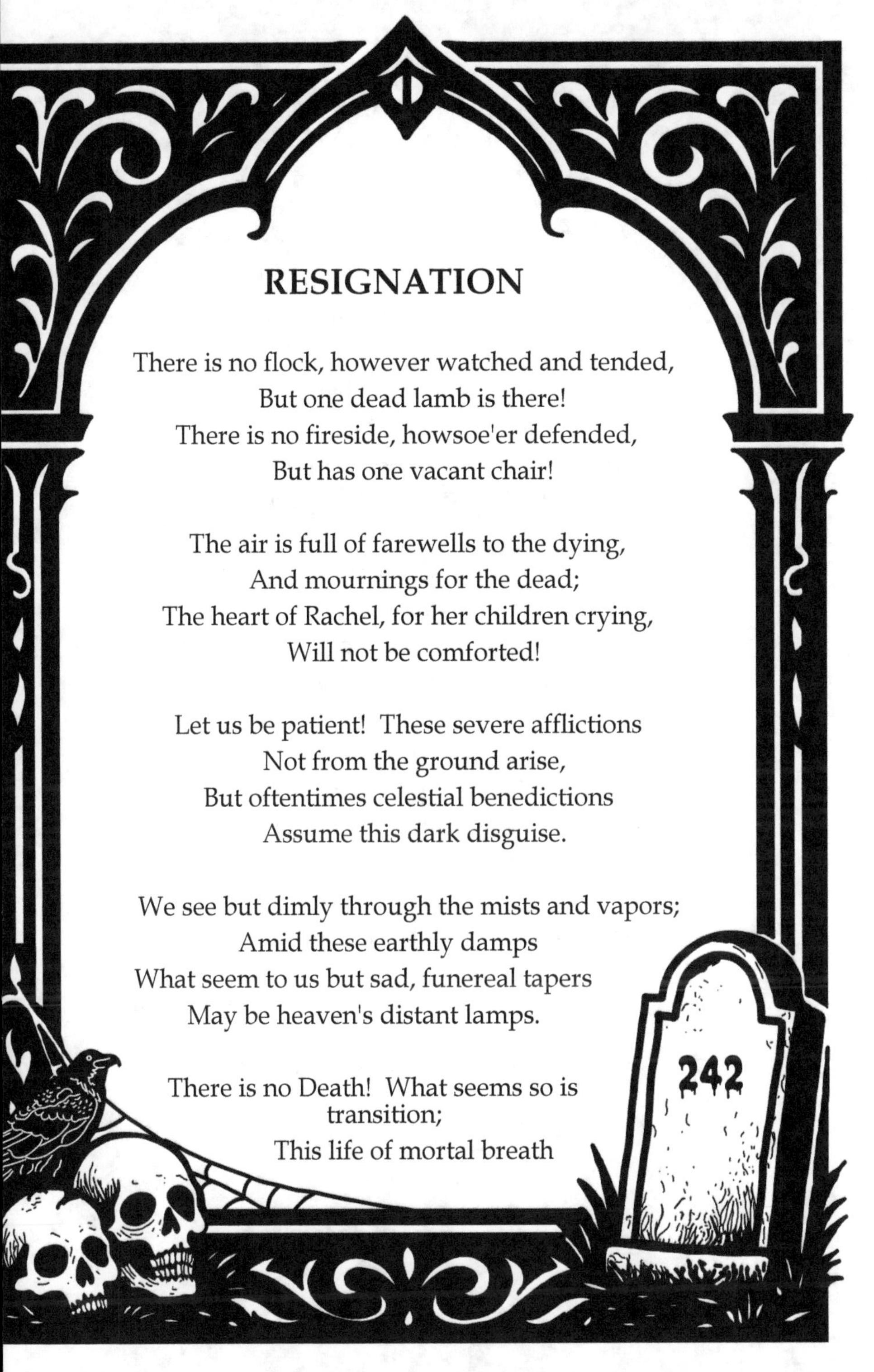

RESIGNATION

There is no flock, however watched and tended,
But one dead lamb is there!
There is no fireside, howsoe'er defended,
But has one vacant chair!

The air is full of farewells to the dying,
And mournings for the dead;
The heart of Rachel, for her children crying,
Will not be comforted!

Let us be patient! These severe afflictions
Not from the ground arise,
But oftentimes celestial benedictions
Assume this dark disguise.

We see but dimly through the mists and vapors;
Amid these earthly damps
What seem to us but sad, funereal tapers
May be heaven's distant lamps.

There is no Death! What seems so is transition;
This life of mortal breath

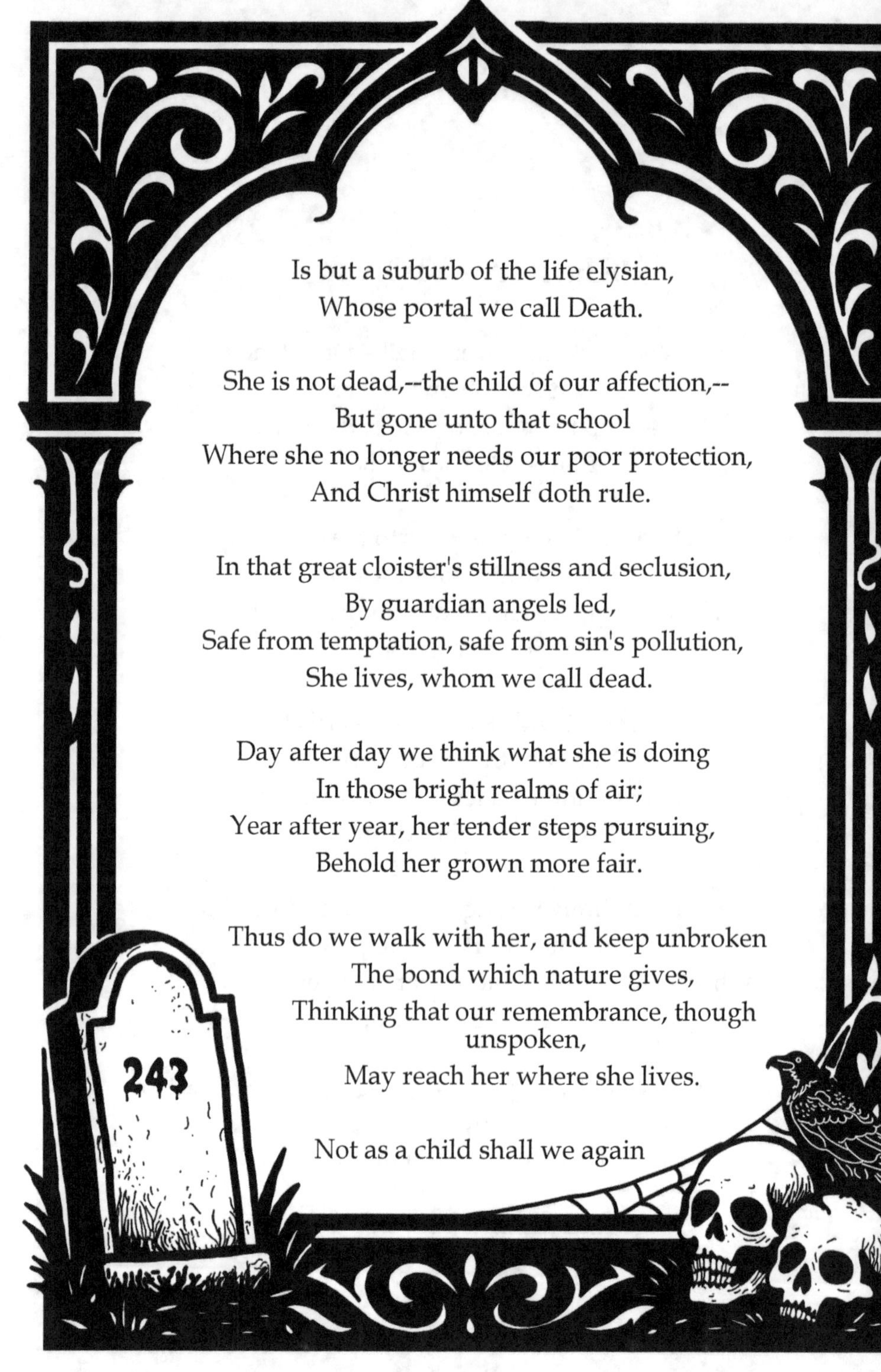

Is but a suburb of the life elysian,
Whose portal we call Death.

She is not dead,--the child of our affection,--
But gone unto that school
Where she no longer needs our poor protection,
And Christ himself doth rule.

In that great cloister's stillness and seclusion,
By guardian angels led,
Safe from temptation, safe from sin's pollution,
She lives, whom we call dead.

Day after day we think what she is doing
In those bright realms of air;
Year after year, her tender steps pursuing,
Behold her grown more fair.

Thus do we walk with her, and keep unbroken
The bond which nature gives,
Thinking that our remembrance, though unspoken,
May reach her where she lives.

Not as a child shall we again

behold her;
For when with raptures wild
In our embraces we again enfold her,
She will not be a child;

But a fair maiden, in her Father's mansion,
Clothed with celestial grace;
And beautiful with all the soul's expansion
Shall we behold her face.

And though at times impetuous with emotion
And anguish long suppressed,
The swelling heart heaves moaning like the ocean,
That cannot be at rest,--

We will be patient, and assuage the feeling
We may not wholly stay;
By silence sanctifying, not concealing,
The grief that must have way.

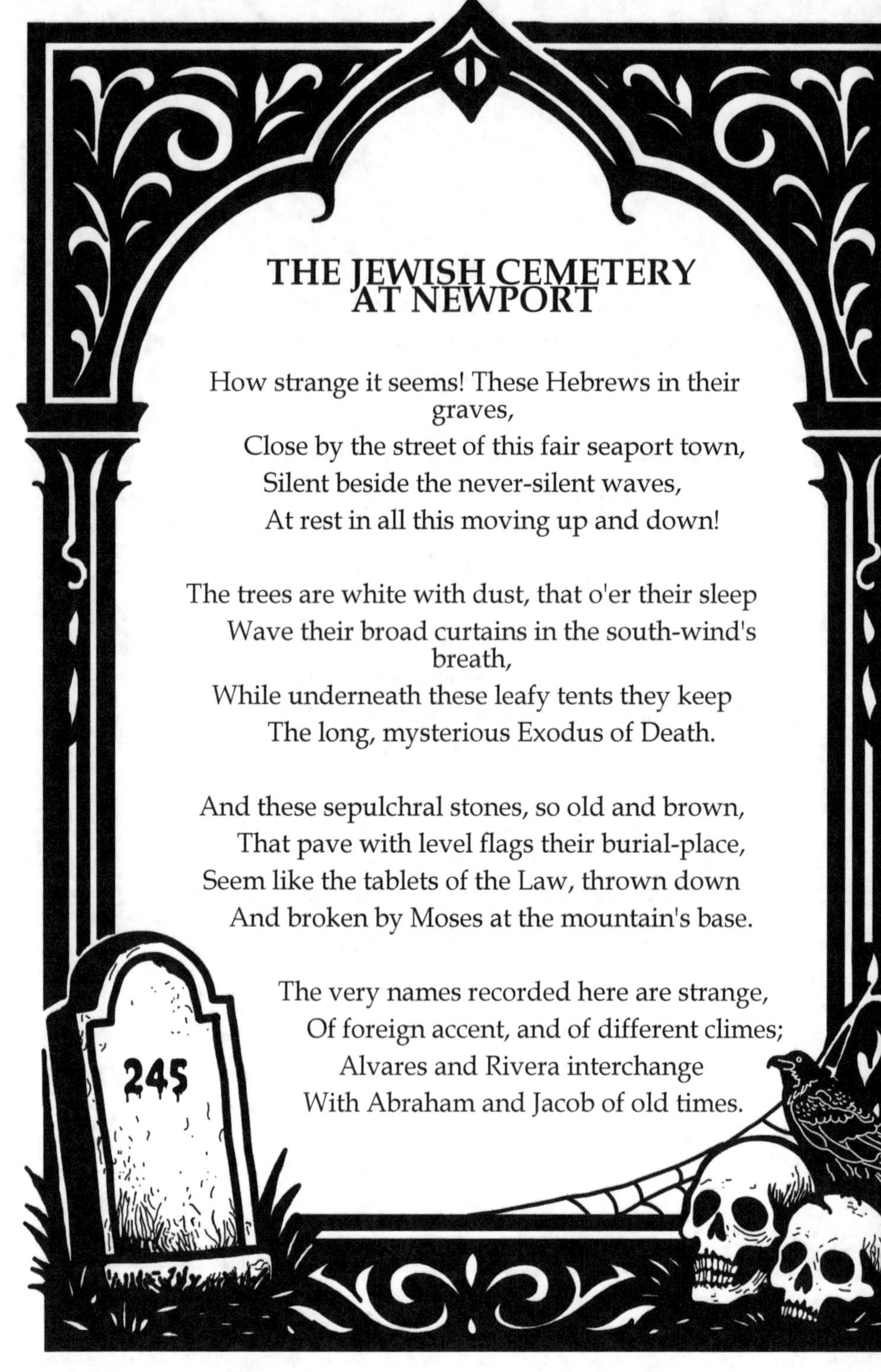

THE JEWISH CEMETERY AT NEWPORT

How strange it seems! These Hebrews in their graves,
Close by the street of this fair seaport town,
Silent beside the never-silent waves,
At rest in all this moving up and down!

The trees are white with dust, that o'er their sleep
Wave their broad curtains in the south-wind's breath,
While underneath these leafy tents they keep
The long, mysterious Exodus of Death.

And these sepulchral stones, so old and brown,
That pave with level flags their burial-place,
Seem like the tablets of the Law, thrown down
And broken by Moses at the mountain's base.

The very names recorded here are strange,
Of foreign accent, and of different climes;
Alvares and Rivera interchange
With Abraham and Jacob of old times.

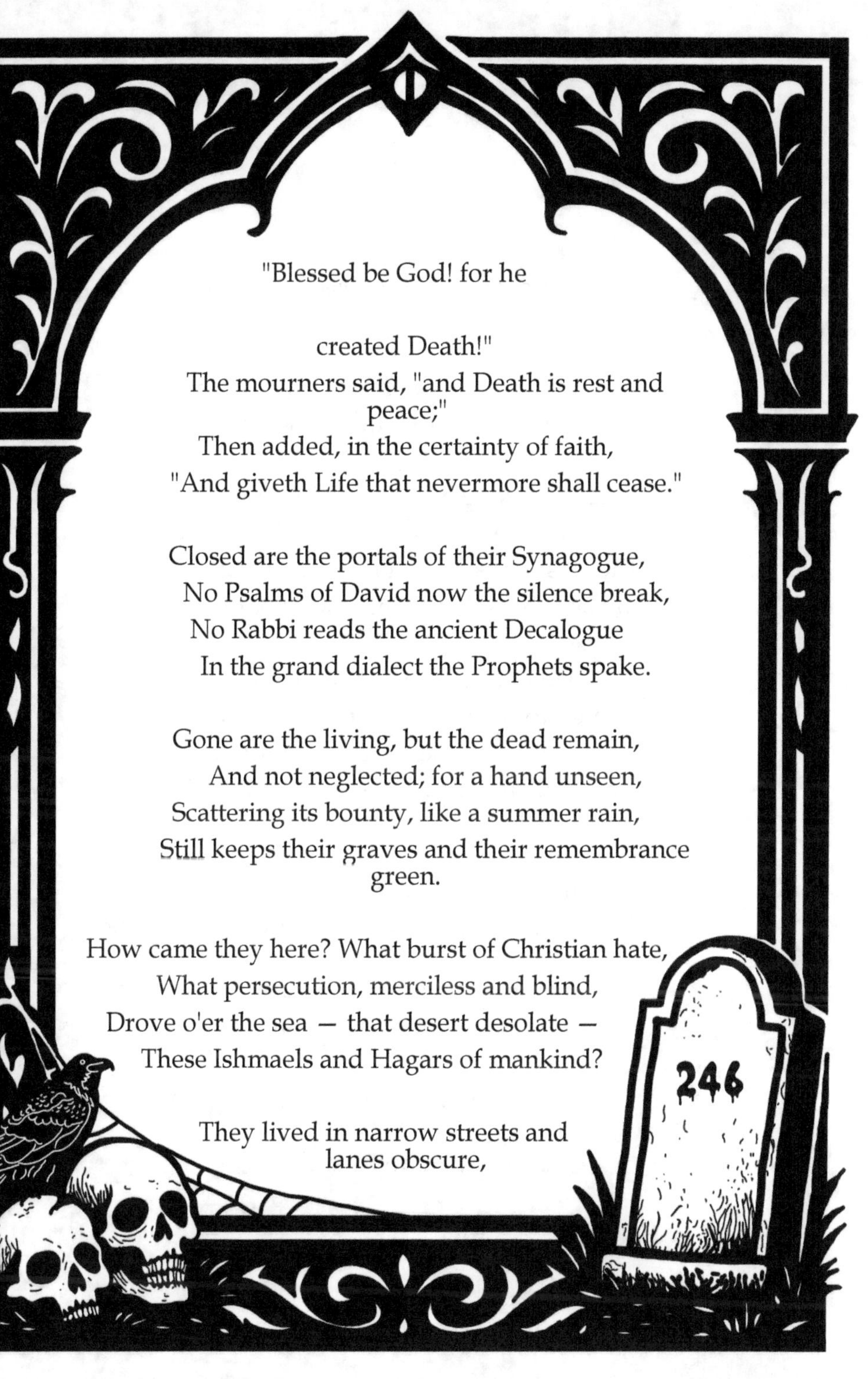

"Blessed be God! for he

created Death!"
The mourners said, "and Death is rest and peace;"
Then added, in the certainty of faith,
"And giveth Life that nevermore shall cease."

Closed are the portals of their Synagogue,
No Psalms of David now the silence break,
No Rabbi reads the ancient Decalogue
In the grand dialect the Prophets spake.

Gone are the living, but the dead remain,
And not neglected; for a hand unseen,
Scattering its bounty, like a summer rain,
Still keeps their graves and their remembrance green.

How came they here? What burst of Christian hate,
What persecution, merciless and blind,
Drove o'er the sea — that desert desolate —
These Ishmaels and Hagars of mankind?

They lived in narrow streets and lanes obscure,

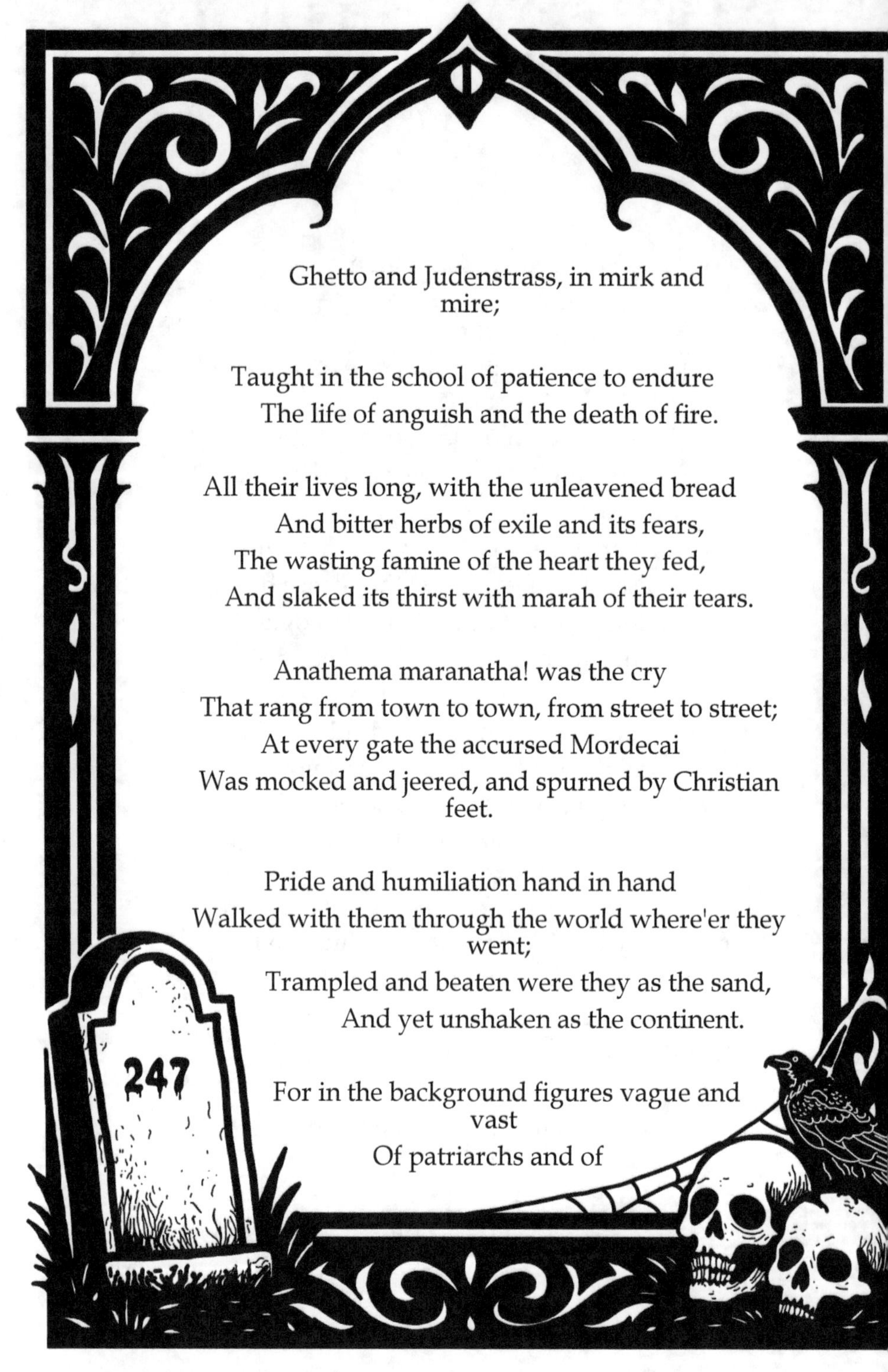

Ghetto and Judenstrass, in mirk and mire;

Taught in the school of patience to endure
The life of anguish and the death of fire.

All their lives long, with the unleavened bread
And bitter herbs of exile and its fears,
The wasting famine of the heart they fed,
And slaked its thirst with marah of their tears.

Anathema maranatha! was the cry
That rang from town to town, from street to street;
At every gate the accursed Mordecai
Was mocked and jeered, and spurned by Christian feet.

Pride and humiliation hand in hand
Walked with them through the world where'er they went;
Trampled and beaten were they as the sand,
And yet unshaken as the continent.

For in the background figures vague and vast
Of patriarchs and of

prophets rose sublime,
And all the great traditions of the Past
They saw reflected in the

coming time.

And thus forever with reverted look
The mystic volume of the world they read,
Spelling it backward, like a Hebrew book,
Till life became a Legend of the Dead.

But ah! what once has been shall be no more!
The groaning earth in travail and in pain
Brings forth its races, but does not restore,
And the dead nations never rise again.

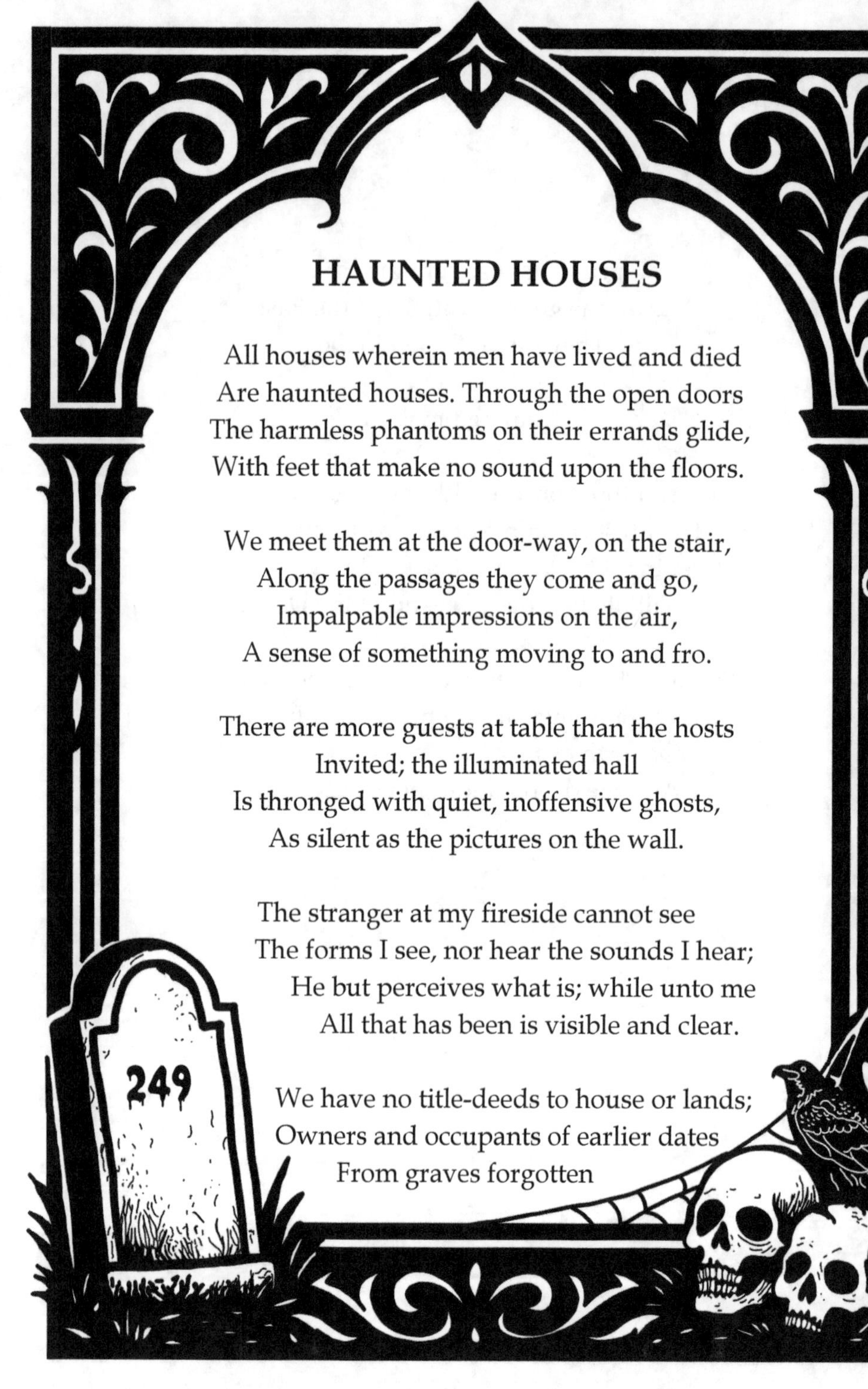

HAUNTED HOUSES

All houses wherein men have lived and died
Are haunted houses. Through the open doors
The harmless phantoms on their errands glide,
With feet that make no sound upon the floors.

We meet them at the door-way, on the stair,
Along the passages they come and go,
Impalpable impressions on the air,
A sense of something moving to and fro.

There are more guests at table than the hosts
Invited; the illuminated hall
Is thronged with quiet, inoffensive ghosts,
As silent as the pictures on the wall.

The stranger at my fireside cannot see
The forms I see, nor hear the sounds I hear;
He but perceives what is; while unto me
All that has been is visible and clear.

We have no title-deeds to house or lands;
Owners and occupants of earlier dates
From graves forgotten

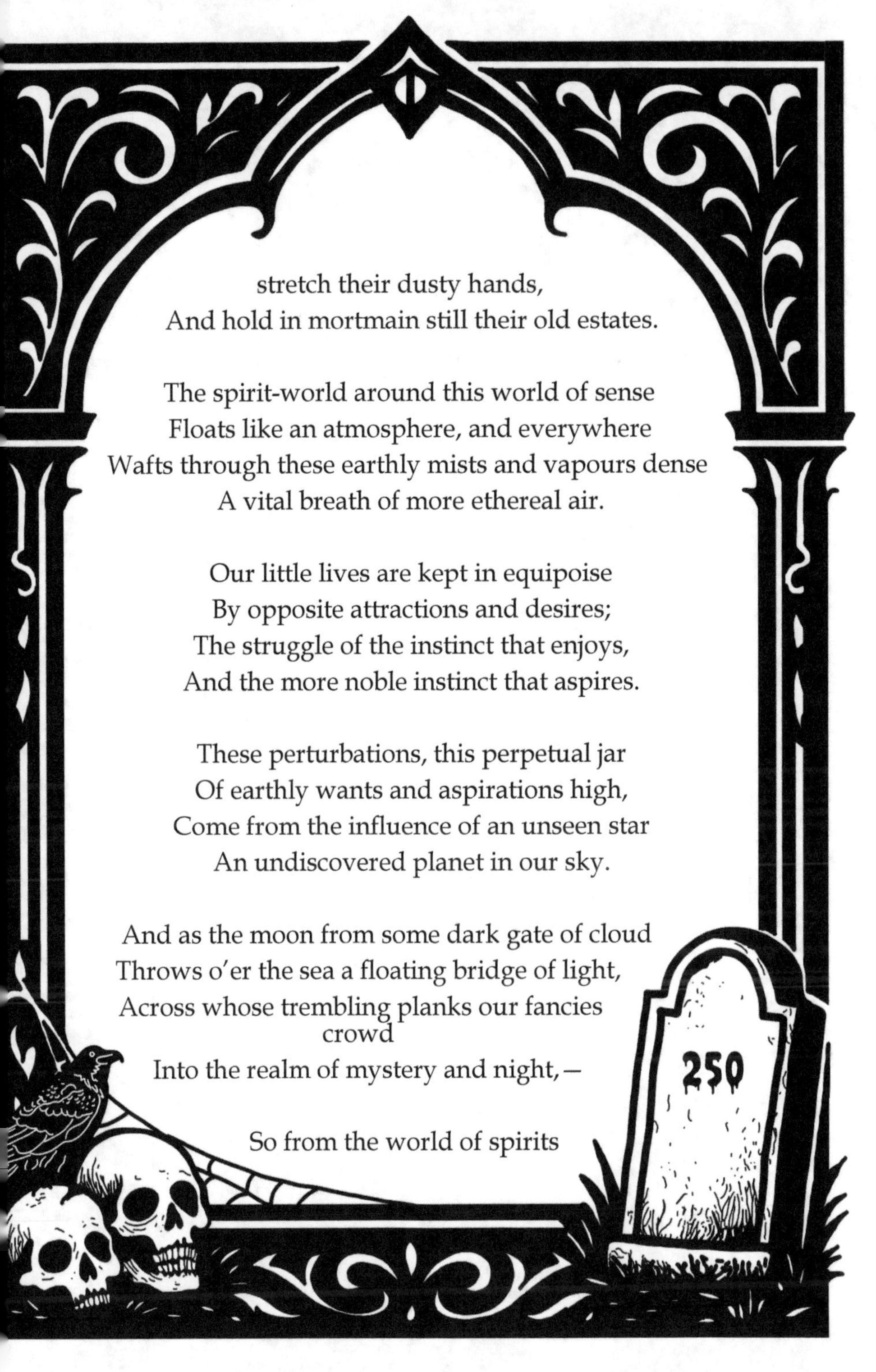

stretch their dusty hands,
And hold in mortmain still their old estates.

The spirit-world around this world of sense
Floats like an atmosphere, and everywhere
Wafts through these earthly mists and vapours dense
A vital breath of more ethereal air.

Our little lives are kept in equipoise
By opposite attractions and desires;
The struggle of the instinct that enjoys,
And the more noble instinct that aspires.

These perturbations, this perpetual jar
Of earthly wants and aspirations high,
Come from the influence of an unseen star
An undiscovered planet in our sky.

And as the moon from some dark gate of cloud
Throws o'er the sea a floating bridge of light,
Across whose trembling planks our fancies crowd
Into the realm of mystery and night,—

So from the world of spirits

there descends
A bridge of light, connecting it with this,
O'er whose unsteady floor, that sways and bends,
Wander our thoughts above the dark abyss.

Nathan Reese Maher

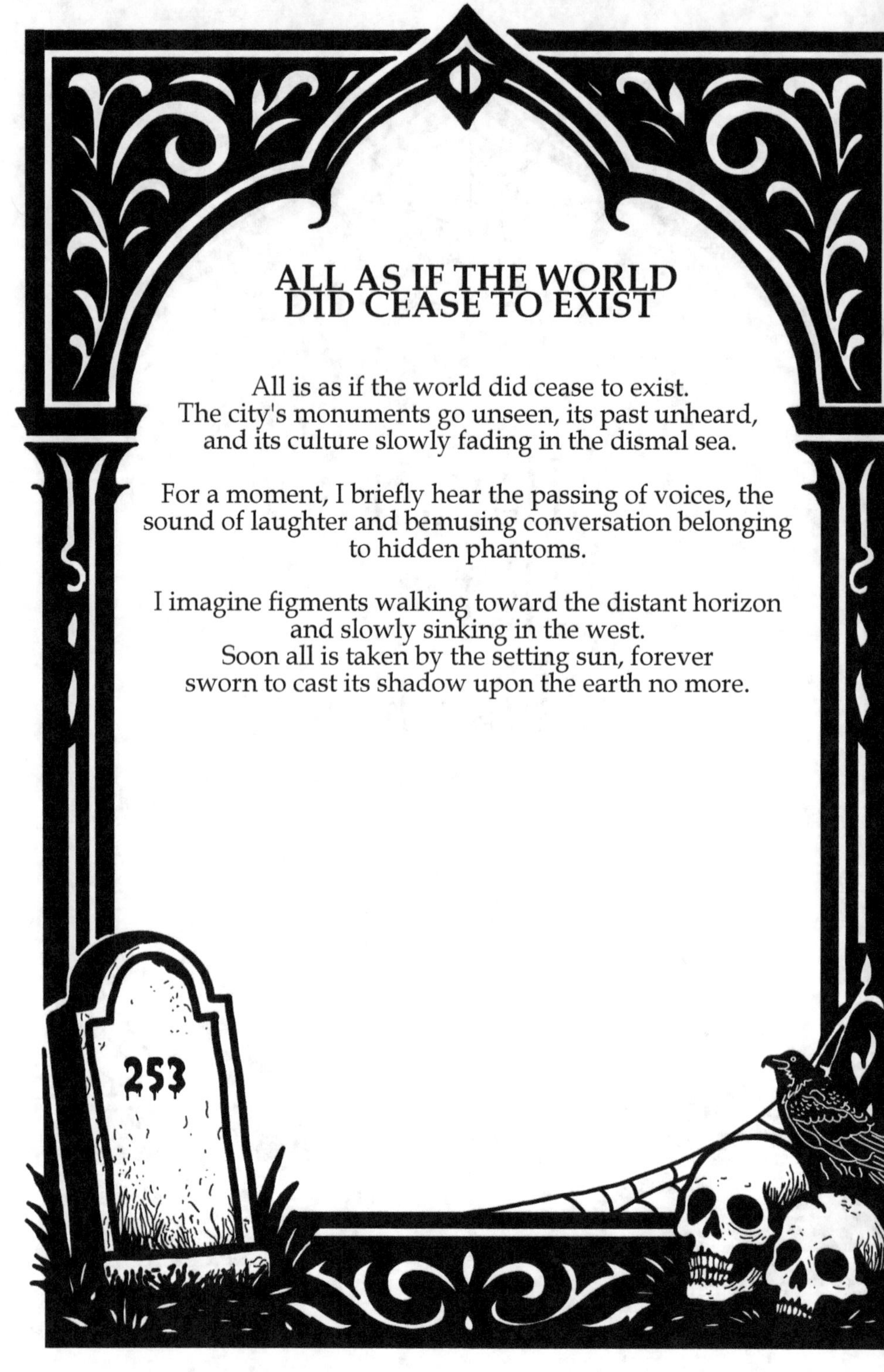

ALL AS IF THE WORLD DID CEASE TO EXIST

All is as if the world did cease to exist.
The city's monuments go unseen, its past unheard,
and its culture slowly fading in the dismal sea.

For a moment, I briefly hear the passing of voices, the
sound of laughter and bemusing conversation belonging
to hidden phantoms.

I imagine figments walking toward the distant horizon
and slowly sinking in the west.
Soon all is taken by the setting sun, forever
sworn to cast its shadow upon the earth no more.

HERE LIES ONE WHOSE NAME WAS WRIT IN WATER

Cry no tears for us, my friend.
Lend no aches to the dreams of yesterday.
Allow the tide sweep free the bay.
And home the ships sailing send.

Bury us low beneath the cold,
Deep in swollen womb, at silent end.
Perched there, the old cypress tree bends
With wing, to carry us westward told.

Slumber we now, beyond the sunlit shown.
Ne'er to wake in favored listless breeze.
Full those sails in silk raised sheaves.
Fare us well, spirit bound for the unknown.

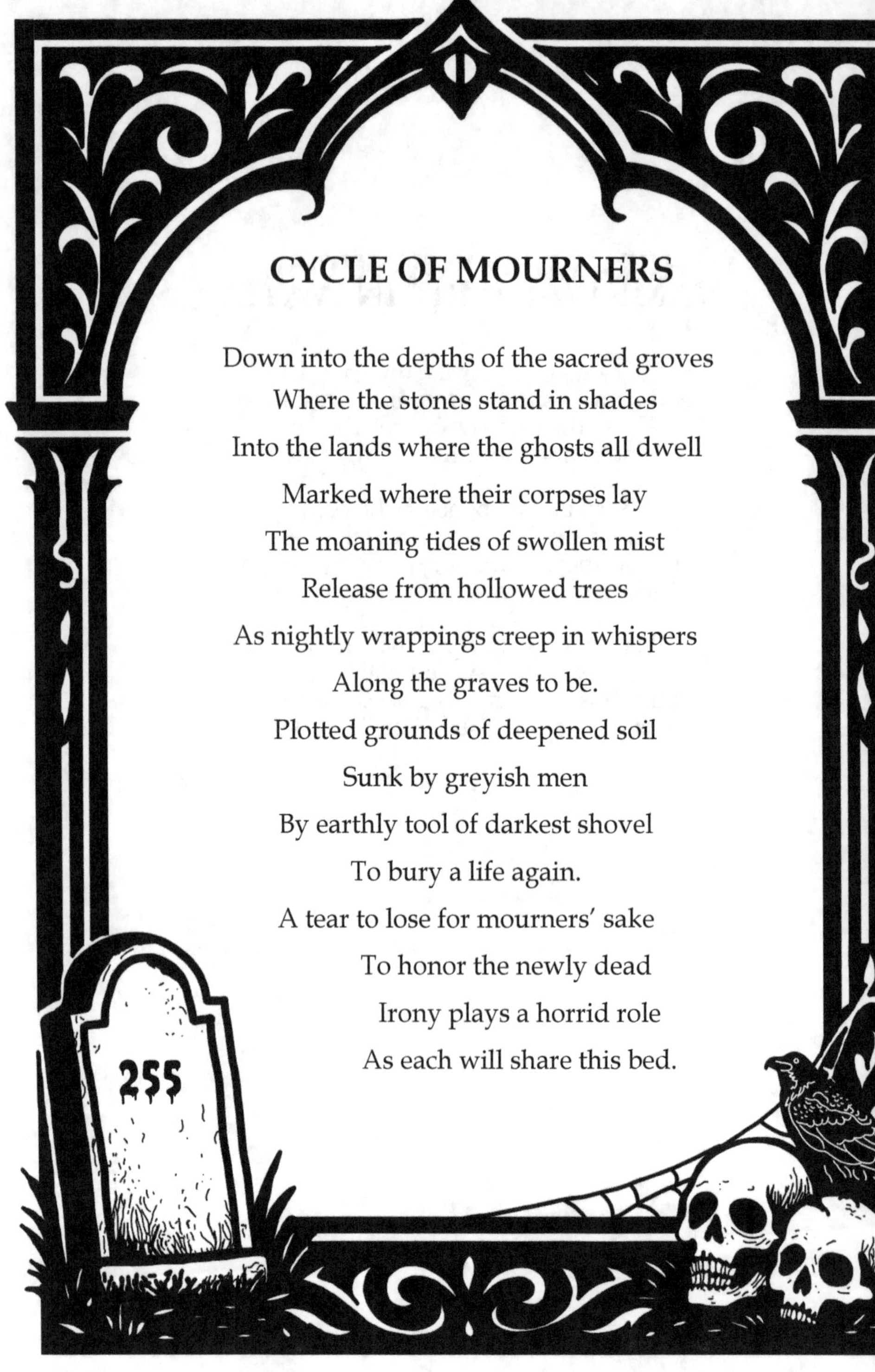

CYCLE OF MOURNERS

Down into the depths of the sacred groves
Where the stones stand in shades
Into the lands where the ghosts all dwell
Marked where their corpses lay
The moaning tides of swollen mist
Release from hollowed trees
As nightly wrappings creep in whispers
Along the graves to be.
Plotted grounds of deepened soil
Sunk by greyish men
By earthly tool of darkest shovel
To bury a life again.
A tear to lose for mourners' sake
To honor the newly dead
Irony plays a horrid role
As each will share this bed.

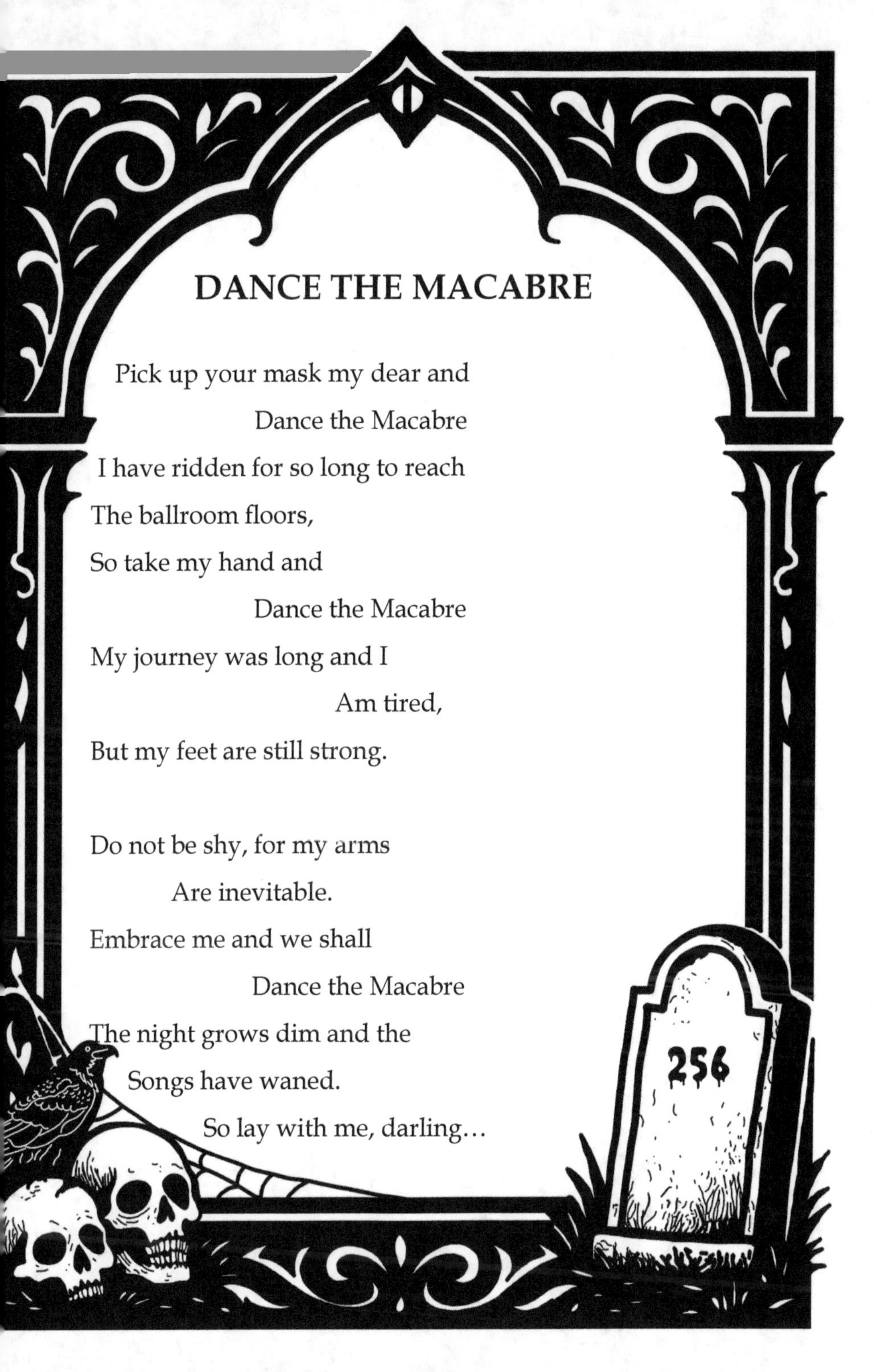

DANCE THE MACABRE

Pick up your mask my dear and
Dance the Macabre
I have ridden for so long to reach
The ballroom floors,
So take my hand and
Dance the Macabre
My journey was long and I
Am tired,
But my feet are still strong.

Do not be shy, for my arms
Are inevitable.
Embrace me and we shall
Dance the Macabre
The night grows dim and the
Songs have waned.
So lay with me, darling…

One last time.

For we have danced the macabre

And now our world grows black.

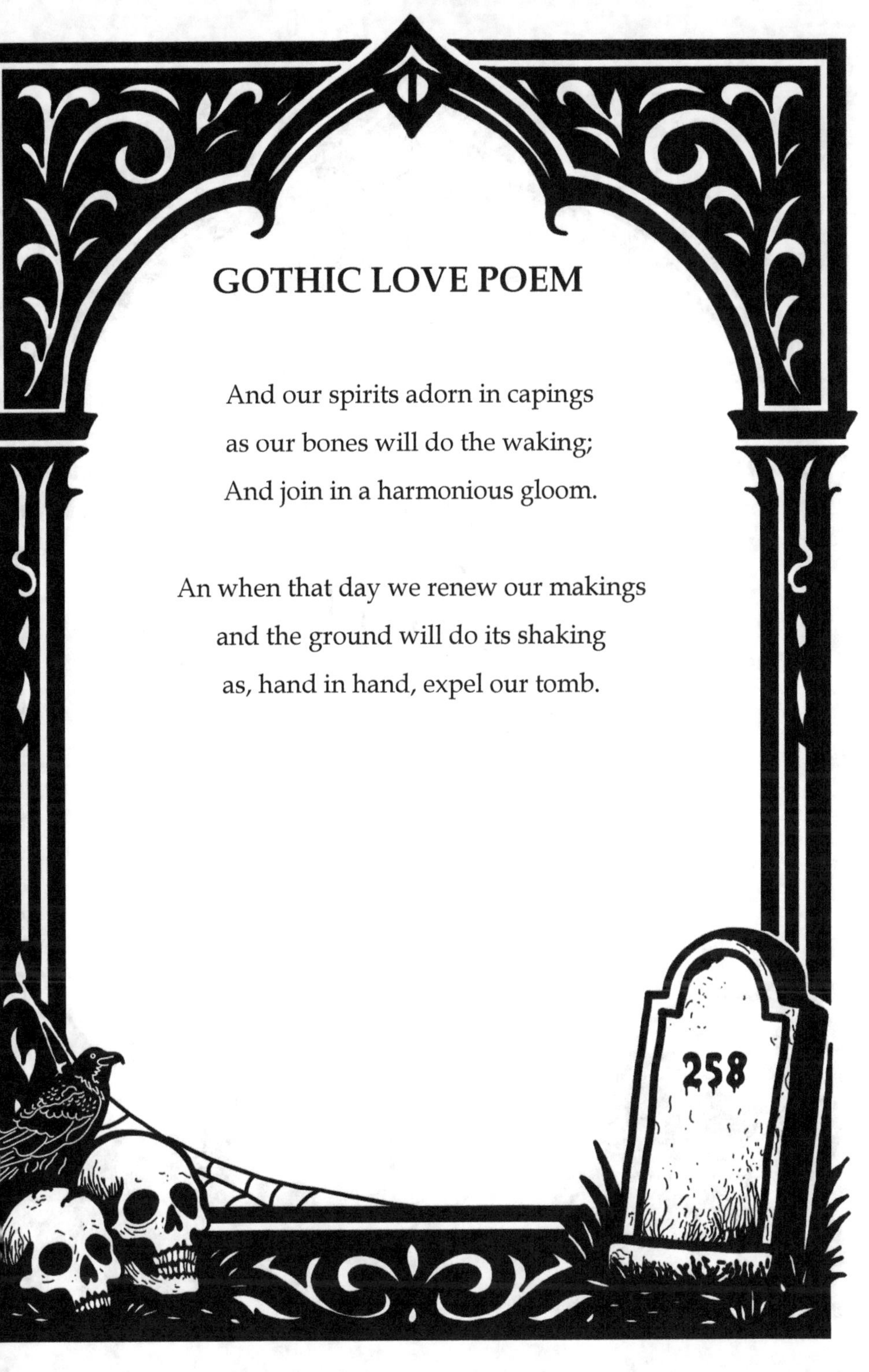

GOTHIC LOVE POEM

And our spirits adorn in capings
as our bones will do the waking;
And join in a harmonious gloom.

An when that day we renew our makings
and the ground will do its shaking
as, hand in hand, expel our tomb.

David Mallet

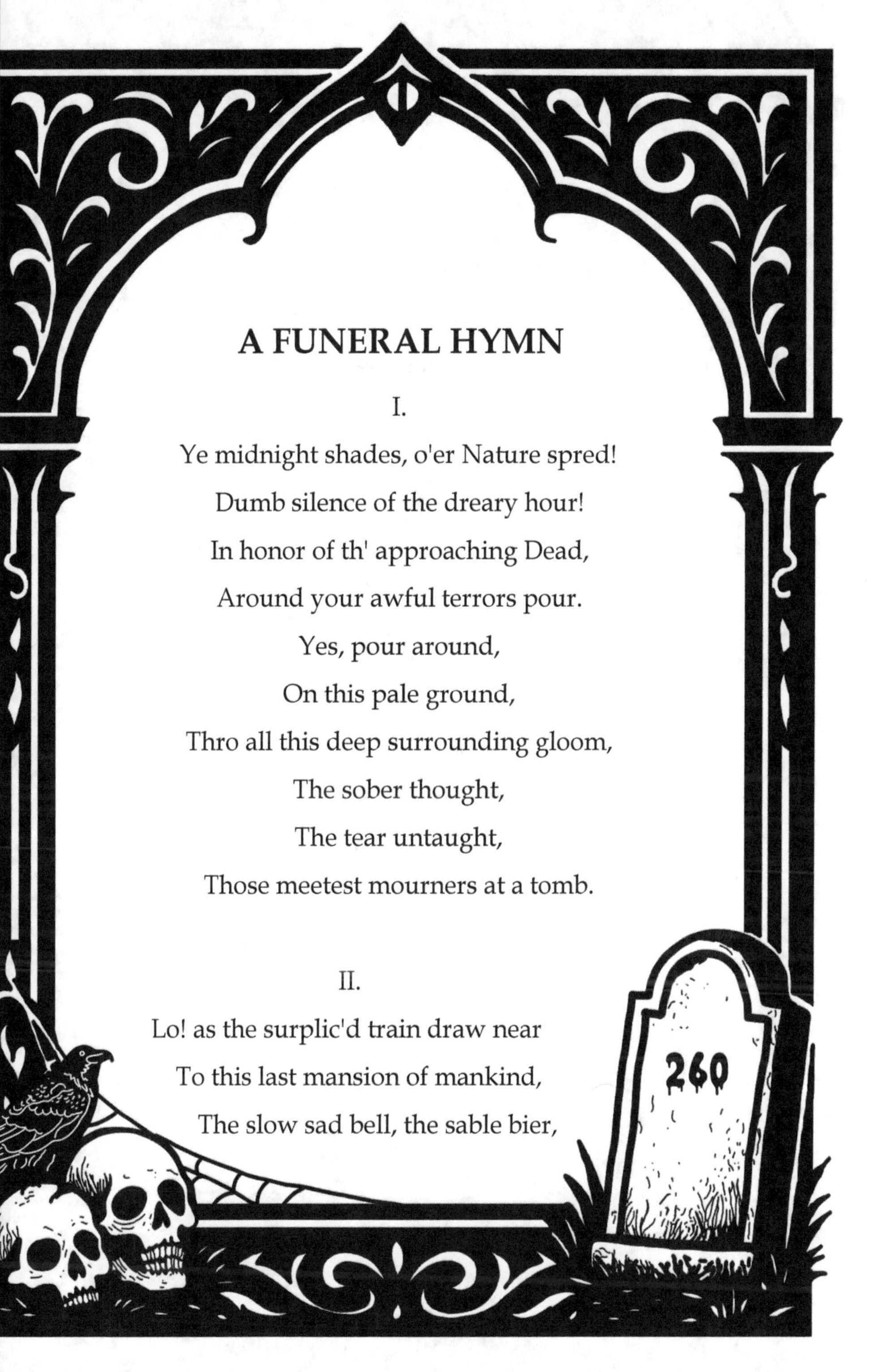

A FUNERAL HYMN

I.

Ye midnight shades, o'er Nature spred!
Dumb silence of the dreary hour!
In honor of th' approaching Dead,
Around your awful terrors pour.
Yes, pour around,
On this pale ground,
Thro all this deep surrounding gloom,
The sober thought,
The tear untaught,
Those meetest mourners at a tomb.

II.

Lo! as the surplic'd train draw near
To this last mansion of mankind,
The slow sad bell, the sable bier,

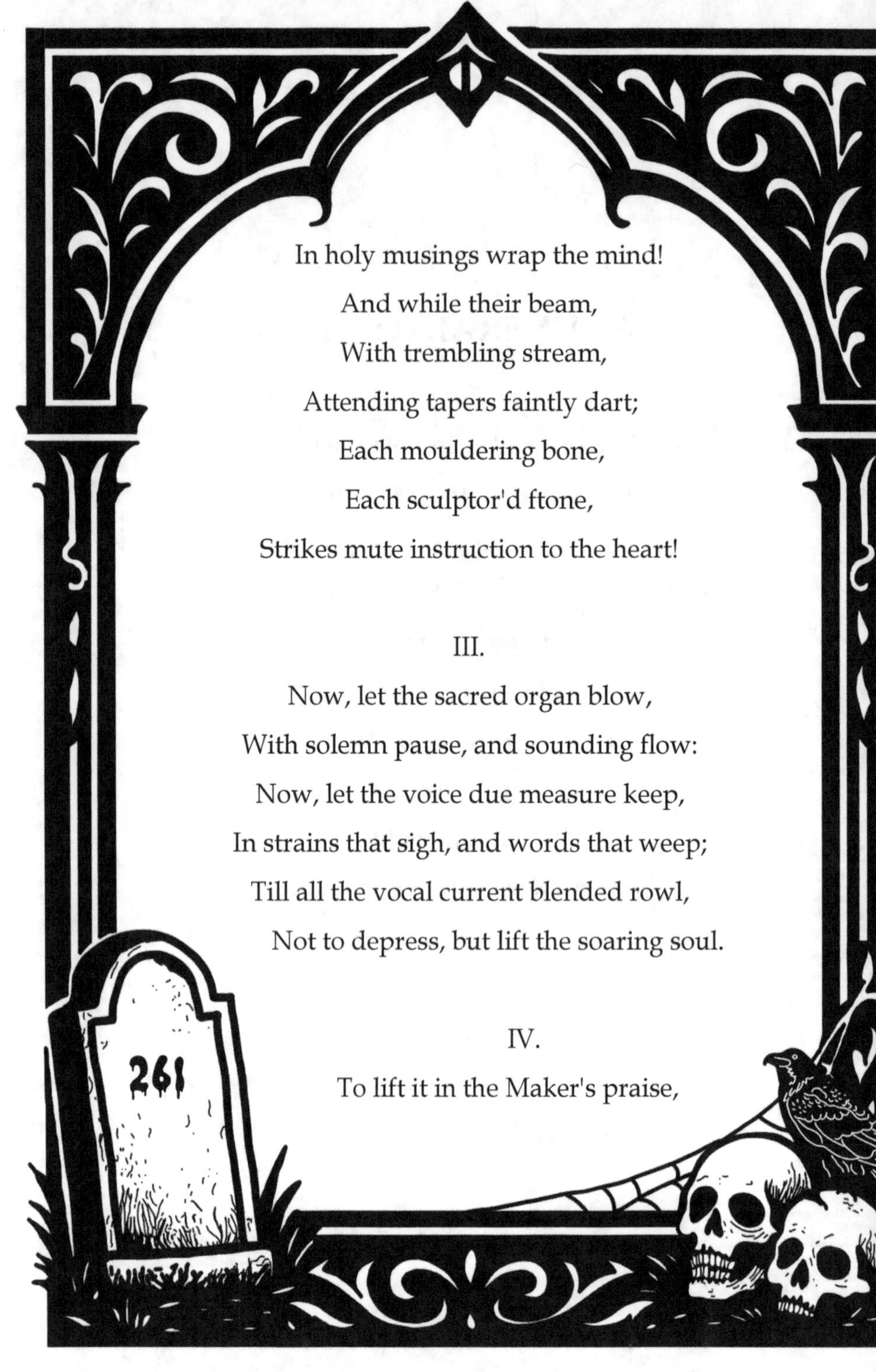

In holy musings wrap the mind!
And while their beam,
With trembling stream,
Attending tapers faintly dart;
Each mouldering bone,
Each sculptor'd ftone,
Strikes mute instruction to the heart!

III.

Now, let the sacred organ blow,
With solemn pause, and sounding flow:
Now, let the voice due measure keep,
In strains that sigh, and words that weep;
Till all the vocal current blended rowl,
Not to depress, but lift the soaring soul.

IV.

To lift it in the Maker's praise,

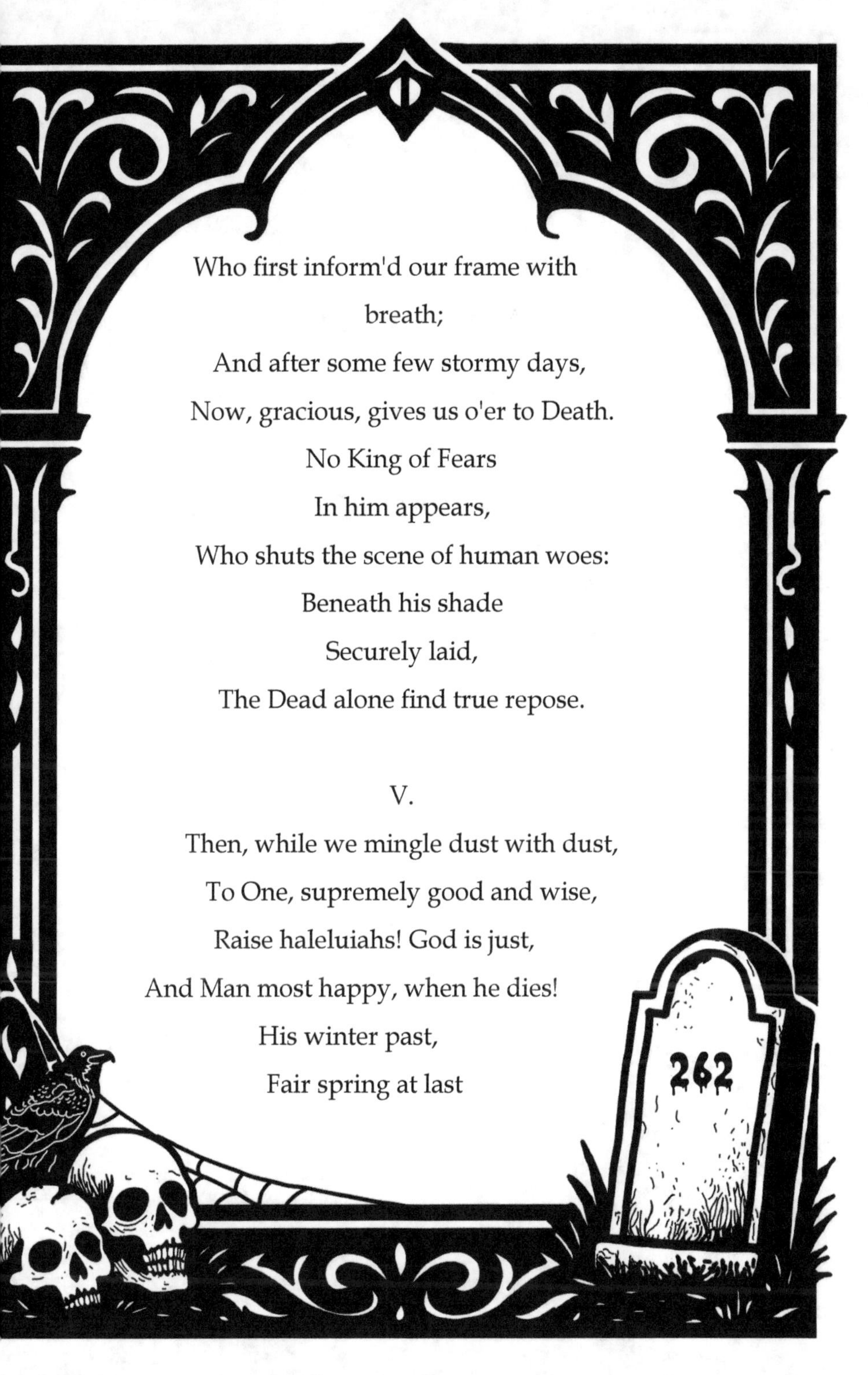

Who first inform'd our frame with
breath;
And after some few stormy days,
Now, gracious, gives us o'er to Death.
No King of Fears
In him appears,
Who shuts the scene of human woes:
Beneath his shade
Securely laid,
The Dead alone find true repose.

V.

Then, while we mingle dust with dust,
To One, supremely good and wise,
Raise haleluiahs! God is just,
And Man most happy, when he dies!
His winter past,
Fair spring at last

Receives him on her flowery shore;
Where Pleasure's rose
Immortal blows,
And sin and sorrow are no more!

THE END.

William Mason

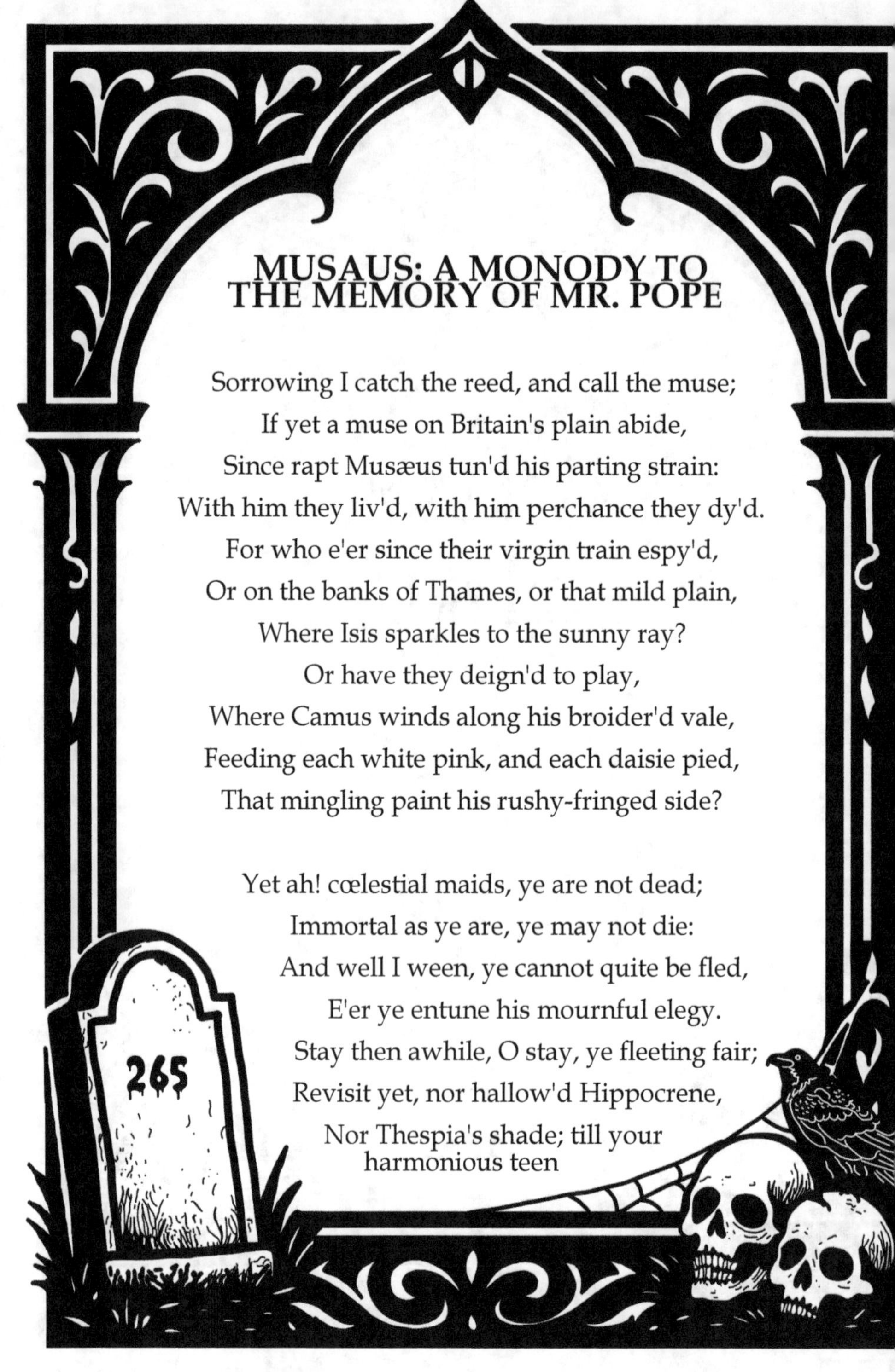

MUSAUS: A MONODY TO THE MEMORY OF MR. POPE

Sorrowing I catch the reed, and call the muse;
If yet a muse on Britain's plain abide,
Since rapt Musæus tun'd his parting strain:
With him they liv'd, with him perchance they dy'd.
For who e'er since their virgin train espy'd,
Or on the banks of Thames, or that mild plain,
Where Isis sparkles to the sunny ray?
Or have they deign'd to play,
Where Camus winds along his broider'd vale,
Feeding each white pink, and each daisie pied,
That mingling paint his rushy-fringed side?

Yet ah! cœlestial maids, ye are not dead;
Immortal as ye are, ye may not die:
And well I ween, ye cannot quite be fled,
E'er ye entune his mournful elegy.
Stay then awhile, O stay, ye fleeting fair;
Revisit yet, nor hallow'd Hippocrene,
Nor Thespia's shade; till your harmonious teen

Be
grateful pour'd in some slow-dittied
air.
Such tribute paid, again ye may repair
To what lov'd haunt you whilom did elect;
Whether Lycæus, or that mountain fair
Trim Mænalus, with piny verdure deckt.
But now it boots you not in these to stray,
Or yet Cyllene's hoary shade to chuse,
Or where mild Ladon's welling waters play.
Forego each vain excuse,
And haste to Thames's shores; for Thames shall join
Our sad society, and passing mourn,
Letting cold tears bedew his silver urn.
And, when the poet's widow'd grot he laves,
His reed-crown'd locks shall shake, his head shall bow,
His tide no more in eddies blith shall rove,
But creep soft by with long-drawn murmurs slow.
For oft the poet rous'd his charmed waves
With martial notes, or lull'd with strain of love.
He must not now in brisk mæanders flow
Gamesome, and kiss the sadly-silent shore,
Without the loan of some poetic woe.

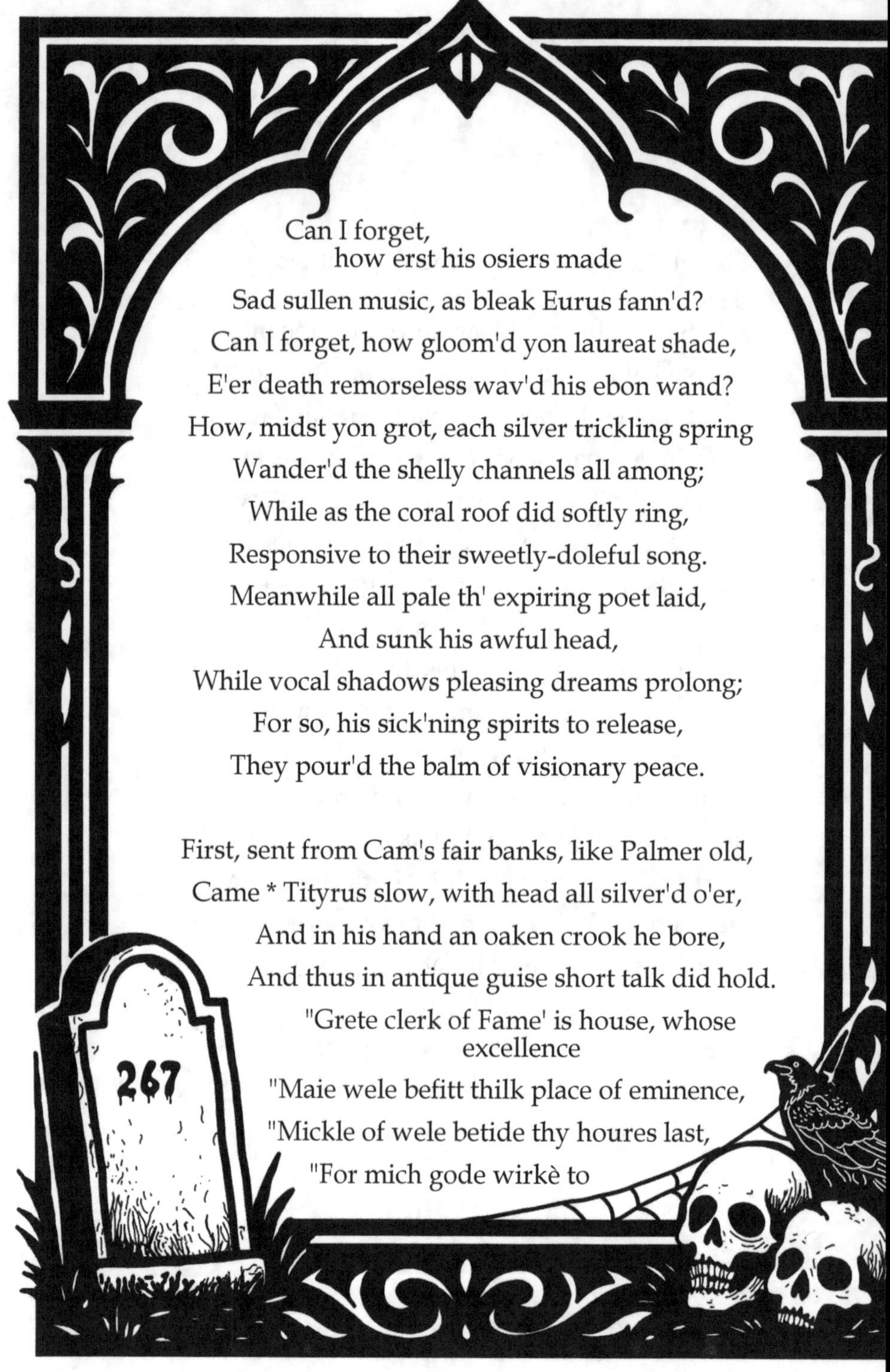

Can I forget,
how erst his osiers made
Sad sullen music, as bleak Eurus fann'd?
Can I forget, how gloom'd yon laureat shade,
E'er death remorseless wav'd his ebon wand?
How, midst yon grot, each silver trickling spring
Wander'd the shelly channels all among;
While as the coral roof did softly ring,
Responsive to their sweetly-doleful song.
Meanwhile all pale th' expiring poet laid,
And sunk his awful head,
While vocal shadows pleasing dreams prolong;
For so, his sick'ning spirits to release,
They pour'd the balm of visionary peace.

First, sent from Cam's fair banks, like Palmer old,
Came * Tityrus slow, with head all silver'd o'er,
And in his hand an oaken crook he bore,
And thus in antique guise short talk did hold.
"Grete clerk of Fame' is house, whose excellence
"Maie wele befitt thilk place of eminence,
"Mickle of wele betide thy houres last,
"For mich gode wirkè to

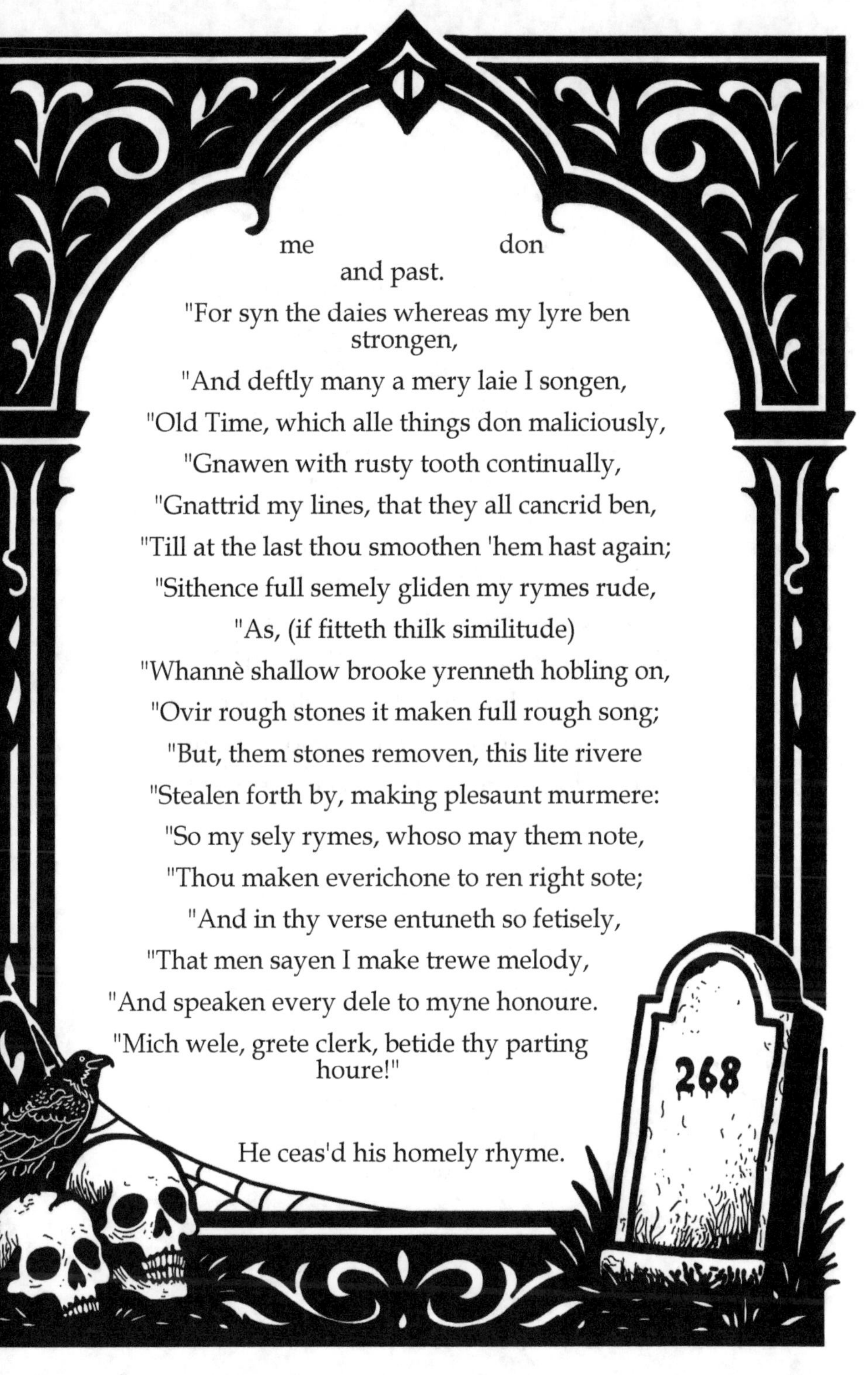

me don
and past.

"For syn the daies whereas my lyre ben strongen,
"And deftly many a mery laie I songen,
"Old Time, which alle things don maliciously,
"Gnawen with rusty tooth continually,
"Gnattrid my lines, that they all cancrid ben,
"Till at the last thou smoothen 'hem hast again;
"Sithence full semely gliden my rymes rude,
"As, (if fitteth thilk similitude)
"Whannè shallow brooke yrenneth hobling on,
"Ovir rough stones it maken full rough song;
"But, them stones removen, this lite rivere
"Stealen forth by, making plesaunt murmere:
"So my sely rymes, whoso may them note,
"Thou maken everichone to ren right sote;
"And in thy verse entuneth so fetisely,
"That men sayen I make trewe melody,
"And speaken every dele to myne honoure.
"Mich wele, grete clerk, betide thy parting houre!"

He ceas'd his homely rhyme.

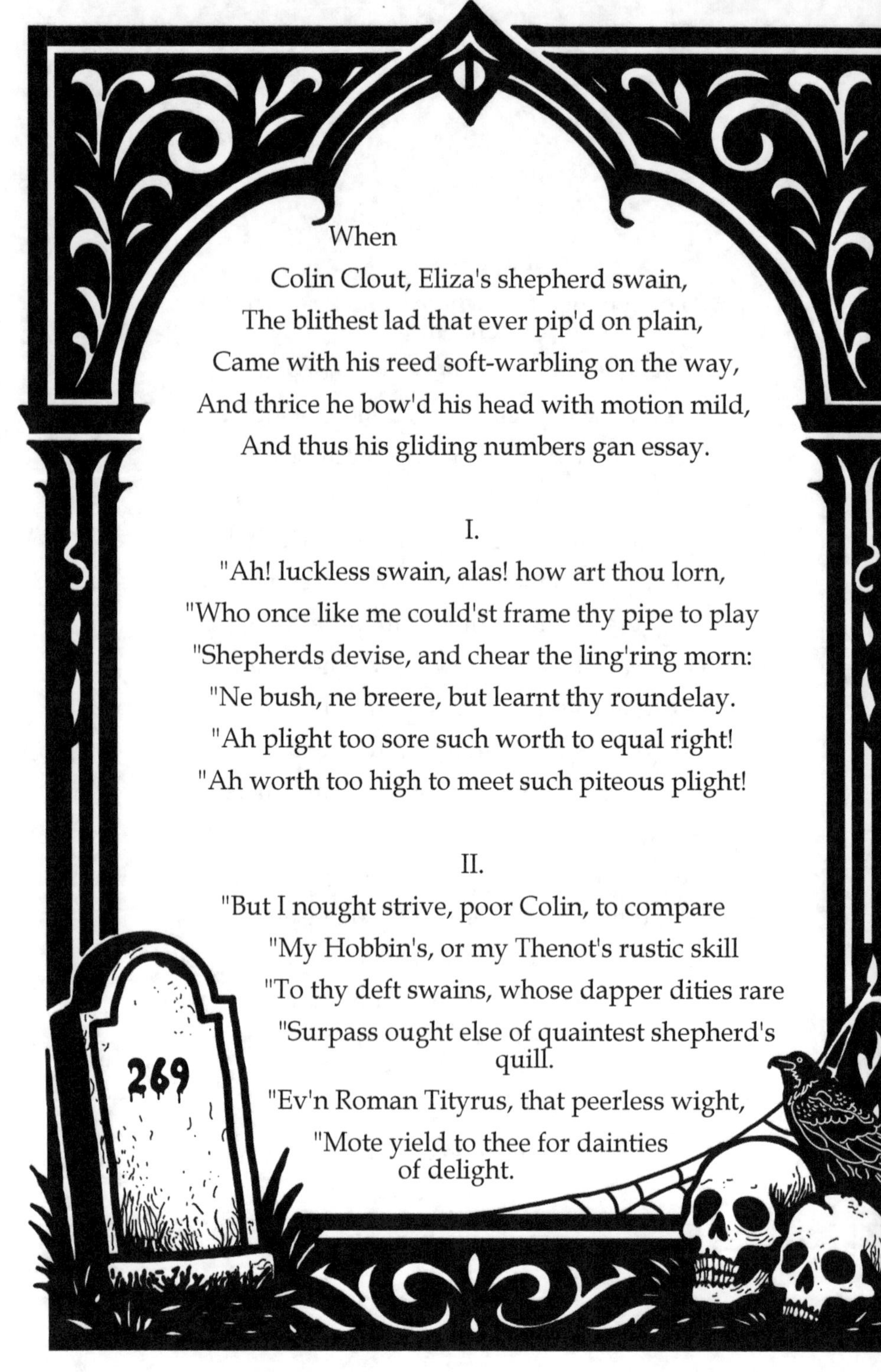

When

Colin Clout, Eliza's shepherd swain,
The blithest lad that ever pip'd on plain,
Came with his reed soft-warbling on the way,
And thrice he bow'd his head with motion mild,
And thus his gliding numbers gan essay.

I.

"Ah! luckless swain, alas! how art thou lorn,
"Who once like me could'st frame thy pipe to play
"Shepherds devise, and chear the ling'ring morn:
"Ne bush, ne breere, but learnt thy roundelay.
"Ah plight too sore such worth to equal right!
"Ah worth too high to meet such piteous plight!

II.

"But I nought strive, poor Colin, to compare
"My Hobbin's, or my Thenot's rustic skill
"To thy deft swains, whose dapper dities rare
"Surpass ought else of quaintest shepherd's quill.
"Ev'n Roman Tityrus, that peerless wight,
"Mote yield to thee for dainties of delight.

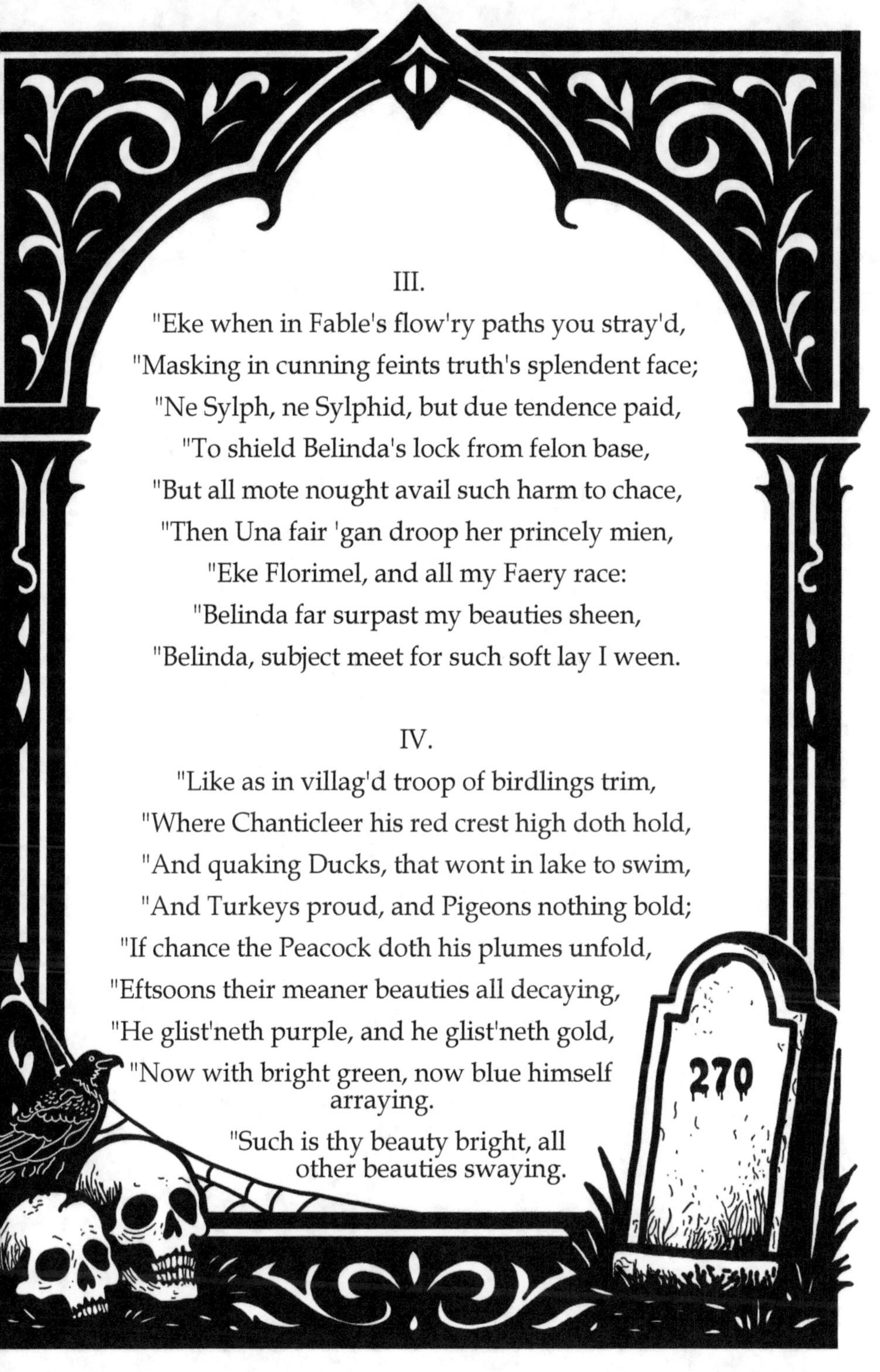

III.

"Eke when in Fable's flow'ry paths you stray'd,
"Masking in cunning feints truth's splendent face;
"Ne Sylph, ne Sylphid, but due tendence paid,
"To shield Belinda's lock from felon base,
"But all mote nought avail such harm to chace,
"Then Una fair 'gan droop her princely mien,
"Eke Florimel, and all my Faery race:
"Belinda far surpast my beauties sheen,
"Belinda, subject meet for such soft lay I ween.

IV.

"Like as in villag'd troop of birdlings trim,
"Where Chanticleer his red crest high doth hold,
"And quaking Ducks, that wont in lake to swim,
"And Turkeys proud, and Pigeons nothing bold;
"If chance the Peacock doth his plumes unfold,
"Eftsoons their meaner beauties all decaying,
"He glist'neth purple, and he glist'neth gold,
"Now with bright green, now blue himself arraying.
"Such is thy beauty bright, all other beauties swaying.

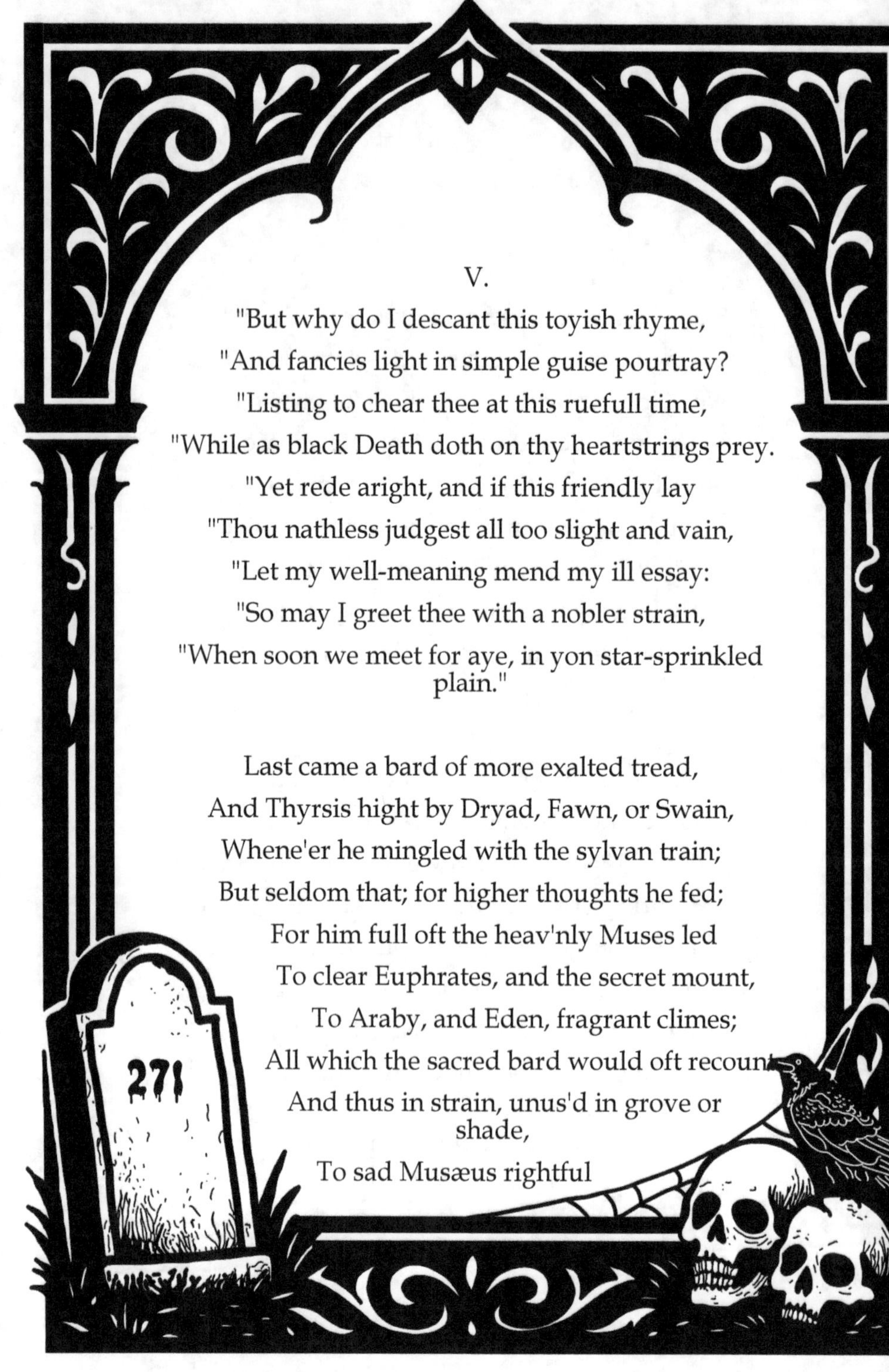

V.

"But why do I descant this toyish rhyme,
"And fancies light in simple guise pourtray?
"Listing to chear thee at this ruefull time,
"While as black Death doth on thy heartstrings prey.
"Yet rede aright, and if this friendly lay
"Thou nathless judgest all too slight and vain,
"Let my well-meaning mend my ill essay:
"So may I greet thee with a nobler strain,
"When soon we meet for aye, in yon star-sprinkled plain."

Last came a bard of more exalted tread,
And Thyrsis hight by Dryad, Fawn, or Swain,
Whene'er he mingled with the sylvan train;
But seldom that; for higher thoughts he fed;
For him full oft the heav'nly Muses led
To clear Euphrates, and the secret mount,
To Araby, and Eden, fragrant climes;
All which the sacred bard would oft recount
And thus in strain, unus'd in grove or shade,
To sad Musæus rightful

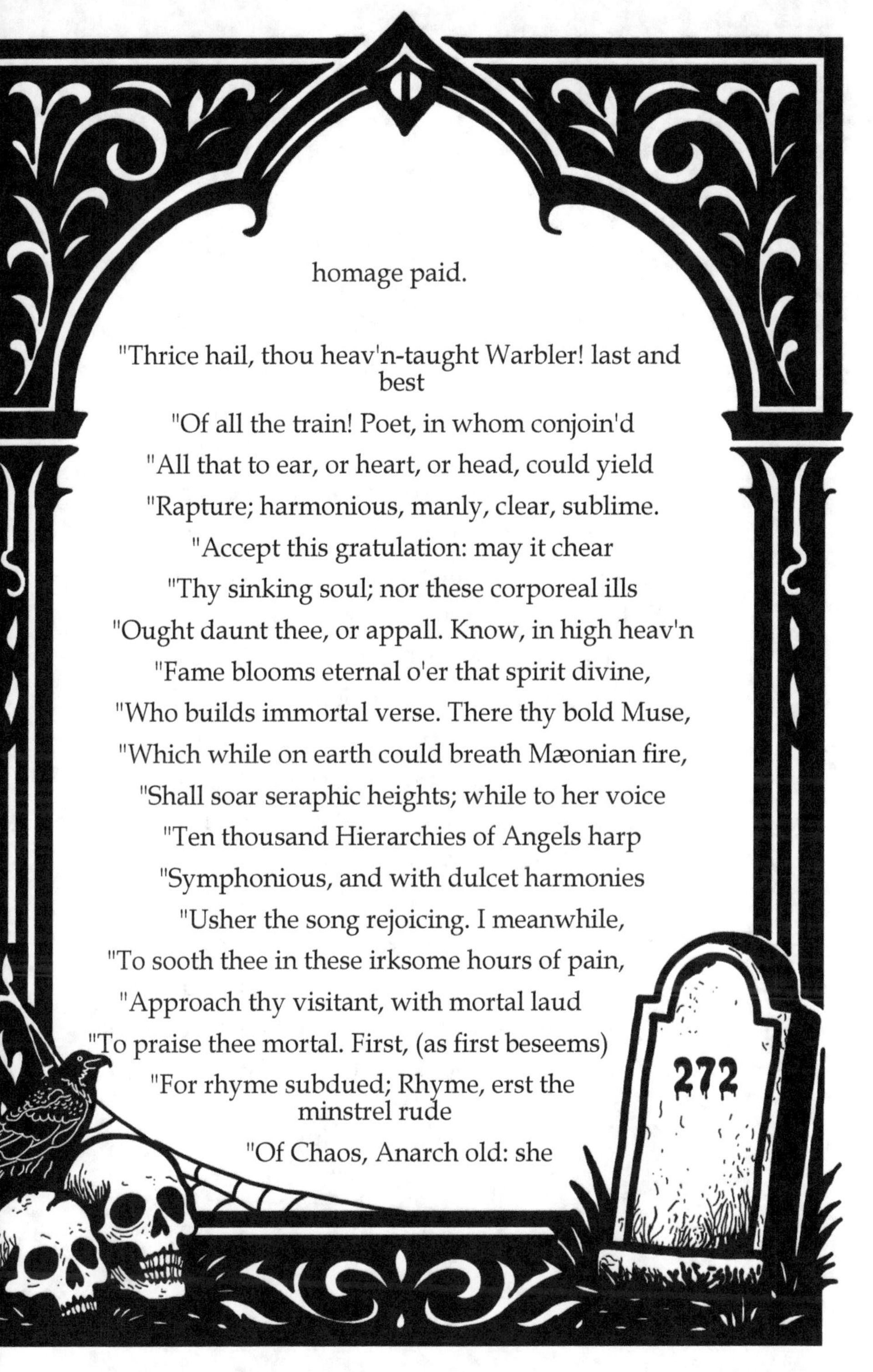

homage paid.

"Thrice hail, thou heav'n-taught Warbler! last and best
"Of all the train! Poet, in whom conjoin'd
"All that to ear, or heart, or head, could yield
"Rapture; harmonious, manly, clear, sublime.
"Accept this gratulation: may it chear
"Thy sinking soul; nor these corporeal ills
"Ought daunt thee, or appall. Know, in high heav'n
"Fame blooms eternal o'er that spirit divine,
"Who builds immortal verse. There thy bold Muse,
"Which while on earth could breath Mæonian fire,
"Shall soar seraphic heights; while to her voice
"Ten thousand Hierarchies of Angels harp
"Symphonious, and with dulcet harmonies
"Usher the song rejoicing. I meanwhile,
"To sooth thee in these irksome hours of pain,
"Approach thy visitant, with mortal laud
"To praise thee mortal. First, (as first beseems)
"For rhyme subdued; Rhyme, erst the minstrel rude
"Of Chaos, Anarch old: she

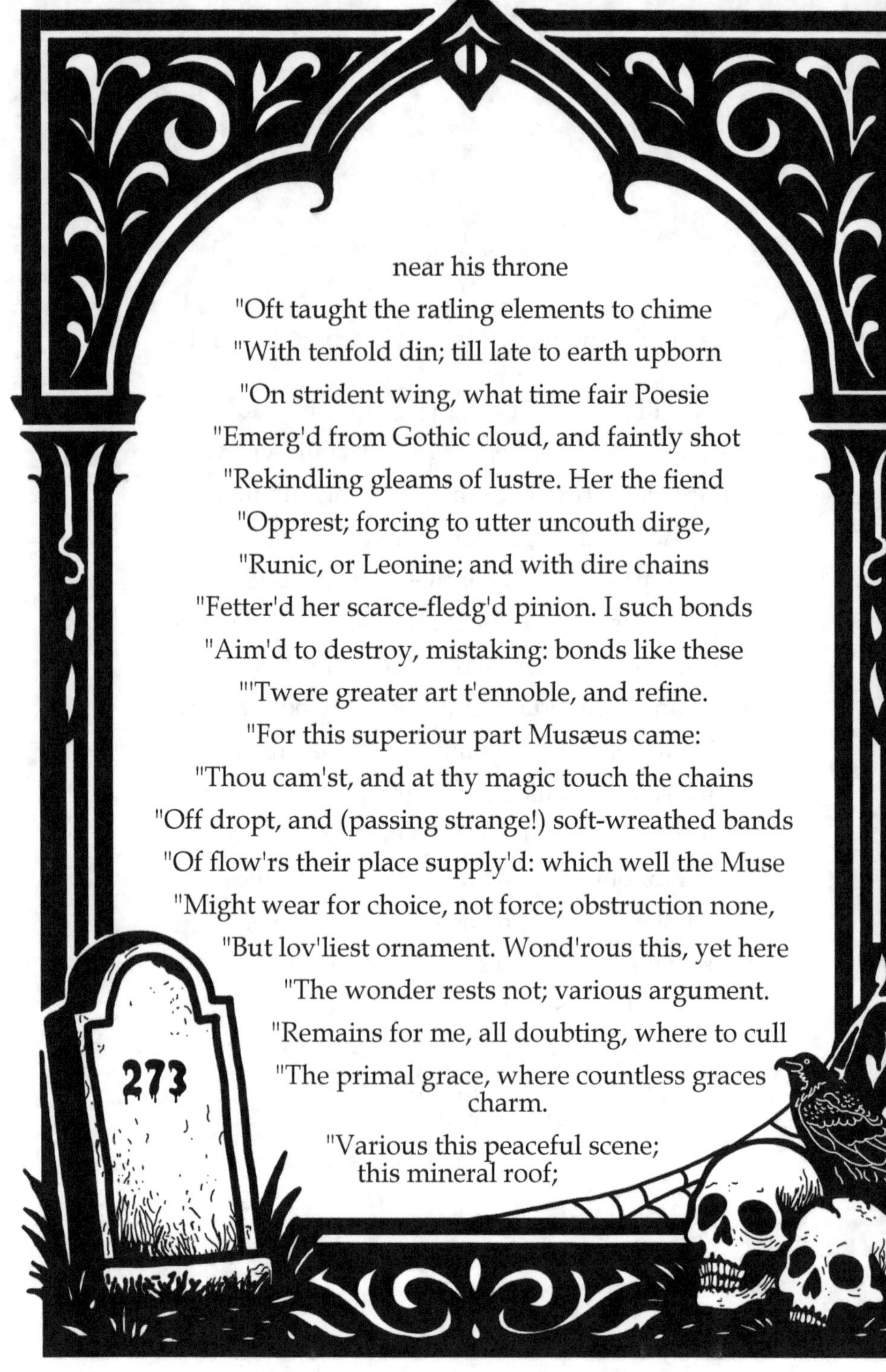

near his throne
"Oft taught the ratling elements to chime
"With tenfold din; till late to earth upborn
"On strident wing, what time fair Poesie
"Emerg'd from Gothic cloud, and faintly shot
"Rekindling gleams of lustre. Her the fiend
"Opprest; forcing to utter uncouth dirge,
"Runic, or Leonine; and with dire chains
"Fetter'd her scarce-fledg'd pinion. I such bonds
"Aim'd to destroy, mistaking: bonds like these
"'Twere greater art t'ennoble, and refine.
"For this superiour part Musæus came:
"Thou cam'st, and at thy magic touch the chains
"Off dropt, and (passing strange!) soft-wreathed bands
"Of flow'rs their place supply'd: which well the Muse
"Might wear for choice, not force; obstruction none,
"But lov'liest ornament. Wond'rous this, yet here
"The wonder rests not; various argument.
"Remains for me, all doubting, where to cull
"The primal grace, where countless graces charm.
"Various this peaceful scene; this mineral roof;

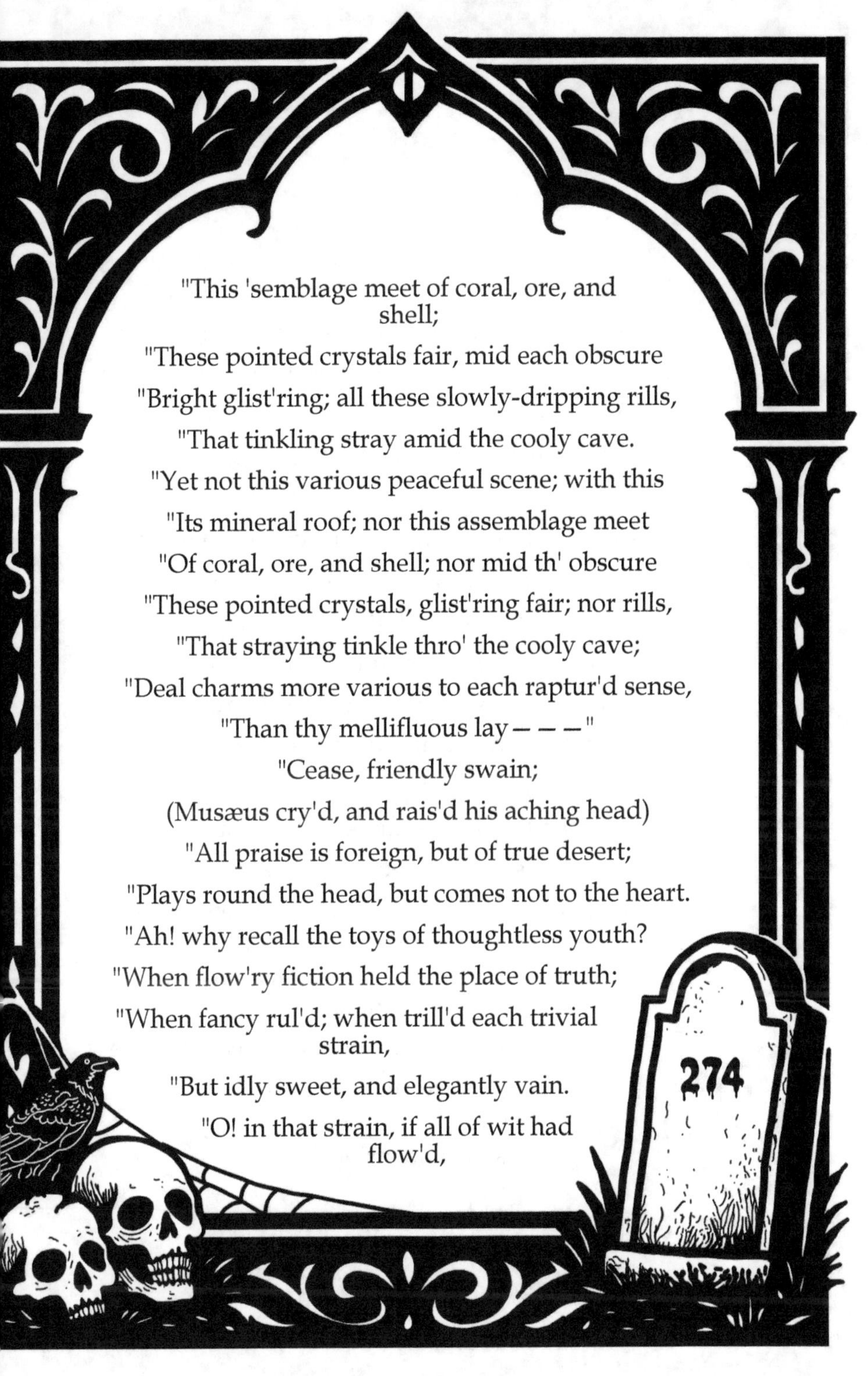

"This 'semblage meet of coral, ore, and shell;
"These pointed crystals fair, mid each obscure
"Bright glist'ring; all these slowly-dripping rills,
"That tinkling stray amid the cooly cave.
"Yet not this various peaceful scene; with this
"Its mineral roof; nor this assemblage meet
"Of coral, ore, and shell; nor mid th' obscure
"These pointed crystals, glist'ring fair; nor rills,
"That straying tinkle thro' the cooly cave;
"Deal charms more various to each raptur'd sense,
"Than thy mellifluous lay— — —"
"Cease, friendly swain;
(Musæus cry'd, and rais'd his aching head)
"All praise is foreign, but of true desert;
"Plays round the head, but comes not to the heart.
"Ah! why recall the toys of thoughtless youth?
"When flow'ry fiction held the place of truth;
"When fancy rul'd; when trill'd each trivial strain,
"But idly sweet, and elegantly vain.
"O! in that strain, if all of wit had flow'd,

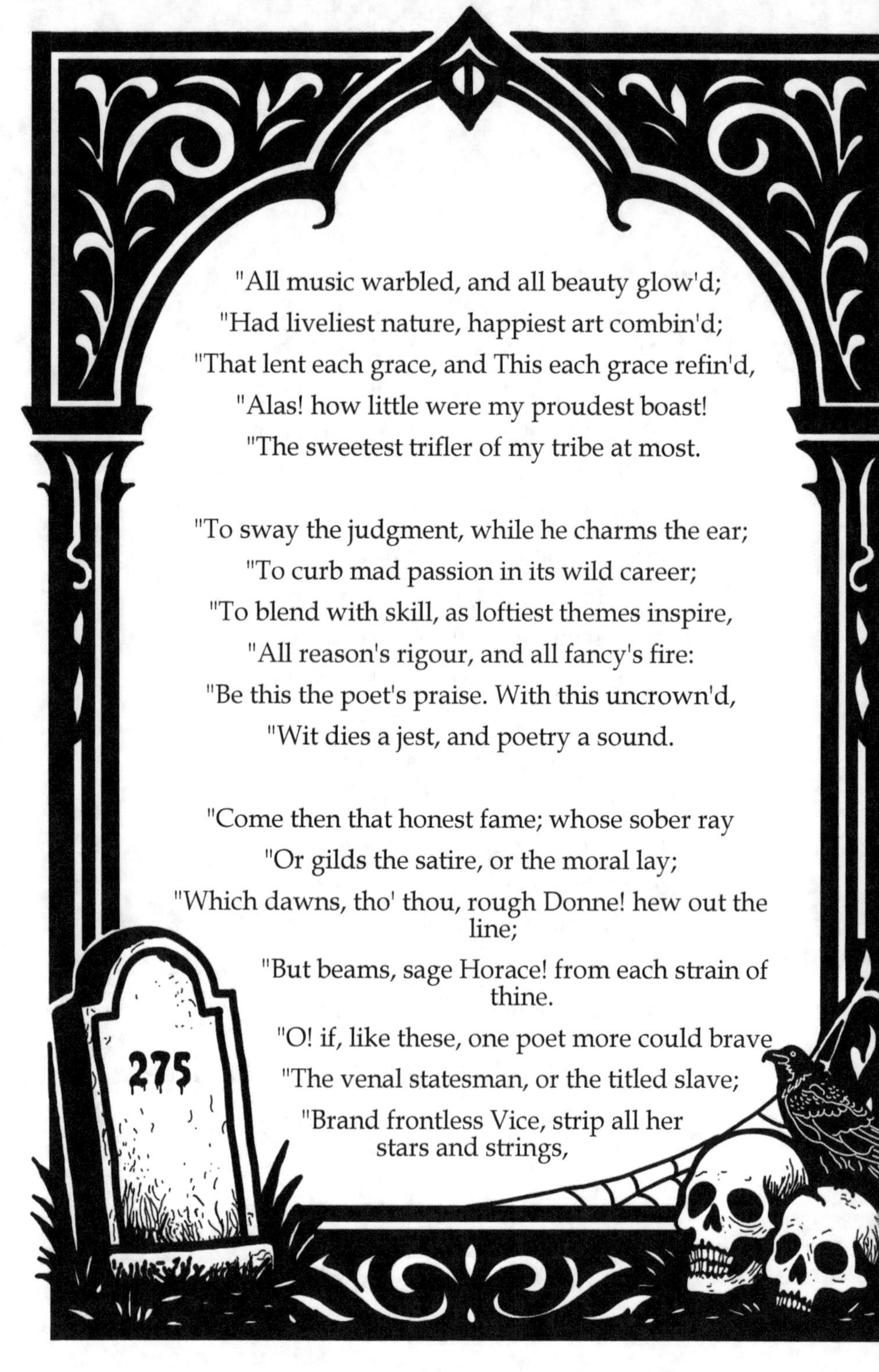

"All music warbled, and all beauty glow'd;
"Had liveliest nature, happiest art combin'd;
"That lent each grace, and This each grace refin'd,
"Alas! how little were my proudest boast!
"The sweetest trifler of my tribe at most.

"To sway the judgment, while he charms the ear;
"To curb mad passion in its wild career;
"To blend with skill, as loftiest themes inspire,
"All reason's rigour, and all fancy's fire:
"Be this the poet's praise. With this uncrown'd,
"Wit dies a jest, and poetry a sound.

"Come then that honest fame; whose sober ray
"Or gilds the satire, or the moral lay;
"Which dawns, tho' thou, rough Donne! hew out the line;
"But beams, sage Horace! from each strain of thine.
"O! if, like these, one poet more could brave
"The venal statesman, or the titled slave;
"Brand frontless Vice, strip all her stars and strings,

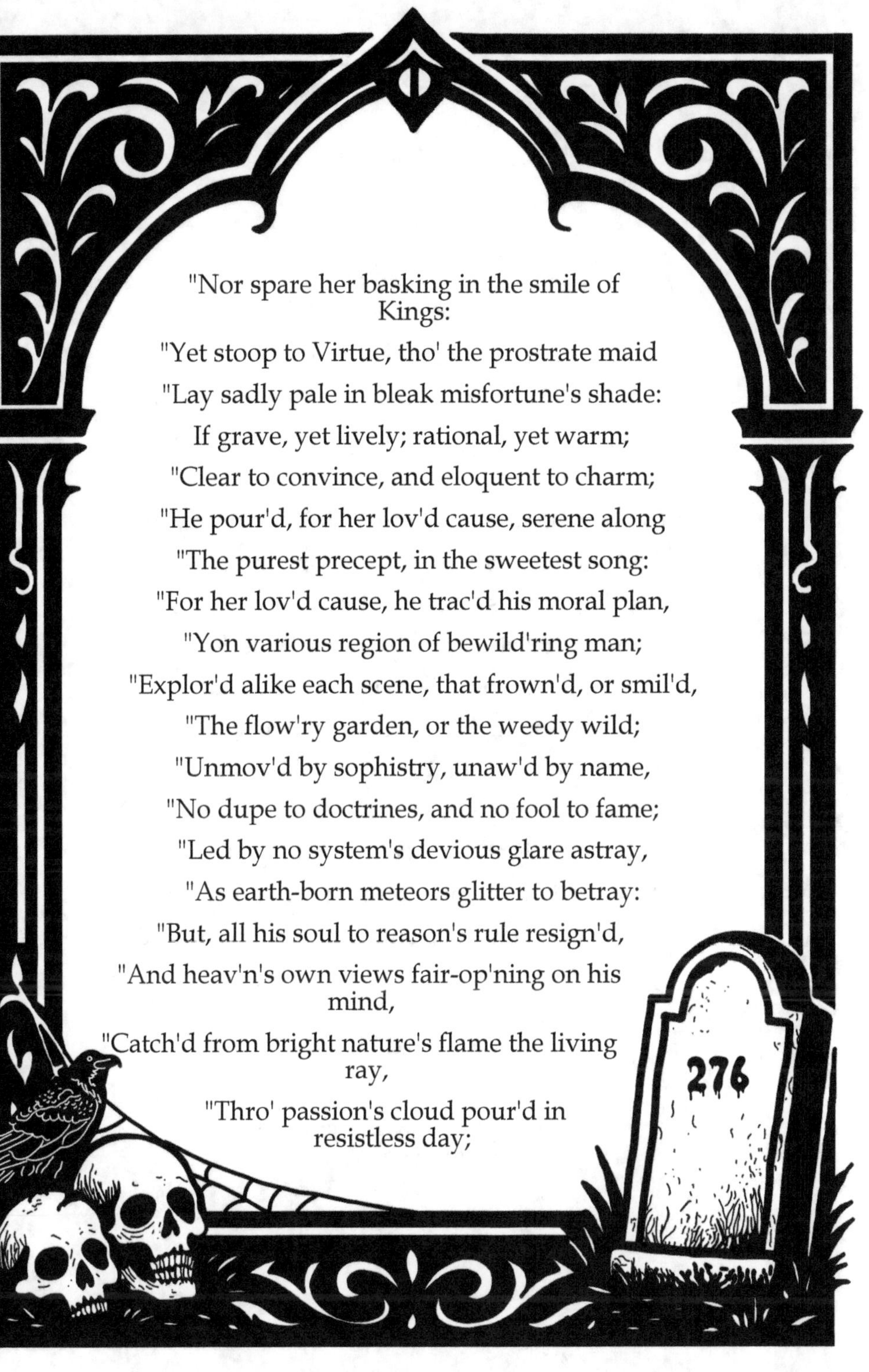

"Nor spare her basking in the smile of Kings:
"Yet stoop to Virtue, tho' the prostrate maid
"Lay sadly pale in bleak misfortune's shade:
If grave, yet lively; rational, yet warm;
"Clear to convince, and eloquent to charm;
"He pour'd, for her lov'd cause, serene along
"The purest precept, in the sweetest song:
"For her lov'd cause, he trac'd his moral plan,
"Yon various region of bewild'ring man;
"Explor'd alike each scene, that frown'd, or smil'd,
"The flow'ry garden, or the weedy wild;
"Unmov'd by sophistry, unaw'd by name,
"No dupe to doctrines, and no fool to fame;
"Led by no system's devious glare astray,
"As earth-born meteors glitter to betray:
"But, all his soul to reason's rule resign'd,
"And heav'n's own views fair-op'ning on his mind,
"Catch'd from bright nature's flame the living ray,
"Thro' passion's cloud pour'd in resistless day;

"And this great truth in all its lustre shew'd,
"That God is wise; and all Creation good:
"If this his boast, pour here the welcome lays;
"Praise less than this is impotence of praise."

"To pour that praise be mine," fair Virtue cry'd;
And shot, all radiant, thro' an op'ning cloud.
But ah! my Muse, how will thy voice express
Th' immortal strain, harmonious, as it flow'd?
Ill suits immortal strain a doric dress:
And far too high already hast thou soar'd.
Enough for thee, that, when the lay was o'er,
The goddess clasp'd him to her throbbing breast.
But what might that avail? Blind Fate before
Had op'd her shears, to slit his vital thread;
And who may hope gainsay her stern behest?
Then thrice he wav'd the hand, thrice bow'd the head,
And sigh'd his soul to rest.

Then wept the Nymphs; witness, ye waving shades!

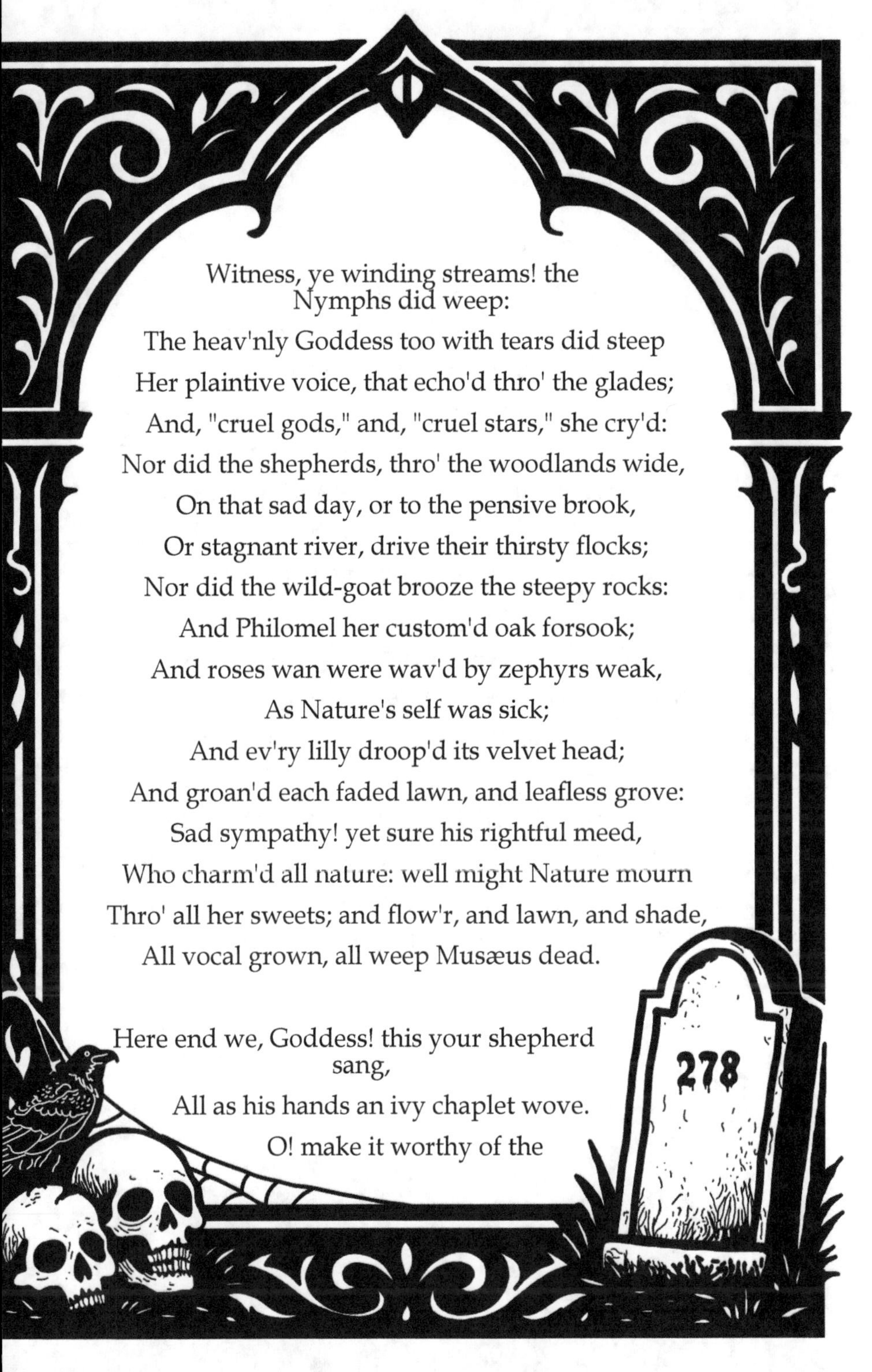

Witness, ye winding streams! the Nymphs did weep:
The heav'nly Goddess too with tears did steep
Her plaintive voice, that echo'd thro' the glades;
And, "cruel gods," and, "cruel stars," she cry'd:
Nor did the shepherds, thro' the woodlands wide,
On that sad day, or to the pensive brook,
Or stagnant river, drive their thirsty flocks;
Nor did the wild-goat brooze the steepy rocks:
And Philomel her custom'd oak forsook;
And roses wan were wav'd by zephyrs weak,
As Nature's self was sick;
And ev'ry lilly droop'd its velvet head;
And groan'd each faded lawn, and leafless grove:
Sad sympathy! yet sure his rightful meed,
Who charm'd all nature: well might Nature mourn
Thro' all her sweets; and flow'r, and lawn, and shade,
All vocal grown, all weep Musæus dead.

Here end we, Goddess! this your shepherd sang,
All as his hands an ivy chaplet wove.
O! make it worthy of the

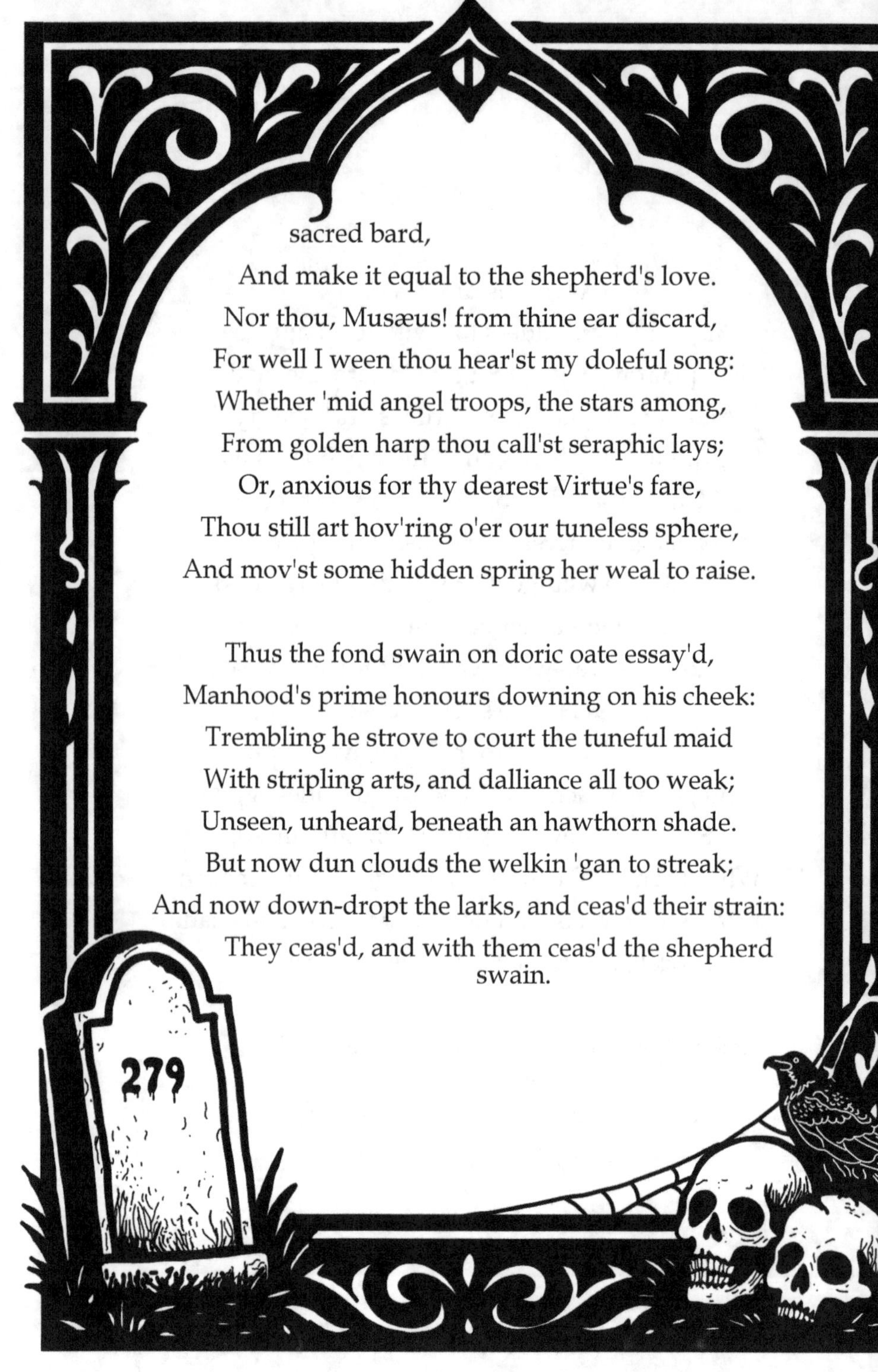

sacred bard,
And make it equal to the shepherd's love.
Nor thou, Musæus! from thine ear discard,
For well I ween thou hear'st my doleful song:
Whether 'mid angel troops, the stars among,
From golden harp thou call'st seraphic lays;
Or, anxious for thy dearest Virtue's fare,
Thou still art hov'ring o'er our tuneless sphere,
And mov'st some hidden spring her weal to raise.

Thus the fond swain on doric oate essay'd,
Manhood's prime honours downing on his cheek:
Trembling he strove to court the tuneful maid
With stripling arts, and dalliance all too weak;
Unseen, unheard, beneath an hawthorn shade.
But now dun clouds the welkin 'gan to streak;
And now down-dropt the larks, and ceas'd their strain:
They ceas'd, and with them ceas'd the shepherd swain.

James MacPherson

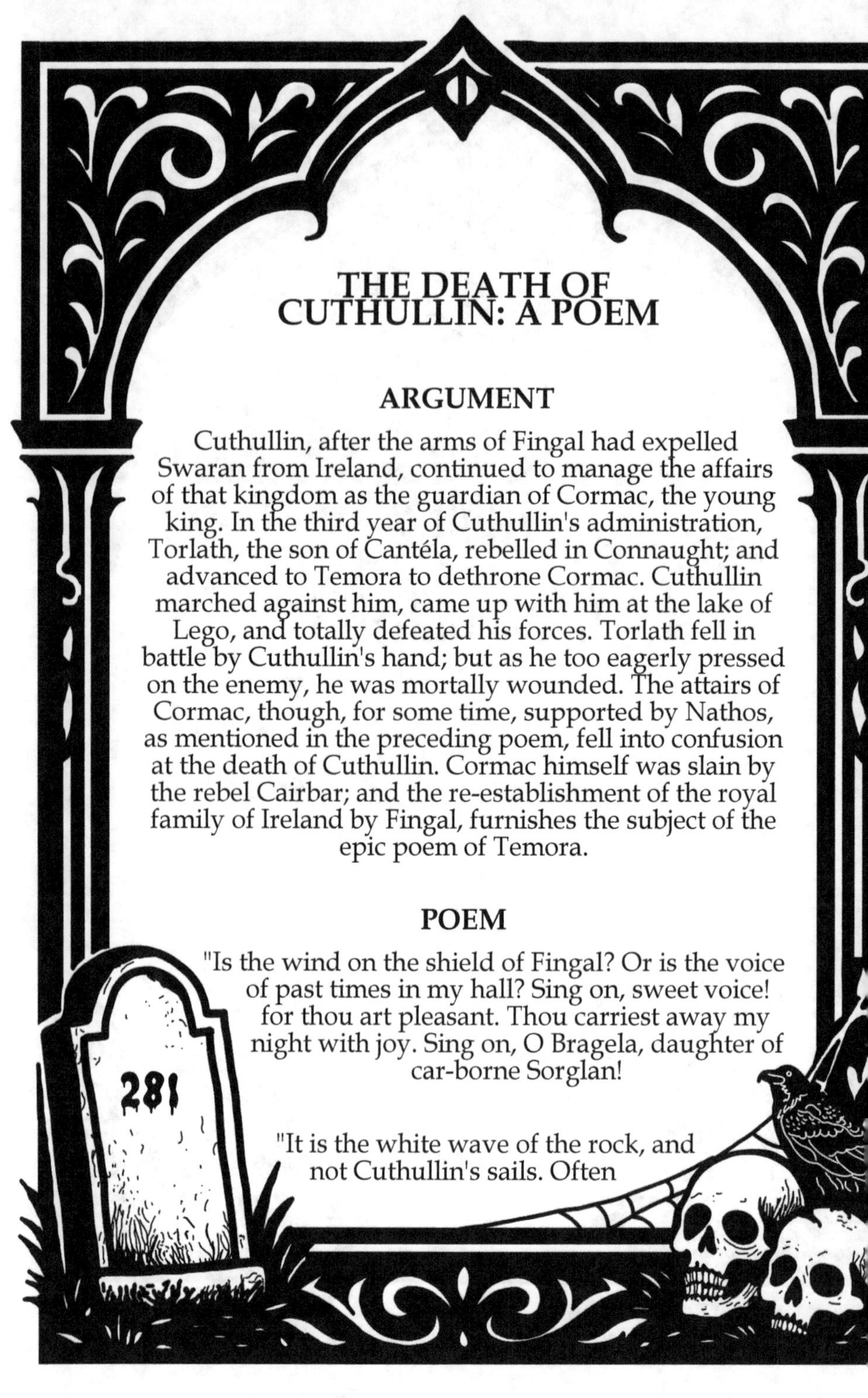

THE DEATH OF CUTHULLIN: A POEM

ARGUMENT

Cuthullin, after the arms of Fingal had expelled Swaran from Ireland, continued to manage the affairs of that kingdom as the guardian of Cormac, the young king. In the third year of Cuthullin's administration, Torlath, the son of Cantéla, rebelled in Connaught; and advanced to Temora to dethrone Cormac. Cuthullin marched against him, came up with him at the lake of Lego, and totally defeated his forces. Torlath fell in battle by Cuthullin's hand; but as he too eagerly pressed on the enemy, he was mortally wounded. The attairs of Cormac, though, for some time, supported by Nathos, as mentioned in the preceding poem, fell into confusion at the death of Cuthullin. Cormac himself was slain by the rebel Cairbar; and the re-establishment of the royal family of Ireland by Fingal, furnishes the subject of the epic poem of Temora.

POEM

"Is the wind on the shield of Fingal? Or is the voice of past times in my hall? Sing on, sweet voice! for thou art pleasant. Thou carriest away my night with joy. Sing on, O Bragela, daughter of car-borne Sorglan!

"It is the white wave of the rock, and not Cuthullin's sails. Often

do the mists deceive me for the ship of my love! when they rise round some ghost, and spread their grey skirts on the wind. Why dost thou delay thy coming, son of the generous Semo? Four times has autumn returned with its winds, and raised the seas of Togorma, since thou hast been in the roar of battles, and Bragéla distant far! Hills of the isle of mist! when will ye answer to his hounds? But ye are dark in your clouds. Sad Bragéla calls in vain! Night comes rolling down. The face of ocean fails. The heath-cock's head is beneath his wing. The hind sleeps, with the hart of the desert. They shall rise with morning's light, and feed by the mossy stream. But my tears return with the sun. My sighs come on with the night. When wilt thou come in thine arms, O chief of Erin's wars?"

Pleasant is thy voice in Ossian's ear, daughter of car-borne Sorglan! But retire to the hall of shells; to the beam of the burning oak. Attend to the murmur of the sea: it rolls at Dunscai's walls: let sleep descend on thy blue eyes. Let the hero arise in thy dreams!

Cuthullin sits at Lego's lake, at the dark rolling of waters. Night is around the hero. His thousands spread on the heath. A hundred oaks burn in the midst. The feast of shells is smoking wide. Carril strikes the harp beneath a tree. His grey locks glitter in the beam. The rustling blast of night is near, and lifts his aged hair. His song is of the blue Togorma, and of its chief, Cuthullin's friend!

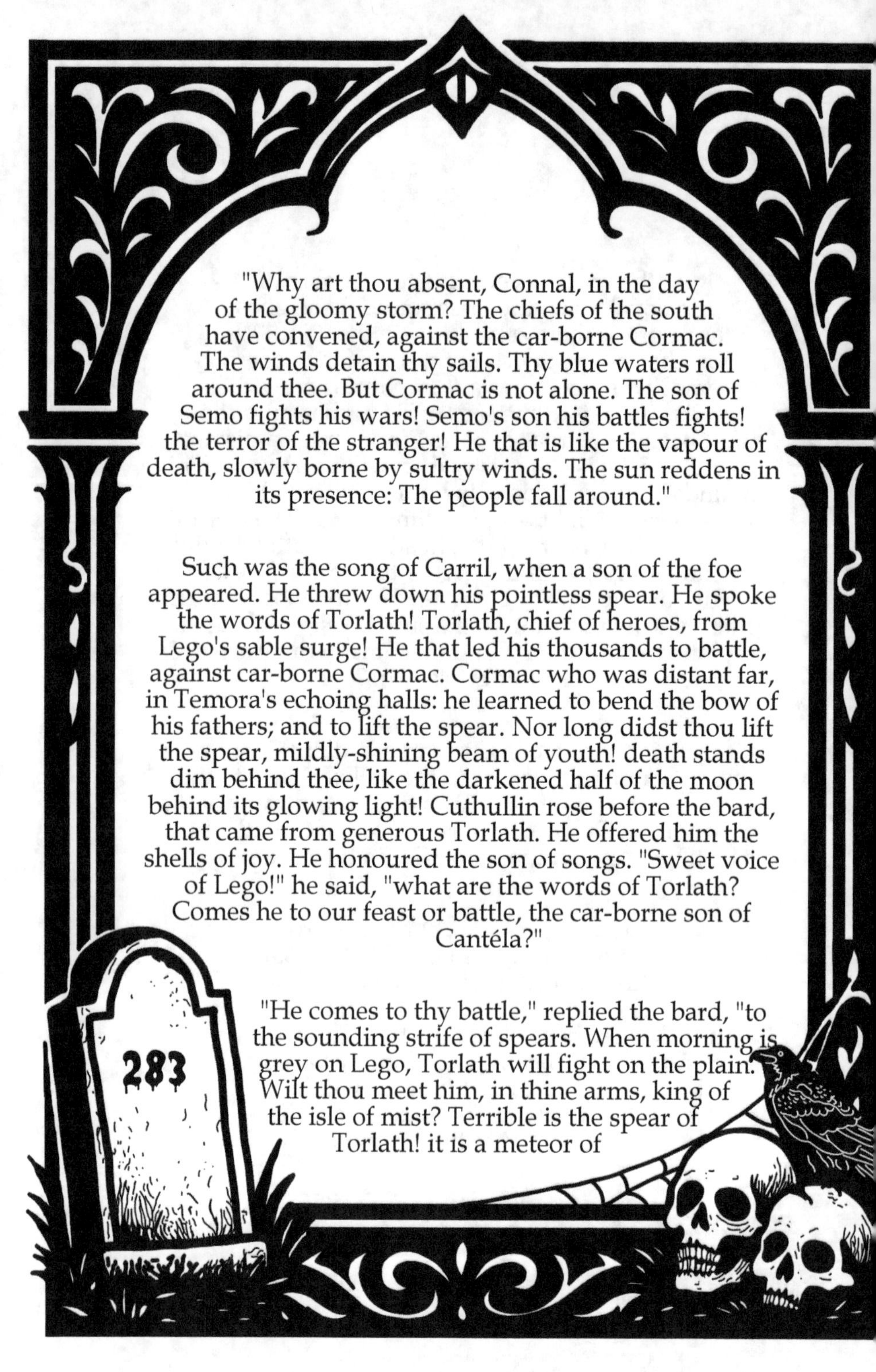

"Why art thou absent, Connal, in the day of the gloomy storm? The chiefs of the south have convened, against the car-borne Cormac. The winds detain thy sails. Thy blue waters roll around thee. But Cormac is not alone. The son of Semo fights his wars! Semo's son his battles fights! the terror of the stranger! He that is like the vapour of death, slowly borne by sultry winds. The sun reddens in its presence: The people fall around."

Such was the song of Carril, when a son of the foe appeared. He threw down his pointless spear. He spoke the words of Torlath! Torlath, chief of heroes, from Lego's sable surge! He that led his thousands to battle, against car-borne Cormac. Cormac who was distant far, in Temora's echoing halls: he learned to bend the bow of his fathers; and to lift the spear. Nor long didst thou lift the spear, mildly-shining beam of youth! death stands dim behind thee, like the darkened half of the moon behind its glowing light! Cuthullin rose before the bard, that came from generous Torlath. He offered him the shells of joy. He honoured the son of songs. "Sweet voice of Lego!" he said, "what are the words of Torlath? Comes he to our feast or battle, the car-borne son of Cantéla?"

"He comes to thy battle," replied the bard, "to the sounding strife of spears. When morning is grey on Lego, Torlath will fight on the plain. Wilt thou meet him, in thine arms, king of the isle of mist? Terrible is the spear of Torlath! it is a meteor of

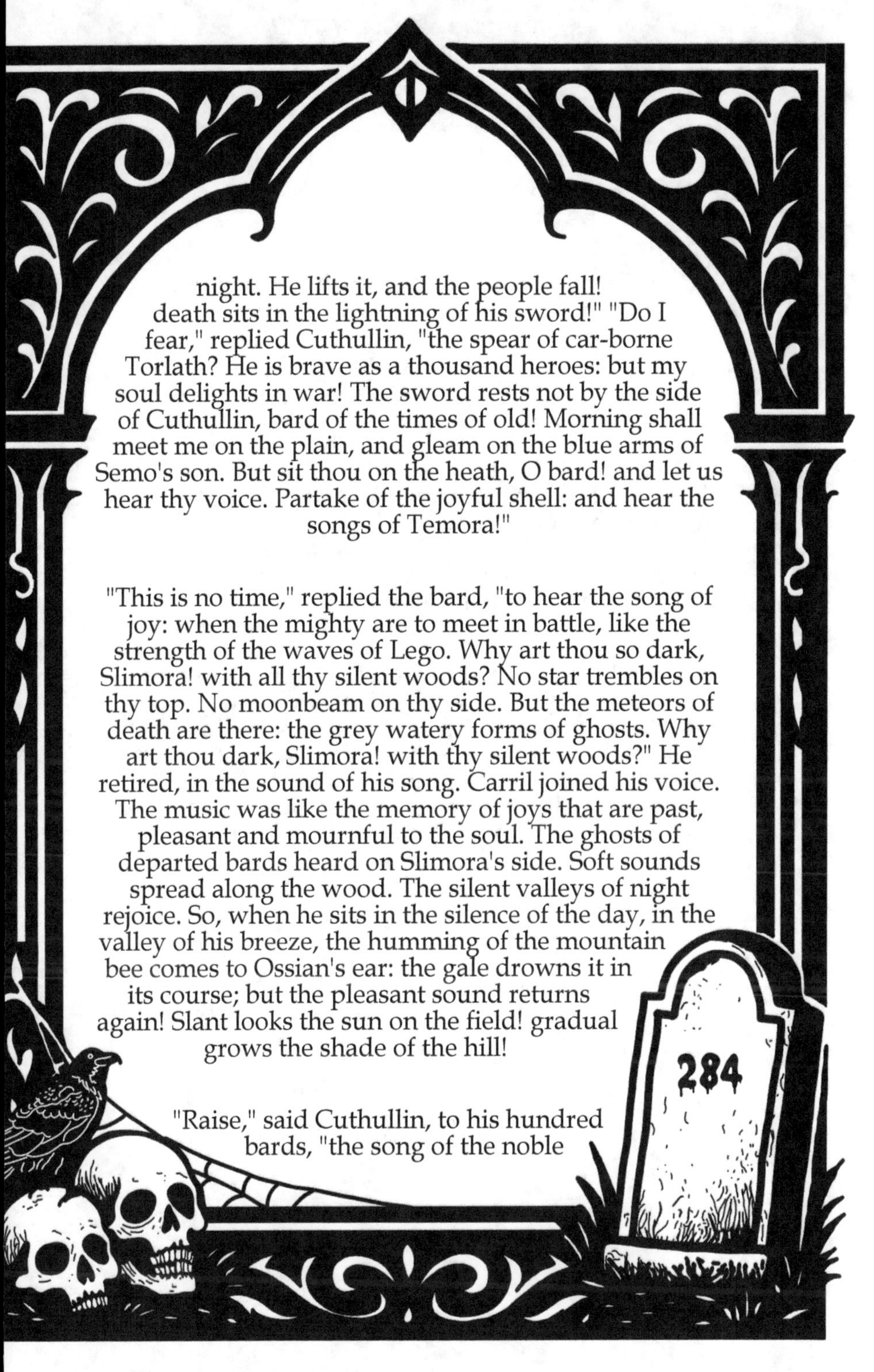

night. He lifts it, and the people fall! death sits in the lightning of his sword!" "Do I fear," replied Cuthullin, "the spear of car-borne Torlath? He is brave as a thousand heroes: but my soul delights in war! The sword rests not by the side of Cuthullin, bard of the times of old! Morning shall meet me on the plain, and gleam on the blue arms of Semo's son. But sit thou on the heath, O bard! and let us hear thy voice. Partake of the joyful shell: and hear the songs of Temora!"

"This is no time," replied the bard, "to hear the song of joy: when the mighty are to meet in battle, like the strength of the waves of Lego. Why art thou so dark, Slimora! with all thy silent woods? No star trembles on thy top. No moonbeam on thy side. But the meteors of death are there: the grey watery forms of ghosts. Why art thou dark, Slimora! with thy silent woods?" He retired, in the sound of his song. Carril joined his voice. The music was like the memory of joys that are past, pleasant and mournful to the soul. The ghosts of departed bards heard on Slimora's side. Soft sounds spread along the wood. The silent valleys of night rejoice. So, when he sits in the silence of the day, in the valley of his breeze, the humming of the mountain bee comes to Ossian's ear: the gale drowns it in its course; but the pleasant sound returns again! Slant looks the sun on the field! gradual grows the shade of the hill!

"Raise," said Cuthullin, to his hundred bards, "the song of the noble

Fingal: that song which he hears at night, when the dreams of his rest descend: when the bards strike the distant harp, and the faint light gleams on Selma's walls. Or let the grief of Lara rise: the sighs of the mother of Calmar, when he was sought, in vain, on his hills; when she beheld his bow in the hall. Carril, place the shield of Caithbat on that branch. Let the spear of Cuthullin be near; that the sound of my battle may rise, with the grey beam of the east." The hero leaned on his father's shield: the song of Lara rose! The hundred bards were distant far: Carril alone is near the chief. The words of the song were his: the sound of his harp was mournful.

"Alclétha with the aged locks! mother of car-borne Calmar! why dost thou look toward the desert, to behold the return of thy son? These are not his heroes dark on the heath: nor is that the voice of Calmar. It is but the distant grove, Alclétha! but the roar of the mountain wind!" "Who bounds over Lara's stream, sister of the noble Calmar? Does not Alclétha behold his spear? But her eyes are dim! Is it not the son of Matha, daughter of my love?"

"It is but an aged oak, Alclétha!" replied the lovely weeping Alona. "It is but an oak, Alclétha, bent over Lara's stream. But who comes along the plain? sorrow is in his speed. He lifts high the spear of Calmar. Alclétha, it is covered with blood!" "But it is covered with the blood of foes, sister of car-borne Calmar! His spear

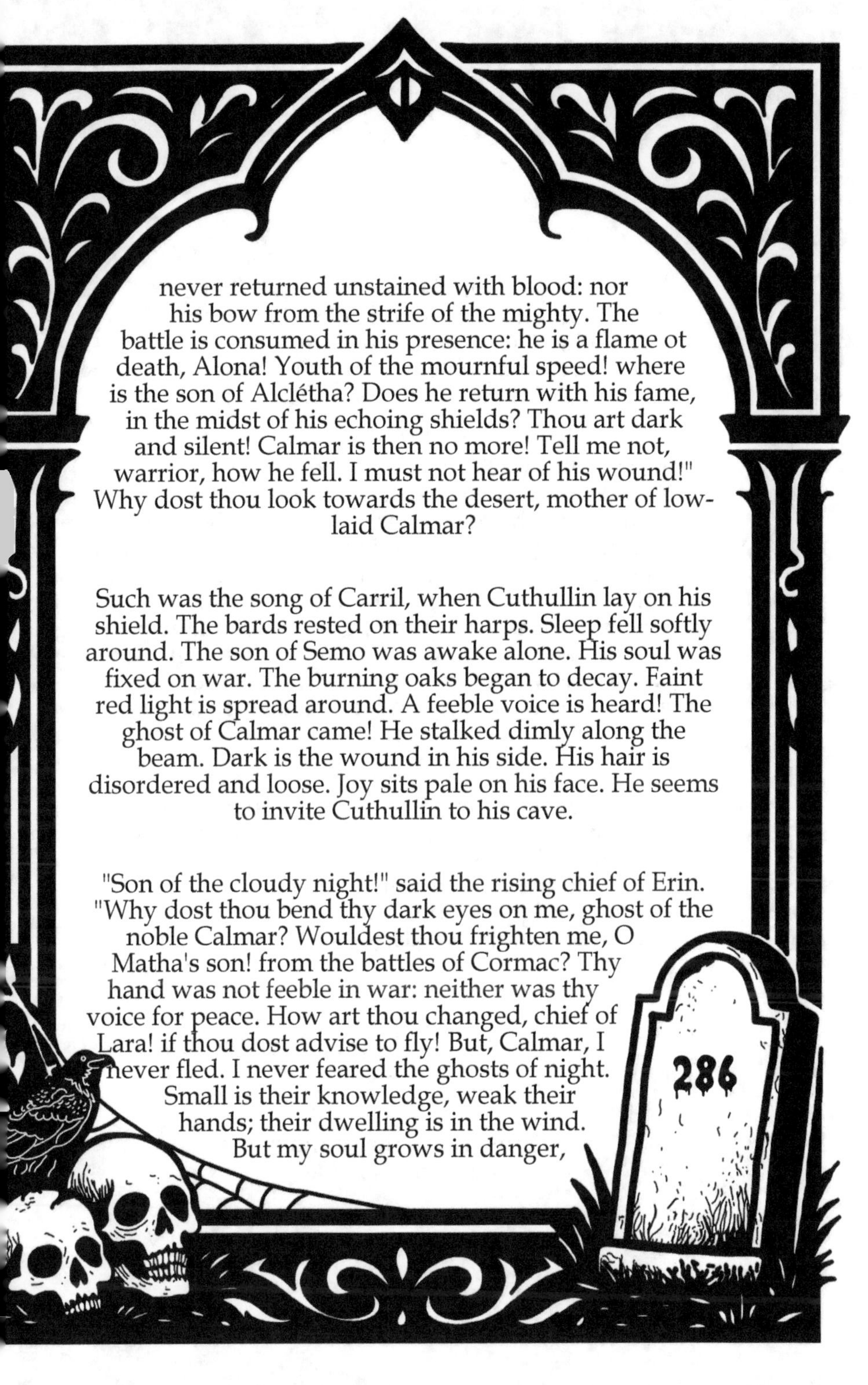

never returned unstained with blood: nor his bow from the strife of the mighty. The battle is consumed in his presence: he is a flame ot death, Alona! Youth of the mournful speed! where is the son of Alclétha? Does he return with his fame, in the midst of his echoing shields? Thou art dark and silent! Calmar is then no more! Tell me not, warrior, how he fell. I must not hear of his wound!" Why dost thou look towards the desert, mother of low-laid Calmar?

Such was the song of Carril, when Cuthullin lay on his shield. The bards rested on their harps. Sleep fell softly around. The son of Semo was awake alone. His soul was fixed on war. The burning oaks began to decay. Faint red light is spread around. A feeble voice is heard! The ghost of Calmar came! He stalked dimly along the beam. Dark is the wound in his side. His hair is disordered and loose. Joy sits pale on his face. He seems to invite Cuthullin to his cave.

"Son of the cloudy night!" said the rising chief of Erin. "Why dost thou bend thy dark eyes on me, ghost of the noble Calmar? Wouldest thou frighten me, O Matha's son! from the battles of Cormac? Thy hand was not feeble in war: neither was thy voice for peace. How art thou changed, chief of Lara! if thou dost advise to fly! But, Calmar, I never fled. I never feared the ghosts of night. Small is their knowledge, weak their hands; their dwelling is in the wind. But my soul grows in danger,

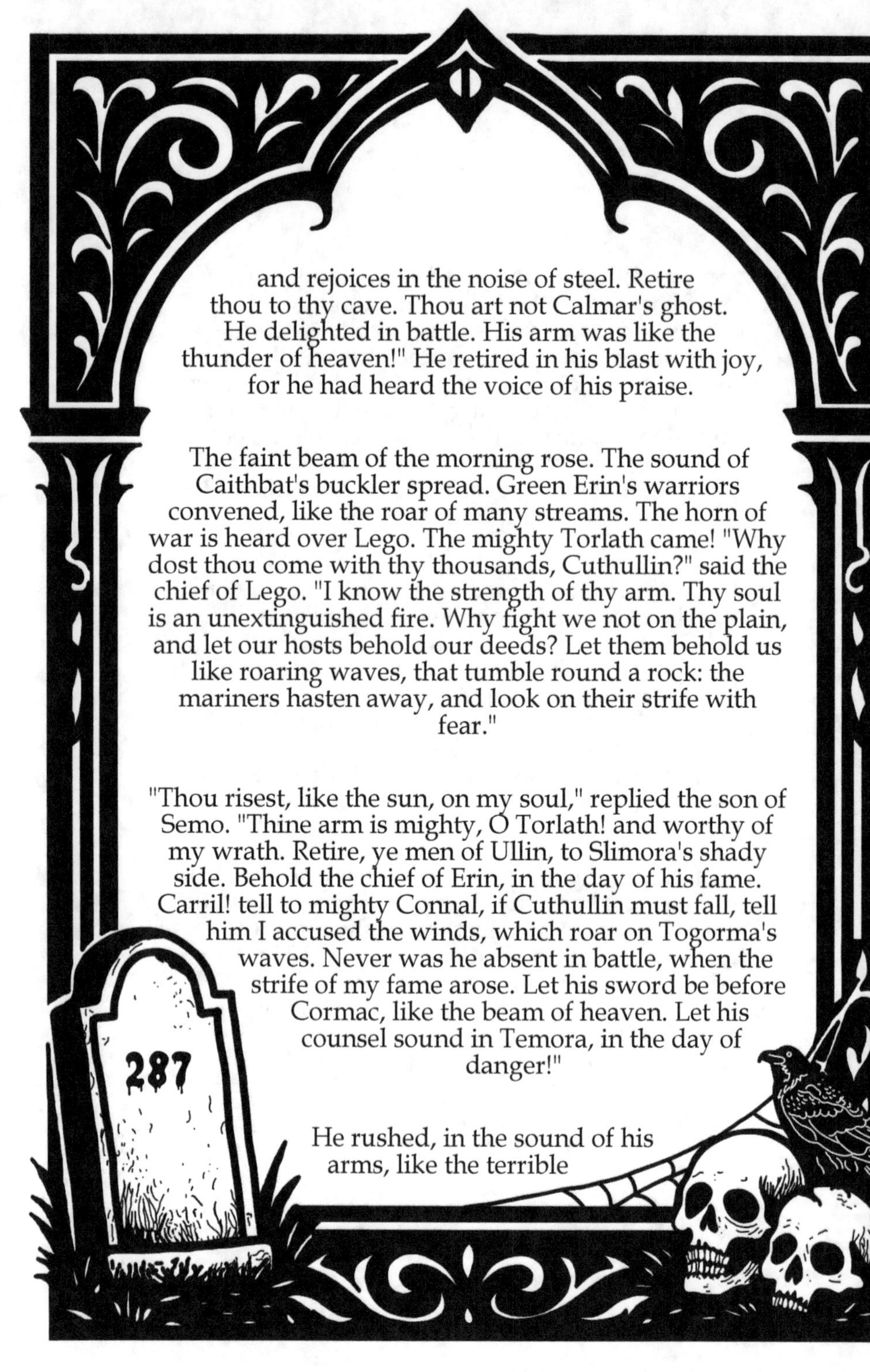

and rejoices in the noise of steel. Retire thou to thy cave. Thou art not Calmar's ghost. He delighted in battle. His arm was like the thunder of heaven!" He retired in his blast with joy, for he had heard the voice of his praise.

The faint beam of the morning rose. The sound of Caithbat's buckler spread. Green Erin's warriors convened, like the roar of many streams. The horn of war is heard over Lego. The mighty Torlath came! "Why dost thou come with thy thousands, Cuthullin?" said the chief of Lego. "I know the strength of thy arm. Thy soul is an unextinguished fire. Why fight we not on the plain, and let our hosts behold our deeds? Let them behold us like roaring waves, that tumble round a rock: the mariners hasten away, and look on their strife with fear."

"Thou risest, like the sun, on my soul," replied the son of Semo. "Thine arm is mighty, O Torlath! and worthy of my wrath. Retire, ye men of Ullin, to Slimora's shady side. Behold the chief of Erin, in the day of his fame. Carril! tell to mighty Connal, if Cuthullin must fall, tell him I accused the winds, which roar on Togorma's waves. Never was he absent in battle, when the strife of my fame arose. Let his sword be before Cormac, like the beam of heaven. Let his counsel sound in Temora, in the day of danger!"

He rushed, in the sound of his arms, like the terrible

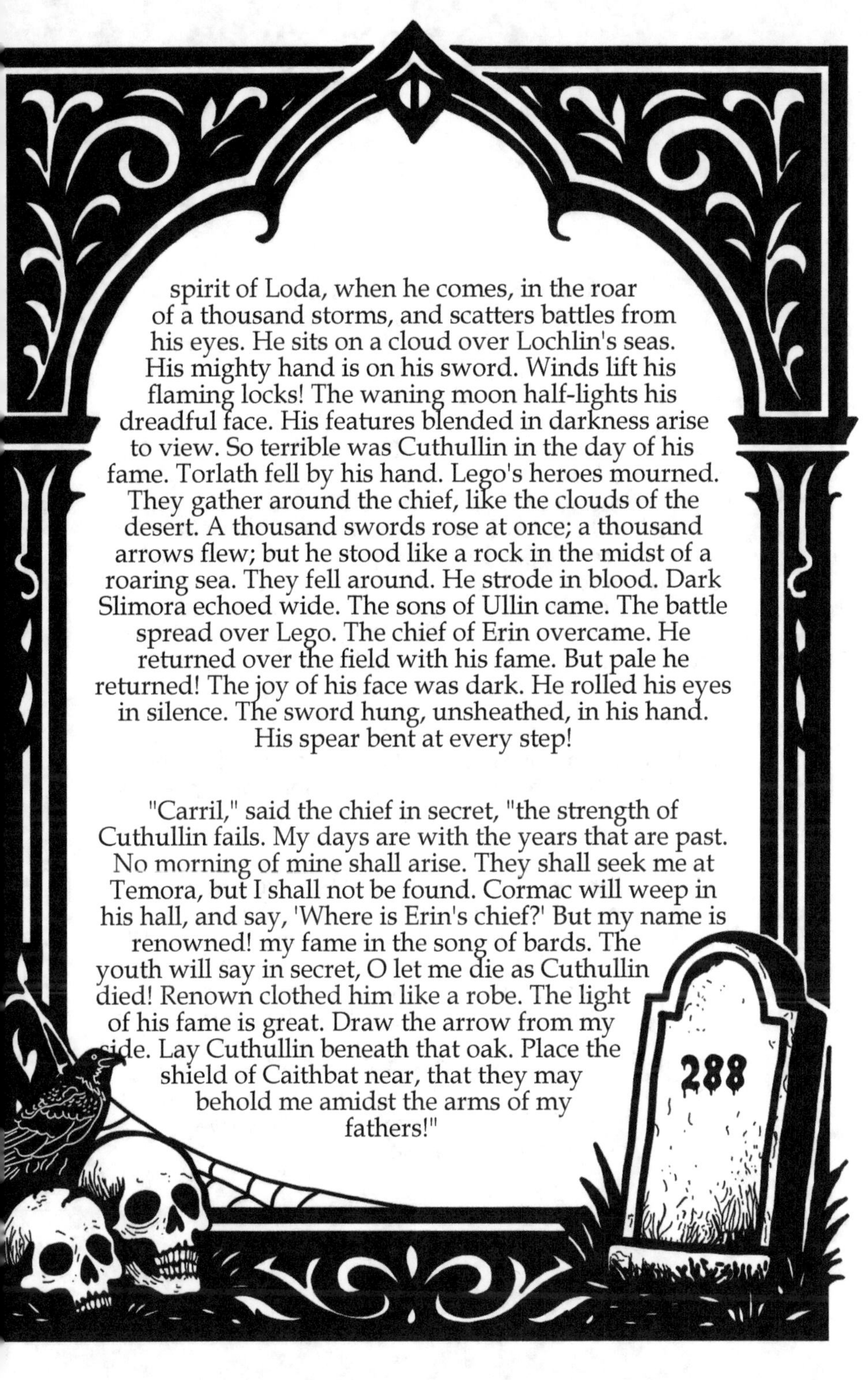

spirit of Loda, when he comes, in the roar of a thousand storms, and scatters battles from his eyes. He sits on a cloud over Lochlin's seas. His mighty hand is on his sword. Winds lift his flaming locks! The waning moon half-lights his dreadful face. His features blended in darkness arise to view. So terrible was Cuthullin in the day of his fame. Torlath fell by his hand. Lego's heroes mourned. They gather around the chief, like the clouds of the desert. A thousand swords rose at once; a thousand arrows flew; but he stood like a rock in the midst of a roaring sea. They fell around. He strode in blood. Dark Slimora echoed wide. The sons of Ullin came. The battle spread over Lego. The chief of Erin overcame. He returned over the field with his fame. But pale he returned! The joy of his face was dark. He rolled his eyes in silence. The sword hung, unsheathed, in his hand. His spear bent at every step!

"Carril," said the chief in secret, "the strength of Cuthullin fails. My days are with the years that are past. No morning of mine shall arise. They shall seek me at Temora, but I shall not be found. Cormac will weep in his hall, and say, 'Where is Erin's chief?' But my name is renowned! my fame in the song of bards. The youth will say in secret, O let me die as Cuthullin died! Renown clothed him like a robe. The light of his fame is great. Draw the arrow from my side. Lay Cuthullin beneath that oak. Place the shield of Caithbat near, that they may behold me amidst the arms of my fathers!"

"And is the son of Semo fallen?" said Carril with a sigh. "Mournful are Tura's walls. Sorrow dwells at Dunscäi. Thy spouse is left alone in her youth. The son of thy love alone! He shall come to Bragéla, and ask her why she weeps? He shall lift his eyes to the wall, and see his father's sword. 'Whose sword is that?' he will say. The soul of his mother is sad. Who is that, like the hart of the desert, in the murmur of his course? His eyes look wildly round in search of his friend. Connal, son of Colgar, where hast thou been, when the mighty fell? Did the seas of Congorma roll around thee? Was the wind of the south in thy sails? The mighty have fallen in battle, and thou wast not there. Let none tell it in Selma, nor in Morven's woody land. Fingal will be sad, and the sons of the desert mourn!"

By the dark rolling waves of Lego they raised the hero's tomb. Luäth, at a distance, lies. The song of bards rose over the dead.

"Blest be thy soul, son of Semo! Thou wert mighty in battle. Thy strength was like the strength of a stream: thy speed like the eagle's wing. Thy path in battle was terrible: the steps of death were behind thy sword. Blest be thy soul, son of Semo, car-borne chief of Dunscäi! Thou hast not fallen by the sword of the mighty, neither was thy blood on the spear of the brave. The arrow came, like the sting of death in a blast: nor did the feeble hand, which drew the bow, perceive it. Peace to thy soul,

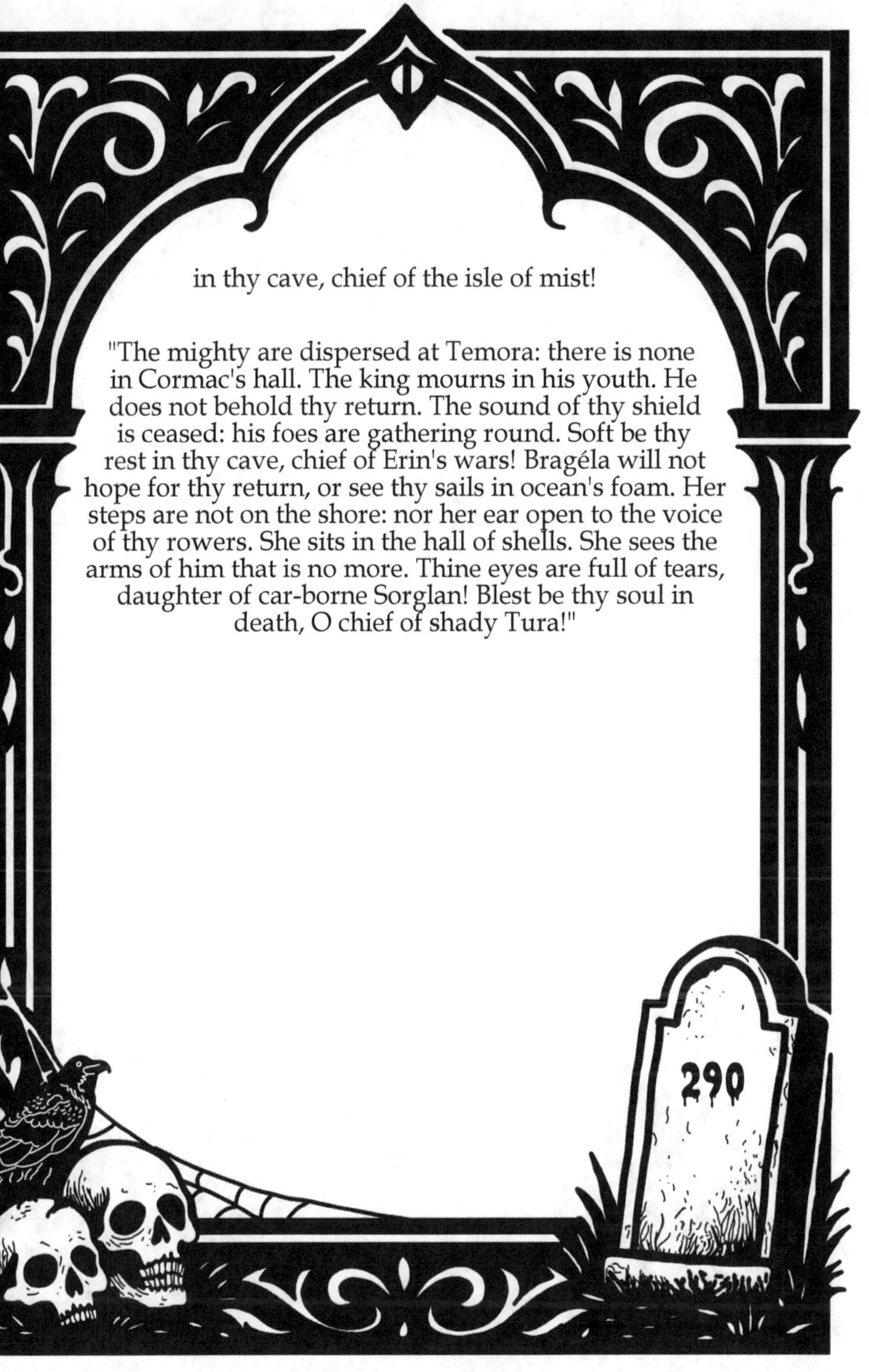

in thy cave, chief of the isle of mist!

"The mighty are dispersed at Temora: there is none in Cormac's hall. The king mourns in his youth. He does not behold thy return. The sound of thy shield is ceased: his foes are gathering round. Soft be thy rest in thy cave, chief of Erin's wars! Bragéla will not hope for thy return, or see thy sails in ocean's foam. Her steps are not on the shore: nor her ear open to the voice of thy rowers. She sits in the hall of shells. She sees the arms of him that is no more. Thine eyes are full of tears, daughter of car-borne Sorglan! Blest be thy soul in death, O chief of shady Tura!"

Thomas Parnell

A NIGHT-PIECE ON DEATH

By the blue taper's trembling light,
No more I waste the wakeful night,
Intent with endless view to pore
The schoolmen and the sages o'er:
Their books from wisdom widely stray,
Or point at best the longest way.
I'll seek a readier path, and go
Where wisdom's surely taught below.
How deep yon azure dyes the sky,
Where orbs of gold unnumbered lie,
While through their ranks in silver pride
The nether crescent seems to glide.
The slumb'ring breeze forgets to breathe,
The lake is smooth and clear beneath,
Where once again the spangled show
Descends to meet our eyes below.
The grounds, which on the right aspire,
In dimness from the view retire:
The left presents a place of graves,
Whose wall the silent water laves.
That steeple guides thy doubtful sight
Among the livid gleams of

night.
There pass, with melancholy state,
By all the solemn heaps of fate,
And think, as softly-sad you tread
Above the venerable dead,
"Time was, like thee they life possessed,
And time shall be, that thou shalt rest."
Those graves, with bending osier bound,
That nameless heave the crumpled ground,
Quick to the glancing thought disclose
Where Toil and Poverty repose.
The flat smooth stones that bear a name,
The chisel's slender help to fame
(Which ere our set of friends decay
Their frequent steps may wear away),
A middle race of mortals own,
Men, half ambitious, all unknown.
The marble tombs that rise on high,
Whose dead in vaulted arches lie,
Whose pillars swell with sculptured stones,
Arms, angels, epitaphs and bones,
These (all the poor remains of state)
Adorn the rich, or praise the great;
Who, while on earth in fame they live,
Are senseless of the fame

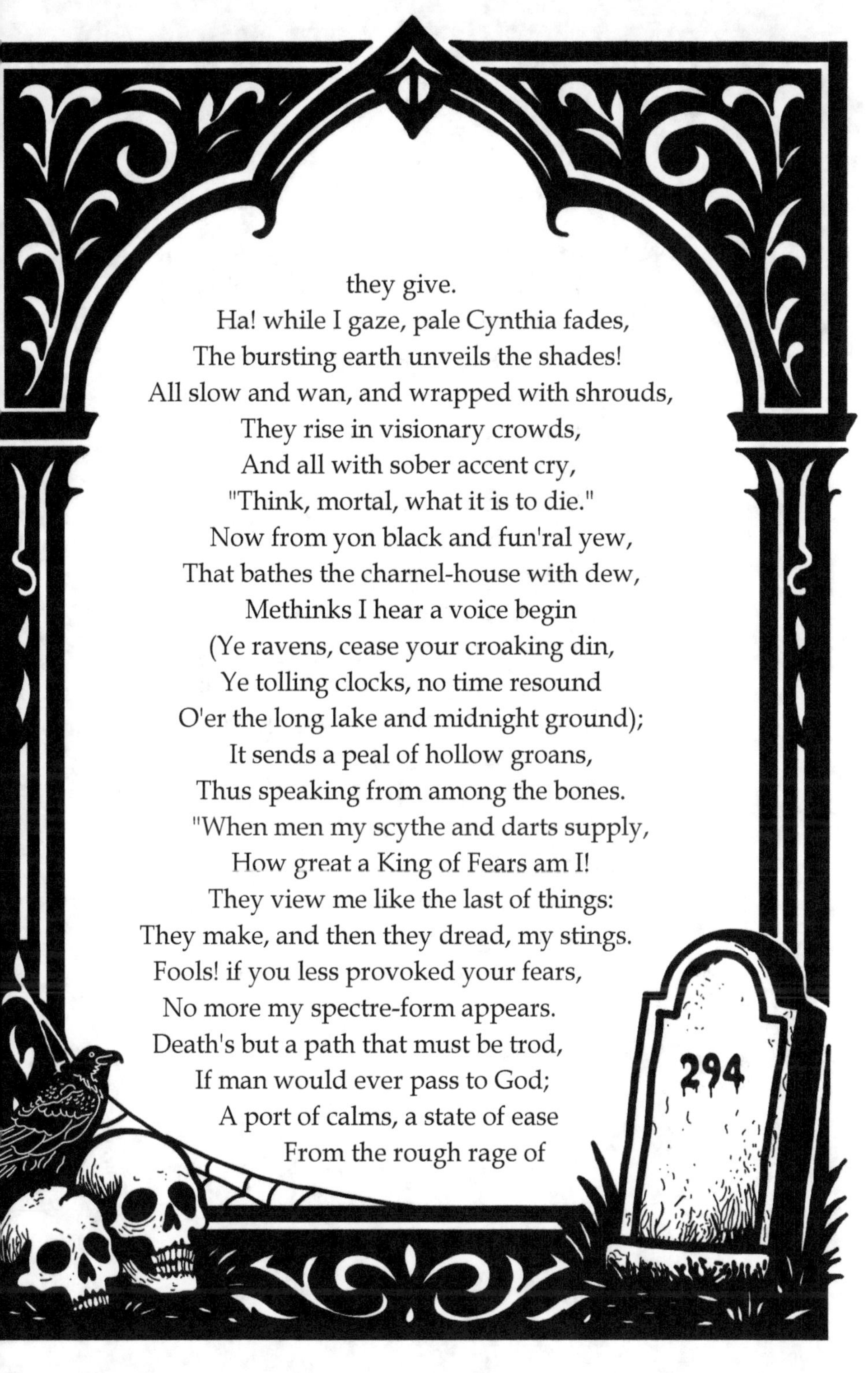

they give.
Ha! while I gaze, pale Cynthia fades,
The bursting earth unveils the shades!
All slow and wan, and wrapped with shrouds,
They rise in visionary crowds,
And all with sober accent cry,
"Think, mortal, what it is to die."
Now from yon black and fun'ral yew,
That bathes the charnel-house with dew,
Methinks I hear a voice begin
(Ye ravens, cease your croaking din,
Ye tolling clocks, no time resound
O'er the long lake and midnight ground);
It sends a peal of hollow groans,
Thus speaking from among the bones.
"When men my scythe and darts supply,
How great a King of Fears am I!
They view me like the last of things:
They make, and then they dread, my stings.
Fools! if you less provoked your fears,
No more my spectre-form appears.
Death's but a path that must be trod,
If man would ever pass to God;
A port of calms, a state of ease
From the rough rage of

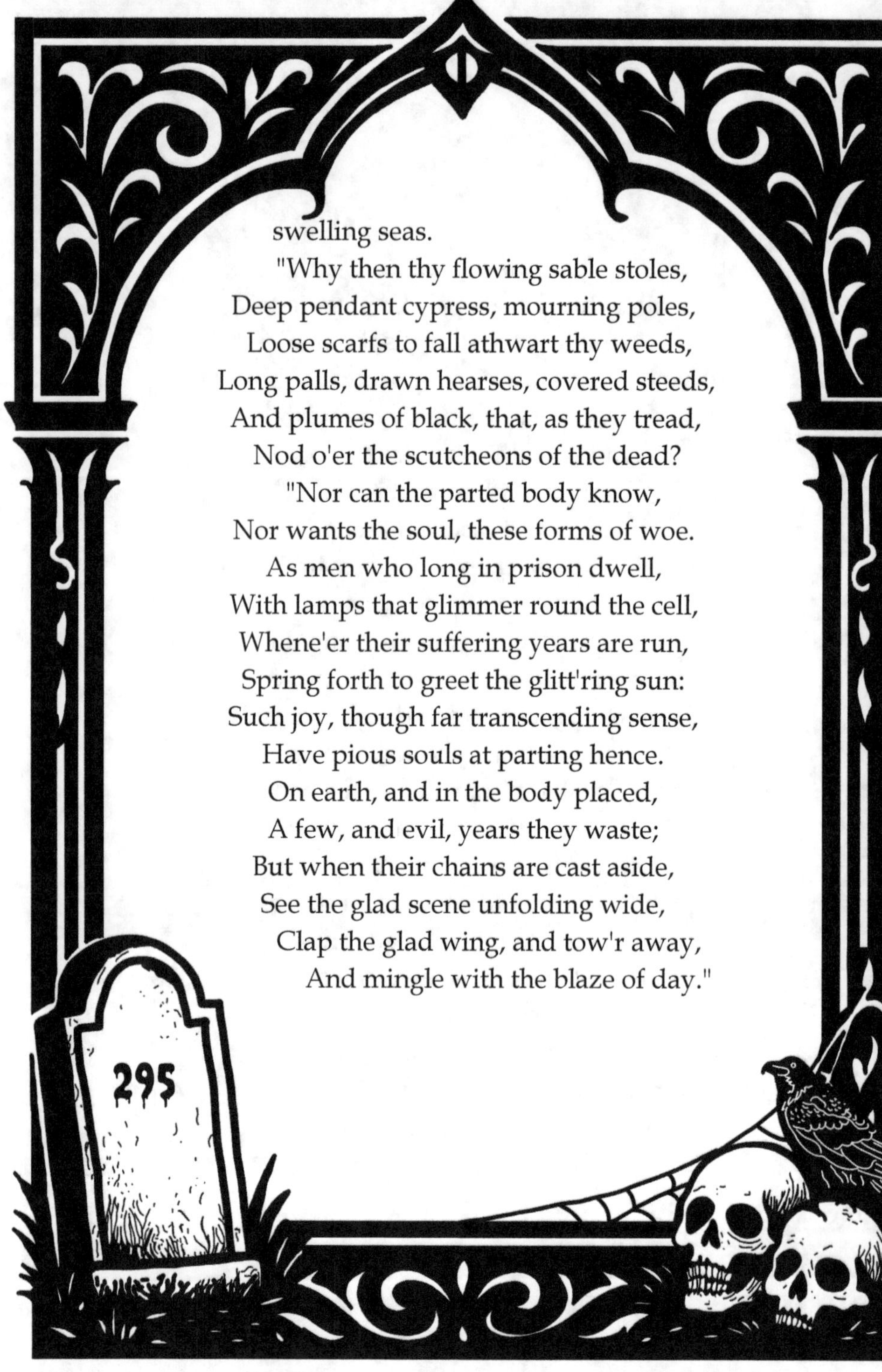

swelling seas.

"Why then thy flowing sable stoles,
Deep pendant cypress, mourning poles,
Loose scarfs to fall athwart thy weeds,
Long palls, drawn hearses, covered steeds,
And plumes of black, that, as they tread,
Nod o'er the scutcheons of the dead?

"Nor can the parted body know,
Nor wants the soul, these forms of woe.
As men who long in prison dwell,
With lamps that glimmer round the cell,
Whene'er their suffering years are run,
Spring forth to greet the glitt'ring sun:
Such joy, though far transcending sense,
Have pious souls at parting hence.
On earth, and in the body placed,
A few, and evil, years they waste;
But when their chains are cast aside,
See the glad scene unfolding wide,
Clap the glad wing, and tow'r away,
And mingle with the blaze of day."

Edgar Allan Poe

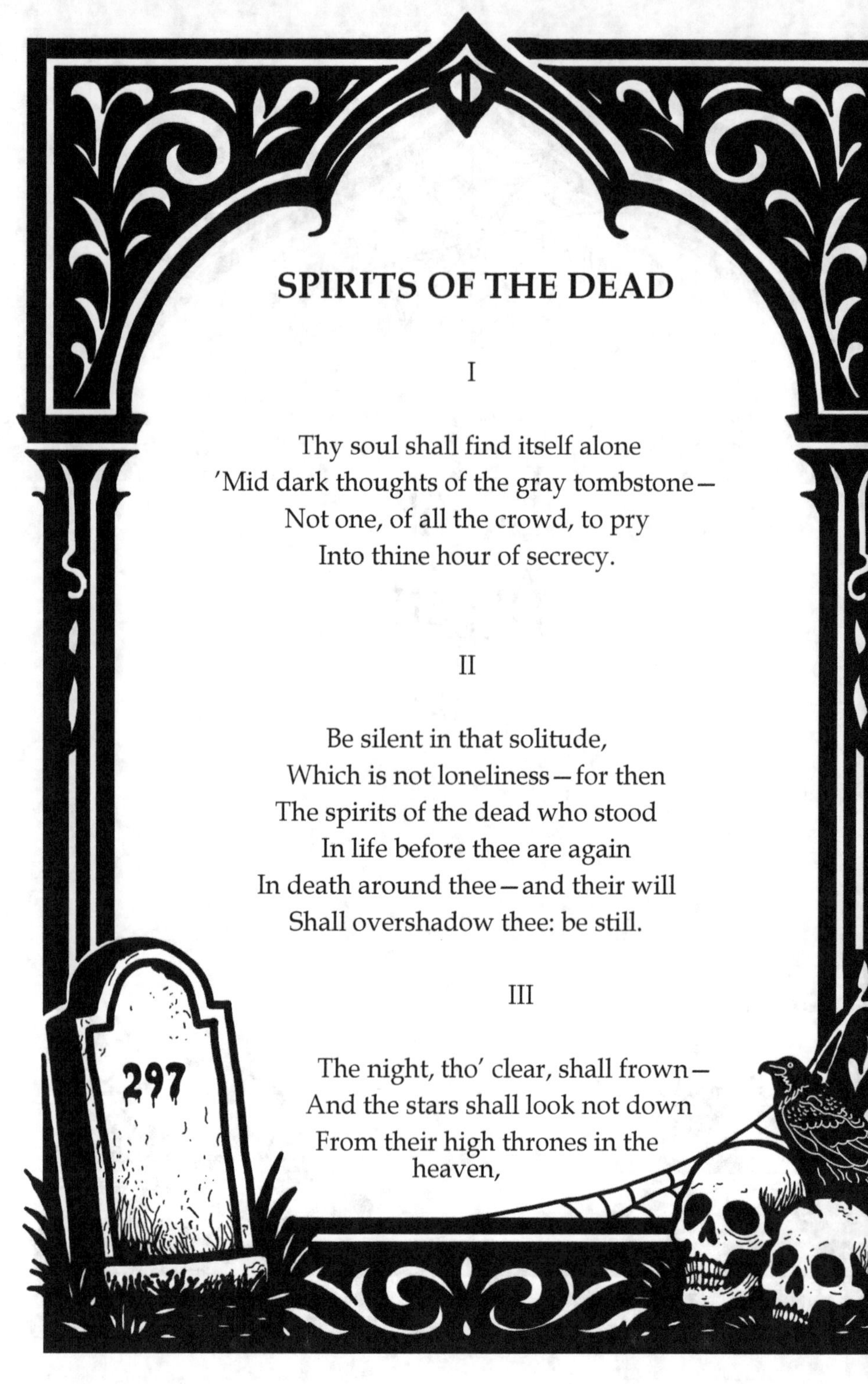

SPIRITS OF THE DEAD

I

Thy soul shall find itself alone
'Mid dark thoughts of the gray tombstone—
Not one, of all the crowd, to pry
Into thine hour of secrecy.

II

Be silent in that solitude,
Which is not loneliness—for then
The spirits of the dead who stood
In life before thee are again
In death around thee—and their will
Shall overshadow thee: be still.

III

The night, tho' clear, shall frown—
And the stars shall look not down
From their high thrones in the heaven,

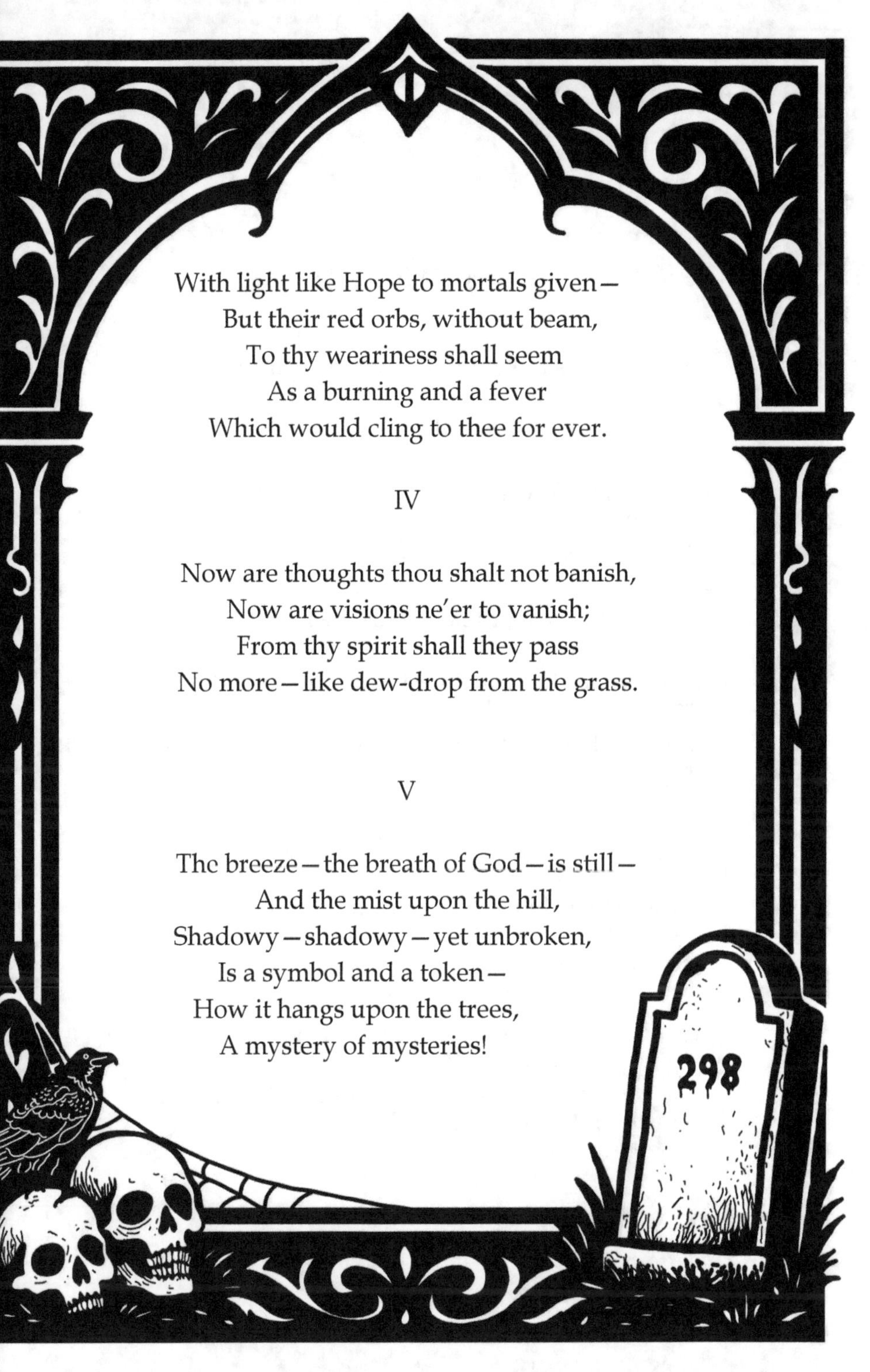

With light like Hope to mortals given—
But their red orbs, without beam,
To thy weariness shall seem
As a burning and a fever
Which would cling to thee for ever.

IV

Now are thoughts thou shalt not banish,
Now are visions ne'er to vanish;
From thy spirit shall they pass
No more—like dew-drop from the grass.

V

Thc breeze—the breath of God—is still—
And the mist upon the hill,
Shadowy—shadowy—yet unbroken,
Is a symbol and a token—
How it hangs upon the trees,
A mystery of mysteries!

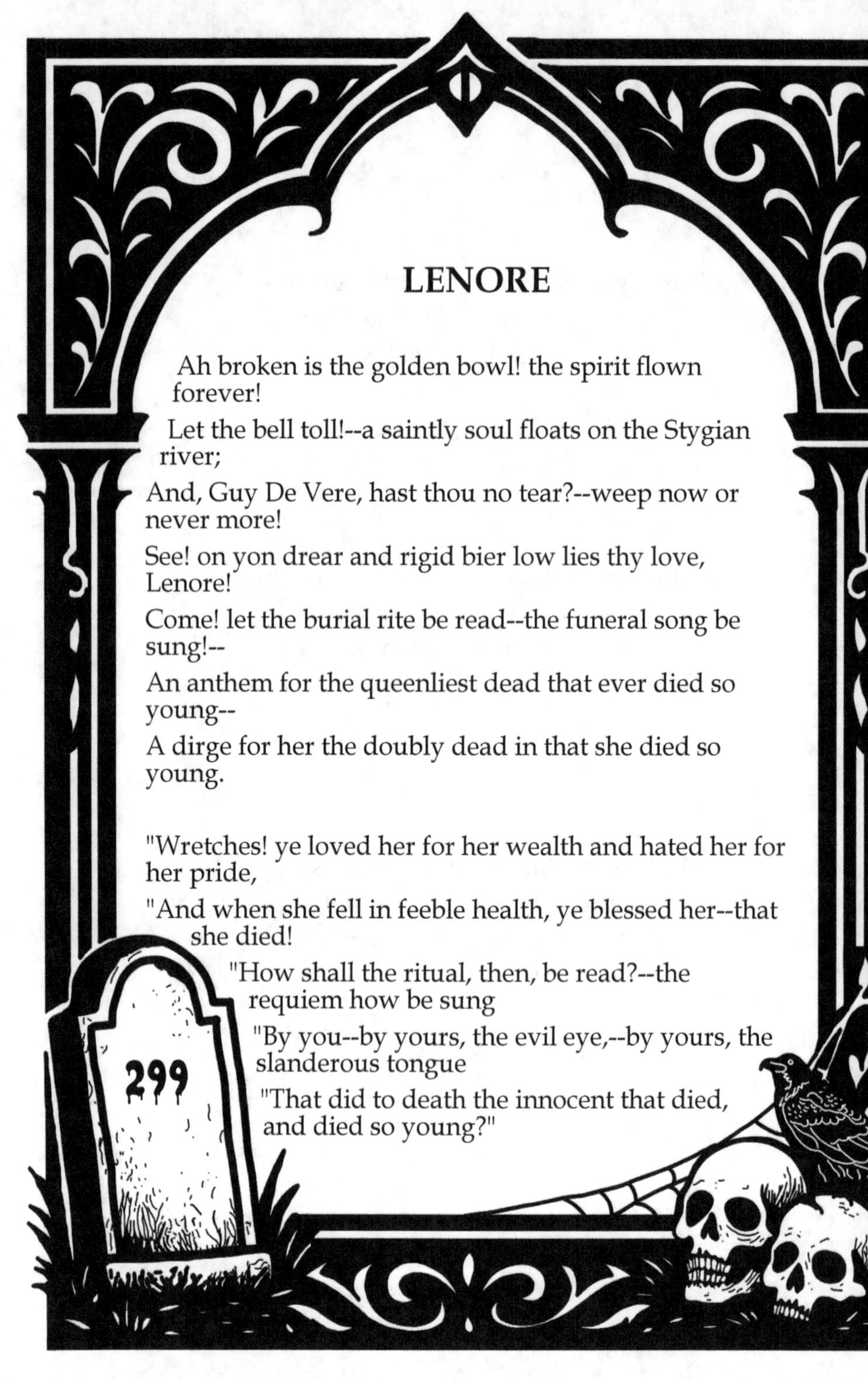

LENORE

Ah broken is the golden bowl! the spirit flown forever!
Let the bell toll!--a saintly soul floats on the Stygian river;
And, Guy De Vere, hast thou no tear?--weep now or never more!
See! on yon drear and rigid bier low lies thy love, Lenore!
Come! let the burial rite be read--the funeral song be sung!--
An anthem for the queenliest dead that ever died so young--
A dirge for her the doubly dead in that she died so young.

"Wretches! ye loved her for her wealth and hated her for her pride,
"And when she fell in feeble health, ye blessed her--that she died!
"How shall the ritual, then, be read?--the requiem how be sung
"By you--by yours, the evil eye,--by yours, the slanderous tongue
"That did to death the innocent that died, and died so young?"

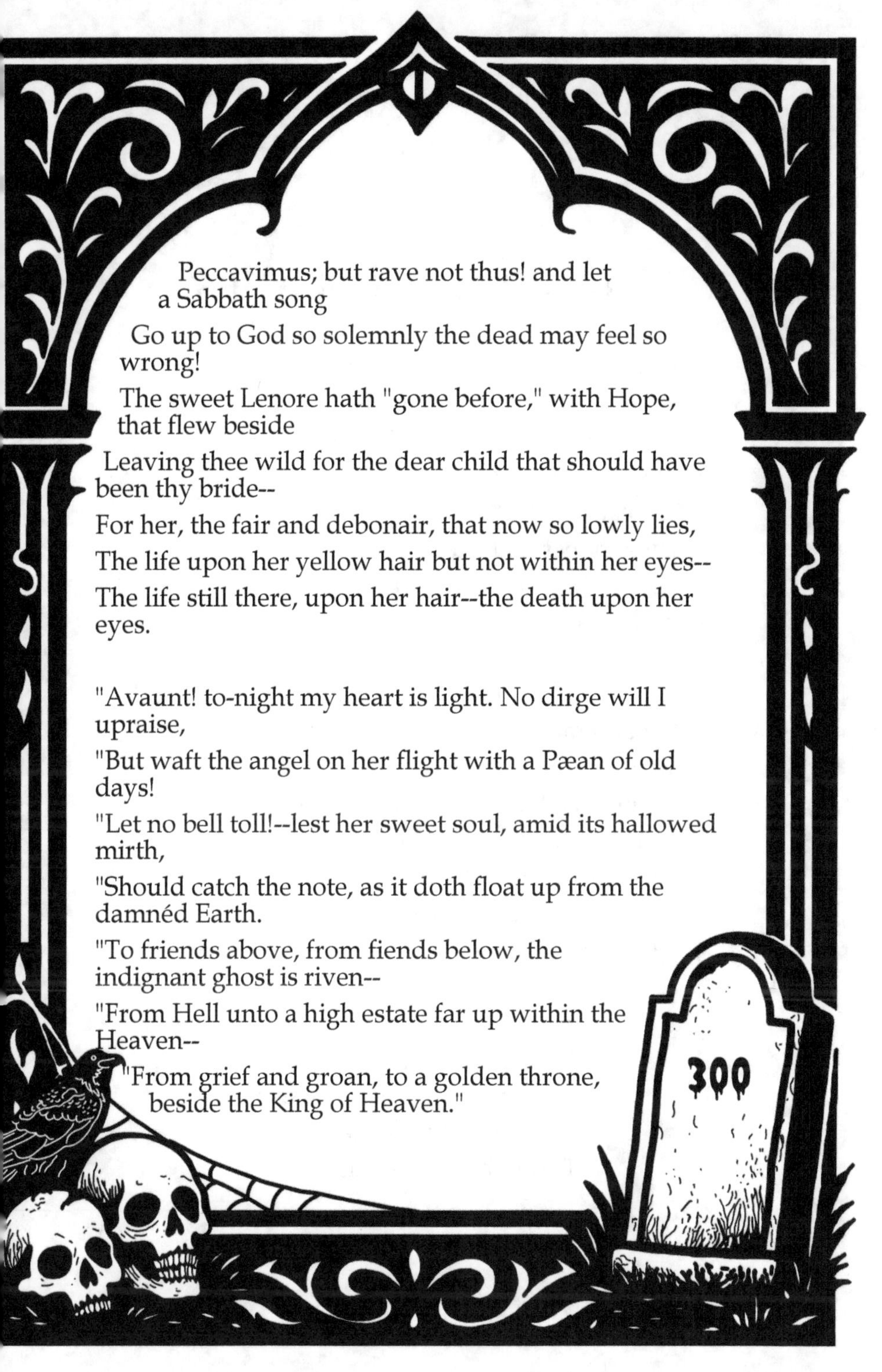

Peccavimus; but rave not thus! and let a Sabbath song
Go up to God so solemnly the dead may feel so wrong!
The sweet Lenore hath "gone before," with Hope, that flew beside
Leaving thee wild for the dear child that should have been thy bride--
For her, the fair and debonair, that now so lowly lies,
The life upon her yellow hair but not within her eyes--
The life still there, upon her hair--the death upon her eyes.

"Avaunt! to-night my heart is light. No dirge will I upraise,
"But waft the angel on her flight with a Pæan of old days!
"Let no bell toll!--lest her sweet soul, amid its hallowed mirth,
"Should catch the note, as it doth float up from the damnéd Earth.
"To friends above, from fiends below, the indignant ghost is riven--
"From Hell unto a high estate far up within the Heaven--
"From grief and groan, to a golden throne, beside the King of Heaven."

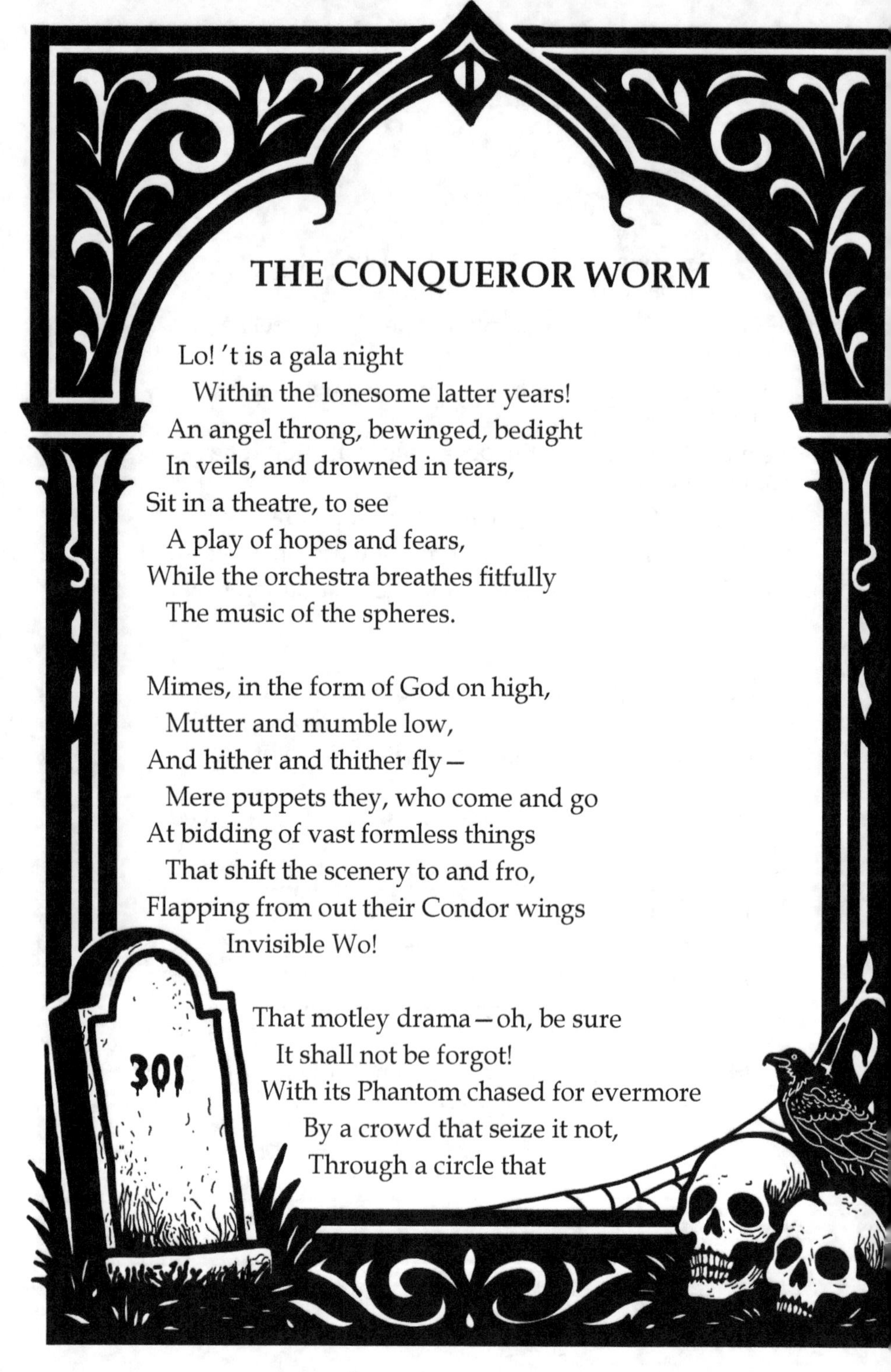

THE CONQUEROR WORM

Lo! 't is a gala night
Within the lonesome latter years!
An angel throng, bewinged, bedight
In veils, and drowned in tears,
Sit in a theatre, to see
A play of hopes and fears,
While the orchestra breathes fitfully
The music of the spheres.

Mimes, in the form of God on high,
Mutter and mumble low,
And hither and thither fly—
Mere puppets they, who come and go
At bidding of vast formless things
That shift the scenery to and fro,
Flapping from out their Condor wings
Invisible Wo!

That motley drama—oh, be sure
It shall not be forgot!
With its Phantom chased for evermore
By a crowd that seize it not,
Through a circle that

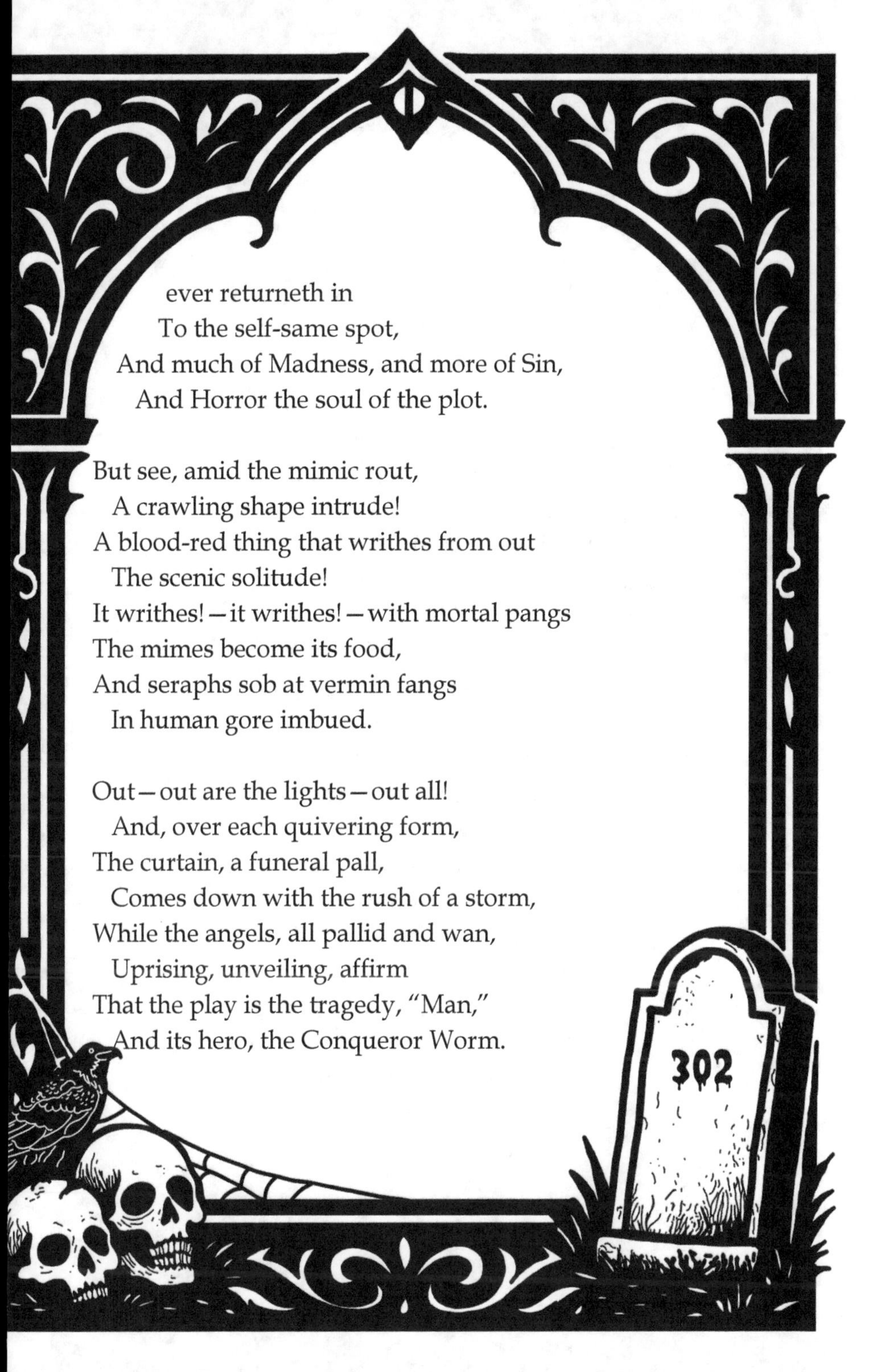

ever returneth in
To the self-same spot,
And much of Madness, and more of Sin,
And Horror the soul of the plot.

But see, amid the mimic rout,
A crawling shape intrude!
A blood-red thing that writhes from out
The scenic solitude!
It writhes! — it writhes! — with mortal pangs
The mimes become its food,
And seraphs sob at vermin fangs
In human gore imbued.

Out — out are the lights — out all!
And, over each quivering form,
The curtain, a funeral pall,
Comes down with the rush of a storm,
While the angels, all pallid and wan,
Uprising, unveiling, affirm
That the play is the tragedy, "Man,"
And its hero, the Conqueror Worm.

TO – – –. ULALUME: A BALLAD

The skies they were ashen and sober;
The leaves they were crispéd and sere –
The leaves they were withering and sere;
It was night in the lonesome October
Of my most immemorial year;
It was hard by the dim lake of Auber,
In the misty mid region of Weir –
It was down by the dank tarn of Auber,
In the ghoul-haunted woodland of Weir.

Here once, through an alley Titanic,
Of cypress, I roamed with my Soul –
Of cypress, with Psyche, my Soul.
These were days when my heart was volcanic
As the scoriac rivers that roll –
As the lavas that restlessly roll
Their sulphurous currents down Yaanek
In the ultimate climes of the pole –
That groan as they roll down Mount Yaanek
In the realms of the boreal pole.

Our talk had been serious

and sober,
But our thoughts they were palsied and sere—
Our memories were treacherous and sere—
For we knew not the month was October,
And we marked not the night of the year—
(Ah, night of all nights in the year!)
We noted not the dim lake of Auber—
(Though once we had journeyed down here)—
We remembered not the dank tarn of Auber,
Nor the ghoul-haunted woodland of Weir.

And now, as the night was senescent
And star-dials pointed to morn—
As the star-dials hinted of morn—
At the end of our path a liquescent
And nebulous lustre was born,
Out of which a miraculous crescent
Arose with a duplicate horn—
Astarte's bediamonded crescent
Distinct with its duplicate horn.

And I said—"She is warmer than Dian:
She rolls through an ether of sighs—
She revels in a region of

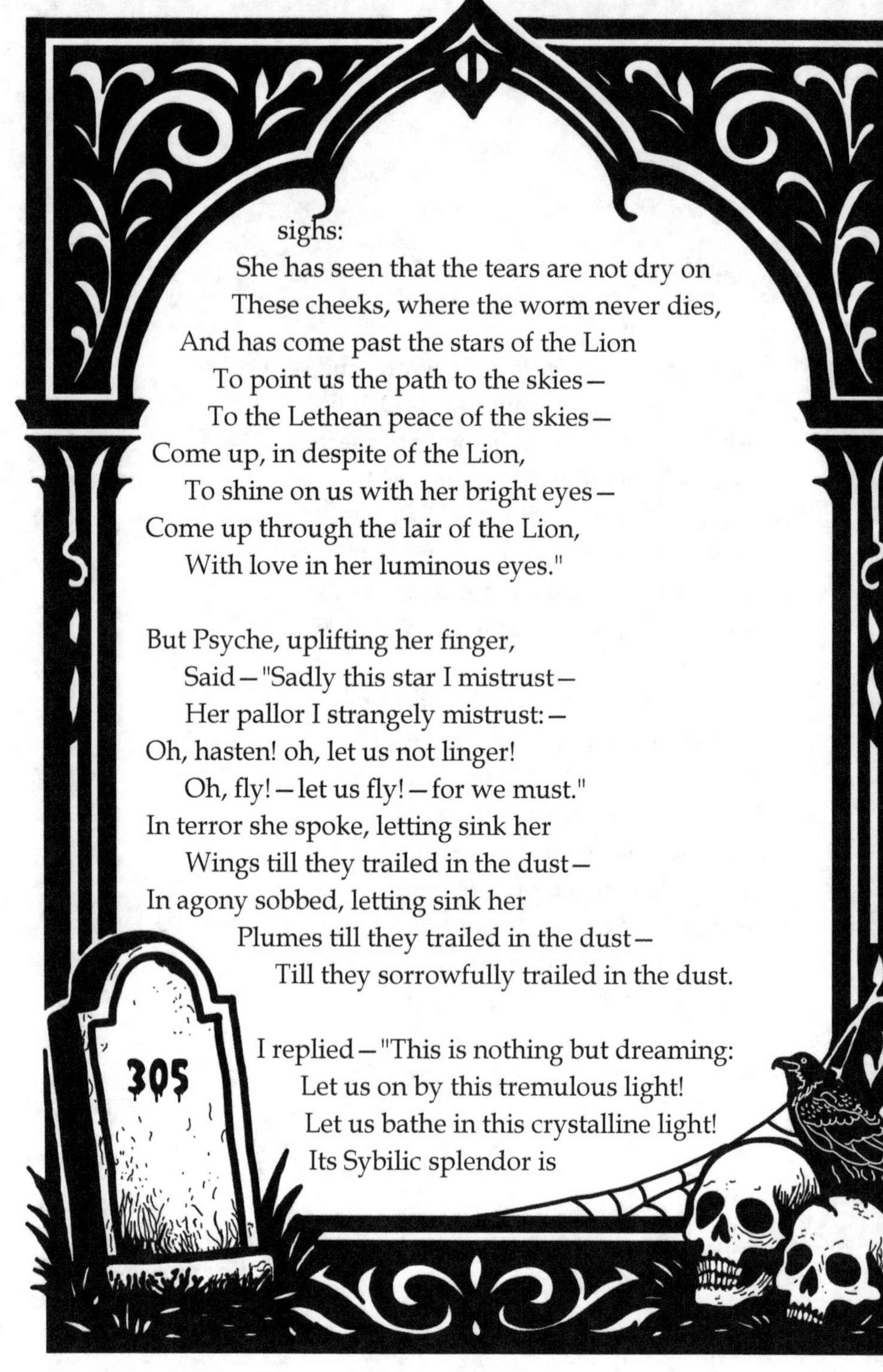

sighs:
She has seen that the tears are not dry on
These cheeks, where the worm never dies,
And has come past the stars of the Lion
To point us the path to the skies—
To the Lethean peace of the skies—
Come up, in despite of the Lion,
To shine on us with her bright eyes—
Come up through the lair of the Lion,
With love in her luminous eyes."

But Psyche, uplifting her finger,
Said—"Sadly this star I mistrust—
Her pallor I strangely mistrust:—
Oh, hasten! oh, let us not linger!
Oh, fly!—let us fly!—for we must."
In terror she spoke, letting sink her
Wings till they trailed in the dust—
In agony sobbed, letting sink her
Plumes till they trailed in the dust—
Till they sorrowfully trailed in the dust.

I replied—"This is nothing but dreaming:
Let us on by this tremulous light!
Let us bathe in this crystalline light!
Its Sybilic splendor is

beaming
With Hope and in Beauty to-night:—
See!—it flickers up the sky through the night!
Ah, we safely may trust to its gleaming,
And be sure it will lead us aright—
We safely may trust to a gleaming
That cannot but guide us aright,
Since it flickers up to Heaven through the night."

Thus I pacified Psyche and kissed her,
And tempted her out of her gloom—
And conquered her scruples and gloom:
And we passed to the end of the vista,
But were stopped by the door of a tomb—
By the door of a legended tomb;
And I said—"What is written, sweet sister,
On the door of this legended tomb?"
She replied—"Ulalume—Ulalume—
'Tis the vault of thy lost Ulalume!"

Then my heart it grew ashen and sober
As the leaves that were crispèd and sere—
As the leaves that were withering and sere,
And I cried—"It was surely October

On this
very night of last year
That I journeyed—I journeyed down
here—
That I brought a dread burden down here—
On this night of all nights in the year,
Oh, what demon has tempted me here?
Well I know, now, this dim lake of Auber—
This misty mid region of Weir—
Well I know, now, this dank tarn of Auber—
In the ghoul-haunted woodland of Weir."

Said we, then—the two, then—"Ah, can it
Have been that the woodlandish ghouls—
The pitiful, the merciful ghouls—
To bar up our way and to ban it
From the secret that lies in these wolds—
From the thing that lies hidden in these wolds—
Had drawn up the spectre of a planet
From the limbo of lunary souls—
This sinfully scintillant planet
From the Hell of the planetary souls?"

ANNABEL LEE

It was many and many a year ago,
In a kingdom by the sea,
That a maiden there lived whom you may know
By the name of Annabel Lee;
And this maiden she lived with no other thought
Than to love and be loved by me.

I was a child and she was a child,
In this kingdom by the sea,
But we loved with a love that was more than love—
I and my Annabel Lee—
With a love that the wingèd seraphs of Heaven
Coveted her and me.

And this was the reason that, long ago,
In this kingdom by the sea,
A wind blew out of a cloud, chilling
My beautiful Annabel Lee;
So that her highborn kinsmen came
And bore her away from me,
To shut her up in a sepulchre
In this kingdom by the sea.

The angels,
not half so happy in Heaven,
Went envying her and me —
Yes! — that was the reason (as all men know,
In this kingdom by the sea)
That the wind came out of the cloud by night,
Chilling and killing my Annabel Lee.

But our love it was stronger by far than the love
Of those who were older than we —
Of many far wiser than we —
And neither the angels in Heaven above
Nor the demons down under the sea
Can ever dissever my soul from the soul
Of the beautiful Annabel Lee;

For the moon never beams, without bringing me dreams
Of the beautiful Annabel Lee;
And the stars never rise, but I feel the bright eyes
Of the beautiful Annabel Lee;
And so, all the night-tide, I lie down by the side
Of my darling — my darling — my life and my bride,
In her sepulchre there by the sea —
In her tomb by the sounding sea.

Alexander Pope

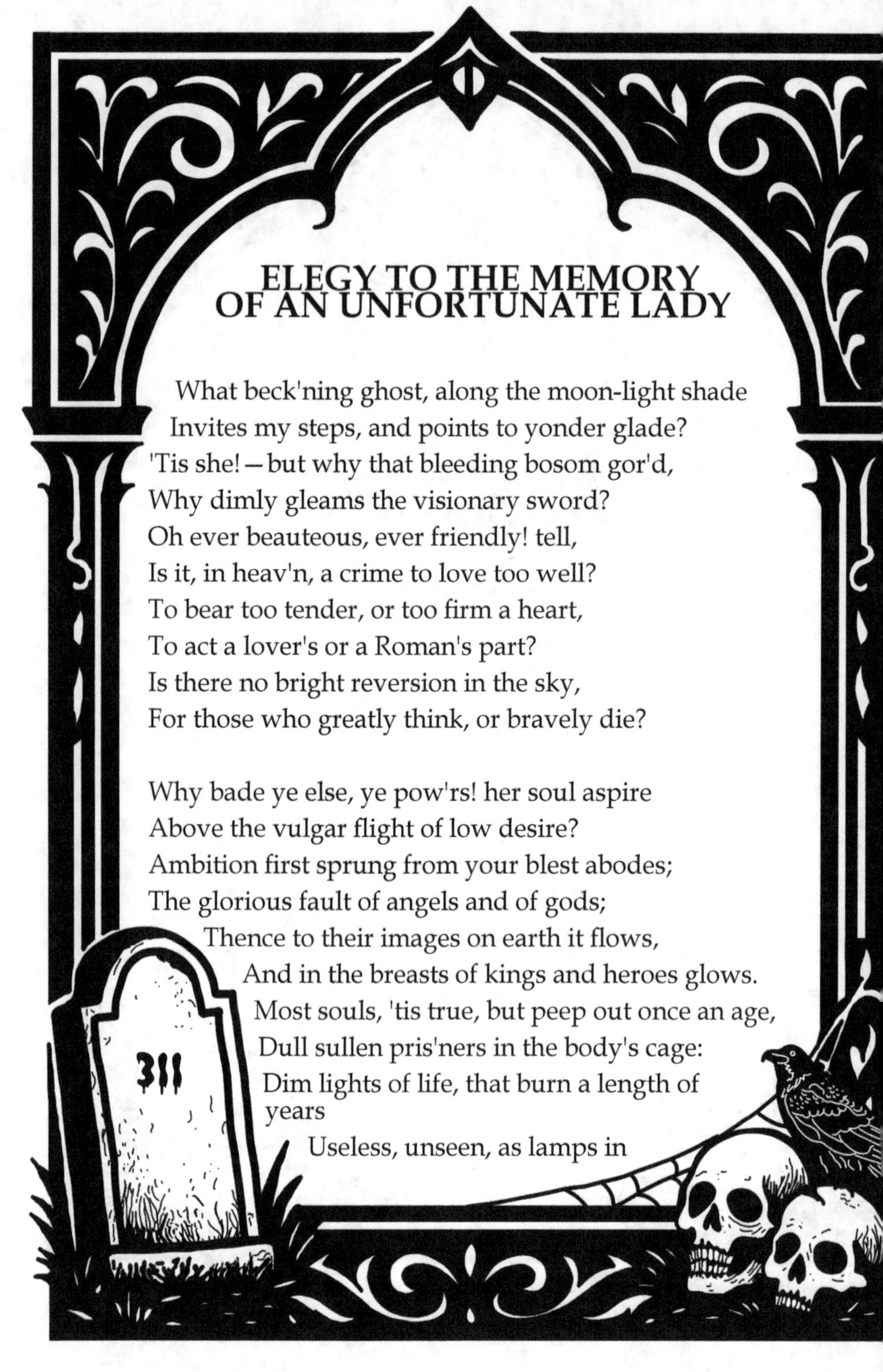

ELEGY TO THE MEMORY OF AN UNFORTUNATE LADY

What beck'ning ghost, along the moon-light shade
Invites my steps, and points to yonder glade?
'Tis she!—but why that bleeding bosom gor'd,
Why dimly gleams the visionary sword?
Oh ever beauteous, ever friendly! tell,
Is it, in heav'n, a crime to love too well?
To bear too tender, or too firm a heart,
To act a lover's or a Roman's part?
Is there no bright reversion in the sky,
For those who greatly think, or bravely die?

Why bade ye else, ye pow'rs! her soul aspire
Above the vulgar flight of low desire?
Ambition first sprung from your blest abodes;
The glorious fault of angels and of gods;
Thence to their images on earth it flows,
And in the breasts of kings and heroes glows.
Most souls, 'tis true, but peep out once an age,
Dull sullen pris'ners in the body's cage:
Dim lights of life, that burn a length of years
Useless, unseen, as lamps in

sepulchres;
Like eastern kings a lazy state they keep,
And close confin'd to their own palace, sleep.

From these perhaps (ere nature bade her die)
Fate snatch'd her early to the pitying sky.
As into air the purer spirits flow,
And sep'rate from their kindred dregs below;
So flew the soul to its congenial place,
Nor left one virtue to redeem her race.

But thou, false guardian of a charge too good,
Thou, mean deserter of thy brother's blood!
See on these ruby lips the trembling breath,
These cheeks now fading at the blast of death:
Cold is that breast which warm'd the world before,
And those love-darting eyes must roll no more.
Thus, if eternal justice rules the ball,
Thus shall your wives, and thus your children fall;
On all the line a sudden vengeance waits,
And frequent hearses shall besiege your gates.
There passengers shall stand, and pointing say,
(While the long fun'rals blacken all the way)
"Lo these were they,

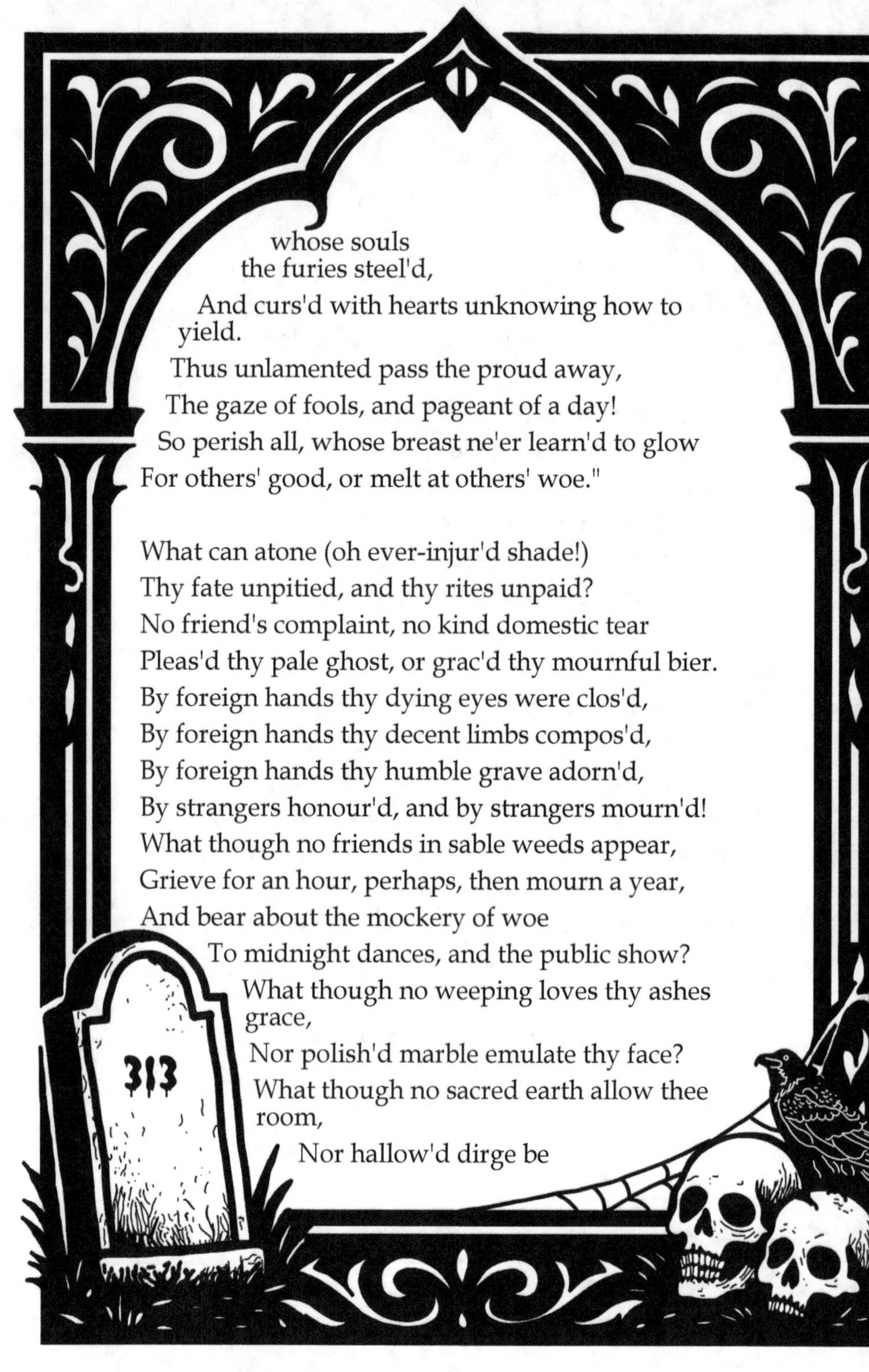

whose souls
the furies steel'd,
And curs'd with hearts unknowing how to yield.
Thus unlamented pass the proud away,
The gaze of fools, and pageant of a day!
So perish all, whose breast ne'er learn'd to glow
For others' good, or melt at others' woe."

What can atone (oh ever-injur'd shade!)
Thy fate unpitied, and thy rites unpaid?
No friend's complaint, no kind domestic tear
Pleas'd thy pale ghost, or grac'd thy mournful bier.
By foreign hands thy dying eyes were clos'd,
By foreign hands thy decent limbs compos'd,
By foreign hands thy humble grave adorn'd,
By strangers honour'd, and by strangers mourn'd!
What though no friends in sable weeds appear,
Grieve for an hour, perhaps, then mourn a year,
And bear about the mockery of woe
To midnight dances, and the public show?
What though no weeping loves thy ashes grace,
Nor polish'd marble emulate thy face?
What though no sacred earth allow thee room,
Nor hallow'd dirge be

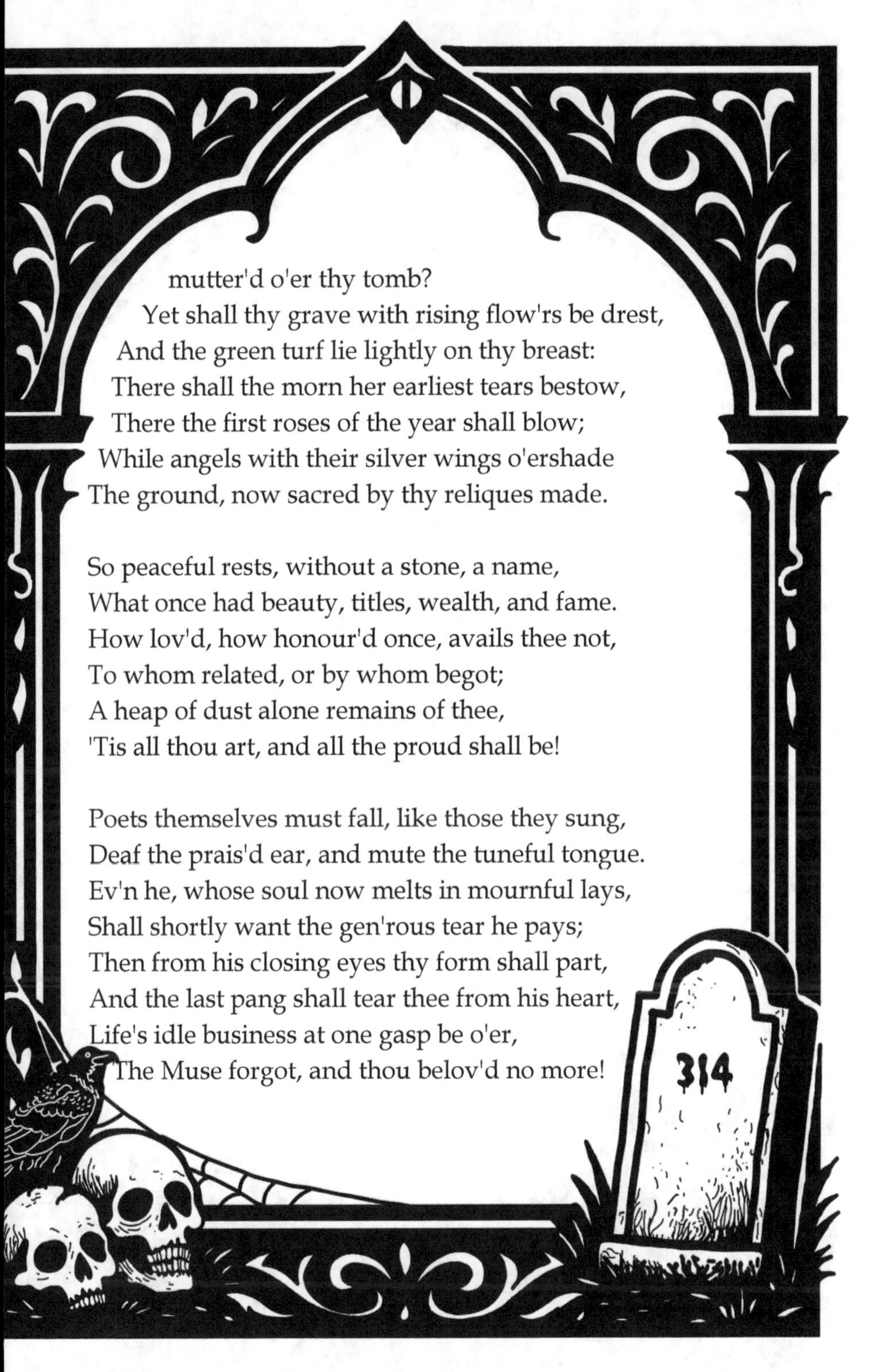

mutter'd o'er thy tomb?
Yet shall thy grave with rising flow'rs be drest,
And the green turf lie lightly on thy breast:
There shall the morn her earliest tears bestow,
There the first roses of the year shall blow;
While angels with their silver wings o'ershade
The ground, now sacred by thy reliques made.

So peaceful rests, without a stone, a name,
What once had beauty, titles, wealth, and fame.
How lov'd, how honour'd once, avails thee not,
To whom related, or by whom begot;
A heap of dust alone remains of thee,
'Tis all thou art, and all the proud shall be!

Poets themselves must fall, like those they sung,
Deaf the prais'd ear, and mute the tuneful tongue.
Ev'n he, whose soul now melts in mournful lays,
Shall shortly want the gen'rous tear he pays;
Then from his closing eyes thy form shall part,
And the last pang shall tear thee from his heart,
Life's idle business at one gasp be o'er,
The Muse forgot, and thou belov'd no more!

Percy Bysshe Shelly

ON DEATH

What beck'ning ghost, along the moon-light shade
THERE IS NO WORK, NOR DEVICE, NOR
KNOWLEDGE, NOR WISDOM,
IN THE GRAVE, WHITHER THOU GOEST.—
Ecclesiastes.

The pale, the cold, and the moony smile
Which the meteor beam of a starless night
Sheds on a lonely and sea-girt isle,
Ere the dawning of morn's undoubted light,
Is the flame of life so fickle and wan
That flits round our steps till their strength is gone.

O man! hold thee on in courage of soul
Through the stormy shades of thy worldly way,
And the billows of cloud that around thee roll
Shall sleep in the light of a wondrous day,
Where Hell and Heaven shall leave thee free
To the universe of destiny.

This world is the nurse of all we know,
This world is the mother of all we feel,
And the coming of death is a

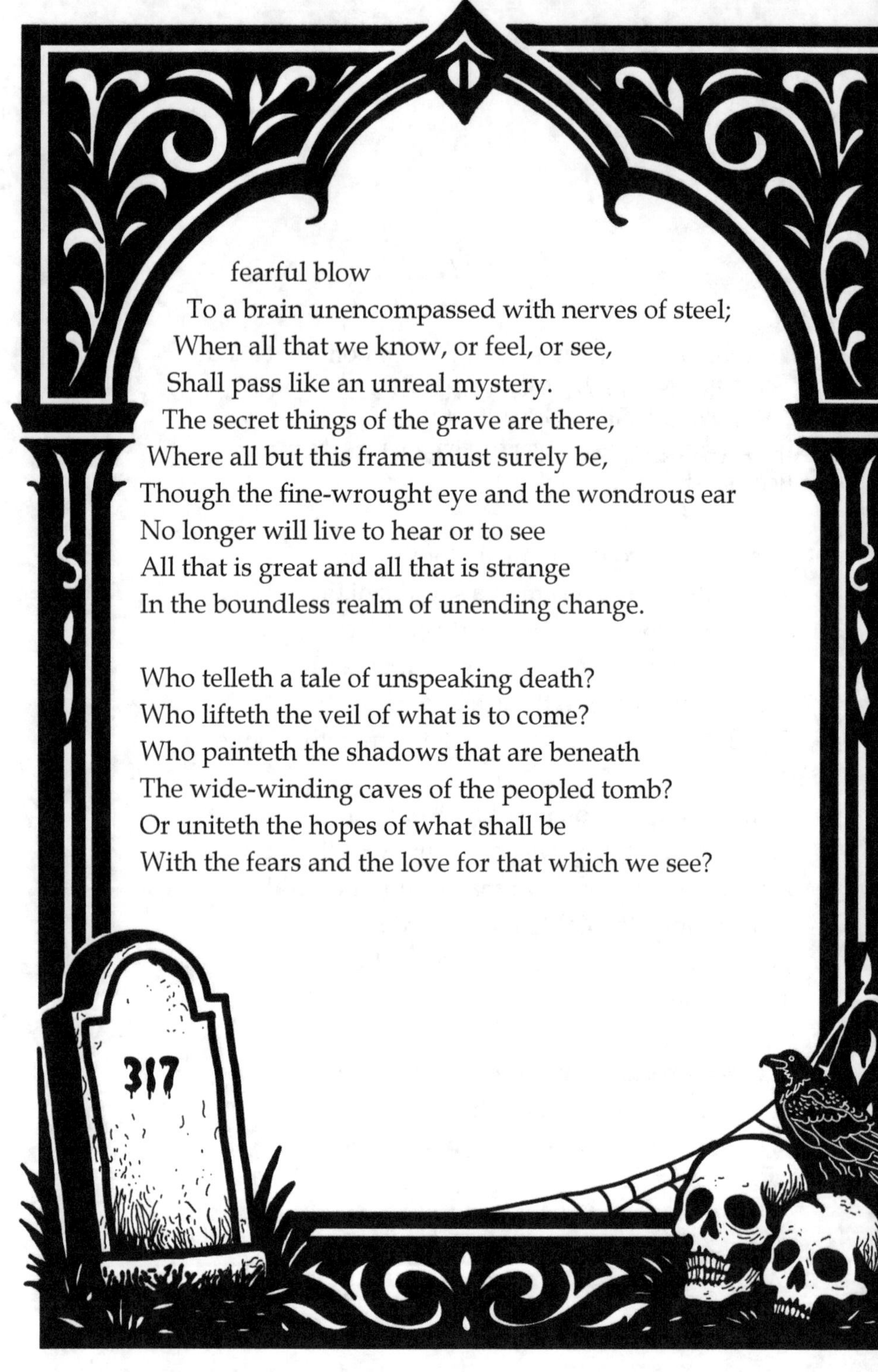

fearful blow
To a brain unencompassed with nerves of steel;
When all that we know, or feel, or see,
Shall pass like an unreal mystery.
The secret things of the grave are there,
Where all but this frame must surely be,
Though the fine-wrought eye and the wondrous ear
No longer will live to hear or to see
All that is great and all that is strange
In the boundless realm of unending change.

Who telleth a tale of unspeaking death?
Who lifteth the veil of what is to come?
Who painteth the shadows that are beneath
The wide-winding caves of the peopled tomb?
Or uniteth the hopes of what shall be
With the fears and the love for that which we see?

Joseph Warton

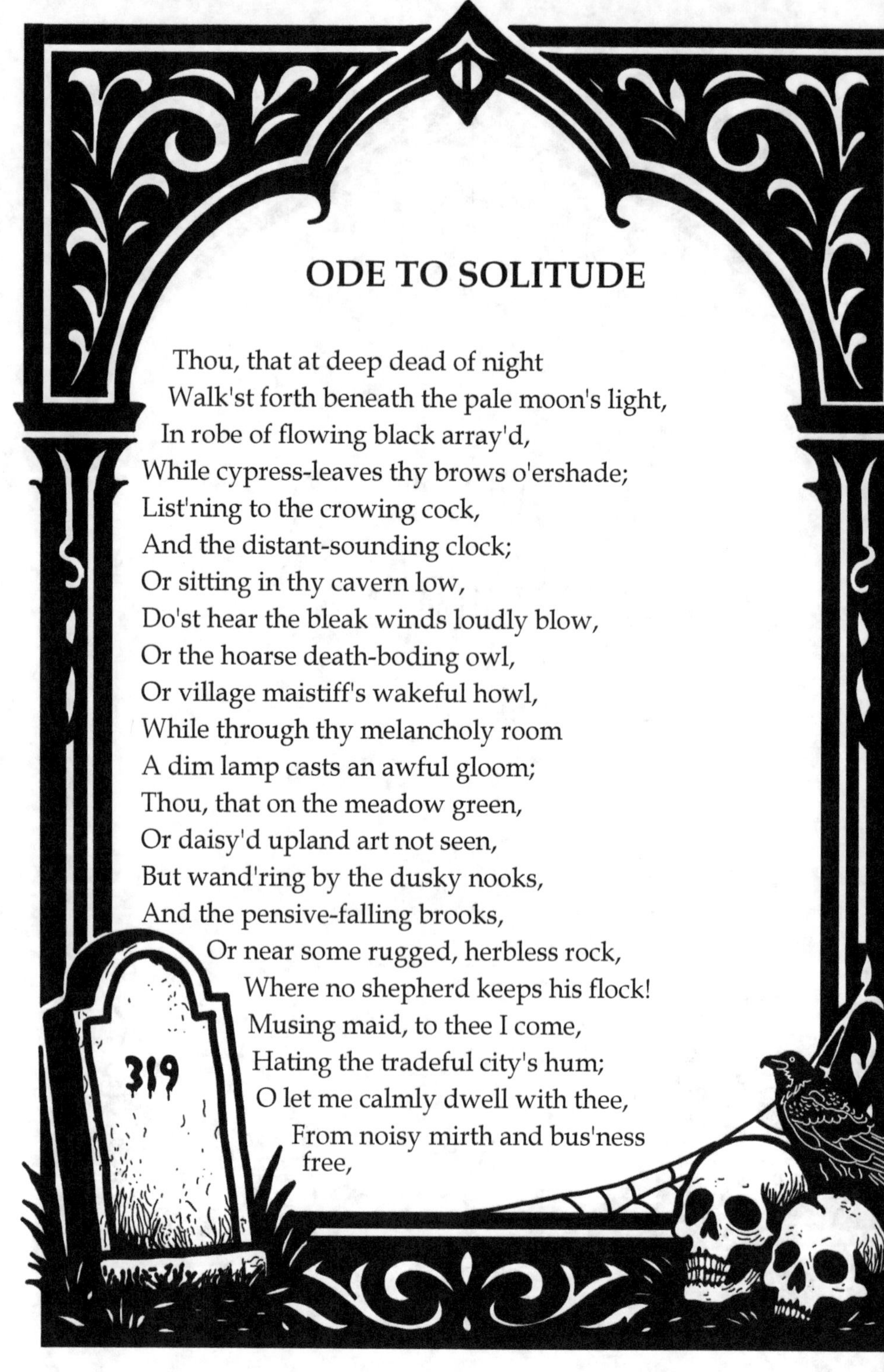

ODE TO SOLITUDE

Thou, that at deep dead of night
Walk'st forth beneath the pale moon's light,
In robe of flowing black array'd,
While cypress-leaves thy brows o'ershade;
List'ning to the crowing cock,
And the distant-sounding clock;
Or sitting in thy cavern low,
Do'st hear the bleak winds loudly blow,
Or the hoarse death-boding owl,
Or village maistiff's wakeful howl,
While through thy melancholy room
A dim lamp casts an awful gloom;
Thou, that on the meadow green,
Or daisy'd upland art not seen,
But wand'ring by the dusky nooks,
And the pensive-falling brooks,
Or near some rugged, herbless rock,
Where no shepherd keeps his flock!
Musing maid, to thee I come,
Hating the tradeful city's hum;
O let me calmly dwell with thee,
From noisy mirth and bus'ness free,

With meditation seek the skies,
This folly-fetter'd world despise!

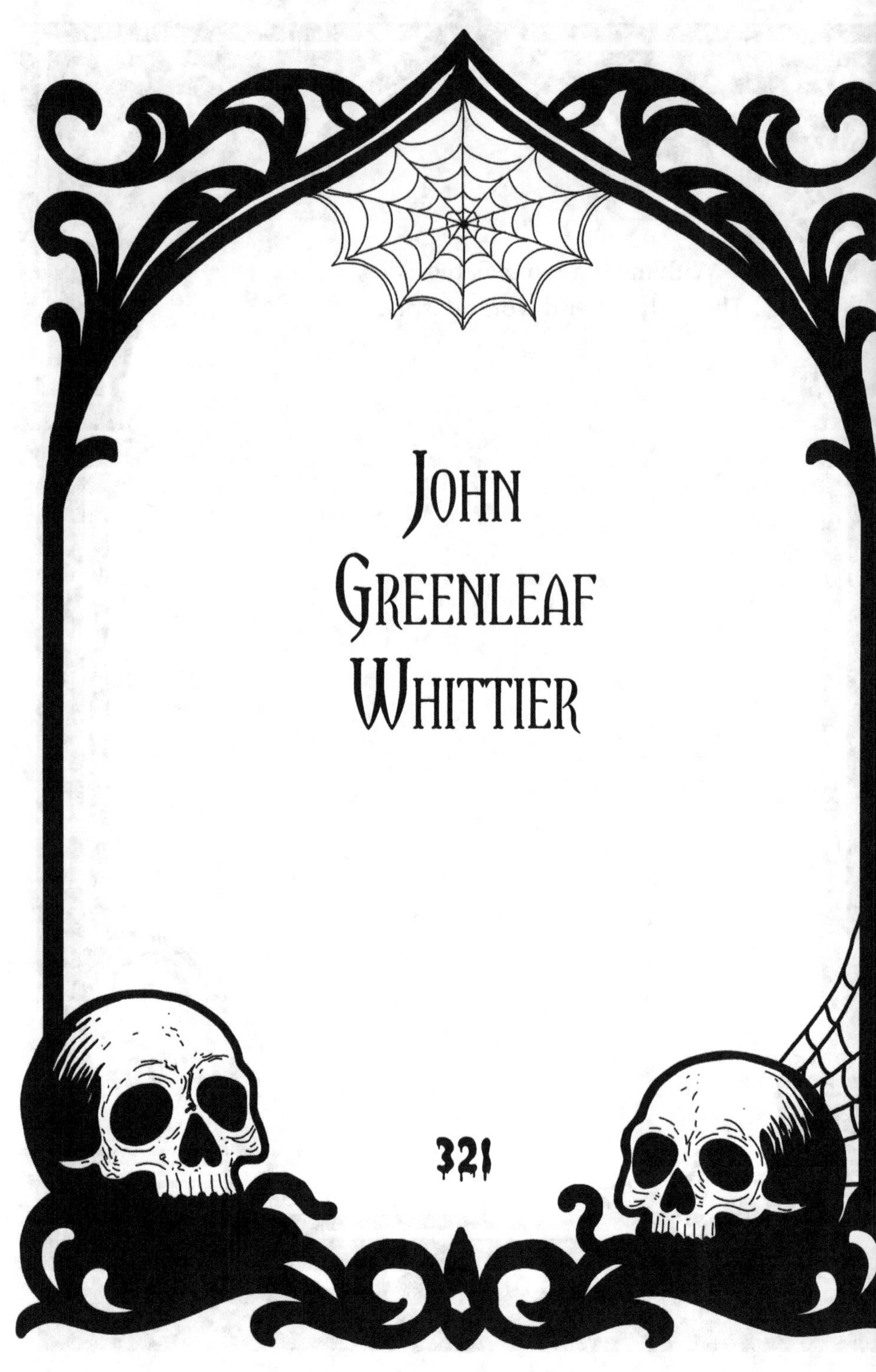

John Greenleaf Whittier

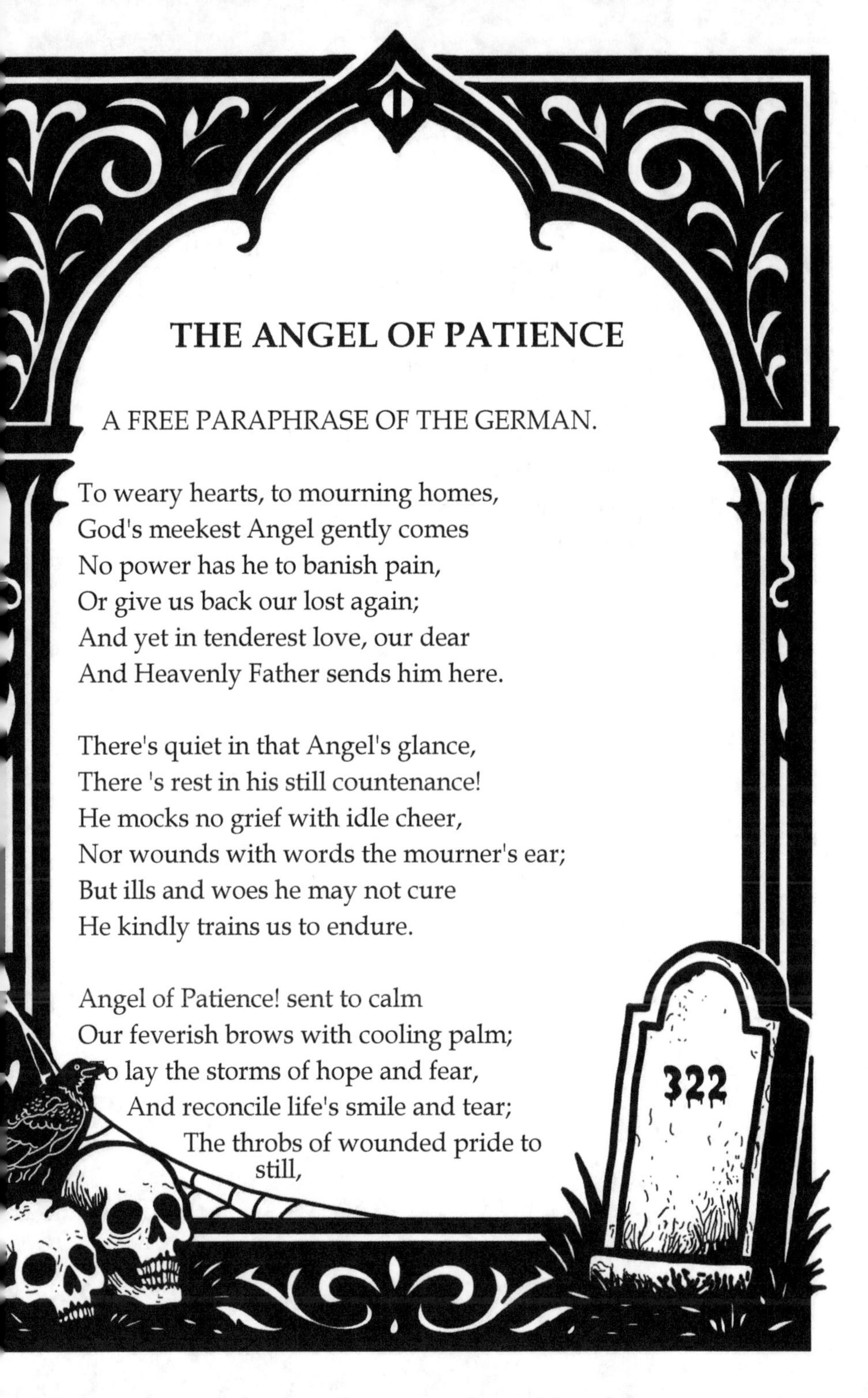

THE ANGEL OF PATIENCE

A FREE PARAPHRASE OF THE GERMAN.

To weary hearts, to mourning homes,
God's meekest Angel gently comes
No power has he to banish pain,
Or give us back our lost again;
And yet in tenderest love, our dear
And Heavenly Father sends him here.

There's quiet in that Angel's glance,
There 's rest in his still countenance!
He mocks no grief with idle cheer,
Nor wounds with words the mourner's ear;
But ills and woes he may not cure
He kindly trains us to endure.

Angel of Patience! sent to calm
Our feverish brows with cooling palm;
To lay the storms of hope and fear,
And reconcile life's smile and tear;
The throbs of wounded pride to still,

And make our
own our Father's will.

O thou who mournest on thy way,
With longings for the close of day;
He walks with thee, that Angel kind,
And gently whispers, 'Be resigned
Bear up, bear on, the end shall tell
The dear Lord ordereth all things well!'

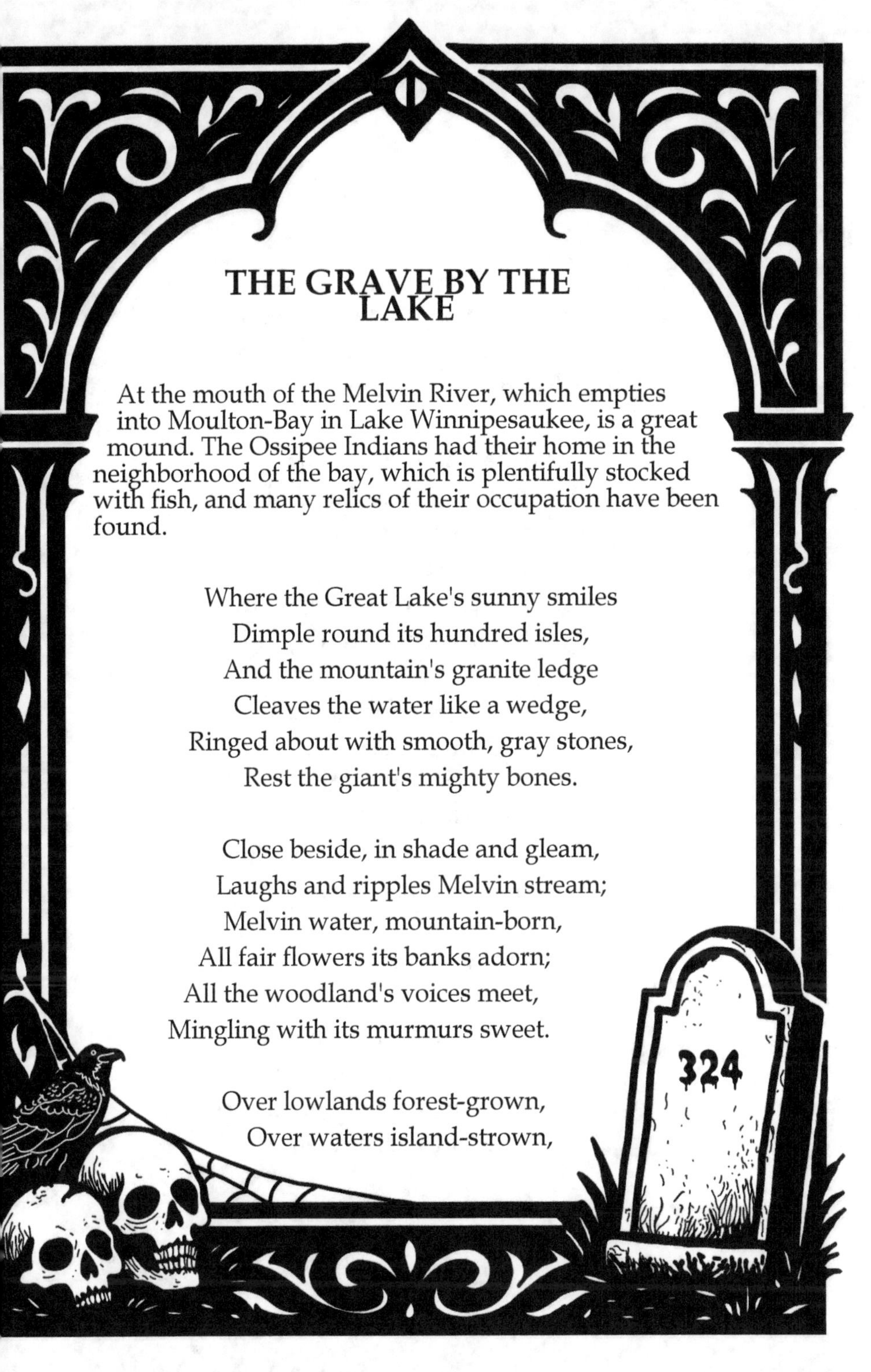

THE GRAVE BY THE LAKE

At the mouth of the Melvin River, which empties into Moulton-Bay in Lake Winnipesaukee, is a great mound. The Ossipee Indians had their home in the neighborhood of the bay, which is plentifully stocked with fish, and many relics of their occupation have been found.

Where the Great Lake's sunny smiles
Dimple round its hundred isles,
And the mountain's granite ledge
Cleaves the water like a wedge,
Ringed about with smooth, gray stones,
Rest the giant's mighty bones.

Close beside, in shade and gleam,
Laughs and ripples Melvin stream;
Melvin water, mountain-born,
All fair flowers its banks adorn;
All the woodland's voices meet,
Mingling with its murmurs sweet.

Over lowlands forest-grown,
Over waters island-strown,

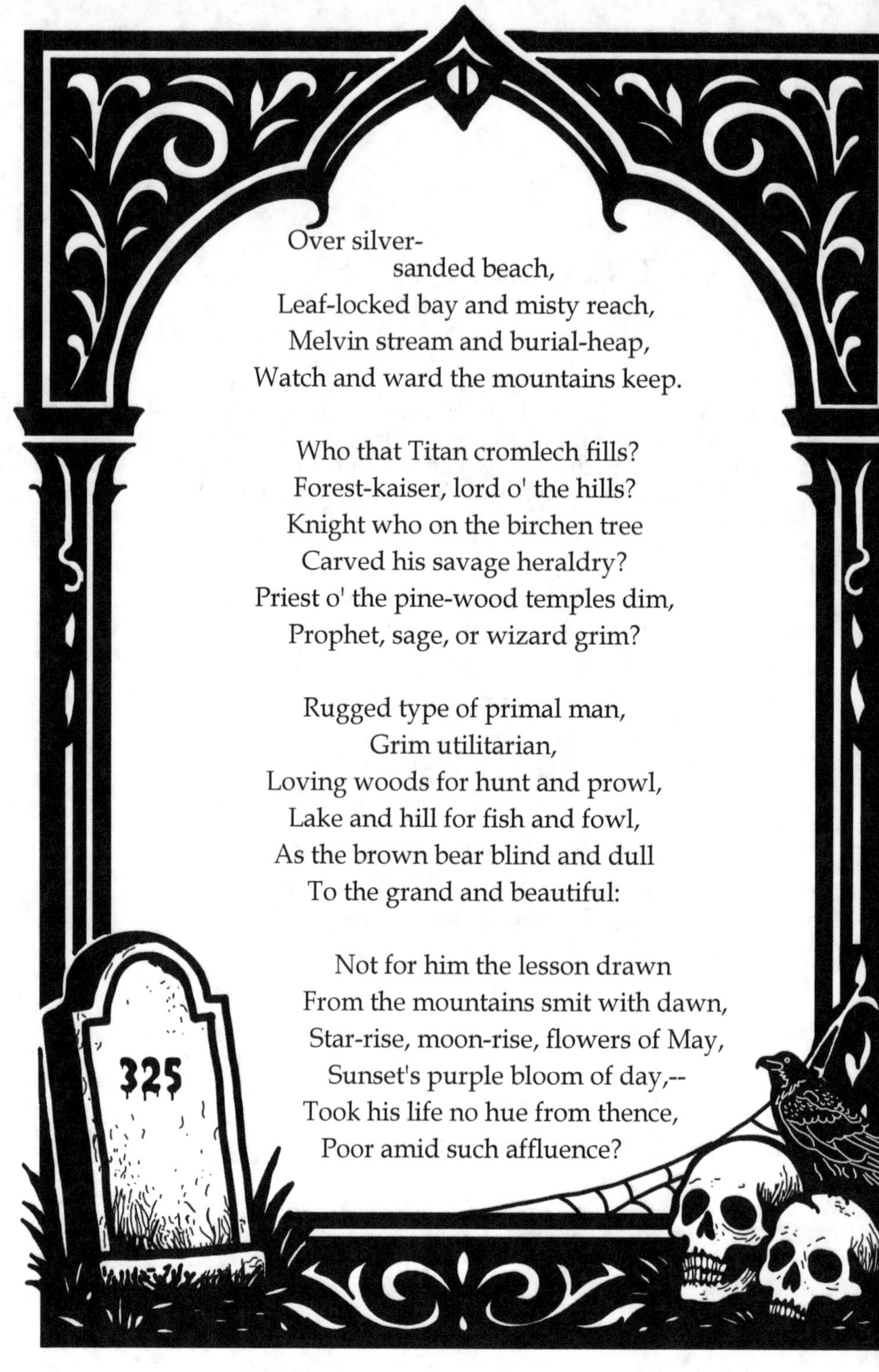

Over silver-
sanded beach,
Leaf-locked bay and misty reach,
Melvin stream and burial-heap,
Watch and ward the mountains keep.

Who that Titan cromlech fills?
Forest-kaiser, lord o' the hills?
Knight who on the birchen tree
Carved his savage heraldry?
Priest o' the pine-wood temples dim,
Prophet, sage, or wizard grim?

Rugged type of primal man,
Grim utilitarian,
Loving woods for hunt and prowl,
Lake and hill for fish and fowl,
As the brown bear blind and dull
To the grand and beautiful:

Not for him the lesson drawn
From the mountains smit with dawn,
Star-rise, moon-rise, flowers of May,
Sunset's purple bloom of day,--
Took his life no hue from thence,
Poor amid such affluence?

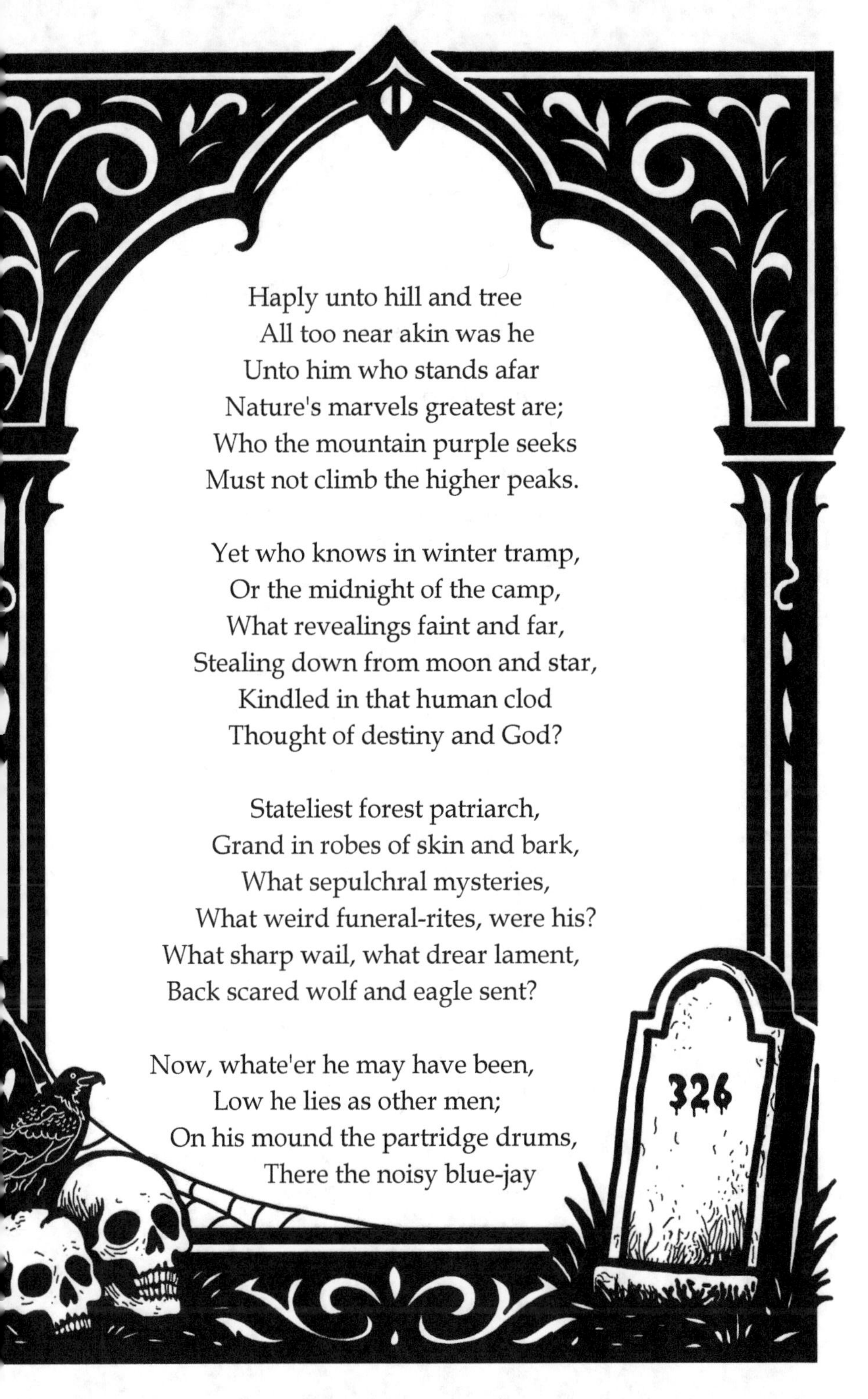

Haply unto hill and tree
All too near akin was he
Unto him who stands afar
Nature's marvels greatest are;
Who the mountain purple seeks
Must not climb the higher peaks.

Yet who knows in winter tramp,
Or the midnight of the camp,
What revealings faint and far,
Stealing down from moon and star,
Kindled in that human clod
Thought of destiny and God?

Stateliest forest patriarch,
Grand in robes of skin and bark,
What sepulchral mysteries,
What weird funeral-rites, were his?
What sharp wail, what drear lament,
Back scared wolf and eagle sent?

Now, whate'er he may have been,
Low he lies as other men;
On his mound the partridge drums,
There the noisy blue-jay

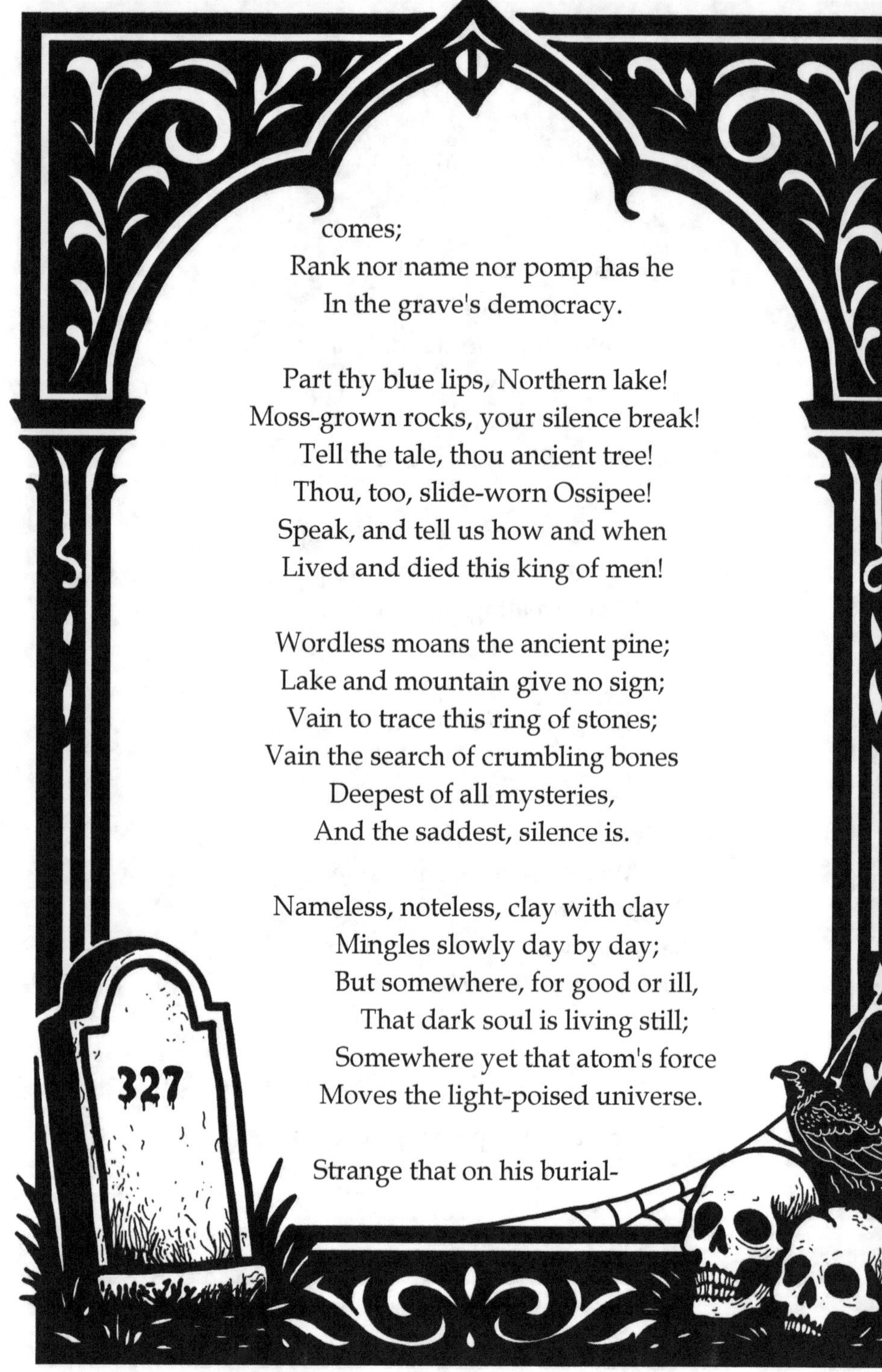

comes;
Rank nor name nor pomp has he
In the grave's democracy.

Part thy blue lips, Northern lake!
Moss-grown rocks, your silence break!
Tell the tale, thou ancient tree!
Thou, too, slide-worn Ossipee!
Speak, and tell us how and when
Lived and died this king of men!

Wordless moans the ancient pine;
Lake and mountain give no sign;
Vain to trace this ring of stones;
Vain the search of crumbling bones
Deepest of all mysteries,
And the saddest, silence is.

Nameless, noteless, clay with clay
Mingles slowly day by day;
But somewhere, for good or ill,
That dark soul is living still;
Somewhere yet that atom's force
Moves the light-poised universe.

Strange that on his burial-

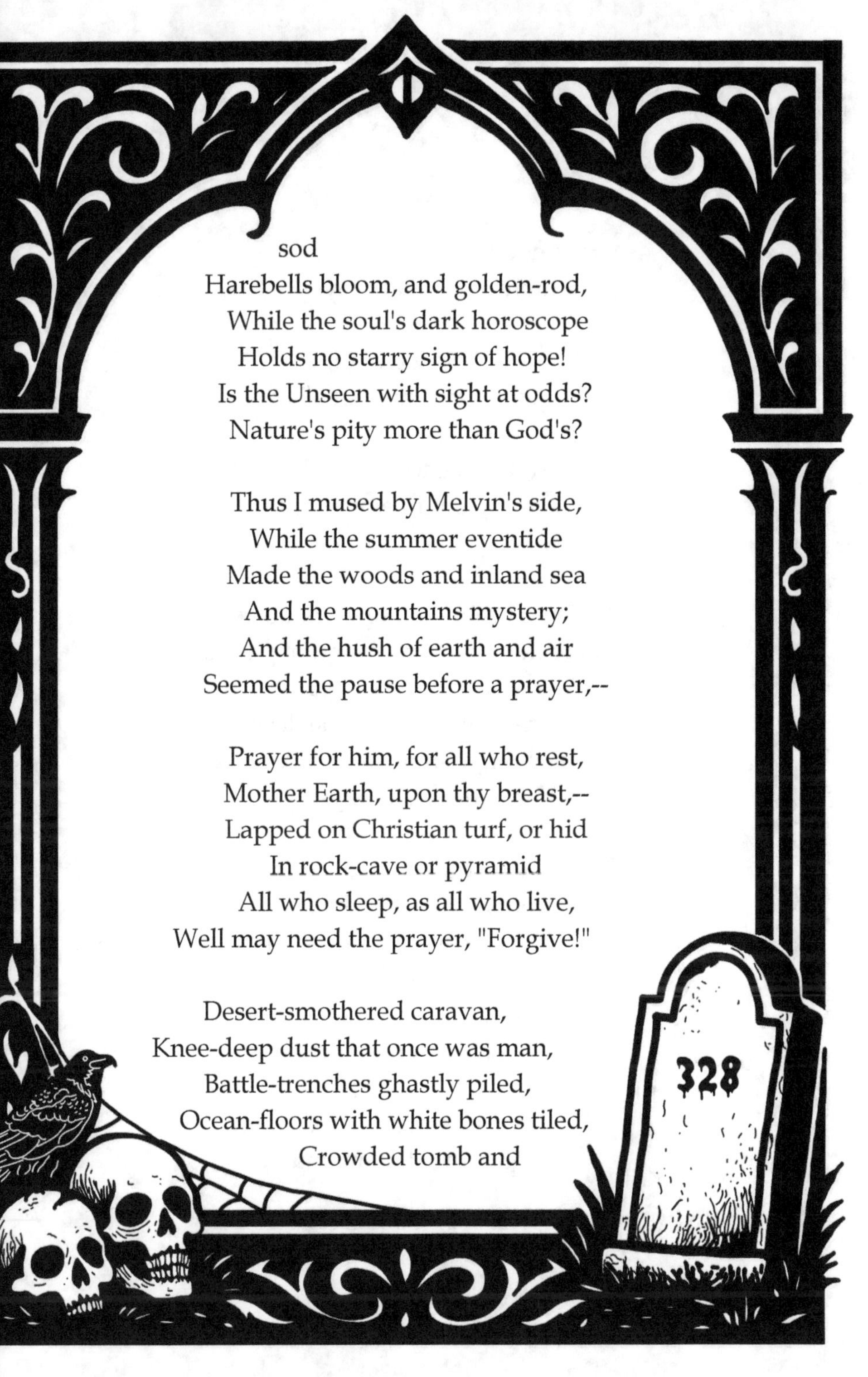

sod
Harebells bloom, and golden-rod,
While the soul's dark horoscope
Holds no starry sign of hope!
Is the Unseen with sight at odds?
Nature's pity more than God's?

Thus I mused by Melvin's side,
While the summer eventide
Made the woods and inland sea
And the mountains mystery;
And the hush of earth and air
Seemed the pause before a prayer,--

Prayer for him, for all who rest,
Mother Earth, upon thy breast,--
Lapped on Christian turf, or hid
In rock-cave or pyramid
All who sleep, as all who live,
Well may need the prayer, "Forgive!"

Desert-smothered caravan,
Knee-deep dust that once was man,
Battle-trenches ghastly piled,
Ocean-floors with white bones tiled,
Crowded tomb and

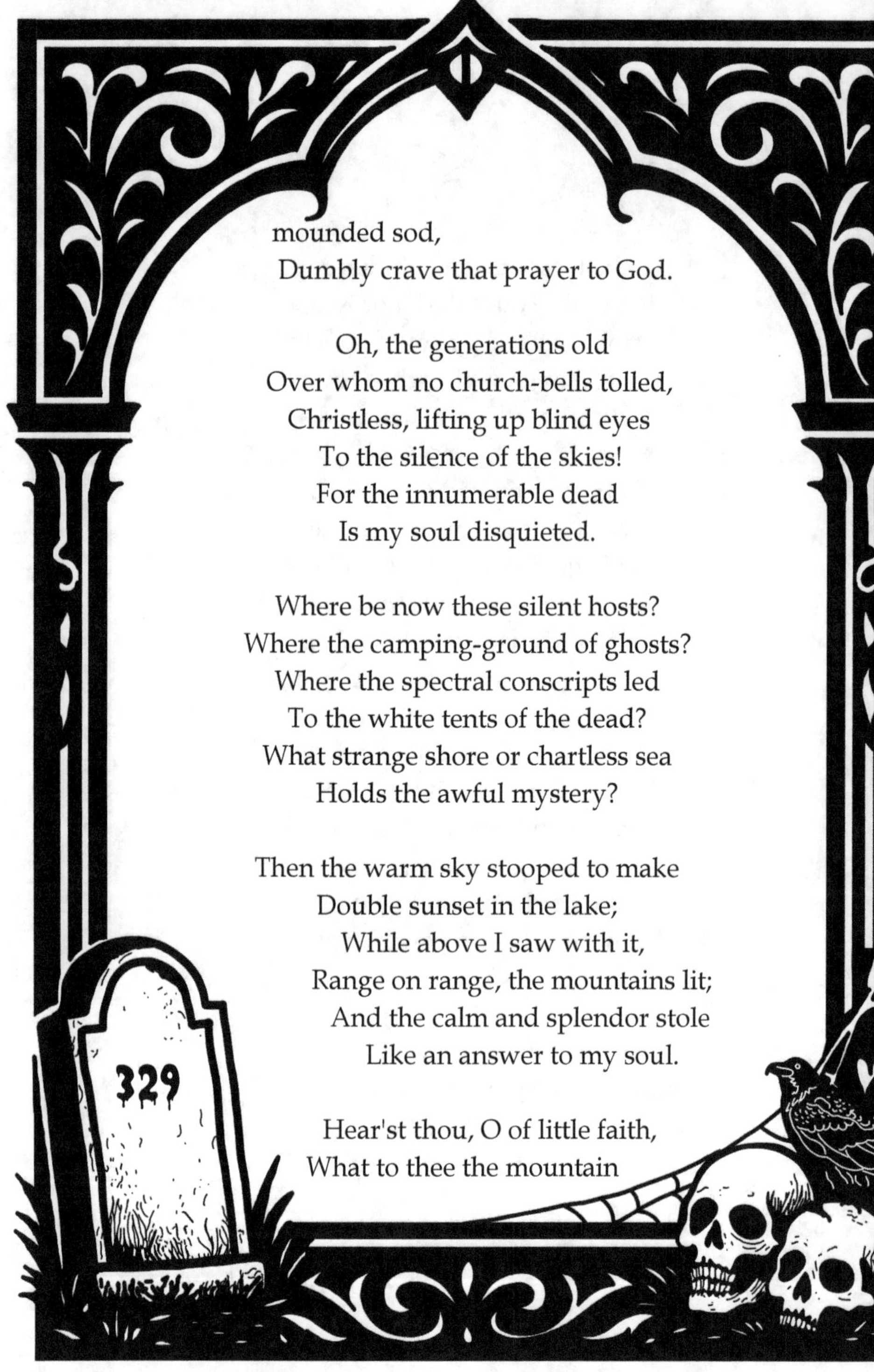

mounded sod,
Dumbly crave that prayer to God.

Oh, the generations old
Over whom no church-bells tolled,
Christless, lifting up blind eyes
To the silence of the skies!
For the innumerable dead
Is my soul disquieted.

Where be now these silent hosts?
Where the camping-ground of ghosts?
Where the spectral conscripts led
To the white tents of the dead?
What strange shore or chartless sea
Holds the awful mystery?

Then the warm sky stooped to make
Double sunset in the lake;
While above I saw with it,
Range on range, the mountains lit;
And the calm and splendor stole
Like an answer to my soul.

Hear'st thou, O of little faith,
What to thee the mountain

saith,
What is whispered by the trees?
Cast on God thy care for these;
Trust Him, if thy sight be dim
Doubt for them is doubt of Him.

"Blind must be their close-shut eyes
Where like night the sunshine lies,
Fiery-linked the self-forged chain
Binding ever sin to pain,
Strong their prison-house of will,
But without He waiteth still.

"Not with hatred's undertow
Doth the Love Eternal flow;
Every chain that spirits wear
Crumbles in the breath of prayer;
And the penitent's desire
Opens every gate of fire.

"Still Thy love, O Christ arisen,
Yearns to reach these souls in prison!
Through all depths of sin and loss
Drops the plummet of Thy cross!
Never yet abyss was found

Deeper than
that cross could sound!"

Therefore well may Nature keep
Equal faith with all who sleep,
Set her watch of hills around
Christian grave and heathen mound,
And to cairn and kirkyard send
Summer's flowery dividend.

Keep, O pleasant Melvin stream,
Thy sweet laugh in shade and gleam
On the Indian's grassy tomb
Swing, O flowers, your bells of bloom!
Deep below, as high above,
Sweeps the circle of God's love.

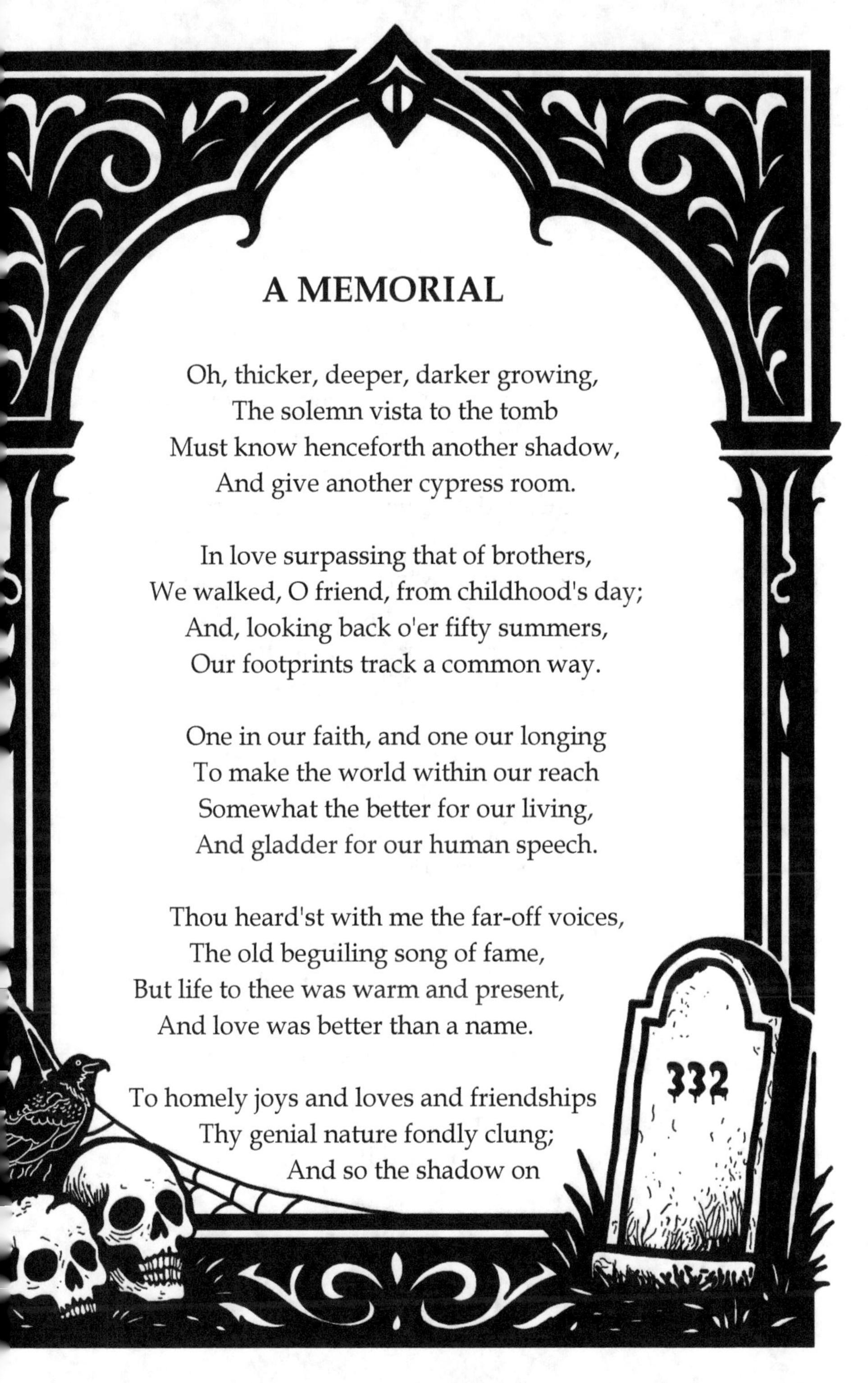

A MEMORIAL

Oh, thicker, deeper, darker growing,
The solemn vista to the tomb
Must know henceforth another shadow,
And give another cypress room.

In love surpassing that of brothers,
We walked, O friend, from childhood's day;
And, looking back o'er fifty summers,
Our footprints track a common way.

One in our faith, and one our longing
To make the world within our reach
Somewhat the better for our living,
And gladder for our human speech.

Thou heard'st with me the far-off voices,
The old beguiling song of fame,
But life to thee was warm and present,
And love was better than a name.

To homely joys and loves and friendships
Thy genial nature fondly clung;
And so the shadow on

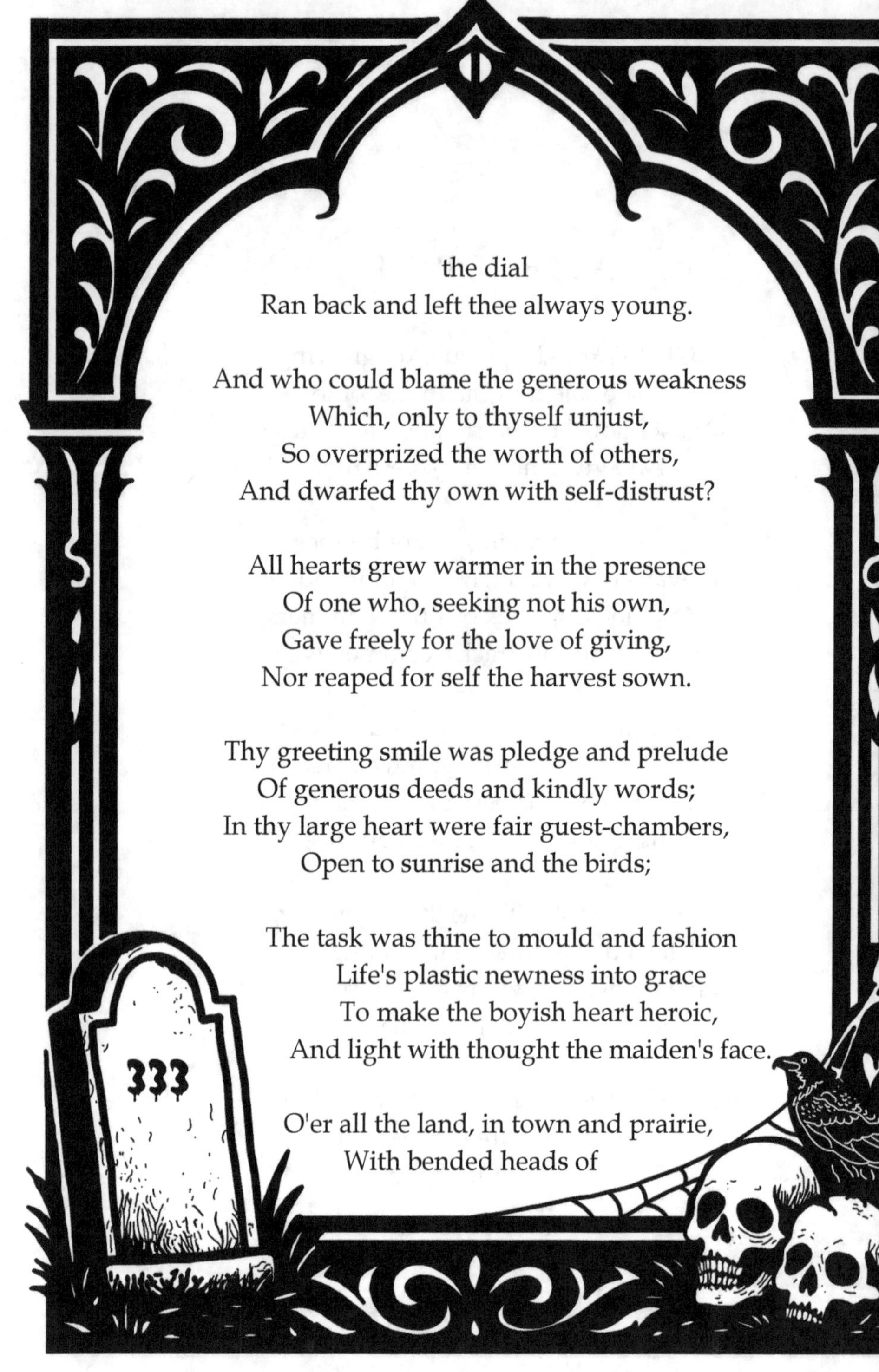

the dial
Ran back and left thee always young.

And who could blame the generous weakness
Which, only to thyself unjust,
So overprized the worth of others,
And dwarfed thy own with self-distrust?

All hearts grew warmer in the presence
Of one who, seeking not his own,
Gave freely for the love of giving,
Nor reaped for self the harvest sown.

Thy greeting smile was pledge and prelude
Of generous deeds and kindly words;
In thy large heart were fair guest-chambers,
Open to sunrise and the birds;

The task was thine to mould and fashion
Life's plastic newness into grace
To make the boyish heart heroic,
And light with thought the maiden's face.

O'er all the land, in town and prairie,
With bended heads of

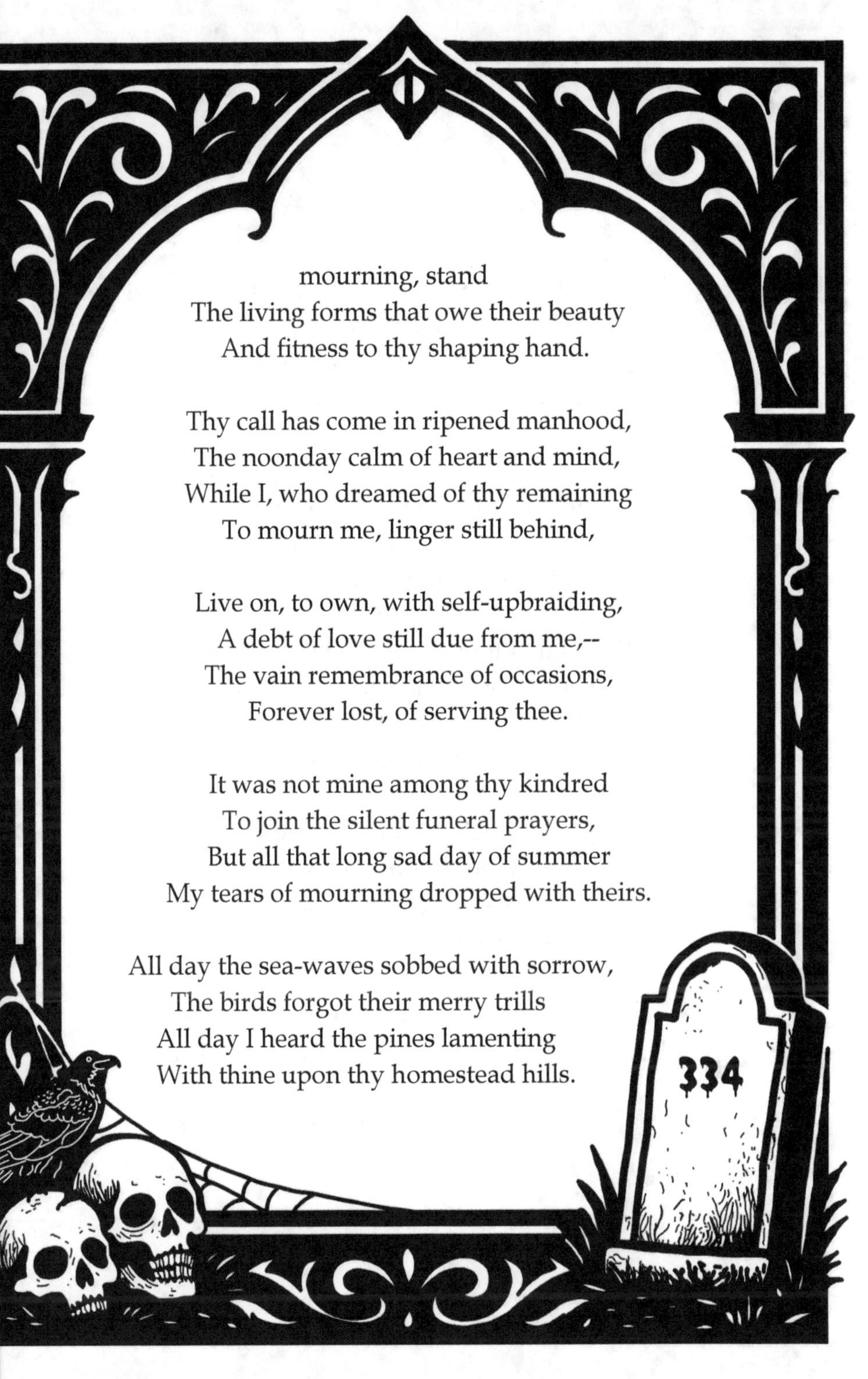

mourning, stand
The living forms that owe their beauty
And fitness to thy shaping hand.

Thy call has come in ripened manhood,
The noonday calm of heart and mind,
While I, who dreamed of thy remaining
To mourn me, linger still behind,

Live on, to own, with self-upbraiding,
A debt of love still due from me,--
The vain remembrance of occasions,
Forever lost, of serving thee.

It was not mine among thy kindred
To join the silent funeral prayers,
But all that long sad day of summer
My tears of mourning dropped with theirs.

All day the sea-waves sobbed with sorrow,
The birds forgot their merry trills
All day I heard the pines lamenting
With thine upon thy homestead hills.

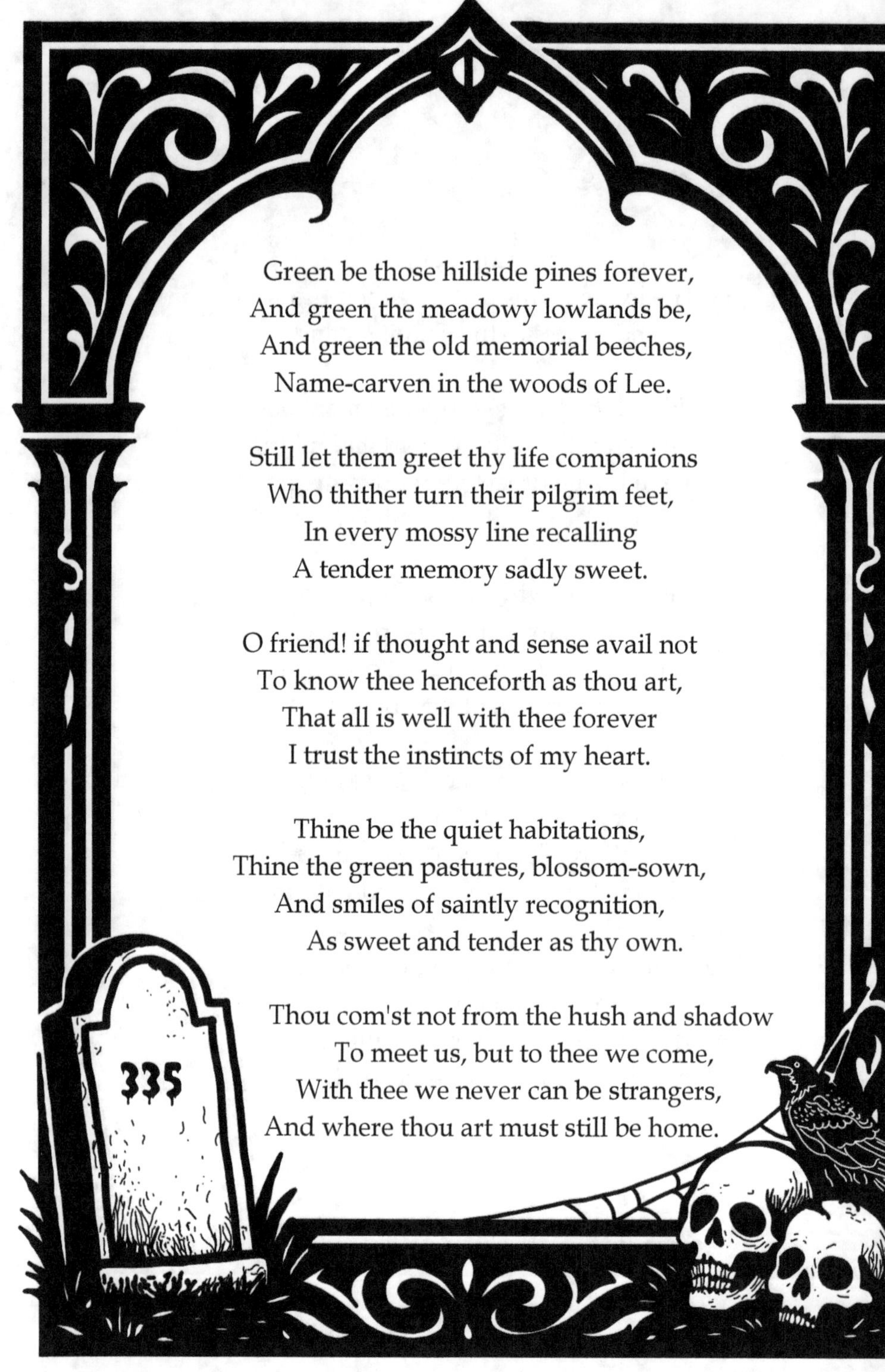

Green be those hillside pines forever,
And green the meadowy lowlands be,
And green the old memorial beeches,
Name-carven in the woods of Lee.

Still let them greet thy life companions
Who thither turn their pilgrim feet,
In every mossy line recalling
A tender memory sadly sweet.

O friend! if thought and sense avail not
To know thee henceforth as thou art,
That all is well with thee forever
I trust the instincts of my heart.

Thine be the quiet habitations,
Thine the green pastures, blossom-sown,
And smiles of saintly recognition,
As sweet and tender as thy own.

Thou com'st not from the hush and shadow
To meet us, but to thee we come,
With thee we never can be strangers,
And where thou art must still be home.

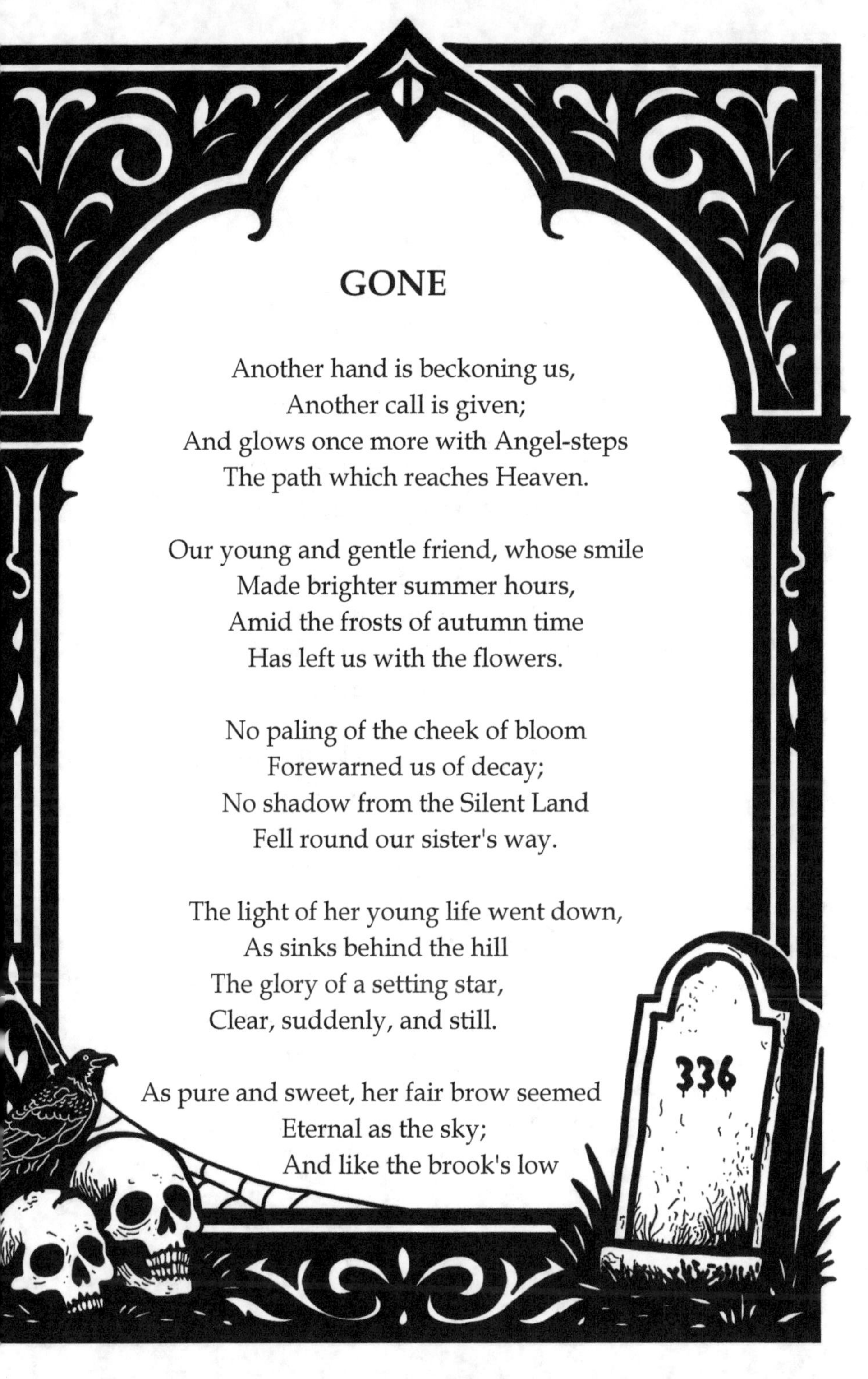

GONE

Another hand is beckoning us,
Another call is given;
And glows once more with Angel-steps
The path which reaches Heaven.

Our young and gentle friend, whose smile
Made brighter summer hours,
Amid the frosts of autumn time
Has left us with the flowers.

No paling of the cheek of bloom
Forewarned us of decay;
No shadow from the Silent Land
Fell round our sister's way.

The light of her young life went down,
As sinks behind the hill
The glory of a setting star,
Clear, suddenly, and still.

As pure and sweet, her fair brow seemed
Eternal as the sky;
And like the brook's low

song, her voice,--
A sound which could not die.

And half we deemed she needed not
The changing of her sphere,
To give to Heaven a Shining One,
Who walked an Angel here.

The blessing of her quiet life
Fell on us like the dew;
And good thoughts where her footsteps pressed
Like fairy blossoms grew.

Sweet promptings unto kindest deeds
Were in her very look;
We read her face, as one who reads
A true and holy book,

The measure of a blessed hymn,
To which our hearts could move;
The breathing of an inward psalm,
A canticle of love.

We miss her in the place of prayer,
And by the hearth-fire's

light;
We pause beside her door to hear
Once more her sweet 'Good-night!'

There seems a shadow on the day,
Her smile no longer cheers;
A dimness on the stars of night,
Like eyes that look through tears.

Alone unto our Father's will
One thought hath reconciled;
That He whose love exceedeth ours
Hath taken home His child.

Fold her, O Father! in Thine arms,
And let her henceforth be
A messenger of love between
Our human hearts and Thee.

Still let her mild rebuking stand
Between us and the wrong,
And her dear memory serve to make
Our faith in Goodness strong.

And grant that she who,

trembling, here
Distrusted all her powers,
May welcome to her holier home
The well-beloved of ours.

Henry Kirke White

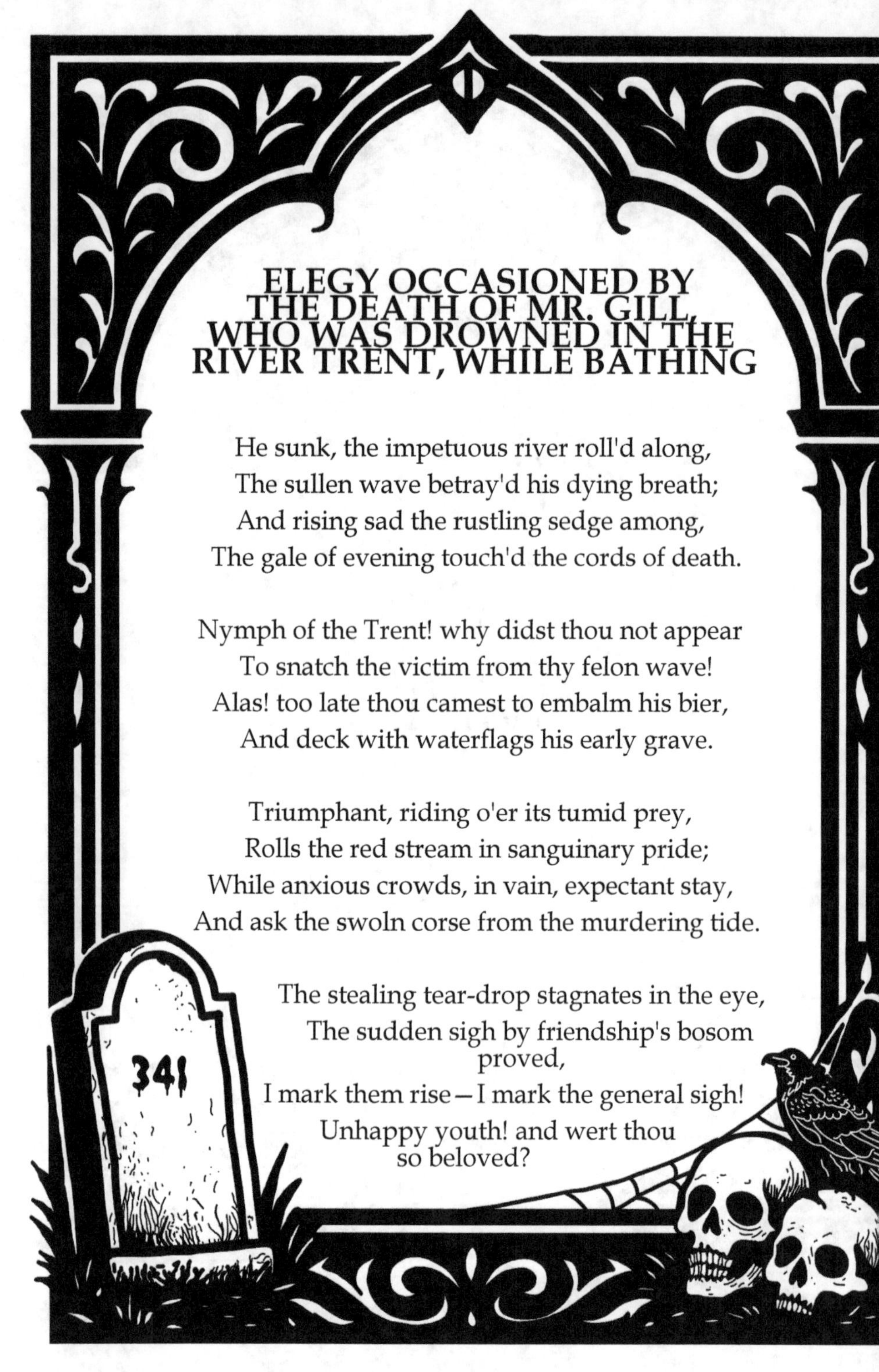

ELEGY OCCASIONED BY THE DEATH OF MR. GILL, WHO WAS DROWNED IN THE RIVER TRENT, WHILE BATHING

He sunk, the impetuous river roll'd along,
The sullen wave betray'd his dying breath;
And rising sad the rustling sedge among,
The gale of evening touch'd the cords of death.

Nymph of the Trent! why didst thou not appear
To snatch the victim from thy felon wave!
Alas! too late thou camest to embalm his bier,
And deck with waterflags his early grave.

Triumphant, riding o'er its tumid prey,
Rolls the red stream in sanguinary pride;
While anxious crowds, in vain, expectant stay,
And ask the swoln corse from the murdering tide.

The stealing tear-drop stagnates in the eye,
The sudden sigh by friendship's bosom proved,
I mark them rise—I mark the general sigh!
Unhappy youth! and wert thou so beloved?

On thee, as lone I trace the Trent's green brink,
When the dim twilight slumbers on the glade;
On thee my thoughts shall dwell, nor Fancy shrink
To hold mysterious converse with thy shade.

Of thee, as early, I, with vagrant feet,
Hail the gray-sandal'd morn in Colwick's vale,
Of thee my sylvan reed shall warble sweet,
And wild-wood echoes shall repeat the tale.

And, oh! ye nymphs of Pæon! who preside
O'er running rill and salutary stream.
Guard ye in future well the halcyon tide
From the rude death-shriek and the dying scream.

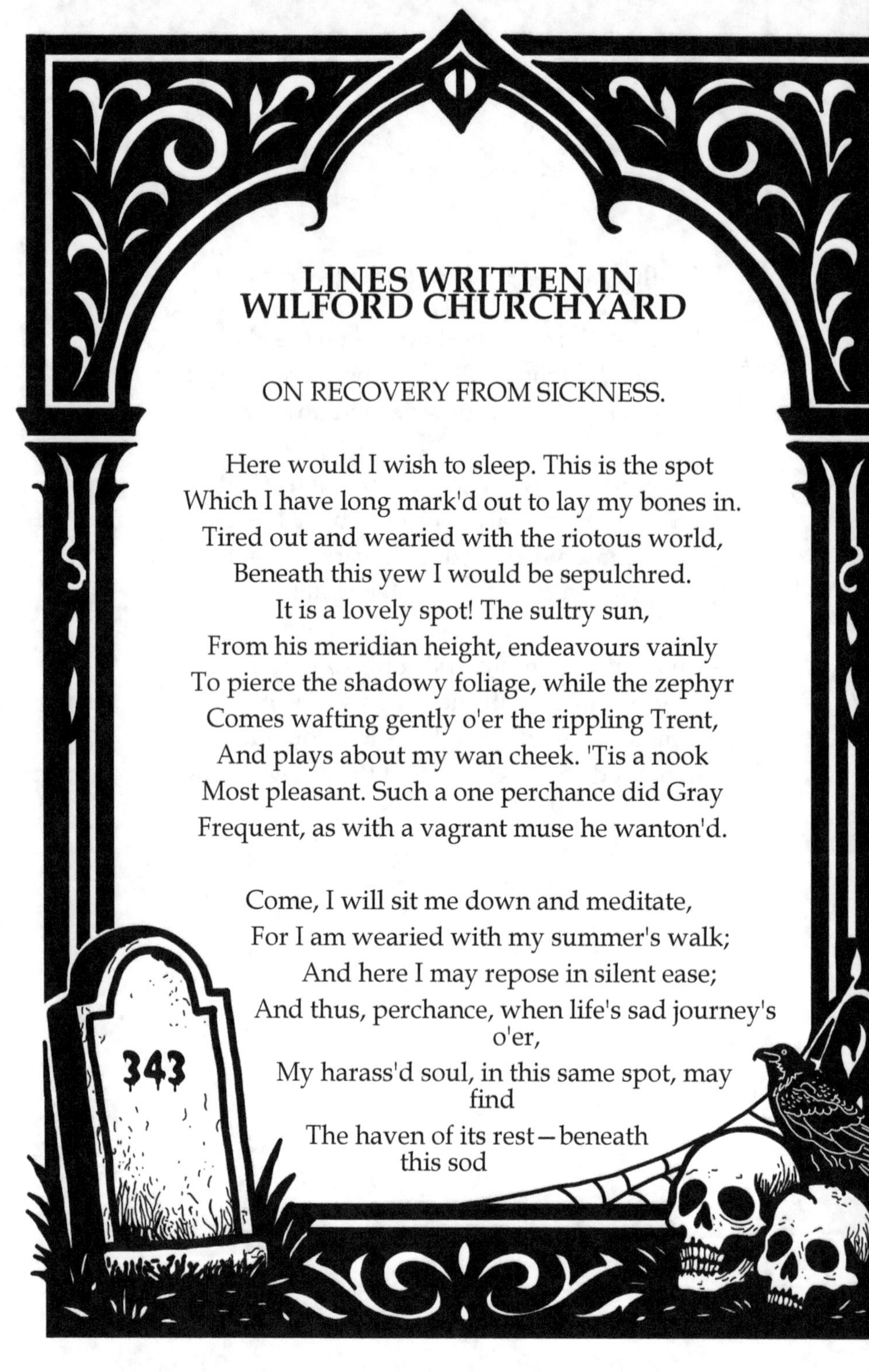

LINES WRITTEN IN WILFORD CHURCHYARD

ON RECOVERY FROM SICKNESS.

Here would I wish to sleep. This is the spot
Which I have long mark'd out to lay my bones in.
Tired out and wearied with the riotous world,
Beneath this yew I would be sepulchred.
It is a lovely spot! The sultry sun,
From his meridian height, endeavours vainly
To pierce the shadowy foliage, while the zephyr
Comes wafting gently o'er the rippling Trent,
And plays about my wan cheek. 'Tis a nook
Most pleasant. Such a one perchance did Gray
Frequent, as with a vagrant muse he wanton'd.

Come, I will sit me down and meditate,
For I am wearied with my summer's walk;
And here I may repose in silent ease;
And thus, perchance, when life's sad journey's o'er,
My harass'd soul, in this same spot, may find
The haven of its rest—beneath this sod

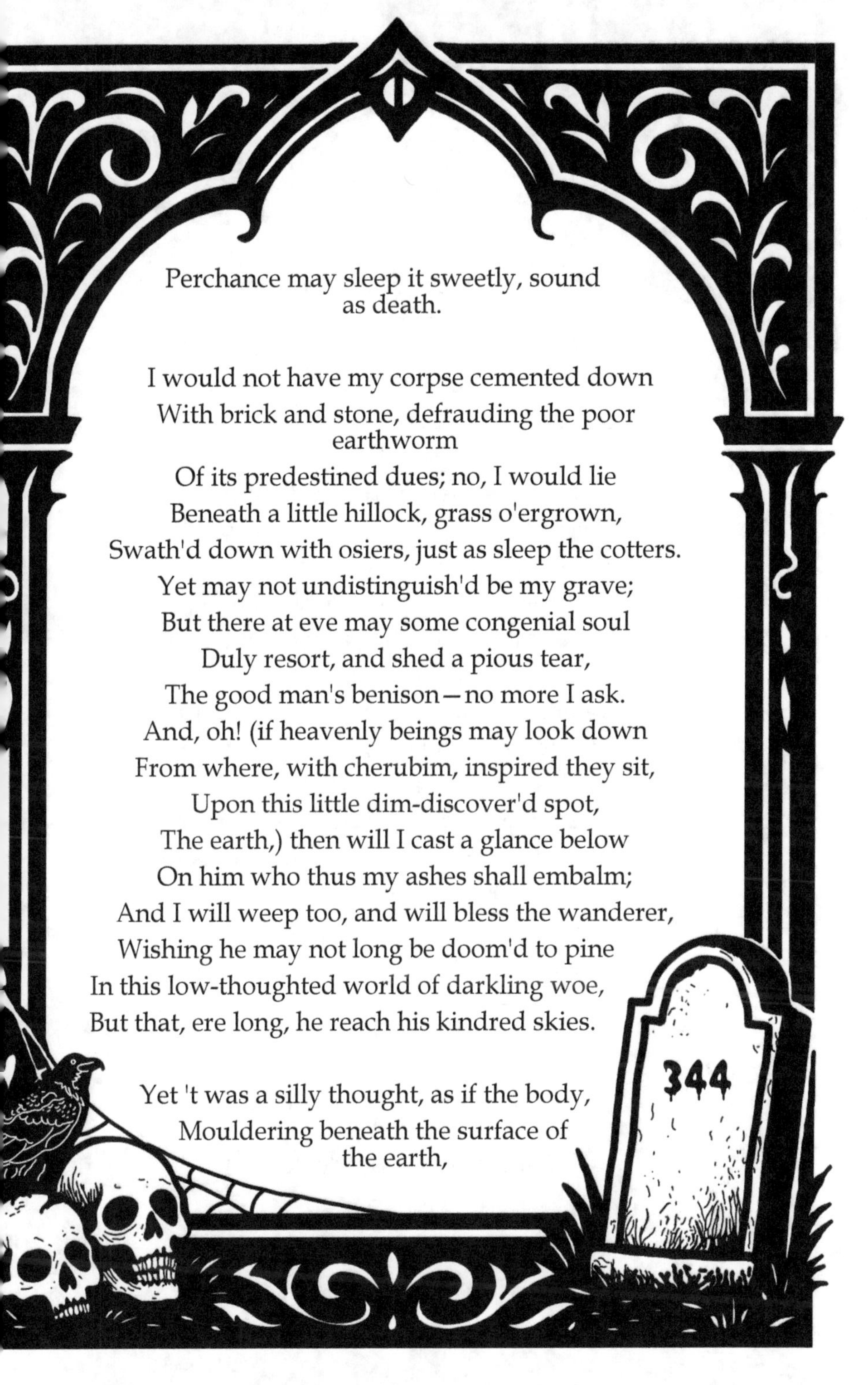

Perchance may sleep it sweetly, sound as death.

I would not have my corpse cemented down
With brick and stone, defrauding the poor earthworm
Of its predestined dues; no, I would lie
Beneath a little hillock, grass o'ergrown,
Swath'd down with osiers, just as sleep the cotters.
Yet may not undistinguish'd be my grave;
But there at eve may some congenial soul
Duly resort, and shed a pious tear,
The good man's benison—no more I ask.
And, oh! (if heavenly beings may look down
From where, with cherubim, inspired they sit,
Upon this little dim-discover'd spot,
The earth,) then will I cast a glance below
On him who thus my ashes shall embalm;
And I will weep too, and will bless the wanderer,
Wishing he may not long be doom'd to pine
In this low-thoughted world of darkling woe,
But that, ere long, he reach his kindred skies.

Yet 't was a silly thought, as if the body,
Mouldering beneath the surface of the earth,

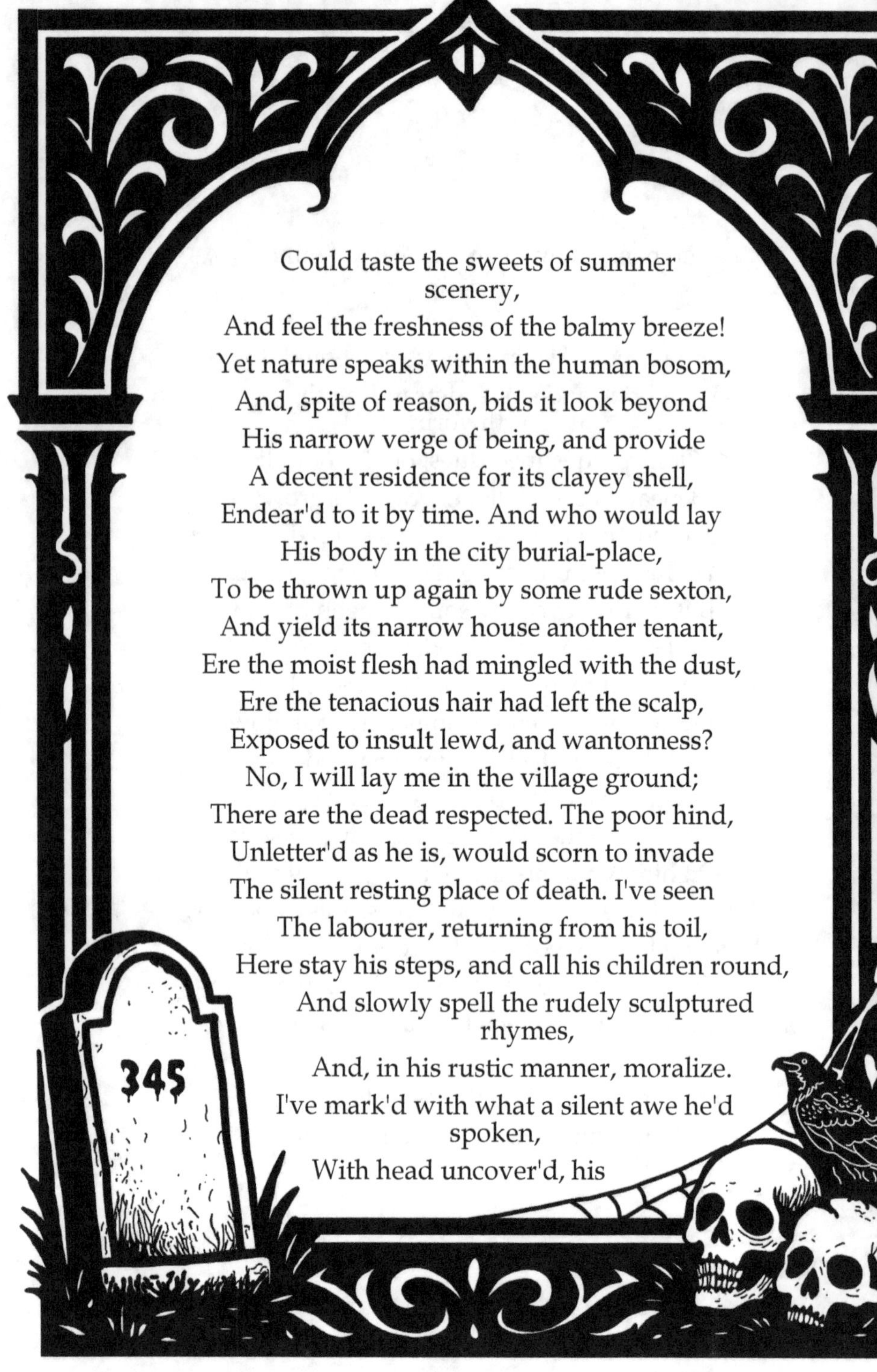

Could taste the sweets of summer scenery,
And feel the freshness of the balmy breeze!
Yet nature speaks within the human bosom,
And, spite of reason, bids it look beyond
His narrow verge of being, and provide
A decent residence for its clayey shell,
Endear'd to it by time. And who would lay
His body in the city burial-place,
To be thrown up again by some rude sexton,
And yield its narrow house another tenant,
Ere the moist flesh had mingled with the dust,
Ere the tenacious hair had left the scalp,
Exposed to insult lewd, and wantonness?
No, I will lay me in the village ground;
There are the dead respected. The poor hind,
Unletter'd as he is, would scorn to invade
The silent resting place of death. I've seen
The labourer, returning from his toil,
Here stay his steps, and call his children round,
And slowly spell the rudely sculptured rhymes,
And, in his rustic manner, moralize.
I've mark'd with what a silent awe he'd spoken,
With head uncover'd, his

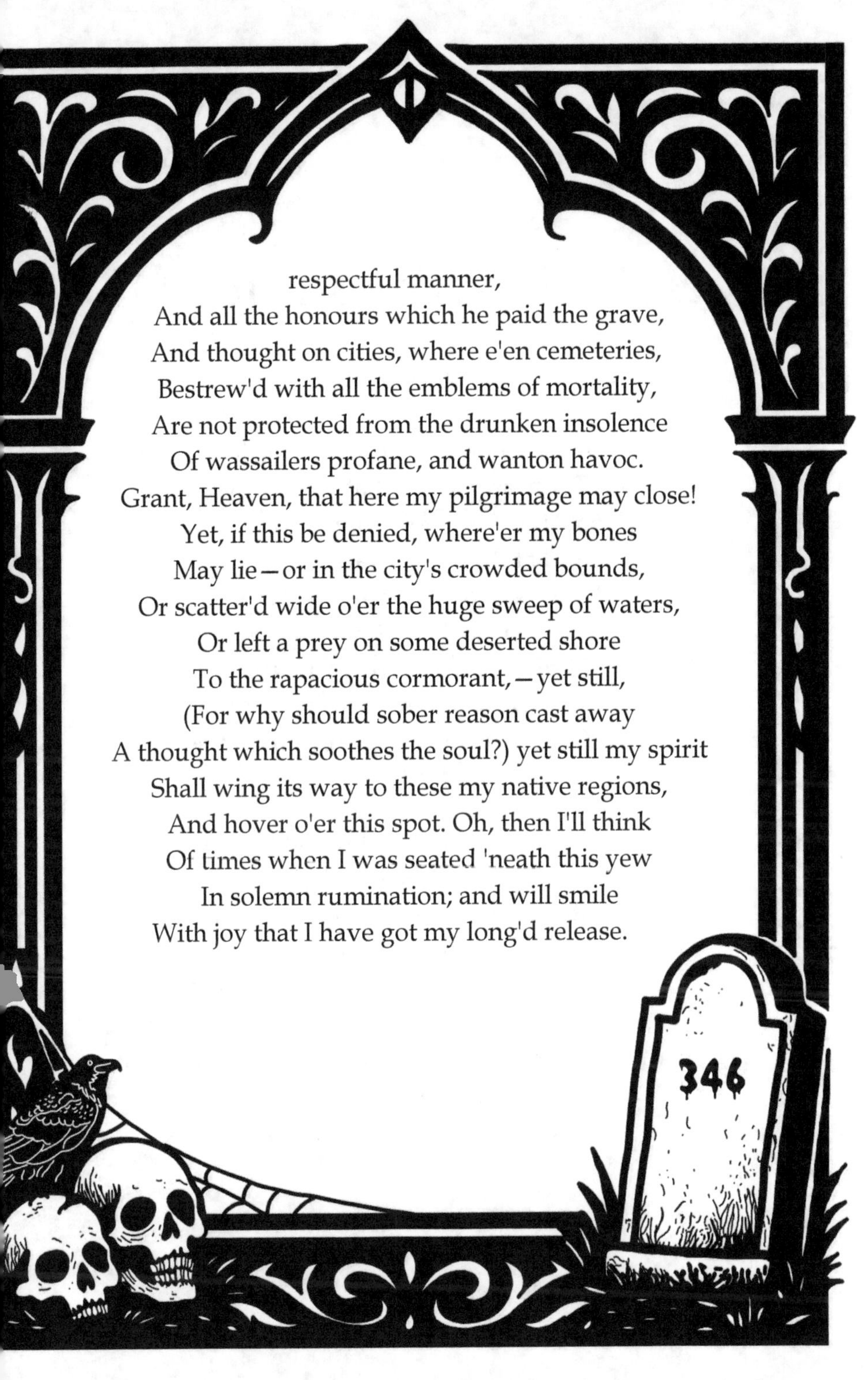

respectful manner,
And all the honours which he paid the grave,
And thought on cities, where e'en cemeteries,
Bestrew'd with all the emblems of mortality,
Are not protected from the drunken insolence
Of wassailers profane, and wanton havoc.
Grant, Heaven, that here my pilgrimage may close!
Yet, if this be denied, where'er my bones
May lie—or in the city's crowded bounds,
Or scatter'd wide o'er the huge sweep of waters,
Or left a prey on some deserted shore
To the rapacious cormorant,—yet still,
(For why should sober reason cast away
A thought which soothes the soul?) yet still my spirit
Shall wing its way to these my native regions,
And hover o'er this spot. Oh, then I'll think
Of times when I was seated 'neath this yew
In solemn rumination; and will smile
With joy that I have got my long'd release.

THE EVE OF DEATH

IRREGULAR.

Silence of death—portentous calm,
Those airy forms that yonder fly
Denote that your void foreruns a storm,
That the hour of fate is nigh.
I see, I see, on the dim mist borne,
The Spirit of battles rear his crest!
I see, I see, that ere the morn,
His spear will forsake its hated rest,
And the widow'd wife of Larrendill will beat her naked breast.

O'er the smooth bosom of the sullen deep,
No softly ruffling zephyrs fly;
But nature sleeps a deathless sleep,
For the hour of battle is nigh.
Not a loose leaf waves on the dusky oak,
But a creeping stillness reigns around;
Except when the raven, with ominous croak
On the ear does unwelcomely sound.
I know, I know what this silence means;

I know what the raven saith—
Strike, oh, ye bards! the melancholy harp,
For this is the eve of death.

Behold, how along the twilight air
The shades of our fathers glide!
There Morven fled, with the blood-drench'd hair,
And Colma with gray side.
No gale around its coolness flings,
Yet sadly sigh the gloomy trees;
And hark! how the harp's unvisited strings
Sound sweet, as if swept by a whispering breeze!
'Tis done! the sun he has set in blood!
He will never set more to the brave;
Let us pour to the hero the dirge of death,
For to-morrow he hies to the grave.

TO MIDNIGHT

Season of general rest, whose solemn still
Strikes to the trembling heart a fearful chill,
But speaks to philosophic souls delight;
Thee do I hail, as at my casement high,
My candle waning melancholy by,
I sit and taste the holy calm of night.

Yon pensive orb, that through the ether sails,
And gilds the misty shadows of the vales,
Hanging in thy dull rear her vestal flame;
To her, while all around in sleep recline,
Wakeful I raise my orisons divine,
And sing the gentle honours of her name;

While Fancy lone o'er me, her votary, bends,
To lift my soul her fairy visions sends,
And pours upon my ear her thrilling song,
And Superstition's gentle terrors come,—
See, see yon dim ghost gliding through the gloom!
See round yon churchyard elm what spectres throng!

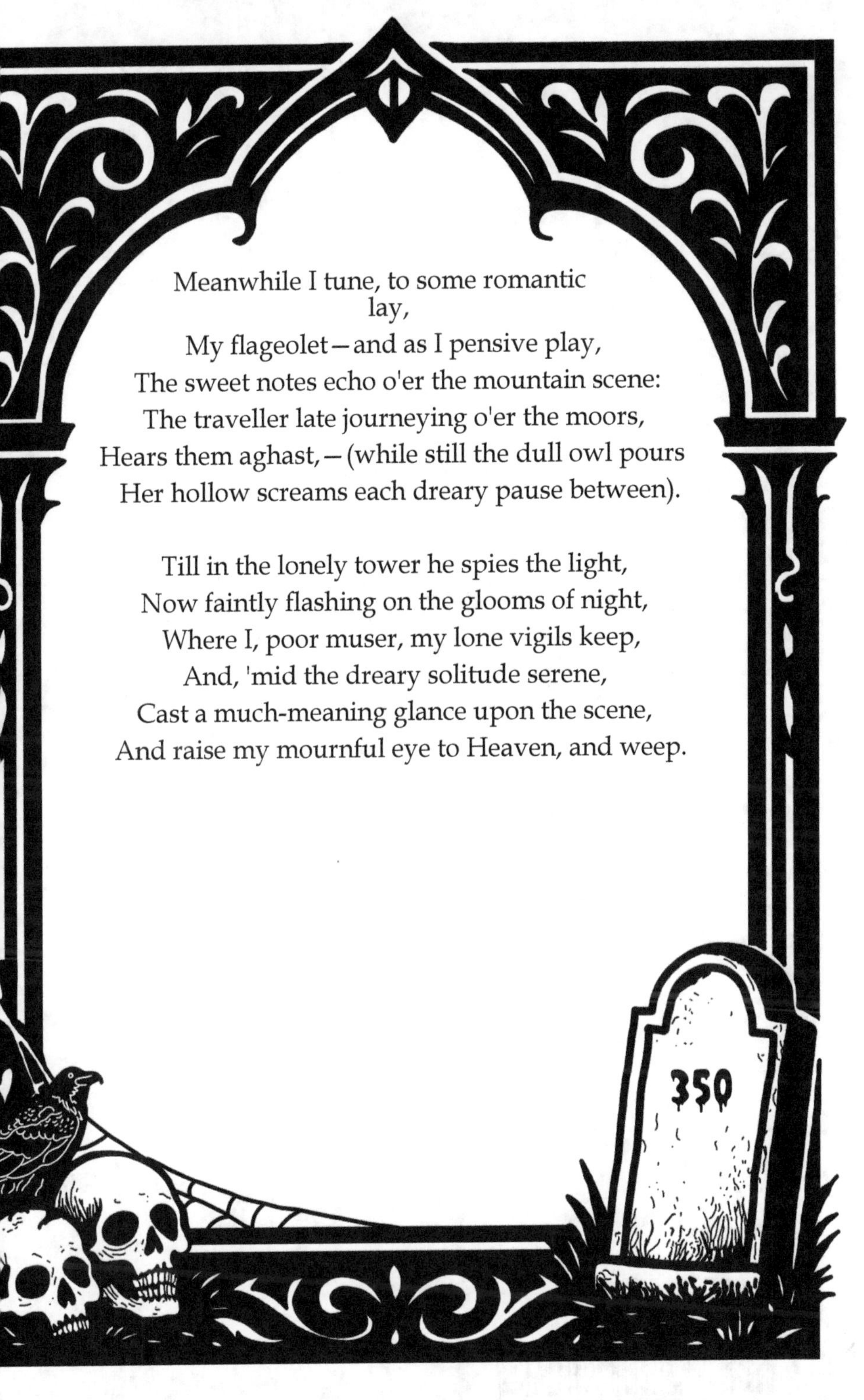

Meanwhile I tune, to some romantic lay,
My flageolet—and as I pensive play,
The sweet notes echo o'er the mountain scene:
The traveller late journeying o'er the moors,
Hears them aghast,—(while still the dull owl pours
Her hollow screams each dreary pause between).

Till in the lonely tower he spies the light,
Now faintly flashing on the glooms of night,
Where I, poor muser, my lone vigils keep,
And, 'mid the dreary solitude serene,
Cast a much-meaning glance upon the scene,
And raise my mournful eye to Heaven, and weep.

www.ingramcontent.com/pod-product-compliance
Lightning Source LLC
Chambersburg PA
CBHW060612310726
48982CB00003B/537